PRINTING, DECEMBER, 1963
PRINTING, APRIL, 1964

TRADEMARK REG. U.S. PAT. OFF. AND FOREIGN COUNTRIES
ED TRADEMARK—MARCA REGISTRADA
N CHICAGO, U.S.A.

T BOOKS are published by
ew American Library of World Literature, Inc.
udison Avenue, New York, New York 10022

ED IN THE UNITED STATES OF AMERICA

"Bawdy, boisterous,
and brilliant
. . . that's Tom Jones."

High-spirited, handsome, and perpetually in
trouble because of his gallantry toward the
opposite sex, young Tom Jones stands at
the center of this great novel of eighteenth-
century England.

Yet he is but one of the book's expertly
realized characters. Tom's amorous misad-
ventures take him from stately manor houses
to the London slums and involve him with
some of the most delightful—and the most
wretched—men and women in all fiction:
the sweet young Sophia, who loves him . . .
the alluring Mrs. Waters, who is determined
to seduce him . . . the kindly and benevolent
squire, who raises him as his adopted son . . .
the contemptible Blifil, who plots to destroy
him.

Tom Jones is one of the marvels of literature.
In its exuberant wit, its perceptive irony, its
constant surprise, the reader views life itself.

SIGNET Play and Movie Tie-Ins

LUTHER *by John Osborne*
A brilliant London and Broadway success about the rebellious priest who challenged, and changed, the spiritual world of his time. By the author of *Look Back in Anger*. (#P2352—60¢)

THE LEOPARD *by Giuseppe di Lampedusa*
A dazzling international bestseller, this novel follows the fortunes of a noble Italian family during fifty eventful years. Now a prize-winning film starring Burt Lancaster. (#T1960—75¢)

CLEOPATRA *by Carlo Maria Franzero*
The spectacular story of the love affair of Marc Antony and Cleopatra. Now a historic motion picture starring Elizabeth Taylor and Richard Burton. (#P2163—60¢)

LAWRENCE OF ARABIA *by Anthony Nutting*
The incredible story of the British Army Officer who led the Arabs to victory over the Turks during World War II, and then mysteriously vanished. Peter O'Toole stars in the title role of the epic motion picture. (#T2106—75¢)

TO OUR READERS: If your dealer does not have the SIGNET and MENTOR books you want, you may order them by mail, enclosing the list price plus 5¢ a copy to cover mailing. If you would like our free catalog, please request it by postcard. The New American Library of World Literature, Inc., P.O. Box 2310, Grand Central Station, New York, N. Y., 10017.

HENRY FIELDING

THE HISTORY OF

TOM JONES

A FOUNDLING

Mores hominum multorum vidit

WITH AN AFTERWORD BY
Frank Kermode

A SIGNET B

Published by THE NEW AN

SIGNE
The N
501 M

PRINT

To the Honourable

GEORGE LYTTLETON, ESQ.,

One of the Lords Commissioners of the Treasury

Sir,

Notwithstanding your constant refusal when I have asked leave to prefix your name to this dedication, I must still insist on my right to desire your protection of this work.

To you, sir, it is owing that this history was ever begun. It was by your desire that I first thought of such a composition. So many years have since passed that you may have, perhaps, forgotten this circumstance, but your desires are to me in the nature of commands, and the impression of them is never to be erased from my memory.

Again, sir, without your assistance this history had never been completed. Be not startled at the assertion. I do not intend to draw on you the suspicion of being a romance-writer. I mean no more than that I partly owe to you my existence during great part of the time which I have employed in composing it: another matter which it may be necessary to remind you of, since there are certain actions of which you are apt to be extremely forgetful; but of these I hope I shall always have a better memory than yourself.

Lastly, it is owing to you that the history appears what it now is. If there be in this work, as some have been pleased to say, a stronger picture of a truly benevolent mind than is to be found in any other, who that knows you and a particular acquaintance of yours will doubt whence that benevolence hath been copied? The world will not, I believe, make me the compliment of thinking I took it from myself. I care not. This they shall own: that the two persons from whom I have taken it, that is to say, two of the best and worthiest men in the world, are strongly and zealously my friends. I might be contented with this, and yet my vanity will add a third to the number, and him one of the greatest and noblest, not only in his rank but in every public and private virtue. But here, whilst my gratitude for the princely benefactions of the Duke of Bed-

ford bursts from my heart, you must forgive my reminding
you that it was you who first recommended me to the notice
of my benefactor.

And what are your objections to the allowance of the honour
which I have solicited? Why, you have commended the book
so warmly that you should be ashamed of reading your name
before the dedication. Indeed, sir, if the book itself doth not
make you ashamed of your commendations, nothing that I can
here write will or ought. I am not to give up my right to your
protection and patronage because you have commended my
book, for though I acknowledge so many obligations to you,
I do not add this to the number; in which friendship, I am
convinced, hath so little share, since that can neither bias your
judgement nor pervert your integrity. An enemy may at any
time obtain your commendation by only deserving it, and the
utmost which the faults of your friends can hope for is
your silence or, perhaps, if too severely accused, your gentle
palliation.

In short, sir, I suspect that your dislike of public praise is
your true objection to granting my request. I have observed
that you have in common with my two other friends an unwillingness to hear the least mention of your own virtues; that, as
a great poet says of one of you (he might justly have said it
of all three), you

> Do good by stealth, and blush to find it fame.

If men of this disposition are as careful to shun applause as
others are to escape censure, how just must be your apprehension of your character falling into my hands, since what would
not a man have reason to dread if attacked by an author who
had received from him injuries equal to my obligations to you!

And will not this dread of censure increase in proportion to
the matter which a man is conscious of having afforded for it?
If his whole life, for instance, should have been one continued
subject of satire, he may well tremble when an incensed satirist takes him in hand. Now, sir, if we apply this to your modest aversion to panegyric, how reasonable will your fears of
me appear!

Yet surely you might have gratified my ambition, from this
single confidence: that I shall always prefer the indulgence of
your inclinations to the satisfaction of my own. A very strong
instance of which I shall give you in this address, in which I
am determined to follow the example of all other dedicators,

and will consider not what my patron really deserves to have written but what he will be best pleased to read.

Without further preface, then, I here present you with the labours of some years of my life. What merit these labours have is already known to yourself. If from your favourable judgement I have conceived some esteem for them, it cannot be imputed to vanity, since I should have agreed as implicitly to your opinion had it been given in favour of any other man's production. Negatively, at least, I may be allowed to say that, had I been sensible of any great demerit in the work, you are the last person to whose protection I would have ventured to recommend it.

From the name of my patron, indeed, I hope my reader will be convinced at his very entrance on this work that he will find in the whole course of it nothing prejudicial to the cause of religion and virtue, nothing inconsistent with the strictest rules of decency, nor which can offend even the chastest eye in the perusal. On the contrary, I declare that to recommend goodness and innocence hath been my sincere endeavour in this history. This honest purpose you have been pleased to think I have attained; and to say the truth, it is likeliest to be attained in books of this kind, for an example is a kind of picture in which virtue becomes, as it were, an object of sight, and strikes us with an idea of that loveliness which Plato asserts there is in her naked charms.

Besides displaying that beauty of virtue which may attract the admiration of mankind, I have attempted to engage a stronger motive to human action in her favour by convincing men that their true interest directs them to a pursuit of her. For this purpose, I have shown that no acquisitions of guilt can compensate the loss of that solid inward comfort of mind which is the sure companion of innocence and virtue, nor can in the least balance the evil of that horror and anxiety which, in their room, guilt introduces into our bosoms. And again, that as these acquisitions are in themselves generally worthless, so are the means to attain them not only base and infamous but at best incertain, and always full of danger. Lastly, I have endeavoured strongly to inculcate that virtue and innocence can scarce ever be injured but by indiscretion, and that it is this alone which often betrays them into the snares that deceit and villainy spread for them. A moral which I have the more industriously laboured, as the teaching it is, of all others, the likeliest to be attended with success, since I believe it is much easier to make good men wise than to make bad men good.

For these purposes I have employed all the wit and humour of which I am master in the following history, wherein I have endeavoured to laugh mankind out of their favourite follies and vices. How far I have succeeded in this good attempt I shall submit to the candid reader, with only two requests: first, that he will not expect to find perfection in this work; and secondly, that he will excuse some parts of it if they fall short of that little merit which I hope may appear in others.

I will detain you, sir, no longer. Indeed I have run into a preface while I professed to write a dedication. But how can it be otherwise? I dare not praise you; and the only means I know of to avoid it, when you are in my thoughts, are either to be entirely silent or to turn my thoughts to some other subject.

Pardon, therefore, what I have said in this epistle, not only without your consent but absolutely against it; and give me at least leave, in this public manner, to declare that I am with the highest respect and gratitude,

SIR,

Your most obliged,

Obedient, humble servant,

HENRY FIELDING.

CONTENTS

BOOK I

Containing as Much of the Birth of the Foundling as Is Necessary or Proper to Acquaint the Reader with the Beginning of This History

BOOK II

*Containing Scenes of Matrimonial Felicity in Different Degrees
of Life, and Various Other Transactions During the First
Two Years After the Marriage Between Captain Blifil and
Miss Bridget Allworthy*

BOOK III

Containing the Most Memorable Transactions Which Passed in the Family of Mr. Allworthy, from the Time When Tommy Jones Arrived at the Age of Fourteen Till He Attained the Age of Nineteen. In This Book the Reader May Pick Up Some Hints Concerning the Education of Children

BOOK IV

Containing the Time of a Year

BOOK V

Containing a Portion of Time Somewhat Longer Than Half a Year

BOOK VI

Containing About Three Weeks

BOOK VII

Containing Three Days

BOOK VIII

Containing Above Two Days

BOOK IX

Containing Twelve Hours

BOOK X

In Which the History Goes Forward About Twelve Hours

BOOK XI

Containing About Three Days

BOOK XII

Containing the Same Individual Time with the Former

BOOK XIII

Containing the Space of Twelve Days

BOOK XIV

Containing Two Days

BOOK XV

In Which the History Advances About Two Days

BOOK XVI

Containing the Space of Five Days

BOOK XVII

Containing Three Days

BOOK XVIII

Containing About Six Days

THE HISTORY OF
TOM JONES

BOOK I

1

THE INTRODUCTION TO THE WORK, OR BILL OF FARE TO THE FEAST

An author ought to consider himself not as a gentleman who gives a private or eleemosynary treat, but rather as one who keeps a public ordinary at which all persons are welcome for their money. In the former case, it is well known that the entertainer provides what fare he pleases, and though this should be very indifferent and utterly disagreeable to the taste of his company, they must not find any fault; nay, on the contrary, good breeding forces them outwardly to approve and to commend whatever is set before them. Now, the contrary of this happens to the master of an ordinary. Men who pay for what they eat will insist on gratifying their palates, however nice and even whimsical these may prove; and, if everything is not agreeable to their taste, will challenge a right to censure, to abuse, and to d—n their dinner without control.

To prevent, therefore, giving offence to their customers by any such disappointment, it hath been usual with the honest and well-meaning host to provide a bill of fare, which all persons may peruse at their first entrance into the house; and, having thence acquainted themselves with the entertainment which they may expect, may either stay and regale with what is provided for them or may depart to some other ordinary better accommodated to their taste.

As we do not disdain to borrow wit or wisdom from any man who is capable of lending us either, we have condescended to take a hint from these honest victuallers and shall prefix not only a general bill of fare to our whole entertainment, but shall likewise give the reader particular bills to every course which is to be served up in this and the ensuing volumes.

The provision, then, which we have here made is no other than HUMAN NATURE. Nor do I fear that my sensible reader, though most luxurious in his taste, will start, cavil, or be offended because I have named but one article. The tortoise, as the Alderman of Bristol, well learned in eating, knows by much experience, besides the delicious calipash and calipee, contains many different kinds of food; nor can the learned reader be ignorant that in Human Nature, though here collected under one general name, is such prodigious variety that a cook will have sooner gone through all the several species of animal and vegetable food in the world than an author will be able to exhaust so extensive a subject.

An objection may perhaps be apprehended from the more delicate that this dish is too common and vulgar; for what else is the subject of all the romances, novels, plays, and poems with which the stalls abound? Many exquisite viands might be rejected by the epicure if it was a sufficient cause for his contemning of them as common and vulgar that something was to be found in the most paltry alleys under the same name. In reality, true nature is as difficult to be met with in authors as the Bayonne ham or Bologna sausage is to be found in the shops.

But the whole, to continue the same metaphor, consists in the cookery of the author; for, as Mr. Pope tells us,

True wit is nature to advantage dressed,
What oft was thought, but ne'er so well expressed.

The same animal which hath the honour to have some part of his flesh eaten at the table of a duke may perhaps be degraded in another part, and some of his limbs gibbeted, as it were, in the vilest stall in town. Where then lies the difference between the food of the nobleman and the porter, if both are at dinner on the same ox or calf, but in the seasoning, the dressing, the garnishing, and the setting forth? Hence, the one provokes and incites the most languid appetite, and the other turns and palls that which is the sharpest and keenest.

In like manner, the excellence of the mental entertainment consists less in the subject than in the author's skill in well dressing it up. How pleased, therefore, will the reader be to find that we have, in the following work, adhered closely to one of the highest principles of the best cook which the present age, or perhaps that of Heliogabalus, hath produced! This great man, as is well known to all polite lovers of eating, begins at first by setting plain things before his hungry guests, rising afterwards by degrees, as their stomachs may be supposed to decrease, to the very quintessence of sauce and spices. In like manner, we shall represent Human Nature at first to the keen appetite of our reader in that more plain and simple manner in which it is found in the country, and shall hereafter hash and ragoo it with all the high French and Italian seasoning of affectation and vice which courts and cities afford. By these means, we doubt not but our reader may be rendered desirous to read on forever, as the great person just above-mentioned is supposed to have made some persons eat.

Having premised thus much, we will now detain those who like our bill of fare no longer from their diet, and shall proceed directly to serve up the first course of our history for their entertainment.

2

A SHORT DESCRIPTION OF SQUIRE ALLWORTHY AND A FULLER
ACCOUNT OF MISS BRIDGET ALLWORTHY, HIS SISTER

In that part of the western division of this kingdom which is commonly called Somersetshire, there lately lived (and perhaps lives still) a gentleman whose name was Allworthy, and who might well be called the favourite of both Nature and Fortune, for both of these seem to have contended which should bless and enrich him most. In this contention Nature may seem to some to have come off victorious, as she bestowed on him many gifts, while Fortune had only one gift in her power; but in pouring forth this, she was so very profuse that others perhaps may think this single endowment to have been more than equivalent to all the various blessings which he enjoyed from Nature. From the former of these he derived an agreeable person, a sound constitution, a solid understanding, and a benevolent heart; by the latter he was decreed to the inheritance of one of the largest estates in the county.

This gentleman had in his youth married a very worthy and beautiful woman, of whom he had been extremely fond; by her he had three children, all of whom died in their infancy. He had likewise had the misfortune of burying this beloved wife herself about five years before the time in which this history chooses to set out. This loss, however great, he bore like a man of sense and constancy, though it must be confessed, he would often talk a little whimsically on this head; for he sometimes said he looked on himself as still married, and considered his wife as only gone a little before him, a journey which he should most certainly, sooner or later, take after her; and that he had not the least doubt of meeting her again in a place where he should never part with her more—sentiments for which his sense was arraigned by one part of his neighbours, his religion by a second, and his sincerity by a third.

He now lived, for the most part, retired in the country, with one sister, for whom he had a very tender affection. This lady was now somewhat past the age of thirty, an era at which, in the opinion of the malicious, the title of old maid may with no impropriety be assumed. She was of that species of women whom you rather commend for good qualities than beauty, and who are generally called by their own sex, very good sort of women—"as good a sort of woman, madam, as you would wish to know." Indeed, she was so far from regretting want of beauty that she never mentioned that perfection (if it can be called one) without contempt; and would often thank God she was not as handsome as Miss Such-a-One, whom perhaps beauty had led into errors which she might have otherwise avoided. Miss Bridget Allworthy (for that was the name of this lady) very rightly conceived the charms of person in a woman to be no better than snares for herself, as well as for others, and yet so discreet was she in her conduct that her prudence was as much on the guard as if she had had all the snares to apprehend, which were ever laid for her whole sex. Indeed, I have observed (though it may seem unaccountable to the reader) that this guard of prudence, like the trained bands, is always readiest to go on duty where there is the least danger. It often basely and cowardly deserts those paragons for whom the men are all wishing, sighing, dying, and spreading every net in their power, and constantly attends at the heels of that higher order of women, for whom the other sex have a more distant and awful respect, and whom (from despair, I suppose, of success) they never venture to attack.

Reader, I think proper, before we proceed any farther together, to acquaint thee that I intend to digress through this whole history as often as I see occasion; of which I am myself a better judge than any pitiful critic whatever. And here I must desire all those critics to mind their own business, and not to intermeddle with affairs or works which no ways concern them; for till they produce the authority by which they are constituted judges, I shall not plead to their jurisdiction.

3

AN ODD ACCIDENT WHICH BEFELL MR. ALLWORTHY AT HIS RETURN HOME. THE DECENT BEHAVIOUR OF MRS. DEBORAH WILKINS, WITH SOME PROPER ANIMADVERSIONS ON BASTARDS

I have told my reader in the preceding chapter that Mr. Allworthy inherited a large fortune, that he had a good heart, and no family. Hence, doubtless, it will be concluded by many that he lived like an honest man, owed no one a shilling, took nothing but what was his own, kept a good house, entertained his neighbours with a hearty welcome at his table, and was charitable to the poor, i.e., to those who had rather beg than work, by giving them the offals from it; that he died immensely rich, and built an hospital.

And true it is that he did many of these things; but, had he done nothing more, I should have left him to have recorded his own merit on some fair free-stone over the door of that hospital. Matters of a much more extraordinary kind are to be the subject of this history, or I should grossly mis-spend my time in writing so voluminous a work; and you, my sagacious friend, might with equal profit and pleasure travel through some pages which certain droll authors have been facetiously pleased to call *The History of England*.

Mr. Allworthy had been absent a full quarter of a year in London on some very particular business, though I know not what it was; but judge of its importance by its having detained him so long from home, whence he had not been absent a month at a time during the space of many years. He came to his house very late in the evening, and after a short supper with his sister, retired much fatigued to his chamber. Here, having spent some minutes on his knees, a custom which he never broke through on any account, he was preparing to step into bed when, upon opening the clothes, to his great surprise he beheld an infant, wrapped up in some coarse linen, in a sweet and profound sleep, between his sheets. He stood some time lost in astonishment at this sight; but, as good nature had always the ascendant in his mind, he soon began to be touched with sentiments of compassion for the little wretch before him. He then rang his bell and ordered an elderly woman-servant to rise immediately and come to him, and in the meantime, was so eager in contemplating the beauty of innocence appearing in those lively colours with which infancy and sleep always display it that his thoughts were too much engaged to reflect that he was in his shirt when the matron came in. She had, indeed, given her master sufficient time to dress himself; for out of respect to him and regard to decency, she had spent many minutes in adjusting her hair at the looking-glass, notwithstanding all the hurry in which she had been summoned by the servant, and though her master, for aught she knew, lay expiring in an apoplexy or in some other fit.

It will not be wondered at that a creature who had so strict a regard to decency in her own person should be shocked at the least deviation from it in another. She therefore no sooner opened the door and saw her master standing by the bedside in his shirt with a candle in his hand than she started back in a most terrible fright, and might perhaps have swooned away had he not now recollected his being undressed and put an end to her terrors by desiring her to stay without the door till he had thrown some clothes over his back and was become incapable of shocking the pure eyes of Mrs. Deborah Wilkins, who, though in the fifty-second year of her age, vowed she had never beheld a man without his coat. Sneerers and profane wits may perhaps laugh at her first fright, yet my graver reader, when he considers the time of night, the summons from her bed, and the situation in which she found her master, will highly justify and applaud her conduct; unless the prudence which must be supposed to attend maidens at that period of life at which Mrs. Deborah had arrived should a little lessen his admiration.

When Mrs. Deborah returned into the room, and was acquainted by her master with the finding the little infant, her consternation was rather greater than his had been; nor could she refrain from crying out, with great horror of accent as well as look, "My good sir! What's to be done?" Mr. All-worthy answered, she must take care of the child that evening, and in the morning he would give orders to provide it a nurse. "Yes, sir," says she, "and I hope your worship will send out your warrant to take up the hussy its mother (for she must be one of the neighbourhood), and I should be glad to see her committed to Bridewell, and whipped at the cart's tail. Indeed, such wicked sluts cannot be too severely punished. I'll warrant 'tis not her first, by her impudence in laying it to your worship." "In laying it to me! Deborah," answered Allworthy, "I can't think she hath any such design. I suppose she hath only taken this method to provide for her child, and truly I am glad she hath not done worse." "I don't know what is worse," cries Deborah, "than for such wicked strumpets to lay their sins at honest men's doors; and though your worship knows your own innocence, yet the world is censorious, and it hath been many an honest man's hap to pass for the father of children he never begot, and if your worship should provide for the child, it may make the people the apter to believe; besides, why should your worship provide for what the parish is obliged to maintain? For my own part, if it was an honest man's child indeed; but for my own part, it goes against me to touch these misbegotten wretches, whom I don't look upon as my fellow creatures. Faugh, how it stinks! It doth not smell like a Christian. If I might be so bold to give my advice, I would have it put in a basket and sent out and laid at the churchwarden's door. It is a good night, only a little rainy and windy; and if it was well wrapped up and put in a warm basket, it is two to one but it lives till it is found in the morning. But if it should not, we have discharged our duty in taking proper care of it; and it is, perhaps, better for such creatures to die in a state of innocence than to grow up and imitate their mothers, for nothing better can be expected of them."

There were some strokes in this speech which, perhaps, would have offended Mr. Allworthy had he strictly attended to it, but he had now got one of his fingers into the infant's hand, which, by its gentle pressure, seeming to implore his assistance, had certainly out-pleaded the eloquence of Mrs. Deborah had it been ten times greater than it was. He now gave Mrs. Deborah positive orders to take the child to her own bed, and to call up a maidservant to provide it pap and other things against it waked. He likewise ordered that proper clothes should be procured for it early in the morning, and that it should be brought to himself as soon as he was stirring.

Such was the discernment of Mrs. Wilkins and such the respect she bore her master, under whom she enjoyed a most excellent place, that her scruples gave way to his peremptory commands, and she took the child under her arms without any apparent disgust at the illegality of its birth, and declaring it was a sweet little infant, walked off with it to her own chamber.

Allworthy here betook himself to those pleasing slumbers which a heart that hungers after goodness is apt to enjoy when thoroughly satisfied; as these are possibly sweeter than what are occasioned by any other hearty meal, I should take more pains to display them to the reader if I knew any air to recommend him to for the procuring such an appetite.

4

THE READER'S NECK BROUGHT INTO DANGER BY A DESCRIPTION; HIS ESCAPE, AND THE GREAT CONDESCENSION OF MISS BRIDGET ALLWORTHY

The Gothic style of building could produce nothing nobler than Mr. Allworthy's house. There was an air of grandeur in it that struck you with awe, and rivalled the beauties of the best Grecian architecture; and it was as commodious within as venerable without.

It stood on the south-east side of a hill; but nearer the bottom than the top of it, so as to be sheltered from the north-east by a grove of old oaks, which rose above it in a gradual ascent of near half a mile, and yet high enough to enjoy a most charming prospect of the valley beneath.

In the midst of the grove was a fine lawn, sloping down towards the house, near the summit of which rose a plentiful spring gushing out of a rock covered with firs and forming a constant cascade of about thirty foot, not carried down a regular flight of steps, but tumbling in a natural fall over the broken and mossy stones till it came to the bottom of the rock; then running off in a pebbly channel that with many lesser falls winded along till it fell into a lake at the foot of the hill, about a quarter of a mile below the house on the south side, and which was seen from every room in the front. Out of this lake, which filled the center of a beautiful plain, embellished with groups of beeches and elms and fed with sheep, issued a river that, for several miles, was seen to meander through an amazing variety of meadows and woods till it emptied itself into the sea; with a large arm of which, and an island beyond it, the prospect was closed.

On the right of this valley opened another of less extent, adorned with several villages and terminated by one of the towers of an old ruined abbey, grown over with ivy, and part of the front, which remained still entire.

The left-hand scene presented the view of a very fine park, composed of very unequal ground and agreeably varied with all the diversity that hills, lawns, wood, and water, laid out with admirable taste, but owing less to art than to Nature, could give. Beyond this the country gradually rose into a ridge of wild mountains, the tops of which were above the clouds.

It was now the middle of May, and the morning was remarkably serene, when Mr. Allworthy walked forth on the terrace, where the dawn opened every minute that lovely prospect we have before described to his eye. And now, having sent forth streams of light, which ascended the blue firmament before him as harbingers preceding his pomp, in the full blaze of his majesty rose the sun; than which one object alone in this lower creation could be more glorious, and that Mr. Allworthy himself presented: a human being replete with benevolence, meditating in what manner he might render himself most acceptable to his Creator by doing most good to his creatures.

Reader, take care; I have unadvisedly led thee to the top of as high a hill as Mr. Allworthy's, and how to get thee down without breaking my neck I do not well know. However, let us e'en venture to slide down together, for Miss Bridget rings her bell and Mr. Allworthy is summoned to breakfast, where I must attend, and, if you please, shall be glad of your company.

The usual compliments having passed between Mr. Allworthy and Miss Bridget, and the tea being poured out, he summoned Mrs. Wilkins and told his sister he had a present for her; for which she thanked him, imagining, I suppose, it had been a gown or some ornament for her person. Indeed, he very often made her such presents, and she, in complaisance to him, spent much time in adorning herself. I say in complaisance to him because she always expressed the greatest contempt for dress and for those ladies who made it their study.

But if such was her expectation, how was she disappointed when Mr. Wilkins, according to the order she had received from her master, produced the little infant! Great surprises, as hath been observed, are apt to be silent; and so was Miss Bridget till her brother began and told her the whole story, which, as the reader knows already, we shall not repeat.

Miss Bridget had always expressed so great a regard for what the ladies are pleased to call virtue, and had herself maintained such a severity of character, that it was expected, especially by Wilkins, that she would have vented much bitterness on this occasion, and would have voted for sending the child, as a kind of noxious animal, immediately out of the house; but, on the contrary, she rather took the good-natured side of the question, intimated some compassion for the helpless little creature, and commended her brother's charity in what he had done.

Perhaps the reader may account for this behaviour from her condescension to Mr. Allworthy when we have informed him that the good man had ended his narrative with owning a resolution to take care of the child and to breed him up as his own; for, to acknowledge the truth, she was always ready to oblige her brother, and very seldom, if ever, contradicted his sentiments; she would indeed sometimes make a few observations, as that men were headstrong and must have their own way, and would wish she had been blessed with an independent fortune; but these were always vented in a low voice, and at the most amounted only to what is called muttering.

However, what she withheld from the infant she bestowed with the utmost profuseness on the poor unknown mother, whom she called an impudent slut, a wanton hussy, an audacious harlot, a wicked jade, a vile strumpet, with every other appellation with which the tongue of virtue never fails to lash those who bring a disgrace on the sex.

A consultation was now entered into how to proceed in order to discover the mother. A scrutiny was first made into the characters of the female servants of the house, who were all acquitted by Mrs. Wilkins, and with apparent merit, for she had collected them herself; and perhaps it would be difficult to find such another set of scarecrows.

The next step was to examine among the inhabitants of the parish; and this was referred to Mrs. Wilkins, who was to inquire with all imaginable diligence and to make her report in the afternoon.

Matters being thus settled, Mr. Allworthy withdrew to his study, as was his custom, and left the child to his sister, who, at his desire, had undertaken the care of it.

5

CONTAINING A FEW COMMON MATTERS, WITH A VERY UN-COMMON OBSERVATION UPON THEM

When her master was departed, Mrs. Deborah stood silent, expecting her cue from Miss Bridget; for as to what had passed before her master, the prudent housekeeper by no means relied upon it, as she had often known the sentiments of the lady in her brother's absence to differ greatly from those which she had expressed in his presence. Miss Bridget did not, however, suffer her to continue long in this doubtful situation; for, having looked some time earnestly at the child as it lay asleep in the lap of Mrs. Deborah, the good lady could not forbear giving it a hearty kiss, at the same time declaring herself wonderfully pleased with its beauty and innocence. Mrs. Deborah no sooner observed this than she fell to squeezing and kissing with as great raptures as sometimes inspire the sage dame of forty and five towards a youthful and vigorous bridegroom, crying out in a shrill voice, "O the dear little creature; the dear, sweet, pretty creature! Well, I vow, it is as fine a boy as ever was seen!"

These exclamations continued till they were interrupted by the lady, who now proceeded to execute the commission given her by her brother, and gave orders for providing all necessaries for the child, appointing a very good room in the house for his nursery. Her orders were indeed so liberal that had it been a child of her own, she could not have exceeded them; but, lest the virtuous reader may condemn her for showing too great regard to a base-born infant, to which all charity is condemned by law as irreligious, we think proper to observe that she concluded the whole with saying since it was her brother's whim to adopt the little brat, she supposed little master must be treated with great tenderness; for her part, she could not help thinking it was an encouragement to vice, but that she knew too much of the obstinacy of mankind to oppose any of their ridiculous humours.

With reflections of this nature she usually, as has been hinted, accompanied every act of compliance with her brother's inclinations; and surely nothing could more contribute to heighten the merit of this compliance than a declaration that she knew, at the same time, the folly and unreasonableness of those inclinations to which she submitted. Tacit obedience implies no force upon the will, and consequently may be easily, and without any pains, preserved; but when a wife, a child, a relation, or a friend performs what we desire with grumbling and reluctance, with expressions of dislike and dissatisfaction, the manifest difficulty which they undergo must greatly enhance the obligation.

As this is one of those deep observations which very few readers can be supposed capable of making themselves, I have thought proper to lend them my assistance; but this is a favour rarely to be expected in the course of my work. Indeed I shall seldom or never so indulge him, unless in such instances as this, where nothing but the inspiration with which we writers are gifted can possibly enable any one to make the discovery.

6

MRS. DEBORAH IS INTRODUCED INTO THE PARISH WITH A SIMILE. A SHORT ACCOUNT OF JENNY JONES, WITH THE DIFFICULTIES AND DISCOURAGEMENTS WHICH MAY ATTEND YOUNG WOMEN IN THE PURSUIT OF LEARNING

Mrs. Deborah, having disposed of the child according to the will of her master, now prepared to visit those habitations which were supposed to conceal its mother.

Not otherwise than when a kite, tremendous bird, is beheld by the feathered generation soaring aloft and hovering over their heads, the amorous dove and every innocent little bird spread wide the alarm, and fly trembling to their hiding-places. He proudly beats the air, conscious of his dignity, and meditates intended mischief.

So when the approach of Mrs. Deborah was proclaimed through the street, all the inhabitants ran trembling into their houses, each matron dreading lest the visit should fall to her lot. She with stately steps proudly advances over the field, aloft she bears her towering head, filled with conceit of her own pre-eminence and schemes to effect her intended discovery.

The sagacious reader will not from this simile imagine these poor people had any apprehension of the design with which Mrs. Wilkins was now coming towards them; but as the great beauty of the simile may possibly sleep these hundred years till some future commentator shall take this work in hand, I think proper to lend the reader a little assistance in this place.

It is my intention therefore to signify that, as it is the nature of a kite to devour little birds, so it is the nature of such persons as Mrs. Wilkins to insult and tyrannize over little people. This being indeed the means which they use to recompense to themselves their extreme servility and condescension to their superiors; for nothing can be more reasonable than that slaves and flatterers should exact the same taxes on all below them which they themselves pay to all above them.

Whenever Mrs. Deborah had had occasion to exert any extraordinary condescension to Mrs. Bridget, and by that means had a little soured her natural disposition, it was usual with her to walk forth among these people in order to refine her temper by venting and, as it were, purging off all ill humours; on which account she was by no means a welcome visitant: to say the truth, she was universally hated and dreaded by them all.

On her arrival in this place, she went immediately to the habitation of an elderly matron, to whom, as this matron had the good fortune to resemble herself in the comeliness of her person as well as in her age, she had generally been more favourable than to any of the rest. To this woman she imparted what had happened and the design upon which she was come thither that morning. These two began presently to scrutinize the characters of the several young girls who lived in any of those houses, and at last fixed their strongest suspicion on one Jenny Jones, who they both agreed was the likeliest person to have committed this fact.

This Jenny Jones was no very comely girl, either in her face or person; but Nature had somewhat compensated the want of beauty with what is generally more esteemed by those ladies whose judgement is arrived at years of perfect maturity, for she had given her a very uncommon share of understanding. This gift Jenny had a good deal improved by erudition. She had lived several years a servant with a schoolmaster, who, discovering a great quickness of parts in the girl and an extraordinary desire of learning (for every leisure hour she was always found reading in the books of scholars), had the good nature, or folly, which the reader pleases to call it, to instruct her so far that she obtained a very competent skill in the Latin language, and was, perhaps, as good a scholar as most of the young men of quality of the age. This advantage, however, like most others of an extraordinary kind, was attended with some small inconveniences; for as it is not to be wondered at that a young woman so well accomplished should have little relish for the society of those whom Fortune had made her equals, but whom education had rendered so much her inferiors, so is it matter of no greater astonishment that this superiority in Jenny, together with that behaviour which is its certain consequence, should produce among the others some little envy and ill will towards her; and these had, perhaps, secretly burnt in the bosoms of her neighbours ever since her return from her service.

Their envy did not, however, display itself openly till poor —— to the surprise of everybody, and to the vexation of all the young women in these parts, had publicly shone forth on a Sunday in a new silk gown, with a laced cap and other proper appendages to these.

The flame, which had before lain in embryo, now burst forth. Jenny had by her learning increased her own pride, which none of her neighbours were kind enough to feed with the honour she seemed to demand; and now, instead of respect and adoration, she gained nothing but hatred and abuse by her finery. The whole parish declared she could not come honestly by such things; and parents, instead of wishing their daughters the same, felicitated themselves that their children had them not.

Hence, perhaps, it was that the good woman first mentioned the name of this poor girl to Mrs. Wilkins; but there was another circumstance that confirmed the latter in her suspicion, for Jenny had lately been often at Mr. Allworthy's house. She had officiated as nurse to Miss Bridget in a violent fit of illness, and had sat up many nights with that lady; besides which, she had been seen there the very day before Mr. Allworthy's return by Mrs. Wilkins herself, though that sagacious person had not at first conceived any suspicion of her on that account; for, as she herself said, she had always esteemed Jenny as a very sober girl (though indeed she knew very little of her) and had rather suspected some of those wanton trollops who gave themselves airs because, forsooth, they thought themselves handsome.

Jenny was now summoned to appear in person before Mrs. Deborah, which she immediately did; when Mrs. Deborah, putting on the gravity of a judge with somewhat more than his austerity, began an oration with the words "You audacious strumpet," in which she proceeded rather to pass sentence on the prisoner than to accuse her.

Though Mrs. Deborah was fully satisfied of the guilt of Jenny, from the reasons above shown, it is possible Mr. Allworthy might have required some stronger evidence to have convicted her; but she saved her accusers any such trouble by freely confessing the whole fact with which she was charged.

This confession, though delivered rather in terms of contrition, as it appeared, did not at all mollify Mrs. Deborah, who now pronounced a second judgement against her in more opprobrious language than before; nor had it any better success with the bystanders, who were now grown very numerous. Many of them cried out they thought what madam's silk gown would end in; others spoke sarcastically of her learning. Not a single female was present but found some means of expressing her abhorrence of poor Jenny, who bore all very patiently, except the malice of one woman, who reflected upon her person and, tossing up her nose, said, "The man must have a good stomach, who would give silk gowns for such sort of trumpery." Jenny replied to this with a bitterness which might have surprised a judicious person who had observed the tranquillity with which she bore all the affronts to her chastity; but her patience was, perhaps, tired out, for this is a virtue which is very apt to be fatigued by exercise.

Mrs. Deborah, having succeeded beyond her hopes in her inquiry, returned with much triumph and, at the appointed hour, made a faithful report to Mr. Allworthy, who was much surprised at the relation; for he had heard of the extraordinary parts and improvements of this girl, whom he intended to have given in marriage, together with a small living, to a neighbouring curate. His concern therefore on this occasion was at least equal to the satisfaction which appeared in Mrs. Deborah, and to many readers may seem much more reasonable.

Miss Bridget blessed herself, and said for her part, she

should never hereafter entertain a good opinion of any woman; for Jenny had likewise had the happiness of being much in her good graces.

The prudent housekeeper was again dispatched to bring the unhappy culprit before Mr. Allworthy in order not, as it was hoped by some and expected by all, to be sent to the House of Correction, but to receive wholesome admonition and reproof, which those who relish that kind of instructive writing may peruse in the next chapter.

7

CONTAINING SUCH GRAVE MATTER THAT THE READER CANNOT LAUGH ONCE THROUGH THE WHOLE CHAPTER, UNLESS PERADVENTURE HE SHOULD LAUGH AT THE AUTHOR

When Jenny appeared, Mr. Allworthy took her into his study and spoke to her as follows:

"You know, child, it is in my power as a magistrate to punish you very rigorously for what you have done; and you will, perhaps, be the more apt to fear I should execute that power because you have in a manner laid your sins at my door.

"But perhaps this is one reason which hath determined me to act in a milder manner with you; for, as no private resentment should ever influence a magistrate, I will be so far from considering your having deposited the infant in my house as an aggravation of your offence that I will suppose, in your favour, this to have proceeded from a natural affection to your child, since you might have some hopes to see it thus better provided for than was in the power of yourself or its wicked father to provide for it. I should indeed have been highly offended with you had you exposed the little wretch in the manner of some inhuman mothers, who seem no less to have abandoned their humanity than to have parted with their chastity. It is the other part of your offence, therefore, upon which I intend to admonish you; I mean the violation of your chastity. A crime, however lightly it may be treated by debauched persons, very heinous in itself and very dreadful in its consequences.

"The heinous nature of this offence must be sufficiently apparent to every Christian, inasmuch as it is committed in defiance of the laws of our religion and of the express commands of Him who founded that religion.

"And here its consequences may well be argued to be dreadful; for what can be more so than to incur the divine displeasure by the breach of the divine commands, and that in an instance against which the highest vengeance is specifically denounced.

"But these things, though too little, I am afraid, regarded, are so plain that mankind, however they may want to be reminded, can never need information on this head. A hint, therefore, to awaken your sense of this matter shall suffice; for I would inspire you with repentance and not drive you to desperation.

"There are other consequences, not indeed so dreadful or replete with horror as this; and yet such as, if attentively considered, must, one would think, deter all of your sex at least from the commission of this crime.

"For by it you are rendered infamous and driven, like lepers of old, out of society; at least from the society of all but wicked and reprobate persons, for no others will associate with you.

"If you have fortunes, you are hereby rendered incapable of enjoying them; if you have none, you are disabled from acquiring any; nay, almost of procuring your sustenance, for no persons of character will receive you into their houses. Thus you are often driven by necessity itself into a state of shame and misery, which unavoidably ends in the destruction of both body and soul.

"Can any pleasure compensate these evils? Can any temptation have sophistry and delusion strong enough to persuade you to so simple a bargain? Or can any carnal appetite so overpower your reason, or so totally lay it asleep, as to prevent your flying with affright and terror from a crime which carries such punishment always with it?

"How base and mean must that woman be, how void of that dignity of mind and decent pride without which we are not worthy the name of human creatures, who can bear to level herself with the lowest animal and to sacrifice all that is great and noble in her, all her heavenly part, to an appetite which she hath in common with the vilest branch of the creation! For no woman, sure, will plead the passion of love for an excuse. This would be to own herself the mere tool and bubble of the man. Love, however barbarously we may corrupt and pervert its meaning, as it is a laudable is
43

a rational passion, and can never be violent but when reciprocal; for though the Scripture bids us love our enemies, it means not with that fervent love which we naturally bear towards our friends; much less that we should sacrifice to them our lives, and what ought to be dearer to us, our innocence. Now in what light but that of an enemy can a reasonable woman regard the man who solicits her to entail on herself all the misery I have above described, and who would purchase to himself a short, trivial, contemptible pleasure so greatly at her expense! For, by the laws of custom, the whole shame, with all its dreadful consequences, falls entirely upon her. Can love, which always seeks the good of its object, attempt to betray a woman into a bargain where she is so greatly to be the loser? If such a corrupter, therefore, should have the impudence to pretend a real affection for her, ought not the woman to regard him not only as an enemy but as the worst of all enemies; a false, designing, treacherous, pretended friend, who intends not only to debauch her body but her understanding at the same time?"

Here, Jenny expressing great concern, Allworthy paused a moment and then proceeded: "I have talked thus to you, child, not to insult you for what is past and irrevocable but to caution and strengthen you for the future. Nor should I have taken this trouble but from some opinion of your good sense, notwithstanding the dreadful slip you have made, and from some hopes of your hearty repentance which are founded on the openness and sincerity of your confession. If these do not deceive me, I will take care to convey you from this scene of your shame, where you shall by being unknown avoid the punishment which, as I have said, is allotted to your crime in this world; and I hope, by repentance, you will avoid the much heavier sentence denounced against it in the other. Be a good girl the rest of your days, and want shall be no motive to your going astray; and believe me, there is more pleasure, even in this world, in an innocent and virtuous life than in one debauched and vicious.

"As to your child, let no thoughts concerning it molest you; I will provide for it in a better manner than you can ever hope. And now nothing remains but that you inform me who was the wicked man that seduced you; for my anger against him will be much greater than you have experienced on this occasion."

Jenny now first lifted her eyes from the ground, and with a modest look and decent voice thus began:

"To know you, sir, and not love your goodness would be an argument of total want of sense or goodness in any one. In me it would amount to the highest ingratitude not to feel in the most sensible manner the great degree of goodness you have been pleased to exert on this occasion. As to my concern for what is past, I know you will spare my blushes the repetition. My future conduct will much better declare my sentiments than any professions I can now make. I beg leave to assure you, sir, that I take your advice much kinder than your generous offer with which you concluded it. For, as you are pleased to say, sir, it is an instance of your opinion of my understanding"—here, her tears flowing apace, she stopped a few moments and then proceeded thus: "Indeed, sir, your kindness overcomes me; but I will endeavour to deserve this good opinion; for, if I have the understanding you are so kindly pleased to allow me, such advice cannot be thrown away upon me. I thank you, sir, heartily, for your intended kindness to my poor helpless child; he is innocent, and, I hope, will live to be grateful for all the favours you shall show him. But now, sir, I must on my knees entreat you not to persist in asking me to declare the father of my infant. I promise you faithfully you shall one day know, but I am under the most solemn ties and engagements of honour, as well as the most religious vows and protestations, to conceal his name at this time. And I know you too well to think you would desire I should sacrifice either my honour or my religion."

Mr. Allworthy, whom the least mention of these sacred words was sufficient to stagger, hesitated a moment before he replied; and then told her she had done wrong to enter into such engagements to a villain, but since she had, he could not insist on her breaking them. He said it was not from a motive of vain curiosity he had inquired but in order to punish the fellow; at least that he might not ignorantly confer favours on the undeserving.

As to these points, Jenny satisfied him by the most solemn assurances that the man was entirely out of his reach and was neither subject to his power nor in any probability of becoming an object of his goodness.

The ingenuity of this behaviour had gained Jenny so much credit with this worthy man that he easily believed what she told him; for as she had disdained to excuse herself by a lie, and had hazarded his farther displeasure in her present situation rather than she would forfeit her honour or integrity by betraying another, he had but little apprehension that she would be guilty of falsehood towards himself.

He therefore dismissed her with assurances that he would very soon remove her out of the reach of that obloquy she had incurred, concluding with some additional documents, in which he recommended repentance, saying, "Consider, child, there is one still to reconcile yourself to, whose favour is of much greater importance to you than mine."

8

A DIALOGUE BETWEEN MESDAMES BRIDGET AND DEBORAH, CONTAINING MORE AMUSEMENT BUT LESS INSTRUCTION THAN THE FORMER

When Mr. Allworthy had retired to his study with Jenny Jones, as hath been seen, Miss Bridget with the good house-keeper had betaken themselves to a post next adjoining to the said study; whence, through the conveyance of a key-hole, they sucked in at their ears the instructive lecture delivered by Mr. Allworthy, together with the answers of Jenny and, indeed, every other particular which passed in the last chapter.

This hole in her brother's study door was, indeed, as well known to Miss Bridget, and had been as frequently applied to by her, as the famous hole in the wall was by Thisbe of old. This served to many good purposes; for by such means Miss Bridget became often acquainted with her brother's inclinations without giving him the trouble of repeating them to her. It is true some inconveniences attended this intercourse, and she had sometimes reason to cry out with Thisbe in Shakespeare, "O wicked, wicked wall!" for as Mr. Allworthy was a justice of peace, certain things occurred in examinations concerning bastards and such like which are apt to give great offence to the chaste ears of virgins, especially when they approach the age of forty, as was the case of Miss Bridget. However, she had on such occasions the advantage of concealing her blushes from the eyes of men, and *De non apparentibus, et nonexistentibus eadem est ratio*. In English: "When a woman is not seen to blush, she doth not blush at all."

Both the good women kept strict silence during the whole scene between Mr. Allworthy and the girl; but as soon as it was ended, and that gentleman out of hearing, Mrs. Deborah could not help exclaiming against the clemency of her master, and especially against his suffering her to conceal the father of the child, which she swore she would have out of her before the sun set.

At these words Miss Bridget discomposed her features with a smile (a thing very unusual to her). Not that I would have my reader imagine that this was one of those wanton smiles which Homer would have you conceive came from Venus when he calls her the laughter-loving goddess; nor was it one of those smiles which Lady Seraphina shoots from the stage-box and which Venus would quit her immortality to be able to equal. No, this was rather one of those smiles which might be supposed to have come from the dimpled cheeks of the august Tisiphone or from one of the misses, her sisters.

With such a smile, then, and with a voice sweet as the evening breeze of Boreas in the pleasant month of November, Miss Bridget gently reproved the curiosity of Mrs. Deborah, a vice with which it seems the latter was too much tainted, and which the former inveighed against with great bitterness, adding that among all her faults, she thanked heaven, her enemies could not accuse her of prying into the affairs of other people.

She then proceeded to commend the honour and spirit with which Jenny had acted. She said she could not help agreeing with her brother that there was some merit in the sincerity of her confession and in her integrity to her lover; that she had always thought her a very good girl and doubted not but she had been seduced by some rascal, who had been infinitely more to blame than herself, and very probably had prevailed with her by a promise of marriage or some other treacherous proceeding.

This behaviour of Miss Bridget greatly surprised Mrs. Deborah; for this well-bred woman seldom opened her lips either to her master or his sister till she had first sounded their inclinations, with which her sentiments were always strictly consonant. Here, however, she thought she might have launched forth with safety; and the sagacious reader will not perhaps accuse her of want of sufficient forecast in so doing, but will rather admire with what wonderful celerity she tacked about when she found herself steering a wrong course.

"Nay, madam," said this able woman and truly great politician, "I must own I cannot help admiring the girl's spirit as well as your ladyship. And, as your ladyship says, if she was deceived by some wicked man, the poor wretch is to be pitied. And to be sure, as your ladyship says, the girl hath always appeared like a good, honest, plain girl, and not vain of her face, forsooth, as some wanton hussies in the neighbourhood are."

"You say true, Deborah," said Miss Bridget. "If the girl had been one of those vain trollops, of which we have too many in the parish, I should have condemned my brother for his lenity towards her. I saw two farmers' daughters at church the other day with bare necks. I protest they shocked me. If wenches will hang out lures for fellows, it is no matter what they suffer. I detest such creatures, and it would be much better for them that their faces had been seamed with the smallpox; but I must confess I never saw any of this wanton behaviour in poor Jenny; some artful villain, I am convinced, hath betrayed, nay perhaps forced her, and I pity the poor wretch with all my heart."

Mrs. Deborah approved all these sentiments; and the dialogue concluded with a general and bitter invective against beauty, and with many compassionate considerations for all honest, plain girls who are deluded by the wicked arts of deceitful men.

9

CONTAINING MATTERS WHICH WILL SURPRISE THE READER

Jenny returned home well pleased with the reception she had met with from Mr. Allworthy, whose indulgence to her she industriously made public; partly perhaps as a sacrifice to her own pride, and partly from the more prudent motive of reconciling her neighbours to her and silencing their clamours.

But though this latter view, if she indeed had it, may appear reasonable enough, yet the event did not answer her expectation; for when she was convened before the justice, and it was universally apprehended that the House of Correction would have been her fate, though some of the young women cried out it was good enough for her, and diverted themselves with the thoughts of her beating hemp in a silk gown, yet there were many others who began to pity her condition; but when it was known in what manner Mr. Allworthy had behaved, the tide turned against her. One said, "I'll assure you, madam hath had good luck." A second cried, "See what it is to be a favourite." A third, "Ay, this comes of her learning." Every person made some malicious comment or other on the occasion, and reflected on the partiality of the justice.

The behaviour of these people may appear impolitic and ungrateful to the reader who considers the power and the benevolence of Mr. Allworthy; but as to his power, he never used it, and as to his benevolence, he exerted so much that he had thereby disobliged all his neighbours; for it is a secret well known to great men that by conferring an obligation they do not always procure a friend, but are certain of creating many enemies.

Jenny was, however, by the care and goodness of Mr. Allworthy soon removed out of the reach of reproach; when malice, being no longer able to vent its rage on her, began to seek another object of its bitterness; and this was no less than Mr. Allworthy himself, for a whisper soon went abroad that he himself was the father of the foundling child.

This supposition so well reconciled his conduct to the general opinion that it met with universal assent; and the outcry against his lenity soon began to take another turn, and was changed into an invective against his cruelty to the poor girl. Very grave and good women exclaimed against men who begot children and then disowned them. Nor were there wanting some who, after the departure of Jenny, insinuated that she was spirited away with a design too black to be mentioned, and who gave frequent hints that a legal inquiry ought to be made into the whole matter and that some people should be forced to produce the girl.

These calumnies might have probably produced ill consequences (at the least might have occasioned some trouble) to a person of a more doubtful and suspicious character than Mr. Allworthy was blessed with; but in his case they had no such effect, and being heartily despised by him, they served only to afford an innocent amusement to the good gossips of the neighbourhood.

But as we cannot possibly divine what complexion our reader may be of, and as it will be some time before he will hear any more of Jenny, we think proper to give him a very early intimation that Mr. Allworthy was, and will hereafter appear to be, absolutely innocent of any criminal intention whatever. He had indeed committed no other than an error in politics by tempering justice with mercy and by refusing to gratify the good-natured disposition of the mob * with an object for their compassion to work on in the person of poor Jenny, whom, in order to pity, they desired to have seen sacrificed to ruin and infamy by a shameful correction in Bridewell.

So far from complying with this their inclination, by which all hopes of reformation would have been abolished, and even the gate shut against her if her own inclinations should ever hereafter lead her to choose the road of virtue, Mr. Allworthy rather chose to encourage the girl to return thither by the only possible means; for too true, I am afraid, it is that many women have become abandoned and have sunk to the last degree of vice by being unable to retrieve the first slip. This will be, I am afraid, always the case while they remain among their former acquaintance; it was therefore wisely done by Mr. Allworthy to remove Jenny to a place where she might enjoy the pleasure of reputation after having tasted the ill consequences of losing it.

To this place, therefore, wherever it was, we will wish her a good journey, and for the present take leave of her and of the little foundling, her child, having matters of much higher importance to communicate to the reader.

10

THE HOSPITALITY OF ALLWORTHY; WITH A SHORT SKETCH OF THE CHARACTERS OF TWO BROTHERS, A DOCTOR AND A CAPTAIN, WHO WERE ENTERTAINED BY THAT GENTLEMAN

Neither Mr. Allworthy's house nor his heart were shut against any part of mankind, but they were both more particularly open to men of merit. To say the truth, this was the only house in the kingdom where you was sure to gain a dinner by deserving it.

Above all others, men of genius and learning shared the principal place in his favour, and in these he had much discernment; for though he had missed the advantage of a learned education, yet being blessed with vast natural abilities, he had so well profited by a vigorous though late application to letters and by much conversation with men of

* Whenever this word occurs in our writings, it intends persons without virtue or sense in all stations, and many of the highest rank are often meant by it.

eminence in this way that he was himself a very competent judge in most kinds of literature.

It is no wonder that in an age when this kind of merit is so little in fashion, and so slenderly provided for, persons possessed of it should very eagerly flock to a place where they were sure of being received with great complaisance; indeed, where they might enjoy almost the same advantages of a liberal fortune as if they were entitled to it in their own right; for Mr. Allworthy was not one of those generous persons who are ready most bountifully to bestow meat, drink, and lodging on men of wit and learning, for which they expect no other return but entertainment, instruction, flattery, and subserviency; in a word, that such persons should be enrolled in the number of domestics, without wearing their master's clothes or receiving wages.

On the contrary, every person in this house was perfect master of his own time; and as he might at his pleasure satisfy all his appetites within the restrictions only of law, virtue, and religion, so he might, if his health required or his inclination prompted him to temperance or even to abstinence, absent himself from any meals or retire from them whenever he was so disposed, without even a solicitation to the contrary; for, indeed, such solicitations from superiors always savour very strongly of commands. But all here were free from such impertinence, not only those whose company is in all other places esteemed a favour from their equality of fortune, but even those whose indigent circumstances make such an eleemosynary abode convenient to them, and who are therefore less welcome to a great man's table because they stand in need of it.

Among others of this kind was Dr. Blifil, a gentleman who had the misfortune of losing the advantage of great talents by the obstinacy of a father who would breed him to a profession he disliked. In obedience to this obstinacy, the doctor had in his youth been obliged to study physic, or rather to say he studied it; for in reality books of this kind were almost the only ones with which he was unacquainted, and unfortunately for him, the doctor was master of almost every other science but that by which he was to get his bread; the consequence of which was that the doctor at the age of forty had no bread to eat.

Such a person as this was certain to find a welcome at Mr. Allworthy's table, to whom misfortunes were ever a recommendation when they were derived from the folly or villainy of others, and not of the unfortunate person himself. Besides this negative merit, the doctor had one positive recommendation. This was a great appearance of religion. Whether his religion was real or consisted only in appearance, I shall not presume to say, as I am not possessed of any touchstone which can distinguish the true from the false.

If this part of his character pleased Mr. Allworthy, it delighted Miss Bridget. She engaged him in many religious controversies, on which occasions she constantly expressed great satisfaction in the doctor's knowledge, and not much less in the compliments which he frequently bestowed on her own. To say the truth, she had read much English divinity, and had puzzled more than one of the neighbouring curates. Indeed her conversation was so pure, her looks so sage, and her whole deportment so grave and solemn that she seemed to deserve the name of saint equally with her namesake or with any other female in the Roman calendar.

As sympathies of all kinds are apt to beget love, so experience teaches us that none have a more direct tendency this way than those of a religious kind between persons of different sexes. The doctor found himself so agreeable to Miss Bridget that he now began to lament an unfortunate accident which had happened to him about ten years before: namely, his marriage with another woman, who was not only still alive but, what was worse, known to be so by Mr. Allworthy. This was a fatal bar to that happiness which he otherwise saw sufficient probability of obtaining with this young lady; for as to criminal indulgences, he certainly never thought of them. This was owing either to his religion, as is most probable, or to the purity of his passion, which was fixed on those things which matrimony only, and not criminal correspondence, could put him in possession of or could give him any title to.

He had not long ruminated on these matters before it occurred to his memory that he had a brother who was under no such unhappy incapacity. This brother he made no doubt would succeed, for he discerned, as he thought, an inclination to marriage in the lady; and the reader, perhaps, when he hears the brother's qualifications, will not blame the confidence which he entertained of his success.

This gentleman was about thirty-five years of age. He was of a middle size and what is called well built. He had a scar on his forehead, which did not so much injure his beauty as it denoted his valour (for he was a half-pay officer). He had good teeth, and something affable, when he pleased, in his smile; though naturally his countenance as well as his air and voice had much of roughness in it, yet he could at any time deposit this and appear all gentleness and good humour. He was not ungenteel nor entirely void of wit, and in his youth had abounded in spriteliness, which, though he had lately put on a more serious character, he could, when he pleased, resume.

He had, as well as the doctor, an academic education, for his father had with the same paternal authority we have mentioned before decreed him for holy orders; but as the old gentleman died before he was ordained, he chose the church militant and preferred the king's commission to the bishop's.

He had purchased the post of lieutenant of dragoons, and afterwards came to be a captain; but having quarrelled with his colonel, was by his interest obliged to sell; from which time he had entirely rusticated himself, had betaken himself to studying the Scriptures, and was not a little suspected of an inclination to Methodism.

It seemed therefore not unlikely that such a person should succeed with a lady of so saint-like a disposition, and whose inclinations were no otherwise engaged than to the married state in general; but why the doctor, who certainly had no great friendship for his brother, should for his sake think of making so ill a return to the hospitality of Allworthy is a matter not so easy to be accounted for.

Is it that some natures delight in evil, as others are thought to delight in virtue? Or is there a pleasure in being accessary to a theft when we cannot commit it ourselves? Or lastly (which experience seems to make probable), have we a satisfaction in aggrandizing our families, even though we have not the least love or respect for them?

Whether any of these motives operated on the doctor, we will not determine; but so the fact was. He sent for his brother and easily found means to introduce him at Allworthy's as a person who intended only a short visit to himself.

The captain had not been in the house a week before the doctor had reason to felicitate himself on his discernment. The captain was indeed as great a master of the art of love as Ovid was formerly. He had, besides, received proper hints from his brother, which he failed not to improve to the best advantage.

11

It hath been observed by wise men or women, I forget which, that all persons are doomed to be in love once in their lives. No particular season is, as I remember, assigned for this; but the age at which Miss Bridget was arrived seems to me as proper a period as any to be fixed on for this purpose; it often indeed happens much earlier, but when it doth not, I have observed, it seldom or never fails about this time. Moreover, we may remark that at this season love is of a more serious and steady nature than what sometimes shows itself in the younger parts of life. The love of girls is uncertain, capricious, and so foolish that we cannot always discover what the young lady would be at; nay, it may almost be doubted whether she always knows this herself.

Now, we are never at a loss to discern this in women about forty; for as such grave, serious, and experienced ladies well know their own meaning, so it is always very easy for a man of the least sagacity to discover it with the utmost certainty.

Miss Bridget is an example of all these observations. She had not been many times in the captain's company before she was seized with this passion. Nor did she go pining and moping about the house like a puny foolish girl, ignorant of her distemper: she felt, she knew, and she enjoyed the pleasing sensation, of which, as she was certain it was not only innocent but laudable, she was neither afraid nor ashamed.

And to say the truth, there is in all points great difference between the reasonable passion which women at this age conceive towards men and the idle and childish liking of a girl to a boy, which is often fixed on the outside only, and on things of little value and no duration: as on cherry cheeks, small lily-white hands, sloe-black eyes, flowing locks, downy chins, dapper shades, nay, sometimes on charms more worthless than these, and less the party's own: such are the outward ornaments of the person, and for which men are beholden to the tailor, the lace-man, the periwig-maker, the hatter, and the milliner, and not to Nature. Such a passion girls may well be ashamed, as they generally are, to own either to themselves or to others.

The love of Miss Bridget was of another kind. The captain owed nothing to any of these fop-makers in his dress, nor was his person much more beholden to Nature. Both his dress and person were such as, had they appeared in an assembly or a drawing-room, would have been the contempt and ridicule of all the fine ladies there. The former of these was indeed neat, but plain, coarse, ill-fancied, and out of fashion. As for the latter, we have expressly described it above. So far was the skin on his cheeks from being cherry-coloured that you could not discern what the natural colour of his cheeks was, they being totally overgrown by a black beard, which ascended to his eyes. His shape and limbs were indeed exactly proportioned, but so large that they denoted the strength rather of a ploughman than any other. His shoulders were broad beyond all size, and the calves of his legs larger than those of a common chairman. In short, his whole person wanted all that elegance and beauty which is the very reverse of clumsy strength, and which so agreeably sets off most of our fine gentlemen; being partly owing to the high blood of their ancestors, viz., blood made of rich sauces and generous wines, and partly to an early town education.

Though Miss Bridget was a woman of the greatest delicacy of taste, yet such were the charms of the captain's conversation that she totally overlooked the defects of his person. She imagined, and perhaps very wisely, that she should enjoy more agreeable minutes with the captain than with a much prettier fellow; and forewent the consideration of pleasing her eyes in order to procure herself much more solid satisfaction.

The captain no sooner perceived the passion of Miss Bridget, in which discovery he was very quick-sighted, than he faithfully returned it. The lady no more than her lover was remarkable for beauty. I would attempt to draw her picture, but that is done already by a more able master, Mr. Hogarth himself, to whom she sat many years ago, and hath been lately exhibited by that gentleman in his print of a winter's morning, of which she was no improper emblem, and may be seen walking (for walk she doth in the print) to Covent Garden church, with a starved footboy behind carrying her prayer-book.

The captain likewise very wisely preferred the more solid enjoyments he expected with this lady to the fleeting charms of person. He was one of those wise men who regard beauty in the other sex as a very worthless and superficial qualification; or, to speak more truly, who rather choose to possess every convenience of life with an ugly woman than a handsome one without any of those conveniences. And having a very good appetite, and but little nicety, he fancied he should play his part very well at the matrimonial banquet without the sauce of beauty.

To deal plainly with the reader, the captain, ever since his arrival, at least from the moment his brother had proposed the match to him, long before he had discovered any flattering symptoms in Miss Bridget, had been greatly enamoured; that is to say, of Mr. Allworthy's house and gardens and of his lands, tenements, and hereditaments; of all which the captain was so passionately fond that he would most probably have contracted marriage with them had he been obliged to have taken the witch of Endor into the bargain.

As Mr. Allworthy, therefore, had declared to the doctor that he never intended to take a second wife, as his sister was his nearest relation, and as the doctor had fished out that his intentions were to make any child of hers his heir, which indeed the law without his interposition would have done for him, the doctor and his brother thought it an act of benevolence to give being to a human creature who would be so plentifully provided with the most essential means of happiness. The whole thoughts, therefore, of both the brothers were how to engage the affections of this amiable lady.

But Fortune, who is a tender parent, and often doth more for her favourite offspring than either they deserve or wish, had been so industrious for the captain that whilst he was laying schemes to execute his purpose the lady conceived the same desires with himself, and was on her side contriving how to give the captain proper encouragement without appearing too forward, for she was a strict observer of all rules of decorum. In this, however, she easily succeeded; for as the captain was always on the look-out, no glance, gesture, or word escaped him.

The satisfaction which the captain received from the kind behaviour of Miss Bridget was not a little abated by his apprehensions of Mr. Allworthy; for, notwithstanding his disinterested professions, the captain imagined he would, when he came to act, follow the example of the rest of the world and refuse his consent to a match so disadvantageous in point of interest to his sister. From what oracle he received this opinion I shall leave the reader to determine; but, however he came by it, it strangely perplexed him how to regulate his conduct so as at once to convey his affection to the lady and to conceal it from her brother. He at length resolved to take all private opportunities of making his addresses, but in the presence of Mr. Allworthy to be as reserved and as much upon his guard as was possible; and this conduct was highly approved by the brother.

He soon found means to make his addresses in express terms to his mistress, from whom he received an answer in the proper form, viz., the answer which was first made some thousands of years ago, and which hath been handed down by tradition from mother to daughter ever since. If I was to translate this into Latin, I should render it by these two words, *Nolo Episcopari*: a phrase likewise of immemorial use on another occasion.

The captain, however he came by his knowledge, perfectly well understood the lady, and very soon after repeated his application with more warmth and earnestness than before, and was again, according to due form, rejected; but as he had increased in the eagerness of his desires, so the lady with the same propriety decreased in the violence of her refusal.

Not to tire the reader by leading him through every scene of this courtship (which, though in the opinion of a certain great author it is the pleasantest scene of life to the actor, is, perhaps, as dull and tiresome as any whatever to the audience), the captain made his advances in form, the citadel was defended in form, and at length, in proper form, surrendered at discretion.

During this whole time, which filled the space of near a month, the captain preserved great distance of behaviour to his lady in the presence of the brother; and the more he succeeded with her in private, the more reserved was he in public. And as for the lady, she had no sooner secured her lover than she behaved to him before company with the highest degree of indifference, so that Mr. Allworthy must have had the insight of the Devil (or perhaps some of his worse qualities) to have entertained the least suspicion of what was going forward.

12

In all bargains, whether to fight or to marry, or concerning any other such business, little previous ceremony is required to bring the matter to an issue when both parties are really in earnest. This was the case at present, and in less than a month the captain and his lady were man and wife.

The great concern now was to break the matter to Mr. Allworthy; and this was undertaken by the doctor.

One day, then, as Allworthy was walking in his garden the doctor came to him and, with great gravity of aspect and all the concern which he could possibly affect in his countenance, said, "I am come, sir, to impart an affair to you of the utmost consequence; but how shall I mention to you what it almost distracts me to think of!" He then launched forth into the most bitter invectives both against men and women, accusing the former of having no attachment but to their interest and the latter of being so addicted to vicious inclinations that they could never be safely trusted with one of the other sex. "Could I," said he, "sir, have suspected that a lady of such prudence, such judgement, such learning, should indulge so indiscreet a passion; or could I have imagined that my brother—why do I call him so? He is no longer a brother of mine——"

"Indeed but he is," said Allworthy, "and a brother of mine too."—"Bless me, sir," said the doctor, "do you know the shocking affair?"—"Look'ee, Mr. Blifil," answered the good man, "it hath been my constant maxim in life to make the best of all matters which happen. My sister, though many years younger than me, is at least old enough to be at the age of discretion. Had he imposed on a child, I should have been more averse to have forgiven him; but a woman upwards of thirty must certainly be supposed to know what will make her most happy. She hath married a gentleman, though perhaps not quite her equal in fortune; and if he hath any perfections in her eye which can make up that deficiency, I see no reason why I should object to her choice of her own happiness, which I, no more than herself, imagine to consist only in immense wealth. I might, perhaps, from the many declarations I have made of complying with almost any proposal, have expected to have been consulted on this occasion; but these matters are of a very delicate nature, and the scruples of modesty, perhaps, are not to be overcome. As to your brother, I have really no anger against him at all. He hath no obligation to me, nor do I think he was under any necessity of asking my consent, since the woman is, as I have said, *sui juris*, and of a proper age to be entirely answerable only to herself for her conduct."

The doctor repeated his accusations against his brother, accused Mr. Allworthy of too great lenity, and declared that he should never more be brought either to see or to own him for his relation. He then launched forth into a panegyric on Allworthy's goodness, into the highest encomiums on his friendship; and concluded by saying he should never forgive his brother for having put the place which he bore in that friendship to a hazard.

Allworthy thus answered: "Had I conceived any displeasure against your brother, I should never have carried that resentment to the innocent, but, I assure you, I have no such displeasure. Your brother appears to me to be a man of sense and honour. I do not disapprove the taste of my sister, nor will I doubt but that she is equally the object of his inclinations. I have always thought love the only foundation of happiness in a married state, as it can only produce that high and tender friendship which should always be the cement of this union; and in my opinion, all those marriages which are contracted from other motives are greatly criminal; they are a profanation of a most holy ceremony and generally end in disquiet and misery; for surely we may call it a profanation to convert this most sacred institution into a wicked sacrifice to lust or avarice, and what better can be said of those matches to which men are induced merely by the consideration of a beautiful person or a great fortune!

"To deny that beauty is an agreeable object to the eye, and even worthy some admiration, would be false and foolish. *Beautiful* is an epithet often used in Scripture, and always mentioned with honour. It was my own fortune to marry a woman whom the world thought handsome, and I can truly say I liked her the better on that account. But to make this the sole consideration of marriage, to lust after it so violently as to overlook all imperfections for its sake, or to require it so absolutely as to reject and disdain religion, virtue, and sense, which are qualities in their nature of much higher perfection, because an elegance of person only is wanting—this is surely inconsistent, either with a wise man or a good Christian. And it is, perhaps, being too charitable to conclude that such persons mean anything more by their marriage than to please their carnal appetites, for the satisfaction of which, we are taught, it was not ordained.

"In the next place, with respect to fortune. Worldly prudence, perhaps, exacts some consideration on this head; nor will I absolutely and altogether condemn it. As the world is constituted, the demands of a married state and the care of posterity require some little regard to what we call circumstances. Yet this provision is greatly increased beyond what is really necessary by folly and vanity, which create abundantly more wants than Nature. Equipage for the wife and large fortunes for the children are by custom enrolled in the list of necessaries, and to procure these, everything truly solid and sweet and virtuous and religious are neglected and overlooked.

"And this in many degrees, the last and greatest of which seems scarce distinguishable from madness. I mean where persons of immense fortunes contract themselves to those who are, and must be, disagreeable to them; to fools and knaves, in order to increase an estate already larger even than the demands of their pleasures. Surely such persons, if they will not be thought mad, must own either that they are incapable of tasting the sweets of the tenderest friendship, or that they sacrifice the greatest happiness of which they are capable to the vain, uncertain, and senseless laws of vulgar opinion, which owe as well their force, as their foundation, to folly."

Here Allworthy concluded his sermon, to which Blifil had listened with the profoundest attention, though it cost him some pains to prevent now and then a small discomposure of his muscles. He now praised every period of what he had heard with the warmth of a young divine who hath the honour to dine with a bishop the same day in which his lordship hath mounted the pulpit.

13

The reader from what hath been said may imagine that the reconciliation (if indeed it could be so called) was only matter of form; we shall therefore pass it over and hasten to what must surely be thought matter of substance.

The doctor had acquainted his brother with what had passed between Mr. Allworthy and him, and added with a smile, "I promise you, I paid you off; nay, I absolutely desired the good gentleman not to forgive you; for you know, after he had made a declaration in your favour, I might with safety venture on such a request with a person of his temper, and I was willing, as well for your sake as for my own, to prevent the least possibility of a suspicion."

Captain Blifil took not the least notice of this, at that time, but he afterwards made a very notable use of it.

One of the maxims which the Devil in a late visit upon earth left to his disciples is, when once you are got up, to kick the stool from under you. In plain English, when you have made your fortune by the good offices of a friend, you are advised to discard him as soon as you can.

Whether the captain acted by this maxim, I will not positively determine; so far, we may confidently say that his actions may be fairly derived from this diabolical principle, and, indeed, it is difficult to assign any other motive to them; for no sooner was he possessed of Miss Bridget and reconciled to Allworthy than he began to show a coldness to his brother, which increased daily, till at length it grew into rudeness and became very visible to every one.

The doctor remonstrated to him privately concerning this behaviour, but could obtain no other satisfaction than the following plain declaration: "If you dislike anything in my brother's house, sir, you know you are at liberty to quit it." This strange, cruel, and almost unaccountable ingratitude in the captain absolutely broke the poor doctor's heart; for ingratitude never so thoroughly pierces the human breast as when it proceeds from those in whose behalf we have been guilty of transgressions. Reflections on great and good actions, however they are received or returned by those in whose favour they are performed, always administer some comfort to us; but what consolation shall we receive under so biting a calamity as the ungrateful behaviour of our friend, when our wounded conscience at the same time flies in our face and upbraids us with having spotted it in the service of one so worthless?

Mr. Allworthy himself spoke to the captain in his brother's behalf, and desired to know what offence the doctor had committed; when the hard-hearted villain had the baseness to say that he should never forgive him for the injury which he had endeavoured to do him in his favour, which, he said, he had pumped out of him, and was such a cruelty that it ought not to be forgiven.

Allworthy spoke in very high terms upon this declaration, which, he said, became not a human creature. He expressed, indeed, so much resentment against unforgiving temper that the captain at last pretended to be convinced by his arguments, and outwardly professed to be reconciled.

As for the bride, she was now in her honeymoon, and so passionately fond of her new husband that he never appeared to her to be in the wrong; and his displeasure against any person was a sufficient reason for her dislike to the same.

The captain at Mr. Allworthy's instance was outwardly, as we have said, reconciled to his brother, yet the same rancour remained in his heart; and he found so many opportunities of giving him private hints of this that the house at last grew insupportable to the poor doctor, and he chose rather to submit to any inconveniences which he might encounter in the world than longer to bear these cruel and ungraceful insults from a brother for whom he had done so much.

He once intended to acquaint Allworthy with the whole; but he could not bring himself to submit to the confession by which he must take to his share so great a portion of guilt. Besides, by how much the worse man he represented his brother to be, so much the greater would his own offence appear to Allworthy, and so much the greater, had he reason to imagine, would be his resentment.

He feigned, therefore, some excuse of business for his departure, and promised to return soon again; and took leave of his brother with so well-dissembled content that, as the captain played his part to the same perfection, Allworthy remained well satisfied with the truth of the reconciliation.

The doctor went directly to London, where he died soon after of a broken heart, a distemper which kills many more than is generally imagined, and would have a fair title to a place in the bill of mortality did it not differ in one instance from all other diseases, viz., that no physician can cure it.

Now, upon the most diligent inquiry into the former lives of these two brothers, I find, besides the cursed and hellish maxim of policy above mentioned, another reason for the captain's conduct: the captain, besides what we have before said of him, was a man of great pride and fierceness, and had always treated his brother, who was of a different complexion and greatly deficient in both these qualities, with the utmost air of superiority. The doctor, however, had much the larger share of learning, and was by many reputed to have the better understanding. This the captain knew and could not bear, for though envy is at best a very malignant passion, yet is its bitterness greatly heightened by mixing with contempt towards the same object; and very much afraid I am that whenever an obligation is joined to these two, indignation and not gratitude will be the product of all three.

BOOK II

CONTAINING SCENES OF MATRIMONIAL FELICITY IN
DIFFERENT DEGREES OF LIFE; AND VARIOUS OTHER
TRANSACTIONS DURING THE FIRST TWO YEARS AFTER
THE MARRIAGE BETWEEN CAPTAIN BLIFIL AND MISS
BRIDGET ALLWORTHY

1

SHOWING WHAT KIND OF A HISTORY THIS IS; WHAT IT IS LIKE,
AND WHAT IT IS NOT LIKE

Though we have properly enough entitled this our work a
history, and not a life, nor an apology for a life, as is
more in fashion, yet we intend in it rather to pursue the
method of those writers who profess to disclose the revolutions of countries than to imitate the painful and voluminous historian, who, to preserve the regularity of his series,
thinks himself obliged to fill up as much paper with the
detail of months and years in which nothing remarkable
happened as he employs upon those notable eras when the
greatest scenes have been transacted on the human stage.

Such histories as these do, in reality, very much resemble a newspaper, which consists of just the same number
of words whether there be any news in it or not. They
may, likewise, be compared to a stage-coach, which performs
constantly the same course empty as well as full. The writer,
indeed, seems to think himself obliged to keep even pace
with time, whose amanuensis he is; and like his master
travels as slowly through centuries of monkish dullness,
when the world seems to have been asleep, as through that
bright and busy age so nobly distinguished by the excellent
Latin poet:

Ad confligendum venientibus undique Pœnis,
Omnia cum belli trepido concussa tumultu
Horrida contremuere sub altis œtheris auris;
In dubioque fuit sub utrorum regna cadendum
Omnibus humanis esset, terraque marique.

Of which we wish we could give our reader a more adequate translation than that by Mr. Creech:

When dreadful Carthage frighted Rome with arms,
And all the world was shook with fierce alarms;
Whilst undecided yet, which part should fall,
Which nation rise the glorious lord of all.

Now, it is our purpose in the ensuing pages to pursue a contrary method. When any extraordinary scene presents itself (as we trust will often be the case), we shall spare no pains nor paper to open it at large to our reader; but if whole years should pass without producing anything worthy his notice, we shall not be afraid of a chasm in our history, but shall hasten on to matters of consequence and leave such periods of time totally unobserved.

These are indeed to be considered as blanks in the grand lottery of time. We therefore who are the registers of that lottery shall imitate those sagacious persons who deal in that which is drawn at guild-hall, and who never trouble the public with the many blanks they dispose of; but when a great prize happens to be drawn, the newspapers are presently filled with it, and the world is sure to be informed at whose office it was sold; indeed, commonly two or three different offices lay claim to the honour of having disposed of it, by which, I suppose, the adventurers are given to understand that certain brokers are in the secrets of Fortune, and indeed of her cabinet council.

My reader, then, is not to be surprised if in the course of this work he shall find some chapters very short, and others altogether as long; some that contain only the time of a single day, and others that comprise years; in a word, if my history sometimes seems to stand still and sometimes to fly. For all which I shall not look on myself as accountable to any court of critical jurisdiction whatever; for as I am, in reality, the founder of a new province of writing, so I am at liberty to make what laws I please therein. And these laws my readers, whom I consider as my subjects, are bound to believe in and to obey; with which that they may readily and cheerfully comply, I do hereby assure them that I shall principally regard their ease and advantage in all such institutions; for I do not, like a *jure divino* tyrant, imagine that they are my slaves or my commodity. I am, indeed, set over them for their own good only, and was created for their use and not they for mine. Nor do I doubt, while I make their interest the great rule of my writings, they will unanimously concur in supporting my dignity and in rendering me all the honour I shall deserve or desire.

2

RELIGIOUS CAUTIONS AGAINST SHOWING TOO MUCH FAVOUR TO
BASTARDS, AND A GREAT DISCOVERY MADE BY MRS. DEBORAH
WILKINS

Eight months after the celebration of the nuptials between Captain Blifil and Miss Bridget Allworthy, a young lady of great beauty, merit, and fortune, was Miss Bridget by reason of a fright delivered of a fine boy. The child was, indeed, to all appearance perfect; but the midwife discovered it was born a month before its full time.

Though the birth of an heir of his beloved sister was a circumstance of great joy to Mr. Allworthy, yet it did not alienate his affections from the little foundling to whom he had been godfather, had given his own name of Thomas, and whom he had hitherto seldom failed of visiting at least once a day in his nursery.

He told his sister, if she pleased, the new-born infant should be bred up together with little Tommy, to which she consented though with some little reluctance; for she had truly a great complaisance for her brother, and hence she had always behaved towards the foundling with rather more kindness than ladies of rigid virtue can sometimes bring themselves to show to these children, who, however innocent, may be truly called the living monuments of incontinence.

The captain could not so easily bring himself to bear what he condemned as a fault in Mr. Allworthy. He gave him frequent hints that to adopt the fruits of sin was to give countenance to it. He quoted several texts (for he was well read in Scripture), such as, "He visits the sins of the fathers upon the children"; and, "The fathers have eaten sour grapes, and the children's teeth are set on edge," etc. Whence he argued the legality of punishing the crime of the parent on the bastard. He said though the law did not positively allow the destroying such base-born children, yet it held them to be the children of nobody; that the Church considered them as the children of nobody; and that at the best they ought to be brought up to the lowest and vilest offices of the commonwealth.

Mr. Allworthy answered to all this and much more which the captain had urged on this subject that, however guilty the parents might be, the children were certainly innocent; that as to the texts he had quoted, the former of them was a particular denunciation against the Jews for the sin of idolatry, of relinquishing and hating their heavenly King, and the latter was parabolically spoken, and rather intended to denote the certain and necessary consequences of sin than any express judgement against it. But to represent the Almighty as avenging the sins of the guilty on the innocent was indecent, if not blasphemous; as it was to represent Him acting against the first principles of natural justice, and against the original notions of right and wrong, which He himself had implanted in our minds, by which we were to judge not only in all matters which were not revealed but even of the truth of Revelation itself. He said he knew many held the same principles with the captain on this head, but he was himself firmly convinced to the contrary, and would provide in the same manner for this poor infant as if a legitimate child had had the fortune to have been found in the same place.

While the captain was taking all opportunities to press these and suchlike arguments to relieve the little foundling from Mr. Allworthy's, of whose fondness for him he began to be jealous, Mrs. Deborah had made a discovery which in its event threatened at least to prove more fatal to poor Tommy than all the reasonings of the captain.

Whether the insatiable curiosity of this good woman had carried her on to that business, or whether she did it to confirm herself in the good graces of Mrs. Blifil, who notwithstanding her outward behaviour to the foundling frequently abused the infant in private, and her brother too for his fondness to it, I will not determine; but she had now, as she conceived, fully detected the father of the foundling.

Now, as this was a discovery of great consequence, it may be necessary to trace it from the fountain-head. We shall therefore very minutely lay open those previous matters by which it was produced; and for that purpose, we shall be obliged to reveal all the secrets of a little family with which my reader is at present entirely unacquainted, and of which the economy was so rare and extraordinary that I fear it will shock the utmost credulity of many married persons.

3

THE DESCRIPTION OF A DOMESTIC GOVERNMENT FOUNDED UPON RULES DIRECTLY CONTRARY TO THOSE OF ARISTOTLE

My reader may please to remember he hath been informed that Jenny Jones had lived some years with a certain schoolmaster, who had at her earnest desire instructed her in Latin, in which, to do justice to her genius, she had so improved herself that she was become a better scholar than her master.

Indeed, though this poor man had undertaken a profession to which learning must be allowed necessary, this was the least of his commendations. He was one of the best-natured fellows in the world, and was at the same time master of so much pleasantry and humour that he was reputed the wit of the country; and all the neighbouring gentlemen were so desirous of his company that, as denying was not his talent, he spent much time at their houses, which he might with more emolument have spent in his school.

It may be imagined that a gentleman so qualified and so disposed was in no danger of becoming formidable to the learned seminaries of Eton or Westminster. To speak plainly, his scholars were divided into two classes: in the upper of which was a young gentleman, the son of a neighbouring squire, who at the age of seventeen was just entered into his Syntaxis; and in the lower was a second son of the same gentleman, who, together with seven parish-boys, was learning to read and write.

The stipend arising hence would hardly have indulged the schoolmaster in the luxuries of life had he not added to this office those of clerk and barber, and had not Mr. Allworthy added to the whole an annuity of ten pound, which the poor man received every Christmas, and with which he was enabled to cheer his heart during that sacred festival.

Among his other treasures the pedagogue had a wife, whom

he had married out of Mr. Allworthy's kitchen for her fortune, viz., twenty pound, which she had there amassed.

This woman was not very amiable in her person. Whether she sat to my friend Hogarth or no, I will not determine, but she exactly resembled the young woman who is pouring out her mistress's tea in the third picture of the *Harlot's Progress*. She was, besides, a professed follower of that notable sect founded by Xantippe of old, by means of which she became more formidable in the school than her husband; for, to confess the truth, he was never master there or anywhere else in her presence.

Though her countenance did not denote much natural sweetness of temper, yet this was, perhaps, somewhat soured by a circumstance which generally poisons matrimonial felicity; for children are rightly called the pledges of love, and her husband, though they had been married nine years, had given her no such pledges; a default for which he had no excuse either from age or health, being not yet thirty years old and what they call a jolly, brisk young man.

Hence arose another evil, which produced no little uneasiness to the poor pedagogue, of whom she maintained so constant a jealousy that he durst hardly speak to one woman in the parish; for the least degree of civility or even correspondence with any female was sure to bring his wife upon her back and his own.

In order to guard herself against matrimonial injuries in her own house, as she kept one maidservant, she always took care to choose her out of that order of females whose faces are taken as a kind of security for their virtue; of which number Jenny Jones, as the reader hath been before informed, was one.

As the face of this young woman might be called pretty good security of the before-mentioned kind, and as her behaviour had been always extremely modest, which is the certain consequence of understanding in women, she had passed above four years at Mr. Partridge's (for that was the schoolmaster's name) without creating the least suspicion in her mistress. Nay, she had been treated with uncommon kindness, and her mistress had permitted Mr. Partridge to give her those instructions which have been before commemorated.

But it is with jealousy as with the gout. When such distempers are in the blood, there is never any security against their breaking out; and that often on the slightest occasions and when least suspected.

Thus it happened to Mrs. Partridge, who had submitted four years to her husband's teaching this young woman, and had suffered her often to neglect her work in order to pursue her learning. For passing by one day as the girl was reading and her master leaning over her, the girl, I know not for what reason, suddenly started up from her chair; and this was the first time that suspicion ever entered into the head of her mistress.

This did not, however, at that time discover itself, but lay lurking in her mind like a concealed enemy, who waits for a reinforcement of additional strength before he openly declares himself and proceeds upon hostile operations; and such additional strength soon arrived to corroborate her suspicion, for not long after, the husband and wife being at dinner, the master said to his maid, *"Da mihi aliquid potum,"* upon which the poor girl smiled, perhaps at the badness of the Latin, and when her mistress cast her eyes on her, blushed, possibly with a consciousness of having laughed at her master. Mrs. Partridge upon this immediately fell into a fury, and discharged the trencher on which she was eating at the head of poor Jenny, crying out, "You impudent whore, do you play tricks with my husband before my face?" and at the same instant rose from her chair with a knife in her hand, with which, most probably, she would have executed very tragical vengeance had not the girl taken the advantage of being nearer the door than her mistress, and avoided her fury by running away; for as to the poor husband, whether surprise had rendered him motionless, or fear (which is full as probable) had restrained him from venturing at any opposition, he sat staring and trembling in his chair; nor did he once offer to move or speak till his wife, returning from the pursuit of Jenny, made some defensive measures necessary for his own preservation, and he likewise was obliged to retreat after the example of the maid.

This good woman was, no more than Othello, of a disposition,

> To make a life of jealousy,
> And follow still the changes of the moon
> With fresh suspicions——

With her, as well as him,

> To be once in doubt,
> Was once to be resolved——

She therefore ordered Jenny immediately to pack up her alls and be gone, for that she was determined she should not sleep that night within her walls.

Mr. Partridge had profited too much by experience to interpose in a matter of this nature. He therefore had recourse to his usual recipe of patience; for though he was not a great adept in Latin, he remembered and well understood the advice contained in these words:

Leve fit, quod bene fertur onus.

In English:

A burden becomes lightest when it is well borne, which he had always in his mouth, and of which, to say the truth, he had often occasion to experience the truth.

Jenny offered to make protestations of her innocence, but the tempest was too strong for her to be heard. She then betook herself to the business of packing, for which a small quantity of brown paper sufficed; and, having received her small pittance of wages, she returned home.

The schoolmaster and his consort passed their time unpleasantly enough that evening, but something or other happened before the next morning which a little abated the fury of Mrs. Partridge, and she at length admitted her husband to make his excuses. To which she gave the readier belief, as he had, instead of desiring her to recall Jenny, professed a satisfaction in her being dismissed, saying she was grown of little use as a servant, spending all her time in reading, and was become, moreover, very pert and obstinate; for, indeed, she and her master had lately had frequent disputes in literature, in which, as hath been said, she was become greatly his superior. This, however, he would by no means allow; and as he called her persisting in the right obstinacy, he began to hate her with no small inveteracy.

4

CONTAINING ONE OF THE MOST BLOODY BATTLES, OR RATHER
DUELS, THAT WERE EVER RECORDED IN DOMESTIC HISTORY

For the reasons mentioned in the preceding chapter, and
from some other matrimonial concessions well known to most
husbands, and which like the secrets of freemasonry should
be divulged to none who are not members of that
honourable fraternity, Mrs. Partridge was pretty well satisfied
that she had condemned her husband without cause, and endeavoured by acts of kindness to make him amends for her
false suspicion. Her passions were, indeed, equally violent
whichever way they inclined; for, as she could be extremely
angry, so could she be altogether as fond.

But though these passions ordinarily succeeded each other,
and scarce twenty-four hours ever passed in which the
pedagogue was not in some degree the object of both, yet on
extraordinary occasions, when the passion of anger had
raged very high, the remission was usually longer; and so was
the case at present; for she continued longer in a state of affability after this fit of jealousy was ended than her husband
had ever known before, and had it not been for some little
exercises, which all the followers of Xantippe are obliged to
perform daily, Mr. Partridge would have enjoyed a perfect
serenity of several months.

Perfect calms at sea are always suspected by the experienced mariner to be the forerunners of a storm; and I
know some persons who, without being generally the dev-
otees of superstition, are apt to apprehend that great and
unusual peace or tranquillity will be attended with its opposite; for which reason the ancients used on such occasions to sacrifice to the goddess Nemesis, a deity who was
thought by them to look with an invidious eye on human
felicity, and to have a peculiar delight in overturning it.

As we are very far from believing in any such heathen goddess or from encouraging any superstition, so we wish Mr.
John Fr——, or some other such philosopher, would bestir
himself a little in order to find out the real cause of this
sudden transition from good to bad fortune, which hath been
so often remarked and of which we shall proceed to give an

instance; for it is our province to relate facts, and we shall leave causes to persons of much higher genius.

Mankind have always taken great delight in knowing and descanting on the actions of others. Hence there have been in all ages and nations certain places set apart for public rendezvous, where the curious might meet and satisfy their mutual curiosity. Among these, the barbers' shops have justly borne the pre-eminence. Among the Greeks, barbers' news was a proverbial expression, and Horace in one of his epistles makes honourable mention of the Roman barbers in the same light.

Those of England are known to be nowise inferior to their Greek or Roman predecessors. You there see foreign affairs discussed in a manner little inferior to that with which they are handled in the coffee-houses, and domestic occurrences are much more largely and freely treated in the former than in the latter. But this serves only for the men. Now, whereas the females of this country, especially those of the lower order, do associate themselves much more than those of other nations, our polity would be highly deficient if they had not some place set apart likewise for the indulgence of their curiosity, seeing they are in this no way inferior to the other half of the species.

In enjoying, therefore, such place of rendezvous, the British fair ought to esteem themselves more happy than any of their foreign sisters, as I do not remember either to have read in history or to have seen in my travels anything of the like kind.

This place, then, is no other than the chandler's shop, the known seat of all the news, or, as it is vulgarly called, gossiping, in every parish in England.

Mrs. Partridge, being one day at this assembly of females, was asked by one of her neighbours if she had heard no news lately of Jenny Jones. To which she answered in the negative. Upon this, the other replied with a smile that the parish was very much obliged to her for having turned Jenny away as she did.

Mrs. Partridge, whose jealousy, as the reader well knows, was long since cured, and who had no other quarrel to her maid, answered boldly she did not know any obligation the parish had to her on that account, for she believed Jenny had scarce left her equal behind her.

"No, truly," said the gossip, "I hope not, though I fancy we have sluts enow too. Then you have not heard, it seems, that she hath been brought to bed of two bastards, but as they are not born here, my husband and the other overseer says we shall not be obliged to keep them."

"Two bastards!" answered Mrs. Partridge hastily. "You surprise me. I don't know whether we must keep them; but I am sure they must have been begotten here, for the wench hath not been nine months gone away."

Nothing can be so quick and sudden as the operations of the mind, especially when hope, or fear, or jealousy to which the two others are but journeymen, set it to work. It occurred instantly to her that Jenny had scarce ever been out of her own house while she lived with her. The leaning over the chair, the sudden starting up, the Latin, the smile, and many other things rushed upon her all at once. The satisfaction her husband expressed in the departure of Jenny appeared now to be only dissembled; again, in the same instant, to be real, and yet to confirm her jealousy as proceeding from satiety and a hundred other bad causes. In a word, she was convinced of her husband's guilt and immediately left the assembly in confusion.

As fair Grimalkin, who though the youngest of the feline family degenerates not in ferocity from the elder branches of her house, and though inferior in strength is equal in fierceness to the nobler tiger himself, when a little mouse, whom it hath long tormented in sport, escapes from her clutches for a while, frets, scolds, growls, swears; but if the trunk or box behind which the mouse lay hid be again removed, she flies like lightning on her prey, and with envenomed wrath bites, scratches, mumbles, and tears the little animal.

Not with less fury did Mrs. Partridge fly on the poor pedagogue. Her tongue, teeth, and hands fell all upon him at once. His wig was in an instant torn from his head, his shirt from his back, and from his face descended five streams of blood, denoting the number of claws with which Nature had unhappily armed the enemy.

Mr. Partridge acted for some time on the defensive only; indeed, he attempted only to guard his face with his hands, but as he found that his antagonist abated nothing of her rage, he thought he might at least endeavour to disarm her, or rather to confine her arms; in doing which, her cap fell off in the struggle, and her hair, being too short to reach her shoulders, erected itself on her head; her stays likewise, which were laced through one single hole at the bottom, burst open, and her breasts, which were much more redundant than her hair, hung down below her middle; her face was likewise marked with the blood of her husband, her teeth gnashed with rage, and fire such as sparkles from a smith's forge darted from her eyes. So that altogether this Amazonian heroine might have been an object of terror to a much bolder man than Mr. Partridge.

He had at length the good fortune, by getting possession of her arms, to render those weapons which she wore at the ends of her fingers useless; which she no sooner perceived than the softness of her sex prevailed over her rage, and she presently dissolved in tears, which soon after concluded in a fit.

That small share of sense which Mr. Partridge had hitherto preserved through this scene of fury, of the cause of which he was hitherto ignorant, now utterly abandoned him. He ran instantly into the street, hallooing out that his wife was in the agonies of death, and beseeching the neighbours to fly with the utmost haste to her assistance. Several good women obeyed his summons, who entering his house and applying the usual remedies on such occasions, Mrs. Partridge was at length to the great joy of her husband brought to herself.

As soon as she had a little recollected her spirits and somewhat composed herself with a cordial, she began to inform the company of the manifold injuries she had received from her husband; who, she said, was not contented to injure her in her bed, but upon her upbraiding him with it had treated her in the cruelest manner imaginable, had tore her cap and hair from her head and her stays from her body, giving her at the same time several blows, the marks of which she should carry to the grave.

The poor man, who bore on his face many more visible marks of the indignation of his wife, stood in silent astonishment at this accusation, which the reader will, I believe, bear witness for him had greatly exceeded the truth; for indeed he had not struck her once, and this silence being interpreted to be a confession of the charge by the whole court, they all began at once, *una voce*, to rebuke and revile him, repeating often that none but a coward ever struck a woman.

Mr. Partridge bore all this patiently; but when his wife appealed to the blood on her face as an evidence of his barbarity, he could not help laying claim to his own blood, for so it really was, as he thought it very unnatural that this should rise up (as we are taught that of a murdered person often doth) in vengeance against him.

To this the women made no other answer than that it was pity it had not come from his heart instead of his face; all declaring that if their husbands should lift their hands against them, they would have their hearts' bloods out of their bodies.

After much admonition for what was past, and much good advice to Mr. Partridge for his future behaviour, the company at length departed and left the husband and wife to a personal conference together, in which Mr. Partridge soon learned the cause of all his sufferings.

5

CONTAINING MUCH MATTER TO EXERCISE THE JUDGEMENT AND REFLECTION OF THE READER

I believe it is a true observation that few secrets are divulged to one person only, but certainly it would be next to a miracle that a fact of this kind should be known to a whole parish and not transpire any farther.

And, indeed, a very few days had passed before the country, to use a common phrase, rung of the schoolmaster of Little Baddington, who was said to have beaten his wife in the most cruel manner. Nay, in some places it was reported he had murdered her; in others that he had broke her arms; in others, her legs; in short, there was scarce an injury which can be done to a human creature but what Mrs. Partridge was somewhere or other affirmed to have received from her husband.

The cause of this quarrel was likewise variously reported; for, as some people said that Mrs. Partridge had caught her husband in bed with his maid, so many other reasons of a very different kind went abroad. Nay, some transferred the guilt to the wife and the jealousy to the husband.

Mrs. Wilkins had long ago heard of this quarrel, but as a different cause from the true one had reached her ears, she thought proper to conceal it; and the rather, perhaps, as the blame was universally laid on Mr. Partridge, and his wife when she was servant to Mr. Allworthy had in something offended Mrs. Wilkins, who was not of a very forgiving temper.

But Mrs. Wilkins, whose eyes could see objects at a distance, and who could very well look forward a few years into futurity, had perceived a strong likelihood of Captain Blifil's being hereafter her master; and as she plainly discerned that the captain bore no great goodwill to the little foundling, she fancied it would be rendering him an agreeable service if she could make any discoveries that might lessen the affection which Mr. Allworthy seemed to have contracted for this child, and which gave visible uneasiness to the captain, who could not entirely conceal it even before Allworthy himself; though his wife, who acted her part much better in public, frequently recommended to him her own example of conniving at the folly of her brother, which, she said, she at least as well perceived and as much resented as any other possibly could.

Mrs. Wilkins, having therefore by accident gotten a true scent of the above story, though long after it had happened, failed not to satisfy herself thoroughly of all the particulars, and then acquainted the captain that she had at last discovered the true father of the little bastard, which she was sorry, she said, to see her master lose his reputation in the country by taking so much notice of.

The captain chid her for the conclusion of her speech as an improper assurance in judging of her master's actions; for if his honour or his understanding would have suffered the captain to make an alliance with Mrs. Wilkins, his pride would by no means have admitted it. And, to say the truth, there is no conduct less politic than to enter into any confederacy with your friend's servants against their master. For by these means you afterwards become the slave of these very servants, by whom you are constantly liable to be betrayed. And this consideration, perhaps, it was which prevented Captain Blifil from being more explicit with Mrs. Wilkins or from encouraging the abuse which she had bestowed on Allworthy.

But though he declared no satisfaction to Mrs. Wilkins at this discovery, he enjoyed not a little from it in his own mind and resolved to make the best use of it he was able.

He kept this matter a long time concealed within his own breast in hopes that Mr. Allworthy might hear it from some other person, but Mrs. Wilkins, whether she resented the captain's behaviour or whether his cunning was beyond her and she feared the discovery might displease him, never afterwards opened her lips about the matter.

I have thought it somewhat strange, upon reflection, that the housekeeper never acquainted Mrs. Blifil with this news, as women are more inclined to communicate all pieces of intelligence to their own sex than to ours. The only way, as it appears to me, of solving this difficulty is by imputing it to that distance which was now grown between the lady and the housekeeper; whether this arose from a jealousy in Mrs. Blifil that Wilkins showed too great a respect to the foundling; for while she was endeavouring to ruin the little infant in order to ingratiate herself with the captain, she was every day more and more commending it before Allworthy as his fondness for it every day increased. This, notwithstanding all the care she took at other times to express the direct contrary to Mrs. Blifil, perhaps offended that delicate lady, who certainly now hated Mrs. Wilkins; and though she did not, or possibly could not, absolutely remove her from her place, she found, however, the means of making her life very uneasy. This Mrs. Wilkins at length so resented that she very openly showed all manner of respect and fondness to little Tommy, in opposition to Mrs. Blifil.

The captain, therefore, finding the story in danger of perishing, he at last took an opportunity to reveal it himself.

He was one day engaged with Mr. Allworthy in a discourse on charity, in which the captain, with great learning, proved to Mr. Allworthy that the word *charity* in Scripture nowhere means beneficence or generosity.

"The Christian religion," he said, "was instituted for much nobler purposes than to enforce a lesson which many heathen philosophers had taught us long before, and which, though it might, perhaps, be called a moral virtue, savoured but little of that sublime Christian-like disposition, that vast elevation of thought, in purity approaching to angelic perfection, to be attained, expressed, and felt only by grace. Those," he said, "came nearer to the Scripture meaning, who understood by it candour, or the forming of a benevolent opinion of our brethren, and passing a favourable judgement on their actions; a virtue much higher and more extensive in its nature than a pitiful distribution of alms, which, though we would never so much prejudice or even ruin our families, could never reach many; whereas charity, in the other and truer sense, might be extended to all mankind."

He said, "Considering who the disciples were, it would be absurd to conceive the doctrine of generosity or giving alms to have been preached to them. And, as we could not well imagine this doctrine should be preached by its divine

Author to men who could not practise it, much less shall we think it understood so by those who can practise it and do not.

"But though," continued he, "there is, I am afraid, little merit in these benefactions, there would, I must confess, be much pleasure in them to a good mind if it was not abated by one consideration: I mean that we are liable to be imposed upon, and to confer our choicest favours often on the undeserving, as you must own was your case in your bounty to that worthless fellow Partridge; for two or three such examples must greatly lessen the inward satisfaction which a good man would otherwise find in generosity; nay, may even make him timorous in bestowing, lest he should be guilty of supporting vice and encouraging the wicked, a crime of a very black dye, and for which it will by no means be a sufficient excuse that we have not actually intended such an encouragement, unless we have used the utmost caution in choosing the objects of our beneficence—a consideration which I make no doubt hath greatly checked the liberality of many a worthy and pious man."

Mr. Allworthy answered he could not dispute with the captain in the Greek language, and therefore could say nothing as to the true sense of the word which is translated *charity*, but that he had always thought it was interpreted to consist in action, and that giving alms constituted at least one branch of that virtue.

As to the meritorious part, he said, he readily agreed with the captain; for where could be the merit of barely discharging a duty which, he said, let the word *charity* have what construction it would, it sufficiently appeared to be from the whole tenor of the New Testament. And as he thought it an indispensable duty, enjoined both by the Christian law and by the law of nature itself, so was it withal so pleasant that if any duty could be said to be its own reward or to pay us while we were discharging it, it was this.

"To confess the truth," said he, "there is one degree of generosity (of charity, I would have called it) which seems to have some show of merit, and that is where, from a principle of benevolence and Christian love, we bestow on another what we really want ourselves; where, in order to lessen the distresses of another, we condescend to share some part of them by giving what even our own necessities cannot well spare. This is, I think, meritorious; but to relieve our brethren only with our superfluities; to be charitable (I must use the word) rather at the expense of our coffers than ourselves; to save several families from misery rather than hang up an extraordinary picture in our houses or to gratify any other idle, ridiculous vanity—this seems to be only being human creatures. Nay, I will venture to go farther, it is being in some degree epicures; for what could the greatest epicure wish rather than to eat with many mouths instead of one, which I think may be predicated of any one who knows that the bread of many is owing to his own largesses.

"As to the apprehension of bestowing bounty on such as may hereafter prove unworthy objects because many have proved such, surely it can never deter a good man from generosity. I do not think a few or many examples of ingratitude can justify a man's hardening his heart against the distresses of his fellow-creatures, nor do I believe it can ever have such effect on a truly benevolent mind. Nothing less than a persuasion of universal depravity can lock up the charity of a good man, and this persuasion must lead him, I think, either into atheism or enthusiasm; but surely it is unfair to argue such universal depravity from a few vicious individuals; nor was this, I believe, ever done by a man who, upon searching his own mind, found one certain exception to the general rule." He then concluded by asking who that Partridge was whom he had called a worthless fellow.

"I mean," said the captain, "Partridge the barber, the schoolmaster, what do you call him? Partridge, the father of the little child which you found in your bed."

Mr. Allworthy expressed great surprise at this account, and the captain as great at his ignorance of it; for, he said, he had known it above a month, and at length recollected with much difficulty that he was told it by Mrs. Wilkins.

Upon this, Wilkins was immediately summoned, who, having confirmed what the captain had said, was by Mr. Allworthy, by and with the captain's advice, dispatched to Little Baddington to inform herself of the truth of the fact; for the captain expressed great dislike at all hasty proceedings in criminal matters, and said he would by no means have Mr. Allworthy take any resolution either to the prejudice of the child or its father before he was satisfied that the latter was guilty; for though he had privately satisfied himself of this from one of Partridge's neighbours, yet he was too generous to give any such evidence to Mr. Allworthy.

6

It may be wondered that a story so well known, and which
had furnished so much matter of conversation, should never
have been mentioned to Mr. Allworthy himself, who was perhaps the only person in that country who had never heard
of it.

To account in some measure for this to the reader, I think
proper to inform him that there was no one in the kingdom
less interested in opposing that doctrine concerning the
meaning of the word *charity* which hath been seen in the
preceding chapter than our good man. Indeed, he was equally
entitled to this virtue in either sense; for as no man was
ever more sensible of the wants or more ready to relieve the
distresses of others, so none could be more tender of their
characters or slower to believe anything to their disadvantage.

Scandal, therefore, never found any access to his table;
for as it hath been long since observed that you may know
a man by his companions, so I will venture to say that by
attending to the conversation at a great man's table you may
satisfy yourself of his religion, his politics, his taste, and
indeed of his entire disposition; for though a few odd fellows
will utter their own sentiments in all places, yet much the
greater part of mankind have enough of the courtier to accommodate their conversation to the taste and inclination of
their superiors.

But to return to Mrs. Wilkins, who, having executed her
commission with great dispatch, though at fifteen miles' distance, brought back such a confirmation of the schoolmaster's guilt that Mr. Allworthy determined to send for the
criminal and examine him *viva voce*. Mr. Partridge, therefore, was summoned to attend in order to his defence (if he
could make any) against this accusation.

At the time appointed, before Mr. Allworthy himself, at
Paradise Hall, came as well the said Partridge, with Anne,
his wife, as Mrs. Wilkins, his accuser.

And now, Mr. Allworthy being seated in the chair of justice, Mr. Partridge was brought before him. Having heard his accusation from the mouth of Mrs. Wilkins, he pleaded not guilty, making many vehement protestations of his innocence.

Mrs. Partridge was then examined, who, after a modest apology for being obliged to speak the truth against her husband, related all the circumstances with which the reader hath already been acquainted, and at last concluded with her husband's confession of his guilt.

Whether she had forgiven him or no, I will not venture to determine, but it is certain she was an unwilling witness in this cause, and it is probable from certain other reasons would never have been brought to depose as she did, had not Mrs. Wilkins with great art fished all out of her at her own house, and had she not indeed made promises in Mr. Allworthy's name that the punishment of her husband should not be such as might anywise affect his family.

Partridge still persisted in asserting his innocence, though he admitted he had made the above-mentioned confession, which he, however, endeavoured to account for by protesting that he was forced into it by the continued importunity she used, who vowed that as she was sure of his guilt, she would never leave tormenting him till he had owned it, and faithfully promised that in such case she would never mention it to him more. Hence, he said, he had been induced falsely to confess himself guilty, though he was innocent; and that he believed he should have confessed a murder from the same motive.

Mrs. Partridge could not bear this imputation with patience; and, having no other remedy in the present place but tears, she called forth a plentiful assistance from them, and then, addressing herself to Mr. Allworthy, she said (or rather cried), "May it please your worship, there never was any poor woman so injured as I am by that base man; for this is not the only instance of his falsehood to me. No, may it please your worship, he hath injured my bed many's the good time and often. I could have put up with his drunkenness and neglect of his business if he had not broke one of the sacred *commandiments*. Besides, if it had been out of doors, I had not mattered it so much, but with my own servant, in my own house, under my own roof; to defile my own chaste bed, which to be sure he hath with his beastly stinking whores. Yes, you villain, you have defiled my own bed, you have; and then you have charged me with *bullocking* you into owning the truth. It is very likely, an't please your worship, that I should *bullock* him. I have marks enow about my body to show of his cruelty to me. If you had been a man, you villain, you would have scorned to injure a woman in that manner. But you an't half a man, you know it. Nor have you been half a husband to me. You need run after whores, you need, when I'm sure— And since he provokes me, I am ready, an't please your worship, to take my bodily oath that I found them abed together. What, you have forgot, I suppose, when you beat me into a fit and made the blood run down my forehead because I only civilly taxed you with your adultery! But I can prove it by all my neighbours. You have almost broke my heart, you have, you have."

Here Mr. Allworthy interrupted and begged her to be pacified, promising her that she should have justice; then, turning to Partridge, who stood aghast, one half of his wits being hurried away by surprise and the other half by fear, he said he was sorry to see there was so wicked a man in the world. He assured him that his prevaricating and lying backward and forward was a great aggravation of his guilt, for which the only atonement he could make was by confession and repentance. He exhorted him, therefore, to begin by immediately confessing the fact, and not to persist in denying what was so plainly proved against him, even by his own wife.

Here, reader, I beg your patience a moment while I make a just compliment to the great wisdom and sagacity of our law, which refuses to admit the evidence of a wife for or against her husband. This, says a certain learned author who, I believe, was never quoted before in any but a law-book, would be the means of creating an eternal dissension between them. It would, indeed, be the means of much perjury, and of much whipping, fining, imprisoning, transporting, and hanging.

Partridge stood awhile silent, till, being bid to speak, he said he had already spoken the truth, and appealed to heaven for his innocence, and lastly to the girl herself, whom he desired his worship immediately to send for; for he was ignorant, or at least pretended to be so, that she had left that part of the country

Mr. Allworthy, whose natural love of justice joined to his coolness of temper made him always a most patient magistrate in hearing all the witnesses which an accused person could produce in his defence, agreed to defer his final determination of this matter till the arrival of Jenny, for whom he immediately dispatched a messenger; and then, having recommended peace between Partridge and his wife (though he addressed himself chiefly to the wrong person), he appointed them to attend again the third day; for he had sent Jenny a whole day's journey from his own house.

At the appointed time the parties all assembled, when the messenger returning brought word that Jenny was not to be found, for that she had left her habitation a few days before in company with a recruiting officer.

Mr. Allworthy then declared that the evidence of such a slut as she appeared to be would have deserved no credit; but he said he could not help thinking that had she been present, and would have declared the truth, she must have confirmed what so many circumstances, together with his own confession and the declaration of his wife that she had caught her husband in the fact, did sufficiently prove. He therefore once more exhorted Partridge to confess, but he still avowing his innocence, Mr. Allworthy declared himself satisfied of his guilt, and that he was too bad a man to receive any encouragement from him. He therefore deprived him of his annuity, and recommended repentance to him on account of another world, and industry to maintain himself and his wife in this.

There were not, perhaps, many more unhappy persons than poor Partridge. He had lost the best part of his income by the evidence of his wife, and yet was daily upbraided by her for having, among other things, been the occasion of depriving her of that benefit; but such was his fortune, and he was obliged to submit to it.

Though I called him poor Partridge in the last paragraph, I would have the reader rather impute that epithet to the compassion of my temper than conceive it to be any declaration of his innocence. Whether he was innocent or not will perhaps appear hereafter; but if the historic Muse hath entrusted me with any secrets, I will by no means be guilty of discovering them till she shall give me leave.

Here, therefore, the reader must suspend his curiosity. Certain it is, that whatever was the truth of the case, there was evidence more than sufficient to convict him before Allworthy; indeed, much less would have satisfied a bench of justices on an order of bastardy; and yet not withstanding the positiveness of Mrs. Partridge, who would have taken the sacrament upon the matter, there is a possibility that the schoolmaster was entirely innocent; for though it appeared clear on comparing the time when Jenny departed from Little Baddington with that of her delivery that she had there conceived this infant, yet it by no means followed of necessity that Partridge must have been its father; for, to omit other particulars, there was in the same house a lad near eighteen, between whom and Jenny there had subsisted sufficient intimacy to found a reasonable suspicion, and yet, so blind is jealousy, this circumstance never once entered into the head of the enraged wife.

Whether Partridge repented or not, according to Mr. Allworthy's advice, is not so apparent. Certain it is, that his wife repented heartily of the evidence she had given against him; especially when she found Mrs. Deborah had deceived her and refused to make any application to Mr. Allworthy on her behalf. She had, however, somewhat better success with Mrs. Blifil, who was, as the reader must have perceived, a much better-tempered woman, and very kindly undertook to solicit her brother to restore the annuity. In which, though good nature might have some share, yet a stronger and more natural motive will appear in the next chapter.

These solicitations were nevertheless unsuccessful; for though Mr. Allworthy did not think, with some late writers, that mercy consists only in punishing offenders, yet he was as far from thinking that it is proper to this excellent quality to pardon great criminals wantonly, without any reason whatever. Any doubtfulness of the fact or any circumstance of mitigation was never disregarded, but the petitions of an offender or the intercessions of others did not in the least affect him. In a word, he never pardoned because the offender himself or his friends were unwilling that he should be punished.

Partridge and his wife were, therefore, both obliged to submit to their fate, which was indeed severe enough; for so far was he from doubling his industry on the account of his lessened income that he did in a manner abandon himself to despair; and as he was by nature indolent, that vice now increased upon him, by which means he lost the little school he had, so that neither his wife nor himself would have had any bread to eat had not the charity of some good Christian interposed and provided them with what was just sufficient for their sustenance.

As this support was conveyed to them by an unknown hand, they imagined, and so, I doubt not, will the reader, that Mr. Allworthy himself was their secret benefactor, who, though he would not openly encourage vice, could yet privately relieve the distresses of the vicious themselves when these became too exquisite and disproportionate to their merit. In which light their wretchedness appeared now to Fortune herself, for she at length took pity on this miserable couple and considerably lessened the wretched state of Partridge by putting a final end to that of his wife, who soon after caught the smallpox and died.

The justice which Mr. Allworthy had executed on Partridge at first met with universal approbation, but no sooner had he felt its consequences than his neighbours began to relent and to compassionate his case, and presently after, to blame that as rigour and severity which they before called justice. They now exclaimed against punishing in cold blood and sang forth the praises of mercy and forgiveness.

These cries were considerably increased by the death of Mrs. Partridge, which, though owing to the distemper above mentioned, which is no consequence of poverty or distress, many were not ashamed to impute to Mr. Allworthy's severity, or, as they now termed it, cruelty.

Partridge, having now lost his wife, his school, and his annuity, and the unknown person having now discontinued the last-mentioned charity, resolved to change the scene, and left the country where he was in danger of starving with the universal compassion of all his neighbours.

7

A SHORT SKETCH OF THAT FELICITY WHICH PRUDENT COUPLES MAY EXTRACT FROM HATRED; WITH A SHORT APOLOGY FOR THOSE PEOPLE WHO OVERLOOK IMPERFECTIONS IN THEIR FRIENDS

Though the captain had effectually demolished poor Partridge, yet had he not reaped the harvest he hoped for, which was to turn the foundling out of Mr. Allworthy's house.

On the contrary, that gentleman grew every day fonder of little Tommy, as if he intended to counterbalance his severity to the father with extraordinary fondness and affection towards the son.

This a good deal soured the captain's temper, as did all the other daily instances of Mr. Allworthy's generosity; for he looked on all such largesses to be diminutions of his own wealth.

In this, we have said, he did not agree with his wife, nor, indeed, in anything else; for though an affection placed on the understanding is by many wise persons thought more durable than that which is founded on beauty, yet it happened otherwise in the present case. Nay, the understandings of this couple were their principal bone of contention and one great cause of many quarrels, which from time to time arose between them, and which at last ended on the side of the lady in a sovereign contempt for her husband, and on the husband's, in an utter abhorrence of his wife.

As these had both exercised their talents chiefly in the study of divinity, this was from their first acquaintance the most common topic of conversation between them. The captain, like a well-bred man, had before marriage always given up his opinion to that of the lady, and this not in the clumsy awkward manner of a conceited blockhead, who while he civilly yields to a superior in an argument is desirous of being still known to think himself in the right. The captain, on the contrary, though one of the proudest fellows in the world, so absolutely yielded the victory to his antagonist that she, who had not the least doubt of his sincerity, retired always from the dispute with an admiration of her own understanding and a love for his.

But though this complaisance to one whom the captain thoroughly despised was not so uneasy to him as it would have been had any hopes of preferment made it necessary to show the same submission to a Hoadley or to some other of great reputation in the science, yet even this cost him too much to be endured without some motive. Matrimony, therefore, having removed all such motives, he grew weary of this condescension, and began to treat the opinions of his wife with that haughtiness and insolence which none but those who deserve some contempt themselves can bestow, and those only who deserve no contempt can bear.

When the first torrent of tenderness was over, and when in the calm and long interval between the fits reason began to open the eyes of the lady, and she saw this alteration of behaviour in the captain, who at length answered all her arguments only with *pish* and *pshaw*, she was far from enduring the indignity with a tame submission. Indeed, it at first so highly provoked her that it might have produced some tragical event had it not taken a more harmless turn by filling her with the utmost contempt for her husband's understanding, which somewhat qualified her hatred towards him; though of this likewise she had a pretty moderate share.

The captain's hatred to her was of a purer kind, for as to any imperfections in her knowledge or understanding, he no more despised her for them than for her not being six feet high. In his opinion of the female sex he exceeded the moroseness of Aristotle himself: he looked on a woman as on an animal of domestic use, of somewhat higher consideration than a cat since her offices were of rather more importance, but the difference between these two was in his estimation so small that in his marriage contracted with Mr. Allworthy's lands and tenements it would have been pretty equal which of them he had taken into the bargain. And yet so tender was his pride that it felt the contempt which his wife now began to express towards him; and this, added to the surfeit he had before taken of her love, created in him a degree of disgust and abhorrence perhaps hardly to be exceeded.

One situation only of the married state is excluded from pleasure, and that is a state of indifference; but as many of my readers, I hope, know what an exquisite delight there is in conveying pleasure to a beloved object, so some few, I am afraid, may have experienced the satisfaction of tormenting one we hate. It is, I apprehend, to come at this latter pleasure that we see both sexes often give up that ease in marriage which they might otherwise possess, though their mate was never so disagreeable to them. Hence the wife often puts on fits of love and jealousy, nay, even denies herself any pleasure, to disturb and prevent those of her husband; and he again in return puts frequent restraints on himself and stays at home in company which he dislikes in order to confine his wife to what she equally detests. Hence, too, must flow those tears which a widow sometimes so plentifully sheds over the ashes of a husband with whom she led a life of constant disquiet and turbulency, and whom now she can never hope to torment any more.

But if ever any couple enjoyed this pleasure, it was at present experienced by the captain and his lady. It was always a sufficient reason to either of them to be obstinate in any opinion that the other had previously asserted the contrary. If the one proposed any amusement, the other constantly objected to it; they never loved or hated, commended or abused, the same person. And for this reason, as the captain looked with an evil eye on the little foundling, his wife began now to caress it almost equally with her own child.

The reader will be apt to conceive that this behaviour between the husband and wife did not greatly contribute to Mr. Allworthy's repose, as it tended so little to that serene happiness which he had proposed to all three from this alliance; but the truth is, though he might be a little disappointed in his sanguine expectations, yet he was far from being acquainted with the whole matter; for, as the captain was from certain obvious reasons much on his guard before him, the lady was obliged for fear of her brother's displeasure to pursue the same conduct. In fact, it is possible for a third person to be very intimate, nay, even to live long in the same house, with a married couple who have any tolerable discretion, and not even guess at the sour sentiments which they bear to each other; for though the whole day may be sometimes too short for hatred as well as for love, yet the many hours which they naturally spend together apart from all observers supply people of tolerable moderation with such ample opportunity for the enjoyment of either passion that, if they love, they can support being a few hours in company without toying, or, if they hate, without spitting in each other's faces.

It is possible, however, that Mr. Allworthy saw enough to render him a little uneasy, for we are not always to conclude that a wise man is not hurt because he doth not cry out and lament himself like those of a childish or effeminate temper. But, indeed, it is possible he might see some faults in the captain without any uneasiness at all; for men of true wisdom and goodness are contented to take persons and things as they are without complaining of their imperfections or attempting to amend them. They can see a fault in a friend, a relation, or an acquaintance without ever mentioning it to the parties themselves or to any others; and this often without the least lessening their affection. Indeed, unless great discernment be tempered with this overlooking disposition, we ought never to contract friendship but with a degree of folly which we can deceive; for I hope my friends will pardon me when I declare I know none of them without a fault, and I should be sorry if I could imagine I had any friend who could not see mine. Forgiveness of this kind we give and demand in turn. It is an exercise of friendship, and perhaps none of the least pleasant. And this forgiveness we must bestow without desire of amendment. There is, perhaps, no surer mark of folly than an attempt to correct the natural infirmities of those we love. The finest composition of human nature, as well as the finest china, may have a flaw in it; and this, I am afraid, in either case is equally incurable, though, nevertheless, the pattern may remain of the highest value.

Upon the whole, then, Mr. Allworthy certainly saw some imperfections in the captain, but as this was a very artful man, and eternally upon his guard before him, these appeared to him no more than blemishes in a good character, which his goodness made him overlook and his wisdom prevented him from discovering to the captain himself. Very different would have been his sentiments had he discovered the whole, which, perhaps, would in time have been the case had the husband and wife long continued this kind of behaviour to each other; but this, kind Fortune took effectual means to prevent by forcing the captain to do that which rendered him again dear to his wife and restored all her tenderness and affection towards him.

8

The captain was made large amends for the unpleasant minutes which he passed in the conversation of his wife (and which were as few as he could contrive to make them) by the pleasant meditations he enjoyed when alone.

These meditations were entirely employed on Mr. Allworthy's fortune; for first, he exercised much thought in calculating as well as he could the exact value of the whole, which calculations he often saw occasion to alter in his own favour; and secondly, and chiefly, he pleased himself with intended alterations in the house and gardens, and in projecting many other schemes, as well for the improvement of the estate as of the grandeur of the place. For this purpose he applied himself to the studies of architecture and gardening, and read over many books on both these subjects; for these sciences, indeed, employed his whole time and formed his only amusement. He at last completed a most excellent plan, and very sorry we are that it is not in our power to present it to our reader, since even the luxury of the present age, I believe, would hardly match it. It had, indeed, in a superlative degree the two principal ingredients which serve to recommend all great and noble designs of this nature; for it required an immoderate expense to execute and a vast length of time to bring it to any sort of perfection. The former of these, the immense wealth of which the captain supposed Mr. Allworthy possessed, and which he thought himself sure of inheriting, promised very effectually to supply; and the latter, the soundness of his own constitution and his time of life, which was only what is called middle age, removed all apprehension of his not living to accomplish.

Nothing was wanting to enable him to enter upon the immediate execution of this plan but the death of Mr. Allworthy, in calculating which he had employed much of his own algebra, besides purchasing every book extant that treats of the value of lives, reversions, &c. From all which he satisfied himself that, as he had every day a chance of this happening, so had he more than an even chance of its happening within a few years.

But while the captain was one day busied in deep contemplations of this kind one of the most unlucky, as well as unseasonable, accidents happened to him. The utmost malice of Fortune could, indeed, have contrived nothing so cruel, so malapropos, so absolutely destructive to all his schemes. In short, not to keep the reader in long suspense, just at the very instant when his heart was exulting in meditations on the happiness which would accrue to him by Mr. Allworthy's death, he himself—died of an apoplexy!

This unfortunately befell the captain as he was taking his evening walk by himself, so that nobody was present to lend him any assistance, if indeed any assistance could have preserved him. He took, therefore, measure of that proportion of soil which was now become adequate to all his future purposes, and he lay dead on the ground, a great (though not a living) example of the truth of that observation of Horace:

> *Tu secanda marmora*
> *Locas sub ipsum fanus; et sepulchri*
> *Immemor, struis domos.*

Which sentiment I shall thus give to the English reader: "You provide the noblest materials for building, when a pickaxe and a spade are only necessary; and build houses of five by a hundred feet, forgetting that of six by two."

9

A PROOF OF THE INFALLIBILITY OF THE FOREGOING RECEIPT
IN THE LAMENTATIONS OF THE WIDOW; WITH OTHER SUIT-
ABLE DECORATIONS OF DEATH, SUCH AS PHYSICIANS, &C., AND
AN EPITAPH IN THE TRUE STYLE

Mr. Allworthy, his sister, and another lady were assembled at the accustomed hour in the supper-room, where, having waited a considerable time longer than usual, Mr. Allworthy first declared he began to grow uneasy at the captain's stay (for he was always most punctual at his meals), and gave orders that the bell should be rung without the doors, and especially towards those walks which the captain was wont to use.

All these summons proving ineffectual (for the captain had by perverse accident betaken himself to a new walk that evening), Mrs. Blifil declared she was seriously frightened. Upon which the other lady, who was one of her most intimate acquaintance and who well knew the true state of her affections, endeavoured all she could to pacify her, telling her—to be sure she could not help being uneasy, but that she should hope the best; that perhaps the sweetness of the evening had enticed the captain to go farther than his usual walk; or he might be detained at some neighbour's. Mrs. Blifil answered no; she was sure some accident had befallen him, for that he would never stay out without sending her word, as he must know how uneasy it would make her. The other lady, having no other arguments to use, betook herself to the entreaties usual on such occasions and begged her not to frighten herself, for it might be of very ill consequence to her own health, and filling out a very large glass of wine, advised and at last prevailed with her to drink it.

Mr. Allworthy now returned into the parlour, for he had been himself in search after the captain. His countenance sufficiently showed the consternation he was under, which, indeed, had a good deal deprived him of speech; but as grief operates variously on different minds, so the same apprehension which depressed his voice elevated that of Mrs.

Blifil. She now began to bewail herself in very bitter terms, and floods of tears accompanied her lamentations, which the lady, her companion, declared she could not blame, but at the same time dissuaded her from indulging; attempting to moderate the grief of her friend by philosophical observations on the many disappointments to which human life is daily subject, which, she said, was a sufficient consideration to fortify our minds against any accidents, how sudden or terrible soever. She said her brother's example ought to teach her patience, who, though indeed he could not be supposed as much concerned as herself, yet was doubtless very uneasy, though his resignation to the divine will had restrained his grief within due bounds.

"Mention not my brother," said Mrs. Blifil. "I alone am the object of your pity. What are the errors of friendship to what a wife feels on these occasions? Oh, he is lost! Somebody hath murdered him—I shall never see him more." Here a torrent of tears had the same consequence with what the suppression had occasioned to Mr. Allworthy, and she remained silent.

At this interval a servant came running in out of breath, and cried out the captain was found; and before he could proceed farther he was followed by two more, bearing the dead body between them.

Here the curious reader may observe another diversity in the operations of grief; for as Mr. Allworthy had been before silent from the same cause which had made his sister vociferous, so did the present sight, which drew tears from the gentleman, put an entire stop to those of the lady, who first gave a violent scream and presently after fell into a fit.

The room was soon full of servants, some of whom, with the lady visitant, were employed in care of the wife, and others, with Mr. Allworthy, assisted in carrying off the captain to a warm bed, where every method was tried in order to restore him to life.

And glad should we be could we inform the reader that both these bodies had been attended with equal success; for those who undertook the care of the lady succeeded so well that after the fit had continued a decent time she again revived, to their great satisfaction; but as to the captain, all experiments of bleeding, chafing, dropping, &c., proved ineffectual. Death, that inexorable judge, had passed sentence on him and refused to grant him a reprieve, though two doctors, who arrived and were fee'd at one and the same instant, were his counsel.

These two doctors, whom to avoid any malicious applications we shall distinguish by the names of Dr. Y. and Dr. Z., having felt his pulse, to wit, Dr. Y. his right arm and Dr. Z. his left, both agreed that he was absolutely dead; but as to the distemper, or cause of his death, they differed, Dr. Y. holding that he died of an apoplexy, and Dr. Z. of an epilepsy.

Hence arose a dispute between the learned men in which each delivered the reasons of their several opinions. These were of such equal force that they served both to confirm either doctor in his own sentiments and made not the least impression on his adversary.

To say the truth, every physician, almost, hath his favourite disease, to which he ascribes all the victories obtained over human nature. The gout, the rheumatism, the stone, the gravel, and the consumption have all their several patrons in the faculty; and none more than the nervous fever, or the fever on the spirits. And here we may account for those disagreements in opinion concerning the cause of a patient's death which sometimes occur between the most learned of the college, and which have greatly surprised that part of the world who have been ignorant of the fact we have above asserted.

The reader may, perhaps, be surprised that instead of endeavouring to revive the patient, the learned gentlemen should fall immediately into a dispute on the occasion of his death, but in reality, all such experiments had been made before their arrival; for the captain was put into a warm bed, had his veins scarified, his forehead chafed, and all sorts of strong drops applied to his lips and nostrils.

The physicians, therefore, finding themselves anticipated in everything they ordered, were at a loss how to apply that portion of time which it is usual and decent to remain for their fee, and were therefore necessitated to find some subject or other for discourse; and what could more naturally present itself than that before mentioned?

Our doctors were about to take their leave when Mr. Allworthy, having given over the captain and acquiesced in the divine will, began to inquire after his sister, whom he desired them to visit before their departure.

This lady was now recovered of her fit and, to use the

common phrase, as well as could be expected for one in her condition. The doctors, therefore, all previous ceremonies being complied with, as this was a new patient, attended according to desire and laid hold on each of her hands, as they had before done on those of the corpse.

The case of the lady was in the other extreme from that of her husband, for as he was past all the assistance of physic, so in reality she required none.

There is nothing more unjust than the vulgar opinion by which physicians are misrepresented as friends to death. On the contrary, I believe, if the number of those who recover by physic could be opposed to that of the martyrs to it, the former would rather exceed the latter. Nay, some are so cautious on this head that to avoid a possibility of killing the patient, they abstain from all methods of curing and prescribe nothing but what can neither do good nor harm. I have heard some of these with great gravity deliver it as a maxim that Nature should be left to do her own work while the physician stands by, as it were, to clap her on the back and encourage her when she doth well.

So little, then, did our doctors delight in death that they discharged the corpse after a single fee; but they were not so disgusted with their living patient, concerning whose case they immediately agreed, and fell to prescribing with great diligence.

Whether, as the lady had at first persuaded her physicians to believe her ill, they had now in return persuaded her to believe herself so, I will not determine, but she continued a whole month with all the decorations of sickness. During this time she was visited by physicians, attended by nurses, and received constant messages from her acquaintance to inquire after her health.

At length, the decent time for sickness and immoderate grief being expired, the doctors were discharged and the lady began to see company; being altered only from what she was before by that colour of sadness in which she had dressed her person and countenance.

The captain was now interred and might, perhaps, have already made a large progress towards oblivion had not the friendship of Mr. Allworthy taken care to preserve his memory by the following epitaph, which was written by a man of as great genius as integrity, and one who perfectly well knew the captain.

HERE LIES,
IN EXPECTATION OF A JOYFUL RISING,
THE BODY OF
CAPTAIN JOHN BLIFIL.
LONDON
HAD THE HONOR OF HIS BIRTH,
OXFORD
OF HIS EDUCATION.
HIS PARTS
WERE AN HONOUR TO HIS PROFESSION
AND TO HIS COUNTRY;
HIS LIFE, TO HIS RELIGION
AND HUMAN NATURE.
HE WAS A DUTIFUL SON,
A TENDER HUSBAND,
AN AFFECTIONATE FATHER,
A SINCERE FRIEND,
A DEVOUT CHRISTIAN,
AND A GOOD MAN.
HIS INCONSOLABLE WIDOW
HATH ERECTED THIS STONE,
THE MONUMENT OF
HIS VIRTUES
AND OF HER AFFECTION.

BOOK III

CONTAINING THE MOST MEMORABLE TRANSACTIONS WHICH PASSED IN THE FAMILY OF MR. ALLWORTHY, FROM THE TIME WHEN TOMMY JONES ARRIVED AT THE AGE OF FOURTEEN TILL HE ATTAINED THE AGE OF NINETEEN. IN THIS BOOK THE READER MAY PICK UP SOME HINTS CONCERNING THE EDUCATION OF CHILDREN.

1

CONTAINING LITTLE OR NOTHING

The reader will be pleased to remember that at the beginning of the second book of this history we gave him a hint of our intention to pass over several large periods of time in which nothing happened worthy of being recorded in a chronicle of this kind.

In so doing, we do not only consult our own dignity and ease but the good and advantage of the reader; for besides that by these means we prevent him from throwing away his time, in reading without either pleasure or emolument, we give him at all such seasons an opportunity of employing that wonderful sagacity of which he is master by filling up these vacant spaces of time with his own conjectures; for which purpose we have taken care to qualify him in the preceding pages.

For instance, what reader but knows that Mr. Allworthy felt at first for the loss of his friend those emotions of grief which, on such occasions, enter into all men whose hearts are not composed of flint or their heads of as solid materials? Again, what reader doth not know that philosophy and religion in time moderated, and at last extinguished, this grief? The former of these teaching the folly and vanity of it, and the latter correcting it as unlawful; and at the same time assuaging it by raising future hopes and assurances, which enable a strong and religious mind to take leave of a friend on his death-bed with little less indifference than if he was preparing for a long journey, and, indeed, with little less hope of seeing him again.

Nor can the judicious reader be at a greater loss on account of Mrs. Bridget Blifil, who, he may be assured, conducted herself through the whole season in which grief is to make its appearance on the outside of the body with the strictest regard to all the rules of custom and decency, suiting the alterations of her countenance to the several alterations of her habit; for as this changed from weeds to black, from black to grey, from grey to white, so did her countenance change from dismal to sorrowful, from sorrowful to sad, and from sad to serious, till the day came in which she was allowed to return to her former serenity.

We have mentioned these two as examples only of the task which may be imposed on readers of the lowest class. Much higher and harder exercises of judgement and penetration may reasonably be expected from the upper graduates in criticism. Many notable discoveries will, I doubt not, be made by such, of the transactions which happened in the family of our worthy man during all the years which we have thought proper to pass over; for though nothing worthy of a place in this history occurred within that period, yet did several incidents happen of equal importance with those reported by the daily and weekly historians of the age, in reading which, great numbers of persons consume a considerable part of their time, very little, I am afraid, to their emolument. Now, in the conjectures here proposed, some of the most excellent faculties of the mind may be employed to much advantage, since it is a more useful capacity to be able to foretell the actions of men in any circumstance from their characters than to judge of their characters from their actions. The former, I own, requires the greater penetration, but may be accomplished by true sagacity with no less certainty than the latter.

As we are sensible that much the greater part of our readers are very eminently possessed of this quality, we have left them a space of twelve years to exert it in, and shall now bring forth our hero at about fourteen years of age, not questioning that many have been long impatient to be introduced to his acquaintance.

THE HERO OF THIS GREAT HISTORY APPEARS WITH VERY BAD
OMENS. A LITTLE TALE OF SO LOW A KIND THAT SOME MAY
THINK IT NOT WORTH THEIR NOTICE. A WORD OR TWO CON-
CERNING A SQUIRE, AND MORE RELATING TO A GAMEKEEPER
AND A SCHOOLMASTER

As we determined when we first sat down to write this history to flatter no man, but to guide our pen throughout by
the directions of truth, we are obliged to bring our hero on
the stage in a much more disadvantageous manner than we
could wish, and to declare honestly, even at his first appearance, that it was the universal opinion of all Mr. Allworthy's
family that he was certainly born to be hanged.

Indeed, I am sorry to say there was too much reason for
this conjecture, the lad having from his earliest years discovered a propensity to many vices, and especially to one,
which hath as direct a tendency as any other to that fate
which we have just now observed to have been prophetically
denounced against him. He had been already convicted of
three robberies: viz., of robbing an orchard, of stealing a
duck out of a farmer's yard, and of picking Master Blifil's
pocket of a ball.

The vices of this young man were, moreover, heightened
by the disadvantageous light in which they appeared when
opposed to the virtues of Master Blifil, his companion, a
youth of so different a cast from little Jones that not only the
family but all the neighbourhood resounded his praises. He
was, indeed, a lad of a remarkable disposition; sober, discreet, and pious beyond his age; qualities which gained him
the love of every one who who knew him, whilst Tom
Jones was universally disliked, and many expressed their
wonder that Mr. Allworthy would suffer such a lad to be
educated with his nephew lest the morals of the latter should
be corrupted by his example.

An incident which happened about this time will set the
character of these two lads more fairly before the discerning
reader than is in the power of the longest dissertation.

Tom Jones, who, bad as he is, must serve for the hero of
this history, had only one friend among the servants of the
family; for, as to Mrs. Wilkins, she had long since given him
up and was perfectly reconciled to her mistress. This friend

was the gamekeeper, a fellow of a loose kind of disposition, and who was thought not to entertain much stricter notions concerning the difference of *meum* and *tuum* than the young gentleman himself. And hence this friendship gave occasion to many sarcastical remarks among the domestics, most of which were either proverbs before, or at least are become so now; and, indeed, the wit of them all may be comprised in that short Latin proverb *Noscitur a socio*, which, I think, is thus expressed in English: "You may know him by the company he keeps."

To say the truth, some of that atrocious wickedness in Jones, of which we have just mentioned three examples, might, perhaps, be derived from the encouragement he had received from this fellow, who in two or three instances had been what the laws calls an accessary after the fact. For the whole duck and great part of the apples were converted to the use of the gamekeeper and his family. Though as Jones alone was discovered, the poor lad bore not only the whole smart but the whole blame, both of which fell again to his lot on the following occasion.

Contiguous to Mr. Allworthy's estate was the manor of one of those gentlemen who are called preservers of the game. This species of men, from the great severity with which they revenge the death of a hare or a partridge, might be thought to cultivate the same superstition with the Bannians in India, many of whom, we are told, dedicate their whole lives to the preservation and protection of certain animals, was it not that our English Bannians, while they preserve them from other enemies, will most unmercifully slaughter whole horse-loads themselves, so that they stand clearly acquitted of any such heathenish superstition.

I have, indeed, a much better opinion of this kind of men than is entertained by some, as I take them to answer the order of Nature and the good purposes for which they were ordained in a more ample manner than many others. Now, as Horace tell us that there are a set of human beings,

Fruges consumere nati,

"born to consume the fruits of the earth," so I make no manner of doubt but that there are others,

Feras consumere nati,

"born to consume the beasts of the field," or, as it is commonly called, the game; and none, I believe, will deny but that those squires fulfil this end of their creation.

Little Jones went one day a-shooting with the gamekeeper when, happening to spring a covey of partridges near the border of that manor over which Fortune, to fulfil the wise purposes of Nature, had planted one of the game-consumers, the birds flew into it, and were *marked* (as it is called) by the two sportsmen in some furze bushes, about two or three hundred paces beyond Mr. Allworthy's dominions.

Mr. Allworthy had given the fellow strict orders, on pain of forfeiting his place, never to trespass on any of his neighbours; no more on those who were less rigid in this matter than on the lord of this manor. With regard to others, indeed, these orders had not been always very scrupulously kept, but as the disposition of the gentleman with whom the partridges had taken sanctuary was well known, the gamekeeper had never yet attempted to invade his territories. Nor had he done it now had not the younger sportsman, who was excessively eager to pursue the flying game, over-persuaded him; but Jones being very importunate, the other, who was himself keen enough after the sport, yielded to his persuasions, entered the manor, and shot one of the partridges.

The gentleman himself was at that time on horseback at a little distance from them, and hearing the gun go off, he immediately made towards the place and discovered poor Tom; for the gamekeeper had leapt into the thickest part of the furze brake, where he had happily concealed himself.

The gentleman, having searched the lad and found the partridge upon him, denounced great vengeance, swearing he would acquaint Mr. Allworthy. He was as good as his word, for he rode immediately to his house and complained of the trespass on his manor in as high terms and as bitter language as if his house had been broken open, and the most valuable furniture stolen out of it. He added that some other person was in his company, though he could not discover him, for that two guns had been discharged almost in the same instant. And, says he, "We have found only this partridge, but the Lord knows what mischief they have done."

At his return home, Tom was presently convened before Mr. Allworthy. He owned the fact and alleged no other excuse but what was really true; viz., that the covey was originally sprung in Mr. Allworthy's own manor.

Tom was then interrogated who was with him, which Mr. Allworthy declared he was resolved to know, acquainting the culprit with the circumstances of the two guns, which had been deposed by the squire and both his servants; but Tom stoutly persisted in asserting that he was alone; yet, to say the truth, he hesitated a little at first, which would have confirmed Mr. Allworthy's belief had what the squire and his servants said wanted any further confirmation.

The gamekeeper, being a suspected person, was now sent for, and the question put to him; but he, relying on the promise which Tom had made him to take all upon himself, very resolutely denied being in company with the young gentleman or, indeed, having seen him the whole afternoon.

Mr. Allworthy then turned towards Tom, with more than usual anger in his countenance, and advised him to confess who was with him, repeating that he was resolved to know. The lad, however, still maintained his resolution, and was dismissed with much wrath by Mr. Allworthy, who told him he should have to the next morning to consider of it, when he should be questioned by another person and in another manner.

Poor Jones spent a very melancholy night, and the more so as he was without his usual companion; for Master Blifil was gone abroad on a visit with his mother. Fear of the punishment he was to suffer was on this occasion his least evil; his chief anxiety being lest his constancy should fail him, and he should be brought to betray the gamekeeper, whose ruin he knew must now be the consequence.

Nor did the gamekeeper pass his time much better. He had the same apprehensions with the youth, for whose honour he had likewise a much tenderer regard than for his skin.

In the morning, when Tom attended the Reverend Mr. Thwackum, the person to whom Mr. Allworthy had committed the instruction of the two boys, he had the same questions put to him by that gentleman which he had been asked the evening before, to which he returned the same answers. The consequence of this was so severe a whipping that it possibly fell little short of the torture with which confessions are in some countries extorted from criminals.

Tom bore his punishment with great resolution, and though his master asked him between every stroke whether he would not confess, he was contented to be flayed rather than betray his friend or break the promise he had made.

The gamekeeper was now relieved from his anxiety, and Mr. Allworthy himself began to be concerned at Tom's sufferings; for besides that Mr. Thwackum, being highly enraged that he was not able to make the boy say what he himself pleased, had carried his severity much beyond the good man's intention, this latter began now to suspect that the squire had been mistaken, which his extreme eagerness and anger seemed to make probable; and as for what the servants had said in confirmation of their master's account, he laid no greater stress upon that. Now, as cruelty and injustice were two ideas of which Mr. Allworthy could by no means support the consciousness a single moment, he sent for Tom and, after many kind and friendly exhortations, said, "I am convinced, my dear child, that my suspicions have wronged you; I am sorry that you have been so severely punished on this account." And at last gave him a little horse to make him amends, again repeating his sorrow for what had passed.

Tom's guilt now flew in his face more than any severity could make it. He could more easily bear the lashes of Thwackum than the generosity of Allworthy. The tears burst from his eyes, and he fell upon his knees, crying, "Oh, sir, you are too good to me! Indeed you are. Indeed, I don't deserve it." And at that very instant, from the fullness of his heart had almost betrayed the secret, but the good genius of the gamekeeper suggested to him what might be the consequence to the poor fellow, and this consideration sealed his lips.

Thwackum did all he could to dissuade Allworthy from showing any compassion or kindness to the boy, saying he had persisted in an untruth, and gave some hints that a second whipping might probably bring the matter to light.

But Mr. Allworthy absolutely refused to consent to the experiment. He said the boy had suffered enough already for concealing the truth, even if he was guilty, seeing that he could have no motive but a mistaken point of honour for so doing.

"Honour!" cried Thwackum, with some warmth. "Mere stubbornness and obstinacy! Can honour teach any one to tell a lie, or can any honour exist independent of religion?"

This discourse happened at table when dinner was just ended, and there were present Mr. Allworthy, Mr. Thwackum, and a third gentleman, who now entered into the debate

and whom, before we proceed any farther, we shall briefly
introduce to our reader's acquaintance.

3

The name of this gentleman, who had then resided some time
at Mr. Allworthy's house, was Mr. Square. His natural parts
were not of the first rate, but he had greatly improved them
by a learned education. He was deeply read in the ancients
and a professed master of all the works of Plato and Aristotle.
Upon which great models he had principally formed himself,
sometimes according with the opinion of the one, and sometimes with that of the other. In morals he was a professed
Platonist, and in religion he inclined to be an Aristotelian.

But though he had, as we have said, formed his morals on
the Platonic model, yet he perfectly agreed with the opinion
of Aristotle in considering that great man rather in the quality of a philosopher or a speculatist than as a legislator. This
sentiment he carried a great way; indeed, so far as to regard
all virtue as matter of theory only. This, it is true, he never
affirmed, as I have heard, to any one; and yet upon the
least attention to his conduct, I cannot help thinking it was
his real opinion, as it will perfectly reconcile some contra-
dictions which might otherwise appear in his character.

This gentleman and Mr. Thwackum scarce ever met without a disputation, for their tenets were indeed diametrically
opposite to each other. Square held human nature to be the
perfection of all virtue, and that vice was a deviation from
our nature in the same manner as deformity of body is.
Thwackum, on the contrary, maintained that the human
mind since the Fall was nothing but a sink of iniquity, till
purified and redeemed by grace. In one point only they
agreed, which was in all their discourses on morality never
to mention the word *goodness*. The favourite phrase of the
former was the natural beauty of virtue; that of the latter
was the divine power of grace. The former measured all actions by the unalterable rule of right and the eternal fitness
of things; the latter decided all matters by authority; but in
doing this he always used the Scriptures and their commenta-

tors, as the lawyer doth his *Coke upon Lyttleton*, where the comment is of equal authority with the text.

After this short introduction, the reader will be pleased to remember that the parson had concluded his speech with a triumphant question, to which he had apprehended no answer: viz., Can any honour exist independent of religion?

To this Square answered that it was impossible to discourse philosophically concerning words till their meaning was first established; that there were scarce any two words of a more vague and uncertain signification than the two he had mentioned; for that there were almost as many different opinions concerning honour as concerning religion. "But," says he, "if by honour you mean the true natural beauty of virtue, I will maintain it may exist independent of any religion whatever. Nay," added he, "you yourself will allow it may exist independent of all but one: so will a Mahometan, a Jew, and all the maintainers of all the different sects in the world."

Thwackum replied this was arguing with the usual malice of all the enemies to the true Church. He said he doubted not but that all the infidels and heretics in the world would, if they could, confine honour to their own absurd errors and damnable deceptions. "But honour," says he, "is not therefore manifold because there are many absurd opinions about it; nor is religion manifold because there are various sects and heresies in the world. When I mention religion, I mean the Christian religion; and not only the Christian religion, but the Protestant religion; and not only the Protestant religion, but the Church of England. And when I mention honour, I mean that mode of divine grace which is not only consistent with but dependent upon this religion, and is consistent with and dependent upon no other. Now, to say that the honour I here mean and which was, I thought, all the honour I could be supposed to mean will uphold, much less dictate, an untruth is to assert an absurdity too shocking to be conceived."

"I purposely avoided," says Square, "drawing a conclusion which I thought evident from what I have said; but if you perceived it, I am sure you have not attempted to answer it. However, to drop the article of religion, I think it is plain from what you have said that we have different ideas of honour; or why do we not agree in the same terms of its explanation? I have asserted that true honour and true virtue are almost synonymous terms, and they are both founded on the unalterable rule of right and the eternal fitness of things; to which an untruth being absolutely repugnant and contrary, it is certain that true honour cannot support an untruth. In this, therefore, I think we are agreed; but that this honour can be said to be founded on religion, to which it is antecedent, if by religion be meant any positive law——"

"I agree," answered Thwackum with great warmth, "with a man who asserts honour to be antecedent to religion! Mr. Allworthy, did I agree——?"

He was proceeding when Mr. Allworthy interposed, telling them very coldly they had both mistaken his meaning, for that he had said nothing of true honour. It is possible, however, he would not have easily quieted the disputants, who were growing equally warm, had not another matter now fallen out which put a final end to the conversation at present.

4

CONTAINING A NECESSARY APOLOGY FOR THE AUTHOR, AND A
CHILDISH INCIDENT, WHICH PERHAPS REQUIRES AN APOLOGY
LIKEWISE

Before I proceed farther, I shall beg leave to obviate some misconstructions into which the zeal of some few readers may lead them; for I would not willingly give offence to any, especially to men who are warm in the cause of virtue or religion.

I hope, therefore, no man will, by the grossest misunderstanding or perversion of my meaning, misrepresent me as endeavouring to cast any ridicule on the greatest perfections of human nature; and which do, indeed, alone purify and ennoble the heart of man and raise him above the brute creation. This, reader, I will venture to say (and by how much the better man you are yourself, by so much the more will you be inclined to believe me): that I would rather have buried the sentiments of these two persons in eternal oblivion than have done any injury to either of these glorious causes.

On the contrary, it is with a view to their service that I have taken upon me to record the lives and actions of two of their false and pretended champions. A treacherous friend is the most dangerous enemy, and I will say boldly that both religion and virtue have received more real discredit from hypocrites than the wittiest profligates or infidels could ever cast upon them; nay, farther, as these two in their purity are rightly called the bands of civil society and are indeed the greatest blessings, so when poisoned and corrupted with fraud, pretence, and affectation, they have become the worst of civil curses and have enabled men to perpetrate the most cruel mischiefs to their own species.

Indeed, I doubt not but this ridicule will in general be allowed; my chief apprehension is, as many true and just sentiments often came from the mouths of these persons, lest the whole should be taken together and I should be conceived to ridicule all alike. Now, the reader will be pleased to consider that as neither of these men were fools, they could not be supposed to have holden none but wrong principles and to have uttered nothing but absurdities; what injustice, therefore, must I have done to their characters had I selected only what was bad, and how horridly wretched and maimed must their arguments have appeared!

Upon the whole, it is not religion or virtue but the want of them which is here exposed. Had not Thwackum too much neglected virtue, and Square religion, in the composition of their several systems, and had not both utterly discarded all natural goodness of heart, they had never been represented as the objects of derision in this history, in which we will now proceed.

This matter, then, which put an end to the debate mentioned in the last chapter was no other than a quarrel between Master Blifil and Tom Jones, the consequence of which had been a bloody nose to the former; for though Master Blifil, notwithstanding he was the younger, was in size above the other's match, yet Tom was much his superior at the noble art of boxing.

Tom, however, cautiously avoided all engagements with that youth; for besides that Tommy Jones was an inoffensive lad amidst all his roguery and really loved Blifil, Mr. Thwackum, being always the second of the latter, would have been sufficient to deter him.

But well says a certain author, no man is wise at all hours; it is therefore no wonder that a boy is not so. A difference arising at play between the two lads, Master Blifil called Tom a beggarly bastard. Upon which the latter, who was somewhat passionate in his disposition, immediately caused that phenomenon in the face of the former which we have above remembered.

Master Blifil now, with his blood running from his nose and the tears galloping after from his eyes, appeared before his uncle and the tremendous Thwackum, in which court an indictment of assault, battery, and wounding was instantly preferred against Tom, who in his excuse only pleaded the provocation, which was indeed all the matter that Master Blifil had omitted.

It is indeed possible that this circumstance might have escaped his memory; for in his reply he positively insisted that he had made use of no such appellation, adding heaven forbid such naughty words should ever come out of his mouth.

Tom, though against all form of law, rejoined in affirmance of the words. Upon which Master Blifil said, "It is no wonder. Those who will tell one fib will hardly stick at another. If I had told my master such a wicked fib as you have done, I should be ashamed to show my face."

"What fib, child?" cries Thwackum pretty eagerly.

"Why, he told you that nobody was with him a-shooting when he killed the partridge; but he knows" (here he burst into a flood of tears), "yes, he knows; for he confessed it to me that Black George, the gamekeeper, was there. Nay, he said—yes you did—deny it if you can, that you would not have confessed the truth though master had cut you to pieces."

At this the fire flashed from Thwackum's eyes and he cried out in triumph, "Oh, oh! This is your mistaken notion of honour! This is the boy who was not to be whipped again!" But Mr. Allworthy with a more gentle aspect turned towards the lad and said, "Is this true, child? How came you to persist so obstinately in a falsehood?"

Tom said he scorned a lie as much as any one, but he thought his honour engaged him to act as he did; for he had promised the poor fellow to conceal him, which, he said, he thought himself farther obliged to, as the gamekeeper had begged him not to go into the gentleman's manor, and had at last gone himself in compliance with his persuasions. He said this was the whole truth of the matter, and he would take his oath of it, and concluded with very passionately begging Mr. Allworthy to have compassion on the poor fellow's family, especially as he himself had been only guilty, and the other had been very difficultly prevailed on to do what he did. "Indeed, sir," said he, "it could hardly be called a lie that I told, for the poor fellow was entirely innocent of the whole matter. I should have gone alone after the birds; nay, I did go first, and he only followed me to prevent more mischief. Do, pray, sir, let me be punished; take my little horse away again, but pray, sir, forgive poor George."

Mr. Allworthy hesitated a few moments and then dismissed the boys, advising them to live more friendly and peaceably together.

5

It is probable that by disclosing this secret, which had been communicated in the utmost confidence to him, young Blifil preserved his companion from a good lashing; for the offence of the bloody nose would have been of itself sufficient cause for Thwackum to have proceeded to correction, but now this was totally absorbed in the consideration of the other matter; and with regard to this, Mr. Allworthy declared privately he thought the boy deserved reward rather than punishment, so that Thwackum's hand was withheld by a general pardon.

Thwackum, whose meditations were full of birch, exclaimed against this weak and, as he said he would venture to call it, wicked lenity. To remit the punishment of such crimes was, he said, to encourage them. He enlarged much on the correction of children and quoted many texts from Solomon and others, which, being to be found in so many other books, shall not be found here. He then applied himself to the vice of lying, on which head he was altogether as learned as he had been on the other.

Square said he had been endeavouring to reconcile the behaviour of Tom with his idea of perfect virtue, but could not. He owned there was something which at first sight appeared like fortitude in the action, but as fortitude was a virtue and falsehood a vice, they could by no means agree or unite together. He added that as this was in some measure to confound virtue and vice, it might be worth Mr. Thwackum's consideration whether a larger castigation might not be laid on upon that account.

As both these learned men concurred in censuring Jones,

so were they no less unanimous in applauding Master Blifil. To bring truth to light was by the parson asserted to be the duty of every religious man; and by the philosopher this was declared to be highly comformable with the rule of right and the eternal and unalterable fitness of things.

All this, however, weighed very little with Mr. Allworthy. He could not be prevailed on to sign the warrant for the execution of Jones. There was something within his own breast with which the invincible fidelity which that youth had preserved corresponded much better than it had done with the religion of Thwackum or with the virtue of Square. He therefore strictly ordered the former of these gentlemen to abstain from laying violent hands on Tom for what had passed. The pedagogue was obliged to obey those orders, but not without great reluctance and frequent mutterings that the boy would be certainly spoiled.

Towards the gamekeeper the good man behaved with more severity. He presently summoned that poor fellow before him, and after many bitter remonstrances paid him his wages and dismissed him from his service; for Mr. Allworthy rightly observed that there was great difference between being guilty of a falsehood to excuse yourself, and to excuse another. He likewise urged, as the principal motive to his inflexible severity against this man, that he had basely suffered Tom Jones to undergo so heavy a punishment for his sake, whereas he ought to have prevented it by making the discovery himself.

When this story became public, many people differed from Square and Thwackum in judging the conduct of the two lads on the occasion. Master Blifil was generally called a sneaking rascal, a poor-spirited wretch, with other epithets of the like kind; whilst Tom was honoured with the appellations of a brave lad, a jolly dog, and an honest fellow. Indeed, his behaviour to Black George much ingratiated him with all the servants; for though that fellow was before universally disliked, yet he was no sooner turned away than he was as universally pitied, and the friendship and gallantry of Tom Jones was celebrated by them all with the highest applause; and they condemned Master Blifil as openly as they durst without incurring the danger of offending his mother. For all this, however, poor Tom smarted in the flesh; for though Thwackum had been inhibited to exercise his arm on the foregoing account, yet, as the proverb says, "It is easy to find a stick, &c." So was it easy to find a rod; and, indeed, the not being able to find one was the only thing which could have kept Thwackum any long time from chastising poor Jones.

Had the bare delight in the sport been the only inducement to the pedagogue, it is probable Master Blifil would likewise have had his share; but though Mr. Allworthy had given him frequent orders to make no difference between the lads, yet was Thwackum altogether as kind and gentle to this youth as he was harsh, nay, even barbarous, to the other. To say the truth, Blifil had greatly gained his master's affections, partly by the profound respect he always showed his person, but much more by the decent reverence with which he received his doctrine; for he had got by heart, and frequently repeated, his phrases, and maintained all his master's religious principles with a zeal which was surprising in one so young and which greatly endeared him to the worthy preceptor.

Tom Jones, on the other hand, was not only deficient in outward tokens of respect, often forgetting to pull off his hat or to bow at his master's approach, but was altogether as unmindful both of his master's precepts and example. He was indeed a thoughtless, giddy youth, with little sobriety in his manners and less in his countenance, and would often very impudently and indecently laugh at his companion for his serious behaviour.

Mr. Square had the same reason for his preference of the former lad, for Tom Jones showed no more regard to the learned discourses which this gentleman would sometimes throw away upon him than to those of Thwackum. He once ventured to make a jest of the rule of right, and at another time said he believed there was no rule in the world capable of making such a man as his father (for so Mr. Allworthy suffered himself to be called).

Master Blifil, on the contrary, had address enough at sixteen to recommend himself at one and the same time to both these opposites. With one he was all religion, with the other he was all virtue. And when both were present he was profoundly silent, which both interpreted in his favour and their own.

Nor was Blifil contented with flattering both these gentlemen to their faces; he took frequent occasions of praising them behind their backs to Allworthy, before whom, when they were alone together and when his uncle commended any religious or virtuous sentiment (for many such came constantly from him), he seldom failed to ascribe it to the good instructions he had received from either Thwackum or Square; for he knew his uncle repeated all such compliments to the persons for whose use they were meant, and he found by experience the great impressions which they made on the philosopher as well as on the divine; for to say the truth, there is no kind of flattery so irresistible as this at second hand.

The young gentleman, moreover, soon perceived how extremely grateful all those panegyrics on his instructors were to Mr. Allworthy himself, as they so loudly resounded the praise of that singular plan of education which he had laid down; for this worthy man, having observed the imperfect institution of our public schools and the many vices which boys were there liable to learn, had resolved to educate his nephew as well as the other lad, whom he had in a manner adopted, in his own house, where he thought their morals would escape all that danger of being corrupted to which they would be unavoidably exposed in any public school or university.

Having therefore determined to commit these two boys to the tuition of a private tutor, Mr. Thwackum was recommended to him for that office by a very particular friend, of whose understanding Mr. Allworthy had a great opinion and in whose integrity he placed much confidence. This Thwackum was fellow of a college, where he almost entirely resided, and had a great reputation for learning, religion, and sobriety of manners. And these were doubtless the qualifications by which Mr. Allworthy's friend had been induced to recommend him, though indeed this friend had some obligations to Thwackum's family, who were the most considerable persons in a borough which that gentleman represented in Parliament.

Thwackum at his first arrival was extremely agreeable to Allworthy; and indeed he perfectly answered the character which had been given of him. Upon longer acquaintance, however, and more intimate conversation, this worthy man saw infirmities in the tutor, which he could have wished him to have been without; though as those seemed greatly overbalanced by his good qualities, they did not incline Mr. Allworthy to part with him; nor would they, indeed, have justified such a proceeding, for the reader is greatly mistaken if he conceives that Thwackum appeared to Mr. Allworthy in the same light as he doth to him in this history; and he is as much deceived if he imagines that the most intimate acquaintance which he himself could have had with that divine would have informed him of those things which we, from our inspiration, are enabled to open and discover. Of readers who from such conceits as these condemn the wisdom or penetration of Mr. Allworthy, I shall not scruple to say that they make a very bad and ungrateful use of that knowledge which we have communicated to them.

These apparent errors in the doctrine of Thwackum served greatly to palliate the contrary errors in that of Square, which our good man no less saw and condemned. He thought, indeed, that the different exuberancies of these gentlemen would correct their different imperfections, and that from both, especially with his assistance, the two lads would derive sufficient precepts of true religion and virtue. If the event happened contrary to his expectations, this possibly proceeded from some fault in the plan itself, which the reader hath my leave to discover if he can; for we do not pretend to introduce any infallible characters into this history, where we hope nothing will be found which hath never yet been seen in human nature.

To return, therefore: the reader will not, I think, wonder that the different behaviour of the two lads above commemorated produced the different effects of which he hath already seen some instance; and besides this, there was another reason for the conduct of the philosopher and the pedagogue, but this being matter of great importance, we shall reveal it in the next chapter.

6

CONTAINING A BETTER REASON STILL FOR THE BEFORE-MENTIONED OPINIONS

It is to be known, then, that those two learned personages, who have lately made a considerable figure on the theatre of this history, had from their first arrival at Mr. Allworthy's house taken so great an affection, the one to his virtue, the other to his religion, that they had meditated the closest alliance with him.

For this purpose they had cast their eyes on that fair widow, whom, though we have not for some time made any mention of her, the reader, we trust, hath not forgot. Mrs. Blifil was indeed the object to which they both aspired.

It may seem remarkable that of four persons whom we have commemorated at Mr. Allworthy's house, three of them should fix their inclinations on a lady who was never greatly celebrated for her beauty, and who was, moreover, now a little descended into the vale of years; but in reality bosom friends and intimate acquaintance have a kind of natural propensity to particular females at the house of a friend: viz., to his grandmother, mother, sister, daughter, aunt, niece, and cousin when they are rich; and to his wife, sister, daughter, niece, cousin, mistress, or servant-maid if they should be handsome.

We would not, however, have our reader imagine that persons of such characters as were supported by Thwackum and Square would undertake a matter of this kind, which hath been a little censured by some rigid moralists, before they had thoroughly examined it and considered whether it was (as Shakespeare phrases it) "Stuff o' th' conscience" or no. Thwackum was encouraged to the undertaking by reflecting that to court your neighbour's sister is nowhere forbidden; and he knew it was a rule in the construction of all laws that *Expressum facit cessare tacitum.* The sense of which is, "When a lawgiver sets down plainly his whole meaning, we are prevented from making him mean what we please ourselves." As some instances of women, therefore, are mentioned in the divine law which forbids us to covet our neighbour's goods, and that of a sister omitted, he concluded it to be lawful. And as to Square, who was in his person what is called a jolly fellow or a widow's man, he easily reconciled his choice to the eternal fitness of things.

Now, as both these gentlemen were industrious in taking every opportunity of recommending themselves to the widow, they apprehended one certain method was by giving her son the constant preference to the other lad; and as they conceived the kindness and affection which Mr. Allworthy showed the latter must be highly disagreeable to her, they doubted not but the laying hold on all occasions to degrade and vilify him would be highly pleasing to her, who, as she hated the boy, must love all those who did him any hurt. In this, Thwackum had the advantage; for while Square could only scarify the poor lad's reputation, he could flay his skin; and, indeed, he considered every lash he gave him as a compliment paid to his mistress, so that he could with the utmost propriety repeat this old flogging line: *Castigo te non quod odio habeam, sed quod AMEM.* "I chastise thee not out of hatred, but out of love." And this, indeed, he often had in his mouth, or rather, according to the old phrase, never more properly applied, at his fingers' ends.

For this reason principally, the two gentlemen concurred, as we have seen above, in their opinion concerning the two lads; this being, indeed, almost the only instance of their concurring on any point; for, beside the difference of their principles, they had both long ago strongly suspected each other's design and hated one another with no little degree of inveteracy.

This mutual animosity was a good deal increased by their alternate successes; for Mrs. Blifil knew what they would be at long before they imagined it, or, indeed, intended she should; for they proceeded with great caution, lest she should be offended and acquaint Mr. Allworthy. But they had no reason for any such fear; she was well enough pleased with a passion of which she intended none should have any fruits but herself. And the only fruits she designed for herself were flattery and courtship; for which purpose she soothed them by turns, and a long time equally. She was, indeed, rather inclined to favour the parson's principles, but Square's person was more agreeable to her eye, for he was a comely man; whereas the pedagogue did in countenance very nearly resemble that gentleman who, in the *Harlot's Progress,* is seen correcting the ladies in Bridewell.

Whether Mrs. Blifil had been surfeited with the sweets of marriage, or disgusted by its bitters, or from other cause it proceeded, I will not determine; but she could never be brought to listen to any second proposals. However, she at last conversed with Square with such a degree of intimacy that malicious tongues began to whisper things of her, to which, as well for the sake of the lady as that they were highly disagreeable to the rule of right and the fitness of things, we will give no credit, and therefore shall not blot our paper with them. The pedagogue, 'tis certain, whipped on without getting a step nearer to his journey's end.

Indeed, he had committed a great error, and that Square discovered much sooner than himself. Mrs. Blifil (as, perhaps, the reader may have formerly guessed) was not over and above pleased with the behaviour of her husband; nay, to be honest, she absolutely hated him till his death, at last, a little reconciled him to her affections. It will not be therefore greatly wondered at if she had not the most violent regard to the offspring she had by him. And, in fact, she had so little of this regard that in his infancy she seldom saw her son or took any notice of him; and hence she acquiesced after a little reluctance in all the favours which Mr. Allworthy showered on the foundling, whom the good man called his own boy, and in all things put on an entire equality with Master Blifil. This acquiescence in Mrs. Blifil was considered by the neighbours and by the family as a mark of her condescension to her brother's humour, and she was imagined by all others, as well as Thwackum and Square, to hate the foundling in her heart; nay, the more civility she showed him, the more they conceived she detested him, and the surer schemes she was laying for his ruin; for as they thought it her interest to hate him, it was very difficult for her to persuade them she did not.

Thwackum was the more confirmed in his opinion as she had more than once slyly caused him to whip Tom Jones when Mr. Allworthy, who was an enemy to this exercise, was abroad; whereas she had never given any such orders concerning young Blifil. And this had likewise imposed upon Square. In reality, though she certainly hated her own son, of which however monstrous it appears I am assured she is not a singular instance, she appeared, notwithstanding all her outward compliance, to be in her heart sufficiently displeased with all the favour shown by Mr. Allworthy to the foundling. She frequently complained of this behind her brother's back, and very sharply censured him for it both to Thwackum and Square; nay, she would throw it in the teeth of Allworthy himself when a little quarrel, or miff, as it is vulgarly called, arose between them.

However, when Tom grew up and gave tokens of that gallantry of temper which greatly recommends men to women, this disinclination which she had discovered to him when a child by degrees abated, and at last she so evidently demonstrated her affection to him to be much stronger than what she bore her own son that it was impossible to mistake her any longer. She was so desirous of often seeing him, and discovered such satisfaction and delight in his company, that before he was eighteen years old he was become a rival to both Square and Thwackum; and what is worse, the whole country began to talk loudly of her inclination to Tom, as they had before done of that which she had shown to

Square, on which account the philosopher conceived the most implacable hatred for our poor hero.

7

IN WHICH THE AUTHOR HIMSELF MAKES HIS APPEARANCE ON THE STAGE

Though Mr. Allworthy was not of himself hasty to see things in a disadvantageous light, and was a stranger to the public voice, which seldom reaches to a brother or a husband though it rings in the ears of all the neighbourhood, yet was this affection of Mrs. Blifil to Tom, and the preference which she too visibly gave him to her own son, of the utmost disadvantage to that youth.

For such was the compassion which inhabited Mr. Allworthy's mind that nothing but the steel of justice could ever subdue it. To be unfortunate in any respect was sufficient, if there was no demerit to counterpoise it, to turn the scale of that good man's pity and to engage his friendship and his benefaction.

When, therefore, he plainly saw Master Blifil was absolutely detested (for that he was) by his own mother, he began on that account only to look with an eye of compassion upon him; and what the effects of compassion are in good and benevolent minds I need not here explain to most of my readers.

Henceforward, he saw every appearance of virtue in the youth through the magnifying end, and viewed all his faults with the glass inverted, so that they became scarce perceptible. And this, perhaps, the amiable temper of pity may make commendable, but the next step the weakness of human nature alone must excuse; for he no sooner perceived that preference which Mrs. Blifil gave to Tom that poor youth (however innocent) began to sink in his affections as he rose in hers. This, it is true, would of itself alone never have been able to eradicate Jones from his bosom, but it was greatly injurious to him, and prepared Mr. Allworthy's mind for those impressions which afterwards produced the mighty events that will be contained hereafter in this history, and to which, it must be confessed, the unfortunate lad by his own wantonness, wildness, and want of caution too much contributed.

In recording some instances of these, we shall if rightly understood afford a very useful lesson to those well-disposed youths who shall hereafter be our readers; for they may here find that goodness of heart and openness of temper, though these may give them great comfort within and administer to an honest pride in their own minds, will by no means—alas!—do their business in the world. Prudence and circumspection are necessary even to the best of men. They are, indeed, as it were, a guard to Virtue, without which she can never be safe. It is not enough that your designs, nay, that your actions, are intrinsically good; you must take care they shall appear so. If your inside be never so beautiful, you must preserve a fair outside also. This must be constantly looked to, or malice and envy will take care to blacken it so that the sagacity and goodness of an All-worthy will not be able to see through it and to discern the beauties within. Let this, my young readers, be your constant maxim: that no man can be good enough to enable him to neglect the rules of prudence, nor will Virtue herself look beautiful unless she be bedecked with the outward ornaments of decency and decorum. And this precept, my worthy disciples, if you read with due attention, you will, I hope, find sufficiently enforced by examples in the following pages.

I ask pardon for this short appearance, by way of chorus, on the stage. It is in reality for my own sake that, while I am discovering the rocks on which innocence and goodness often split, I may not be misunderstood to recommend the very means to my worthy readers by which I intend to show them they will be undone. And this, as I could not prevail on any of my actors to speak, I was obliged to declare myself.

8

A CHILDISH INCIDENT, IN WHICH, HOWEVER, IS SEEN A GOOD-NATURED DISPOSITION IN TOM JONES

The reader may remember that Mr. Allworthy gave Tom Jones a little horse, as a kind of smart-money for the punishment which he imagined he had suffered innocently.

This horse Tom kept above half a year, and then rode him to a neighbouring fair and sold him.

At his return, being questioned by Thwackum what he had done with the money for which the horse was sold, he frankly declared he would not tell him.

"Oho!" says Thwackum. "You will not! Then I will have it out of your br——h"—that being the place to which he always applied for information on every doubtful occasion.

Tom was now mounted on the back of a footman and everything prepared for execution, when Mr. Allworthy, entering the room, gave the criminal a reprieve and took him with him into another apartment, where, Mr. Allworthy being only present with Tom, he put the same question to him which Thwackum had before asked him.

Tom answered he could in duty refuse him nothing, but as for that tyrannical rascal, he would never make him any other answer than with a cudgel, with which he hoped soon to be able to pay him for all his barbarities.

Mr. Allworthy very severely reprimanded the lad for his indecent and disrespectful expressions concerning his master, but much more for his avowing an intention of revenge. He threatened him with the entire loss of his favour if he ever heard such another word from his mouth; for, he said, he would never support or befriend a reprobate. By these and the like declarations he extorted some compunction from Tom, in which that youth was not over-sincere, for he really meditated some return for all the smarting favours he had received at the hands of the pedagogue. He was, however, brought by Mr. Allworthy to express a concern for his resentment against Thwackum; and then the good man, after some wholesome admonition, permitted him to proceed, which he did as follows:

"Indeed, my dear sir, I love and honour you more than all the world. I know the great obligations I have to you, and should detest myself if I thought my heart was capable of ingratitude. Could the little horse you gave me speak, I am sure he could tell you how fond I was of your present; for I had more pleasure in feeding him than in riding him. Indeed, sir, it went to my heart to part with him; nor would I have sold him upon any other account in the world than what I did. You yourself, sir, I am convinced, in my case would have done the same; for none ever so sensibly felt the misfortunes of others. What would you feel, dear sir, if you thought yourself the occasion of them? Indeed, sir, there never was any misery like theirs."—"Like whose, child?" says Allworthy. "What do you mean?"—"Oh, sir," answered Tom, "your poor gamekeeper with all his large family, ever since your discarding him, have been perishing with all the miseries of cold and hunger. I could not bear to see these poor wretches naked and starving, and at the same time know myself to have been the occasion of all their sufferings. I could not bear it, sir, upon my soul, I could not." Here the tears run down his cheeks, and he thus proceeded: "It was to save them from absolute destruction I parted with your dear present, notwithstanding all the value I had for it. I sold the horse for them, and they have every farthing of the money."

Mr. Allworthy now stood silent for some moments, and before he spoke the tears started from his eyes. He at length dismissed Tom with a gentle rebuke, advising him for the future to apply to him in cases of distress rather than to use extraordinary means of relieving them himself.

This affair was afterwards the subject of much debate between Thwackum and Square. Thwackum held that this was flying in Mr. Allworthy's face, who had intended to punish the fellow for his disobedience. He said in some instances what the world called charity appeared to him to be opposing the will of the Almighty, which had marked some particular persons for destruction, and that this was in like manner acting in opposition to Mr. Allworthy—concluding as usual with a hearty recommendation of birch.

Square argued strongly on the other side, in opposition, perhaps, to Thwackum, or in compliance with Mr. Allworthy, who seemed very much to approve what Jones had done. As to what he urged on this occasion, as I am convinced most of my readers will be much abler advocates for poor Jones, it would be impertinent to relate it. Indeed, it was not difficult to reconcile to the rule of right an action which it would have been impossible to deduce from the rule of wrong.

9

CONTAINING AN INCIDENT OF A MORE HEINOUS KIND, WITH THE COMMENTS OF THWACKUM AND SQUARE

It hath been observed by some man of much greater reputation for wisdom than myself that misfortunes seldom come single. An instance of this may, I believe, be seen in those gentlemen who have the misfortune to have any of their rogueries detected, for here discovery seldom stops till the whole is come out. Thus it happened to poor Tom, who was no sooner pardoned for selling the horse than he was discovered to have some time before sold a fine Bible which Mr. Allworthy gave him, the money arising from which sale he had disposed in the same manner. This Bible Master Blifil had purchased, though he had already such another of his own, partly out of respect for the book and partly out of friendship to Tom, being unwilling that the Bible should be sold out of the family at half-price. He therefore deposited the said half-price himself; for he was a very prudent lad and so careful of his money that he had laid up almost every penny which he had received from Mr. Allworthy.

Some people had been noted to be able to read in no book but their own. On the contrary, from the time when Master Blifil was first possessed of this Bible he never used any other. Nay, he was seen reading in it much oftener than he had before been in his own. Now, as he frequently asked Thwackum to explain difficult passages to him, that gentleman unfortunately took notice of Tom's name, which was written in many parts of the book. This brought on an inquiry, which obliged Master Blifil to discover the whole matter.

Thwackum was resolved a crime of this kind, which he called sacrilege, should not go unpunished. He therefore proceeded immediately to castigation, and not contented with that, he acquainted Mr. Allworthy at their next meeting with this monstrous crime, as it appeared to him, inveighing against Tom in the most bitter terms and likening him to the buyers and sellers who were driven out of the temple.

Square saw this matter in a very different light. He said he could not perceive any higher crime in selling one book than in selling another; that to sell Bibles was strictly lawful by all laws, both divine and human, and consequently there was no unfitness in it. He told Thwackum that his great concern on this occasion brought to his mind the story of a very devout woman who, out of pure regard to religion, stole Tillotson's *Sermons* from a lady of her acquaintance.

This story caused a vast quantity of blood to rush into the parson's face, which of itself was none of the palest, and he was going to reply with great warmth and anger had not

Mrs. Blifil, who was present at this debate, interposed. That lady declared herself absolutely of Mr. Square's side. She argued, indeed, very learnedly in support of his opinion, and concluded with saying if Tom had been guilty of any fault, she must confess her own son appeared to be equally culpable; for that she could see no difference between the buyer and the seller, both of whom were alike to be driven out of the temple.

Mrs. Bilfil, having declared her opinion, put an end to the debate. Square's triumph would almost have stopped his words, had he needed them; and Thwackum, besides that for reasons before mentioned he durst not venture at disobliging the lady, was almost choked with indignation. As to Mr. Allworthy, he said since the boy had been already punished, he would not deliver his sentiments on the occasion; and whether he was or was not angry with the lad, I must leave to the reader's own conjecture.

Soon after this, an action was brought against the gamekeeper by Squire Western (the gentleman in whose manor the partridge was killed) for depredations of the like kind. This was a most unfortunate circumstance for the fellow, as it not only of itself threatened his ruin but actually prevented Mr. Allworthy from restoring him to his favour; for as that gentleman was walking out one evening with Master Blifil and young Jones, the latter slyly drew him to the habitation of Black George, where the family of that poor wretch, namely, his wife and children, were found in all the misery with which cold, hunger, and nakedness can affect human creatures; for as to the money they had received from Jones, former debts had consumed almost the whole.

Such a scene as this could not fail of affecting the heart of Mr. Allworthy. He immediately gave the mother a couple of guineas, with which he bid her clothe her children. The poor woman burst into tears at this goodness, and while she was thanking him could not refrain from expressing her gratitude to Tom, who had, she said, long preserved both her and hers from starving. "We have not," says she, "had a morsel to eat, nor have these poor children had a rag to put on, but what his goodness hath bestowed on us." For indeed, besides the horse and the Bible, Tom had sacrificed a night-gown and other things to the use of this distressed family.

On their return home, Tom made use of all his eloquence to display the wretchedness of these people and the penitence of Black George himself; and in this he succeeded so well that Mr. Allworthy said he thought the man had suffered enough for what was past; that he would forgive him, and think of some means of providing for him and his family.

Jones was so delighted with this news that though it was dark when they returned home, he could not help going back a mile, in a shower of rain, to acquaint the poor woman with the glad tidings; but, like other hasty divulgers of news, he only brought on himself the trouble of contradicting it; for the ill fortune of Black George made use of the very opportunity of his friend's absence to overturn all again.

10

IN WHICH MASTER BLIFIL AND JONES APPEAR IN DIFFERENT
LIGHTS

Master Blifil fell very short of his companion in the amiable quality of mercy, but he as greatly exceeded him in one of a much higher kind, namely, in justice, in which he followed both the precepts and example of Thwackum and Square; for though they would both make frequent use of the word mercy, yet it was plain that in reality Square held it to be inconsistent with the rule of right, and Thwackum was for doing justice and leaving mercy to heaven. The two gentlemen did indeed somewhat differ in opinion concerning the objects of this sublime virtue, by which Thwackum would probably have destroyed one half of mankind and Square the other half.

Master Blifil, then, though he had kept silence in the presence of Jones, yet when he had better considered the matter could by no means endure the thought of suffering his uncle to confer favours on the undeserving. He therefore resolved immediately to acquaint him with the fact which we have above slightly hinted to the readers. The truth of which was as follows:

The gamekeeper, about a year after he was dismissed from Mr. Allworthy's service and before Tom's selling the horse, being in want of bread either to fill his own mouth or those of his family, as he passed through a field belonging to Mr. Western, espied a hare sitting in her form. This hare he had basely and barbarously knocked on the head, against the laws of the land and no less against the laws of sportsmen.

The higgler to whom the hare was sold, being unfortunately taken many months after with a quantity of game upon him, was obliged to make his peace with the squire by becoming evidence against some poacher. And now Black George was pitched upon by him as being a person already obnoxious to Mr. Western and one of no good fame in the country. He was, besides, the best sacrifice the higgler could make, as he had supplied him with no game since, and by this means the witness had an opportunity of screening his better customers; for the squire, being charmed with the power of punishing Black George, whom a single transgression was sufficient to ruin, made no further inquiry.

Had this fact been truly laid before Mr. Allworthy, it might probably have done the gamekeeper very little mischief. But there is no zeal blinder than that which is inspired with the love of justice against offenders. Master Blifil had forgot the distance of the time. He varied likewise in the manner of the fact, and by the hasty addition of the single letter *S*, he considerably altered the story, for he said that George had wired hares. These alterations might probably have been set right had not Master Blifil unluckily insisted on a promise of secrecy from Mr. Allworthy before he revealed the matter to him; but by that means the poor gamekeeper was condemned without having any opportunity to defend himself; for as the fact of killing the hare and of the action brought were certainly true, Mr. Allworthy had no doubt concerning the rest.

Short-lived, then, was the joy of these poor people; for Mr. Allworthy the next morning declared he had fresh reason, without assigning it, for his anger, and strictly forbade Tom to mention George any more; though as for his family, he said he would endeavour to keep them from starving, but as to the fellow himself, he would leave him to the laws, which nothing could keep him from breaking.

Tom could by no means divine what had incensed Mr. Allworthy, for of Master Blifil he had not the least suspicion. However, as his friendship was to be tired out by no disappointments, he now determined to try another method of preserving the poor gamekeeper from ruin.

Jones was lately grown very intimate with Mr. Western. He had so greatly recommended himself to that gentleman by leaping over five-barred gates and by other acts of sportsmanship that the squire had declared Tom would certainly make a great man if he had sufficient encouragement. He often wished he had himself a son with such parts, and one day very solemnly asserted at a drinking bout that Tom should hunt a pack of hounds for a thousand pound of his money with any huntsman in the whole county.

By such kind of talents he had so ingratiated himself with the squire that he was a most welcome guest at his table and a favourite companion in his sport; everything which the squire held most dear, to wit, his guns, dogs, and horses, were now as much at the command of Jones as if they had been his own. He resolved, therefore, to make use of this favour on behalf of his friend Black George, whom he hoped to introduce into Mr. Western's family in the same capacity in which he had before served Mr. Allworthy.

The reader, if he considers that this fellow was already obnoxious to Mr. Western, and if he considers farther the weighty business by which that gentleman's displeasure had been incurred, will perhaps condemn this as a foolish and desperate undertaking; but if he should not totally condemn young Jones on that account, he will greatly applaud him for strengthening himself with all imaginable interest on so arduous an occasion.

For this purpose, then, Tom applied to Mr. Western's daughter, a young lady of about seventeen years of age, whom her father, next after those necessary implements of sport just before mentioned, loved and esteemed above all the world. Now, as she had some influence on the squire, so Tom had some little influence on her. But this being the intended heroine of this work, a lady with whom we are ourselves greatly in love and with whom many of our readers will probably be in love too before we part, it is by no means proper she should make her appearance at the end of a book.

BOOK IV

1

CONTAINING FIVE PAGES OF PAPER

As truth distinguishes our writings from those idle romances which are filled with monsters, the productions not of Nature but of distempered brains, and which have been therefore recommended by an eminent critic to the sole use of the pastry-cook, so, on the other hand, we would avoid any resemblance to that kind of history which a celebrated poet seems to think is no less calculated for the emolument of the brewer as the reading it should be always attended with a tankard of good ale:

> While—history with her comrade ale,
> Soothes the sad series of her serious tale.

For as this is the liquor of modern historians, nay, perhaps their muse if we may believe the opinion of Butler, who attributes inspiration to ale, it ought likewise to be the potation of their readers, since every book ought to be read with the same spirit and in the same manner as it is writ. Thus the famous author of *Hurlothrumbo* told a learned bishop that the reason his lordship could not taste the excellence of his piece was that he did not read it with a fiddle in his hand, which instrument he himself had always had in his own when he composed it.

That our work, therefore, might be in no danger of being likened to the labours of these historians, we have taken every occasion of interspersing through the whole sundry similes, descriptions, and other kind of poetical embellishments. These are, indeed, designed to supply the place of the said ale, and to refresh the mind whenever those slumbers which in a long work are apt to invade the reader as well as the writer shall begin to creep upon him. Without interruptions of this kind, the best narrative of plain matter of fact must overpower every reader; for nothing but the everlasting watchfulness which Homer hath ascribed to Jove himself can be proof against a newspaper of many volumes.

We shall leave to the reader to determine with what judgement we have chosen the several occasions for inserting these ornamental parts of our work. Surely it will be allowed that none could be more proper than the present, where we are about to introduce a considerable character on the scene, no less, indeed, than the heroine of this heroic, historical, prosaic poem. Here, therefore, we have thought proper to prepare the mind of the reader for her reception by filling it with every pleasing image which we can draw from the face of Nature. And for this method we plead many precedents: first, this is an art well known to, and much practised by, our tragic poets, who seldom fail to prepare their audience for the reception of their principal characters.

Thus the hero is always introduced with a flourish of drums and trumpets, in order to rouse a martial spirit in the audience and to accommodate their ears to bombast and fustian, which Mr. Locke's blind man would not have grossly erred in likening to the sound of a trumpet. Again, when lovers are coming forth, soft music often conducts them on the stage, either to soothe the audience with all the softness of the tender passion or to lull and prepare them for that gentle slumber in which they will most probably be composed by the ensuing scene.

And not only the poets but the masters of these poets, the managers of playhouses, seem to be in this secret; for, besides the aforesaid kettledrums, &c., which denote the hero's approach, he is generally ushered on the stage by a large troop of half a dozen scene-shifters; and how necessary these are imagined to his appearance may be concluded from the following theatrical story:

King Pyrrhus was at dinner at an ale-house bordering on the theatre when he was summoned to go on the stage. The hero, being unwilling to quit his shoulder of mutton and as unwilling to draw on himself the indignation of Mr. Wilks (his brother-manager) for making the audience wait, had bribed these his harbingers to be out of the way. While Mr. Wilks, therefore, was thundering out, "Where are the carpenters to walk on before King Pyrrhus?" that monarch very quietly ate his mutton, and the audience, however impatient, were obliged to entertain themselves with music in his absence.

To be plain, I much questioned whether the politician, who hath generally a good nose, hath not scented out somewhat of the utility of this practice. I am convinced that awful magistrate my Lord Mayor contracts a good deal of that reverence which attends him through the year by the several pageants which precede his pomp. Nay, I must confess, that even I myself, who am not remarkably liable to be captivated with show, have yielded not a little to the impressions of much preceding state. When I have seen a man strutting in a procession after others whose business hath been only to walk before him, I have conceived a higher notion of his dignity than I have felt on seeing him in a common situation. But there is one instance which comes exactly up to my purpose. This is the custom of sending on a basket-woman who is to precede the pomp at a coronation and to strew the stage with flowers before the great personages begin their procession. The ancients would certainly have invoked the goddess Flora for this purpose, and it would have been no difficulty for their priests or politicians to have persuaded the people of the real presence of the deity, though a plain mortal had personated her and performed her office. But we have no such design of imposing on our reader, and therefore, those who object to the heathen theology may, if they please, change our goddess into the above-mentioned basket-woman. Our intention, in short, is to introduce our heroine with the utmost solemnity in our power, with an elevation of style and all other circumstances proper to raise the veneration of our reader. Indeed we would, for certain causes, advise those of our male readers who have any hearts to read no farther, were we not well assured that how amiable soever the picture of our heroine will appear, as it is really a copy from Nature, many of our fair country-women will be found worthy to satisfy any passion and to answer any idea of female perfection which our pencil will be able to raise.

And now, without any further preface, we proceed to our next chapter.

A SHORT HINT OF WHAT WE CAN DO IN THE SUBLIME, AND A DESCRIPTION OF MISS SOPHIA WESTERN

Hushed be every ruder breath. May the heathen ruler of the winds confine in iron chains the boisterous limbs of noisy Boreas and the sharp-pointed nose of bitter-biting Eurus. Do thou, sweet Zephyrus, rising from thy fragrant bed, mount the western sky and lead on those delicious gales, the charms of which call forth the lovely Flora from her chamber, perfumed with pearly dews, when on the first of June, her birthday, the blooming maid in loose attire gently tips it over the verdant mead, where every flower rises to do her homage till the whole field becomes enamelled and colours contend with sweets which shall ravish her most.

So charming may she now appear; and you, the feathered choristers of Nature, whose sweetest notes not even Handel can excel, tune your melodious throats to celebrate her appearance. From love proceeds your music, and to love it returns. Awaken therefore that gentle passion in every swain; for lo, adorned with all the charms in which Nature can array her, bedecked with beauty, youth, sprightliness, innocence, modesty, and tenderness, breathing sweetness from her rosy lips, and darting brightness from her sparkling eyes, the lovely Sophia comes!

Reader, perhaps thou hast seen the statue of the Venus de Medicis. Perhaps, too, thou hast seen the gallery of beauties at Hampton Court. Thou mayest remember each bright Churchill of the galaxy, and all the toasts of the Kit-cat. Or if their reign was before thy times, at least thou hast seen their daughters, the no less dazzling beauties of the present age, whose names, should we here insert, we apprehend they would fill the whole volume.

Now, if thou hast seen all these, be not afraid of the rude answer which Lord Rochester once gave to a man who had seen many things. No. If thou hast seen all these without knowing what beauty is, thou hast no eyes; if without feeling its power, thou hast no heart.

Yet it is possible, my friend, that thou mayest have seen all these without being able to form an exact idea of Sophia; for she did not exactly resemble any of them. She was most like the picture of Lady Ranelagh, and, I have heard, more still to the famous Duchess of Mazarine; but most of all she resembled one whose image never can depart from my breast, and whom if thou dost remember, thou hast then, my friend, an adequate idea of Sophia.

But lest this should not have been thy fortune, we will endeavour with our utmost skill to describe this paragon, though we are sensible that our highest abilities are very inadequate to the task.

Sophia, then, the only daughter of Mr. Western, was a middle-sized woman, but rather inclining to tall. Her shape was not only exact but extremely delicate, and the nice proportion of her arms promised the truest symmetry in her limbs. Her hair, which was black, was so luxuriant that it reached her middle before she cut it to comply with the modern fashion, and it was now curled so gracefully in her neck that few would believe it to be her own. If envy could find any part of her face which demanded less commendation than the rest, it might possibly think her forehead might have been higher without prejudice to her. Her eyebrows were full, even, and arched beyond the power of art to imitate. Her black eyes had a lustre in them which all her softness could not extinguish. Her nose was exactly regular, and her mouth, in which were two rows of ivory, exactly answered Sir John Suckling's description in those lines:

> Her lips were red, and one was thin,
> Compared to that was next her chin.
> Some bee had stung it newly.

Her cheeks were of the oval kind, and in her right she had a dimple which the least smile discovered. Her chin had certainly its share in forming the beauty of her face, but it was difficult to say it was either large or small, though perhaps it was rather of the former kind. Her complexion had rather more of the lily than of the rose, but when exercise or modesty increased her natural colour, no vermilion could equal it. Then one might indeed cry out with the celebrated Dr. Donne,

> ——Her pure and eloquent blood
> Spoke in her cheeks, and so distinctly wrought,
> That one might almost say her body thought.

Her neck was long and finely turned; and here, if I was not afraid of offending her delicacy, I might justly say the highest beauties of the famous *Venus de Medicis* were outdone. Here was whiteness which no lilies, ivory, nor alabaster could match. The finest cambric might indeed be supposed from envy to cover that bosom, which was much whiter than itself. It was, indeed,

Nitor splendens Pario marmore purius,

"a gloss shining beyond the purest brightness of Parian marble."

Such was the outside of Sophia; nor was this beautiful frame disgraced by an inhabitant unworthy of it. Her mind was every way equal to her person; nay, the latter borrowed some charms from the former, for when she smiled, the sweetness of her temper diffused that glory over her countenance which no regularity of features can give. But as there are no perfections of the mind which do not discover themselves in that perfect intimacy to which we intend to introduce our reader with this charming young creature, so it is needless to mention them here; nay, it is a kind of tacit affront to our reader's understanding, and may also rob him of that pleasure which he will receive in forming his own judgement of her character.

It may, however, be proper to say that whatever mental accomplishments she had derived from Nature, they were somewhat improved and cultivated by art; for she had been educated under the care of an aunt, who was a lady of great discretion and was thoroughly acquainted with the world, having lived in her youth about the court, whence she had retired some years since into the country. By her conversation and instructions, Sophia was perfectly well bred, though perhaps she wanted a little of that ease in her behaviour which is to be acquired only by habit and living within what is called the polite circle. But this, to say the truth, is often too dearly purchased; and though it hath charms so inexpressible that the French, perhaps, among other qualities, mean to express this when they declare they know not what it is, yet its absence is well compensated by innocence, nor can good sense and a natural gentility ever stand in need of it.

WHEREIN THE HISTORY GOES BACK TO COMMEMORATE A
TRIFLING INCIDENT THAT HAPPENED SOME YEARS SINCE; BUT
WHICH, TRIFLING AS IT WAS, HAD SOME FUTURE CON-
SEQUENCES

The amiable Sophia was now in her eighteenth year when she
is introduced into this history. Her father, as hath been said,
was fonder of her than of any other human creature. To
her, therefore, Tom Jones applied in order to engage her
interest on the behalf of his friend of the gamekeeper.

But before we proceed to this business, a short recapitula-
tion of some previous matters may be necessary.

Though the different tempers of Mr. Allworthy and of Mr.
Western did not admit of a very intimate correspondence,
yet they lived upon what is called a decent footing together;
by which means the young people of both families had been
acquainted from their infancy, and as they were all near
of the same age, had been frequent playmates together.

The gaiety of Tom's temper suited better with Sophia
than the grave and sober disposition of Master Blifil. And
the preference which she gave the former of these would
often appear so plainly that a lad of more passionate turn
than Master Blifil was might have shown some displeasure
at it.

As he did not, however, outwardly express any such disgust, it would be an ill office in us to pay a visit to the
inmost recesses of his mind, as some scandalous people search
into the most secret affairs of their friends and often pry into
their closets and cupboards only to discover their poverty and
meanness to the world.

However, as persons who suspect they have given others
cause of offence are apt to conclude they are offended, so
Sophia imputed an action of Master Blifil to his anger
which the superior sagacity of Thwackum and Square discerned to have arisen from a much better principle.

Tom Jones, when very young, had presented Sophia with
a little bird which he had taken from the nest, had nursed
up, and taught to sing.

Of this bird, Sophia, then about thirteen years old, was
so extremely fond that her chief business was to feed and

tend it and her chief pleasure to play with it. By these means little Tommy, for so the bird was called, was become so tame that it would feed out of the hand of its mistress, would perch upon her finger, and lie contented in her bosom, where it seemed almost sensible of its own happiness, though she always kept a small string about its leg, nor would ever trust it with the liberty of flying away.

One day, when Mr. Allworthy and his whole family dined at Mr. Western's, Master Blifil, being in the garden with little Sophia and observing the extreme fondness that she showed for her little bird, desired her to trust it for a moment in his hands. Sophia presently complied with the young gentleman's request and, after some previous caution, delivered him her bird; of which he was no sooner in possession than he slipped the string from its leg and tossed it into the air.

The foolish animal no sooner perceived itself at liberty than, forgetting all the favours it had received from Sophia, it flew directly from her and perched on a bough at some distance.

Sophia, seeing her bird gone, screamed out so loud that Tom Jones, who was at a little distance, immediately ran to her assistance.

He was no sooner informed of what had happened than he cursed Blifil for a pitiful, malicious rascal, and then immediately stripping off his coat, he applied himself to climbing the tree to which the bird escaped.

Tom had almost recovered his little namesake when the branch on which it was perched and that hung over a canal broke, and the poor lad plumped over head and ears into the water.

Sophia's concern now changed its object. And as she apprehended the boy's life was in danger, she screamed ten times louder than before; and, indeed, Master Blifil himself now seconded her with all the vociferation in his power.

The company, who were sitting in a room next the garden, were instantly alarmed and came all forth, but just as they reached the canal, Tom (for the water was luckily pretty shallow in that part) arrived safely on shore.

Thwackum fell violently on poor Tom, who stood dripping and shivering before him, when Mr. Allworthy desired him to have patience, and, turning to Master Blifil, said, "Pray, child, what is the reason of all this disturbance?"

Master Blifil answered, "Indeed, uncle, I am very sorry for

what I have done; I have been unhappily the occasion of it all. I had Miss Sophia's bird in my hand and, thinking the poor creature languished for liberty, I own I could not forbear giving it what it desired, for I always thought there was something very cruel in confining anything. It seemed to me against the law of Nature, by which everything hath a right to liberty; nay, it is even unchristian, for it is not doing what we would be done by; but if I had imagined Miss Sophia would have been so much concerned at it, I am sure I would never have done it; nay, if I had known what would have happened to the bird itself; for when Master Jones, who climbed up that tree after it, fell into the water, the bird took a second flight, and presently a nasty hawk carried it away."

Poor Sophia, who now first heard of her little Tommy's fate, for her concern for Jones had prevented her perceiving it when it happened, shed a shower of tears. These Mr. Allworthy endeavoured to assuage, promising her a much finer bird, but she declared she would never have another. Her father chid her for crying so for a foolish bird, but could not help telling young Blifil, if he was a son of his, his backside should be well flayed.

Sophia now returned to her chamber, the two young gentlemen were sent home, and the rest of the company returned to their bottle, where a conversation ensued on the subject of the bird, so curious that we think it deserves a chapter by itself.

4

CONTAINING SUCH VERY DEEP AND GRAVE MATTERS THAT
SOME READERS, PERHAPS, MAY NOT RELISH IT

Square had no sooner lighted his pipe than, addressing himself to Allworthy, he thus began: "Sir, I cannot help congratulating you on your nephew, who, at an age when few lads have any ideas but of sensible objects, is arrived at a capacity of distinguishing right from wrong. To confine anything seems to me against the law of Nature, by which everything hath a right to liberty. These were his words; and the impression they have made on me is never to be eradicated. Can any man have a higher notion of the rule of right and the eternal fitness of things? I cannot help promising myself from such a dawn that the meridian of this youth will be equal to that of either the elder or the younger Brutus."

Here Thwackum hastily interrupted and, spilling some of his wine and swallowing the rest with great eagerness, answered, "From another expression he made use of, I hope he will resemble much better men. The law of Nature is a jargon of words which means nothing. I know not of any such law, nor of any right which can be derived from it. To do as we would be done by is indeed a Christian motive, as the boy well expressed himself, and I am glad to find my instructions have borne so good fruit."

"If vanity was a thing fit," says Square, "I might indulge some on the same occasion, for whence he can only have learnt his notions of right or wrong I think is pretty apparent. If there be no law of Nature, there is no right nor wrong."

"How!" says the parson. "Do you then banish revelation? Am I talking with a deist or an atheist?"

"Drink about," says Western; "Pox of your laws of Nature! I don't know what you mean, either of you, by right and wrong. To take away my girl's bird was wrong in my opinion, and my neighbour Allworthy may do as he pleases, but to encourage boys in such practices is to breed them up to the gallows."

Allworthy answered that he was sorry for what his nephew had done, but could not consent to punish him, as he acted rather from a generous than unworthy motive. He said if the boy had stolen the bird, none would have been more ready to vote for a severe chastisement than himself, but it was plain that was not his design. And, indeed, it was as apparent to him that he could have no other view but what he had himself confessed. (For as to that malicious purpose which Sophia suspected, it never once entered into the head of Mr. Allworthy.) He at length concluded with again blaming the action as inconsiderate, and which, he said, was only pardonable in a child.

Square had delivered his opinion so openly that if he was now silent, he must submit to have his judgement censured. He said, therefore, with some warmth that Mr. Allworthy had too much respect to the dirty consideration of property; that in passing our judgements on great and mighty actions, all private regards should be laid aside; for by adhering to those narrow rules the younger Brutus had been condemned of ingratitude and the elder of parricide.

"And if they had been hanged too for those crimes," cried

Thwackum, "they would have had no more than their deserts. A couple of heathenish villains! Heaven be praised we have no Brutus's nowadays. I wish, Mr. Square, you would desist from filling the minds of my pupils with such antichristian stuff; for the consequence must be, while they are under my care, its being well scourged out of them again. There is your disciple, Tom, almost spoiled already. I overheard him the other day disputing with Master Blifil that there was no merit in faith without works. I know that is one of your tenets, and I suppose he had it from you."

"Don't accuse me of spoiling him," says Square. "Who taught him to laugh at whatever is virtuous and decent and fit and right in the nature of things? He is your own scholar, and I disclaim him. No, no, Master Blifil is my boy. Young as he is, that lad's notions of moral rectitude I defy you ever to eradicate."

Thwackum put on a contemptuous sneer at this and replied, "Ah, ay, I will venture him with you. He is too well grounded for all your philosophical cant to hurt. No, no, I have taken care to instil such principles into him——"

"And I have instilled principles into him too," cries Square; "what but the sublime idea of virtue could inspire a human mind with the generous thought of giving liberty? And I repeat to you again, if it was a fit thing to be proud, I might claim the honour of having infused that idea."

"And if pride was not forbidden," said Thwackum, "I might boast of having taught him that duty which he himself assigned as his motive."

"So, between you both," says the squire, "the young gentleman hath been taught to rob my daughter of her bird. I find I must take care of my partridge mew. I shall have some virtuous religious man or other set all my partridges at liberty." Then, slapping a gentleman of the law who was present on the back, he cried out, "What say you to this, Mr. Counsellor? Is not this against law?"

The lawyer, with great gravity, delivered himself as follows:

"If the case be put of a partridge, there can be no doubt but an action would lie; for though this be *feræ naturæ*, yet being reclaimed, property vests; but being the case of a singing bird, though reclaimed, as it is a thing of base nature, it must be considered as *nullius in bonis*. In this case, therefore, I conceive the plaintiff must be nonsuited, and I should disadvise the bringing any such action."

"Well," says the squire, "if it be *nulus bonus*, let us drink about and talk a little of the state of the nation or some such discourse that we all understand; for I am sure I don't understand a word of this. It may be learning and sense for aught I know, but you shall never persuade me into it. Pox! You have neither of you mentioned a word of that poor lad who deserves to be commended. To venture breaking his neck to oblige my girl was a generous-spirited action; I have learning enough to see that. D——n me, here's Tom's health. I shall love the boy for it the longest day I have to live."

Thus was the debate interrupted; but it would probably have been soon resumed had not Mr. Allworthy presently called for his coach and carried off the two combatants.

Such was the conclusion of this adventure of the bird and the dialogue occasioned by it, which we could not help recounting to our reader, though it happened some years before that stage or period of time at which our history is now arrived.

5

CONTAINING MATTER ACCOMMODATED TO EVERY TASTE

Parva leves capiunt animos—"Small things affect light minds"—was the sentiment of a great master of the passion of love. And certain it is, that from this day Sophia began to have some little kindness for Tom Jones and no little aversion for his companion.

Many accidents from time to time improved both these passions in her breast, which, without our recounting, the reader may well conclude from what we have before hinted of the different tempers of these lads, and how much the one suited with her own inclinations more than the other. To say the truth, Sophia, when very young, discerned that Tom, though an idle, thoughtless, rattling rascal, was nobody's enemy but his own; and that Master Blifil, though a prudent, discreet, sober young gentleman, was at the same time strongly attached to the interest only of one single person; and who that single person was the reader will be able to divine without any assistance of ours.

These two characters are not always received in the world

137

with the different regard which seems severally due to either, and which one would imagine mankind from self-interest should show towards them. But perhaps there may be a political reason for it: in finding one of a truly benevolent disposition, men may very reasonably suppose they have found a treasure and be desirous of keeping it, like all other good things, to themselves. Hence they may imagine that to trumpet forth the praises of such a person would, in the vulgar phrase, be "crying roast meat" and calling in par-takers of what they intend to apply solely to their own use. If this reason does not satisfy the reader, I know no other means of accounting for the little respect which I have com-monly seen paid to a character which really does great hon-our to human nature and is productive of the highest good to society. But it was otherwise with Sophia. She honoured Tom Jones and scorned Master Blifil almost as soon as she knew the meaning of those two words.

Sophia had been absent upwards of three years with her aunt, during all which time she had seldom seen either of these young gentlemen. She dined, however, once together with her aunt at Mr. Allworthy's. This was a few days after the adventure of the partridge before commemorated. Sophia heard the whole story at table, where she said nothing; nor, indeed, could her aunt get many words from her as she re-turned home, but her maid, when undressing her, happening to say, "Well, miss, I suppose you have seen young Master Blifil to-day," she answered with much passion, "I hate the name of Master Blifil, as I do whatever is base and treacher-ous; and I wonder Mr. Allworthy would suffer that old bar-barous schoolmaster to punish a poor boy so cruelly for what was only the effect of his good nature." She then re-counted the story to her maid and concluded with saying, "Don't you think he is a boy of a noble spirit?"

This young lady was now returned to her father, who gave her the command of his house and placed her at the upper end of his table, where Tom (who from his great love of hunting was become a great favourite of the squire) often dined. Young men of open, generous dispositions are natural-ly inclined to gallantry, which, if they have good under-standings, as was in reality Tom's case, exerts itself in an obliging, complaisant behaviour to all women in general. This greatly distinguished Tom from the boisterous brutality of mere country squires, on the one hand, and from the solemn and somewhat sullen deportment of Master Blifil, on the other; and he began now at twenty to have the name of a pretty fellow among all the women in the neighbourhood.

Tom behaved to Sophia with no particularity, unless, perhaps, by showing her a higher respect than he paid to any other. This distinction her beauty, fortune, sense, and amiable carriage seemed to demand; but as to design upon her person, he had none; for which we shall at present suffer the reader to condemn him of stupidity, but perhaps we shall be able indifferently well to account for it hereafter.

Sophia, with the highest degree of innocence and modesty, had a remarkable sprightliness in her temper. This was so greatly increased whenever she was in company with Tom that, had he not been very young and thoughtless, he must have observed it; or had not Mr. Western's thoughts been generally either in the field, the stable, or the dog-kennel, it might have, perhaps, created some jealousy in him, but so far was the good gentleman from entertaining any such suspicions that he gave Tom every opportunity with his daughter which any lover could have wished. And these Tom innocently improved to better advantage by following only the dictates of his natural gallantry and good nature than he might, perhaps, have done had he had the deepest designs on the young lady.

But, indeed, it can occasion little wonder that this matter escaped the observation of others, since poor Sophia herself never remarked it, and her heart was irretrievably lost before she suspected it was in danger.

Matters were in this situation when Tom, one afternoon, finding Sophia alone, began, after a short apology, with a very serious face, to acquaint her that he had a favour to ask of her, which he hoped her goodness would comply with.

Though neither the young man's behaviour nor, indeed, his manner of opening this business were such as could give her any just cause of suspecting he intended to make love to her, yet—whether Nature whispered something into her ear or from what cause it arose I will not determine—certain it is, some idea of that kind must have intruded itself, for her colour forsook her cheeks, her limbs trembled, and her tongue would have faltered had Tom stopped for an answer; but he soon relieved her from her perplexity by proceeding to inform her of his request, which was to solicit her interest on behalf of the gamekeeper, whose own ruin and that of a large family must be, he said, the consequence of Mr. Western's pursuing his action against him.

Sophia presently recovered her confusion and, with a smile full of sweetness, said, "Is this the mighty favour you asked with so much gravity? I will do it with all my heart. I really pity the poor fellow, and no longer ago than yesterday sent a small matter to his wife." This small matter was one of her gowns, some linen, and ten shillings in money, of which Tom had heard; and it had, in reality, put this solicitation into his head.

Our youth, now emboldened with his success, resolved to push the matter farther, and ventured even to beg her recommendation of him to her father's service, protesting that he thought him one of the honestest fellows in the country and extremely well qualified for the place of a gamekeeper, which luckily then happened to be vacant.

Sophia answered, "Well, I will undertake this too; but I cannot promise you as much success as in the former part, which I assure you I will not quit my father without obtaining. However, I will do what I can for the poor fellow, for I sincerely look upon him and his family as objects of great compassion. And now, Mr. Jones, I must ask you a favour."

"A favour, madam," cries Tom; "if you knew the pleasure you have given me in the hopes of receiving a command from you, you would think by mentioning it you must confer the greatest favour on me; for, by this dear hand, I would sacrifice my life to oblige you."

He then snatched her hand and eagerly kissed it, which was the first time his lips had ever touched her. The blood, which before had forsaken her cheeks, now made her sufficient amends by rushing all over her face and neck with such violence that they became all of a scarlet colour. She now first felt a sensation to which she had been before a stranger, and which, when she had leisure to reflect on it, began to acquaint her with some secrets which the reader, if he does not already guess them, will know in due time.

Sophia, as soon as she could speak (which was not instantly), informed him that the favour she had to desire of him was not to lead her father through so many dangers in hunting; for that, from what she had heard, she was terribly frightened every time they went out together, and expected some day or other to see her father brought home with broken limbs. She therefore begged him for her sake to be more cautious, and, as he well knew Mr. Western would follow him, not to ride so madly nor to take those dangerous leaps for the future.

Tom faithfully promised to obey her commands and, after thanking her for her kind compliance with his request, took his leave and departed highly charmed with his success.

Poor Sophia was charmed too; but in a very different way. Her sensations, however, the reader's heart (if he or she have any) will better represent than I can if I had as many mouths as ever poet wished for, to eat, I suppose, those many dainties with which he was so plentifully provided.

It was Mr. Western's custom every afternoon as soon as he was drunk to hear his daughter play on the harpsichord; for he was a great lover of music and, perhaps, had he lived in town, might have passed for a connoisseur, for he always excepted against the finest compositions of Mr. Handel. He never relished any music but what was light and airy and, indeed, his most favourite tunes were "Old Sir Simon the King," "St. George He Was for England," "Bobbing Joan," and some others.

His daughter, though she was a perfect mistress of music and would never willingly have played any but Handel's, was so devoted to her father's pleasure that she learnt all those tunes to oblige him. However, she would now and then endeavour to lead him into her own taste, and when he required the repetition of his ballads would answer with a "Nay, dear sir," and would often beg him to suffer her to play something else.

This evening, however, when the gentleman was retired from his bottle, she played all his favourites three times over without any solicitation. This so pleased the good squire that he started from his couch, gave his daughter a kiss, and swore her hand was greatly improved. She took this opportunity to execute her promise to Tom, in which she succeeded so well that the squire declared if she would give him t'other bout of "Old Sir Simon," he would give the gamekeeper his deputation the next morning. "Sir Simon" was played again and again till the charms of the music soothed Mr. Western to sleep. In the morning Sophia did not fail to remind him of his engagement, and his attorney was immediately sent for, ordered to stop any further proceedings in the action, and to make out the deputation.

Tom's success in this affair soon began to ring over the country, and various were the censures passed upon it, some greatly applauding it as an act of good nature, others sneering, and saying no wonder that one idle fellow should love another. Young Blifil was greatly enraged at it. He had long hated Black George in the same proportion as Jones delighted in him, not from any offence which he had ever received but from his great love to religion and virtue; for Black George had the reputation of a loose kind of a fellow. Blifil therefore represented this as flying in Mr. Allworthy's face, and declared with great concern that it was impossible to find any other motive for doing good to such a wretch.

Thwackum and Square likewise sung to the same tune: they were now (especially the latter) become greatly jealous of young Jones with the widow; for he now approached the age of twenty, was really a fine young fellow, and that lady by her encouragements to him seemed daily more and more to think him so.

Allworthy was not, however, moved with their malice. He declared himself very well satisfied with what Jones had done. He said the perseverance and integrity of his friendship was highly commendable, and he wished he could see more frequent instances of that virtue.

But Fortune, who seldom greatly relishes such sparks as my friend Tom, perhaps because they do not pay more ardent addresses to her, gave now a very different turn to all his actions, and showed them to Mr. Allworthy in a light far less agreeable than that gentleman's goodness had hitherto seen them in.

6

AN APOLOGY FOR THE INSENSIBILITY OF MR. JONES TO ALL THE CHARMS OF THE LOVELY SOPHIA; IN WHICH, POSSIBLY, WE MAY IN A CONSIDERABLE DEGREE LOWER HIS CHARACTER IN THE ESTIMATION OF THOSE MEN OF WIT AND GALLANTRY WHO APPROVE THE HEROES IN MOST OF OUR MODERN COMEDIES

There are two sorts of people who, I am afraid, have already conceived some contempt for my hero on account of his behaviour to Sophia. The former of these will blame his prudence in neglecting an opportunity to possess himself of Mr. Western's fortune; and the latter will no less despise him for his backwardness to so fine a girl, who seemed ready to fly into his arms if he would open them to receive her.

Now, though I shall not, perhaps, be able absolutely to acquit him of either of these charges (for want of prudence admits of no excuse, and what I shall produce against the latter charge will, I apprehend, be scarce satisfactory), yet, as evidence may sometimes be offered in mitigation, I shall set forth the plain matter of fact and leave the whole to the reader's determination.

Mr. Jones had somewhat about him, which, though I think writers are not thoroughly agreed in its name, doth certainly inhabit some human beasts; whose use is not so properly to distinguish right from wrong as to prompt and incite them to the former and to restrain and withhold them from the latter.

This somewhat may be indeed resembled to the famous trunk-maker in the playhouse; for whenever the person who is possessed of it doth what is right, no ravished or friendly spectator is so eager or so loud in his applause; on the contrary, when he doth wrong, no critic is so apt to hiss and explode him.

To give a higher idea of the principle I mean, as well as one more familiar to the present age, it may be considered as sitting on its throne in the mind like the Lord High Chancellor of this kingdom in his court, where it presides, governs, directs, judges, acquits, and condemns according to merit and justice, with a knowledge which nothing escapes, a penetration which nothing can deceive, and an integrity which nothing can corrupt.

This active principle may perhaps be said to constitute the most essential barrier between us and our neighbours the brutes; for if there be some in the human shape who are not under any such dominion, I choose rather to consider them as deserters from us to our neighbours, among whom they will have the fate of deserters, and not be placed in the first rank.

Our hero, whether he derived it from Thwackum or Square I will not determine, was very strongly under the guidance of this principle; for though he did not always act rightly, yet he never did otherwise without feeling and suffering for it. It was this which taught him that to repay the civilities and little friendships of hospitality by robbing the house where you have received them is to be the basest and meanest of thieves. He did not think the baseness of this offence lessened by the height of the injury committed; on the contrary, if to steal another's plate deserved death and infamy, it seemed to him difficult to assign a punishment adequate to the robbing a man of his whole fortune and of his child into the bargain.

This principle therefore prevented him from any thought of making his fortune by such means (for this, as I have said, is an active principle, and doth not content itself with knowledge or belief only). Had he been greatly enamoured of Sophia, he possibly might have thought otherwise; but give me leave to say there is great difference between running away with a man's daughter from the motive of love, and doing the same thing from the motive of theft.

Now, though this young gentleman was not insensible of the charms of Sophia, though he greatly liked her beauty and esteemed all her other qualifications, she had made, however, no deep impression on his heart; for which, as it renders him liable to the charge of stupidity, or at least of want of taste, we shall now proceed to account.

The truth, then, is, his heart was in the possession of another woman. Here I question not but the reader will be surprised at our long taciturnity as to this matter, and at no less loss to divine who this woman was, since we have hitherto not dropped a hint of any one likely to be a rival to Sophia; for as to Mrs. Blifil, though we have been obliged to mention some suspicions of her affection for Tom, we have not hitherto given the least latitude for imagining that he had any for her; and, indeed, I am sorry to say it, but the youth of both sexes are too apt to be deficient in their gratitude for that regard with which persons more advanced in years are sometimes so kind to honour them.

That the reader may be no longer in suspense, he will be pleased to remember that we have often mentioned the family of George Seagrim, commonly called Black George, the gamekeeper, which consisted at present of a wife and five children.

The second of these children was a daughter whose name was Molly, and who was esteemed one of the handsomest girls in the whole country.

Congreve well says, "There is in true beauty something which vulgar souls cannot admire"; so can no dirt or rags hide this something from those souls which are not of the vulgar stamp.

The beauty of this girl made, however, no impression on Tom till she grew towards the age of sixteen, when Tom, who was near three years older, began first to cast the eyes of affection upon her. And this affection he had fixed on the girl long before he could bring himself to attempt the possession of her person; for though his constitution urged him greatly to this, his principles no less forcibly restrained him. To debauch a young woman, however low her condition was, appeared to him a very heinous crime, and the goodwill he bore the father, with the compassion he had for his family, very strongly corroborated all such sober reflections; so that he once resolved to get the better of his inclinations, and he actually abstained three whole months without ever going to Seagrim's house or seeing his daughter.

Now, though Molly was, as we have said, generally thought a very fine girl, and in reality she was so, yet her beauty was not of the most amiable kind. It had indeed very little of feminine in it, and would at least have become a man as well as a woman; for to say the truth, youth and florid health had a very considerable share in the composition.

Nor was her mind more effeminate than her person. As this was tall and robust, so was that bold and forward. So little had she of modesty that Jones had more regard for her virtue than she herself. And as most probably she liked Tom as well as he liked her, so when she perceived his backwardness she herself grew proportionately forward; and when she saw he had entirely deserted the house, she found means of throwing herself in his way and behaved in such a manner that the youth must have had very much or very little of the hero if her endeavours had proved unsuccessful. In a word, she soon triumphed over all the virtuous resolutions of Jones; for though she behaved at last with all decent reluctance, yet I rather choose to attribute the triumph to her, since, in fact, it was her design which succeeded.

In the conduct of this matter Molly so well played her part that Jones attributed the conquest entirely to himself, and considered the young woman as one who had yielded to the violent attacks of his passion. He likewise imputed her yielding to the ungovernable force of her love towards him; and this the reader will allow to have been a very natural and probable supposition, as we have more than once mentioned the uncommon comeliness of his person, and indeed, he was one of the handsomest young fellows in the world.

As there are some minds whose affections, like Master Blifil's, are solely placed on one single person, whose interest and indulgence alone they consider on every occasion, regarding the good and ill of all others as merely indifferent any farther than as they contribute to the pleasure or advantage of that person, so there is a different temper of mind which borrows a degree of virtue even from self-love; such can never receive any kind of satisfaction from another without loving the creature to whom that satisfaction is owing, and without making its well-being in some sort necessary to their own ease.

Of this latter species was our hero. He considered this poor girl as one whose happiness or misery he had caused to be dependent on himself. Her beauty was still the object of desire, though greater beauty or a fresher object might have been more so; but the little abatement which fruition had occasioned to this was highly overbalanced by the considerations of the affection which she visibly bore him, and of the situation into which he had brought her. The former of these created gratitude, the latter compassion; and both, together with his desire for her person, raised in him a passion which might without any great violence to the word be called Love, though, perhaps, it was at first not very judiciously placed.

This, then, was the true reason of that insensibility which he had shown of the charms of Sophia, and of that behaviour in her which might have been reasonably enough interpreted as an encouragement to his addresses; for as he could not think of abandoning his Molly, poor and destitute as she was, so no more could he entertain a notion of betraying such a creature as Sophia. And surely, had he given the least encouragement to any passion for that young lady, he must have been absolutely guilty of one or other of those crimes, either of which would, in my opinion, have very justly subjected him to that fate which at his first introduction into this history I mentioned to have been generally predicted as his certain destiny.

7

BEING THE SHORTEST CHAPTER IN THIS BOOK

Her mother first perceived the alteration in the shape of Molly, and in order to hide it from her neighbours, she foolishly clothed her in that sack which Sophia had sent her, though indeed that young lady had little apprehension

146

that the poor woman would have been weak enough to let any of her daughters wear it in that form.

Molly was charmed with the first opportunity she had ever had of showing her beauty to advantage; for though she could very well bear to contemplate herself in the glass, even when dressed in rags, and though she had in that dress conquered the heart of Jones and perhaps of some others, yet she thought the addition of finery would much improve her charms and extend her conquests.

Molly, therefore, having dressed herself out in this sack, with a new laced cap and some other ornaments which Tom had given her, repairs to church with her fan in her hand the very next Sunday. The great are deceived if they imagine they have appropriated ambition and vanity to themselves. These noble qualities flourish as notably in a country church and churchyard as in the drawing-room or in the closet. Schemes have, indeed, been laid in the vestry which would hardly disgrace the conclave. Here is a ministry, and here is an opposition. Here are plots and circumventions, parties and factions, equal to those which are to be found in courts.

Nor are the women here less practised in the highest feminine arts than their fair superiors in quality and fortune. Here are prudes and coquettes. Here are dressing and ogling, falsehood, envy, malice, scandal; in short, everything which is common to the most splendid assembly or politest circle. Let those of high life, therefore, no longer despise the ignorance of their inferiors, nor the vulgar any longer rail at the vices of their betters.

Molly had seated herself some time before she was known by her neighbours, and a whisper ran through the whole congregation, "Who is she?" But when she was discovered, such sneering, giggling, tittering, and laughing ensued among the women that Mr. Allworthy was obliged to exert his authority to preserve any decency among them.

8

A BATTLE SUNG BY THE MUSE IN THE HOMERICAN STYLE, AND WHICH NONE BUT THE CLASSICAL READER CAN TASTE

Mr. Western had an estate in this parish, and as his house stood at little greater distance from this church than from his own, he very often came to divine service here; and both he and the charming Sophia happened to be present at this time.

Sophia was much pleased with the beauty of the girl, whom she pitied for her simplicity, in having dressed herself in that manner, as she saw the envy which it had occasioned among her equals. She no sooner came home than she sent for the gamekeeper and ordered him to bring his daughter to her, saying she would provide for her in the family, and might possibly place the girl about her own person when her own maid, who was now going away, had left her.

Poor Seagrim was thunderstruck at this; for he was no stranger to the fault in the shape of his daughter. He answered in a stammering voice that he was afraid Molly would be too awkward to wait on her ladyship, as she had never been at service. "No matter for that," says Sophia. "She will soon improve. I am pleased with the girl and am resolved to try her."

Black George now repaired to his wife, on whose prudent council he depended to extricate him out of this dilemma, but when he came thither he found his house in some confusion. So great envy had this sack occasioned that when Mr. Allworthy and the other gentry were gone from church, the rage, which had hitherto been confined, burst into an uproar and, having vented itself at first in opprobrious words, laughs, hisses, and gestures, betook itself at last to certain missile weapons, which, though from their plastic nature they threatened neither the loss of life or of limb, were however sufficiently dreadful to a well-dressed lady. Molly had too much spirit to bear this treatment tamely. Having therefore—but hold, as we are diffident of our own abilities, let us here invite a superior power to our assistance.

Ye Muses, then, whoever ye are, who love to sing battles, and principally thou, who whilom didst recount the slaughter in those fields where Hudibras and Trulla fought, if thou wert not starved with thy friend Butler, assist me on this great occasion. All things are not in the power of all.

As a vast herd of cows in a rich farmer's yard if while they are milked they hear their calves at a distance, lamenting the robbery which is then committing, roar and bellow, so roared forth the Somersetshire mob an hallaloo, made up of almost as many squawls, screams, and other different sounds as there were persons, or indeed passions, among them; some were inspired by rage, others alarmed by fear, and others had nothing in their heads but the love of fun, but chiefly envy, the sister of Satan and his constant companion, rushed among the crowd and blew up the fury of the women, who no sooner came up to Molly than they pelted her with dirt and rubbish.

Molly, having endeavoured in vain to make a handsome retreat, faced about, and laying hold of ragged Bess, who advanced in the front of the enemy, she at one blow felled her to the ground. The whole army of the enemy (though near a hundred in number), seeing the fate of their general, gave back many paces and retired behind a new-dug grave; for the churchyard was the field of battle where there was to be a funeral that very evening. Molly pursued her victory and, catching up a skull which lay on the side of the grave, discharged it with such fury that, having hit a tailor on the head, the two skulls sent equally forth a hollow sound at their meeting, and the tailor took presently measure of his length on the ground, where the skulls lay side by side, and it was doubtful which was the most valuable of the two. Molly then taking a thigh-bone in her hand fell in among the flying ranks, and dealing her blows with great liberality on either side, overthrew the carcass of many a mighty hero and heroine.

Recount, O Muse, the names of those who fell on this fatal day. First, Jemmy Tweedle felt on his hinder head the direful bone. Him the pleasant banks of sweetly winding Stour had nourished, where he first learnt the vocal art with which, wandering up and down at wakes and fairs, he cheered the rural nymphs and swains, when upon the green they interweave the sprightly dance, while he himself stood fiddling and jumping to his own music. How little now avails his fiddle? He thumps the verdant floor with his carcass. Next, old Echepole, the sow-gelder, received a blow in his forehead from our Amazonian heroine, and immediately fell to the ground. He was a swinging fat fellow, and fell with almost as much noise as a horse. His tobacco-box dropped at the same time from his pocket, which Molly took up as lawful spoils. Then Kate of the Mill tumbled unfortunately over a tombstone, which, catching hold of her ungartered stocking, inverted the order of nature and gave her heels the superiority to her head. Betty Pippin, with young Roger, her lover, fell both to the ground, where, O perverse fate, she salutes the earth and he the sky. Tom Freckle, the smith's son, was the next victim to her rage. He was an ingenious workman and made excellent pattens; nay, the very patten with which he was knocked down was his own workmanship. Had he been at that time singing psalms in the church, he would have avoided a broken head. Miss Crow, the daughter of a farmer; John Giddish, himself a farmer; Nan Slouch, Esther Codling, Will Spray, Tom Bennet; the three Misses Potter, whose father keeps the sign of the Red Lion; Betty Chambermaid, Jack Ostler, and many others of inferior note lay rolling among the graves.

Not that the strenuous arm of Molly reached all these, for many of them in their flight overthrew each other.

But now Fortune, fearing she had acted out of character and had inclined too long to the same side, especially as it was the right side, hastily turned about: for now Goody Brown, whom Zekiel Brown caresses in his arms; nor he alone, but half the parish besides, so famous was she in the fields of Venus; nor indeed less in those of Mars. The trophies of both these her husband always bore about on his head and face; for if ever human head did by its horns display the amorous glories of a wife, Zekiel's did; nor did his well-scratched face less denote her talents (or rather talons) of a different kind.

No longer bore this Amazon the shameful flight of her party. She stopped short and, calling aloud to all who fled, spoke as follows: "Ye Somersetshire men, or rather ye Somersetshire women, are ye not ashamed thus to fly from a single woman? But if no other will oppose her, I myself and Joan Top, here, will have the honour of the victory." Having thus said, she flew at Molly Seagrim and easily wrenched the thigh-bone from her hand, at the same time clawing off her cap from her head. Then, laying hold of the hair of Molly with her left hand, she attacked her so furiously in the face with the right that the blood soon began to trickle from her nose. Molly was not idle this while. She soon removed the clout from the head of Goody Brown, and then, fastening on her hair with one hand, with the other she caused the same bloody stream to issue forth from the nostrils of the enemy.

When each of the combatants had borne off sufficient spoils of hair from the head of her antagonist, the next rage was against their garments. In this attack they exerted so much violence that in a very few minutes they were both naked to the middle.

It is lucky for the women that the seat of fisticuff-war is

not the same with them as among men; but though they may seem a little to deviate from their sex when they go forth to battle, yet I have observed they never so far forget it as to assail the bosoms of each other, where a few blows would be fatal to most of them. This, I know, some derive from their being of a more bloody inclination than the males. On which account they apply to the nose as to the part whence blood may most easily be drawn; but this seems a far-fetched as well as ill-natured supposition.

Goody Brown had great advantage of Molly in this particular; for the former had indeed no breasts, her bosom (if it may be so called) as well in colour as in many other properties exactly resembling an ancient piece of parchment, upon which any one might have drummed a considerable while without doing her any great damage.

Molly, beside her present unhappy condition, was differently formed in those parts, and might, perhaps, have tempted the envy of Brown to give her a fatal blow had not the lucky arrival of Tom Jones at this instant put an immediate end to the bloody scene.

This accident was luckily owing to Mr. Square; for he, Master Blifil, and Jones had mounted their horses after church to take the air, and had ridden about a quarter of a mile when Square, changing his mind (not idly, but for a reason which we shall unfold as soon as we have leisure), desired the young gentlemen to ride with him another way than they had at first proposed. This motion being complied with brought them of necessity back again to the churchyard.

Master Blifil, who rode first, seeing such a mob assembled and two women in the posture in which we left the combatants, stopped his horse to inquire what was the matter. A country fellow, scratching his head, answered him, "I don't know, measter, un't I; an't please your honour, here hath been a vight, I think, between Goody Brown and Moll Seagrim." "Who, who?" cries Tom, but without waiting for an answer, having discovered the features of his Molly through all the discomposure in which they now were, he hastily alighted, turned his horse loose, and, leaping over the wall, ran to her. She now, first bursting into tears, told him how barbarously she had been treated. Upon which, forgetting the sex of Goody Brown, or perhaps not knowing it in his rage (for in reality she had no feminine appearance but a petticoat, which he might not observe), he gave her a lash or two with his horsewhip; and then flying at the mob, who were all accused by Molly, he dealt his blows so profusely on all sides that unless I would invoke the Muse (which the good-natured reader may think a little too hard upon her, as she hath so lately been violently sweated), it would be impossible for me to recount the horsewhipping of that day.

Having scoured the whole coast of the enemy as well as any of Homer's heroes ever did, or as Don Quixote or any knight-errant in the world could have done, he returned to Molly, whom he found in a condition which must give both me and my reader pain was it to be described here. Tom raved like a madman, beat his breast, tore his hair, stamped on the ground, and vowed the utmost vengeance on all who had been concerned. He then pulled off his coat and buttoned it round her, put his hat upon her head, wiped the blood from her face as well as he could with his handkerchief, and called out to the servant to ride as fast as possible for a sidesaddle, or a pillion, that he might carry her safe home.

Master Blifil objected to the sending away the servant, as they had only one with them; but as Square seconded the order of Jones, he was obliged to comply.

The servant returned in a very short time with the pillion; and Molly, having collected her rags as well as she could, was placed behind him, in which manner she was carried home, Square, Blifil, and Jones attending.

Here, Jones, having received his coat, given her a sly kiss, and whispered her that he would return in the evening, quitted his Molly and rode on after his companions.

9

CONTAINING MATTERS OF NO VERY PEACEABLE COLOUR

Molly had no sooner apparelled herself in her accustomed rags than her sisters began to fall violently upon her, particularly her elder sister, who told her she was well enough served. How had she the assurance to wear a gown which young Madam Western had given to Mother! "If one of us was to wear it, I think," says she, "I myself have the best right; but I warrant you think it belongs to your beauty. I suppose you think yourself more handsomer than any of us."—

"Hand her down the bit of glass from over the cupboard," cries another; "I'd wash the blood from my face before I tawked of my beauty."—"You'd better have minded what the parson says," cries the eldest, "and not a-harkened after men voke."—"Indeed, child, and so she had," says the mother sobbing. "She hath brought a disgrace upon us all. She's the vurst of the vamily that ever was a whore."—"You need not upbraid me with that, Mother," cries Molly; "you yourself was brought to bed of sister there within a week after you was married."—"Yes, hussy," answered the enraged mother, "so I was, and what was the mighty matter of that? I was made an honest woman then, and if you was to be made an honest woman, I should not be angry; but you must have to doing with a gentleman, you nasty slut; you will have a bastard, hussy, you will, and that I defy any one to say of me."

In this situation Black George found his family when he came home for the purpose before mentioned. As his wife and three daughters were all of them talking together, and most of them crying, it was some time before he could get an opportunity of being heard, but as soon as such an interval occurred, he acquainted the company with what Sophia had said to him.

Goody Seagrim then began to revile her daughter afresh. "Here," says she, "you have brought us into a fine quandary indeed. What will madam say to that big belly? Oh, that ever I should live to see this day!"

Molly answered with great spirit, "And what is this mighty place which you have got for me, Father?" (for he had not well understood the phrase used by Sophia of being about her person). "I suppose it is to be under the cook; but I shan't wash dishes for anybody. My gentleman will provide better for me. See what he hath given me this afternoon; he hath promised I shall never want money, and you shan't want money neither, Mother, if you will hold your tongue and know when you are well." And so saying, she pulled out several guineas and gave her mother one of them.

The good woman no sooner felt the gold within her palm than her temper began (such is the efficacy of that panacea) to be mollified. "Why, husband," says she, "would any but such a blockhead as you not have inquired what place this was before he had accepted it? Perhaps, as Molly says, it may be in the kitchen, and truly I don't care my daughter should be a scullion wench; for poor as I am, I am a gentlewoman. And thof I was obliged, as my father, who was a clergyman, died worse than nothing and so could not give me a shilling of *potion,* to undervalue myself by marrying a poor man, yet I would have you to know that I have a spirit above all *them* things. Marry come up, it would better become Madam Western to look at home and remember who her own grandfather was. Some of my family, for aught I know, might ride in their coaches when the grandfathers of some voke walked a-voot. I warrant she fancies she did a mighty matter when she sent us that old *gownd;* some of my family would not have picked up such rags in the street; but poor people are always trampled upon. The parish need not have been in such a flutter with Molly. You might have told them, child, your grandmother wore better things new out of the shop."

"Well, but consider," cried George, "what answer shall I make to madam?"—"I don't know what answer," says she; "you are always bringing your family into one quandary or other. Do you remember when you shot the partridge, the occasion of all our misfortunes? Did not I advise you never to go into Squire Western's manor? Did not I tell you many a good year ago what would come of it? But you would have your own headstrong ways; yes you would, you villain."

Black George was in the main a peaceable kind of fellow, and nothing choleric nor rash, yet did he bear about him something of what the ancients called the irascible, and which his wife, if she had been endowed with much wisdom, would have feared. He had long experienced that when the storm grew very high, arguments were but wind, which served rather to increase than to abate it. He was therefore seldom unprovided with a small switch, a remedy of wonderful force, as he had often essayed, and which the word *villain* served as a hint for his applying.

No sooner, therefore, had this sympton appeared than he had immediate recourse to the said remedy, which though, as it is usual in all very efficacious medicines, it at first seemed to heighten and inflame the disease, soon produced a total calm and restored the patient to perfect ease and tranquillity.

This is, however, a kind of horse medicine, which requires a very robust constitution to digest and is therefore only proper for the vulgar, unless in one single instance, viz., where superiority of birth breaks out; in which case we should not think it very improperly applied by any husband whatever if the application was not in itself so base that, like certain applications of the physical kind which need not be mentioned, it so much degrades and contaminates the hand employed in it that no gentleman should endure the thought of anything so low and detestable.

The whole family were soon reduced to a state of perfect quiet; for the virtue of this medicine, like that of electricity, is often communicated through one person to many others who are not touched by the instrument. To say the truth, as they both operate by friction, it may be doubted whether there is not something analogous between them, of which Mr. Freke would do well to inquire before he publishes the next edition of his book.

A council was now called, in which after many debates Molly still persisting that she would not go to service, it was at length resolved that Goody Seagrim herself should wait on Miss Western and endeavour to procure the place for her elder daughter, who declared great readiness to accept it; but Fortune, who seems to have been an enemy of this little family, afterwards put a stop to her promotion.

10

A STORY TOLD BY MR. SUPPLE, THE CURATE. THE PENE-
TRATION OF SQUIRE WESTERN. HIS GREAT LOVE FOR HIS
DAUGHTER, AND THE RETURN TO IT MADE BY HER

The next morning Tom Jones hunted with Mr. Western, and was at his return invited by that gentleman to dinner.

The lovely Sophia shone forth that day with more gaiety and sprightliness than usual. Her battery was certainly levelled at our hero, though I believe she herself scarce yet knew her own intention; but if she had any design of charming him, she now succeeded.

Mr. Supple, the curate of Mr. Allworthy's parish, made one of the company. He was a good-natured, worthy man, but chiefly remarkable for his great taciturnity at table, though his mouth was never shut at it. In short, he had one of the best appetites in the world. However, the cloth was no sooner taken away than he always made sufficient amends for his silence, for he was a very hearty fellow and his conversation was often entertaining, never offensive.

At his first arrival, which was immediately before the entrance of the roast beef, he had given an intimation that he had brought some news with him, and was beginning to tell that he came that moment from Mr. Allworthy's when the sight of the roast beef struck him dumb, permitting him only to say grace and to declare he must pay his respect to the baronet, for so he called the sirloin.

When dinner was over, being reminded by Sophia of his news, he began as follows: "I believe, lady, your ladyship observed a young woman at church yesterday at evensong who was dressed in one of your outlandish garments; I think I have seen your ladyship in such a one. However, in the country such dresses are

Rara avis in terris, nigroque simillima cygno.

That is, madam, as much as to say, 'A rare bird upon the earth, and very like a black swan.'

"The verse is in Juvenal. But to return to what I was relating. I was saying such garments are rare sights in the country, and perchance too it was thought the more rare, respect being had to the person who wore it, who, they tell me, is the daughter of Black George, your worship's gamekeeper, whose sufferings, I should have opined, might have taught him more wit than to dress forth his wenches in such gaudy apparel. She created so much confusion in the congregation that if Squire Allworthy had not silenced it, it would have interrupted the service, for I was once about to stop in the middle of the first lesson. Howbeit, nevertheless, after prayer was over and I was departed home, this occasioned a battle in the churchyard, where amongst other mischief the head of a travelling fiddler was very much braken. This morning the fiddler came to Squire Allworthy for a warrant, and the wench was brought before him. The squire was inclined to have compounded matters, when, lo, on a sudden the wench appeared (I ask your ladyship pardon) to be, as it were, at the eve of bringing forth a bastard! The squire demanded of her who was the father, but she pertinaciously refused to make any response. So that he was about to make her mittimus to Bridewell when I departed."

"And is a wench having a bastard all your news, Doctor?" cries Western. "I thought it might have been some public matter, something about the nation."

"I am afraid it is too common, indeed," answered the parson, "but I thought the whole story all together deserved commemorating. As to national matters, your worship knows them best. My concerns extend no farther than my own parish."

"Why, ay," says the squire, "I believe I do know a little of that matter, as you say; but come, Tommy, drink about, the bottle stands with you."

Tom begged to be excused, for that he had particular business, and getting up from table, escaped the clutches of the squire, who was rising to stop him, and went off with very little ceremony.

The squire gave him a good curse at his departure, and then turning to the parson, he cried out, "I smoke it; I smoke it. Tom is certainly the father of this bastard. Zooks, Parson, you remember how he recommended the veather o' her to me. D——n un, what a sly b——ch 'tis. Ay, ay, as sure as twopence, Tom is the veather of the vastard."

"I should be very sorry for that," says the parson.

"Why sorry," cries the squire, "where is the mighty matter o't? What, I suppose, dost pretend that thee hast never got a bastard? Pox! More good luck's thine; for I warrant hast a-done therefore many's the good time and often."

"Your worship is pleased to be jocular," answered the parson, "but I do not only animadvert on the sinfulness of the action, though that surely is to be greatly deprecated, but I fear his unrighteousness may injure him with Mr. Allworthy. And truly I must say, though he hath the character of being a little wild, I never saw any harm in the young man; nor can I say I have heard any, save what your worship now mentions. I wish, indeed, he was a little more regular in his responses at church, but altogether he seems

Ingenui vultus puer ingenuique pudoris.

That is a classical line, young lady, and being rendered into English is, 'A lad of an ingenuous countenance, and of an ingenuous modesty,' for this was a virtue in great repute both among the Latins and Greeks. I must say the young gentleman (for so I think I may call him, notwithstanding his birth) appears to me a very modest, civil lad, and I should be sorry that he should do himself any injury in Squire Allworthy's opinion."

"Pooh!" says the squire. "Injury with Allworthy! Why, Allworthy loves a wench himself. Doth not all the country know whose son Tom is? You must talk to another person in that manner. I remember Allworthy at college."

"I thought," said the parson, "he had never been at the University."

"Yes, yes, he was," says the squire, "and many a wench have we two had together. As errant a whore-master as any within five miles o'un. No, no. It will do'n no harm with he, assure yourself; nor with anybody else. Ask Sophy there—you have not the worse opinion of a young fellow for getting a bastard, have you, girl? No, no, the women will like un the better for't."

This was a cruel question to poor Sophia. She had observed Tom's colour change at the parson's story, and that, with his hasty and abrupt departure, gave her sufficient reason to think her father's suspicion not groundless. Her heart now at once discovered the great secret to her which it had been so long disclosing by little and little, and she found herself highly interested in this matter. In such a situation, her father's malapert question, rushing suddenly upon her, produced some symptoms which might have alarmed a suspicious heart, but to do the squire justice, that was not his fault. When she rose, therefore, from her chair, and told him a hint from him was always sufficient to make her withdraw, he suffered her to leave the room; and then with great gravity of countenance remarked that it was better to see a daughter over-modest than over-forward, a sentiment which was highly applauded by the parson.

There now ensued between the squire and the parson a most excellent political discourse, framed out of newspapers and political pamphlets, in which they made a libation of four bottles of wine to the good of their country; and then, the squire being fast asleep, the parson lighted his pipe, mounted his horse, and rode home.

When the squire had finished his half-hour's nap, he summoned his daughter to her harpsichord, but she begged to be excused that evening on account of a violent headache. This remission was presently granted; for indeed she seldom had occasion to ask him twice, as he loved her with such ardent affection that by gratifying her he commonly conveyed the highest gratification to himself. She was really what he frequently called her, his little darling, and she well deserved to be so, for she returned all his affection in the most ample manner. She had preserved the most inviolable duty to him in all things, and this her love made not only easy but so delightful that, when one of her companions laughed at her for placing so much merit in such scrupulous obedience, as that young lady called it, Sophia answered, "You mistake me, madam, if you think I value myself upon this account; for besides that I am barely discharging my duty, I am likewise pleasing myself. I can truly say I have no delight equal to that of contributing to my father's happiness, and if I value myself, my dear, it is on having this power, and not on executing it."

This was a satisfaction, however, which poor Sophia was incapable of tasting this evening. She therefore not only desired to be excused from her attendance at the harpsichord but likewise begged that he would suffer her to absent herself from supper. To this request likewise the squire agreed, though not without some reluctance, for he scarce ever permitted her to be out of his sight unless when he was engaged with his horses, dogs, or bottle. Nevertheless, he yielded to the desire of his daughter, though the poor man was at the same time obliged to avoid his own company (if I may so express myself) by sending for a neighbouring farmer to sit with him.

11

THE NARROW ESCAPE OF MOLLY SEAGRIM, WITH SOME OBSERVATIONS FOR WHICH WE HAVE BEEN FORCED TO DIVE PRETTY DEEP INTO NATURE

Tom Jones had ridden one of Mr. Western's horses that morning in the chase, so that having no horse of his own in the squire's stable, he was obliged to go home on foot; this he did so expeditiously that he ran upwards of three miles within the half-hour.

Just as he arrived at Mr. Allworthy's outward gate he met the constable and company with Molly in their possession, whom they were conducting to that house where the inferior sort of people may learn one good lesson: viz., respect and deference to their superiors; since it must show them the wide distinction Fortune intends between those persons who are to be corrected for their faults and those who are not; which lesson if they do not learn, I am afraid they very rarely learn any other good lesson or improve their morals at the House of Correction.

A lawyer may, perhaps, think Mr. Allworthy exceeded his authority a little in this instance. And, to say the truth, I question, as here was no regular information before him, whether his conduct was strictly regular. However, as his intention was truly upright, he ought to be excused *in foro conscientiæ*, since so many arbitrary acts are daily committed by magistrates, who have not this excuse to plead for themselves.

Tom was no sooner informed by the constable whither they were proceeding (indeed he pretty well guessed it of himself) than he caught Molly in his arms, and embracing her tenderly before them all, swore he would murder the first man who offered to lay hold of her. He bid her dry her eyes and be comforted, for wherever she went he would accompany her. Then, turning to the constable, who stood trembling with his hat off, he desired him in a very mild voice to return with him for a moment only to his father (so he now called Allworthy); for he durst, he said, be assured that when he had alleged what he had to say in her favour, the girl would be discharged.

The constable, who, I make no doubt, would have surrendered his prisoner had Tom demanded her, very readily consented to this request. So back they all went into Mr. Allworthy's hall, where Tom desired them to stay till his return, and then went himself in pursuit of the good man. As soon as he was found Tom threw himself at his feet and, having begged a patient hearing, confessed himself to be the father of the child of which Molly was then big. He entreated him to have compassion on the poor girl, and to consider if there was any guilt in the case, it lay principally at his door.

"If there is any guilt in the case!" answered Allworthy warmly. "Are you, then, so profligate and abandoned a libertine to doubt whether the breaking the laws of God and man, the corrupting and ruining a poor girl, be guilt? I own, indeed, it doth lie principally upon you, and so heavy it is that you ought to expect it should crush you."

"Whatever may be my fate," says Tom, "let me succeed in my intercessions for the poor girl. I confess I have corrupted her, but whether she shall be ruined depends on you. For heaven's sake, sir, revoke your warrant, and do not send her to a place which must unavoidably prove her destruction."

Allworthy bid him immediately call a servant. Tom answered there was no occasion, for he had luckily met them at the gate and, relying upon his goodness, had brought them all back into his hall, where they now waited his final resolution, which upon his knees he besought him might be in favour of the girl; that she might be permitted to go home to her parents, and not to be exposed to a greater degree of shame and scorn than must necessarily fall upon her. "I know," said he, "that is too much. I know I am the wicked occasion of it. I will endeavour to make amends if possible; and if you shall have hereafter the goodness to forgive me, I hope I shall deserve it."

Allworthy hesitated some time, and at last said, "Well, I will discharge my mittimus. You may send the constable to me." He was instantly called, discharged, and so was the girl.

It will be believed that Mr. Allworthy failed not to read Tom a very severe lecture on this occasion, but it is unnecessary to insert it here, as we have faithfully transcribed what he said to Jenny Jones in the first book, most of which may be applied to the men equally with the women. So sensible an effect had these reproofs on the young man, who was no hardened sinner, that he retired to his own room, where he passed the evening alone in much melancholy contemplation.

Allworthy was sufficiently offended by this transgression of Jones; for, notwithstanding the assertions of Mr. Western, it is certain this worthy man had never indulged himself in any loose pleasures with women, and greatly condemned the vice of incontinence in others. Indeed, there is much reason to imagine that there was not the least truth in what Mr. Western affirmed, especially as he laid the scene of those impurities at the University, where Mr. Allworthy had never been. In fact, the good squire was a little too apt to indulge that kind of pleasantry which is generally called *rodomontade*, but which may with as much propriety be expressed by a much shorter word; and, perhaps, we too often supply the use of this little monosyllable by others, since very much of what frequently passes in the world for wit and humour should, in the strictest purity of language, receive that short appellation which, in conformity to the well-bred laws of custom, I here suppress.

But whatever detestation Mr. Allworthy had to this or to any other vice, he was not so blinded by it but that he could discern any virtue in the guilty person as clearly, indeed, as if there had been no mixture of vice in the same character. While he was angry, therefore, with the incontinence of Jones, he was no less pleased with the honour and honesty of his self-accusation. He began now to form in his mind the same opinion of this young fellow which, we hope, our reader may have conceived. And in balancing his faults with his perfections, the latter seemed rather to preponderate.

It was to no purpose, therefore, that Thwackum, who was immediately charged by Mr. Blifil with the story, unbended all his rancour against poor Tom. Allworthy gave a patient hearing to these invectives and then answered coldly that young men of Tom's complexion were too generally addicted to this vice, but he believed that youth was sincerely affected with what he had said to him on the occasion, and he hoped he would not transgress again. So that as the days of whipping were at an end, the tutor had no other vent but his own mouth for his gall, the usual poor resource of impotent revenge.

But Square, who was a less violent, was a much more artful man; and as he hated Jones more, perhaps, than Thwackum himself, so he contrived to do him more mischief in the mind of Mr. Allworthy.

The reader must remember the several little incidents of the partridge, the horse, and the Bible which were recounted in the second book. By all which Jones had rather improved than injured the affection which Mr. Allworthy was inclined to entertain for him. The same, I believe, must have happened to him with every other person who hath any idea of friendship, generosity, and greatness of spirit; that is to say, who hath any traces of goodness in his mind.

Square himself was not unacquainted with the true impression which those several instances of goodness had made on the excellent heart of Allworthy; for the philosopher very well knew what virtue was, though he was not always, perhaps, steady in its pursuit; but as for Thwackum, from what reason I will not determine, no such thoughts ever entered into his head: he saw Jones in a bad light, and he imagined Allworthy saw him in the same, but that he was resolved from pride and stubbornness of spirit not to give up the boy whom he had once cherished, since by so doing he must tacitly acknowledge that his former opinion of him had been wrong.

Square therefore embraced this opportunity of injuring Jones in the tenderest part by giving a very bad turn to all

these before-mentioned occurrences. "I am sorry, sir," said
he, "to own I have been deceived as well as yourself. I
could not, I confess, help being pleased with what I ascribed to the motive of friendship, though it was carried to
an excess, and all excess is faulty and vicious; but in this
I made allowance for youth. Little did I suspect that the
sacrifice of truth, which we both imagined to have been made
to friendship, was in reality a prostitution of it to a depraved and debauched appetite. You now plainly see whence
all the seeming generosity of this young man to the family
of the gamekeeper proceeded. He supported the father in
order to corrupt the daughter, and preserved the family from
starving to bring one of them to shame and ruin. This is
friendship! This is generosity! As Sir Richard Steele says,
'Gluttons, who give high prices for delicacies, are very
worthy to be called generous.' In short, I am resolved
from this instance never to give way to the weakness of
human nature more, nor to think anything virtue which
doth not exactly quadrate with the unerring rule of right."

The goodness of Allworthy had prevented those considerations from occurring to himself, yet were they too plausible
to be absolutely and hastily rejected when laid before his
eyes by another. Indeed what Square had said sunk very
deeply into his mind, and the uneasiness which it there
created was very visible to the other, though the good man
would not acknowledge this, but made a very slight answer
and forcibly drove off the discourse to some other subject.
It was well, perhaps, for poor Tom that no such suggestions
had been made before he was pardoned, for they certainly
stamped in the mind of Allworthy the first bad impression
concerning Jones.

12

CONTAINING MUCH CLEARER MATTERS; BUT WHICH FLOW FROM THE SAME FOUNTAIN WITH THOSE IN THE PRECEDING CHAPTER

The reader will be pleased, I believe, to return with me to
Sophia. She passed the night after we saw her last in no
very agreeable manner. Sleep befriended her but little, and
dreams less. In the morning, when Mrs. Honour, her maid,

attended her at the usual hour, she was found already up and dressed.

Persons who live two or three miles' distance in the country are considered as next-door neighbours, and transactions at the one house fly with incredible celerity to the other. Mrs. Honour, therefore, had heard the whole story of Molly's shame, which she, being of a very communicative temper, had no sooner entered the apartment of her mistress than she began to relate in the following manner:

"La, ma'am, what doth your la'ship think? The girl that your la'ship saw at church on Sunday, whom you thought so handsome, though you would not have thought her so handsome neither if you had seen her nearer, but to be sure, she hath been carried before the Justice for being big with child. She seemed to me to look like a confident slut, and to be sure, she hath laid the child to young Mr. Jones. And all the parish says Mr. Allworthy is so angry with young Mr. Jones that he won't see him. To be sure, one can't help pitying the poor young man, and yet he doth not deserve much pity neither for demeaning himself with such kind of trumpery. Yet he is so pretty a gentleman I should be sorry to have him turned out of doors. I dares to swear the wench was as willing as he, for she was always a forward kind of body. And when wenches are so coming, young men are not so much to be blamed neither; for to be sure, they do no more than what is natural. Indeed, it is beneath them to meddle with such dirty draggle-tails, and whatever happens to them it is good enough for them. And yet, to be sure, the vile baggages are most in fault. I wishes with all my heart they were well to be whipped at the cart's tail; for it is pity they should be the ruin of a pretty young gentleman, and nobody can deny but that Mr. Jones is one of the most handsomest young men that ever——"

She was running on thus when Sophia, with a more peevish voice than she had ever spoken to her in before, cried, "Prithee, why dost thou trouble me with all this stuff? What concern have I in what Mr. Jones doth? I suppose you are all alike. And you seem to me to be angry it was not your own case."

"I, ma'am!" answered Mrs. Honour. "I am sorry your ladyship should have such an opinion of me. I am sure nobody can say any such thing of me. All the young fellows in the world may go to the divil for me. Because I said he was a handsome man! Everybody says it as well as I. To be sure, I never thought as it was any harm to say a young man was handsome; but to be sure, I shall never think him so any more now, for handsome is that handsome does. A beggar wench!———"

"Stop thy torrent of impertinence," cries Sophia, "and see whether my father wants me at breakfast."

Mrs. Honour then flung out of the room muttering much to herself, of which "Marry come up, I assure you," was all that could be plainly distinguished.

Whether Mrs. Honour really deserved that suspicion of which her mistress gave her a hint is a matter which we cannot indulge our reader's curiosity by resolving. We will, however, make him amends in disclosing what passed in the mind of Sophia.

The reader will be pleased to recollect that a secret affection for Mr. Jones had insensibly stolen into the bosom of this young lady; that it had there grown to a pretty great height before she herself had discovered it. When she first began to perceive its symptoms, the sensations were so sweet and pleasing that she had not resolution sufficient to check or repel them; and thus she went on cherishing a passion of which she never once considered the consequences.

This incident relating to Molly first opened her eyes. She now first perceived the weakness of which she had been guilty, and though it caused the utmost perturbation in her mind, yet it had the effect of other nauseous physic and for the time expelled her distemper. Its operation indeed was most wonderfully quick, and in the short interval while her maid was absent so entirely removed all symptoms that when Mrs. Honour returned with a summons from her father, she was become perfectly easy and had brought herself to a thorough indifference for Mr. Jones.

The diseases of the mind do in almost every particular imitate those of the body. For which reason, we hope that learned Faculty, for whom we have so profound a respect, will pardon us the violent hands we have been necessitated to lay on several words and phrases which of right belong to them, and without which our descriptions must have been often unintelligible.

Now, there is no one circumstance in which the distempers of the mind bear a more exact analogy to those which are called bodily than that aptness which both have

165

to a relapse. This is plain in the violent diseases of ambition and avarice. I have known ambition, when cured at court by frequent disappointments (which are the only physic for it), to break out again in a contest for foreman of the grand jury at an assizes; and have heard of a man who had so far conquered avarice as to give away many a sixpence that comforted himself at last on his death-bed by making a crafty and advantageous bargain concerning his ensuing funeral with an undertaker who had married his only child.

In the affair of love, which out of strict conformity with the Stoic philosophy we shall here treat as a disease, this proneness to relapse is no less conspicuous. Thus it happened to poor Sophia, upon whom, the very next time she saw young Jones, all the former symptoms returned, and from that time cold and hot fits alternately seized her heart.

The situation of this young lady was now very different from what it had ever been before. That passion, which had formerly been so exquisitely delicious, became now a scorpion in her bosom. She resisted it, therefore, with her utmost force, and summoned every argument her reason (which was surprisingly strong for her age) could suggest to subdue and expel it. In this she so far succeeded that she began to hope from time and absence a perfect cure. She resolved therefore to avoid Tom Jones as much as possible; for which purpose she began to conceive a design of visiting her aunt, to which she made no doubt of obtaining her father's consent.

But Fortune, who had other designs in her head, put an immediate stop to any such proceeding by introducing an accident, which will be related in the next chapter.

13

A DREADFUL ACCIDENT WHICH BEFELL SOPHIA. THE GALLANT
BEHAVIOUR OF JONES, AND THE MORE DREADFUL CON-
SEQUENCE OF THAT BEHAVIOUR TO THE YOUNG LADY; WITH
A SHORT DIGRESSION IN FAVOUR OF THE FEMALE SEX

Mr. Western grew every day fonder and fonder of Sophia, insomuch that his beloved dogs themselves almost gave place to her in his affections; but as he could not prevail on himself to abandon these, he contrived very cunningly to enjoy their company together with that of his daughter by insisting on her riding a-hunting with him.

Sophia, to whom her father's word was a law, readily complied with his desires, though she had not the least delight in a sport which was of too rough and masculine a nature to suit with her disposition. She had, however, another motive beside her obedience to accompany the old gentleman in the chase; for by her presence she hoped in some measure to restrain his impetuosity, and to prevent him from so frequently exposing his neck to the utmost hazard.

The strongest objection was that which would have formerly been an inducement to her, namely, the frequent meeting with young Jones, whom she had determined to avoid; but as the end of the hunting season now approached, she hoped by a short absence with her aunt to reason herself entirely out of her unfortunate passion, and had not any doubt of being able to meet him in the field the subsequent season without the least danger.

On the second day of her hunting, as she was returning from the chase and was arrived within a little distance from Mr. Western's house, her horse, whose mettlesome spirit required a better rider, fell suddenly to prancing and capering in such a manner that she was in the most imminent peril of falling. Tom Jones, who was at a little distance behind, saw this, and immediately galloped up to her assistance. As soon as he came up, he immediately leapt from his own horse and caught hold of hers by the bridle. The unruly beast presently reared himself on end on his hind legs and threw his lovely burden from his back, and Jones caught her in his arms.

She was so affected with the fright that she was not immediately able to satisfy Jones, who was very solicitous to know whether she had received any hurt. She soon after, however, recovered her spirits, assured him she was safe, and thanked him for the care he had taken of her. Jones answered, "If I have preserved you, madam, I am sufficiently repaid; for I promise you I would have secured you from the least harm, at the expense of a much greater misfortune to myself than I have suffered on this occasion."

"What misfortune?" replied Sophia, eagerly. "I hope you have come to no mischief."

"Be not concerned, madam," answered Jones. "Heaven be praised you have escaped so well, considering the danger you was in. If I have broke my arm, I consider it as a trifle in comparison of what I feared upon your account."

Sophia then screamed out, "Broke your arm! Heaven forbid."

"I am afraid I have, madam," says Jones, "but I beg you will suffer me first to take care of you. I have a right hand yet at your service to help you into the next field, where we have but a very little walk to your father's house."

Sophia, seeing his left arm dangling by his side while he was using the other to lead her, no longer doubted of the truth. She now grew much paler than her fears for herself had made her before. All her limbs were seized with a trembling, insomuch that Jones could scarce support her; and as her thoughts were in no less agitation, she could not refrain from giving Jones a look so full of tenderness that it almost argued a stronger sensation in her mind than even gratitude and pity united can raise in the gentlest female bosom without the assistance of a third more powerful passion.

Mr. Western, who was advanced at some distance when this accident happened, was now returned, as were the rest of the horsemen. Sophia immediately acquainted them with what had befallen Jones and begged them to take care of him. Upon which Western, who had been much alarmed by meeting his daughter's horse without its rider, and was now overjoyed to find her unhurt, cried out, "I am glad it is no worse; if Tom hath broken his arm, we will get a joiner to mend un again."

The squire alighted from his horse, and proceeded to his house on foot with his daughter and Jones. An impartial spectator who had met them on the way would, on viewing their several countenances, have concluded Sophia alone to have been the object of compassion; for as to Jones, he exulted in having probably saved the life of the young lady at the price only of a broken bone; and Mr. Western, though he was not unconcerned at the accident which had befallen Jones, was, however, delighted in a much higher degree with the fortunate escape of his daughter.

The generosity of Sophia's temper construed this behaviour of Jones into great bravery, and it made a deep impression on her heart; for certain it is, that there is no one quality which so generally recommends men to women as this, proceeding, if we believe the common opinion, from that natural timidity of the sex, which is, says Mr. Osborne, so great that a woman

is "the most cowardly of all the creatures God ever made"
—a sentiment more remarkable for its bluntness than for
its truth. Aristotle in his *Politics* doth them, I believe, more
justice when he says, "The modesty and fortitude of men differ from those virtues in women; for the fortitude which
becomes a woman would be cowardice in a man, and the
modesty which becomes a man would be pertness in a woman." Nor is there, perhaps, more of truth in the opinion of
those who derive the partiality which women are inclined to
show to the brave from this excess of their fear. Mr. Bayle
(I think in his article of Helen) imputes this, and with
greater probability, to their violent love of glory; for the
truth of which we have the authority of him who of all
others saw farthest into human nature, and who introduces the heroine of his *Odyssey*, the great pattern of matrimonial love and constancy, assigning the glory of her husband as the only source of her affection towards him.*

However this be, certain it is that the accident operated
very strongly on Sophia; and indeed after much inquiry into
the matter I am inclined to believe that at this very time
the charming Sophia made no less impression on the heart
of Jones; to say truth, he had for some time become sensible of the irresistible power of her charms.

14

THE ARRIVAL OF A SURGEON. HIS OPERATIONS, AND A LONG
DIALOGUE BETWEEN SOPHIA AND HER MAID

When they arrived in Mr. Western's hall, Sophia, who had
tottered along with much difficulty, sunk down in a chair;
but by the assistance of hartshorn and water she was prevented from fainting away, and had pretty well recovered
her spirits when the surgeon, who was sent for to Jones,
appeared. Mr. Western, who imputed these symptoms in his
daughter to her fall, advised her to be presently blooded
by way of prevention. In this opinion he was seconded by
the surgeon, who gave so many reasons for bleeding and
quoted so many cases where persons had miscarried for
want of it that the squire became very importunate, and in-

* The English reader will not find this in the poem, for the sentiment is entirely left out in the translation.

deed insisted peremptorily that his daughter should be blooded.

Sophia soon yielded to the commands of her father, though entirely contrary to her own inclinations; for she suspected, I believe, less danger from the fright than either the squire or the surgeon. She then stretched out her beautiful arm, and the operator began to prepare for his work.

While the servants were busied in providing materials, the surgeon, who imputed the backwardness which had appeared in Sophia to her fears, began to comfort her with assurances that there was not the least danger; for no accident, he said, could ever happen in bleeding but from the monstrous ignorance of pretenders to surgery, which he pretty plainly insinuated was not at present to be apprehended. Sophia declared she was not under the least apprehension, adding, "If you open an artery, I promise you I'll forgive you." "Will you?" cries Western. "D—n me if I will; if he does thee the least mischief, d—n me if I don't ha' the heart's blood o'un out." The surgeon assented to bleed her upon these conditions, and then proceeded to his operation, which he performed with as much dexterity as he had promised; and with as much quickness, for he took but little blood from her, saying it was much safer to bleed again and again than to take away too much at once.

Sophia, when her arm was bound up, retired; for she was not willing (nor was it, perhaps, strictly decent) to be present at the operation on Jones. Indeed one objection which she had to bleeding (though she did not make it) was the delay which it would occasion to dressing the broken bone. For Western, when Sophia was concerned, had no consideration but for her; and as for Jones himself, he "sat like patience on a monument, smiling at grief." To say the truth, when he saw the blood springing from the lovely arm of Sophia, he scarce thought of what had happened to himself.

The surgeon now ordered his patient to be stripped to his shirt, and then, entirely baring the arm, he began to stretch and examine it in such a manner that the tortures he put him to caused Jones to make several wry faces; which the surgeon, observing, greatly wondered at, crying, "What is the matter, sir? I am sure it is impossible I should hurt you." And then holding forth the broken arm, he began a long and very learned lecture of anatomy in which simple and double fractures were most accurately considered, and the several ways in which Jones might have broken his arm were discussed, with proper annotations showing how many of these would have been better and how many worse than the present case.

Having at length finished his laboured harangue, with which the audience, though it had greatly raised their attention and admiration, were not much edified, as they really understood not a single syllable of all he had said, he proceeded to business, which he was more expeditious in finishing than he had been in beginning.

Jones was then ordered into bed, which Mr. Western compelled him to accept at his own house, and sentence of water-gruel was passed upon him.

Among the good company which had attended in the hall during the bone-setting Mrs. Honour was one, who, being summoned to her mistress as soon as it was over and asked by her how the young gentleman did, presently launched into extravagant praises on the *magnimity*, as she called it, of his behaviour, which, she said, "was so charming in so pretty a creature." She then burst forth into much warmer encomiums on the beauty of his person, enumerating many particulars and ending with the whiteness of his skin.

This discourse had an effect on Sophia's countenance, which would not, perhaps, have escaped the observance of the sagacious waiting-woman had she once looked her mistress in the face all the time she was speaking; but as a looking-glass, which was most commodiously placed opposite to her, gave her an opportunity of surveying those features in which of all others she took most delight, so she had not once removed her eyes from that amiable object during her whole speech.

Mrs. Honour was so entirely wrapped up in the subject on which she exercised her tongue, and the object before her eyes, that she gave her mistress time to conquer her confusion; which having done, she smiled on her maid and told her she was certainly in love with this young fellow. "I in love, madam!" answers she. "Upon my word, ma'am, I assure you, ma'am, upon my soul, ma'am, I am not." "Why, if you was," cries her mistress, "I see no reason that you should be ashamed of it, for he is certainly a pretty fellow" "Yes, ma'am," answered the other, "that he is, the most handsomest man I ever saw in my life. Yes, to be sure, that he is, and as your ladyship says, I don't know why I should be ashamed of loving him, though he is my betters. To be sure, gentlefolks are but flesh and blood no more than us servants. Besides, as for Mr. Jones thof Squire Allworthy hath made

z
171

a gentleman of him, he was not so good as myself by birth; for thof I am a poor body, I am an honest person's child, and my father and mother were married, which is more than some people can say, as high as they hold their heads. Marry, come up! I assure you, my dirty cousin! Thof his skin be so white, and to be sure, it is the most whitest that ever was seen, I am a Christian as well as he, and nobody can say that I am base born; my grandfather was a clergyman,* and would have been very angry, I believe, to have thought any of his family should have taken up with Molly Seagrim's dirty leavings."

Perhaps Sophia might have suffered her maid to run on in this manner from wanting sufficient spirits to stop her tongue, which the reader may probably conjecture was no very easy task; for certainly there were some passages in her speech which were far from being agreeable to the lady. However, she now checked the torrent, as there seemed no end of its flowing. "I wonder," says she, "at your assurance in daring to talk thus of one of my father's friends. As to the wench, I order you never to mention her name to me. And with regard to the young gentleman's birth, those who can say nothing more to his disadvantage may as well be silent on that head, as I desire you will be for the future."

"I am sorry I have offended your ladyship," answered Mrs. Honour. "I am sure I hate Molly Seagrim as much as your ladyship can, and as for abusing Squire Jones, I can call all the servants in the house to witness that whenever any talk hath been about bastards I have always taken his part; 'for which of you,' says I to the footmen, 'would not be a bastard if he could, to be made a gentleman of? And,' says I, 'I am sure he is a very fine gentleman, and he hath one of the whitest hands in the world; for to be sure, so he hath; and,' says I, 'one of the sweetest-temperedest, best-naturedest men in the world he is, and,' says I, 'all the servants and neighbours all round the country loves him.' And to be sure, I could tell your ladyship something, but that I am afraid it would offend you." "What could you tell me, Honour?" says Sophia. "Nay, ma'am, to be sure, he meant nothing by it; therefore I would not have your ladyship be offended."

---

* This is the second person of low condition whom we have recorded in this history to have sprung from the clergy. It is to be hoped such instances will in future ages, when some provision is made for the families of the inferior clergy, appear stranger than they can be thought at present.

"Prithee tell me," says Sophia. "I will know it this instant." "Why, ma'am," answered Mrs. Honour, "he came into the room one day last week when I was at work, and there lay your ladyship's muff on a chair, and to be sure, he puts his hands into it, that very muff your ladyship gave me but yesterday. 'La,' says I, 'Mr. Jones, you will stretch my lady's muff and spoil it'; but he still kept his hands in it, and then he kissed it. To be sure, I hardly ever saw such a kiss in my life as he gave it." "I suppose he did not know it was mine," replied Sophia. "Your ladyship shall hear, ma'am. He kissed it again and again, and said it was the prettiest muff in the world. 'La, sir,' says I, 'you have seen it a hundred times!' 'Yes, Mrs. Honour,' cried he, 'but who can see anything beautiful in the presence of your lady but herself'; nay, that's not all neither, but I hope your ladyship won't be offended, for to be sure, he meant nothing. One day, as your ladyship was playing on the harpsichord to my master, Mr. Jones was sitting in the next room, and methought he looked melancholy. 'La,' says I, 'Mr. Jones, what's the matter? A penny for your thoughts,' says I. 'Why, hussy,' says he, starting up from a dream, 'what can I be thinking of when that angel, your mistress, is playing?' And then squeezing me by the hand: 'Oh, Mrs. Honour,' says he, 'how happy will that man be!' And then he sighed; upon my troth, his breath is as sweet as a nosegay—but to be sure, he meant no harm by it. So I hope your ladyship will not mention a word; for he gave me a crown never to mention it, and made me swear upon a book, but I believe, indeed, it was not the Bible."

Till something of a more beautiful red than vermilion be found out, I shall say nothing of Sophia's colour on this occasion. "Ho—nour," says she, "I—if you will not mention this any more to me—nor to anybody else, I will not betray you —I mean I will not be angry; but I am afraid of your tongue. Why, my girl, will you give it such liberties?" "Nay, ma'am," answered she, "to be sure, I would sooner cut out my tongue than offend your ladyship—to be sure, I shall never mention a word that your ladyship would not have me." "Why, I would not have you mention this any more," said Sophia, "for it may come to my father's ears and he would be angry with Mr. Jones, though I really believe, as you say, he meant nothing. I should be very angry myself if I imagined——" "Nay, ma'am," says Honour, "I protest I believe he meant nothing. I thought he talked as if he was out of his senses; nay, he said he believed he was beside himself when he had spoken the words. 'Ay, sir,' says I, 'I believe so too.' 'Yes,' says he, 'Honour,'—but I ask your ladyship's pardon; I could tear my tongue out for offending you." "Go on," says Sophia, "you may mention anything you have not told me before." " 'Yes, Honour,' says he (this was some time afterwards, when he gave me the crown), 'I am neither such a coxcomb or such a villain as to think of her in any other *delight* but as my goddess; as such I will always worship and adore her while I have breath.' This was all, ma'am, I will be sworn, to the best of my remembrance. I was in a passion with him myself, till I found he meant no harm." "Indeed, Honour," says Sophia, "I believe you have a real affection for me; I was provoked the other day when I gave you warning, but if you have a desire to stay with me, you shall." "To be sure, ma'am," answered Mrs. Honour, "I shall never desire to part with your ladyship. To be sure, I almost cried my eyes out when you gave me warning. It would be very ungrateful in me to desire to leave your ladyship, because as why, I should never get so good a place again. I am sure I would live and die with your ladyship; for, as poor Mr. Jones said, happy is the man——"

Here the dinner-bell interrupted a conversation which had wrought such an effect on Sophia that she was, perhaps, more obliged to her bleeding in the morning than she at the time had apprehended she should be. As to the present situation of her mind, I shall adhere to a rule of Horace by not attempting to describe it from despair of success. Most of my readers will suggest it easily to themselves, and the few who cannot would not understand the picture, or at least would deny it to be natural if ever so well drawn.

BOOK V

1

OF THE *serious* IN WRITING, AND FOR WHAT PURPOSE IT IS INTRODUCED

Peradventure there may be no parts in this prodigious work which will give the reader less pleasure in perusing than those which have given the author the greatest pains in composing. Among these, probably, may be reckoned those initial essays which we have prefixed to the historical matter contained in every book, and which we have determined to be essentially necessary to this kind of writing, of which we have set ourselves at the head.

For this our determination we do not hold ourselves strictly bound to assign any reason, it being abundantly sufficient that we have laid it down as a rule necessary to be observed in all prosai-comi-epic writing. Who ever demanded the reasons of that nice unity of time or place which is now established to be so essential to dramatic poetry? What critic hath been ever asked why a play may not contain two days as well as one? Or why the audience (provided they travel, like electors, without any expense) may not be wafted fifty miles as well as five? Hath any commentator well accounted for the limitation which an ancient critic hath set to the drama, which he will have contain neither more nor less than five acts? Or hath any one living attempted to explain what the modern judges of our theatres mean by that word *low*, by which they have happily succeeded in banishing all humour from the stage and have made the theatre as dull as a drawing-room? Upon all these occasions, the world seems to have embraced a maxim of our law: vis., *Cuicunque in arte sua perito credendum est;* for it seems, perhaps, difficult to conceive that any one should have had enough of impudence to lay down dogmatical rules in any art or science without the least foundation. In such cases, therefore, we are apt to conclude there are sound and good reasons at the bottom, though we are unfortunately not able to see so far.

Now, in reality, the world have paid too great a compliment to critics, and have imagined them men of much greater profundity than they really are. From this complaisance the critics have been emboldened to assume a dictatorial power, and have so far succeeded that they are now become the masters and have the assurance to give laws to those authors from whose predecessors they originally received them.

The critic, rightly considered, is no more than the clerk, whose office it is to transcribe the rules and laws laid down by those great judges whose vast strength of genius hath placed them in the light of legislators in the several sciences over which they presided. This office was all which the critics of old aspired to, nor did they ever dare to advance a sentence without supporting it by the authority of the judge from whence it was borrowed.

But in the process of time, and in ages of ignorance, the clerk began to invade the power and assume the dignity of his master. The laws of writing were no longer founded on the practice of the author but on the dictates of the critic. The clerk became the legislator, and those very peremptorily gave laws whose business it was at first only to transcribe them.

Hence arose an obvious and, perhaps, an unavoidable error; for these critics, being men of shallow capacities, very easily mistook mere form for substance. They acted as a judge would who should adhere to the lifeless letter of law and reject the spirit. Little circumstances which were, perhaps, accidental in a great author were by these critics considered to constitute his chief merit, and transmitted as essentials to be observed by all his successors. To these encroachments time and ignorance, the two great supporters of imposture, gave authority; and thus many rules for good writing have been established which have not the least foundation in truth or nature, and which commonly serve for no other purpose than to curb and restrain genius, in the same manner as it would have restrained the dancing-master had the many excellent treatises on that art laid it down as an essential rule that every man must dance in chains.

To avoid, therefore, all imputation of laying down a rule for posterity founded only on the authority of *ipse dixit,* for which, to say the truth, we have not the profoundest veneration, we shall here waive the privilege above contended for and proceed to lay before the reader the reasons which have induced us to intersperse these several digressive essays in the course of this work.

And here we shall of necessity be led to open a new vein of knowledge which, if it hath been discovered, hath not to our remembrance been wrought on by any ancient or modern writer. This vein is no other than that of contrast, which runs through all the works of the Creation and may probably have a large share in constituting in us the idea of all beauty, as well natural as artificial; for what demonstrates the beauty and excellence of anything but its reverse? Thus the beauty of day and that of summer is set off by the horrors of night and winter. And, I believe, if it was possible for a man to have seen only the two former, he would have a very imperfect idea of their beauty.

But to avoid too serious an air: can it be doubted but that the finest woman in the world would lose all benefit of her charms in the eye of a man who had never seen one of another cast? The ladies themselves seem so sensible of this that they are all industrious to procure foils; nay, they will become foils to themselves; for I have observed (at Bath particularly) that they endeavour to appear as ugly as possible in the morning, in order to set off that beauty which they intend to show you in the evening.

Most artists have this secret in practice, though some, perhaps, have not much studied the theory. The jeweller knows that the finest brilliant requires a foil, and the painter by the contrast of his figures often acquires great applause.

A great genius among us will illustrate this matter fully. I cannot, indeed, range him under any general head of common artists, as he hath a title to be placed among those

> *Inventas qui vitam excoluere per artes.*

> Who by invented arts have life improved.

I mean here the inventor of that most exquisite entertainment called the English Pantomime.

This entertainment consisted of two parts, which the inventor distinguished by the names of the *serious* and the *comic*. The serious exhibited a certain number of heathen gods and heroes, who were certainly the worst and dullest company into which an audience was ever introduced, and (which was a secret known to few) were actually intended so to be, in order to contrast the *comic* part of the entertainment, and to display the tricks of Harlequin to the better advantage.

This was, perhaps, no very civil use of such personages, but the contrivance was nevertheless ingenious enough, and had its effect. And this will now plainly appear if instead of *serious* and *comic* we supply the words *duller* and *dullest;* for the *comic* was certainly duller than anything before shown on the stage, and could only be set off by that superlative degree of dullness which composed the *serious*. So intolerably serious, indeed, were these gods and heroes that Harlequin (though the English gentleman of that name is not at all related to the French family, for he is of a much more serious disposition) was always welcome on the stage, as he relieved the audience from worse company.

Judicious writers have always practised this art of contrast with great success. I have been surprised that Horace should cavil at this art in Homer, but indeed he contradicts himself in the very next line:

> *Indignor quandoque bonus dormitat Homerus;*
> *Verum operi longo fas est obrepere somnum.*

> I grieve if e'er great Homer chance to sleep,
> Yet slumbers on long works have right to creep.

For we are not here to understand, as perhaps some have, that an author actually falls asleep while he is writing. It is true that readers are too apt to be so overtaken; but if the work was as long as any of Oldmixon, the author himself is too well entertained to be subject to the least drowsiness. He is, as Mr. Pope observes,

> Sleepless himself to give his readers sleep.

To say the truth, these soporific parts are so many scenes of *serious* artfully interwoven in order to contrast and set off the rest; and this is the true meaning of a late facetious writer who told the public that whenever he was dull, they might be assured there was a design in it.

In this light, then, or rather in this darkness, I would have the reader to consider these initial essays. And after this warning, if he shall be of opinion that he can find enough of *serious* in other parts of this history, he may pass over these, in which we profess to be laboriously dull, and begin the following books at the second chapter.

2

IN WHICH MR. JONES RECEIVES MANY FRIENDLY VISITS DURING HIS CONFINEMENT; WITH SOME FINE TOUCHES OF THE PASSION OF LOVE SCARCE VISIBLE TO THE NAKED EYE

Tom Jones had many visitors during his confinement, though some, perhaps, were not very agreeable to him. Mr. Allworthy saw him almost every day, but though he pitied Tom's sufferings and greatly approved the gallant behaviour which had occasioned them, yet he thought this was a favourable opportunity to bring him to a sober sense of his indiscreet conduct, and that wholesome advice for that purpose could never be applied at a more proper season than at the present, when the mind was softened by pain and sickness and alarmed by danger, and when its attention was unembarrassed with those turbulent passions which engage us in the pursuit of pleasure.

At all seasons, therefore, when the good man was alone with the youth, especially when the latter was totally at ease, he took occasion to remind him of his former miscarriages, but in the mildest and tenderest manner, and only in order to introduce the caution which he prescribed for his future behaviour; on which alone, he assured him, would depend his own felicity and the kindness which he might yet promise himself to receive at the hands of his father by adoption unless he should hereafter forfeit his good opinion; for as to what had passed, he said, it should be all forgotten and forgiven. He therefore advised him to make a good use of this accident, that so in the end it might prove a visitation for his own good.

Thwackum was likewise pretty assiduous in his visits, and he too considered a sick-bed to be a convenient scene for lectures. His style, however, was more severe than Mr. Allworthy's: He told his pupil that he ought to look on his broken limb as a judgement from heaven on his sins; that it would become him to be daily on his knees, pouring forth thanksgivings that he had broken his arm only and not his neck, which latter, he said, was very probably reserved for some future occasion, and that, perhaps, not very remote. For his part, he said, he had often wondered some judgement had not overtaken him before, but it might be perceived by this that divine punishments, though slow, are always sure. Hence, likewise, he advised him to foresee with equal certainty the greater evils which were yet behind, and which were as sure as this of overtaking him in his state of reprobacy. "These are," said he, "to be averted only by such a thorough and sincere repentance as is not to be expected or hoped for from one so abandoned in his youth, and whose mind, I am afraid, is totally corrupted. It is my duty, however, to exhort you to this repentance, though I too well know all exhortations will be vain and fruitless. But *liberavi animam meam*. I can accuse my own conscience of no neglect; though it is at the same time with the utmost concern I see you travelling on to certain misery in this world, and to as certain damnation in the next."

Square talked in a very different strain: he said such accidents as a broken bone were below the consideration of a wise man; that it was abundantly sufficient to reconcile the mind to any of these mischances to reflect that they are liable to befall the wisest of mankind, and are undoubtedly for the good of the whole. He said it was a mere abuse of words to call those things evils in which there was no moral unfitness; that pain, which was the worst consequence of such accidents, was the most contemptible thing in the world; with more of the like sentences, extracted out of the second book of Tully's *Tusculan Questions* and from the great Lord Shaftesbury. In pronouncing these, he was one day so eager that he unfortunately bit his tongue, and in such a manner that it not only put an end to his discourse but created much emotion in him, and caused him to mutter an oath or two; but what was worst of all, this accident gave Thwackum, who was present, and who held such doctrine to be heathenish and atheistical, an opportunity to clap a judgement on his back. Now, this was done with so malicious a sneer that it totally unhinged (if I may so say) the temper of the philosopher, which the bite of his tongue had somewhat ruffled; and as he was disabled from venting his wrath at his lips, he had possibly found a more violent method of revenging himself had not the surgeon, who was then luckily in the room, contrary to his own interest interposed and preserved the peace.

Mr. Blifil visited his friend Jones but seldom, and never alone. This worthy young man, however, professed much regard for him and as great concern at his misfortune, but cautiously avoided any intimacy lest, as he frequently hinted, it might contaminate the sobriety of his own character; for which purpose he had constantly in his mouth that proverb in which Solomon speaks against evil communication. Not that he was so bitter as Thwackum; for he always expressed some hopes of Tom's reformation, which, he said, the unparalleled goodness shown by his uncle on this occasion must certainly effect in one not absolutely abandoned; but concluded, "If Mr. Jones ever offends hereafter, I shall not be able to say a syllable in his favour."

As to Squire Western, he was seldom out of the sick-room, unless when he was engaged either in the field or over his bottle. Nay, he would sometimes retire hither to take his beer, and it was not without difficulty that he was prevented from forcing Jones to take his beer too; for no quack ever held his nostrum to be a more general panacea than he did this, which, he said, had more virtues in it than was in all the physic in an apothecary's shop. He was, however, by much entreaty prevailed on to forbear the application of this medicine; but from serenading his patient every hunting morning with the horn under his window it was impossible to withhold him, nor did he ever lay aside that halloo with which he entered into all companies, when he visited Jones, without any regard to the sick person's being at that time either awake or asleep.

This boisterous behaviour, as it meant no harm, so happily it effected none, and was abundantly compensated to Jones as soon as he was able to sit up by the company of Sophia, whom the squire then brought to visit him; nor was it, indeed, long before Jones was able to attend her to the harpsichord, where she would kindly condescend for hours together to charm him with the most delicious music, unless when the squire thought proper to interrupt her by insisting on "Old Sir Simon" or some other of his favourite pieces.

Notwithstanding the nicest guard which Sophia endeavoured to set on her behaviour, she could not avoid letting some appearances now and then slip forth; for love may again be likened to a disease in this: that when it is denied a vent in one part, it will certainly break out in another. What her lips therefore concealed, her eyes, her blushes, and many little involuntary actions betrayed.

One day when Sophia was playing on the harpsichord and Jones was attending, the squire came into the room, crying, "There, Tom, I have had a battle for thee below-stairs with thick Parson Thwackum. He hath been a-telling Allworthy before my face that the broken bone was a judgement upon thee. 'D——n it,' says I, 'how can that be? Did not he come by it in defence of a young woman? A judgement indeed! Pox, if he never doth anything worse, he will go to heaven sooner than all the parsons in the country. He hath more reason to glory in it than to be ashamed of it.'" "Indeed, sir," says Jones, "I have no reason for either; but if it preserved Miss Western, I shall always think it the happiest accident of my life." "And to gu," said the squire, "to zet Allworthy against thee vor it. D——n un, if the parson had unt had his petticoats on, I should ha' lent un a flick; for I love thee dearly, my boy, and d——n me if there is anything in my power which I won't do for thee. Sha't take thy choice of all the horses in my stable to-morrow morning, except only the Chevalier and Miss Slouch." Jones thanked him, but declined accepting the offer. "Nay," added the squire, "sha't ha' the sorrel mare that Sophy rode. She cost me fifty guineas, and comes six years old this grass." "If she had cost me a thousand," cries Jones passionately, "I would have given her to the dogs." "Pooh, pooh!" answered Western. "What! Because she broke thy arm? Shouldst forget and forgive. I thought hadst been more a man than to bear malice against a dumb creature." Here Sophia interposed and put an end to the conversation by desiring her father's leave to play to him a request which he never refused.

The countenance of Sophia had undergone more than one change during the foregoing speeches, and probably she imputed the passionate resentment which Jones had expressed against the mare to a different motive from that from which her father had derived it. Her spirits were at this time in a visible flutter, and she played so intolerably ill that had not Western soon fallen asleep, he must have remarked it. Jones, however, who was sufficiently awake and was not without an ear any more than without eyes, made some observations, which, being joined to all which the reader may remember to have passed formerly, gave him pretty strong assurances when he came to reflect on the whole that all was not well in the tender bosom of Sophia—an opinion which many young gentlemen will, I doubt not, extremely wonder at his not having been well confirmed in long ago. To confess the truth, he had rather too much diffidence in himself, and was not forward enough in seeing the advances of a young lady, a misfortune which can only be cured by that early town education which is at present so generally in fashion.

When these thoughts had fully taken possession of Jones, they occasioned a perturbation in his mind, which in a constitution less pure and firm than his might have been at such a season attended with very dangerous consequences. He was truly sensible of the great worth of Sophia. He extremely liked her person, no less admired her accomplishments, and tenderly loved her goodness. In reality, as he had never once entertained any thought of possessing her, nor had ever the least voluntary indulgence to his inclinations, he had a much stronger passion for her than he himself was acquainted with. His heart now brought forth the full secret at the same time that it assured him the adorable object returned his affection.

3

WHICH ALL WHO HAVE NO HEART WILL THINK TO CONTAIN MUCH ADO ABOUT NOTHING

The reader will perhaps imagine the sensations which now arose in Jones to have been so sweet and delicious that they would rather tend to produce a cheerful serenity in the mind than any of those dangerous effects which we have mentioned; but in fact, sensations of this kind, however delicious, are at their first recognition of a very tumultous nature, and have very little of the opiate in them. They were, moreover, in the present case embittered with certain circumstances which, being mixed with sweeter ingredients, tended altogether to compose a draught that might be termed bitter-sweet; than which, as nothing can be more disagreeable to the palate, so nothing in the metaphorical sense can be so injurious to the mind.

For first, though he had sufficient foundation to flatter himself on what he had observed in Sophia, he was not yet free from doubt of misconstruing compassion, or at best esteem, into a warmer regard. He was far from a sanguine assurance that Sophia had any such affection towards him as might promise his inclinations that harvest which, if they were encouraged and nursed, they would finally grow up to require. Besides, if he could hope to find no bar to his happiness from the daughter, he thought himself certain of meeting an effectual bar in the father, who, though he was a country squire in his diversions, was perfectly a man of the world in whatever regarded his fortune, had the most violent affection for this only daughter, and had often signified in his cups the pleasure he proposed in seeing her married to one of the richest men in the county. Jones was not so vain and senseless a coxcomb as to expect from any regard which Western had professed for him that he would ever be induced to lay aside these views of advancing his daughter. He well knew that fortune is generally the principal, if not the sole, consideration which operates on the best of parents in these matters; for friendship makes us warmly espouse the interests of others, but is very cold to the gratification of their passions. Indeed, to feel the happiness which may result from this, it is necessary we should possess the passion ourselves. As he had, therefore, no hopes of obtaining her father's consent, so he thought to endeavour to succeed without it, and by such means to frustrate the great point of Mr. Western's life was to make a very ill use of his hospitality and a very ungrateful return to the many little favours received (however roughly) at his hands. If he saw such a consequence with horror and disdain, how much more was he shocked with what regarded Mr. Allworthy, to whom, as he had more than filial obligations, so had he for him more than filial piety. He knew the nature of that good man to be so averse to any baseness or treachery that the least attempt of such a kind would make the guilty person forever odious to his eyes, and the name of that person a detestable sound in his ears. The appearance of such unsurmountable difficulties was sufficient to have inspired him with despair, however ardent his wishes had been, but even these were controlled by compassion for another woman. The idea of lovely Molly now intruded itself before him. He had sworn eternal constancy in her arms, and she had as often vowed never to outlive his deserting her. He now saw her in all the most shocking postures of death; nay, he considered all the miseries of prostitution, to which she would be liable and of which he would be doubly the occasion: first by seducing and then by deserting her; for he well knew the hatred which all her neighbours and even her own sisters bore her, and how ready they would all be to tear her to pieces. Indeed he had exposed her to more envy than shame, or rather to the latter by means of the former; for many women abused her for being a whore while they envied her her lover and her finery, and would have been themselves glad to have purchased these at the same rate. The ruin, therefore, of the poor girl must, he foresaw, unavoidably attend his deserting her; and this thought stung him to the soul. Poverty and distress seemed to him to give none a right of aggravating those misfortunes. The meanness of her condition did not represent her misery as of little consequence in his eyes, nor did it appear to justify, or even to palliate, his guilt in bringing that misery upon her. But why do I mention justification? His own heart would not suffer him to destroy a human creature who, he thought, loved him, and had to that love sacrificed her innocence. His own good heart pleaded her cause, not as a cold venal advocate but as one interested in the event, and which must itself deeply share in all the agonies its owner brought on another.

When this cunning advocate had sufficiently raised the pity of Jones by painting poor Molly in all the circumstances of wretchedness, it artfully called in the assistance of another passion, and represented the girl in all the amiable colours of youth, health, and beauty; as one greatly the object of desire, and much more so, at least to a good mind, from being at the same time the object of compassion.

Amidst these thoughts poor Jones passed a long sleepless night, and in the morning the result of the whole was to abide by Molly and to think no more of Sophia.

In this virtuous resolution he continued all the next day till the evening, cherishing the idea of Molly and driving Sophia from his thoughts, but in the fatal evening, a very trifling accident set all his passions again on float, and worked so total a change in his mind that we think it decent to communicate it in a fresh chapter.

4

A LITTLE CHAPTER, IN WHICH IS CONTAINED A LITTLE
INCIDENT

Among other visitants who paid their compliments to the
young gentleman in his confinement Mrs. Honour was one.
The reader, perhaps, when he reflects on some expressions
which have formerly dropped from her, may conceive that
she herself had a very particular affection for Mr. Jones, but in
reality it was no such thing. Tom was a handsome young
fellow, and for that species of men Mrs. Honour had some
regard; but this was perfectly indiscriminate; for having been
crossed in the love which she bore a certain nobleman's footman, who had basely deserted her after a promise of marriage, she had so securely kept together the broken remains
of her heart that no man had ever since been able to possess
himself of any single fragment. She viewed all handsome
men with that equal regard and benevolence which a sober
and virtuous mind bears to all the good. She might, indeed,
be called a lover of men, as Socrates was a lover of mankind, preferring one to another for corporeal, as he for
mental, qualifications; but never carrying this preference so
far as to cause any perturbation in the philosophical serenity
of her temper.

The day after Mr. Jones had had that conflict with himself
which we have seen in the preceding chapter, Mrs. Honour
came into his room and, finding him alone, began in the
following manner: "La, sir, where do you think I have been?
I warrants you, you would not guess in fifty years; but if you
did guess, to be sure, I must not tell you neither." "Nay, if it
be something which you must not tell me," said Jones, "I
shall have the curiosity to inquire, and I know you will not
be so barbarous to refuse me." "I don't know," cries she,
"why I should refuse you neither, for that matter; for to be
sure, you won't mention it any more. And for that matter,
if you knew where I had been, unless you knew what I had
been about, it would not signify much. Nay, I don't see why
it should be kept a secret, for my part; for to be sure, she
is the best lady in the world." Upon this Jones began to beg
earnestly to be let into this secret, and faithfully promised
not to divulge it. She then proceeded thus: "Why, you must

186

know, sir, my young lady sent me to inquire after Molly Sea-grim, and to see whether the wench wanted anything; to be sure, I did not care to go, methinks, but servants must do what they are ordered. How could you undervalue your-self so, Mr. Jones? So my lady bid me go and carry her some linen and other things. She is too good. If such for-ward sluts were sent to Bridewell, it would be better for them. I told my lady, says I, 'Madam, your la'ship is en-couraging idleness.' " "And was my Sophia so good?" says Jones. "My Sophia! I assure you, marry come up," an-swered Honour. "And yet if you knew all—indeed, if I was as Mr. Jones, I should look a little higher than such trum-pery as Molly Seagrim." "What do you mean by these words," replied Jones, "if I knew all?" "I mean what I mean," says Honour. "Don't you remember putting your hands in my lady's muff once? I vow I could almost find in my heart to tell if I was certain my lady would never come to the hearing on't." Jones then made several solemn protestations. And Honour proceeded, "Then, to be sure, my lady gave me that muff; and afterwards, upon hearing what you had done——" "Then you told her what I had done!" interrupted Jones. "If I did, sir," answered she, "you need not be angry with me. Many's the man would have given his head to have had my lady told, if they had known—for, to be sure, the biggest lord in the land might be proud—but I protest I have a great mind not to tell you." Jones fell to entreaties, and soon prevailed on her to go on thus: "You must know, then, sir, that my lady had given this muff to me, but about a day or two after I had told her the story, she quarrels with her new muff, and, to be sure, it is the prettiest that ever was seen. 'Honour,' says she, 'this is an odious muff; it is too big for me—I can't wear it—till I can get another, you must let me have my old one again, and you may have this in the room on't.' For she's a good lady, and scorns to give a thing and take a thing, I promise you that. So to be sure, I fetched it her back again, and I believe she hath worn it upon her arm almost ever since, and I warrants hath given it many a kiss when nobody hath seen her."

Here the conversation was interrupted by Mr. Western himself, who came to summon Jones to the harpsichord; whither the poor young fellow went all pale and trembling. This Western observed, but on seeing Mrs. Honour imputed it to a wrong cause; and having given Jones a hearty curse between jest and earnest, he bid him beat abroad and not poach up the game in his warren.

Sophia looked this evening with more than usual beauty, and we may believe it was no small addition to her charms in the eye of Mr. Jones that she now happened to have on her right arm this very muff.

She was playing one of her father's favourite tunes, and he was leaning on her chair, when the muff fell over her fingers and put her out. This so disconcerted the squire that he snatched the muff from her, and with a hearty curse threw it into the fire. Sophia instantly started up, and with the utmost eagerness recovered it from the flames.

Though this incident will probably appear of little consequence to many of our readers, yet trifling as it was, it had so violent an effect on poor Jones that we thought it our duty to relate it. In reality, there are many little circumstances too often omitted by injudicious historians, from which events of the utmost importance arise. The world may indeed be considered as a vast machine in which the great wheels are originally set in motion by those which are very minute and almost imperceptible to any but the strongest eyes.

Thus, not all the charms of the incomparable Sophia, not all the dazzling brightness and languishing softness of her eyes, the harmony of her voice, and of her person; not all her wit, good humour, greatness of mind, or sweetness of disposition had been able so absolutely to conquer and enslave the heart of poor Jones as this little incident of the muff. Thus the poet sweetly sings of Troy:

> ——*Captique dolis lachrymisque coacti*
> *Quos neque Tydides, nec Larissæus Achilles,*
> *Non anni domuere decem, non mille carinæ.*

> What Diomede, or Thetis' greater son,
> A thousand ships, nor ten years siege had done,
> False fears and fawning words the city won.
>
> DRYDEN.

The citadel of Jones was now taken by surprise. All those considerations of honour and prudence which our hero had lately with so much military wisdom placed as guards over the avenues of his heart ran away from their posts, and the God of Love marched in, in triumph.

A VERY LONG CHAPTER, CONTAINING A VERY GREAT INCIDENT

But though this victorious deity easily expelled his avowed enemies from the heart of Jones, he found it more difficult to supplant the garrison which he himself had placed there. To lay aside all allegory, the concern for what must become of poor Molly greatly disturbed and perplexed the mind of the worthy youth. The superior merit of Sophia totally eclipsed, or rather extinguished, all the beauties of the poor girl; but compassion instead of contempt succeeded to love. He was convinced the girl had placed all her affections and all her prospect of future happiness in him only. For this he had, he knew, given sufficient occasion by the utmost profusion of tenderness towards her, a tenderness which he had taken every means to persuade her he would always maintain. She on her side had assured him of her firm belief in his promise, and had with the most solemn vows declared that on his fulfilling or breaking these promises it depended whether she should be the happiest or most miserable of womankind. And to be the author of this highest degree of misery to a human being was a thought on which he could not bear to ruminate a single moment. He considered this poor girl as having sacrificed to him everything in her little power, as having been at her own expense the object of his pleasure, as sighing and languishing for him even at that very instant. "Shall, then," says he, "my recovery, for which she hath so ardently wished; shall my presence, which she hath so eagerly expected, instead of giving her that joy with which she hath flattered herself cast her at once down into misery and despair? Can I be such a villain?" Here, when the genius of poor Molly seemed triumphant, the love of Sophia towards him, which now appeared no longer dubious, rushed upon his mind and bore away every obstacle before it.

At length it occurred to him that he might possibly be able to make Molly amends another way: namely, by giving her a sum of money. This, nevertheless, he almost despaired of her accepting when he recollected the frequent and vehement assurances he had received from her that the world put in balance with him would make her no amends for his loss. However, her extreme poverty, and chiefly her egregious vanity (somewhat of which hath been already hinted to the reader), gave him some little hope that notwithstanding all her avowed tenderness she might in time be brought to content herself with a fortune superior to her expectation, and which might indulge her vanity by setting her above all her equals. He resolved, therefore, to take the first opportunity of making a proposal of this kind.

One day, accordingly, when his arm was so well recovered that he could walk easily with it slung in a sash, he stole forth at a season when the squire was engaged in his field exercises, and visited his fair one. Her mother and sisters, whom he found taking their tea, informed him first that Molly was not at home, but afterwards the elder sister acquainted him with a malicious smile that she was above-stairs abed. Tom had no objection to this situation of his mistress, and immediately ascended the ladder which led towards her bedchamber; but when he came to the top, he to his great surprise found the door fast, nor could he for some time obtain any answer from within; for Molly, as she herself afterwards informed him, was fast asleep.

The extremes of grief and joy have been remarked to produce very similar effects, and when either of these rushes on us by surprise, it is apt to create such a total perturbation and confusion that we are often thereby deprived of the use of all our faculties. It cannot therefore be wondered at that the unexpected sight of Mr. Jones should so strongly operate on the mind of Molly and should overwhelm her with such confusion that for some minutes she was unable to express the great raptures with which the reader will suppose she was affected on this occasion. As for Jones, he was so entirely possessed and, as it were, enchanted by the presence of his beloved object that he for a while forgot Sophia, and consequently the principal purpose of his visit.

This, however, soon recurred to his memory; and after the first transports of their meeting were over, he found means by degrees to introduce a discourse on the fatal consequences which must attend their amour if Mr. Allworthy, who had strictly forbidden him ever seeing her more, should discover that he still carried on this commerce. Such a discovery, which his enemies gave him reason to think would be unavoidable, must, he said, end in his ruin and consequently in hers. Since, therefore, their hard fates had determined that they must separate, he advised her to bear it with resolution, and swore he would never omit any opportunity through the course of his life of showing her the sincerity of his affection by providing for her in a manner beyond her utmost expectation or even beyond her wishes if ever that should be in his power; concluding at last that she might soon find some man who would marry her, and who would make her much happier than she could be by leading a disreputable life with him.

Molly remained a few moments in silence, and then, bursting into a flood of tears, she began to upbraid him in the following words: "And this is your love for me, to forsake me in this manner now you have ruined me? How often, when I have told you that all men are false and perjury alike, and grow tired of us as soon as ever they have had their wicked wills of us, how often have you sworn you would never forsake me? And can you be such a perjury man after all? What signifies all the riches in the world to me without you, now you have gained my heart, so you have—you have—? Why do you mention another man to me? I can never love any other man as long as I live. All other men are nothing to me. If the greatest squire in all the country would come a-suiting to me to-morrow, I would not give my company to him. No, I shall always hate and despise the whole sex for your sake——"

She was proceeding thus when an accident put a stop to her tongue before it had run out half its career. The room, or rather garret, in which Molly lay, being up one pair of stairs, that is to say, at the top of the house, was of a sloping figure resembling the great Delta of the Greeks. The English reader may, perhaps, form a better idea of it by being told that it was impossible to stand upright anywhere but in the middle. Now, as this room wanted the conveniency of a closet, Molly had, to supply that defect, nailed up an old rug against the rafters of the house, which enclosed a little hole where her best apparel, such as the remains of that sack which we have formerly mentioned, some caps, and other things with which she had lately provided herself were hung up and secured from the dust.

This enclosed place exactly fronted the foot of the bed, to which, indeed, the rug hung so near that it served in a manner to supply the want of curtains. Now, whether Molly in the agonies of her rage pushed this rug with her feet, or Jones might touch it, or whether the pin or nail gave way of its own accord, I am not certain; but as Molly pronounced those last words, which are recorded above, the wicked rug got loose from its fastening and discovered everything hid behind it; where, among other female utensils, appeared (with shame I write it, and with sorrow will it be read) the philosopher Square, in a posture (for the place would not near admit his standing upright) as ridiculous as can possibly be conceived.

The posture, indeed, in which he stood was not greatly unlike that of a soldier who is tied neck and heels, or rather resembling the attitude in which we often see fellows in the public streets of London who are not suffering but deserving punishment by so standing. He had a night-cap belonging to Molly on his head, and his two large eyes, the moment the rug fell, stared directly at Jones; so that when the idea of philosophy was added to the figure now discovered, it would have been very difficult for any spectator to have refrained from immoderate laughter.

I question not but the surprise of the reader will be here equal to that of Jones, as the suspicions which must arise from the appearance of this wise and grave man in such a place may seem so inconsistent with that character which he hath, doubtless, maintained hitherto in the opinion of every one.

But to confess the truth, this inconsistency is rather imaginary than real. Philosophers are composed of flesh and blood as well as other human creatures, and however sublimated and refined the theory of these may be, a little practical frailty is as incident to them as to other mortals. It is, indeed, in theory only and not in practice, as we have before hinted, that consists the difference; for though such great beings think much better and more wisely, they always act exactly like other men. They know very well how to subdue all appetites and passions and to despise both pain and pleasure, and this knowledge affords much delightful contemplation, and is easily acquired; but the practice would be vexatious and troublesome, and, therefore, the same wisdom which teaches them to know this teaches them to avoid carrying it into execution.

Mr. Square happened to be at church on that Sunday when, as the reader may be pleased to remember, the appearance of Molly in her sack had caused all that disturbance. Here he first observed her, and was so pleased with her beauty that he prevailed with the young gentlemen to change their intended ride that evening that he might pass by the habitation of Molly and, by that means, might obtain a second chance of seeing her. This reason, however, as he did not at that time mention to any, so neither did we think proper to communicate it then to the reader.

Among other particulars which constituted the unfitness of things in Mr. Square's opinion, danger and difficulty were two. The difficulty, therefore, which he apprehended there might be in corrupting this young wench and the danger which would accrue to his character on the discovery were such strong dissuasives that it is probable he at first intended to have contented himself with the pleasing ideas which the sight of beauty furnishes us with. These the gravest men, after a full meal of serious meditation, often allow themselves by way of desert; for which purpose certain books and pictures find their way into the most private recesses of their study, and a certain lecherous part of natural philosophy is often the principal subject of their conversation.

But when the philosopher heard a day or two afterwards that the fortress of virtue had already been subdued, he began to give a larger scope to his desires. His appetite was not of that squeamish kind which cannot feed on a dainty because another hath tasted it. In short, he liked the girl the better for the want of that chastity which, if she had possessed it, must have been a bar to his pleasures; he pursued and obtained her.

The reader will be mistaken if he thinks Molly gave Square the preference to her younger lover. On the contrary, had she been confined to the choice of one only, Tom Jones would undoubtedly have been of the two the victorious person. Nor was it solely the consideration that two are better than one (though this had its proper weight) to which Mr. Square owed his success; the absence of Jones during his confinement was an unlucky circumstance; and in that interval, some well-chosen presents from the philosopher so softened and unguarded the girl's heart that a favourable opportunity became irresistible, and Square triumphed over the poor remains of virtue which subsisted in the bosom of Molly.

It was now about a fortnight since this conquest when Jones paid the above-mentioned visit to his mistress, at a time when she and Square were in bed together. This was the true reason why the mother denied her as we have seen; for as the old woman shared in the profits arising from the iniquity of her daughter, she encouraged and protected her in it to the utmost of her power; but such was the envy and hatred which the elder sister bore towards Molly that, notwithstanding she had some part of the booty, she would willingly have parted with this to ruin her sister and spoil her trade. Hence she had acquainted Jones with her being above-stairs in bed in hopes that he might have caught her in Square's arms. This, however, Molly found means to prevent, as the door was fastened, which gave her an opportunity of conveying her lover behind that rug or blanket where he now was unhappily discovered.

Square no sooner made his appearance than Molly flung herself back in her bed, cried out she was undone, and abandoned herself to despair. This poor girl, who was yet but a novice in her business, had not arrived to that perfection of assurance which helps off a town lady in any extremity, and either prompts her with an excuse or else inspires her to brazen out the matter with her husband, who from love of quiet or out of fear of his reputation and sometimes, perhaps, from fear of the gallant, who like Mr. Constant in the play wears a sword, is glad to shut his eyes and contented to put his horns in his pocket. Molly, on the contrary, was silenced by this evidence, and very fairly gave up a cause which she had hitherto with so many tears and with such solemn and vehement protestations of the purest love and constancy maintained.

As to the gentleman behind the arras, he was not in much less consternation. He stood for a while motionless, and seemed equally at a loss what to say or whither to direct his eyes. Jones, though perhaps the most astonished of the three, first found his tongue; and being immediately recovered from those uneasy sensations which Molly by her upbraidings had occasioned, he burst into a loud laughter and then, saluting Mr. Square, advanced to take him by the hand and to relieve him from his place of confinement.

Square, being now arrived in the middle of the room, in which part only he could stand upright, looked at Jones with a very grave countenance and said to him, "Well, sir, I see you enjoy this mighty discovery and, I dare swear, taste great delight in the thoughts of exposing me; but if you will consider the matter fairly, you will find you are yourself only to blame. I am not guilty of corrupting innocence. I have done nothing for which that part of the world which judges of matters by the rule of right will condemn me. Fitness is governed by the nature of things, and not by customs, forms, or municipal laws. Nothing is, indeed, unfit which is not unnatural." "Well reasoned, old boy," answered Jones, "but why dost thou think that I should desire to expose thee? I promise thee, I was never better pleased with thee in my life; and unless thou hast a mind to discover it thyself, this affair may remain a profound secret for me." "Nay, Mr. Jones," replied Square, "I would not be thought to undervalue reputation. Good fame is a species of the *Kalon*, and it is by no means fitting to neglect it. Besides, to murder one's own reputation is a kind of suicide, a detestable and odious vice. If you think proper, therefore, to conceal any infirmity of mine (for such I may have, since no man is perfectly perfect), I promise you I will not betray myself. Things may be fitting to be done which are not fitting to be boasted of; for by the perverse judgement of the world, that often becomes the subject of censure which is, in truth, not only innocent but laudable." "Right!" cries Jones. "What can be more innocent than the indulgence of a natural appetite? Or what more laudable than the propagation of our species?" "To be serious with you," answered Square, "I profess they always appeared so to me." "And yet," said Jones, "you was of a different opinion when my affair with this girl was first discovered." "Why, I must confess," says Square, "as the matter was misrepresented to me by that person Thwackum, I might condemn the corruption of innocence; it was that, sir, it was that—and that: for you must know, Mr. Jones, in the consideration of fitness very minute circumstances, sir, very minute circumstances cause great alteration." "Well," cries Jones, "be that as it will, it shall be your own fault as I have promised you if you ever hear any more of this adventure. Behave kindly to the girl, and I will never open my lips concerning the matter to any one. And, Molly, do you be faithful to your friend, and I will not only forgive your infidelity to me but will do you all the service I can." So saying, he took a hasty leave and, slipping down the ladder, retired with much expedition.

Square was rejoiced to find this adventure was likely to have no worse conclusion, and as for Molly, being recovered from her confusion, she began at first to upbraid Square with having been the occasion of her loss of Jones; but that gentleman soon found the means of mitigating her anger, partly by caresses and partly by a small nostrum from his purse of wonderful and approved efficacy in purging off the ill humours of the mind and in restoring it to a good temper.

She then poured forth a vast profusion of tenderness towards her new lover, turned all she had said to Jones, and Jones himself, into ridicule, and vowed, though he had had the possession of her person, that none but Square had ever been master of her heart.

6

BY COMPARING WHICH WITH THE FORMER, THE READER MAY POSSIBLY CORRECT SOME ABUSE WHICH HE HATH FORMERLY BEEN GUILTY OF IN THE APPLICATION OF THE WORD LOVE

The infidelity of Molly, which Jones had now discovered, would perhaps have vindicated a much greater degree of resentment than he expressed on the occasion, and if he had abandoned her directly from that moment, very few, I believe, would have blamed him.

Certain, however, it is, that he saw her in the light of compassion, and though his love to her was not of that kind which could give him any great uneasiness at her inconstancy, yet was he not a little shocked on reflecting that he had himself originally corrupted her innocence; for to this corruption he imputed all the vice into which she appeared now so likely to plunge herself.

This consideration gave him no little uneasiness till Betty, the elder sister, was so kind some time afterwards entirely to cure him by a hint that one Will Barnes, and not himself, had been the first seducer of Molly; and that the little child, which he had hitherto so certainly concluded to be his own, might very probably have an equal title at least to claim Barnes for its father.

Jones eagerly pursued this scent when he had first received it, and in a very short time was sufficiently assured that the girl had told him truth, not only by the confession of the fellow but at last by that of Molly herself.

This Will Barnes was a country gallant, and had acquired as many trophies of this kind as any ensign or attorney's clerk in the kingdom. He had, indeed, reduced several women to a state of utter profligacy, had broken the hearts of some, and had the honour of occasioning the violent death of one poor girl, who had either drowned herself or, what was rather more probable, had been drowned by him.

Among other of his conquests, this fellow had triumphed

over the heart of Betty Seagrim. He had made love to her long before Molly was grown to be a fit object of that pastime, but had afterwards deserted her and applied to her sister, with whom he had almost immediate success. Now, Will had in reality the sole possession of Molly's affection, while Jones and Square were almost equally sacrifices to her interest and to her pride.

Hence had grown that implacable hatred which we have before seen raging in the mind of Betty, though we did not think it necessary to assign this cause sooner, as envy itself was alone adequate to all the effects we have mentioned.

Jones was become perfectly easy by possession of this secret with regard to Molly, but as to Sophia, he was far from being in a state of tranquillity; nay, indeed, he was under the most violent perturbation; his heart was now, if I may use the metaphor, entirely evacuated, and Sophia took absolute possession of it. He loved her with an unbounded passion and plainly saw the tender sentiments she had for him, yet could not this assurance lessen his despair of obtaining the consent of her father, nor the horrors which attended his pursuit of her by any base or treacherous method.

The injury which he must thus do to Mr. Western and the concern which would accrue to Mr. Allworthy were circumstances that tormented him all day and haunted him on his pillow at night. His life was a constant struggle between honour and inclination, which alternately triumphed over each other in his mind. He often resolved in the absence of Sophia to leave her father's house, and to see her no more; and as often in her presence forgot all those resolutions, and determined to pursue her at the hazard of his life and at the forfeiture of what was much dearer to him.

This conflict began soon to produce very strong and visible effects; for he lost all his usual sprightliness and gaiety of temper, and became not only melancholy when alone but dejected and absent in company; nay, if ever he put on a forced mirth to comply with Mr. Western's humour, the constraint appeared so plain that he may seem to have been giving the strongest evidence of what he endeavoured to conceal by such ostentation.

It may, perhaps, be a question whether the art which he used to conceal his passion or the means which honest nature employed to reveal it betrayed him most; for while art made him more than ever reserved to Sophia and forbade him to address any of his discourse to her, nay, to avoid meeting her eyes, with the utmost caution, nature was no less busy in counterplotting him. Hence, at the approach of the young lady he grew pale; and if this was sudden, started. If his eyes accidentally met hers, the blood rushed into his cheeks and his countenance became all over scarlet. If common civility ever obliged him to speak to her, as to drink her health at table, his tongue was sure to falter. If he touched her, his hand, nay, his whole frame, trembled. And if any discourse tended, however remotely, to raise the idea of love, an involuntary sigh seldom failed to steal from his bosom. Most of which accidents nature was wonderfully industrious to throw daily in his way.

All these symptoms escaped the notice of the squire, but not so of Sophia. She soon perceived these agitations of mind in Jones, and was at no loss to discover the cause, for indeed she recognized it in her own breast. And this recognition is, I suppose, that sympathy which hath been so often noted in lovers and which will sufficiently account for her being so much quicker-sighted than her father.

But, to say the truth, there is a more simple and plain method of accounting for that prodigious superiority of penetration which we must observe in some men over the rest of the human species, and one which will not only serve in the case of lovers but of all others. For whence is it that the knave is generally so quick-sighted to those symptoms and operations of knavery which often dupe an honest man of a much better understanding? There surely is no general sympathy among knaves, nor have they like freemasons any common sign of communication. In reality, it is only because they have the same thing in their heads, and their thoughts are turned the same way. Thus, that Sophia saw and that Western did not see the plain symptoms of love in Jones can be no wonder when we consider that the idea of love never entered into the head of the father, whereas the daughter at present thought of nothing else.

When Sophia was well satisfied of the violent passion which tormented poor Jones, and no less certain that she herself was its object, she had not the least difficulty in discovering the true cause of his present behaviour. This highly endeared him to her and raised in her mind two of the best affections which any lover can wish to raise in a mistress. These were esteem and pity; for sure, the most outrageously rigid among her sex will excuse her pitying a man whom she saw miserable on her own account; nor can they blame her for esteeming one who visibly from the most honourable motives endeavoured to smother a flame in his own bosom, which, like the famous Spartan theft, was preying upon and consuming his very vitals. Thus his backwardness, his shunning her, his coldness, and his silence were the forwardest, the most diligent, the warmest, and most eloquent advocates; and wrought so violently on her sensible and tender heart that she soon felt for him all those gentle sensations which are consistent with a virtuous and elevated female mind. In short, all which esteem, gratitude, and pity can inspire in such towards an agreeable man—indeed, all which the nicest delicacy can allow. In a word—she was in love with him to distraction.

One day this young couple accidentally met in the garden at the end of two walks which were both bounded by that canal in which Jones had formerly risked drowning to retrieve the little bird that Sophia had there lost.

This place had been of late much frequented by Sophia. Here she used to ruminate with a mixture of pain and pleasure on an incident which, however trifling itself, had possibly sown the first seeds of that affection which was now arrived to such maturity in her heart.

Here, then, this young couple met. They were almost close together before either of them knew anything of the other's approach. A bystander would have discovered sufficient marks of confusion in the countenance of each, but they felt too much themselves to make any observation. As soon as Jones had a little recovered his first surprise, he accosted the young lady with some of the ordinary forms of salutation, which she in the same manner returned, and their conversation began, as usual, on the delicious beauty of the morning. Hence they passed to the beauty of the place, on which Jones launched forth very high encomiums. When they came to the tree whence he had formerly tumbled into the canal, Sophia could not help reminding him of that accident and said, "I fancy, Mr. Jones, you have some little shuddering when you see that water." "I assure you, madam," answered Jones, "the concern you felt at the loss of your little bird will always appear to me the highest circumstance in that adventure. Poor little Tommy, there is the branch he stood upon. How could the little wretch have the folly to fly away from that state of happiness in which

I had the honour to place him? His fate was a just punishment for his ingratitude." "Upon my word, Mr. Jones," said she, "your gallantry very narrowly escaped as severe a fate. Sure, the remembrance must affect you." "Indeed, madam," answered he, "if I have any reason to reflect with sorrow on it, it is perhaps that the water had not been a little deeper, by which I might have escaped many bitter heartaches that Fortune seems to have in store for me." "Fie, Mr. Jones," replied Sophia, "I am sure you cannot be in earnest now. This affected contempt of life is only an excess of your complaisance to me. You would endeavour to lessen the obligation of having twice ventured it for my sake. Beware the third time." She spoke these last words with a smile and softness inexpressible. Jones answered with a sigh he feared it was already too late for caution, and then, looking tenderly and steadfastly on her, he cried, "Oh, Miss Western! Can you desire me to live? Can you wish me so ill?" Sophia, looking down on the ground, answered with some hesitation, "Indeed, Mr. Jones, I do not wish you ill." "Oh! I know too well that heavenly temper," cries Jones, "that divine goodness which is beyond every other charm." "Nay, now," answered she, "I understand you not. I can stay no longer—I——" "I would not be understood," cries he; "nay, I can't be understood. I know not what I say. Meeting you here so unexpectedly—I have been unguarded—for heaven's sake pardon me if I have said anything to offend you—I did not mean it—indeed, I would rather have died—nay, the very thought would kill me." "You surprise me," answered she. "How can you possibly think you have offended me?" "Fear, madam," says he, "easily runs into madness; and there is no degree of fear like that which I feel of offending you. How can I speak, then? Nay, don't look angrily at me, one frown will destroy me. I mean nothing—blame my eyes, or blame those beauties. What am I saying? Pardon me if I have said too much. My heart overflowed. I have struggled with my love to the utmost and have endeavoured to conceal a fever which preys on my vitals and will, I hope, soon make it impossible for me ever to offend you more."

Mr. Jones now fell a-trembling as if he had been shaken with the fit of an ague. Sophia, who was in a situation not very different from his, answered in these words: "Mr. Jones, I will not affect to misunderstand you; indeed, I understand you too well; but for heaven's sake, if you have any affection for me, let me make the best of my way into the house. I wish I may be able to support myself thither."

Jones, who was hardly able to support himself, offered her his arm, which she condescended to accept, but begged he would not mention a word more to her of this nature at present. He promised he would not, insisting only on her forgiveness of what love without the leave of his will had forced from him; this, she told him, he knew how to obtain by his future behaviour; and thus this young pair tottered and trembled along, the lover not once daring to squeeze the hand of his mistress though it was locked in his.

Sophia immediately retired to her chamber, where Mrs. Honour and the hartshorn were summoned to her assistance. As to poor Jones, the only relief to his distempered mind was an unwelcome piece of news, which, as it opens a scene of a different nature from those in which the reader hath lately been conversant, will be communicated to him in the next chapter.

7

IN WHICH MR. ALLWORTHY APPEARS ON A SICK-BED

Mr. Western was become so fond of Jones that he was unwilling to part with him, though his arm had been long since cured, and Jones, either from his love of sport or from some other reason, was easily persuaded to continue at his house, which he did sometimes for a fortnight together without paying a single visit at Mr. Allworthy's; nay, without ever hearing from thence.

Mr. Allworthy had been for some days indisposed with a cold, which had been attended with a little fever. This he had, however, neglected, as it was usual with him to do all manner of disorders which did not confine him to his bed or prevent his several faculties from performing their ordinary functions—a conduct which we would by no means be thought to approve or recommend to imitation; for surely the gentlemen of the Æsculapian art are in the right in advising that the moment the disease is entered at one door, the physician should be introduced at the other. What else is meant by that old adage *Venienti occurrite morbo?* "Oppose a distemper at its first approach." Thus the doctor and the disease meet in fair and equal conflict; whereas by giving time to the latter we often suffer him to fortify and entrench himself like a French army, so that the learned gentleman finds it very difficult, and sometimes impossible, to come at the enemy. Nay, sometimes by gaining time the disease applies to the French military politics, and corrupts nature over to his side; and then all the powers of physics must arrive too late. Agreeable to these observations was, I remember, the complaint of the great Doctor Misaubin, who used very pathetically to lament the late applications which were made to his skill, saying, "Bygar, me believe my pation take me for de undertaker; for dey never send for me till de physicion have kill dem."

Mr. Allworthy's distemper by means of this neglect gained such ground that when the increase of his fever obliged him to send for assistance, the doctor at his first arrival shook his head, wished he had been sent for sooner, and intimated that he thought him in very imminent danger. Mr. Allworthy, who had settled all his affairs in this world and was as well prepared as it is possible for human nature to be for the other, received this information with the utmost calmness and unconcern. He could, indeed, whenever he laid himself down to rest say with Cato in the tragical poem:

> ———Let guilt or fear
> Disturb man's rest: Cato knows neither of them;
> Indifferent in his choice to sleep or die.

In reality, he could say this with ten times more reason and confidence than Cato, or any other proud fellow among the ancient or modern heroes; for he was not only devoid of fear but might be considered as a faithful labourer when at the end of harvest he is summoned to receive his reward at the hands of a bountiful master.

The good man gave immediate orders for all his family to be summoned round him. None of these were then abroad but Mrs. Blifil, who had been some time in London, and Mr. Jones, whom the reader hath just parted from at Mr. Western's, and who received this summons just as Sophia had left him.

The news of Mr. Allworthy's danger (for the servant told him he was dying) drove all thoughts of love out of his head. He hurried instantly into the chariot which was sent for him and ordered the coachman to drive with all imaginable haste; nor did the idea of Sophia, I believe, once occur to him on the way.

And now, the whole family—namely, Mr. Blifil, Mr. Jones, Mr. Thwackum, Mr. Square, and some of the servants (for such were Mr. Allworthy's orders)—being all assembled round his bed, the good man sat up in it and was beginning to speak when Blifil fell to blubbering, and began to express very loud and bitter lamentations. Upon this Mr. Allworthy shook him by the hand and said, "Do not sorrow thus, my dear nephew, at the most ordinary of all human occurrences. When misfortunes befall our friends we are justly grieved; for those are accidents which might often have been avoided, and which may seem to render the lot of one man more peculiarly unhappy than that of others; but death is certainly unavoidable, and is that common lot in which alone the fortunes of all men agree; nor is the time when this happens to us material. If the wisest of men hath compared life to a span, surely we may be allowed to consider it as a day. It is my fate to leave it in the evening, but those who are taken away earlier have only lost a few hours, at the best little worth lamenting, and much oftener hours of labour and fatigue, of pain and sorrow. One of the Roman poets, I remember, likens our leaving life to our departure from a feast—a thought which hath often occurred to me when I have seen men struggling to protract an entertainment and to enjoy the company of their friends a few moments longer. Alas! How short is the most protracted of such enjoyments! How immaterial the difference between him who retires the soonest and him who stays the latest! This is seeing life in the best view, and this unwillingness to quit our friends is the most amiable motive from which we can derive the fear of death; and yet the longest enjoyment which we can hope for of this kind is of so trivial a duration that it is to a wise man truly contemptible. Few men, I own, think in this manner; for indeed few men think of death till they are in its jaws. However gigantic and terrible an object this may appear when it approaches them, they are nevertheless incapable of seeing it at any distance; nay, though they have been ever so much frightened and alarmed when they have apprehended themselves in danger of dying, they are no sooner cleared from this apprehension than even the fears of it are erased from their minds. But alas! He who escapes from death is not pardoned; he is only reprieved, and reprieved to a short day.

"Grieve, therefore, no more, my dear child, on this occasion; an event which may happen every hour, which every element, nay, almost every particle of matter that surrounds us, is capable of producing and which must and will most unavoidably reach us all at last ought neither to occasion our surprise nor our lamentation.

"My physician having acquainted me (which I take very kindly of him) that I am in danger of leaving you all very shortly, I have determined to say a few words to you at this our parting before my distemper, which I find grows very fast upon me, puts it out of my power.

"But I shall waste my strength too much. I intended to speak concerning my will, which, though I have settled long ago, I think proper to mention such heads of as concern any of you, that I may have the comfort of perceiving you are all satisfied with the provision I have there made for you.

"Nephew Blifil, I leave you the heir to my whole estate, except only £500 a year, which is to revert to you after the death of your mother, and except one other estate of £500 a year and the sum of £6000, which I have bestowed in the following manner:

"The estate of £500 a year I have given to you, Mr. Jones. And as I know the inconvenience which attends the want of ready money, I have added £1000 in specie. In this I know not whether I have exceeded or fallen short of your expectation. Perhaps you will think I have given you too little, and the world will be as ready to condemn me for giving you too much; but the latter censure I despise, and as to the former, unless you should entertain that common error which I have often heard in my life pleaded as an excuse for total want of charity: namely, that instead of raising gratitude by voluntary acts of bounty we are apt to raise demands which of all others are the most boundless and most difficult to satisfy. Pardon me the bare mention of this; I will not suspect any such thing."

Jones flung himself at his benefactor's feet and, taking eagerly hold of his hand, assured him his goodness to him, both now and at all other times, had so infinitely exceeded not only his merit but his hopes that no words could express his sense of it. "And I assure you, sir," said he, "your present generosity hath left me no other concern than for the present melancholy occasion. Oh, my friend! My father!" Here his words choked him, and he turned away to hide a tear which was starting from his eyes.

Allworthy then gently squeezed his hand and proceeded thus: "I am convinced, my child, that you have much goodness, generosity, and honour in your temper; if you will add prudence and religion to these, you must be happy; for the three former qualities, I admit, make you worthy of happiness, but they are the latter only which will put you in possession of it.

"One thousand pound I have given to you, Mr. Thwackum; a sum, I am convinced, which greatly exceeds your desires as well as your wants. However, you will receive it as a memorial of my friendship, and whatever superfluities may redound to you, that piety which you so rigidly maintain will instruct you how to dispose of it.

"A like sum, Mr. Square, I have bequeathed to you. This, I hope, will enable you to pursue your profession with better success than hitherto. I have often observed with concern that distress is more apt to excite contempt than commiseration, especially among men of business, with whom poverty is understood to indicate want of ability. But the little I have been able to leave you will extricate you from those difficulties with which you have formerly struggled, and then I doubt not but you will meet with sufficient prosperity to supply what a man of your philosophical temper will require.

"I find myself growing faint, so I shall refer you to my will for my disposition of the residue. My servants will there find some tokens to remember me by, and there are a few charities which, I trust, my executors will see faithfully performed. Bless you all. I am setting out a little before you——"

Here a footman came hastily into the room and said there was an attorney from Salisbury who had a particular message, which he said he must communicate to Mr. Allworthy himself; that he seemed in a violent hurry and protested he had so much business to do that if he could cut himself into four quarters, all would not be sufficient.

"Go, child," said Allworthy to Blifil. "See what the gentleman wants. I am not able to do any business now, nor can he have any with me in which you are not at present more concerned than myself. Besides I really am—I am incapable of seeing any one at present, or of any longer attention." He then saluted them all, saying perhaps he should be able to see them again, but he should be now glad to compose himself a little, finding that he had too much exhausted his spirits in discourse.

Some of the company shed tears at their parting; and even the philosopher, Square, wiped his eyes, albeit unused to the melting mood. As to Mrs. Wilkins, she dropped her pearls as fast as the Arabian trees their medicinal gums; for this was a ceremonial which that gentlewoman never omitted on a proper occasion.

After this Mr. Allworthy again laid himself down on his pillow and endeavoured to compose himself to rest.

8

CONTAINING MATTER RATHER NATURAL THAN PLEASING

Besides grief for her master, there was another source for that briny stream which so plentifully rose above the two mountainous cheek-bones of the housekeeper. She was no sooner retired than she began to mutter to herself in the following pleasant strain: "Sure master might have made some difference, methinks, between me and the other servants. I suppose he hath left me mourning; but i' fackins, if that be all, the devil shall wear it for him for me! I'd have his worship know I am no beggar. I have saved five hundred pound in his service, and after all to be used in this manner. It is a fine encouragement to servants to be honest; and to be sure, if I have taken a little something now and then, others have taken ten times as much; and now we are all put in a lump together. If so be that it be so, the legacy may go to the devil with him that gave it. No, I won't give it up neither because that will please some folks. No, I'll buy the gayest gown I can get and dance over the old curmudgeon's grave in it. This is my reward for taking his part so often when all the country have cried shame of him for breeding up his bastard in that manner; but he is going now where he must pay for all. It would have becomed him better to have repented of his sins on his death-bed than to glory in them and give away his estate out of his own family to a misbegotten child. Found in his bed, forsooth! A pretty story! Ay, ay, those that hide know where to find. Lord forgive him, I warrant he hath many more bastards to answer for if the truth was known. One comfort is they will be all known where he is a-going now. 'The servants will find some token to remember me by.' Those were the very words; I shall never forget them if I was to live a thousand years. Ay, ay, I shall remember you for huddling me among the servants. One would have thought he might have mentioned my name as well as that of Square; but he is a gentleman forsooth, though he had not clothes on his back when he came hither first. Marry come up with such gentlemen! Though he hath lived here these many years, I don't believe there is *arrow* a servant in the house ever saw the colour of his money. The devil shall wait upon such gentlemen for me." Much more of the like kind she muttered to herself, but this taste shall suffice to the reader.

Neither Thwackum nor Square were much better satisfied with their legacies. Though they breathed not their resentment so loud, yet from the discontent which appeared in their countenances, as well as from the following dialogue, we collect that no great pleasure reigned in their minds.

About an hour after they had left the sick-room, Square met Thwackum in the hall and accosted him thus, "Well, sir, have you heard any news of your friend since we parted from him?" "If you mean Mr. Allworthy," answered Thwackum, "I think you might rather give him the appellation of your friend; for he seems to me to have deserved that title." "The title is as good on your side," replied Square, "for his bounty, such as it is, hath been equal to both." "I should not have mentioned it first," cries Thwackum, "but since you begin, I must inform you I am of a different opinion. There is a wide distinction between voluntary favours and rewards. The duty I have done in his family and the care I have taken in the education of his two boys are services for which some men might have expected a greater return. I would not have you imagine I am therefore dissatisfied, for St. Paul hath taught me to be content with the little I have. Had the modicum been less, I should have known my duty. But though the Scripture obliges me to remain contented, it doth not enjoin me to shut my eyes to my own merit nor restrain me from seeing when I am injured by an unjust comparison." "Since you provoke me," returned Square, "that injury is done to me; nor did I ever imagine Mr. Allworthy had held my friendship so light as to put me in balance with one who received his wages. I know to what it is owing: it proceeds from those narrow principles which you have been so long endeavouring to infuse into him in contempt of everything which is great and noble. The beauty and loveliness of friendship is too strong for dim eyes, nor can it be perceived by any other medium than that unerring rule of right, which you have so often endeavoured to ridicule that you have perverted my friend's understanding." "I wish," cries Thwackum in a rage, "I wish for the sake of his soul your damnable doctrines have not perverted his faith. It is to this I impute his present behaviour, so unbecoming a Christian. Who but an atheist could think of leaving the world without having first made up his account? Without confessing his sins, and receiving that absolution which he knew he had one in the house duly authorized to give him? He will feel the want of these necessaries when it is too late, when he is arrived at that place where there is wailing and gnashing of teeth. It is then he will find in what mighty stead that heathen goddess, that virtue, which you and all other deists of the age adore, will stand him. He will then summon his priest when there is none to be found, and will lament the want of that absolution without which no sinner can be safe." "If it be so material," says Square, "why don't you present it him of your own accord?" "It hath no virtue," cries Thwackum, "but to those who have sufficient grace to require it. But why do I talk thus to a heathen and an unbeliever? It is you who have taught him this lesson, for which you have been well rewarded in this world, as I doubt not your disciple will soon be in the other." "I know not what you mean by my reward," said Square, "but if you hint at that pitiful memorial of our friendship which he hath thought fit to bequeath me, I despise it, and nothing but the unfortunate situation of my circumstances should prevail on me to accept it."

The physician now arrived and began to inquire of the two disputants how we all did above-stairs. "In a miserable way," answered Thwackum. "It is no more than I expected," cries the doctor. "But, pray, what symptoms have appeared since I left you?" "No good ones, I am afraid," replied Thwackum; "after what passed at our departure, I think there were little hopes." The bodily physician, perhaps, misunderstood the curer of souls, and before they came to an explanation Mr. Blifil came to them with a most melancholy countenance and acquainted them that he brought sad news, for that his mother was dead at Salisbury; that she had been seized on the road home with the gout in her head and stomach, which had carried her off in a few hours. "Good-lackaday," says the doctor, "one cannot answer for events; but I wish I had been at hand to have been called in. The gout is a distemper which it is difficult to treat, yet I have been remarkably successful in it." Thwackum and Square both condoled with Mr. Blifil for the loss of his mother, which the one advised him to bear like a man, and the other like a Christian. The young gentleman said he knew very well we were all mortal, and he would endeavour to submit to his loss as well as he could. That he could not, however, help complaining a little against the peculiar severity of his fate, which brought the news of so great a calamity to him by surprise, and that at a time when he hourly expected the severest blow he was capable of feeling from the malice of Fortune. He said the present occasion would put to the test those excellent rudiments which he had learnt from Mr. Thwackum and Mr. Square, and it would be entirely owing to them if he was enabled to survive such misfortunes.

It was now debated whether Mr. Allworthy should be informed of the death of his sister; this the doctor violently opposed, in which, I believe, the whole College would agree with him; but Mr. Blifil said he had received such positive and repeated orders from his uncle never to keep any secret from him, for fear of the disquietude which it might give him, that he durst not think of disobedience, whatever might be the consequence. He said for his part, considering the religious and philosophic temper of his uncle, he could not agree with the doctor in his apprehensions. He was therefore resolved to communicate it to him; for if his uncle recovered (as he heartily prayed he might), he knew he would never forgive an endeavour to keep a secret of this kind from him.

The physician was forced to submit to these resolutions, which the two other learned gentlemen very highly commended. So together moved Mr. Blifil and the doctor towards the sickroom, where the physician first entered and approached the bed in order to feel his patient's pulse, which he had no sooner done than he declared he was much better; that the last application had succeeded to a miracle and had brought the fever to intermit; so that, he said, there appeared now to be as little danger as he had before apprehended there were hopes.

To say the truth, Mr. Allworthy's situation had never been so bad as the great caution of the doctor had represented it; but as a wise general never despises his enemy however inferior his force may be, so neither doth a wise physician ever despise a distemper however inconsiderable. As the former preserves the same strict discipline, places the same guards, and employs the same scouts, though the enemy be never so weak, so the latter maintains the same gravity of countenance and shakes his head with the same significant air, let the distemper be never so trifling. And both, among many other good ones, may assign this solid reason for their conduct: that by these means the greater glory redounds to them if they gain the victory, and the less disgrace if by any unlucky accident they should happen to be conquered.

Mr. Allworthy had no sooner lifted up his eyes and thanked heaven for these hopes of his recovery than Mr. Blifil drew near with a very dejected aspect, and having applied his handkerchief to his eye, either to wipe away his tears or, as Ovid somewhere expresses himself on another occasion,

> *Si nullus erit, tamen excute nullum*
> (If there be none, wipe away that none),

he communicated to his uncle what the reader hath been just before acquainted with.

Allworthy received the news with concern, with patience, and with resignation. He dropped a tender tear, then composed his countenance, and at last cried, "The Lord's will be done in everything."

He now inquired for the messenger, but Blifil told him it had been impossible to detain him a moment; for he appeared by the great hurry he was in to have some business of importance on his hands; that he complained of being hurried and driven and torn out of his life, and repeated many times that if he could divide himself into four quarters, he knew how to dispose of every one.

Allworthy then desired Blifil to take care of the funeral. He said he would have his sister deposited in his own chapel, and as to the particulars, he left them to his own discretion, only mentioning the person whom he would have employed on this occasion.

9

WHICH, AMONG OTHER THINGS, MAY SERVE AS A COMMENT ON THAT SAYING OF AESCHINES THAT "DRUNKENNESS SHOWS THE MIND OF A MAN, AS A MIRROR REFLECTS HIS PERSON"

The reader may, perhaps, wonder at hearing nothing of Mr.

Jones in the last chapter. In fact, his behaviour was so different from that of the persons there mentioned that we chose not to confound his name with theirs.

When the good man had ended his speech, Jones was the last who deserted the room. Thence he retired to his own apartment to give vent to his concern, but the restlessness of his mind would not suffer him to remain long there; he slipped softly, therefore, to Allworthy's chamber door, where he listened a considerable time without hearing any kind of motion within unless a violent snoring, which at last his fears misrepresented as groans. This so alarmed him that he could not forbear entering the room, where he found the good man in the bed, in a sweet composed sleep, and his nurse snoring in the above-mentioned hearty manner at the bed's feet. He immediately took the only method of silencing this thorough-bass, whose music he feared might disturb Mr. Allworthy; and then, sitting down by the nurse, he remained motionless till Blifil and the doctor came in together and waked the sick man in order that the doctor might feel his pulse and that the other might communicate to him that piece of news which, had Jones been apprised of it, would have had great difficulty of finding its way to Mr. Allworthy's ear at such a season.

When he first heard Blifil tell his uncle this story, Jones could hardly contain the wrath which kindled in him at the other's indiscretion, especially as the doctor shook his head and declared his unwillingness to have the matter mentioned to his patient. But as his passion did not so far deprive him of all use of his understanding as to hide from him the consequences which any violent expressions toward Blifil might have on the sick, this apprehension stilled his rage at the present; and he grew afterwards so satisfied with finding that this news had, in fact, produced no mischief that he suffered his anger to die in his own bosom without ever mentioning it to Blifil.

The physician dined that day at Mr. Allworthy's, and having after dinner visited his patient, he returned to the company and told them that he had now the satisfaction to say with assurance that his patient was out of all danger; that he had brought his fever to a perfect intermission, and doubted not by throwing in the bark to prevent its return.

This account so pleased Jones and threw him into such immoderate excess of rapture that he might be truly said to be drunk with joy—an intoxication which greatly forwards the effects of wine; and as he was very free too with the bottle on this occasion, (for he drank many bumpers to the doctor's health as well as to other toasts), he became very soon literally drunk.

Jones had naturally violent animal spirits; these being set on float and augmented by the spirit of wine produced most extravagant effects. He kissed the doctor, and embraced him with the most passionate endearments, swearing that next to Mr. Allworthy himself, he loved him of all men living. "Doctor," added he, "you deserve a statue to be erected to you at the public expense for having preserved a man who is not only the darling of all good men who know him but a blessing to society, the glory of his country, and an honour to human nature. D——n me if I don't love him better than my own soul."

"More shame for you," cried Thwackum. "Though I think you have reason to love him, for he hath provided very well for you. And, perhaps, it might have been better for some folks that he had not lived to see just reason of revoking his gift."

Jones now, looking on Thwackum with inconceivable disdain, answered, "And doth thy mean soul imagine that any such considerations could weigh with me? No, let the earth open and swallow her own dirt (if I had millions of acres I would say it) rather than swallow up my dear glorious friend."

> *Quis desiderio sit pudor aut modus*
> *Tam chari capitis?* *

The doctor now interposed and prevented the effects of a wrath which was kindling between Jones and Thwackum; after which the former gave a loose to mirth, sang two or three amorous songs, and fell into every frantic disorder which unbridled joy is apt to inspire; but so far was he from any disposition to quarrel that he was ten times better humoured, if possible, than when he was sober.

To say truth, nothing is more erroneous than the common observation that men who are ill natured and quarrelsome when they are drunk are very worthy persons when they are

---

* "What modesty or measure can set bounds to our desire of so dear a friend." The word *desiderium* here cannot be easily translated. It includes our desire of enjoying our friend again and the grief which attends that desire.

sober; for drink, in reality, doth not reverse nature or create passions in men which did not exist in them before. It takes away the guard of reason, and consequently forces us to produce those symptoms which many when sober have art enough to conceal. It heightens and inflames our passions (generally, indeed, that passion which is uppermost in our mind), so that the angry temper, the amorous, the generous, the good-humoured, the avaricious, and all other dispositions of men are in their cups heightened and exposed.

And yet, as no nation produces so many drunken quarrels, especially among the lower people, as England (for, indeed, with them to drink and to fight together are almost synonymous terms), I would not, methinks, have it thence concluded, that the English are the worst-natured people alive. Perhaps the love of glory only is at the bottom of this; so that the fair conclusion seems to be that our countrymen have more of that love and more of bravery than any other plebeians. And this the rather as there is seldom anything ungenerous, unfair, or ill natured exercised on those occasions; nay, it is common for the combatants to express goodwill for each other even at the time of the conflict; and as their drunken mirth generally ends in a battle, so do most of their battles end in friendship.

But to return to our history. Though Jones had shown no design of giving offence, yet Mr. Blifil was highly offended at a behaviour which was so inconsistent with the sober and prudent reserve of his own temper. He bore it too with the greater impatience, as it appeared to him very indecent at this season, when, as he said, the house was a house of mourning on the account of his dear mother; and if it had pleased heaven to give him some prospect of Mr. Allworthy's recovery, it would become them better to express the exultations of their hearts in thanksgiving than in drunkenness and riots, which were properer methods to increase the divine wrath than to avert it. Thwackum, who had swallowed more liquor than Jones, but without any ill effect on his brain, seconded the pious harangue of Blifil; but Square, for reasons which the reader may probably guess, was totally silent.

Wine had not so totally overpowered Jones as to prevent his recollecting Mr. Blifil's loss the moment it was mentioned. As no person, therefore, was more ready to confess and condemn his own errors, he offered to shake Mr. Blifil by the hand, and begged his pardon, saying his excessive joy for Mr. Allworthy's recovery had driven every other thought out of his mind.

Blifil scornfully rejected his hand and with much indignation answered it was little to be wondered at if tragical spectacles made no impression on the blind; but, for his part, he had the misfortune to know who his parents were, and consequently must be affected with their loss.

Jones, who notwithstanding his good humour had some mixture of the irascible in his constitution, leaped hastily from his chair and, catching hold of Blifil's collar, cried out, "D—n you for a rascal. Do you insult me with the misfortune of my birth?" He accompanied these words with such rough actions that they soon got the better of Mr. Blifil's peaceful temper, and a scuffle immediately ensued, which might have produced mischief had it not been prevented by the interposition of Thwackum and the physician; for the philosophy of Square rendered him superior to all emotions, and he very calmly smoked his pipe, as was his custom in all broils, unless when he apprehended some danger of having it broken in his mouth.

The combatants, being now prevented from executing present vengeance on each other, betook themselves to the common resources of disappointed rage and vented their wrath in threats and defiance. In this kind of conflict, Fortune, which in the personal attack seemed to incline to Jones, was now altogether as favourable to his enemy.

A truce, nevertheless, was at length agreed on by the mediation of the neutral parties, and the whole company again sat down at the table, where, Jones being prevailed on to ask pardon and Blifil to give it, peace was restored and every thing seemed in *statu quo*.

But though the quarrel was in all appearance perfectly reconciled, the good humour which had been interrupted by it was by no means restored. All merriment was now at an end, and the subsequent discourse consisted only of grave relations of matters of fact, and of as grave observations upon them. A species of conversation in which, though there is much dignity and instruction, there is but little entertainment. As we presume, therefore, only to convey this last to the reader, we shall pass by whatever was said, till the rest of the company, having by degrees dropped off, left Square and the physician only together; at which time the conversation was a little heightened by some comments on what had happened between the two young gentlemen, both of whom the doctor declared to be no better than scoundrels; to which appellation the philosopher, very sagaciously shaking his head, agreed.

10

SHOWING THE TRUTH OF MANY OBSERVATIONS OF OVID AND OF OTHER MORE GRAVE WRITERS WHO HAVE PROVED BEYOND CONTRADICTION THAT WINE IS OFTEN THE FORERUNNER OF INCONTINENCY

Jones retired from the company in which we have seen him engaged into the fields, where he intended to cool himself by a walk in the open air before he attended Mr. Allworthy. There, whilst he renewed those meditations on his dear Sophia which the dangerous illness of his friend and benefactor had for some time interrupted, an accident happened, which with sorrow we relate, and with sorrow, doubtless, will it be read; however, that historic truth to which we profess so inviolable an attachment obliges us to communicate it to posterity.

It was now a pleasant evening in the latter end of June when our hero was walking in a most delicious grove, where the gentle breezes fanning the leaves, together with the sweet trilling of a murmuring stream and the melodious notes of nightingales, formed altogether the most enchanting harmony. In this scene, so sweetly accommodated to love, he meditated on his dear Sophia. While his wanton fancy roved unbounded over all her beauties and his lively imagination painted the charming maid in various ravishing forms, his warm heart melted with tenderness, and at length, throwing himself on the ground by the side of a gently murmuring brook, he broke forth into the following ejaculation:

"O Sophia, would heaven give thee to my arms, how blessed would be my condition! Cursed be that fortune which sets a distance between us! Was I but possessed of thee, one only suit of rags thy whole estate, is there a man on earth whom I would envy! How contemptible would the brightest Circassian beauty dressed in all the jewels of the Indies appear to my eyes! But why do I mention another woman? Could I think my eyes capable of looking at any other with tenderness, these hands should tear them from my head. No, my Sophia, if cruel Fortune separates us forever, my soul shall dote on thee alone. The chastest constancy will I ever preserve to thy image. Though I should never have possession of thy charming person, still shalt thou alone have possession of my thoughts, my love, my soul. Oh, my fond heart is so wrapped in that tender bosom that the brightest beauties would for me have no charms, nor would a hermit be colder in their embraces. Sophia, Sophia alone shall be mine. What raptures are in that name! I will engrave it on every tree."

At these words he started up, and beheld—not his Sophia, no, nor a Circassian maid richly and elegantly attired for the Grand Signior's seraglio. No; without a gown, in a shift that was somewhat of the coarsest and none of the cleanest, bedewed likewise with some odoriferous effluvia, the produce of the day's labour, with a pitchfork in her hand Molly Seagrim approached. Our hero had his penknife in his his hand, which he had drawn for the before-mentioned purpose of carving on the bark; when the girl coming near him cried out with a smile, "You don't intend to kill me, squire, I hope!" "Why should you think I would kill you?" answered Jones. "Nay," replied she, "after your cruel usage of me when I saw you last, killing me would, perhaps, be too great kindness for me to expect."

Here ensued a parley, which, as I do not think myself obliged to relate, I shall omit. It is sufficient that it lasted a full quarter of an hour, at the conclusion of which they retired into the thickest part of the grove.

Some of my readers may be inclined to think this event unnatural. However, the fact is true; and, perhaps, may be sufficiently accounted for by suggesting that Jones probably thought one woman better than none, and Molly as probably imagined two men to be better than one. Besides the before-mentioned motive assigned to the present behaviour of Jones, the reader will be likewise pleased to recollect in his favour that he was not at this time perfect master of that wonderful power of Reason, which so well enables grave and wise men to subdue their unruly passions and to decline any of these prohibited amusements. Wine now had totally subdued this power in Jones. He was, indeed, in a condition in which if Reason had interposed, though only to advise, she might have received the answer which one Cleostratus gave many years ago to a silly fellow who asked him if he was not ashamed to be drunk. "Are not you," said Cleostratus, "ashamed to admonish a drunken man?" To say the truth, in a court of justice drunkenness must not be an excuse, yet in a court of conscience it is greatly so; and therefore Aristotle, who commends the laws of Pittacus, by which drunken men received double punishment for their crimes, allows there is more of policy than justice in that law. Now, if there are any transgressions pardonable from drunkenness, they are certainly such as Mr. Jones was at present guilty of; on which head I could could pour forth a vast profusion of learning if I imagined it would either entertain my reader or teach him anything more than he knows already. For his sake, therefore, I shall keep my learning to myself and return to my history.

It hath been observed that Fortune seldom doth things by halves. To say truth, there is no end to her freaks whenever she is disposed to gratify or displease. No sooner had our hero retired with his Dido, but

> *Speluncam* Blifil *dux et divinus eandem*
> *Deveniunt.*

The parson and the young squire, who were taking a serious walk, arrived at the stile which leads into the grove, and the latter caught a view of the lovers just as they were sinking out of sight.

Blifil knew Jones very well, though he was at above a hundred yards' distance, and he was as positive to the sex of his companion, though not to the individual person. He started; blessed himself, and uttered a very solemn ejaculation.

Thwackum expressed some surprise at these sudden emotions, and asked the reason of them. To which Blifil answered he was certain he had seen a fellow and wench retire together among the bushes, which he doubted not was with some wicked purpose. As to the name of Jones, he thought proper to conceal it, and why he did so must be left to the judgement of the sagacious reader; for we never choose to assign motives to the actions of men when there is any possibility of our being mistaken.

The parson, who was not only strictly chaste in his own person but a great enemy to the opposite vice in all others, fired at this information. He desired Mr. Blifil to conduct him immediately to the place, which as he approached he breathed forth vengeance mixed with lamentations; nor did he refrain from casting some oblique reflections on Mr. Allworthy, insinuating that the wickedness of the country was principally owing to the encouragement he had given to vice by having exerted such kindness to a bastard, and by having mitigated that just and wholesome rigour of the law which allots a very severe punishment to loose wenches.

The way through which our hunters were to pass in pursuit of their game was so beset with briars that it greatly obstructed their walk, and caused, besides, such a rustling that Jones had sufficient warning of their arrival before they could surprise him; nay, indeed, so incapable was Thwackum of concealing his indignation, and such vengeance did he mutter forth every step he took, that this alone must have abundantly satisfied Jones that he was (to use the language of sportsmen) *found sitting*.

11

IN WHICH A SIMILE IN MR. POPE'S PERIOD OF A MILE
INTRODUCES AS BLOODY A BATTLE AS CAN POSSIBLY BE
FOUGHT WITHOUT THE ASSISTANCE OF STEEL OR COLD IRON

As in the season of RUTTING (an uncouth phrase by which the vulgar denote that gentle dalliance which in the well-wooded * forest of Hampshire passes between lovers of the ferine kind), if while the lofty-crested stag meditates the amorous sport, a couple of puppies or any other beasts of hostile note should wander so near the temple of Venus Ferina that the fair hind should shrink from the place, touched with that somewhat, either of fear or frolic, of nicety or skittishness, with which Nature hath bedecked all females, or hath at least instructed them how themselves to put on; lest, through the indelicacy of males, the Samean mysteries should be pryed into by unhallowed eyes; for at the celebration of these rites the female priestess cries out with her in Virgil (who was then probably hard at work on such celebration),

      —*Procul, O procul este, profani;*
      Proclamat vates, totoque absistite luco.

      —Far hence be souls profane,

---

* This is an ambiguous phrase, and may mean either a forest well clothed with wood or well stripped of it.

218

The sibyl cried, and from the grove abstain.

DRYDEN.

If, I say, while these sacred rites, which are in common to *genus omne animantium*, are in agitation between the stag and his mistress any hostile beasts should venture too near, on the first hint given by the frighted hind, fierce and tremendous rushes forth the stag to the entrance of the thicket; there stands he sentinel over his love, stamps the ground with his foot, and with his horns brandished aloft in air proudly provokes the apprehended foe to combat.

Thus, and more terrible, when he perceived the enemy's approach, leaped forth our hero. Many a step advanced he forwards in order to conceal the trembling hind and if possible to secure her retreat. And now Thwackum, having first darted some livid lightning from his fiery eyes, began to thunder forth, "Fie upon it! Fie upon it, Mr. Jones! Is it possible you should be the person!" "You see," answered Jones, "it is possible I should be here." "And who," said Thwackum, "is that wicked slut with you?" "If I have any wicked slut with me," cries Jones, "it is possible I shall not let you know who she is." "I command you to tell me immediately," says Thwackum, "and I would not have you imagine, young man, that your age, though it hath somewhat abridged the purpose of tuition, hath totally taken away the authority of the master. The relation of the master and scholar is indelible, as indeed all other relations are, for they all derive their original from heaven. I would have you think yourself, therefore, as much obliged to obey me now as when I taught you your first rudiments." "I believe you would," cries Jones, "but that will not happen unless you had the same birchen argument to convince me." "Then I must tell you plainly," said Thwackum, "I am resolved to discover the wicked wretch." "And I must tell you plainly," returned Jones, "I am resolved you shall not." Thwackum then offered to advance, and Jones laid hold of his arms; which Mr. Blifil endeavoured to rescue, declaring he would not see his old master insulted.

Jones, now finding himself engaged with two, thought it necessary to rid himself of one of his antagonists as soon as possible. He therefore applied to the weakest first; and letting the parson go, he directed a blow at the young squire's breast, which luckily taking place reduced him to measure his length on the ground.

Thwackum was so intent on the discovery that the moment he found himself at liberty he stepped forward directly into the fern, without any great consideration of what might in the meantime befall his friend; but he had advanced a very few paces into the thicket before Jones, having defeated Blifil, overtook the parson and dragged him backward by the skirt of his coat.

This parson had been a champion in his youth and had won much honour by his fist both at school and at the University. He had now, indeed, for a great number of years declined the practice of that noble art, yet was his courage full as strong as his faith, and his body no less strong than either. He was, moreover, as the reader may perhaps have conceived, somewhat irascible in his nature. When he looked back, therefore, and saw his friend stretched out on the ground, and found himself at the same time so roughly handled by one who had formerly been only passive in all conflicts between them (a circumstance which highly aggravated the whole), his patience at length gave way; he threw himself into a posture of offence and, collecting all his force, attacked Jones in the front with as much impetuosity as he had formerly attacked him in the rear.

Our hero received the enemy's attack with the most undaunted intrepidity, and his bosom resounded with the blow. This he presently returned with no less violence, aiming likewise at the parson's breast; but he dextrously drove down the fist of Jones so that it reached only his belly, where two pounds of beef and as many of pudding were then deposited, and whence consequently no hollow sound could proceed. Many lusty blows, much more pleasant as well as easy to have seen than to read or describe, were given on both sides; at last, a violent fall in which Jones had thrown his knees into Thwackum's breast so weakened the latter that victory had been no longer dubious had not Blifil, who had now recovered his strength, again renewed the fight and, by engaging with Jones, given the parson a moment's time to shake his ears and to regain his breath.

And now both together attacked our hero, whose blows did not retain that force with which they had fallen at first, so weakened was he by his combat with Thwackum; for though the pedagogue chose rather to play *solos* on the human instrument and had been lately used to those only, yet he still retained enough of his ancient knowledge to perform his part very well in a *duet*.

The victory, according to modern custom, was like to be decided by numbers when on a sudden a fourth pair of fists appeared in the battle, and immediately paid their compliments to the parson; and the owner of them at the same time crying out, "Are not you ashamed, and be d—ned to you, to fall two of you upon one?"

The battle, which was of the kind that for distinction's sake is called ROYAL, now raged with the utmost violence during a few minutes; till Blifil being a second time laid sprawling by Jones, Thwackum condescended to apply for quarter to his new antagonist, who was now found to be Mr. Western himself; for in the heat of the action none of the combatants had recognized him.

In fact, that honest squire, happening in his afternoon's walk with some company to pass through the field where the bloody battle was fought, and having concluded from seeing three men engaged that two of them must be on a side, he hastened from his companions, and with more gallantry than policy espoused the cause of the weaker party. By which generous proceeding he very probably prevented Mr. Jones from becoming a victim to the wrath of Thwackum and to the pious friendship which Blifil bore his old master; for besides the disadvantage of such odds, Jones had not yet sufficiently recovered the former strength of his broken arm. This reinforcement, however, soon put an end to the action, and Jones with his ally obtained the victory.

12

IN WHICH IS SEEN A MORE MOVING SPECTACLE THAN ALL THE
BLOOD IN THE BODIES OF THWACKUM AND BLIFIL, AND OF
TWENTY OTHER SUCH, IS CAPABLE OF PRODUCING

The rest of Mr. Western's company were now come up, being just at the instant when the action was over. These were the honest clergyman, whom we have formerly seen at Mr. Western's table; Mrs. Western, the aunt of Sophia; and lastly, the lovely Sophia herself.

At this time the following was the aspect of the bloody field: In one place lay on the ground, all pale and almost breathless, the vanquished Blifil. Near him stood the conqueror Jones, almost covered with blood, part of which was naturally his own, and part had been lately the property of the Reverend Mr. Thwackum. In a third place stood the said Thwackum like King Porus, sullenly submitting to the conqueror. The last figure in the piece was Western the Great, most gloriously forbearing the vanquished foe.

Blifil, in whom there was little sign of life, was at first the principal object of the concern of every one, and particularly of Mrs. Western, who had drawn from her pocket a bottle of hartshorn, and was herself about to apply it to his nostrils, when, on a sudden, the attention of the whole company was diverted from poor Blifil, whose spirit if it had any such design might have now taken an opportunity of stealing off to the other world without any ceremony.

For now a more melancholy as more lovely object lay motionless before them. This was no other than the charming Sophia herself, who, from the sight of blood, or from fear for her father, or from some other reason, had fallen down in a swoon before any one could get to her assistance.

Mrs. Western first saw her, and screamed. Immediately two or three voices cried out, "Miss Western is dead." Hartshorn, water, every remedy, were called for almost at one and the same instant.

The reader may remember that in our description of this grove we mentioned a murmuring brook, which brook did not come there as such gentle streams flow through vulgar romances with no other purpose than to murmur. No; Fortune had decreed to ennoble this little brook with a higher honour than any of those which wash the plains of Arcadia ever deserved.

Jones was rubbing Blifil's temples, for he began to fear he had given him a blow too much, when the words *Miss Western* and *dead* rushed at once on his ear. He started up, left Blifil to his fate, and flew to Sophia, whom, while all the rest were running against each other backward and forward looking for water in the dry paths, he caught up in his arms, and then ran away with her over the field to the rivulet above mentioned, where, plunging himself into the water, he contrived to besprinkle her face, head, and neck very plentifully.

Happy was it for Sophia that the same confusion which prevented her other friends from serving her prevented them likewise from obstructing Jones. He had carried her halfways before they knew what he was doing, and he had actually restored her to life before they reached the waterside; she stretched out her arms, opened her eyes, and cried, "O heavens!" just as her father, aunt, and the parson came up.

Jones, who had hitherto held this lovely burden in his arms, now relinquished his hold, but gave her at the same instant a tender caress, which had her senses been then perfectly restored could not have escaped her observation. As she expressed, therefore, no displeasure at this freedom, we suppose she was not sufficiently recovered from her swoon at the time.

This tragical scene was now converted into a sudden scene of joy. In this, our hero was most certainly the principal character; for as he probably felt more ecstatic delight in having saved Sophia than she herself received from being saved, so neither were the congratulations paid to her equal to what were conferred on Jones, especially by Mr. Western himself, who after having once or twice embraced his daughter fell to hugging and kissing Jones. He called him the preserver of Sophia, and declared there was nothing except her or his estate which he would not give him; but upon recollection, he afterwards excepted his fox-hounds, the Chevalier, and Miss Slouch (for so he called his favourite mare.)

All fears for Sophia being now removed, Jones became the object of the squire's consideration. "Come, my lad," says Western, "Doff thy quoat and wash thy feace; for att in a devilish pickle, I promise thee. Come, come, wash thyself, and shat go huome with me; and we'll zee to vind thee another quoat."

Jones immediately complied, threw off his coat, went down to the water, and washed both his face and bosom; for the latter was as much exposed and as bloody as the former; but though the water could clear off the blood, it could not remove the black and blue marks which Thwackum had imprinted on both his face and breast, and which, being discerned by Sophia, drew from her a sigh and a look full of inexpressible tenderness.

Jones received this full in his eyes, and it had infinitely a stronger effect on him than all the contusions which he had received before. An effect, however, widely different; for so soft and balmy was it that had all his former blows been stabs it would for some minutes have prevented his feeling their smart.

The company now moved backwards and soon arrived where Thwackum had got Mr. Blifil again on his legs. Here we cannot suppress a pious wish that all quarrels were to be decided by those weapons only with which Nature, knowing what is proper for us, hath supplied us; and that cold iron was to be used in digging no bowels but those of the earth. Then would war, the pastime of monarchs, be almost inoffensive, and battles between great armies might be fought at the particular desire of several ladies of quality, who, together with the kings themselves, might be actual spectators of the conflict. Then might the field be this moment well strewed with human carcasses, and the next, the dead men or infinitely the greatest part of them might get up like Mr. Bayes's troops, and march off either at the sound of a drum or fiddle, as should be previously agreed on.

I would avoid, if possible, treating this matter ludicrously, lest grave men and politicians, whom I know to be offended at a jest, may cry pish at it; but, in reality, might not a battle be as well decided by the greater number of broken heads, bloody noses, and black eyes as by the greater heaps of mangled and murdered human bodies? Might not towns be contended for in the same manner? Indeed, this may be thought too detrimental a scheme to the French interest, since they would thus lose the advantage they have over other nations in the superiority of their engineers; but when I consider the gallantry and generosity of that people, I am persuaded they would never decline putting themselves upon a par with their adversary, or, as the phrase is, *making themselves his match*.

But such reformations are rather to be wished than hoped for; I shall content myself, therefore, with this short hint, and return to my narrative.

Western began now to inquire into the original rise of this quarrel. To which neither Blifil nor Jones gave any answer, but Thwackum said surlily, "I believe the cause is not far off; if you beat the bushes well, you may find her." "Find her!" replied Western. "What, have you been fighting for a wench?" "Ask the gentleman in his waistcoat there," said Thwackum. "He best knows." "Nay, then," cries Western, "it is a wench certainly. Ah, Tom, Tom, thou art a lecherous dog. But come, gentlemen, be all friends and go home with me, and make final peace over a bottle." "I ask your pardon, sir," says Thwackum; "it is no such slight matter for a man of my character to be thus injuriously treated and buffeted by a boy only because I would have done my duty in endeavouring to detect and bring to justice a wanton harlot; but, indeed, the principal fault lies in Mr. Allworthy and yourself, for if you put the laws in execution, as you ought to do, you would soon rid the country of these vermin."

"I would as soon rid the country of foxes," cries Western. "I think we ought to encourage the recruiting those numbers which we are every day losing in the war; but where is she? Prithee, Tom, show me." He then began to beat about in the same language and in the same manner as if he had been beating for a hare, and at last cried out, "Soho! Puss is not far off. Here's her form, upon my soul; I believe I may cry stole away." And indeed so he might, for he had now discovered the place whence the poor girl had at the beginning of the fray stolen away upon as many feet as a hare generally uses in travelling.

Sophia now desired her father to return home, saying she found herself very faint and apprehended a relapse. The squire immediately complied with his daughter's request (for he was the fondest of parents). He earnestly endeavoured to prevail with the whole company to go and sup with him, but Blifil and Thwackum absolutely refused; the former saying there were more reasons than he could then mention why he must decline this honour, and the latter declaring (perhaps rightly) that it was not proper for a person of his function to be seen at any place in his present condition.

Jones was incapable of refusing the pleasure of being with his Sophia. So on he marched with Squire Western and his ladies, the parson bringing up the rear. This had, indeed, offered to tarry with his brother Thwackum, professing his regard for the cloth would not permit him to depart; but Thwackum would not accept the favour, and with no great civility pushed him after Mr. Western.

Thus ended this bloody fray; and thus shall end the fifth book of this history.

BOOK VI

1

OF LOVE

In our last book we have been obliged to deal pretty much with the passion of love, and in our succeeding book shall be forced to handle this subject still more largely. It may not, therefore, in this place be improper to apply ourselves to the examination of that modern doctrine which certain philosophers among many other wonderful discoveries pretend to have found out: that there is no such passion in the human breast.

Whether these philosophers be the same with that surprising sect who are honourably mentioned by the late Dr. Swift as having by the mere force of genius alone, without the least assistance of any kind of learning or even reading, discovered that profound and invaluable secret that there was no God; or whether they are not rather the same with those who some years since very much alarmed the world by showing that there were no such things as virtue or goodness really existing in human nature, and who deduced our best actions from pride, I will not here presume to determine. In reality, I am inclined to suspect that all these several finders of truth are the very identical men who are by others called the Finders of Gold; the method used in both these searches after truth and after gold being indeed one and the same: viz., the searching, rummaging, and examining into a nasty place, indeed, in the former instances, into the nastiest of all places, A BAD MIND.

But though in this particular, and perhaps in their success, the truth-finder and the gold-finder may very properly be compared together, yet in modesty, surely, there can be no comparison between the two; for who ever heard of a gold-finder that had the impudence or folly to assert from the ill success of his search that there was no such thing as gold in the world? Whereas the truth-finder, having raked out that jakes, his own mind, and being there capable of tracing no ray of divinity, nor anything virtuous, or good, or lovely, or loving, very fairly, honestly, and logically concludes that no such things exist in the whole creation.

To avoid, however, all contention if possible with these philosophers, if they will be called so, and to show our own disposition to accommodate matters peaceably between us, we shall here make them some concessions which may possibly put an end to the dispute.

First, we will grant that many minds, and perhaps those of the philosophers, are entirely free from the least traces of such a passion.

Secondly, that what is commonly called love, namely, the desire of satisfying a voracious appetite with a certain quantity of delicate white human flesh, is by no means that passion for which I here contend. This is indeed more properly hunger; and as no glutton is ashamed to apply the word *love* to his appetite, and to say he LOVES such and such dishes, so may the lover of this kind with equal propriety say he HUNGERS after such and such women.

Thirdly, I will grant, which I believe will be a most acceptable concession, that this love for which I am an advocate, though it satisfies itself in a much more delicate manner, doth nevertheless seek its own satisfaction as much as the grossest of all our appetites.

And lastly, that this love when it operates towards one of a different sex is very apt towards its complete gratification to call in the aid of that hunger which I have mentioned above; and which it is so far from abating that it heightens all its delights to a degree scarce imaginable by those who have never been susceptible of any other emotions than what have proceeded from appetite alone.

In return to all these concessions, I desire of the philosophers to grant that there is in some (I believe in many) human breasts a kind and benevolent disposition, which is gratified by contributing to the happiness of others. That in this gratification alone, as in friendship, in parental and filial affection, and indeed in general philanthropy, there is a great and exquisite delight. That if we will not call such disposition love, we have no name for it. That though the pleasures arising from such pure love may be heightened and sweetened by the assistance of amorous desires, yet the former can subsist alone, nor are they destroyed by the intervention of the latter. Lastly, that esteem and gratitude are the proper motives to love, as youth and beauty are to desire; and, therefore, though such desire may naturally cease when age or sickness overtake its object, yet these can have no effect on love, nor ever shake or remove from a good mind that sensation or passion which hath gratitude and esteem for its basis.

To deny the existence of a passion of which we often see manifest instances seems to be very strange and absurd, and can indeed proceed only from that self-admonition which we have mentioned above: but how unfair is this? Doth the man who recognizes in his own heart no traces of avarice or ambition conclude therefore that there are no such passions in human nature? Why will we not modestly observe the same rule in judging of the good as well as the evil of others? Or why, in any case, will we, as Shakespeare phrases it, "put the world in our own person"?

Predominant vanity is, I am afraid, too much concerned here. This is one instance of that adulation which we bestow on our own minds, and this almost universally. For there is scarce any man, how much soever he may despise the character of a flatterer, but will condescend in the meanest manner to flatter himself.

To those, therefore, I apply for the truth of the above observations, whose minds can bear testimony to what I have advanced.

Examine your heart, my good reader, and resolve whether you do believe these matters with me. If you do, you may now proceed to their exemplification in the following pages; if you do not, you have, I assure you, already read more than you have understood, and it would be wiser to pursue your business or your pleasures (such as they are) than to throw away any more of your time in reading what you can neither taste nor comprehend. To treat of the effects of love to you must be as absurd as to discourse on colours to a man born blind, since possibly your idea of love may be as absurd as that which we are told such blind man once entertained of the colour red: that colour seemed to him to be very much like the sound of a trumpet, and love probably may, in your opinion, very greatly resemble a dish of soup or a sirloin of roast beef.

2

The reader hath seen Mr. Western, his sister, and daughter with young Jones and the parson going together to Mr. Western's house, where the greater part of the company spent the evening with much joy and festivity. Sophia was indeed the only grave person; for as to Jones, though love had now gotten entire possession of his heart, yet the pleasing reflection on Mr. Allworthy's recovery and the presence of his mistress, joined to some tender looks which she now and then could not refrain from giving him, so elevated our hero that he joined the mirth of the other three, who were perhaps as good-humoured people as any in the world.

Sophia retained the same gravity of countenance the next morning at breakfast, whence she retired likewise earlier than usual, leaving her father and aunt together. The squire took no notice of this change in his daughter's disposition. To say the truth, though he was somewhat of a politician and had been twice a candidate in the country interest at an election, he was a man of no great observation. His sister was a lady of a different turn. She had lived about the court and had seen the world. Hence she had acquired all that knowledge which the said world usually communicates, and was a perfect mistress of manners, customs, ceremonies, and fashions; nor did her erudition stop here. She had considerably improved her mind by study; she had not only read all the modern plays, operas, oratorios, poems and romances, in all which she was a critic, but had gone through Rapin's *History of England*, Eachard's *Roman History*, and many French *Mémoires pour servir à l'Histoire;* to these she had added most of the political pamphlets and journals published within the last twenty years. From which she had attained a very competent skill in politics, and could discourse very learnedly on the affairs of Europe. She was, moreover, excellently well skilled in the doctrine of Amour, and knew better than anybody who and who were together: a knowledge which she the more easily attained as her pursuit of it was never diverted by any affairs of her own; for either she had no inclinations or they had never been solicited; which last is indeed very probable, for her masculine person, which was near six foot high, added to her manner and learning, possibly prevented the other sex from regarding her, notwithstanding her petticoats, in the light of a woman. However, as she had considered the matter scientifically, she perfectly well knew, though she had never practised them, all the arts which fine ladies use when they desire to give encouragement or to conceal liking, with all the long appendage of smiles, ogles, glances, &c., as they are at present practised in the *beau-monde*. To sum the whole, no species of disguise or affectation had escaped her notice; but as to the plain simple workings of honest nature, as she had never seen any such, she could know but little of them.

By means of this wonderful sagacity, Mrs. Western had now, as she thought, made a discovery of something in the mind of Sophia. The first hint of this she took from the behaviour of the young lady in the field of battle, and the suspicion which she then conceived was greatly corroborated by some observations which she had made that evening and the next morning. However, being greatly cautious to avoid being found in a mistake, she carried the secret a whole fortnight in her bosom, giving only some oblique hints by simperings, winks, nods, and now and then dropping an obscure word, which indeed sufficiently alarmed Sophia but did not at all affect her brother.

Being at length, however, thoroughly satisfied of the truth of her observation, she took an opportunity one morning when she was alone with her brother to interrupt one of his whistles in the following manner.

"Pray, brother, have you not observed something very extraordinary in my niece lately?" "No, not I," answered Western. "Is anything the matter with the girl?" "I think there is," replies she, "and something of much consequence too." "Why, she doth not complain of anything," cries Western, "and she hath had the smallpox." "Brother," returned she, "girls are liable to other distempers besides the smallpox, and sometimes possibly to much worse." Here Western interrupted her with much earnestness, and begged her if anything ailed his daughter to acquaint him immediately, adding she knew he loved her more than his own soul, and that he would send to the world's end for the best physician to her. "Nay, nay," answered she, smiling, "the distemper is not so terrible; but I believe, brother, you are convinced I know the world, and I promise you I was never more deceived in my life if my niece be not most desperately in love." "How! In love," cries Western in a passion, "in love without acquainting me! I'll disinherit her; I'll turn her out of doors, stark naked, without a farthing. Is all my kindness vor ur, and vondness o' ur come to this, to fall in love without asking me leave!" "But you will not," answered Mrs. Western, "turn this daughter, whom you love better than your own soul, out of doors before you know whether you shall approve her choice. Suppose she should have fixed on the very person whom you yourself would wish, I hope you would not be angry then." "No, no," cries Western, "that would make a difference. If she marries the man I would ha' her, she may love whom she pleases; I shan't trouble my head about that." "That is spoken," answered the sister, "like a sensible man, but I believe the very person she hath chosen would be the very person you would choose for her. I will disclaim all knowledge of the world if it is not so; and I believe, brother, you will allow I have some." "Why, lookee, sister," said Western, "I do believe you have as much as any woman, and to be sure, those are women's matters. You know I don't love to hear you talk about politics; they belong to us, and petticoats should not meddle; but come, who is the man?" "Marry!" said she. "You may find him out yourself if you please. You who are so great a politician can be at no great loss. The judgement which can penetrate into the cabinets of princes and discover the secret springs which move the great state wheels in all the political machines of Europe must surely with very little difficulty find out what passes in the rude uninformed mind of a girl." "Sister," cries the squire, "I have often warned you not to talk the court gibberish to me. I tell you, I don't understand the lingo; but I can read a journal or the *London Evening Post*. Perhaps, indeed, there may be now and tan a verse which I can't make much of because half the letters are left out; yet I know very well what is meant by that, and that our affairs don't go so well as they should do because of bribery and corruption." "I pity your country ignorance from my heart," cries the lady. "Do you?" answered Western. "And I pity your town learning; I had rather be anything than a courtier, and a Presbyterian, and a Hanoverian too, as some people, I believe, are." "If you mean me," answered she, "you know I am a woman, brother; and it signifies nothing what I am. Besides——" "I do know you are a woman," cries the squire, "and it's well for thee that a't one; if hadst been a man, I promise thee I had lent thee a flick long ago." "Ay, there," said she, "in that flick lies all your fancied superiority. Your bodies, and not your brains, are stronger than ours. Believe me, it is well for you that you are able to beat us, or such is the superiority of our understanding we should make all of you what the brave, and wise, and witty, and polite are already—our slaves." "I am glad I know your mind," answered the squire, "but we'll talk more of this matter another time. At present, do tell me what man it is you mean about my daughter." "Hold a moment," said she, "while I digest that sovereign contempt I have for your sex; or else I ought to be too angry with you. There—I have made a shift to gulp it down. And now, good politic sir, what think you of Mr. Blifil? Did she not faint away on seeing him lie breathless on the ground? Did she not after he was recovered turn pale again the moment we came up to that part of the field where he stood? And, pray, what else should be the occasion of her melancholy that night at supper, the next morning, and indeed ever since?" " 'Fore George!" cries the squire. "Now you mind me on't, I remember it all. It is certainly so, and I am glad on't, with all my heart. I knew Sophy was a good girl and would not fall in love to make me angry. I was never more rejoiced in my life; for nothing can lie so handy together as our two estates. I had this matter in my head some time ago; for certainly the two estates are in a manner joined together in matrimony already, and it would be a thousand pities to part them. It is true, indeed, there be larger estates in the kingdom, but not in this county, and I had rather bate something than marry my daughter among strangers and foreigners. Besides, most o' zuch great estates be in the hands of lords, and I heate the very name of *themmun*. Well, but sister, what would you advise me to do; for I tell you women know these matters better than we do?" "Oh, your humble servant, sir," answered the lady, "we are obliged to you for allowing us a capacity in anything. Since you are pleased, then, most politic sir, to ask my advice, I think you may propose the match to Allworthy yourself. There is no indecorum in the proposal's coming from the parent of either side. King Alcinous, in Mr. Pope's *Odyssey*, offers his daughter to Ulysses. I need not caution so politic a person not to say that your daughter is in love; that would indeed be against all rules." "Well," said the squire, "I will propose it, but I shall certainly lend un a flick if he should refuse me." "Fear not," cries Mrs. Western; "the match is too advantageous to be refused." "I don't know that," answered the squire; "Allworthy is a queer b—ch, and money hath no effect o' un." "Brother," said the lady, "your politics astonish me. Are you really to be imposed on by professions? Do you think Mr. Allworthy hath more contempt for money than other men because he professes more? Such credulity would better become one of us weak women than that wise sex which heaven hath formed for politicians. Indeed, brother, you would make a fine plenipo to negotiate with the French. They would soon persuade you that they take towns out of mere defensive principles." "Sister," answered the squire, with much scorn, "let your friends at court answer for the towns taken; as you are a woman, I shall lay no blame upon you, for I suppose they are wiser than to trust women with secrets." He accompanied this with so sarcastical a laugh that Mrs. Western could bear no longer. She had been all this time fretted in a tender part (for she was indeed very deeply skilled in these matters, and very violent in them) and therefore burst forth in a rage, declared her brother to be both a clown and a blockhead, and that she would stay no longer in his house.

The squire, though perhaps he had never read Machiavel, was, however, in many points a perfect politician. He strongly held all those wise tenets which are so well inculcated in that politico-peripatetic school of Exchange Alley. He knew the just value and only use of money: viz., to play it up. He was likewise well skilled in the exact value of reversions, expectations, &c., and had often considered the amount of his sister's fortune and the chance which he or his posterity had of inheriting it. This he was infinitely too wise to sacrifice to a trifling resentment. When he found, therefore, he had carried matters too far, he began to think of reconciling them, which was no very difficult task, as the lady had great affection for her brother and still greater for her niece; and though too susceptible of an affront offered to her skill in politics, on which she much valued herself, was a woman of a very extraordinary good and sweet disposition.

Having first, therefore, laid violent hands on the horses, for whose escape from the stable no place but the window was left open, he next applied himself to his sister, softened and soothed her by unsaying all he had said and by assertions directly contrary to those which had incensed her. Lastly, he summoned the eloquence of Sophia to his assistance, who besides a most graceful and winning address had the advantage of being heard with great favour and partiality by her aunt.

The result of the whole was a kind of smile from Mrs. Western, who said, "Brother, you are absolutely a perfect Croat, but as those have their use in the army of the Empress Queen, so you likewise have some good in you. I will therefore once more sign a treaty of peace with you, and see that you do not infringe it on your side; at least, as you are so excellent a politician, I may expect you will keep your leagues, like the French, till your interest calls upon you to break them."

3

CONTAINING TWO DEFIANCES TO THE CRITICS

The squire, having settled matters with his sister, as we have seen in the last chapter, was so greatly impatient to communicate the proposal to Allworthy that Mrs. Western had the utmost difficulty to prevent him from visiting that gentleman in his sickness for this purpose.

Mr. Allworthy had been engaged to dine with Mr. Western at the time when he was taken ill. He was, therefore, no sooner discharged out of the custody of physic but he thought (as was usual with him on all occasions, both the highest and the lowest) of fulfilling his engagement.

In the interval between the time of the dialogue in the last chapter and this day of public entertainment, Sophia had from certain obscure hints thrown out by her aunt collected some apprehension that the sagacious lady suspected her passion for Jones. She now resolved to take this opportunity of wiping out all suspicion, and for that purpose to put an entire constraint on her behaviour.

First, she endeavoured to conceal a throbbing, melancholy heart with the utmost sprightliness in her countenance and the highest gaiety in her manner. Secondly, she addressed her whole discourse to Mr. Blifil, and took not the least notice of poor Jones the whole day.

The squire was so delighted with this conduct of his daughter that he scarce eat any dinner, and spent almost his whole time in watching opportunities of conveying signs of his approbation by winks and nods to his sister, who was not at first altogether so pleased with what she saw as was her brother.

In short, Sophia so greatly overacted her part that her aunt was at first staggered, and began to suspect some affectation in her niece; but as she was herself a woman of great art, so she soon attributed this to extreme art in Sophia. She remembered the many hints she had given her niece concerning her being in love, and imagined the young lady had taken this way to rally her out of her opinion by an overacted civility; a notion that was greatly corroborated by the excessive gaiety with which the whole was accompanied. We cannot here avoid remarking that this conjecture would have been better founded had Sophia lived ten years in the air of Grosvenor Square, where young ladies do learn a wonderful knack of rallying and playing with that passion which is a mighty serious thing in woods and groves a hundred miles distant from London.

To say the truth, in discovering the deceit of others it matters much that our own art be wound up, if I may use the expression, in the same key with theirs; for very artful men sometimes miscarry by fancying others wiser or, in other words, greater knaves, than they really are. As this observation is pretty deep, I will illustrate it by the following short story. Three countrymen were pursuing a Wiltshire thief through Brentford. The simplest of them, seeing the Wiltshire House written under a sign, advised his companions to enter it, for there most probably they would find their countryman. The second, who was wiser, laughed at this simplicity; but the third, who was wiser still, answered, "Let us go in, however, for he may think we should not suspect him of going amongst his own countrymen." They accordingly went in and searched the house, and by that means missed overtaking the thief, who was at that time but a little way before them, and who, as they all knew but had never once reflected, could not read.

The reader will pardon a digression in which so invaluable a secret is communicated, since every gamester will agree how necessary it is to know exactly the play of another in order to countermine him. This will, moreover, afford a reason why the wiser man, as is often seen, is the bubble of the weaker, and why many simple and innocent characters are so generally misunderstood and misrepresented; but what is most material, this will account for the deceit which Sophia put on her politic aunt.

Dinner being ended and the company retired into the garden, Mr. Western, who was thoroughly convinced of the certainty of what his sister had told him, took Mr. Allworthy aside and very bluntly proposed a match between Sophia and young Mr. Blifil.

Mr. Allworthy was not one of those men whose hearts flutter at any unexpected and sudden tidings of worldly profit. His mind was, indeed, tempered with that philosophy which becomes a man and a Christian. He affected no absolute superiority to all pleasure and pain, to all joy and grief, but was not at the same time to be discomposed and ruffled by every accidental blast, by every smile or frown of Fortune. He received, therefore, Mr. Western's proposal without any visible emotion or without any alteration of countenance. He said the alliance was such as he sincerely wished; then launched forth into a very just encomium on the young lady's merit, acknowledged the offer to be advantageous in point of fortune, and after thanking Mr. Western for the good opinion he had professed of his nephew, concluded that if the young people liked each other, he should be very desirous to complete the affair.

Western was a little disappointed at Mr. Allworthy's answer, which was not so warm as he expected. He treated the doubt whether the young people might like one another with great contempt, saying that parents were the best judges of proper matches for their children; that for his part he should insist on the most resigned obedience from his daughter; and if any young fellow could refuse such a bedfellow, he was his humble servant and hoped there was no harm done.

Allworthy endeavoured to soften this resentment by many eulogiums on Sophia, declaring he had no doubt but that Mr. Blifil would very gladly receive the offer, but all was ineffectual: he could obtain no other answer from the squire but—"I say no more—I humbly hope there's no harm done —that's all." Which words he repeated at least a hundred times before they parted.

Allworthy was too well acquainted with his neighbour to

be offended at this behaviour; and though he was so averse to the rigour which some parents exercise on their children in the article of marriage that he had resolved never to force his nephew's inclinations, he was nevertheless much pleased with the prospect of this union; for the whole county resounded the praises of Sophia, and he had himself greatly admired the uncommon endowments of both her mind and person. To which I believe we may add the consideration of her vast fortune, which, though he was too sober to be intoxicated with, he was too sensible to despise.

And here, in defiance of all the barking critics in the world, I must and will introduce a digression concerning true wisdom, of which Mr. Allworthy was in reality as great a pattern as he was of goodness.

True wisdom, then, notwithstanding all which Mr. Hogarth's poor poet may have writ against riches, and in spite of all which any rich, well-fed divine may have preached against pleasure, consists not in the contempt of either of these. A man may have as much wisdom in the possession of an affluent fortune as any beggar in the streets, or may enjoy a handsome wife or a hearty friend and still remain as wise as any sour popish recluse who buries all his social faculties and starves his belly while he well lashes his back.

To say the truth, the wisest man is the likeliest to possess all worldly blessings in an eminent degree; for as that moderation which wisdom prescribes is the surest way to useful wealth, so can it alone qualify us to taste many pleasures. The wise man gratifies every appetite and every passion while the fool sacrifices all the rest to pall and satiate one.

It may be objected that very wise men have been notoriously avaricious. I answer, "Not in that instance." It may likewise be said that the wisest men have been in their youth immoderately fond of pleasure. I answer, "They were not wise then."

Wisdom, in short, whose lessons have been represented as so hard to learn by those who never were at her school, teaches us only to extend a simple maxim universally known and followed even in the lowest life a little farther than that life carries it. And this is not to buy at too dear a price.

Now, whoever takes this maxim abroad with him into the grand market of the world and constantly applies it to honours, to riches, to pleasures, and to every other commodity which that market affords is, I will venture to affirm, a wise man, and must be so acknowledged in the worldly sense of the word; for he makes the best of bargains, since in reality he purchases everything at the price only of a little trouble, and carries home all the good things I have mentioned while he keeps his health, his innocence, and his reputation, the common prices which are paid for them by others, entire and to himself.

From this moderation, likewise, he learns two other lessons, which complete his character. First, never to be intoxicated when he hath made the best bargain, nor dejected when the market is empty or when its commodities are too dear for his purpose.

But I must remember on what subject I am writing, and not trespass too far on the patience of a good-natured critic. Here, therefore, I put an end to the chapter.

4

CONTAINING SUNDRY CURIOUS MATTERS

As soon as Mr. Allworthy returned home, he took Mr. Blifil apart, and after some preface communicated to him the proposal which had been made by Mr. Western, and at the same time informed him how agreeable this match would be to himself.

The charms of Sophia had not made the least impression on Blifil; not that his heart was pre-engaged, neither was he totally insensible of beauty, or had any aversion to women; but his appetites were by nature so moderate that he was easily able by philosophy, or by study, or by some other method to subdue them; and as to that passion which we have treated of in the first chapter of this book, he had not the least tincture of it in his whole composition.

But though he was so entirely free from that mixed passion of which we there treated, and of which the virtues and beauty of Sophia formed so notable an object, yet was he altogether as well furnished with some other passions that promised themselves very full gratification in the young lady's fortune. Such were avarice and ambition, which divided the dominion of his mind between them. He had more than once considered the possession of this fortune as a very desirable thing, and had entertained some distant views concerning it, but his own youth and that of the young lady, and indeed, principally a reflection that Mr. Western might marry again and have more children, had restrained him from too hasty or eager a pursuit.

This last and most material objection was now in great measure removed, as the proposal came from Mr. Western himself. Blifil, therefore, after a very short hesitation answered Mr. Allworthy that matrimony was a subject on which he had not yet thought, but that he was so sensible of his friendly and fatherly care that he should in all things submit himself to his pleasure.

Allworthy was naturally a man of spirit, and his present gravity arose from true wisdom and philosophy, not from any original phlegm in his disposition; for he had possessed much fire in his youth and had married a beautiful woman for love. He was not, therefore, greatly pleased with this cold answer of his nephew, nor could he help launching forth into the praises of Sophia and expressing some wonder that the heart of a young man could be impregnable to the force of such charms unless it was guarded by some prior affection.

Blifil assured him he had no such guard, and then proceeded to discourse so wisely and religiously on love and marriage that he would have stopped the mouth of a parent much less devoutly inclined than was his uncle. In the end the good man was satisfied that his nephew, far from having any objections to Sophia, had that esteem for her which in sober and virtuous minds is the sure foundation of friendship and love. And as he doubted not but the lover would in a little time become altogether as agreeable to his mistress, he foresaw great happiness arising to all parties by so proper and desirable a union. With Mr. Blifil's consent, therefore, he wrote the next morning to Mr. Western, acquainting him that his nephew had very thankfully and gladly received the proposal, and would be ready to wait on the young lady whenever she should be pleased to accept his visit.

Western was much pleased with this letter, and immediately returned an answer, in which without having mentioned a word to his daughter he appointed that very afternoon for opening the scene of courtship.

As soon as he had dispatched this messenger, he went in quest of his sister, whom he found reading and expounding the *Gazette* to Parson Supple. To this exposition he was obliged to attend near a quarter of an hour, though with great violence to his natural impetuosity, before he was suffered to speak. At length, however, he found an opportunity of acquainting the lady that he had business of great consequence to impart to her; to which she answered, "Brother, I am entirely at your service. Things look so well in the north that I was never in a better humour."

The parson then withdrawing, Western acquainted her with all which had passed and desired her to communicate the affair to Sophia, which she readily and cheerfully undertook; though perhaps her brother was a little obliged to that agreeable northern aspect which had so delighted her that he heard no comment on his proceedings, for they were certainly somewhat too hasty and violent.

5

IN WHICH IS RELATED WHAT PASSED BETWEEN SOPHIA AND HER AUNT

Sophia was in her chamber reading when her aunt came in. The moment she saw Mrs. Western she shut the book with so much eagerness that the good lady could not forbear asking her what book that was which she seemed so much afraid of showing. "Upon my word, madam," answered Sophia, "it is a book which I am neither ashamed nor afraid to own I have read. It is the production of a young lady of fashion, whose good understanding, I think, doth honour to her sex, and whose good heart is an honour to human nature." Mrs. Western then took up the book, and immediately after threw it down, saying, "Yes, the author is of a very good family, but she is not much among people one knows. I have never read it; for the best judges say there is not much in it." "I dare not, madam, set up my own opinion," says Sophia, "against the best judges, but there appears to me a great deal of human nature in it, and in many parts so much true tenderness and delicacy that it hath cost me many a tear." "Ay, and do you love to cry, then?" says the aunt. "I love a tender sensation," answered the niece, "and would pay the price of a tear for it any time." "Well, but show me," said the aunt, "what you was reading when I came in; there was something very tender in that, I believe, and very loving too. You blush, my dear Sophia. Ah, child, you should read books which would teach you a little hypocrisy, which would instruct you how to hide your thoughts a little better." "I hope, madam," answered Sophia, "I have no thoughts which I ought to be ashamed of discovering." "Ashamed, no!" cries the aunt. "I don't think you have any thoughts which you ought to be ashamed of; and yet, child, you blushed just now when I mentioned the word *loving*. Dear Sophy, be assured you have not one thought which I am not well acquainted with, as well, child, as the French are with our motions long before we put them in execution. Did you think, child, because you have been able to impose upon your father that you could impose upon me? Do you imagine I did not know the reason of your overacting all that friendship for Mr. Blifil yesterday? I have seen a little too much of the world to be so deceived. Nay, nay, do not blush again. I tell you it is a passion you need not be ashamed of. It is a passion I myself approve, and have already brought your father into the approbation of. Indeed, I solely consider your inclination; for I would always have that gratified if possible, though one may sacrifice higher prospects. Come, I have news which will delight your very soul. Make me your confidante, and I will undertake you shall be happy to the very extent of your wishes." "La, madam," says Sophia, looking more foolishly than ever she did in her life, "I know not what to say. Why, madam, should you suspect?" "Nay, no dishonesty," returned Mrs. Western. "Consider you are speaking to one of your own sex, to an aunt, and I hope you are convinced you speak to a friend. Consider you are only revealing to me what I know already, and what I plainly saw yesterday through that most artful of all disguises which you had put on, and which must have deceived any one who had not perfectly known the world. Lastly, consider it is a passion which I highly approve." "La, madam," says Sophia, "you come upon one so unawares, and on a sudden. To be sure, madam, I am not blind—and certainly, if it be a fault to see all human perfections assembled together—but is it possible my father and you, madam, can see with my eyes?" "I tell you," answered the aunt, "we do entirely approve; and this very afternoon your father hath appointed for you to receive your lover." "My father, this afternoon!" cries Sophia with the blood starting from her face. "Yes, child," said the aunt, "this afternoon. You know the impetuosity of my brother's temper. I acquainted him with the passion which I first discovered in you that evening when you fainted away in the field. I saw it in your fainting. I saw it immediately upon your recovery. I saw it that evening at supper, and the next morning at breakfast (you know, child, I have seen the world). Well, I no sooner acquainted my brother but he immediately wanted to propose it to Allworthy. He proposed it yesterday, Allworthy consented (as to be sure he must with joy), and this afternoon, I tell you, you are to put on all your best airs." "This afternoon!" cries Sophia. "Dear aunt, you frighten me out of my senses." "Oh, my dear," said the aunt, "you will soon come to yourself again; for he is a charming young fellow, that's the truth on't." "Nay, I will own," says Sophia, "I know none with such perfections. So brave, and yet so gentle; so witty, yet so inoffensive; so humane, so civil, so genteel, so handsome! What signifies his being base born when compared with such qualifications as these?" "Base born! What do you mean?" said the aunt. "Mr. Blifil base born!" Sophia turned instantly pale at this name, and faintly repeated it. Upon which the aunt cried, "Mr. Blifil, ay, Mr. Blifil, of whom else have we been talking?" "Good heavens," answered Sophia, ready to sink, "of Mr. Jones I thought; I am sure I know no other who deserves——" "I protest," cries the aunt, "you frighten me in your turn. Is it Mr. Jones and not Mr. Blifil who is the object of your affection?" "Mr. Blifil!" repeated Sophia. "Sure it is impossible you can be in earnest; if you are, I am the most miserable woman alive." Mrs. Western now stood a few moments silent while sparks of fiery rage flashed from her eyes. At length, collecting all her force of voice, she thundered forth in the following articulate sounds:

"And is it possible you can think of disgracing your family by allying yourself to a bastard? Can the blood of the Westerns submit to such contamination! If you have not sense sufficient to restrain such monstrous inclinations, I thought the pride of our family would have prevented you from giving the least encouragement to so base an affection; much less did I imagine you would ever have had the assurance to own it to my face."

"Madam," answered Sophia, trembling, "what I have said you have extorted from me. I do not remember to have ever mentioned the name of Mr. Jones with approbation to any one before; nor should I now had I not conceived he had had your approbation. Whatever were my thoughts of that poor unhappy young man I intended to have carried them with me to my grave—to that grave where now, I find, I am only to seek repose." Here she sunk down in her chair, drowned in her tears, and in all the moving silence of unutterable grief presented a spectacle which must have affected almost the hardest heart.

All this tender sorrow, however, raised no compassion in her aunt. On the contrary, she now fell into the most violent rage. "And I would rather," she cried in a most vehement voice, "follow you to your grave than I would see you disgrace yourself and your family by such a match. O heavens! Could I have ever suspected that I should live to hear a niece of mine declare a passion for such a fellow? You are the first—yes, Miss Western—you are the first of your name who ever entertained so grovelling a thought. A family so noted for the prudence of its women . . ." Here she run on a full quarter of an hour till, having exhausted her breath rather than her rage, she concluded with threatening to go immediately and acquaint her brother.

Sophia then threw herself at her feet and, laying hold of her hands, begged her with tears to conceal what she had drawn from her; urging the violence of her father's temper, and protesting that no inclinations of hers should ever prevail with her to do anything which might offend him.

Mrs. Western stood a moment looking at her, and then, having recollected herself, said that on one consideration only she would keep the secret from her brother, and this was that Sophia should promise to entertain Mr. Blifil that very afternoon as her lover, and to regard him as the person who was to be her husband.

Poor Sophia was too much in her aunt's power to deny her anything positively; she was obliged to promise that she would see Mr. Blifil and be as civil to him as possible, but begged her aunt that the match might not be hurried on. She said Mr. Blifil was by no means agreeable to her, and she hoped her father would be prevailed on not to make her the most wretched of women.

Mrs. Western assured her that the match was entirely agreed upon, and that nothing could or should prevent it. "I must own," said she, "I looked on it as on a matter of indifference; nay, perhaps, had some scruples about it before, which were actually got over by my thinking it highly agreeable to your own inclinations; but now I regard it as the most eligible thing in the world, nor shall there be, if I can prevent it, a moment of time lost on the occasion."

Sophia replied, "Delay at least, madam, I may expect from both your goodness and my father's. Surely you will give me time to endeavour to get the better of so strong a disinclination as I have at present to this person."

The aunt answered she knew too much of the world to be so deceived; that as she was sensible another man had her affections, she should persuade Mr. Western to hasten the match as much as possible. "It would be bad politics indeed," added she, "to protract a siege when the enemy's army is at hand and in danger of relieving it. No, no, Sophy," said she, "as I am convinced you have a violent passion which you can never satisfy with honour, I will do all I can to put your honour out of the care of your family; for when you are married those matters will belong only to the consideration of your husband. I hope, child, you will always have prudence enough to act as becomes you, but if you should not, marriage hath saved many a woman from ruin."

Sophia well understood what her aunt meant, but did not think proper to make her an answer. However, she took a resolution to see Mr. Blifil and to behave to him as civilly as she could; for on that condition only she obtained a promise from her aunt to keep secret the liking which her ill fortune, rather than any scheme of Mrs. Western, had unhappily drawn from her.

6

CONTAINING A DIALOGUE BETWEEN SOPHIA AND MRS. HONOUR, WHICH MAY A LITTLE RELIEVE THOSE TENDER AFFECTIONS WHICH THE FOREGOING SCENE MAY HAVE RAISED IN THE MIND OF A GOOD-NATURED READER

Mrs. Western, having obtained that promise from her niece which we have seen in the last chapter, withdrew, and presently after arrived Mrs. Honour. She was at work in a neighbouring apartment, and had been summoned to the keyhole by some vociferation in the preceding dialogue, where she had continued during the remaining part of it. At her entry into the room she found Sophia standing motionless, with the tears trickling from her eyes. Upon which she immediately ordered a proper quantity of tears into her own eyes, and then began, "Oh, Gemini, my dear lady, what is the matter?" "Nothing," cries Sophia. "Nothing!" "Oh, dear madam," answers Mrs. Honour, "you must not tell me that when your ladyship is in this taking, and when there hath been such a preamble between your ladyship and Madam Western." "Don't tease me," cries Sophia; "I tell you nothing is the matter. Good heavens! Why was I born?" "Nay, madam," says Mrs. Honour, "you shall never persuade me that your la'ship can lament yourself so for nothing. To be sure, I am but a servant; but to be sure, I have been always faithful to your ladyship, and to be sure, I would serve your la'ship with my life." "My dear Honour," says Sophia, "'tis not in thy power to be of any service to me. I am irretrievably undone." "Heaven forbid," answered the waiting-woman; "but if I can't be of any service to you, pray tell me, madam; it will be some comfort to me to know; pray, dear ma'am, tell me what's the matter." "My father," cries Sophia, "is going to marry me to a man I both despise and hate." "Oh, dear ma'am," answered the other, "who is this wicked man? For to be sure, he is very bad or your la'ship would not despise him." "His name is poison to my tongue," replied Sophia. "Thou wilt know it too soon." Indeed, to confess the truth, she knew it already, and therefore was not very inquisitive as to that point. She then proceeded thus: "I don't pretend to give your la'ship advice, whereof your la'ship knows much better than I can pretend to, being but a servant, but, i' fackins, no father in England should marry me against my consent! And to be sure, the squire is so good that if he did but know your la'ship despises and hates the young man, to be sure, he would not desire you to marry him. And if your la'ship would but give me leave to tell my master so— to be sure, it would be more properer to come from your own mouth; but as your la'ship doth not care to foul your tongue with his nasty name——" "You are mistaken, Honour," says Sophia, "my father was determined before he ever thought fit to mention it to me." "More shame for him," cries Honour; "you are to go to bed to him, and not master. And thof a man may be a very proper man, yet every woman mayn't think him handsome alike. I am sure my master would never act in this manner of his own head. I wish some people would trouble themselves only with what belongs to them; they would not, I believe, like to be served so if it was their own case; for though I am a maid, I can easily believe as how all men are not equally agreeable. And what signifies your la'ship having so great a fortune if you can't please yourself with the man you think most handsomest? Well, I say nothing, but to be sure, it is pity some folks had not been better born; nay, as for that matter, I should not mind it myself, but then there is not so much money. And what of that? Your la'ship hath money enough for both, and where can your la'ship bestow your fortune better? For to be sure, everyone must allow that he is the most handsomest, charmingest, finest, tallest, properest man in the world." "What do you mean by running on in this manner to me?" cries Sophia with a very grave countenance. "Have I ever given any encouragement for these liberties?" "Nay, ma'am, I ask pardon; I meant no harm," answered she; "but to be sure, the poor gentleman hath run in my head ever since I saw him this morning. To be sure, if your ladyship had but seen him just now you must have pitied him. Poor gentleman! I wishes some misfortune hath not happened to him; for he hath been walking about with his arms across, and looking so melancholy all this morning; I vow and protest it made me almost cry to see him." "To see whom?" says Sophia. "Poor Mr. Jones," answered Honour. "See him! Why, where did you see him?" cries Sophia. "By the canal, ma'am," says Honour. "There he hath been walking all this morning, and at last there he laid himself down; I believe he lies there still. To be sure, if it had not been for my modesty, being a maid as I am, I should have gone and spoke to him. Do, ma'am, let me go and see, only for a fancy, whether he is there still." "Pugh!" says Sophia. "There! No, no, what should he do there? He is gone before this time, to be sure. Besides, why—what— why should you go to see? Besides, I want you for something else. Go, fetch me my hat and gloves. I shall walk with my aunt in the grove before dinner." Honour did immediately as she was bid, and Sophia put her hat on; when looking in the glass, she fancied the ribbon with which her hat was tied did not become her, and so sent her maid back again for a ribbon of a different colour; and then, giving Mrs. Honour repeated charges not to leave her work on any account, as she said it was in violent haste and must be finished that very day, she muttered something more about going to the grove, and then sallied out the contrary way and walked as fast as her tender, trembling limbs could carry her directly towards the canal.

Jones had been there, as Mrs. Honour had told her; he had indeed spent two hours there that morning in melancholy contemplation on his Sophia, and had gone out from the garden at one door the moment she entered it at another. So that those unlucky minutes which had been spent in changing the ribbons had prevented the lovers from meeting at this time. A most unfortunate accident, from which my fair readers will not fail to draw a very wholesome lesson. And here I strictly forbid all male critics to intermeddle with a circumstance which I have recounted only for the sake of the ladies, and upon which they only are at liberty to comment.

7

A PICTURE OF FORMAL COURTSHIP IN MINIATURE, AS IT ALWAYS OUGHT TO BE DRAWN, AND A SCENE OF A TENDERER KIND, PAINTED AT FULL LENGTH

It was well remarked by one (and perhaps by more) that misfortunes do not come single. This wise maxim was now verified by Sophia, who was not only disappointed of seeing the man she loved but had the vexation of being obliged to dress herself out in order to receive a visit from the man she hated.

That afternoon, Mr. Western for the first time acquainted his daughter with his intention, telling her he knew very well that she had heard it before from her aunt. Sophia looked very grave upon this, nor could she prevent a few pearls from stealing into her eyes. "Come, come," says Western, "none of your maidenish airs; I know all; I assure you, sister hath told me all."

"Is it possible," says Sophia, "that my aunt can have betrayed me already?" "Ay, ay," says Western, "betrayed you, ay! Why, you betrayed yourself yesterday at dinner. You showed your fancy very plainly, I think. But you young girls never know what you would be at. So you cry because I am going to marry you to the man you are in love with! Your mother, I remember, whimpered and whined just in the same manner, but it was all over within twenty-four hours after we were married; Mr. Blifil is a brisk young man, and will soon put an end to your squeamishness. Come, cheer up, cheer up, I expect un every minute."

Sophia was now convinced that her aunt had behaved honourably to her; and she determined to go through that disagreeable afternoon with as much resolution as possible, and without giving the least suspicion in the world to her father.

Mr. Blifil soon arrived, and Mr. Western, soon after withdrawing, left the young couple together.

Here a long silence of near a quarter of an hour ensued; for the gentleman, who was to begin the conversation, had all that unbecoming modesty which consists in bashfulness. He often attempted to speak and as often suppressed his words just at that very point of utterance. At last out they broke in a torrent of far-fetched and high-strained compliments, which were answered on her side by downcast looks, half-bows, and civil monosyllables. Blifil from his inexperience in the ways of women, and from his conceit of himself, took this behaviour for a modest assent to his courtship, and when to shorten a scene which she could no longer support Sophia rose up and left the room, he imputed that, too, merely to bashfulness, and comforted himself that he should soon have enough of her company.

He was indeed perfectly well satisfied with his prospect of success; for as to that entire and absolute possession of the heart of his mistress, which romantic lovers require, the very idea of it never entered his head. Her fortune and her person were the sole objects of his wishes, of which he made no doubt soon to obtain the absolute property, as Mr. Western's mind was so earnestly bent on the match, and as he well knew the strict obedience which Sophia was always ready to pay to her father's will, and the greater still which her father would exact if there was occasion. This authority, therefore, together with the charms which he fancied in his own person and conversation, could not fail, he thought, of succeeding with a young lady whose inclinations were, he doubted not, entirely disengaged.

Of Jones he certainly had not even the least jealousy, and I have often thought it wonderful that he had not. Perhaps he imagined the character which Jones bore all over the country (how justly let the reader determine), of being one of the wildest fellows in England, might render him odious to a lady of the most exemplary modesty. Perhaps his suspicions might be laid asleep by the behaviour of Sophia and of Jones himself when they were all in company together. Lastly, and indeed principally, he was well assured there was not another self in the case. He fancied that he knew Jones to the bottom, and had in reality a great contempt for his understanding for not being more attached to his own interest. He had no apprehension that Jones was in love with Sophia, and as for any lucrative motives, he imagined they would sway very little with so silly a fellow. Blifil, moreover, thought the affair of Molly Seagrim still went on, and indeed believed it would end in marriage; for Jones really loved him from his childhood and had kept no secret from him till his behaviour on the sickness of Mr. Allworthy had entirely alienated his heart; and it was by means of the quarrel which had ensued on this occasion, and which was not yet reconciled, that Mr. Blifil knew nothing of the alteration in the affection which Jones had formerly borne towards Molly.

From these reasons, therefore, Mr. Blifil saw no bar to his success with Sophia. He concluded her behaviour was like that of all other young ladies on a first visit from a lover, and it had indeed entirely answered his expectations.

Mr. Western took care to waylay the lover at his exit from his mistress. He found him so elevated with his success, so enamoured with his daughter, and so satisfied with her reception of him that the old gentleman began to caper and dance about his hall and by many other antic actions to express the extravagance of his joy; for he had not the least command over any of his passions, and that which had at any time the ascendant in his mind hurried him to the wildest excesses.

As soon as Blifil was departed, which was not till after many hearty kisses and embraces bestowed on him by Western, the good squire went instantly in quest of his daughter, whom he no sooner found than he poured forth the most extravagant raptures, bidding her choose what clothes and jewels she pleased, and declaring that he had no other use for fortune but to make her happy. He then caressed her again and again with the utmost profusion of fondness, called her by the most endearing names, and protested she was his only joy on earth.

Sophia, perceiving her father in this fit of affection, which she did not absolutely know the reason of (for fits of fondness were not unusual to him, though this was rather more violent than ordinary), thought she should never have a better opportunity of disclosing herself than at present, as far at least as regarded Mr. Blifil; and she too well foresaw the necessity which she should soon be under of coming to a full explanation. After having thanked the squire, therefore, for all his professions of kindness, she added, with a look full of inexpressible softness, "And is it possible my papa can be so good to place all his joy in his Sophy's happiness?" which Western having confirmed by a great oath and a kiss, she then laid hold of his hand, and, falling on her knees, after many warm and passionate declarations of affection and duty, she begged him not to make her the most miserable creature on earth by forcing her to marry a man whom she detested. "This I entreat of you, dear sir," said she, "for your sake as well as my own, since you are so very kind to tell me your happiness depends on mine." "How! What!" says Western, staring wildly. "Oh, sir," continued she, "not only your poor Sophy's happiness, her very life, her being, depends upon your granting her request. I cannot live with Mr. Blifil. To force me into this marriage would be killing me." "You can't live with Mr. Blifil!" says Western. "No, upon my soul I can't," answered Sophia. "Then die and be d—ned," cries he, spurning her from him. "Oh, sir," cries Sophia, catching hold of the skirt of his coat, "take pity on me, I beseech you! Don't look and say such cruel— Can you be unmoved while you see your Sophy in this dreadful condition? Can the best of fathers break my heart? Will he kill me by the most painful, cruel, lingering death?" "Pooh! Pooh!" cries the squire. "All stuff and nonsense, all maidenish tricks. Kill you indeed! Will marriage kill you?" "Oh, sir," answered Sophia, "such a marriage is worse than death. He is not even indifferent; I hate and detest him." "If you detest un never so much," cries Western, "you shall ha 'un." This he bound by an oath too shocking to repeat, and after many violent asseverations concluded in these words: "I am resolved upon the match, and unless you consent to it, I will not give you a groat, not a single farthing; no, though I saw you expiring with famine in the street, I would not relieve you with a morsel of bread. This is my fixed resolution, and so I leave you to consider on it." He then broke from her with such violence that her face dashed against the floor, and he burst directly out of the room, leaving poor Sophia prostrate on the ground.

When Western came into the hall he found Jones, who, seeing his friend looking wild, pale, and almost breathless, could not forbear inquiring the reason of all these melancholy appearances. Upon which the squire immediately acquainted him with the whole matter, concluding with bitter denunciations against Sophia and very pathetic lamentations of the misery of all fathers who are so unfortunate to have daughters.

Jones, to whom all the resolutions which had been taken in

favour of Blifil were yet a secret, was at first almost struck dead with this relation; but recovering his spirits a little, mere despair, as he afterwards said, inspired him to mention a matter to Mr. Western which seemed to require more impudence than a human forehead was ever gifted with. He desired leave to go to Sophia that he might endeavour to obtain her concurrence with her father's inclinations.

If the squire had been as quick-sighted as he was remarkable for the contrary, passion might at present very well have blinded him. He thanked Jones for offering to undertake the office, and said, "Go, go; prithee, try what canst do," and then swore many execrable oaths that he would turn her out of doors unless she consented to the match.

8

THE MEETING BETWEEN JONES AND SOPHIA

Jones departed instantly in quest of Sophia, whom he found just risen from the ground where her father had left her, with the tears trickling from her eyes and the blood running from her lips. He presently ran to her, and with a voice full at once of tenderness and terror cried, "Oh, my Sophia, what means this dreadful sight!" She looked softly at him for a moment before she spoke, and then said, "Mr. Jones, for heaven's sake, how came you here? Leave me, I beseech you, this moment." "Do not," says he, "impose so harsh a command upon me—my heart bleeds faster than those lips. Oh, Sophia, how easily could I drain my veins to preserve one drop of that dear blood!" "I have too many obligations to you already," answered she, "for sure you meant them such." Here she looked at him tenderly almost a minute and then, bursting into an agony, cried, "Oh, Mr. Jones, why did you save my life? My death would have been happier for us both." "Happier for us both!" cried he. "Could racks or wheels kill me so painfully as Sophia's! I cannot bear the dreadful sound. Do I live but for her?" Both his voice and look were full of inexpressible tenderness when he spoke these words, and at the same time he laid gentle hold on her hand, which she did not withdraw from him; to say the truth, she hardly knew what she did or suffered. A few moments now passed in silence between these lovers while his eyes were eagerly fixed on Sophia and hers declining towards the ground; at last she recovered strength enough to desire him again to leave her, for that her certain ruin would be the consequence of their being found together; adding, "Oh, Mr. Jones, you know not, you know not what hath passed this cruel afternoon." "I know all, my Sophia," answered he; "your cruel father hath told me all, and he himself hath sent me hither to you." "My father sent you to me!" replied she. "Sure you dream." "Would to heaven," cries he, "it was but a dream. Oh, Sophia, your father hath sent me to you to be an advocate for my odious rival, to solicit you in his favour. I took any means to get access to you. Oh, speak to me, Sophia; comfort my bleeding heart. Sure no one ever loved, ever doted like me. Do not unkindly withhold this dear, this soft, this gentle hand. One moment, perhaps, tears you forever from me. Nothing less than this cruel occasion could, I believe, have ever conquered the respect and awe with which you have inspired me." She stood a moment silent and covered with confusion, then, lifting up her eyes gently towards him, she cried, "What would Mr. Jones have me say?" "Oh, do but promise," cries he, "that you never will give yourself to Blifil." "Name not," answered she, "the destested sound. Be assured I will never give him what it is in my power to withhold from him." "Now, then," cries he, "while you are so perfectly kind go a little farther and add that I may hope." "Alas," says she, "Mr. Jones, whither will you drive me? What hope have I to bestow? You know my father's intentions." "But I know," answered he, "your compliance with them cannot be compelled." "What," says she, "must be the dreadful consequence of my disobedience? My own ruin is my least concern. I cannot bear the thoughts of being the cause of my father's misery." "He is himself the cause," cries Jones, "by exacting a power over you which Nature hath not given him. Think on the misery which I am to suffer if I am to lose you, and see on which side pity will turn the balance." "Think of it!" replied she. "Can you imagine I do not feel the ruin which I must bring on you should I comply with your desire? It is that thought which gives me resolution to bid you fly from me forever and avoid your own destruction." "I fear no destruction," cries he, "but the loss of Sophia; if you would save me from the most bitter agonies, recall that cruel sentence. Indeed I can never part with you; indeed I cannot."

The lovers now stood both silent and trembling, Sophia

being unable to withdraw her hand from Jones and he almost as unable to hold it, when the scene, which I believe some of my readers will think had lasted long enough, was interrupted by one of so different a nature that we shall reserve the relation of it for a different chapter.

9

BEING OF A MUCH MORE TEMPESTUOUS KIND THAN THE FORMER

Before we proceed with what now happened to our lovers, it may be proper to recount what had passed in the hall during their tender interview.

Soon after Jones had left Mr. Western in the manner above mentioned, his sister came to him, and was presently informed of all that had passed between her brother and Sophia relating to Blifil.

This behaviour in her niece the good lady construed to be an absolute breach of the condition on which she had engaged to keep her love for Mr. Jones a secret. She considered herself, therefore, at full liberty to reveal all she knew to the squire, which she immediately did in the most explicit terms and without any ceremony or preface.

The idea of a marriage between Jones and his daughter had never once entered into the squire's head, either in the warmest minutes of his affection towards that young man, or from suspicion, or on any other occasion. He did indeed consider a parity of fortune and circumstances to be physically as necessary an ingredient in marriage as difference of sexes or any other essential; and had no more apprehension of his daughter's falling in love with a poor man than with any animal of a different species.

He became, therefore, like one thunderstruck at his sister's relation. He was, at first, incapable of making any answer, having been almost deprived of his breath by the violence of the surprise. This, however, soon returned and, as is usual in other cases after an intermission, with redoubled force and fury.

The first use he made of the power of speech after his recovery from the sudden effects of his astonishment was to discharge a round volley of oaths and imprecations. After which he proceeded hastily to the apartment where he expected to find the lovers and murmured, or, indeed, rather roared forth intentions of revenge every step he went.

As when two doves, or two wood-pigeons, or as when Strephon and Phyllis (for that comes nearest to the mark) are retired into some pleasant solitary grove to enjoy the delightful conversation of Love, that bashful boy who cannot speak in public and is never a good companion to more than two at a time; here, while every object is serene, should hoarse thunder burst suddenly through the shattered clouds and rumbling roll along the sky, the frightened maid starts from the mossy bank or verdant turf, the pale livery of death succeeds the red regimentals in which Love had before dressed her cheeks, fear shakes her whole frame, and her lover scarce supports her trembling, tottering limbs.

Or as when the two gentlemen, strangers to the wondrous wit of the place, are cracking a bottle together at some inn or tavern at Salisbury, if the great Dowdy, who acts the part of a madman as well as some of his setters-on do that of a fool, should rattle his chains and dreadfully hum forth the grumbling catch along the gallery, the frightened strangers stand aghast, scared at the horrid sound; they seek some place of shelter from the approaching danger, and if the well-barred windows did admit their exit, would venture their necks to escape the threatening fury now coming upon them.

So trembled poor Sophia, so turned she pale at the noise of her father, who in a voice most dreadful to hear came on swearing, cursing, and vowing the destruction of Jones. To say the truth, I believe the youth himself would, from some prudent considerations, have preferred another place of abode at this time had his terror on Sophia's account given him liberty to reflect a moment on what any otherways concerned himself than as his love made him partake whatever affected her.

And now the squire, having burst open the door, beheld an object which instantly suspended all his fury against Jones: this was the ghastly appearance of Sophia, who had fainted away in her lover's arms. This tragical sight Mr. Western no sooner beheld than all his rage forsook him; he roared for help with his utmost violence, ran first to his daughter, then back to the door calling for water, and then back again to Sophia, never considering in whose arms she then was, nor perhaps once recollecting that there was such a person in the world as Jones; for indeed I believe the present circumstances of his daughter were now the sole consideration which employed his thoughts.

Mrs. Western and a great number of servants soon came to the assistance of Sophia with water, cordials, and everything necessary on those occasions. These were applied with such success that Sophia in a very few minutes began to recover and all the symptoms of life to return. Upon which she was presently led off by her own maid and Mrs. Western; nor did that good lady depart without leaving some wholesome admonitions with her brother on the dreadful effects of his passion, or, as she pleased to call it, madness.

The squire perhaps did not understand this good advice, as it was delivered in obscure hints, shrugs, and notes of admiration; at least, if he did understand it, he profited very little by it; for no sooner was he cured of his immediate fears for his daughter than he relapsed into his former frenzy, which must have produced an immediate battle with Jones had not Parson Supple, who was a very strong man, been present, and by mere force restrained the squire from acts of hostility.

The moment Sophia was departed Jones advanced in a very suppliant manner to Mr. Western, whom the parson held in his arms, and begged him to be pacified; for that while he continued in such a passion it would be impossible to give him any satisfaction.

"I wull have satisfaction o' thee," answered the squire. "So doff thy clothes. *At unt* half a man, and I'll lick thee as well as wast ever licked in thy life." He then bespattered the youth with abundance of that language which passes between country gentlemen who embrace opposite sides of the question, with frequent applications to him to salute that part which is generally introduced into all controversies that arise among the low orders of the English gentry, at horse-races, cock-matches, and other public places. Allusions to this part are likewise often made for the sake of the jest. And here, I believe, the wit is generally misunderstood. In reality, it lies in desiring another to kiss your a— for having just before threatened to kick his; for I have observed very accurately that no one ever desires you to kick that which belongs to himself, nor offers to kiss this part in another.

It may likewise seem surprising that in the many thousand kind invitations of this sort, which every one who hath conversed with country gentlemen must have heard, no one, I believe, hath ever seen a single instance where the desire hath been complied with. A great instance of their want of politeness; for in town nothing can be more common than for the finest gentlemen to perform this ceremony every day to their superiors without having that favour once requested of them.

To all such wit Jones very calmly answered, "Sir, this usage may perhaps cancel every other obligation you have conferred on me, but there is one you can never cancel; nor will I be provoked by your abuse to lift my hand against the father of Sophia."

At these words the squire grew still more outrageous than before, so that the parson begged Jones to retire, saying, "You behold, sir, how he waxeth wroth at your abode here; therefore, let me pray you not to tarry any longer. His anger is too much kindled for you to commune with him at present. You had better therefore conclude your visit and refer what matters you have to urge in your behalf to some other opportunity."

Jones accepted this advice with thanks, and immediately departed. The squire now regained the liberty of his hands, and so much temper as to express some satisfaction in the restraint which had been laid upon him, declaring that he should certainly have beat his brains out, and adding, "It would have vexed one confoundedly to have been hanged for such a rascal."

The parson now began to triumph in the success of his peace-making endeavours, and proceeded to read a lecture against anger, which might perhaps rather have tended to raise than to quiet that passion in some hasty minds. This lecture he enriched with many valuable quotations from the ancients, particularly from Seneca, who hath, indeed, so well handled this passion that none but a very angry man can read him without great pleasure and profit. The doctor concluded his harangue with the famous story of Alexander and Clitus, but as I find that entered in my commonplace under title "Drunkenness," I shall not insert in here.

The squire took no notice of this story, nor perhaps of anything he said; for he interrupted him before he had finished by calling for a tankard of beer, observing (which is perhaps as true as any observation on this fever of the mind) that anger makes a man dry.

No sooner had the squire swallowed a large draught than he renewed the discourse on Jones, and declared a resolution of going the next morning early to acquaint Mr. Allworthy. His friend would have dissuaded him from this, from the mere motive of good nature, but his dissuasion had no other effect than to produce a large volley of oaths and curses, which greatly shocked the pious ears of Supple; but he did not dare to remonstrate against a privilege which the squire claimed as a free-born Englishman. To say truth, the parson submitted to please his palate at the squire's table at the expense of suffering this violence now and then to his ears. He contented himself with thinking he did not promote this evil practice, and that the squire would not swear an oath the less if he never entered within his gates. However, though he was not guilty of ill manners by rebuking a gentleman in his own house, he paid him off obliquely in the pulpit; which had not, indeed, the good effect of working a reformation in the squire himself; yet it so far operated on his conscience that he put the laws very severely in execution against others, and the magistrate was the only person in the parish who could swear with impunity.

10

IN WHICH MR. WESTERN VISITS ALLWORTHY

Mr. Allworthy was now retired from breakfast with his nephew, well satisfied with the report of the young gentleman's successful visit to Sophia (for he greatly desired the match, more on account of the young lady's character than of her riches), when Mr. Western broke abruptly in upon them and without any ceremony began as follows:

"There, you have done a fine piece of work, truly. You have brought up your bastard to a fine purpose; not that I believe you have had any hand in it neither, that is, as a man may say, designedly; but there is a fine kettle of fish made o't up at our house." "What can be the matter, Mr. Western?" said Allworthy. "Oh, matter enow of all conscience; my daughter hath fallen in love with your bastard, that's all; but I won't ge her a ha'penny, not the twentieth part of a brass farthing. I always thought what would come o' breeding up a bastard like a gentleman and letting un come about to volk's houses. It's well vor un I could not get at un; I'd a-licked un; I'd a-spoiled his caterwauling, I'd a-taught the son of a whore to meddle with meat for his master. He shan't ever have a morsel of meat of mine, or a farthing to buy it; if she will ha' un, one smock shall be her portion. I'll sooner ge my esteate to the zinking fund, that it may be sent to Hanover to corrupt our nation with." "I am heartily sorry," cries Allworthy. "Pox o' your sorrow," says Western. "It will do me abundance of good when I have lost my only child, my poor Sophy, that was the joy of my heart and all the hope and comfort of my age; but I am resolved I will turn her out o' doors; she shall beg and starve and rot in the streets. Not one ha'penny, not a ha'penny, shall she ever hae o' mine. The son of a bitch was always good at finding a hare sitting; an' be rotted to'n, I little thought what puss he was looking after, but it shall be the worst he ever vound in his life. She shall be no better than carrion; the skin o'er is all he shall ha', and zu you may tell un." "I am in amazement," cries Allworthy, "at what you tell me, after what passed between my nephew and the young lady no longer ago than yesterday." "Yes, sir," answered Western, "it was after what passed between your nephew and she that the whole matter came out. Mr. Blifil there was no sooner gone than the son of a whore came lurching about the house. Little did I think when I used to love him for a sportsman that he was all the while a-poaching after my daughter." "Why, truly," says Allworthy, "I could wish you had not given him so many opportunities with her, and you will do me the justice to acknowledge that I have always been averse to his staying so much at your house, though I own I had no suspicion of this kind." "Why, zounds!" cries Western. "Who could have thought it? What the devil had she to do wi'n? He did not come there a-courting to her; he came there a-hunting with me." "But was it possible," says Allworthy, "that you should never discern any symptoms of love between them when you have seen them so often together?" "Never in my life, as I hope to be saved," cries Western. "I never so much as seed him kiss her in all my life, and so far from courting her, he used rather to be more silent when she was in company than at any other time; and as for the girl, she was always less civil to'n than to any young man that came to the house. As to that matter, I am not more easy to be deceived than another; I would not have you think I am, neighbour." Allworthy could scarce refrain laughter at this, but he resolved to do a violence to himself; for he perfectly well knew mankind and had too much good breeding and good nature to offend the squire in his present circumstances.

He then asked Western what he would have him do upon this occasion. To which the other answered that he would have him keep the rascal away from his house, and that he would go and lock up the wench; for he was resolved to make her marry Mr. Blifil in spite of her teeth. He then shook Blifil by the hand and swore he would have no other son-in-law. Presently after which he took his leave, saying his house was in such disorder that it was necessary for him to make haste home to take care his daughter did not give him the slip; and as for Jones, he swore if he caught him at his house, he would qualify him to run for the geldings' plate.

When Allworthy and Blifil were again left together, a long silence ensued between them; all which interval the young gentleman filled up with sighs, which proceeded partly from disappointment but more from hatred, for the success of Jones was much more grievous to him than the loss of Sophia.

At length his uncle asked him what he was determined to do, and he answered in the following words: "Alas, sir, can it be a question what step a lover will take when reason and passion point different ways? I am afraid it is too certain he will in that dilemma always follow the latter. Reason dictates to me to quit all thoughts of a woman who places her affections on another; my passion bids me hope she may in time change her inclinations in my favour. Here, however, I conceive an objection may be raised, which if it could not fully be answered, would totally deter me from any further pursuit. I mean the injustice of endeavouring to supplant another in a heart of which he seems already in possession; but the determined resolution of Mr. Western shows that in this case I shall by so doing promote the happiness of every party; not only that of the parent, who will thus be preserved from the highest degree of misery, but of both the others, who must be undone by this match. The lady, I am sure, will be undone in every sense; for besides the loss of most part of her own fortune, she will be married not only to a beggar, but the little fortune which her father cannot withhold from her will be squandered on that wench with whom I know he yet converses. Nay, that is a trifle; for I know him to be one of the worst men in the world; for had my dear uncle known what I have hitherto endeavoured to conceal, he must have long since abandoned so profligate a wretch." "How," said Allworthy, "hath he done anything worse than I already know? Tell me, I beseech you." "No," replied Blifil, "it is now past, and perhaps he may have repented of it." "I command you on your duty," said Allworthy, "to tell me what you mean." "You know, sir," says Blifil, "I never disobeyed you; but I am sorry I mentioned it, since it may now look like revenge, whereas I thank heaven no such motive ever entered my heart; and if you oblige me to discover it, I must be his petitioner to you for your forgiveness." "I will have no conditions," answered Allworthy; "I think I have shown tenderness enough towards him, and more perhaps than you ought to thank me for." "More, indeed, I fear than he deserved," cries Blifil, "for in the very day of your utmost danger, when myself and all the family were in tears, he filled the house with riot and debauchery. He drank and sung and roared, and when I gave him a gentle hint of the indecency of his actions, he fell into a violent passion, swore many oaths, called me rascal, and struck me." "How!" cries Allworthy. "Did he dare to strike you?" "I am sure," cries Blifil, "I have forgiven him that long ago. I wish I could so easily forget his ingratitude to the best of benefactors, and yet, even that I hope you will forgive him, since he must have certainly been possessed with the devil; for that very evening, as Mr. Thwackum and myself were taking the air in the fields and exulting in the good symptoms which then first began to discover themselves, we unluckily saw him engaged with a wench in a manner not fit to be mentioned. Mr. Thwackum, with more boldness than prudence, advanced to rebuke him, when (I am sorry to say it) he fell upon the worthy man and beat him so outrageously that I wish he may have yet recovered the bruises. Nor was I without my share of the effects of his malice while I endeavoured to protect my tutor; but that I have long forgiven; nay, I prevailed with Mr. Thwackum to forgive him too, and not to inform you of a secret which I feared might be fatal to him. And now, sir, since I have unadvisedly dropped a hint of this matter, and your commands have obliged me to discover the whole, let me intercede with you for him." "Oh, child," said Allworthy, "I know not whether I should blame or applaud your goodness in concealing such villainy a moment. But where is Mr. Thwackum? Not that I want any confirmation of what you say, but I will examine all the evidence of this matter to justify to the world the example I am resolved to make of such a monster."

Thwackum was now sent for, and presently appeared. He corroborated every circumstance which the other had deposed; nay, he produced the record upon his breast, where the handwriting of Mr. Jones remained very legible in black and blue. He concluded with declaring to Mr. Allworthy that he should have long since informed him of this matter had not Mr. Blifil by the most earnest interpositions prevented him. "He is," says he, "an excellent youth; though such forgiveness of enemies is carrying the matter too far."

In reality, Blifil had taken some pains to prevail with the parson, and to prevent the discovery at that time; for which he had many reasons. He knew that the minds of men are apt to be softened and relaxed from their usual severity by sickness. Besides, he imagined that if the story was told when the fact was so so recent, and the physician about the house, who might have unravelled the real truth, he should never be able to give it the malicious turn which he intended. Again, he resolved to hoard up this business till the indiscretion of Jones should afford some additional complaints; for he thought the joint weight of many facts falling upon him together would be the most likely to crush him; and he watched therefore some such opportunity as that which Fortune had now kindly presented him. Lastly, by prevailing with Thwackum to conceal the matter for a time, he knew he should confirm an opinion of his friendship to Jones, which he had greatly laboured to establish in Mr. Allworthy.

11

A SHORT CHAPTER; BUT WHICH CONTAINS SUFFICIENT MATTER
TO AFFECT THE GOOD-NATURED READER

It was Mr. Allworthy's custom never to punish any one, not even to turn away a servant, in a passion. He resolved, therefore, to delay passing sentence on Jones till the afternoon.

The poor young man attended at dinner as usual, but his heart was too much loaded to suffer him to eat. His grief too was a good deal aggravated by the unkind looks of Mr. Allworthy, whence he concluded that Western had discovered the whole affair between him and Sophia; but as to Mr. Blifil's story, he had not the least apprehension; for of much the greater part he was entirely innocent, and for the residue, as he had forgiven and forgotten it himself, so he suspected no remembrance on the other side. When dinner was over and the servants departed, Mr. Allworthy began to harangue.

He set forth in a long speech the many iniquities of which Jones had been guilty, particularly those which this day had brought to light, and concluded by telling him that unless he could clear himself of the charge, he was resolved to banish him from his sight forever.

Many disadvantages attended poor Jones in making his defence; nay, indeed, he hardly knew his accusation; for as Mr. Allworthy, in recounting the drunkenness, &c., while he lay ill, out of modesty sunk everything that related particularly to himself, which indeed principally constituted the crime, Jones could not deny the charge. His heart was, besides, almost broken already; and his spirits were so sunk that he could say nothing for himself, but acknowledge the whole and, like a criminal in despair, threw himself upon mercy, concluding that though he must own himself guilty of many follies and inadvertencies, he hoped he had done nothing to deserve what would be to him the greatest punishment in the world.

Allworthy answered that he had forgiven him too often already, in compassion to his youth and in hopes of his amendment; that he now found he was an abandoned reprobate, and such as it would be criminal in any one to support and encourage. "Nay," said Mr. Allworthy to him, "your audacious attempt to steal away the young lady calls upon me to justify my own character in punishing you. The world, who have already censured the regard I have shown for you, may think with some colour at least of justice that I connive at so base and barbarous an action—an action of which you must have known my abhorrence, and which, had you had any concern for my ease and honour as well as for my friendship, you would never have thought of undertaking. Fie upon it, young man! Indeed, there is scarce any punishment equal to your crimes, and I can scarce think myself justifiable in what I am now going to bestow on you. However, as I have educated you like a child of my own, I will not turn you naked into the world. When you open this paper, therefore, you will find something which may enable you with industry to get an honest livelihood, but if you employ it to worse purposes, I shall not think myself obliged to supply you farther, being resolved from this day forward to converse no more with you on any account. I cannot avoid saying there is no part of your conduct which I resent more than your ill treatment of that good young man," meaning

Blifil, "who hath behaved with so much tenderness and honour towards you."

These last words were a dose almost too bitter to be swallowed. A flood of tears now gushed from the eyes of Jones, and every faculty of speech and motion seemed to have deserted him. It was some time before he was able to obey Allworthy's peremptory commands of departing, which he at length did, having first kissed his hands with a passion difficult to be affected and as difficult to be described.

The reader must be very weak if, when he considers the light in which Jones then appeared to Mr. Allworthy, he should blame the rigour of his sentence. And yet all the neighbourhood, either from this weakness or from some worse motive, condemned this justice and severity as the highest cruelty. Nay, the very persons who had before censured the good man for the kindness and tenderness shown to a bastard (his own, according to the general opinion) now cried out as loudly against turning his own child out of doors. The women especially were unanimous in taking the part of Jones, and raised more stories on the occasion than I have room in this chapter to set down.

One thing must not be omitted: that in their censures on this occasion none ever mentioned the sum contained in the paper which Allworthy gave Jones, which was no less than five hundred pounds, but all agreed that he was sent away penniless, and some said naked, from the house of his inhuman father.

12

CONTAINING LOVE-LETTERS, &C.

Jones was commanded to leave the house immediately and told that his clothes and everything else should be sent to him whithersoever he should order them.

He accordingly set out and walked above a mile, not regarding, and indeed scarce knowing, whither he went. At length, a little brook obstructing his passage, he threw himself down by the side of it, nor could he help muttering with some little indignation, "Sure my father will not deny me this place to rest in?"

Here he presently fell into the most violent agonies, tearing his hair from his head and using most other actions which generally accompany fits of madness, rage, and despair.

When he had in this manner vented the first emotions of passion, he began to come a little to himself. His grief now took another turn and discharged itself in a gentler way till he became, at last, cool enough to reason with his passion and to consider what steps were proper to be taken in his deplorable condition.

And now the great doubt was how to act with regard to Sophia. The thoughts of leaving her almost rent his heart asunder, but the consideration of reducing her to ruin and beggary still racked him, if possible, more; and if the violent desire of possessing her person could have induced him to listen one moment to this alternative, still he was by no means certain of her resolution to indulge his wishes at so high an expense. The resentment of Mr. Allworthy and the injury he must do to his quiet argued strongly against this latter; and lastly, the apparent impossibility of his success, even if he would sacrifice all these considerations to it, came to his assistance; and thus honour at last, backed with despair, with gratitude to his benefactor, and with real love to his mistress, got the better of burning desire, and he resolved rather to quit Sophia than to pursue her to her ruin.

It is difficult for any who have not felt it to conceive the glowing warmth which filled his breast on the first contemplation of this victory over his passion. Pride flattered him so agreeably that his mind perhaps enjoyed perfect happiness, but this was only momentary; Sophia soon returned to his imagination and allayed the joy of his triumph with no less bitter pangs than a good-natured general must feel when he surveys the bleeding heaps at the price of whose blood he hath purchased his laurels; for thousands of tender ideas lay murdered before our conqueror.

Being resolved, however, to pursue the paths of this Giant Honour, as the gigantic poet Lee calls it, he determined to write a farewell letter to Sophia, and accordingly proceeded to a house not far off where, being furnished with proper materials, he wrote as follows:

MADAM,

When you reflect on the situation in which I write, I am sure your good nature will pardon any inconsistency or absurdity which my letter contains; for everything here flows from a heart so full that no language can express its dictates.

I have resolved, madam, to obey your commands in flying forever from your dear, your lovely, sight. Cruel indeed those commands are; but it is a cruelty which proceeds from Fortune, not from my Sophia. Fortune hath made it necessary, necessary to your preservation, to forget there ever was such a wretch as I am.

Believe me, I would not hint all my sufferings to you if I imagined they could possibly escape your ears. I know the goodness and tenderness of your heart, and would avoid giving you any of those pains which you always feel for the miserable. Oh, let nothing which you shall hear of my hard fortune cause a moment's concern; for after the loss of you everything is to me a trifle.

Oh, my Sophia! It is hard to leave you; it is harder still to desire you to forget me; yet the sincerest love obliges me to both. Pardon my conceiving that any remembrance of me can give you disquiet; but if I am so gloriously wretched, sacrifice me every way to your relief. Think I never loved you; or think truly how little I deserve you; and learn to scorn me for a presumption which can never be too severely punished. I am unable to say more. May guardian angels protect you forever.

He was now searching his pockets for his wax, but found none, nor indeed anything else therein; for in truth he had in his frantic disposition tossed everything from him, and amongst the rest his pocket-book which he had received from Mr. Allworthy, which he had never opened, and which now first occurred to his memory.

The house supplied him with a wafer for his present purpose, with which, having sealed his letter, he returned hastily towards the brook-side in order to search for the things which he had there lost. In his way he met his old friend Black George, who heartily condoled with him on his misfortune; for this had already reached his ears and, indeed, those of all the neighbourhood.

Jones acquainted the gamekeeper with his loss, and he as readily went back with him to the brook, where they searched every tuft of grass in the meadow, as well where Jones had not been as where he had been; but all to no purpose, for they found nothing; for indeed, though the things were then in the meadow, they omitted to search the only place where they were deposited: to wit, in the pockets of the said George; for he had just before found them and being luckily apprised of their value, had very carefully put them up for his own use.

The gamekeeper, having exerted as much diligence in quest of the lost goods as if he had hoped to find them, desired Mr. Jones to recollect if he had been in no other place. "For sure," said he, "if you had lost them here so lately, the things must have been here still, for this is a very unlikely place for any one to pass by"; and indeed, it was by great accident that he himself had passed through that field in order to lay wires for hares, with which he was to supply a poulterer at Bath the next morning.

Jones now gave over all hopes of recovering his loss and almost all thoughts concerning it, and, turning to Black George, asked him earnestly if he would do him the greatest favour in the world.

George answered with some hesitation, "Sir, you know you may command me whatever is in my power, and I heartily wish it was in my power to do you any service." In fact, the question staggered him; for he had by selling game amassed a pretty good sum of money in Mr. Western's service, and was afraid that Jones wanted to borrow some small matter of him; but he was presently relieved from his anxiety by being desired to convey a letter to Sophia, which with great pleasure he promised to do. And indeed I believe there are few favours which he would not have gladly conferred on Mr. Jones; for he bore as much gratitude towards him as he could, and was as honest as men who love money better than any other thing in the universe generally are.

Mrs. Honour was agreed by both to be the proper means by which this letter should pass to Sophia. Then they separated; the gamekeeper returned home to Mr. Western's, and Jones walked to an ale-house at half a mile's distance to wait for his messenger's return.

George no sooner came home to his master's house than he met with Mrs. Honour, to whom, having first sounded her with a few previous questions, he delivered the letter for her mistress, and received at the same time another from her for Mr. Jones, which Honour told him she had carried all that day in her bosom and began to despair of finding any means of delivering it.

The gamekeeper returned hastily and joyfully to Jones, who, having received Sophia's letter from him, instantly withdrew and, eagerly breaking it open, read as follows:

Sir,

It is impossible to express what I have felt since I saw you. Your submitting on my account to such cruel insults from my father lays me under an obligation I shall ever own. As you know his temper, I beg you will for my sake avoid him. I wish I had any comfort to send you; but believe this: that nothing but the last violence shall ever give my hand or heart where you would be sorry to see them bestowed.

Jones read this letter a hundred times over and kissed it a hundred times as often. His passion now brought all tender desires back into his mind. He repented that he had writ to Sophia in the manner we have seen above; but he repented more that he had made use of the interval of his messenger's absence to write and dispatch a letter to Mr. Allworthy, in which he had faithfully promised and bound himself to quit all thoughts of his love. However, when his cool reflections returned, he plainly perceived that his case was neither mended nor altered by Sophia's billet, unless to give him some little glimpse of hope from her constancy of some favourable accident hereafter. He therefore resumed his resolution and, taking leave of Black George, set forward to a town about five miles distant, whither he had desired Mr. Allworthy, unless he pleased to revoke his sentence, to send his things after him.

13

THE BEHAVIOUR OF SOPHIA ON THE PRESENT OCCASION, WHICH NONE OF HER SEX WILL BLAME WHO ARE CAPABLE OF BEHAVING IN THE SAME MANNER. AND THE DISCUSSION OF A KNOTTY POINT IN THE COURT OF CONSCIENCE

Sophia had passed the last twenty-four hours in no very desirable manner. During a large part of them she had been entertained by her aunt with lectures of prudence, recommending to her the example of the polite world, where love (so the good lady said) is at present entirely laughed at, and where women consider matrimony as men do offices of public trust, only as the means of making their fortunes and of advancing themselves in the world. In commenting on which text Mrs. Western had displayed her eloquence during several hours.

These sagacious lectures, though little suited either to the taste or inclination of Sophia, were, however, less irksome to her than her own thoughts, that formed the entertainment of the night, during which she never once closed her eyes.

But though she could neither sleep nor rest in her bed, yet, having no avocation from it, she was found there by her father at his return from Allworthy's, which was not till past ten o'clock in the morning. He went directly up to her apartment, opened the door, and seeing she was not up, cried, "Oh, you are safe, then! and I am resolved to keep you so." He then locked the door and delivered the key to Honour, having first given her the strictest charge, with great promises of rewards for her fidelity and most dreadful menaces of punishment in case she should betray her trust.

Honour's orders were not to suffer her mistress to come out of her room without the authority of the squire himself, and to admit none to her but him and her aunt, but she was herself to attend her with whatever Sophia pleased, except only pen, ink, and paper, of which she was forbidden the use.

The squire ordered his daughter to dress herself and attend him at dinner, which she obeyed; and, having sat the usual time, was again conducted to her prison.

In the evening the gaoler, Honour, brought her the letter which she received from the gamekeeper. Sophia read it very attentively twice or thrice over, and then threw herself upon the bed and burst into a flood of tears. Mrs. Honour expressed great astonishment at this behaviour in her mistress, nor could she forbear very eagerly begging to know the cause of this passion. Sophia made her no answer for some time, and then, starting suddenly up, caught her maid by the hand and cried, "O, Honour! I am undone." "Marry forbid," cries Honour. "I wish the letter had been burnt before I had brought it to your la'ship. I'm sure I thought it would have comforted your la'ship, or I would have seen it at the devil before I would have touched it." "Honour," says Sophia, "you are a good girl, and it is vain to attempt concealing longer my weakness from you: I have thrown away my heart on a man who hath forsaken me." "And is Mr. Jones," answered the maid, "such a perfidy man?" "He hath taken his leave of me," says Sophia, "forever in that letter. Nay, he hath desired me to forget him. Could he have desired that if he had loved me? Could he have borne such a thought? Could he have written such a word?" "No certainly, ma'am," cries Honour; "and to be sure, if the best man in England was to desire me to forget him, I'd take him at his word. Marry come up! I am sure your la'ship hath done him too much honour ever to think on him—a young lady who may take her choice of all the young men in the county. And to be sure, if I may be so presumptuous as to offer my poor opinion, there is young Mr. Blifil, who besides that he is come of honest parents and will be one of the greatest squires all hereabouts, he is to be sure, in my poor opinion, a more handsomer and a more politer man by half; and besides he is a young gentleman of a sober character, and who may defy any of the neighbours to say black is his eye: he follows no dirty trollops, nor can any bastards be laid at his door. Forget him indeed! I thank heaven I myself am not so much at my last prayers as to suffer any man to bid me forget him twice. If the best he that wears a head was for to go for to offer to say such an affronting word to me, I would never give him my company afterwards if there was another young man in the kingdom. And as I was a-saying, to be sure, there is young Mr. Blifil." "Name not his detested name," cries Sophia. "Nay, ma'am," says Honour, "if your la'ship doth not like him, there be more jolly handsome young men that would court your la'ship if they had but the least encouragement. I don't believe there is arrow young gentleman in this county or in the next to it that if your la'ship was but to look as if you had a mind to him would not come about to make his offers directly." "What a wretch dost thou imagine me," cries Sophia, "by affronting my ears with such stuff! I detest all mankind." "Nay, to be sure, ma'am," answered Honour, "your la'ship hath had enough to give you a surfeit of them. To be used ill by such a poor beggarly bastardly fellow." "Hold your blasphemous tongue," cries Sophia; "how dare you mention his name with disrespect before me! He use me ill? No, his poor bleeding heart suffered more when he writ the cruel words than mine from reading them. Oh, he is all heroic virtue and angelic goodness! I am ashamed of the weakness of my own passion for blaming what I ought to admire. Oh, Honour, it is my good only which he consults! To my interest he sacrifices both himself and me. The apprehension of ruining me hath driven him to despair." "I am very glad," says Honour, "to hear your la'ship takes that into your consideration; for to be sure, it must be nothing less than ruin to give your mind to one that is turned out of doors and is not worth a farthing in the world." "Turned out of doors!" cries Sophia hastily. "How! What dost thou mean?" "Why, to be sure ma'am, my master no sooner told Squire Allworthy about Mr. Jones having offered to make love to your ladyship than the squire stripped him stark naked and turned him out of doors." "Ha!" says Sophia. "Have I been the cursed, wretched cause of his destruction? Turned naked out of doors! Here, Honour, take all the money I have; take the rings from my fingers. Here, my watch, carry him all. Go, find him immediately." "For heaven's sake, ma'am," answered Mrs. Honour, "do but consider; if my master should miss any of these things, I should be made to answer for them. Therefore let me beg your ladyship not to part with your watch and jewels. Besides, the money, I think, is enough of all conscience; and as for that, my master can never know anything of the matter." "Here, then," cries Sophia, "take every farthing I am worth; find him out immediately and give it him. Go, go, lose not a moment."

Mrs. Honour departed according to orders and, finding Black George below stairs, delivered him the purse, which contained sixteen guineas, being indeed the whole stock of Sophia; for though her father was very liberal to her, she was much too generous herself to be rich.

Black George, having received the purse, set forward towards the ale-house, but in the way a thought occurred to him, whether he should not detain this money likewise. His conscience, however, immediately started at this suggestion, and began to upbraid him with ingratitude to his benefactor. To this his avarice answered that his conscience should have considered the matter before, when he deprived poor Jones of his £500; that, having quietly acquiesced in what was of so much greater importance, it was absurd, if not downright hypocrisy, to affect any qualms at this trifle. In return to which, conscience like a good lawyer attempted to distinguish between an absolute breach of trust, as here where the goods were delivered, and a bare concealment of what was found, as in the former case. Avarice presently treated this with ridicule, called it a distinction without a difference, and absolutely insisted that when once all pretensions of honour and virtue were given up in any one instance, that there was no precedent for resorting to them upon a second occasion. In short, poor conscience had certainly been defeated in the argument had not fear stepped in to her assistance and very strenuously urged that the real distinction between the two actions did not lie in the different degrees of honour, but of safety; for that the secreting the £500 was a matter of very little hazard, whereas the detaining the sixteen guineas was liable to the utmost danger of discovery.

By this friendly aid of fear, conscience obtained a complete victory in the mind of Black George and, after making him a few compliments on his honesty, forced him to deliver the money to Jones.

14

A SHORT CHAPTER, CONTAINING A SHORT DIALOGUE BETWEEN
SQUIRE WESTERN AND HIS SISTER

Mrs. Western had been engaged abroad all that day. The squire met her at her return home, and when she inquired after Sophia, he acquainted her that he had secured her safe enough. "She is locked up in chamber," cries he, "and Honour keeps the key." As his looks were full of prodigious wisdom and sagacity when he gave his sister this information, it is probable he expected much applause from her for what he had done; but how was he disappointed when with a most disdainful aspect she cried, "Sure, brother, you are the weakest of all men. Why will you not confide in me for the management of my niece? Why will you interpose? You have now undone all that I have been spending my breath in order to bring about. While I have been endeavouring to fill her mind with maxims of prudence, you have been provoking her to reject them. English women, brother, I thank heaven, are no slaves. We are not to be locked up like the Spanish and Italian wives. We have as good a right to liberty as yourselves. We are to be convinced by reason and persuasion only, and not governed by force. I have seen the world, brother, and know what arguments to make use of; and, if your folly had not prevented me, should have prevailed with her to form her conduct by those rules of prudence and discretion which I formerly taught her." "To be sure," said the squire, "I am always in the wrong." "Brother," answered the lady, "you are not in the wrong unless when you meddle with matters beyond your knowledge. You must agree that I have seen most of the world, and happy had it been for my niece if she had not been taken from under my care. It is by living at home with you that she hath learned romantic notions of love and nonsense." "You don't imagine, I hope," cries the squire, "that I have taught her any such things." "Your ignorance, brother," returned she, "as the great Milton says, almost subdues my patience." * "D—n Milton," answered the squire, "if he had the impudence to say so to my face, I'd lend him a douse, thof he was never so great a man. Patience! An' you come to that, sister, I have more occasion of patience to be used like an overgrown schoolboy as I am by you. Do you think no one hath any understanding unless he hath been about at court? Pox! The world is come to a fine pass, indeed, if we are all fools except a parcel of Roundheads and Hanover rats. Pox! I hope the times are a-coming that we shall make fools of them, and every man shall enjoy his own. That's all, sister, and every man shall enjoy his own. I hope to zee it, sister, before the Hanover rats have eat all our corn and left us nothing but turneps to feed upon." "I protest, brother," cries she, "you are now got beyond my understanding. Your jargon of turneps and Hanover rats is to me perfectly unintelligible." "I believe," cries he, "you don't care to hear o' em, but the country interest may succeed one day or other for all that." "I wish," answered the lady, "you would think a little of your daughter's interest; for believe me, she is in greater danger than the nation." "Just now," said he, "you chid me for thinking on her, and would ha' her left to you." "And if you will promise to interpose no more," answered she, "I will out of my regard for my niece undertake the charge." "Well, do then," said the squire, "for you know I always agreed that women are the properest to manage women."

Mrs. Western then departed, muttering something with an air of disdain concerning women and the management of the nation. She immediately repaired to Sophia's apartment, who was now after a day's confinement released again from her captivity.

* The reader may perhaps subdue his own patience if he searches for this in Milton.

BOOK VII

1

A COMPARISON BETWEEN THE WORLD AND THE STAGE

The world hath been often compared to the theatre, and many grave writers as well as the poets have considered human life as a great drama, resembling in almost every particular those scenical representations which Thespis is first reported to have invented and which have been since received with so much approbation and delight in all polite countries.

This thought hath been carried so far, and become so general, that some words proper to the theatre, and which were at first metaphorically applied to the world, are now indiscriminately and literally spoken of both: thus, stage and scene are by common use grown as familiar to us when we speak of life in general as when we confine ourselves to dramatic performances; and when we mention transactions behind the curtain, St. James's is more likely to occur to our thoughts than Drury Lane.

It may seem easy enough to account for all this by reflecting that the theatrical stage is nothing more than a representation, or, as Aristotle calls it, an imitation, of what really exists; and hence, perhaps, we might fairly pay a very high compliment to those who by their writings or actions have been so capable of imitating life as to have their pictures in a manner confounded with or mistaken for the originals.

But in reality we are not so fond of paying compliments to these people, whom we use as children frequently do the instruments of their amusements, and have much more pleasure in hissing and buffeting them than in admiring their excellence. There are many other reasons which have induced us to see this analogy between the world and the stage.

Some have considered the larger part of mankind in the light of actors, as personating characters no more their own, and to which, in fact, they have no better title than the player hath to be in earnest thought the king or emperor whom he represents. Thus, the hypocrite may be said to be a player, and indeed the Greeks called them both by one and the same name.

The brevity of life hath likewise given occasion to this comparison. So the immortal Shakespeare:

> ——Life's . . . a poor player,
> That struts and frets his hour upon the stage,
> And then is heard no more.

For which hackneyed quotation I will make the reader amends by a very noble one, which few, I believe, have read. It is taken from a poem called the *Deity,* published about nine years ago and long since buried in oblivion—a proof that good books no more than good men do always survive the bad.

> From Thee* all human actions take their springs,
> The rise of empires, and the fall of kings!
> See the *vast theatre of time* displayed,
> While o'er the scene succeeding heroes tread!
> With pomp the shining images succeed,
> What leaders triumph, and what monarchs bleed!
> Perform the parts Thy providence assigned,
> Their pride, their passions to Thy ends inclined:
> Awhile they glitter in the face of day,
> Then at Thy nod the phantoms pass away;
> No traces left of all the busy scene,
> But that remembrance says—*the things have been!*

In all these, however, and in every other similitude of life to the theatre, the resemblance hath been always taken from the stage only. None, as I remember, have at all considered the audience at this great drama.

But as Nature often exhibits some of her best performances to a very full house, so will the behaviour of her spectators no less admit the above-mentioned comparison than that of

* The Deity.

274

her actors. In this vast theatre of time are seated the friend and the critic; here are claps and shouts, hisses and groans; in short, everything which was ever seen or heard at the Theatre Royal.

Let us examine this in one example: for instance, in the behaviour of the great audience on that scene which Nature was pleased to exhibit in the twelfth chapter of the preceding book, where she introduced Black George running away with the £500 from his friend and benefactor.

Those who sat in the world's upper gallery treated that incident, I am well convinced, with their usual vociferation, and every term of scurrilous reproach was most probably vented on that occasion.

If we had descended to the next order of spectators, we should have found an equal degree of abhorrence, though less of noise and scurrility; yet here the good women gave Black George to the Devil, and many of them expected every minute that the cloven-footed gentleman would fetch his own.

The pit as usual was no doubt divided. Those who delight in heroic virtue and perfect character objected to the producing such instances of villainy without punishing them very severely for the sake of example. Some of the author's friends cried, "Lookee, gentlemen, the man is a villain; but it is nature for all that." And all the young critics of the age, the clerks, apprentices, &c., called it low and fell a-groaning.

As for the boxes, they behaved with their accustomed politeness. Most of them were attending to something else. Some of those few who regarded the scene at all declared he was a bad kind of man; while others refused to give their opinion till they had heard that of the best judges.

Now we, who are admitted behind the scenes of this great theatre of Nature (and no author ought to write anything besides dictionaries and spelling-books who hath not this privilege), can censure the action without conceiving any absolute detestation of the person, whom, perhaps, Nature may not have designed to act an ill part in all her dramas; for in this instance life most exactly resembles the stage, since it is often the same person who represents the villain and the hero, and he who engages your admiration to-day will probably attract your contempt to-morrow. As Garrick, whom I regard in tragedy to be the greatest genius the world hath ever produced, sometimes condescends to play the fool, so did Scipio the Great and Laelius the Wise, according to Horace, many years ago; nay, Cicero reports them to have been "incredibly childish." These, it is true, played the fool, like my friend Garrick, in jest only; but several eminent characters have in numberless instances of their lives played the fool egregiously in earnest, so far as to render it a matter of some doubt whether their wisdom or folly was predominant, or whether they were better entitled to the applause or censure, the admiration or contempt, the love or hatred, of mankind.

Those persons, indeed, who have passed any time behind the scenes of this great theatre, and are thoroughly acquainted not only with the several disguises which are there put on but also with the fantastic and capricious behaviour of the Passions, who are the managers and directors of this theatre (for as to Reason the patentee, he is known to be a very idle fellow and seldom to exert himself), may most probably have learned to construe the famous *Nil admirari* of Horace, or in the English phrase, "to stare at nothing."

A single bad act no more constitutes a villain in life than a single bad part on the stage. The passions, like the managers of a playhouse, often force men upon parts without consulting their judgement, and sometimes without any regard to their talents. Thus the man as well as the player may condemn what he himself acts; nay, it is common to see vice sit as awkwardly on some men as the character of Iago would on the honest face of Mr. William Mills.

Upon the whole, then, the man of candour and of true understanding is never hasty to condemn. He can censure an imperfection or even a vice without rage against the guilty party. In a word, they are the same folly, the same childishness, the same ill breeding, and the same ill nature which raise all the clamours and uproars both in life and on the stage. The worst of men generally have the words *rogue* and *villain* most in their mouths, as the lowest of all wretches are the aptest to cry out *low* in the pit.

2

CONTAINING A CONVERSATION WHICH MR. JONES HAD WITH
HIMSELF

Jones received his effects from Mr. Allworthy's early in the
morning with the following answer to his letter:

SIR,

I am commanded by my uncle to acquaint you that as
he did not proceed to those measures he hath taken with
you without the greatest deliberation and after the fullest
evidence of your unworthiness, so will it be always out of
your power to cause the least alteration in his resolution.
He expresses great surprise at your presumption in saying
you have resigned all pretensions to a young lady to whom
it is impossible you should ever have had any, her birth
and fortune having made her so infinitely your superior.
Lastly, I am commanded to tell you that the only instance
of your compliance with my uncle's inclinations which
he requires is your immediately quitting this country. I
cannot conclude this without offering you my advice as a
Christian that you would seriously think of amending your
life; that you may be assisted with grace so to do will be
always the prayer of

Your humble servant,
W. BLIFIL.

Many contending passions were raised in our hero's
mind by this letter, but the tender prevailed at last over
the indignant and irascible, and a flood of tears came sea-
sonably to his assistance and possibly prevented his misfortunes from either turning his head or bursting his heart.

He grew, however, soon ashamed of indulging this remedy
and, starting up, he cried, "Well, then, I will give Mr. Allworthy the only instance he requires of my obedience. I will
go this moment. But whither? Why, let Fortune direct;
since there is no other who thinks it of any consequence
what becomes of this wretched person, it shall be a matter of
equal indifference to myself. Shall I alone regard what no
other—ha, have I not reason to think there is another?
One whose value is above that of the whole world! I may, I
must imagine my Sophia is not indifferent to what becomes
of me. Shall I then leave this only friend—and such a

friend? Shall I not stay with her? Where? How can I stay with her? Have I any hopes of even seeing her, though she was as desirous as myself, without exposing her to the wrath of her father? And to what purpose? Can I think of soliciting such a creature to consent to her own ruin? Shall I indulge any passion of mine at such a price? Shall I lurk about this country like a thief, with such intentions? No, I disdain, I detest the thought. Farewell, Sophia; far 'l most lovely, most beloved—" Here passion stopped his mouth and found a vent at his eyes.

And now, having taken a resolution to leave the country, he began to debate with himself whither he should go. The world, as Milton phrases it, lay all before him; and Jones no more than Adam had any man to whom he might resort for comfort or assistance. All his acquaintance were the acquaintance of Mr. Allworthy, and he had no reason to expect any countenance from them, as that gentleman had withdrawn his favour from him. Men of great and good characters should indeed be very cautious how they discard their dependents, for the consequence to the unhappy sufferer is being discarded by all others.

What course of life to pursue or to what business to apply himself was a second consideration; and here the prospect was all a melancholy void. Every profession and every trade required length of time, and what was worse, money; for matters are so constituted that "nothing out of nothing" is not a truer maxim in physics than in politics, and every man who is greatly destitute of money is on that account entirely excluded from all means of acquiring it.

At last the Ocean, that hospitable friend to the wretched, opened her capacious arms to receive him; and he instantly resolved to accept her kind invitation. To express myself less figuratively, he determined to go to sea.

This thought indeed no sooner suggested itself than he eagerly embraced it, and having presently hired horses, he set out for Bristol to put it in execution.

But before we attend him on his expedition, we shall resort a while to Mr. Western's and see what farther happened to the charming Sophia.

CONTAINING SEVERAL DIALOGUES

The morning in which Mr. Jones departed, Mrs. Western summoned Sophia into her apartment; and having first acquainted her that she had obtained her liberty of her father, she proceeded to read her a long lecture on the subject of matrimony, which she treated not as a romantic scheme of happiness arising from love, as it hath been described by the poets, nor did she mention any of those purposes for which we are taught by divines to regard it as instituted by sacred authority; she considered it rather as a fund in which prudent women deposit their fortunes to the best advantage in order to receive a larger interest for them than they could have elsewhere.

When Mrs. Western had finished, Sophia answered that she was very incapable of arguing with a lady of her aunt's superior knowledge and experience, especially on a subject which she had so very little considered, as this of matrimony.

"Argue with me, child!" replied the older. "I do not indeed expect it. I should have seen the world to very little purpose truly if I am to argue with one of your years. I have taken this trouble in order to instruct you. The ancient philosophers, such as Socrates, Alcibiades, and others, did not use to argue with their scholars. You are to consider me, child, as Socrates, not asking your opinion but only informing you of mine." From which last words the reader may possibly imagine that this lady had read no more of the philosophy of Socrates than she had of that of Alcibiades; and indeed we cannot resolve his curiosity as to this point.

"Madam," cries Sophia, "I have never presumed to controvert any opinion of yours; and this subject, as I have said, I have never yet thought of and perhaps never may."

"Indeed, Sophy," replied the aunt, "this dissimulation with me is very foolish. The French shall as soon persuade me that they take foreign towns in defence only of their own country as you can impose on me to believe you have never yet thought seriously of matrimony. How can you, child, affect to deny that you have considered of contracting an alliance when you so well know I am acquainted with the party with whom you desire to contract it. An alliance as unnatural and contrary to your interest as a separate league with the French would be to the interest of the Dutch! But however, if you have not hitherto considered of this matter, I promise you it is now high time; for my brother is resolved immediately to conclude the treaty with Mr. Blifil, and indeed I am a sort of guarantee in the affair, and have promised your concurrence."

"Indeed, madam," cries Sophia, "this is the only instance in which I must disobey both yourself and my father; for this is a match which requires very little consideration in me to refuse."

"If I was not as great a philosopher as Socrates himself," returned Mrs. Western, "you would overcome my patience. What objection can you have to the young gentleman?"

"A very solid objection, in my opinion," says Sophia. "I hate him."

"Will you never learn a proper use of words?" answered the aunt. "Indeed, child, you should consult Bailey's *Dictionary*. It is impossible you should hate a man from whom you have received no injury. By hatred, therefore, you mean no more than dislike, which is no sufficient objection against your marrying of him. I have known many couples who have entirely disliked each other lead very comfortable, genteel lives. Believe me, child, I know these things better than you. You will allow me, I think, to have seen the world, in which I have not an acquaintance who would not rather be thought to dislike her husband than to like him. The contrary is such out-of-fashion romantic nonsense that the very imagination of it is shocking."

"Indeed, madam," replied Sophia, "I shall never marry a man I dislike. If I promise my father never to consent to any marriage contrary to his inclinations, I think I may hope he will never force me into that state contrary to my own."

"Inclinations!" cries the aunt with some warmth. "Inclinations! I am astonished at your assurance. A young woman of your age, and unmarried, to talk of inclinations! But whatever your inclinations may be my brother is resolved; nay, since you talk of inclinations, I shall advise him to hasten the treaty. Inclinations!"

Sophia then flung herself upon her knees, and tears began to trickle from her shining eyes. She entreated her aunt to have mercy upon her, and not to resent so cruelly her unwillingness to make herself miserable; often urging that she alone was concerned and that her happiness only was at stake.

As a bailiff, when well authorized by his writ, having possessed himself of the person of some unhappy debtor, views all his tears without concern; in vain the wretched captive attempts to raise compassion; in vain the tender wife, bereft of her companion, the little prattling boy or frighted girl, are mentioned as inducements to reluctance. The noble bumtrap, blind and deaf to every circumstance of distress, greatly rises above all the motives to humanity and into the hands of the gaoler resolves to deliver his miserable prey.

Not less blind to the tears or less deaf to every entreaty of Sophia was the politic aunt, nor less determined was she to deliver over the trembling maid into the arms of the gaoler, Blifil. She answered with great impetuosity, "So far, madam, from your being concerned alone, your concern is the least, or surely the least important. It is the honour of your family which is concerned in this alliance; you are only the instrument. Do you conceive, mistress, that in an intermarriage between kingdoms, as when a daughter of France is married into Spain, the princess herself is alone considered in the match? No, it is a match between two kingdoms rather than between two persons. The same happens in great families such as ours. The alliance between the families is the principal matter. You ought to have a greater regard for the honour of your family than for your own person; and if the example of a princess cannot inspire you with these noble thoughts, you cannot surely complain at being used no worse than all princesses are used."

"I hope, madam," cries Sophia with a little elevation of voice, "I shall never do anything to dishonour my family; but as for Mr. Blifil, whatever may be the consequence I am resolved against him, and no force shall prevail in his favour."

Western, who had been within hearing during the greater part of the preceding dialogue, had now exhausted all his patience; he therefore entered the room in a violent passion, crying, "D—n me, then, if shatunt ha' un, d—n me if shatunt, that's all—that's all. D—n me if shatunt."

Mrs. Western had collected a sufficient quantity of wrath for the use of Sophia, but she now transferred it all to the squire. "Brother," said she, "it is astonishing that you will interfere in a matter which you had totally left to my negotiation. Regard to my family hath made me take upon myself to be the mediating power in order to rectify those mistakes in policy which you have committed in your daughter's education. For, brother, it is you, it is your preposterous conduct, which hath eradicated all the seeds that I had formerly sown in her tender mind. It is you yourself who have taught her disobedience." "Blood!" cries the squire, foaming at the mouth. "You are enough to conquer the patience of the Devil! Have I ever taught my daughter disobedience? Here she stands; speak honestly, girl, did ever I bid you be disobedient to me? Have not I done everything to humour and to gratify you, and to make you obedient to me? And very obedient to me she was when a little child, before you took her hand and spoiled her by filling her head with a pack of court notions. Why—why—why—did not I overhear you telling her she must behave like a princess? You have made a Whig of the girl; and how should her father or anybody else expect any obedience from her?" "Brother," answered Mrs. Western with an air of great disdain, "I cannot express the contempt I have for your politics of all kinds; but I will appeal likewise to the young lady herself whether I have ever taught her any principles of disobedience. On the contrary, niece, have I not endeavoured to inspire you with a true idea of the several relations in which a human creature stands in society? Have I not taken infinite pains to show you that the law of Nature hath enjoined a duty on children to their parents? Have I not told you what Plato says on that subject? A subject on which you was so notoriously ignorant when you came first under my care that I verily believe you did not know the relation between a daughter and a father." "'Tis a lie," answered Western. "The girl is no such fool as to live to eleven years old without knowing that she was her father's relation." "Oh, more than Gothic ignorance," answered the lady. "And as for your manners, brother, I must tell you they deserve a cane." "Why, then, you may gi' it me if you think you are able," cries the squire; "nay, I suppose your niece there will be ready enough to help you." "Brother," said Mrs. Western, "though I despise you beyond expression, yet I shall endure your insolence no longer; so I desire my coach may be got ready immediately, for I am resolved to leave your house this very morning." "And a good riddance too," answered he; "I can bear your insolence no longer, an' you come to that. Blood! It is almost enough of itself to make my daughter undervalue my sense when she hears you telling me every minute you despise me."

"It is impossible, it is impossible," cries the aunt; "no one can undervalue such a boor." "Boar," answered the squire, "I am no boar; no, nor ass; no, nor rat neither, madam. Remember that—I am no rat. I am a true Englishman, and not of your Hanover breed, that have eat up the nation." "Thou art one of those wise men," cries she, "whose nonsensical principles have undone the nation by weakening the hands of our government at home and by discouraging our friends and encouraging our enemies abroad." "Ho, are you come back to your politics!" cries the squire. "As for those, I despise them as much as I do a f—t." Which last word he accompanied and graced with the very action which, of all others, was the most proper to it. And whether it was this word or the contempt expressed for her politics which most affected Mrs. Western I will not determine, but she flew into the most violent rage, uttered phrases improper to be here related, and instantly burst out of the house. Nor did her brother or her niece think proper either to stop or to follow her; for the one was so much possessed by concern and the other by anger that they were rendered almost motionless.

The squire, however, sent after his sister the same holla which attends the departure of a hare when she is first started before the hounds. He was indeed a great master of this kind of vociferation, and had a holla proper for most occasions in life.

Women who, like Mrs. Western, know the world, and have applied themselves to philosophy and politics, would have immediately availed themselves of the present disposition of Mr. Western's mind by throwing in a few artful compliments to his understanding at the expense of his absent adversary; but poor Sophia was all simplicity. By which word we do not intend to insinuate to the reader that she was silly, which is generally understood as a synonymous term with simple; for she was indeed a most sensible girl, and her understanding was of the first rate, but she wanted all that useful art which females convert to so many good purposes in life and which, as it rather arises from the heart than from the head, is often the property of the silliest of women.

A PICTURE OF A COUNTRY GENTLEWOMAN TAKEN FROM LIFE

Mr. Western, having finished his holla and taken a little breath, began to lament in very pathetic terms the unfortunate condition of men, who are, says he, "always whipped in by the humours of some d—ned b— or other. I think I was hard run enough by your mother for one man; but after giving her a dodge, here's another b— follows me upon the foil; but curse my jacket if I will be run down in this manner by any o' um."

Sophia never had a single dispute with her father till this unlucky affair of Blifil on any account, except in defence of her mother, whom she had loved most tenderly, though she lost her in the eleventh year of her age. The squire, to whom that poor woman had been a faithful upper servant all the time of their marriage, had returned that behaviour by making what the world calls a good husband. He very seldom swore at her (perhaps not above once a week) and never beat her; she had not the least occasion for jealousy, and was perfect mistress of her time; for she was never interrupted by her husband, who was engaged all the morning in his field exercises and all the evening with bottle companions. She scarce, indeed, ever saw him but at meals, where she had the pleasure of carving those dishes which she had before attended at the dressing. From these meals she retired about five minutes after the other servants, having only stayed to drink "the king over the water." Such were, it seems, Mr. Western's orders; for it was a maxim with him that women should come in with the first dish and go out after the first glass. Obedience to these orders was perhaps no difficult task, for the conversation (if it may be called so) was seldom such as could entertain a lady. It consisted chiefly of hallooing, singing, relations of sporting adventures, b—d—y, and abuse of women and of the government.

These, however, were the only seasons when Mr. Western saw his wife; for when he repaired to her bed he was generally so drunk that he could not see, and in the sporting season he always rose from her before it was light. Thus was she perfect mistress of her time, and had, besides, a coach and four usually at her command, though unhappily, indeed, the badness of the neighbourhood and of the roads made this of little use; for none who had set much value on their necks would have passed through the one, or who had set any value on their hours would have visited the other. Now, to deal honestly with the reader, she did not make all the return expected to so much indulgence; for she had been married against her will by a fond father, the match having been rather advantageous on her side; for the squire's estate was upwards of £3000 a year and her fortune no more than a bare £8000. Hence, perhaps, she had contracted a little gloominess of temper, for she was rather a good servant than a good wife; nor had she always the gratitude to return the extraordinary degree of roaring mirth with which the squire received her even with a good-humoured smile. She would, moreover, sometimes interfere with matters which did not concern her, as the violent drinking of her husband, which in the gentlest terms she would take some of the few opportunities he gave her of remonstrating against. And once in her life she very earnestly entreated him to carry her for two months to London, which he peremptorily denied; nay, was angry with his wife for the request ever after, being well assured that all the husbands in London are cuckolds.

For this last, and many other good reasons, Western at length heartily hated his wife; and as he never concealed this hatred before her death, so he never forgot it afterwards, but when anything in the least soured him, as a bad scenting day, or a distemper among his hounds, or any other such misfortune, he constantly vented his spleen by invectives against the deceased, saying, "If my wife was alive now, she would be glad of this."

These invectives he was especially desirous of throwing forth before Sophia; for as he loved her more than he did any other, so he was really jealous that she had loved her mother better than him. And this jealousy Sophia seldom failed of heightening on these occasions; for he was not contented with violating her ears with the abuse of her mother, but endeavoured to force an explicit approbation of all this abuse, with which desire he never could prevail upon her by any promise or threats to comply.

Hence some of my readers will, perhaps, wonder that the squire had not hated Sophia as much as he had hated her mother; but I must inform them that hatred is not the effect of love, even through the medium of jealousy. It is, indeed, very possible for jealous persons to kill the objects of their jealousy, but not to hate them. Which sentiment being a pretty hard morsel, and bearing something of the air of a paradox, we shall leave the reader to chew the cud upon it to the end of the chapter.

5

THE GENEROUS BEHAVIOUR OF SOPHIA TOWARDS HER AUNT

Sophia kept silence during the foregoing speech of her father, nor did she once answer otherwise than with a sigh; but as he understood none of the language, or, as he called it, lingo, of the eyes, so he was not satisfied without some further approbation of his sentiments, which he now demanded in the usual way of his daughter, telling her he expected she was ready to take the part of everybody against him, as she had always done that of the b— her mother. Sophia remaining still silent, he cried out, "What, art dumb? Why dost unt speak. Was not thy mother a d—d b— to me? Answer me that. What, I suppose, you despise your father too, and don't think him good enough to speak to?"

"For heaven's sake, sir," answered Sophia, "do not give so cruel a turn to my silence. I am sure I would sooner die than be guilty of any disrespect towards you, but how can I venture to speak when every word must either offend my dear papa or convict me of the blackest ingratitude, as well as impiety, to the memory of the best of mothers? For such, I am certain, my mamma was always to me."

"And your aunt, I suppose, is the best of sisters too!" replied the squire. "Will you be so kind as to allow that she is a b—? I may fairly insist upon that, I think."

"Indeed, sir," says Sophia, "I have great obligations to my aunt. She hath been a second mother to me."

"And a second wife to me too," returned Western. "So you will take her part too! You won't confess that she hath acted the part of the vilest sister in the world?"

"Upon my word, sir," cries Sophia, "I must belie my heart wickedly if I did. I know my aunt and you differ very much in your ways of thinking, but I have heard her a thousand times express the greatest affection for you; and I am convinced, so far from her being the worst sister in the world, there are very few who love a brother better."

"The English of all which is," answered the squire, "that I am in the wrong. Ay, certainly. Ay, to be sure, the woman is in the right, and the man in the wrong always."

"Pardon me, sir," cries Sophia. "I do not say so."

"What don't you say?" answered the father. "You have the impudence to say she's in the right; doth it not follow, then, of course that I'm in the wrong? And perhaps I am in the wrong to suffer such a Presbyterian Hanoverian b— to come into my house. She may 'dite me of a plot for anything I know, and give my estate to the government."

"So far, sir, from injuring you or your estate," says Sophia, "if my aunt had died yesterday, I am convinced she would have left you her whole fortune."

Whether Sophia intended it or no I shall not presume to assert, but certain it is, these last words penetrated very deep into the ears of her father and produced a much more sensible effect than all she had said before. He received the sound with much the same action as a man receives a bullet in his head. He started, staggered, and turned pale. After which he remained silent above a minute, and then began in the following hesitating manner: "Yesterday! She would have left me her esteate yesterday! Would she? Why yesterday of all the days in the year? I suppose if she dies to-morrow, she will leave it to somebody else, and perhaps out of the vamily." "My aunt, sir," cries Sophia, "hath very violent passions, and I can't answer what she may do under their influence."

"You can't!" returned the father. "And, pray, who hath been the occasion of putting her into those violent passions? Nay, who hath actually put her into them? Was not you and she hard at it before I came into the room? Besides, was not all our quarrel about you? I have not quarrelled with sister these many years but upon your account, and now you would throw the whole blame upon me, as thof I should be the occasion of her leaving her esteate out o' the family. I could have expected no better, indeed; this is like the return you make to all the rest of my fondness."

"I beseech you, then," cries Sophia, "upon my knees I beseech you, if I have been the unhappy occasion of this difference, that you will endeavour to make it up with my aunt and not suffer her to leave your house in this violent rage of anger; she is a very good-natured woman, and a few civil words will satisfy her. Let me entreat you, sir."

"So, I must go and ask pardon for your fault, must I?"

answered Western. "You have lost the hare, and I must draw every way to find her again? Indeed if I was certain—" Here he stopped, and Sophia, throwing in more entreaties, at length prevailed upon him; and after venting two or three bitter sarcastical expressions against his daughter, he departed as fast as he could to recover his sister before her equipage could be gotten ready.

Sophia then retired to her chamber of mourning, where she indulged herself (if the phrase may be allowed me) in all the luxury of tender grief. She read over the letter which she had received from Jones more than once; her muff too was used on this occasion, and she bathed both these, as well as herself, with her tears. In this situation the friendly Mrs. Honour exerted her utmost abilities to comfort her afflicted mistress. She ran over the names of many young gentlemen and, having greatly commended their parts and persons, assured Sophia that she might take her choice of any. These methods must have certainly been used with some success in disorders of the like kind, or so skilful a practitioner as Mrs. Honour would never have ventured to apply them; nay, I have heard that the College of Chambermaids hold them to be as sovereign remedies as any in the female dispensary; but whether it was that Sophia's disease differed inwardly from those cases with which it agreed in external symptoms I will not assert, but in fact the good waiting-woman did more harm than good, and at last so incensed her mistress (which was no easy matter) that with an angry voice she dismissed her from her presence.

6

CONTAINING GREAT VARIETY OF MATTER

The squire overtook his sister just as she was stepping into the coach, and partly by force and partly by solicitations prevailed upon her to order her horses back into their quarters. He succeeded in this attempt without much difficulty; for the lady was, as we have already hinted, of a most placable disposition and greatly loved her brother, though she despised his parts, or rather his little knowledge of the world.

Poor Sophia, who had first set on foot this reconciliation, was now made the sacrifice to it. They both concurred in their censures on her conduct, jointly declared war against her, and directly proceeded to council how to carry it on in the most vigorous manner. For this purpose Mrs. Western proposed not only an immediate conclusion of the treaty with Allworthy but as immediately to carry it into execution, saying that there was no other way to succeed with her niece but by violent methods, which she was convinced Sophia had not sufficient resolution to resist. "By violent," says she, "I mean, rather, hasty measures; for as to confinement or absolute force, no such things must or can be attempted. Our plan must be concerted for a surprise and not for a storm."

These matters were resolved on when Mr. Blifil came to pay a visit to his mistress. The squire no sooner heard of his arrival than he stepped aside, by his sister's advice, to give his daughter orders for the proper reception of her lover, which he did with the most bitter execrations and denunciations of judgement on her refusal.

The impetuosity of the squire bore down all before him, and Sophia, as her aunt very wisely foresaw, was not able to resist him. She agreed, therefore, to see Blifil, though she had scarce spirits or strength sufficient to utter her assent. Indeed, to give a peremptory denial to a father whom she so tenderly loved was no easy task. Had this circumstance been out of the case, much less resolution than what she was really mistress of would, perhaps, have served her; but it is no unusual thing to ascribe those actions entirely to fear which are in a great measure produced by love.

In pursuance, therefore, of her father's peremptory command, Sophia now admitted Mr. Blifil's visit. Scenes like this when painted at large afford, as we have observed, very little entertainment to the reader. Here, therefore, we shall strictly adhere to a rule of Horace, by which writers are directed to pass over all those matters which they despair of placing in a shining light—a rule, we conceive, of excellent use as well to the historian as to the poet; and which if followed must at least have this good effect: that many a great evil (for so all great books are called) would thus be reduced to a small one.

It is possible the great art used by Blifil at this interview would have prevailed on Sophia to have made another man in his circumstances her confidant, and to have revealed the whole secret of her heart to him, but she had contracted so ill an opinion of this young gentleman that she was resolved to place no confidence in him; for simplicity when set on its guard is often a match for cunning. Her behaviour to him, therefore, was entirely forced, and indeed such as is generally prescribed to virgins upon the second formal visit from one who is appointed for their husband.

But though Blifil declared himself perfectly satisfied with his reception to the squire, yet that gentleman, who in company with his sister had overheard all, was not so well pleased. He resolved, in pursuance of the advice of the sage lady, to push matters as forward as possible, and addressing himself to his intended son-in-law in the hunting phrase, he cried after a loud holla, "Follow her, boy, follow her; run in, run in, that's it, honeys. Dead, dead, dead. Never be bashful, nor stand shall I, shall I? Allworthy and I can finish all matters between us this afternoon, and let us ha' the wedding to-morrow."

Blifil, having conveyed the utmost satisfaction into his countenance, answered, "As there is nothing, sir, in this world which I so eagerly desire as an alliance with your family, except my union with the most amiable and deserving Sophia, you may easily imagine how impatient I must be to see myself in possession of my two highest wishes. If I have not therefore importuned you on this head, you will impute it only to my fear of offending the lady by endeavouring to hurry on so blessed an event faster than a strict compliance with all the rules of decency and decorum will permit. But if by your interest, sir, she might be induced to dispense with any formalities——"

"Formalities! With a pox!" answered the squire. "Pooh, all stuff and nonsense! I tell thee she shall ha' thee to-morrow; you will know the world better hereafter when you come to my age. Women never gi' their consent, man, if they can help it; 'tis not the fashion. If I had stayed for her mother's consent, I might have been a bachelor to this day. To her, to her, co to her; that's it, you jolly dog. I tell thee shat ha' her to-morrow morning."

Blifil suffered himself to be overpowered by the forcible rhetoric of the squire, and it being agreed that Western should close with Allworthy that very afternoon, the lover departed home, having first earnestly begged that no violence might be offered to the lady by his haste, in the same manner as a popish inquisitor begs the lay power to do no violence to the heretic delivered over to it, and against whom the Church hath passed sentence.

And to say the truth, Blifil had passed sentence against Sophia; for however pleased he had declared himself to Western with his reception, he was by no means satisfied, unless it was that he was convinced of the hatred and scorn of his mistress; and this had produced no less reciprocal hatred and scorn in him. It may, perhaps, be asked, Why, then, did he not put an immediate end to all further courtship? I answer, for that very reason, as well as for several others equally good, which we shall now proceed to open to the reader.

Though Mr. Blifil was not of the complexion of Jones, nor ready to eat every woman he saw, yet he was far from being destitute of that appetite which is said to be the common property of all animals. With this he had likewise that distinguishing taste which serves to direct men in their choice of the objects, or food, of their several appetites; and this taught him to consider Sophia as a most delicious morsel, indeed to regard her with the same desires which an ortolan inspires into the soul of an epicure. Now, the agonies which affected the mind of Sophia rather augmented than impaired her beauty; for her tears added brightness to her eyes, and her breasts rose higher with her sighs. Indeed no one hath seen beauty in its highest lustre who hath never seen it in distress. Blifil therefore looked on this human ortolan with greater desire than when he had viewed her last, nor was his desire at all lessened by the aversion which he discovered in her to himself. On the contrary, this served rather to heighten the pleasure he proposed in rifling her charms, as it added triumph to lust; nay, he had some further views, from obtaining the absolute possession of her person, which we detest too much even to mention; and revenge itself was not without its share in the gratifications which he promised himself. The rivalling poor Jones and supplanting him in her affections added another spur to his pursuit and promised another additional rapture to his enjoyment.

Besides all these views, which to some scrupulous persons may seem to savour too much of malevolence, he had one prospect which few readers will regard with any great abhorrence. And this was the estate of Mr. Western, which was all to be settled on his daughter and her issue; for so extravagant was the affection of that fond parent that provided his child would but consent to be miserable with the husband he chose, he cared not at what price he purchased him.

For these reasons Mr. Blifil was so desirous of the match that he intended to deceive Sophia by pretending to love her, and to deceive her father and his own uncle by pretending he was beloved by her. In doing this, he availed himself of the piety of Thwackum, who held that if the end proposed was religious (as surely matrimony is), it mattered not how wicked were the means. As to other occasions, he used to apply the philosophy of Square, which taught that the end was immaterial so that the means were fair and consistent with moral rectitude. To say truth, there were few occurrences in life on which he could not draw advantage from the precepts of one or other of those great masters.

Little deceit was indeed necessary to be practised on Mr. Western, who thought the inclinations of his daughter of as little consequence as Blifil himself conceived them to be; but as the sentiments of Mr. Allworthy were of a very different kind, so it was absolutely necessary to impose on him. In this, however, Blifil was so well assisted by Western that he succeeded without difficulty; for as Mr. Allworthy had been assured by her father that Sophia had a proper affection for Blifil and that all which he had suspected concerning Jones was entirely false, Blifil had nothing more to do than to confirm these assertions; which he did with such equivocations that he preserved a salvo for his conscience, and had the satisfaction of conveying a lie to his uncle without the guilt of telling one. When he was examined touching the inclinations of Sophia by Allworthy, who said he would on no account be accessary to forcing a young lady into a marriage contrary to her own will, he answered that the real sentiments of young ladies were very difficult to be understood, that her behaviour to him was full as forward as he wished it, and that if he could believe her father, she had all the affection for him which any lover could desire. "As for Jones," said he, "whom I am loath to call villain, though his behaviour to you, sir, sufficiently justifies the appellation, his own vanity or perhaps some wicked views might make him boast of a falsehood; for if there had been any reality in Miss Western's love to him, the greatness of her fortune would never have suffered him to desert her, as you are well informed he hath. Lastly, sir, I promise you I would not myself for any consideration, no, not for the whole world, consent to marry this young lady if I was not persuaded she had all the passion for me which I desire she should have."

This excellent method of conveying a falsehood with the heart only without making the tongue guilty of an untruth, by the means of equivocation and imposture, hath quieted the conscience of many a notable deceiver; and yet when we consider that it is Omniscience on which these endeavour to impose, it may possibly seem capable only of affording a very superficial comfort, and that this artful and refined distinction between communicating a lie and telling one is hardly worth the pains it costs them.

Allworthy was pretty well satisfied with what Mr. Western and Mr. Blifil told him, and the treaty was now, at the end of two days, concluded. Nothing then remained previous to the office of the priest but the office of the lawyers, which threatened to take up so much time that Western offered to bind himself by all manner of covenants rather than to defer the happiness of the young couple. Indeed he was so very earnest and pressing that an indifferent person might have concluded he was more a principal in this match than he really was; but this eagerness was natural to him on all occasions, and he conducted every scheme he under-took in such a manner, as if the success of that alone was sufficient to constitute the whole happiness of his life.

The joint importunities of both father and son-in-law would probably have prevailed on Mr. Allworthy, who brooked but ill any delay of giving happiness to others, had not Sophia herself prevented it, and taken measures to put a final end to the whole treaty and to rob both Church and Law of those taxes which these wise bodies have thought proper to receive from the propagation of the human species in a lawful manner. Of which in the next chapter.

7

A STRANGE RESOLUTION OF SOPHIA, AND A MORE STRANGE
STRATAGEM OF MRS. HONOUR

Though Mrs. Honour was principally attached to her own interest, she was not without some little attachment to Sophia. To say truth, it was very difficult for any one to know that young lady without loving her. She no sooner, therefore, heard a piece of news, which she imagined to be of great importance to her mistress, than, quite forgetting the anger which she had conceived two days before at her unpleasant dismission from Sophia's presence, she ran hastily to inform her of this news.

The beginning of her discourse was as abrupt as her entrance into the room: "Oh, dear ma'am," says she, "what doth your la'ship think? To be sure, I am frightened out of my wits; and yet I thought it my duty to tell your la'ship, though perhaps it may make you angry, for we servants don't always know what will make our ladies angry; for to be sure, everything is always laid to the charge of a servant. When our ladies are out of humour, to be sure, we must be scolded; and to be sure, I should not wonder if your la'ship should be out of humour; nay, it must surprise you certainly, ay, and shock you too." "Good Honour, let me know it without any longer preface!" says Sophia. "There are few things, I promise you, which will surprise, and fewer which will shock me." "Dear ma'am," answered Honour, "to be sure, I overheard my master talking to Parson Supple about getting a licence this very afternoon, and to be sure, I heard him say your la'ship should be married to-morrow morning." Sophia turned pale at these words and repeated eagerly, "To-morrow morning!" "Yes, madam," replied the trusty waiting-woman, "I will take my oath I heard my master say so." "Honour," says Sophia, "you have both surprised and shocked me to such a degree that I have scarce any breath or spirits left. What is to be done in my dreadful situation?" "I wish I was able to advise your la'ship," says she. "Do advise me," cries Sophia; "pray, dear Honour, advise me. Think what you would attempt if it was your own case." "Indeed, ma'am," cries Honour, "I wish your la'ship and I could change situations; that is, I mean, without hurting your la'ship, for to be sure I don't wish you so bad as to be a servant; but because that if so be it was my case, I should find no manner of difficulty in it; for in my poor opinion young Squire Blifil is a charming, sweet, handsome man." "Don't mention such stuff," cries Sophia. "Such stuff," repeated Honour, "why, there—well, to be sure, what's one man's meat is another man's poison, and the same is altogether as true of women." "Honour," says Sophia, "rather than submit to be the wife of that contemptible wretch, I would plunge a dagger into my heart." "Oh, lud, ma'am," answered the other, "I am sure you frighten me out of my wits now. Let me beseech your la'ship not to suffer such wicked thoughts to come into your head. Oh, lud, to be sure I tremble every inch of me. Dear ma'am, consider—that to be denied Christian burial, and to have your corpse buried in the highway, and a stake drove through you, as Farmer Halfpenny was served at Ox Cross; and to be sure, his ghost hath walked there ever since; for several people have seen him. To be sure it can be nothing but the Devil which can put such wicked thoughts into the head of anybody; for certainly it is less wicked to hurt all the world than one's own dear self, and so I have heard said by more parsons than one. If your la'ship hath such a violent aversion and hates the young gentleman so very bad that you can't bear to think of going into bed to him; for to be sure, there may be such antipathies in nature, and one had lieverer touch a toad than the flesh of some people——"

Sophia had been too much wrapped in contemplation to pay any great attention to the foregoing excellent discourse of her maid; interrupting her, therefore, without making any answer to it, she said, "Honour, I am come to a resolution. I am determined to leave my father's house this very night, and if you have the friendship for me which you have often professed, you will keep me company." "That I will, ma'am, to the world's end," answered Honour; "but I beg your la'ship to consider the consequence before you undertake any rash action. Where can your la'ship possibly go?" "There is," replied Sophia, "a lady of quality in London, a relation of mine, who spent several months with my aunt in the country, during all which time she treated me with great kindness and expressed so much pleasure in my company that she earnestly desired my aunt to suffer me to go with her to London. As she is a woman of very great note, I shall easily find her out, and I make no doubt of being very well and kindly received by her." "I would not have your la'ship too confident of that," cries Honour; "for the first lady I lived with used to invite people very earnestly to her house, but if she heard afterwards they were coming, she used to get out of the way. Besides, though this lady would be very glad to see your la'ship, as to be sure anybody would be glad to see your la'ship, yet when she hears your la'ship is run away from my master——" "You are mistaken, Honour," says Sophia; "she looks upon the authority of a father in a much lower light than I do; for she pressed me violently to go to London with her, and when I refused to go without my father's consent she laughed me to scorn, called me silly country girl, and said I should make a pure loving wife since I could be so dutiful a daughter. So I have no doubt but she will both receive me and protect me too till my father, finding me out of his power, can be brought to some reason."

"Well, but ma'am," answered Honour, "how doth your la'ship think of making your escape? Where will you get any horses or conveyance? For as for your own horse, as all the servants know a little how matters stand between my master and your la'ship, Robin will be hanged before he will suffer it to go out of the stable without my master's express orders." "I intend to escape," said Sophia, "by walking out of the doors when they are open. I thank heaven my legs are very able to carry me. They have supported me many a long evening after a fiddle with no very agreeable partner, and surely they will assist me in running from so detestable a partner for life." "Oh, heavens, ma'am, doth your la'ship know what you are saying?" cries Honour. "Would you think of walking about the country by night and alone?" "Not alone," answered the lady; "you have promised to bear me company." "Yes, to be sure," cries Honour, "I will follow your la'ship through the world; but your la'ship had almost as good be alone, for I shall not be able to defend you if any robbers or other villains should meet with you. Nay, I should be in as horrible a fright as your la'ship; for to be certain, they would ravish us both. Besides, ma'am, consider how cold the nights are now; we shall be frozen to death." "A good brisk pace," answered Sophia, "will preserve us from the cold, and if you cannot defend me from a villain, Honour, I will defend you, for I will take a pistol with me. There are two always charged in the hall." "Dear ma'am, you frighten me more and more," cries Honour; "sure your la'ship would not venture to fire it off! I had rather run any chance than your la'ship should do that." "Why so?" says Sophia, smiling. "Would not you, Honour, fire a pistol at any one who should attack your virtue?" "To be sure, ma'am," cries Honour, "one's virtue is a dear thing, especially to us poor servants, for it is our livelihood, as a body may say; yet I mortally hate firearms, for so many accidents happen by them." "Well, well," says Sophia, "I believe I may ensure your virtue at a very cheap rate without carrying any arms with us; for I intend to take horses at the very first town we come to, and we shall hardly be attacked in our way thither. Look'ee, Honour, I am resolved to go, and if you will attend me, I promise you I will reward you to the very utmost of my power."

This last argument had a stronger effect on Honour than all the preceding. And since she saw her mistress so determined, she desisted from any further dissuasions. They then entered into a debate on ways and means of executing their project. Here a very stubborn difficulty occurred, and this was the removal of their effects, which was much more easily got over by the mistress than by the maid; for when a lady hath once taken a resolution to run to a lover or to run from him, all obstacles are considered as trifles. But Honour was inspired by no such motive; she had no raptures to expect nor any terrors to shun; and besides the real value of her clothes, in which consisted great part of her fortune, she had a capricious fondness for several gowns and other things, either because they became her or because they were given her by such a particular person; because she had bought them lately or because she had had them long; or for some other reasons equally good, so that she could not endure the thought of leaving the poor things behind her exposed to the mercy of Western, who, she doubted not, would make them suffer martyrdom in his rage.

The ingenious Mrs. Honour, having applied all her oratory to dissuade her mistress from her purpose, when she found her positively determined, at last started the following expedient to remove her clothes: viz., to get herself turned out of doors that very evening. Sophia highly approved this method, but doubted how it might be brought about. "Oh, ma'am," cries Honour, "your la'ship may trust that to me; we servants very well know how to obtain this favour of our masters and mistresses, though sometimes indeed where they owe us more wages than they can readily pay, they will put up with all our affronts and will hardly take any warning we can give them; but the squire is none of those, and since your la'ship is resolved upon setting out to-night, I warrant I get discharged this afternoon." It was then resolved that she should pack up some linen and a nightgown for Sophia with her own things; and as for all her other clothes, the young lady abandoned them with no more remorse than the sailor feels when he throws over the goods of others in order to save his own life.

CONTAINING SCENES OF ALTERCATION OF NO VERY UNCOMMON KIND

Mrs. Honour had scarce sooner parted from her young lady than something (for I would not, like the old woman in Quevedo, injure the Devil by any false accusation, and possibly he might have no hand in it), but something, I say, suggested to her that by sacrificing Sophia and all her secrets to Mr. Western she might probably make her fortune. Many considerations urged this discovery. The fair prospect of a handsome reward for so great and acceptable a service to the squire tempted her avarice; and again, the danger of the enterprise she had undertaken, the uncertainty of its success, night, cold, robbers, ravishers—all alarmed her fears. So forcibly did all these operate upon her that she was almost determined to go directly to the squire and to lay open the whole affair. She was, however, too upright a judge to decree on one side before she had heard the other. And here, first, a journey to London appeared very strongly in support of Sophia. She eagerly longed to see a place in which she fancied charms short only of those which a raptured saint imagines in heaven. In the next place, as she knew Sophia to have much more generosity than her master, so her fidelity promised her a greater reward than she could gain by treachery. She then cross-examined all the articles which had raised her fears on the other side and found, on fairly sifting the matter, that there was very little in them. And now both scales being reduced to a pretty even balance, her love to her mistress being thrown into the scale of her integrity made that rather preponderate, when a circumstance struck upon her imagination which might have had a dangerous effect had its whole weight been fairly put into the other scale. This was the length of time which must intervene before Sophia would be able to fulfil her promises; for though she was entitled to her mother's fortune at the death of her father, and to the sum of £3000 left her by an uncle when she came of age, yet these were distant days, and many accidents might prevent the intended generosity of the young lady, whereas the rewards she might expect from Mr. Western were immediate. But while she was pursuing this thought the good genius of Sophia, or that which presided over the integrity of Mrs. Honour, or perhaps mere chance, sent an accident in her way which at once preserved her fidelity and even facilitated the intended business.

Mrs. Western's maid claimed great superiority over Mrs. Honour on several accounts. First, her birth was higher, for her great-grandmother by the mother's side was a cousin not far removed to an Irish peer. Secondly, her wages were greater. And lastly, she had been at London and had of consequence seen more of the world. She had always behaved, therefore, to Mrs. Honour with that reserve and had always exacted of her those marks of distinction which every order of females preserves and requires in conversation with those of an inferior order. Now, as Honour did not at all times agree with this doctrine, but would frequently break in upon the respect which the other demanded, Mrs. Western's maid was not at all pleased with her company; indeed, she earnestly longed to return home to the house of her mistress, where she domineered at will over all the other servants. She had been greatly, therefore, disappointed in the morning when Mrs. Western had changed her mind on the very point of departure, and had been in what is vulgarly called a glouting humour ever since.

In this humour, which was none of the sweetest, she came into the room where Honour was debating with herself in the manner we have above related. Honour no sooner saw her than she addressed her in the following obliging phrase: "Soh, madam, I find we are to have the pleasure of your company longer, which I was afraid the quarrel between my master and your lady would have robbed us of." "I don't know, madam," answered the other, "who you mean by we and us. I assure you I do not look on any of the servants in this house to be proper company for me. I am company, I hope, for their betters every day in the week. I do not speak on your account, Mrs. Honour; for you are a civilized young woman, and when you have seen a little more of the world, I should not be ashamed to walk with you in St. James's Park." "Hoity-toity!" cries Honour. "Madam is in her airs, I protest. Mrs. Honour, forsooth! Sure, madam, you might call me by my sir-name; for though my lady calls me Honour, I have a sir-name as well as other folks. Ashamed to walk with me, quotha! Marry, as good as yourself, I hope." "Since you make such a return to my civility," said the other, "I must acquaint you, Mrs. Honour, that you are not so good as me. In the country one is indeed obliged to take up with all kind of trumpery, but in town I visit none but the women of women of quality. Indeed, Mrs. Honour, there is some difference, I hope, between you and me." "I hope so, too," answered Honour; "there is some difference in our ages, and—I think in our persons." Upon speaking which last words, she strutted by Mrs. Western's maid with the most provoking air of contempt, turning up her nose, tossing her head, and violently brushing the hoop of her competitor with her own. The other lady put on one of her most malicious sneers and said, "Creature! You are below my anger, and it is beneath me to give ill words to such an audacious saucy trollop; but, hussy, I must tell you your breeding shows the meanness of your birth as well as of your education, and both very properly qualify you to be the mean serving-woman of a country-girl." "Don't abuse my lady," cries Honour; "I won't take that of you; she's as much better than yours as she is younger, and ten thousand times more handsomer."

Here ill luck, or rather good luck, sent Mrs. Western to see her maid in tears, which began to flow plentifully at her approach; and of which being asked the reason by her mistress, she presently acquainted her that her tears were occasioned by the rude treatment of the creature there, meaning Honour. "And, madam," continued she, "I could have despised all she said to me, but she hath had the audacity to affront your ladyship and to call you ugly. Yes, madam, she called you ugly old cat to my face. I could not bear to hear your ladyship called ugly." "Why do you repeat her impudence so often?" said Mrs. Western. And then turning to Mrs. Honour, she asked her how she had the assurance to mention her name with disrespect? "Disrespect, madam!" answered Honour. "I never mentioned your name at all; I said somebody was not as handsome as my mistress, and to be sure you know that as well as I." "Hussy," replied the lady, "I will make such a saucy trollop as yourself know that I am not a proper subject of your discourse. And if my brother doth not discharge you this moment, I will never sleep in his house again. I will find him out and have you discharged this moment." "Discharged!" cries Honour. "And suppose I am: there are more places in the world than one. Thank heaven, good servants need not want places, and if you turn away all who do not think you handsome, you will want servants very soon, let me tell you that."

Mrs. Western spoke, or rather thundered, in answer, but as she was hardly articulate, we cannot be very certain of the identical words; we shall therefore omit inserting a speech which at best would not greatly redound to her honour. She then departed in search of her brother with a countenance so full of rage that she resembled one of the Furies rather than a human creature.

The two chambermaids, being again left alone, began a second bout at altercation, which soon produced a combat of a more active kind. In this the victory belonged to the lady of inferior rank, but not without some loss of blood, of hair, and of lawn and muslin.

9

THE WISE DEMEANOUR OF MR. WESTERN IN THE CHARACTER OF A MAGISTRATE. A HINT TO JUSTICES OF PEACE CONCERNING THE NECESSARY QUALIFICATIONS OF A CLERK; WITH EXTRAORDINARY INSTANCES OF PATERNAL MADNESS AND FILIAL AFFECTION

Logicians sometimes prove too much by an argument, and politicians often overreach themselves in a scheme. Thus had it like to have happened to Mrs. Honour, who instead of recovering the rest of her clothes had liked to have stopped even those she had on her back from escaping; for the squire no sooner heard of her having abused his sister than he swore twenty oaths he would send her to Bridewell.

Mrs. Western was a very good-natured woman and ordinarily of a forgiving temper. She had lately remitted the trespass of a stage-coachman who had overturned her postchaise into a ditch; nay, she had even broken the law in refusing to prosecute a highwayman who had robbed her not only of a sum of money but of her ear-rings, at the same time d—ning her and saying, "Such handsome b—s as you don't want jewels to set them off, and be d—ned to you." But now, so uncertain are our tempers and so much do we at different times differ from ourselves, she would hear of no mitigation; nor could all the affected penitence of Honour nor all the entreaties of Sophia for her own servant prevail with her to desist from earnestly desiring her brother to execute justiceship (for it was indeed a syllable more than justice) on the wench.

But luckily the clerk had a qualification which no clerk to a justice of peace ought ever to be without: namely, some understanding in the law of this realm. He therefore whispered in the ear of the justice that he would exceed his authority by committing the girl to Bridewell, as there had been no attempt to break the peace; "for I am afraid, sir," says he, "you cannot legally commit any one to Bridewell only for ill breeding."

In matters of high importance, particularly in cases relating to the game, the justice was not always attentive to these admonitions of his clerk, for indeed, in executing the laws under that head, many justices of peace suppose they have a large discretionary power. By virtue of which, under the notion of searching for and taking away engines for the destruction of the game, they often commit trespasses, and sometimes felony, at their pleasure.

But this offence was not of quite so high a nature, nor so dangerous to the society. Here, therefore, the justice behaved with some attention to the advice of his clerk; for in fact he had already had two informations exhibited against him in the King's Bench and had no curiosity to try a third.

The squire, therefore, putting on a most wise and significant countenance, after a preface of several hums and ha's, told his sister that upon more mature deliberation he was of opinion that as there was no breaking up of the peace, such as the law, says he, calls breaking open a door, or breaking a hedge, or breaking a head, or any such sort of breaking, the matter did not amount to a felonious kind of a thing, nor trespass, nor damages, and, therefore, there was no punishment in the law for it.

Mrs. Western said she knew the law much better; that she had known servants very severely punished for affronting their masters; and then named a certain justice of the peace in London who, she said, would commit a servant to Bridewell at any time when a master or mistress desired it.

"Like enough," cries the squire, "it may be so in London, but the law is different in the country." Here followed a very learned dispute between the brother and sister concerning the law, which we would insert if we imagined many of our readers could understand it. This was, however, at length referred by both parties to the clerk, who decided it in favour of the magistrate; and Mrs. Western was in the end obliged to content herself with the satisfaction of having Honour turned away, to which Sophia herself very readily and cheerfully consented.

Thus Fortune, after having diverted herself according to custom with two or three frolics, at last disposed all matters to the advantage of our heroine, who, indeed, succeeded admirably well in her deceit, considering it was the first she had ever practised. And to say the truth, I have often concluded that the honest part of mankind would be much too hard for the knavish if they could bring themselves to incur the guilt or thought it worth their while to take the trouble.

Honour acted her part to the utmost perfection. She no sooner saw herself secure from all danger of Bridewell, a word which had raised most horrible ideas in her mind, than she resumed those airs which her terrors before had a little abated, and laid down her place with as much affectation of content and, indeed, of contempt as was ever practised at the resignation of places of a much greater importance. If the reader pleases, therefore, we choose rather to say she resigned—which hath, indeed, been always held a synonymous expression with being turned out or turned away.

Mr. Western ordered her to be very expeditious in packing; for his sister declared she would not sleep another night under the same roof with so impudent a slut. To work, therefore, she went, and that so earnestly that everything was ready early in the evening, when, having received her wages, away packed bag and baggage to the great satisfaction of every one; but of none more than of Sophia, who, having appointed her maid to meet at a certain place not far from the house exactly at the dreadful and ghostly hour of twelve, began to prepare for her own departure.

But first she was obliged to give two painful audiences, the one to her aunt, and the other to her father. In these Mrs. Western herself began to talk to her in a more peremptory style than before, but her father treated her in so violent and outrageous a manner that he frightened her into an affected compliance with his will, which so highly pleased the good squire that he changed his frowns into smiles and his menaces into promises; he vowed his whole soul was wrapped in hers, that her consent (for so he construed the words "You know, sir, I must not, nor can, refuse to obey any absolute command of yours") had made him the happiest of mankind. He then gave her a large bank-bill to dispose of in any trinkets she pleased, and kissed and embraced her in the fondest manner, while tears of joy trickled from those eyes which a few moments before had darted fire and rage against the dear object of all his affection.

Instances of this behaviour in parents are so common that the reader, I doubt not, will be very little astonished at the whole conduct of Mr. Western. If he should, I own I am not able to account for it, since that he loved his daughter most tenderly is, I think, beyond dispute. So indeed have many others who have rendered their children most completely miserable by the same conduct, which, though it is almost universal in parents, hath always appeared to me to be the most unaccountable of all the absurdities which ever entered into the brain of that strange prodigious creature man.

The latter part of Mr. Western's behaviour had so strong an effect on the tender heart of Sophia that it suggested a thought to her which not all the politic sophistry of her aunt nor all the menaces of her father had ever once brought into her head. She reverenced her father so piously and loved him so passionately that she had scarce ever felt more pleasing sensations than what arose from the share she frequently had of contributing to his amusement; and sometimes, perhaps, to higher gratifications; for he never could contain the delight of hearing her commended, which he had the satisfaction of hearing almost every day of her life. The idea, therefore, of the immense happiness she should convey to her father by her consent to this match made a strong impression on her mind. Again, the extreme piety of such an act of obedience worked very forcibly, as she had a very deep sense of religion. Lastly, when she reflected how much she herself was to suffer, being indeed to become little less than a sacrifice or a martyr to filial love and duty, she felt an agreeable tickling in a certain little passion which, though it bears no immediate affinity either to religion or virtue, is often so kind as to lend great assistance in executing the purposes of both.

Sophia was charmed with the contemplation of so heroic an action and began to compliment herself with much premature flattery when Cupid, who lay hid in her muff, suddenly crept out and, like Punchinello in a puppet-show kicked all out before him. In truth (for we scorn to deceive our readers or to vindicate the character of our heroine by ascribing her actions to supernatural impulse), the thoughts of her beloved Jones and some hopes (however distant) in which he was very particularly concerned immediately destroyed all which filial love, piety, and pride had with their joint endeavours been labouring to bring about.

But before we proceed any farther with Sophia, we must now look back to Mr. Jones.

10

CONTAINING SEVERAL MATTERS NATURAL ENOUGH, PERHAPS, BUT LOW

The reader will be pleased to remember that we left Mr. Jones, in the beginning of this book, on his road to Bristol, being determined to seek his fortune at sea, or rather, indeed, to fly away from his fortune on shore.

It happened (a thing not very unusual) that the guide who undertook to conduct him on his way was unluckily unacquainted with the road, so that having missed his right track and being ashamed to ask information, he rambled about backwards and forwards till night came on and it began to grow dark. Jones, suspecting what had happened, acquainted the guide with his apprehensions, but he insisted on it, that they were in the right road, and added it would be very strange if he should not know the road to Bristol; though in reality it would have been much stranger if he had known it, having never passed through it in his life before.

Jones had not such implicit faith in his guide but that on their arrival at a village he inquired of the first fellow he saw whether they were in the road to Bristol. "Whence did you come?" cries the fellow. "No matter," says Jones a little hastily; "I want to know if this be the road to Bristol." "The road to Bristol!" cries the fellow, scratching his head, "Why, measter, I believe you will hardly get to Bristol this way to-night." "Prithee, friend, then," answered Jones, "do tell us which is the way." "Why, measter," cries the fellow, "you must be come out of your road the Lord knows whither; for thick way goeth to Gloucester." "Well, and which way goes to Bristol?" said Jones. "Why, you be going away from Bristol," answered the fellow. "Then," said Jones, "we must go back again." "Ay, you must," said the fellow. "Well, and when we come back to the top of the hill, which way must we take?" "Why, you must keep the straight road." "But I remember there are two roads, one to the right and the other

305

to the left." "Why, you must keep the right-hand road, and then gu straight vorwards; only, remember to turn first to your right, and then to your left again, and then to your right; and that brings you to the squire's, and then you must keep straight vorwards, and turn to the left."

Another fellow now came up and asked which way the gentlemen were going—of which being informed by Jones, he first scratched his head and then, leaning upon a pole he had in his hand, began to tell him that he must keep the right-hand road for about a mile, or a mile and a half, or zuch a matter, and then he must turn short to the left, which would bring him round by Measter Jin Bearnes's." "But which is Mr. John Bearnes's?" says Jones. "Oh, Lord," cries the fellow, "why, don't you know Measter Jin Bearnes? Whence, then, did you come?"

These two fellows had almost conquered the patience of Jones when a plain, well-looking man (who was indeed a Quaker) accosted him thus: "Friend, I perceive thou hast lost thy way, and if thou wilt take my advice, thou wilt not attempt to find it to-night. It is almost dark, and the road is difficult to hit; besides, there have been several robberies committed lately between this and Bristol. Here is a very creditable house just by, where thou mayest find good entertainment for thyself and thy cattle till morning." Jones after a little persuasion agreed to stay in this place till the morning, and was conducted by his friend to the public-house.

The landlord, who was a very civil fellow, told Jones he hoped he would excuse the badness of his accommodation; for that his wife was gone from home, and had locked up almost everything and carried the keys along with her. Indeed, the fact was that a favourite daughter of hers was just married, and gone that morning home with her husband; and that she and her mother together had almost stripped the poor man of all his goods, as well as money; for though he had several children, this daughter only, who was the mother's favourite, was the object of her consideration, and to the humour of this one child she would with pleasure have sacrificed all the rest, and her husband into the bargain.

Though Jones was very unfit for any kind of company and would have preferred being alone, yet he could not resist the importunities of the honest Quaker, who was the more desirous of sitting with him from having remarked the melancholy which appeared both in his countenance and behaviour, and which the poor Quaker thought his conversation might in some measure relieve.

After they had passed some time together in such a manner that my honest friend might have thought himself at one of his silent meetings, the Quaker began to be moved by some spirit or other, probably that of curiosity, and said, "Friend, I perceive some sad disaster hath befallen thee; but pray be of comfort. Perhaps thou hast lost a friend. If so, thou must consider we are all mortal. And why shouldst thou grieve when thou knowest thy grief will do thy friend no good. We are all born to affliction. I myself have my sorrows as well as thee, and most probably greater sorrows. Though I have a clear estate of £100 a year, which is as much as I want, and I have a conscience, I thank the Lord, void of offence; my constitution is sound and strong, and there is no man can demand a debt of me nor accuse me of an injury —yet, friend, I should be concerned to think thee as miserable as myself."

Here the Quaker ended with a deep sigh, and Jones presently answered, "I am very sorry, sir, for your unhappiness, whatever is the occasion of it." "Ah, friend," replied the Quaker, "one only daughter is the occasion. One who was my greatest delight upon earth, and who within this week is run away from me and is married against my consent. I had provided her a proper match, a sober man, and one of substance; but she, forsooth, would choose for herself, and away she is gone with a young fellow not worth a groat. If she had been dead, as I suppose thy friend is, I should have been happy!" "That is very strange, sir," said Jones. "Why, would it not be better for her to be dead than to be a beggar?" replied the Quaker; "for, as I told you, the fellow is not worth a groat, and surely she cannot expect that I shall ever give her a shilling. No, as she hath married for love, let her live on love if she can; let her carry her love to market and see whether any one will change it into silver, or even into halfpence." "You know your own concerns best, sir," said Jones. "It must have been," continued the Quaker, "a long premeditated scheme to cheat me; for they have known one another from their infancy, and I have always preached to her against love—and told her a thousand times over it was all folly and wickedness. Nay, the cunning slut pretended to hearken to me and to despise all wantonness of the flesh; and yet, at last, to break out at a window two pair of stairs; for I began, indeed, a little to suspect her, and had locked her up carefully, intending the very next morning to have married her up to my liking. But she disappointed me within a few hours and escaped away to the lover of her own choosing, who lost no time; for they were married and bedded, and all within an hour.

"But it shall be the worst hour's work for them both that they ever did, for they may starve, or beg, or steal together for me. I will never give either of them a farthing." Here Jones, starting up, cried, "I really must be excused; I wish you would leave me." "Come, come, friend," said the Quaker "don't give way to concern. You see there are other people miserable besides yourself." "I see there are madmen and fools and villains in the world," cries Jones. "But let me give you a piece of advice: Send for your daughter and son-in-law home, and don't be yourself the only cause of misery to one you pretend to love." "Send for her and her husband home!" cries the Quaker loudly. "I would sooner send for the two greatest enemies I have in the world!" "Well, go home yourself, or where you please," said Jones; "for I will sit no longer in such company." "Nay, friend," answered the Quaker, "I scorn to impose my company on any one." He then offered to pull money from his pocket, but Jones pushed him with some violence out of the room.

The subject of the Quaker's discourse had so deeply affected Jones that he stared very wildly all the time he was speaking. This the Quaker had observed, and this, added to the rest of his behaviour, inspired honest Broadbrim with a conceit that his companion was in reality out of his senses. Instead of resenting the affront, therefore, the Quaker was moved with compassion for his unhappy circumstances, and having communicated his opinion to the landlord, he desired him to take great care of his guest and to treat him with the highest civility.

"Indeed," says the landlord, "I shall use no such civility towards him; for it seems, for all his laced waistcoat there, he is no more a gentleman than myself, but a poor parish bastard bred up at a great squire's about thirty miles off, and now turned out of doors (not for any good to be sure). I shall get him out of my house as soon as possible. If I do lose my reckoning, the first loss is always the best. It is not above a year ago that I lost a silver spoon."

"What dost thou talk of a parish bastard, Robin?" answered the Quaker. "Thou must certainly be mistaken in thy man."

"Not at all," replied Robin; "the guide, who knows him very well, told it me." For indeed the guide had no sooner taken his place at the kitchen fire than he acquainted the whole company with all he knew or had ever heard concerning Jones.

The Quaker was no sooner assured by this fellow of the birth and low fortune of Jones than all compassion for him vanished, and the honest, plain man went home fired with no less indignation than a duke would have felt at receiving an affront from such a person.

The landlord himself conceived an equal disdain for his guest, so that when Jones rung the bell in order to retire to bed, he was acquainted that he could have no bed there. Besides disdain of the mean condition of his guest, Robin entertained violent suspicion of his intentions, which were, he supposed, to watch some favourable opportunity of robbing the house. In reality he might have been very well eased of these apprehensions by the prudent precautions of his wife and daughter, who had already removed everything which was not fixed to the freehold, but he was by nature suspicious, and had been more particularly so since the loss of his spoon. In short, the dread of being robbed totally absorbed the comfortable consideration that he had nothing to lose.

Jones, being assured that he could have no bed, very contentedly betook himself to a great chair made with rushes, when sleep, which had lately shunned his company in much better apartments, generously paid him a visit in his humble cell.

As for the landlord, he was prevented by his fears from retiring to rest. He returned, therefore, to the kitchen fire, whence he could survey the only door which opened into the parlour, or rather hole, where Jones was seated; and as for the window to that room, it was impossible for any creature larger than a cat to have made his escape through it.

11

THE ADVENTURE OF A COMPANY OF SOLDIERS

The landlord, having taken his seat directly opposite to the door of the parlour, determined to keep guard there the whole night. The guide and another fellow remained long on duty with him, though they neither knew his suspicions nor had any of their own. The true cause of their watching did indeed at length put an end to it; for this was no other than the strength and goodness of the beer, of which having tippled a very large quantity, they grew at first very noisy and vociferous, and afterwards fell both asleep.

But it was not in the power of liquor to compose the fears of Robin. He continued still waking in his chair with his eyes fixed steadfastly on the door which led into the apartment of Mr. Jones, till a violent thundering at his outward gate called him from his seat and obliged him to open it; which he had no sooner done than his kitchen was immediately full of gentlemen in red coats, who all rushed upon him in as tumultuous a manner as if they intended to take his little castle by storm.

The landlord was now forced from his post to furnish his numerous guests with beer, which they called for with great eagerness, and upon his second or third return from the cellar he saw Mr. Jones standing before the fire in the midst of the soldiers; for it may easily be believed that the arrival of so much good company should put an end to any sleep, unless that from which we are only to be awakened by the last trumpet.

The company having now pretty well satisfied their thirst, nothing remained but to pay the reckoning, a circumstance often productive of much mischief and discontent among the inferior rank of gentry, who are apt to find great difficulty in assessing the sum with exact regard to distributive justice, which directs that every man shall pay according to the quantity which he drinks. This difficulty occurred upon the present occasion; and it was the greater as some gentlemen had in their extreme hurry marched off after their first draught, and had entirely forgot to contribute anything towards the said reckoning.

A violent dispute arose, in which every word may be said to have been deposed upon oath; for the oaths were at least equal to all the other words spoken. In this controversy the whole company spoke together, and every man seemed wholly bent to extenuate the sum which fell to his share, so that the most probable conclusion which could be foreseen was that a large portion of the reckoning would fall to the landlord's share to pay, or (what is much the same thing) would remain unpaid.

All this while Mr. Jones was engaged in conversation with the sergeant; for that officer was entirely unconcerned in the present dispute, being privileged by immemorial custom from all contribution.

The dispute now grew so very warm that it seemed to draw towards a military decision, when Jones, stepping forward, silenced all their clamours at once by declaring that he would pay the whole reckoning, which indeed amounted to no more than three shillings and fourpence.

This declaration procured Jones the thanks and applause of the whole company. The terms *honourable, noble,* and *worthy gentleman* resounded through the room; nay, my landlord himself began to have a better opinion of him and almost to disbelieve the account which the guide had given.

The sergeant had informed Mr. Jones that they were marching against the rebels, and expected to be commanded by the glorious Duke of Cumberland. By which the reader may perceive (a circumstance which we have not thought necessary to communicate before) that this was the very time when the late rebellion was at the highest; and indeed the banditti were now marched into England, intending, as it was thought, to fight the King's forces and to attempt pushing forward to the metropolis.

Jones had some heroic ingredients in his composition, and was a hearty well-wisher to the glorious cause of liberty and of the Protestant religion. It is no wonder, therefore, that in circumstances which would have warranted a much more romantic and wild undertaking, it should occur to him to serve as a volunteer in this expedition.

Our commanding officer had said all in his power to encourage and promote this good disposition from the first moment he had been acquainted with it. He now proclaimed the noble resolution aloud, which was received with great pleasure by the whole company, who all cried out, "God bless King George and your honour"; and then added with many oaths, "We will stand by you both to the last drops of our blood."

The gentleman who had been all night tippling at the alehouse was prevailed on by some arguments which a corporal had put into his hand to undertake the same expedition. And now, the portmanteau belonging to Mr. Jones being put up in the baggage-cart, the forces were about to move forward when the guide, stepping up to Jones, said, "Sir, I hope you will consider that the horses have been kept out all night, and we have travelled a great ways out of our way."

Jones was surprised at the impudence of this demand, and acquainted the soldiers with the merits of his cause, who were all unanimous in condemning the guide for his endeavours to put upon a gentleman. Some said he ought to be tied neck and heels; others, that he deserved to run the gauntlet; and the sergeant shook his cane at him and wished he had him under his command, swearing heartily he would make an example of him.

Jones contented himself, however, with a negative punishment, and walked off with his new comrades, leaving the guide to the poor revenge of cursing and reviling him, in which latter the landlord joined, saying, "Ay, ay, he is a pure one, I warrant you. A pretty gentleman, indeed, to go for a soldier. He shall wear a laced waistcoat truly. It is an old proverb and a true one: all is not gold that glisters. I am glad my house is well rid of him."

All that day the sergeant and the young soldier marched together, and the former, who was an arch fellow, told the latter many entertaining stories of his campaigns, though in reality he had never made any; for he was but lately come into the service, and had by his own dexterity so well ingratiated himself with his officers that he had promoted himself to a halberd, chiefly, indeed, by his merit in recruiting, in which he was most excellently well skilled.

Much mirth and festivity passed among the soldiers during their march. In which the many occurrences that had passed at their last quarters were remembered, and everyone with great freedom made what jokes he pleased on his officers, some of which were of the coarser kind and very near bordering on scandal. This brought to our hero's mind the custom which he had read of among the Greeks and Romans of indulging on certain festivals and solemn occasions the liberty of slaves of using an uncontrolled freedom of speech towards their masters.

Our little army, which consisted of two companies of foot, were now arrived at the place where they were to halt that evening. The sergeant then acquainted his lieutenant, who was the commanding officer, that they had picked up two fellows in that day's march, one of which, he said, was as fine a man as ever he saw (meaning the tippler), for that he was near six feet, well proportioned, and strongly limbed; and the other (meaning Jones) would do well enough for the rear rank.

The new soldiers were now produced before the officer,

who, having examined the six-foot man, he being first produced, came next to survey Jones; at the first sight of whom the lieutenant could not help showing some surprise; for, besides that he was very well dressed and was naturally genteel, he had a remarkable air of dignity in his look, which is rarely seen among the vulgar and is, indeed, not inseparably annexed to the features of their superiors.

"Sir," said the lieutenant, "my sergeant informed me that you are desirous of enlisting in the company I have at present under my command; if so, sir, we shall very gladly receive a gentleman who promises to do much honour to the company by bearing arms in it."

Jones answered that he had not mentioned anything of enlisting himself; that he was most zealously attached to the glorious cause for which they were going to fight, and was very desirous of serving as a volunteer; concluding with some compliments to the lieutenant, and expressing the great satisfaction he should have in being under his command.

The lieutenant returned his civility, commended his resolution, shook him by the hand, and invited him to dine with himself and the rest of the officers.

12

THE ADVENTURE OF A COMPANY OF OFFICERS

The lieutenant whom we mentioned in the preceding chapter, and who commanded this party, was now near sixty years of age. He had entered very young into the army, and had served in the capacity of an ensign at the Battle of Tannieres; here he had received two wounds and had so well distinguished himself that he was by the Duke of Marlborough advanced to be a lieutenant, immediately after that battle.

In this commission he had continued ever since: viz., near forty years, during which time he had seen vast numbers preferred over his head, and had now the mortification to be commanded by boys whose fathers were at nurse when he had first entered into the service.

Nor was this ill success in his profession solely owing to his having no friends among the men in power. He had the misfortune to incur the displeasure of his colonel who for many years continued in the command of this regiment. Nor did he owe the implacable ill will which this man bore him to any neglect or deficiency as an officer, nor indeed to any fault in himself, but solely to the indiscretion of his wife, who was a very beautiful woman and who though she was remarkably fond of her husband would not purchase his preferment at the expense of certain favours which the colonel required of her.

The poor lieutenant was more peculiarly unhappy in this: that while he felt the effects of the enmity of his colonel, he neither knew nor suspected that he really bore him any; for he could not suspect an ill will for which he was not conscious of giving any cause, and his wife, fearing what her husband's nice regard to his honour might have occasioned, contented herself with preserving her virtue without enjoying the triumphs of her conquest.

This unfortunate officer (for so I think he may be called) had many good qualities besides his merit in his profession; for he was a religious, honest, good-natured man, and had behaved so well in his command that he was highly esteemed and beloved not only by the soldiers of his own company but by the whole regiment.

The other officers who marched with him were a French lieutenant, who had been long enough out of France to forget his own language, but not long enough in England to learn ours, so that he really spoke no language at all and could barely make himself understood on the most ordinary occasions. There were likewise two ensigns, both very young fellows, one of whom had been bred under an attorney and the other was son to the wife of a nobleman's butler.

As soon as dinner was ended, Jones informed the company of the merriment which had passed among the soldiers upon their march; "and yet," says he, "notwithstanding all their vociferation, I dare swear they will behave more like Grecians than Trojans when they come to the enemy." "Grecians and Trojans!" says one of the ensigns. "Who the devil are they? I have heard of all the troops in Europe, but never of any such as these."

"Don't pretend to more ignorance than you have, Mr. Northerton," said the worthy lieutenant; "I suppose you have heard of the Greeks and Trojans, though perhaps you never read Pope's *Homer*, who, I remember, now the gentleman mentions it, compares the march of the Trojans to the cackling of geese and greatly commends the silence of the Gre-

314

cians. And upon my honour, there is great justice in the cadet's observation."

"Begar, me remember dem ver well," said the French lieutenant; "me ave read dem at school in dans Madam Dacière; des Greek, des Trojan, dey fight for von woman—ouy, ouy, me ave read all dat."

"D—n Homo with all my heart," says Northerton; "I have the marks of him in my a— yet. There's Thomas of our regiment, always carries a Homo in his pocket; d—n me if ever I come at it if I don't burn it. And there's Corderius, another d—ned son of a whore that hath got me many a flogging."

'Then you have been at school, Mr. Northerton?" said the lieutenant.

"Ay, d—n, me have I," answered he; "the devil take my father for sending me thither. The old put wanted to make a parson of me, but d—n me, thinks I to myself, I'll nick you there, old cull; the devil a smack of your nonsense shall you ever get into me. There's Jimmy Oliver of our regiment— he narrowly escaped being a pimp too; and that would have been a thousand pities, for d—n me if he is not one of the prettiest fellows in the whole world; but he went farther than I with the old cull, for Jimmey can neither write nor read."

"You give your friend a very good character," said the lieutenant, "and a very deserved one, I dare say; but prithee, Northerton, leave off that foolish as well as wicked custom of swearing; for you are deceived, I promise you, if you think there is wit or politeness in it. I wish too you would take my advice and desist from abusing the clergy. Scandalous names and reflections cast on any body of men must be always unjustifiable, but especially so when thrown on so sacred a function; for to abuse the body is to abuse the function itself, and I leave it to you to judge how inconsistent such a behaviour is in men who are going to fight in defence of the Protestant religion."

Mr. Adderley, which was the name of the other ensign, had sat hitherto kicking his heels and humming a tune without seeming to listen to the discourse; he now answered, *"Oh, monsieur, on ne parle pas de la religion dans la guerre."* "Well said, Jack," cries Northerton, "if *la religion* was the only matter, the parsons should fight their own battles for me."

"I don't know, gentlemen," says Jones, "what may be your

315

opinion, but I think no man can engage in a nobler cause than that of his religion; and I have observed in the little I have read of history that no soldiers have fought so bravely as those who have been inspired with a religious zeal; for my own part, though I love my king and country, I hope, as well as any man in it, yet the Protestant interest is no small motive to my becoming a volunteer in the cause."

Northerton now winked on Adderley and whispered to him slyly, "Smoke the prig, Adderley, smoke him"; then, turning to Jones, said to him, "I am very glad, sir, you have chosen our regiment to be a volunteer in; for if our parson should at any time take a cup too much, I find you can supply his place. I presume, sir, you have been at the University; may I crave the favour to know what college?"

"Sir," answered Jones, "so far from having been at the University, I have even had the advantage of yourself, for I was never at school."

"I presumed," cries the ensign, "only upon the information of your great learning——" "Oh, sir," answered Jones, "it is as possible for a man to know something without having been at school as it is to have been at school and to know nothing!"

"Well said, young volunteer," cries the lieutenant; "upon my word, Northerton, you had better let him alone, for he will be too hard for you."

Northerton did not very well relish the sarcasm of Jones, but he thought the provocation was scarce sufficient to justify a blow, or a rascal, or scoundrel, which were the only repartees that suggested themselves. He was therefore silent at present but resolved to take the first opportunity of returning the jest by abuse.

It now came to the turn of Mr. Jones to give a toast, as it is called, who could not refrain from mentioning his dear Sophia. This he did the more readily as he imagined it utterly impossible that any one present should guess the person he meant.

But the lieutenant, who was the toast-master, was not contented with Sophia only. He said he must have her surname; upon which Jones hesitated a little and presently after named Miss Sophia Western. Ensign Northerton declared he would not drink her health in the same round with his own toast unless somebody would vouch for her. "I knew one Sophy Western," says he, "that was lain with by half the young fellows at Bath, and perhaps this is the same woman." Jones very solemnly assured him of the contrary, asserting that the young lady he named was one of great fashion and fortune. "Ay, ay," says the ensign, "and so she is; d—n me, it is the same woman, and I'll hold half a dozen of burgundy Tom French of our regiment brings her into company with us at any tavern in Bridges Street." He then proceeded to describe her person exactly (for he had seen her with her aunt), and concluded with saying that her father had a great estate in Somersetshire.

The tenderness of lovers can ill brook the least jesting with the names of their mistresses. However, Jones, though he had enough of the lover and of the hero too in his disposition, did not resent these slanders as hastily as perhaps he ought to have done. To say the truth, having seen but little of this kind of wit, he did not readily understand it, and for a long time imagined Mr. Northerton had really mistaken his charmer for some other. But now, turning to the ensign with a stern aspect, he said, "Pray, sir, choose some other subject for your wit; for I promise you I will bear no jesting with this lady's character." "Jesting," cries the other, "d—n me if ever I was more in earnest in my life. Tom French of our regiment had both her and her aunt at Bath." "Then I must tell you in earnest," cries Jones, "that you are one of the most impudent rascals upon earth."

He had no sooner spoken these words than the ensign, together with a volley of curses, discharged a bottleful at the head of Jones, which, hitting him a little above the right temple, brought him instantly to the ground.

The conqueror, perceiving the enemy to lie motionless before him, and blood beginning to flow pretty plentifully from his wound, began now to think of quitting the field of battle, where no more honour was to be gotten; but the lieutenant interposed by stepping before the door and thus cut off his retreat.

Northerton was very importunate with the lieutenant for his liberty, urging the ill consequences of his stay, asking him what he could have done less! "Zounds!" says he. "I was but in jest with the fellow. I never heard any harm of Miss Western in my life." "Have not you?" said the lieutenant. "Then you richly deserve to be hanged, as well for making such jests as for using such a weapon. You are my prisoner, sir; nor shall you stir from hence till a proper guard comes to secure you."

Such an ascendant had our lieutenant over this ensign that

all that fervency of courage which had levelled our poor hero with the floor would scarce have animated the said ensign to have drawn his sword against the lieutenant had he then had one dangling at his side; but all the swords, being hung up in the room, were at the very beginning of the fray secured by the French officer. So that Mr. Northerton was obliged to attend the final issue of this affair.

The French gentleman and Mr. Adderley at the desire of their commanding officer had raised up the body of Jones, but as they could perceive but little (if any) sign of life in him, they again let him fall, Adderley damning him for having blooded his waistcoat, and the Frenchman declaring, "Begar, me no tush de Engliseman de mort, me ave heard de Englise ley, law, what you call, hang up de man dat tush him last."

When the good lieutenant applied himself to the door, he applied himself likewise to the bell; and the drawer immediately attending, he dispatched him for a file of musketeers and a surgeon. These commands, together with the drawer's report of what he had himself seen, not only produced the soldiers but presently drew up the landlord of the house, his wife and servants, and indeed every one else who happened at that time to be in the inn.

To describe every particular and to relate the whole conversation of the ensuing scene is not within my power, unless I had forty pens and could at once write them all together as the company now spoke. The reader must therefore content himself with the most remarkable incidents, and perhaps he may very well excuse the rest.

The first thing done was securing the body of Northerton, who, being delivered into the custody of six men with a corporal at their head, was by them conducted from a place which he was very willing to leave, but it was unluckily to a place whither he was very unwilling to go. To say the truth, so whimsical are the desires of ambition, the very moment this youth had attained the above-mentioned honour, he would have been well contented to have retired to some corner of the world where the fame of it should never have reached his ears.

It surprises us, and so perhaps it may the reader, that the lieutenant, a worthy and good man, should have applied his chief care rather to secure the offender than to preserve the life of the wounded person. We mention this observation not with any view of pretending to account for so odd a behaviour, but lest some critic should hereafter plume himself on discovering it. We would have these gentlemen know we can see what is odd in characters as well as themselves, but it is our business to relate facts as they are; which, when we have done, it is the part of the learned and sagacious reader to consult that original book of nature, whence every passage in our work is transcribed, though we quote not always the particular page for its authority.

The company which now arrived were of different disposition. They suspended their curiosity concerning the person of the ensign till they should see him hereafter in a more engaging attitude. At present their whole concern and attention were employed about the bloody object on the floor, which, being placed upright in a chair, soon began to discover some symptoms of life and motion. These were no sooner perceived by the company (for Jones was at first generally concluded to be dead) than they all fell at once to prescribing for him (for as none of the physical order was present, every one there took that office upon him).

Bleeding was the unanimous voice of the whole room, but unluckily there was no operator at hand; every one then cried, "Call the barber"; but none stirred a step. Several cordials were likewise prescribed in the same ineffective manner till the landlord ordered up a tankard of his strong beer, with a toast, which he said was the best cordial in England.

The person principally assistant on this occasion, indeed the only one who did any service or seemed likely to do any, was the landlady. She cut off some of her hair and applied it to the wound to stop the blood. She fell to chafing the youth's temples with her hand, and having expressed great contempt for her husband's prescription of beer, she dispatched one of her maids to her own closet for a bottle of brandy, of which as soon as it was brought she prevailed upon Jones, who was just returned to his senses, to drink a very large and plentiful draught.

Soon afterwards arrived the surgeon, who, having viewed the wound, having shaken his head, and blamed everything which was done, ordered his patient instantly to bed; in which place we think proper to leave him some time to his repose, and shall here, therefore, put an end to this chapter.

13

CONTAINING THE GREAT ADDRESS OF THE LANDLADY, THE
GREAT LEARNING OF A SURGEON, AND THE SOLID SKILL IN
CASUISTRY OF THE WORTHY LIEUTENANT

When the wounded man was carried to his bed, and the
house began again to clear up from the hurry which this
accident had occasioned, the landlady thus addressed the
commanding officer, "I am afraid, sir," said she, "this young
man did not behave himself as well as he should do to your
honours, and if he had been killed, I suppose he had but his
desarts; to be sure, when gentlemen admit inferior *parsons*
into their company, they *oft* to keep their distance; but as
my first husband used to say, few of 'em know how to do it.
For my own part, I am sure, I should not have suffered any
fellows to *include* themselves into gentlemen's company; but I
thoft he had been an officer himself till the sergeant told me
he was but a recruit."

"Landlady," answered the lieutenant, "you mistake the
whole matter. The young man behaved himself extremely
well and is, I believe, a much better gentleman than the ensign who abused him. If the young fellow dies, the man who
struck him will have most reason to be sorry for it; for the
regiment will get rid of a very troublesome fellow, who is a
scandal to the army, and if he escapes from the hands of
justice, blame me, madam, that's all."

"Ay! Ay! Good lackaday!" said the landlady. "Who could
have *thoft* it? Ay, ay, ay, I am satisfied your honour will see
justice done; and to be sure it *oft* to be to every one. Gentlemen *oft* not to kill poor folks without answering for it. A
poor man hath a soul to be saved as well as his betters."

"Indeed, madam," said the lieutenant, "you do the volunteer wrong; I dare swear he is more of a gentleman than the
officer."

"Ay," cries the landlady, "why, look you there, now; well,
my first husband was a wise man; he used to say you can't
always know the inside by the outside. Nay, that might have
been well enough too, for I never *sawed* him till he was all
over blood. Who would have *thoft* it! Mayhap, some young
gentleman crossed in love. Good lackaday! If he should die,
what a concern it would be to his parents! Why, sure the

Devil must possess the wicked wretch to do such an act. To be sure, he is a scandal to the army, as your honour says; for most of the gentlemen of the army that ever I saw are quite different sort of people, and look as if they would scorn to spill any Christian blood as much as any men, I mean, that is, in a civil way, as my first husband used to say. To be sure, when they come into the wars there must be bloodshed, but that they are not to be blamed for. The more of our enemies they kill there, the better, and I wish with all my heart they could kill every mother's son of them."

"Oh fie, madam!" said the lieutenant, smiling. *"All* is rather too bloody-minded a wish."

"Not at all, sir," answered she, "I am not at all bloody-minded, only to our enemies, and there is no harm in that. To be sure, it is natural for us to wish our enemies dead, that the wars may be at an end and our taxes be lowered, for it is a dreadful thing to pay as we do. Why now, there is above forty shillings for window-lights, and yet we have stopped up all we could; we have almost blinded the house, I am sure; says I to the exciseman, says I, I think you *oft* to favour us; I am sure we are very good friends to the government; and so we are for *sartain*, for we pay a mint of money to 'um. And yet I often think to myself the government doth not imagine itself more obliged to us than to those that don't pay 'um a farthing. Ay, ay; it is the way of the world."

She was proceeding in this manner when the surgeon entered the room. The lieutenant immediately asked how his patient did. But he resolved him only by saying, "Better, I believe, than he would have been this time if I had not been called; and even as it is, perhaps it would have been lucky if I could have been called sooner." "I hope, sir," said the lieutenant, "the skull is not fractured." "Hum," cries the surgeon, "fractures are not always the most dangerous symptoms. Contusions and lacerations are often attended with worse phenomena and with more fatal consequences than fractures. People who know nothing of the matter conclude if the skull is not fractured, all is well; whereas I had rather see a man's skull broke all to pieces than some contusions I have met with." "I hope," says the lieutenant, "there are no such symptoms here." "Symptoms," answered the surgeon, "are not always regular nor constant. I have known very unfavourable symptoms in the morning change to favourable ones at noon, and return to unfavourable again at night. Of wounds, indeed, it is rightly and truly said, *Nemo repente fuit turpissimus.* I was once, I remember, called to a patient who had received a violent contusion in his tibia, by which the exterior cutis was lacerated, so that there was a profuse sanguinary discharge; and the interior membranes were so divellicated that the os, or bone, very plainly appeared through the aperture of the vulnus, or wound. Some febrile symptoms intervening at the same time (for the pulse was exuberant and indicated much phlebotomy), I apprehended an immediate mortification. To prevent which I presently made a large orifice in the vein of the left arm, whence I drew twenty ounces of bood, which I expected to have found extremely sizy and glutinous, or indeed coagulated, as it is in pleuritic complaints; but to my surprise it appeared rosy and florid, and its consistency differed little from the blood of those in perfect health. I then applied a fomentation to the part, which highly answered the intention; and after three or four times dressing, the wound began to discharge a thick pus, or matter, by which means the cohesion— But perhaps I do not make myself perfectly well understood." "No, really," answered the lieutenant, "I cannot say I understand a syllable." "Well, sir," said the surgeon, "then I shall not tire your patience; in short, within six weeks my patient was able to walk upon his legs as perfectly as he could have done before he received the contusion." "I wish, sir," said the lieutenant, "you would be so kind only to inform me whether the wound this young gentleman hath had the misfortune to receive is likely to prove mortal." "Sir," answered the surgeon, "to say whether a wound will prove mortal or not at first dressing would be very weak and foolish presumption; we are all mortal, and symptoms often occur in a cure which the greatest of our profession could never foresee." "But do you think him in danger?" says the other. "In danger! Ay, surely," cries the doctor; "who is there among us who in the most perfect health can be said not to be in danger? Can a man, therefore, with so bad a wound as this be said to be out of danger? All I can say at present is that it is well I was called as I was, and perhaps it would have been better if I had been called sooner. I will see him again early in the morning, and in the meantime let him be kept extremely quiet and drink liberally of water-gruel." "Won't you allow him sack-whey?" said the landlady. "Ay, ay, sack-whey," cries the doctor, "if you will, provided it be very small." "And a little chicken broth too?" added she. "Yes, yes, chicken broth," said the doctor, "is very good." "Mayn't

I make him some jellies too?" said the landlady. "Ay, ay," answered the doctor, "jellies are very good for wounds, for they promote cohesion." And indeed it was lucky she had not named soup or high sauces, for the doctor would have complied rather than have lost the custom of the house.

The doctor was no sooner gone than the landlady began to trumpet forth his fame to the lieutenant, who had not from their short acquaintance conceived quite so favourable an opinion of his physical abilities as the good woman and all the neighbourhood entertained (and indeed very rightly); for though I am afraid the doctor was a little of a coxcomb, he might be nevertheless very much of a surgeon.

The lieutenant, having collected from the learned discourse of the surgeon that Mr. Jones was in great danger, gave orders for keeping Mr. Northerton under a very strict guard, intending in the morning to attend him to a justice of peace and to commit the conducting the troops to Gloucester to the French lieutenant, who, though he could neither read, write, nor speak any language, was, however, a good officer.

In the evening our commander sent a message to Mr. Jones that if a visit would not be troublesome he would wait on him. This civility was very kindly and thankfully received by Jones, and the lieutenant accordingly went up to his room, where he found the wounded man much better than he expected; nay, Jones assured his friend that if he had not received express orders to the contrary from the surgeon, he should have got up long ago; for he appeared to himself to be as well as ever, and felt no other inconvenience from his wound but an extreme soreness on that side of his head.

"I should be very glad," quoth the lieutenant, "that you was as well as you fancy yourself, for then you would be able to do yourself justice immediately; for when a matter can't be made up, as in case of a blow, the sooner you take him out, the better; but I am afraid you think yourself better than you are, and he would have too much advantage over you."

"I'll try, however," answered Jones, "if you please, and will be so kind to lend me a sword, for I have none here of my own."

"My sword is heartily at your service, my dear boy," cries the lieutenant, kissing him; "you are a brave lad and I love your spirit; but I fear your strength; for such a blow and so much loss of blood must have very much weakened you, and though you feel no want of strength in your bed, yet you most probably would after a thrust or two. I can't consent to your taking him out to-night, but I hope you will be able to come up with us before we get many days' march advance; and I give you my honour you shall have satisfaction, or the man who hath injured you shan't stay in our regiment."

"I wish," said Jones, "it was possible to decide this matter to-night; now you have mentioned it to me, I shall not be able to rest."

"Oh, never think of it," returned the other; "a few days will make no difference. The wounds of honour are not like those in your body. They suffer nothing by the delay of cure. It will be altogether as well for you to receive satisfaction a week hence as now."

"But suppose," says Jones, "I should grow worse and die of the consequences of my present wound."

"Then your honour," answered the lieutenant, "will require no reparation at all. I myself will do justice to your character, and will testify to the world your intention to have acted properly if you had recovered."

"Still," replied Jones, "I am concerned at the delay. I am almost afraid to mention it to you who are a soldier, but though I have been a very wild young fellow, still in my most serious moments and at the bottom I am really a Christian."

"So am I too, I assure you," said the officer; "and so zealous a one that I was pleased with you at dinner for taking up the cause of your religion; and I am a little offended with you now, young gentleman, that you should express a fear of declaring your faith before any one."

"But how terrible must it be," cries Jones, "to any one who is really a Christian to cherish malice in his breast, in opposition to the command of Him who hath expressly forbid it! How can I bear to do this on a sick-bed? Or how shall I make up my account with such an article as this in my bosom against me?"

"Why, I believe there is such a command," cries the lieutenant, "but a man of honour can't keep it. And you must be a man of honour if you will be in the army. I remember I once put the case to our chaplain over a bowl of punch, and he confessed there was much difficulty in it, but said he hoped there might be a latitude granted to soldiers in this one instance; and to be sure, it is our duty to hope so, for who would bear to live without his honour? No, no, my dear boy; be a good Christian as long as you live, but be a man of honour too and never put up an affront; not all the books nor all the parsons in the world shall ever persuade me to that. I love my religion very well, but I love my honour more. There must be some mistake in the wording the text, or in the translation, or in the understanding it, or somewhere or other. But however that be, a man must run the risk, for he must preserve his honour. So compose yourself to-night, and I promise you, you shall have an opportunity of doing yourself justice." Here he gave Jones a hearty buss, shook him by the hand, and took his leave.

But though the lieutenant's reasoning was very satisfactory to himself, it was not entirely so to his friend. Jones, therefore, having revolved this matter much in his thoughts, at last came to a resolution, which the reader will find in the next chapter.

14

Jones swallowed a large mess of chicken, or rather cock, broth, with a very good appetite, as indeed he would have done the cock it was made of, with a pound of bacon into the bargain; and now, finding in himself no deficiency of either health or spirit, he resolved to get up and seek his enemy.

But first he sent for the sergeant, who was his first acquaintance among these military gentlemen. Unluckily, that worthy officer, having in a literal sense taken his fill of liquor, had been some time retired to his bolster, where he was snoring so loud that it was not easy to convey a noise in at his ears capable of drowning that which issued from his nostrils.

However, as Jones persisted in his desire of seeing him, a vociferous drawer at length found means to disturb his slumbers and to acquaint him with the message. Of which the sergeant was no sooner made sensible than he arose from his bed, and, having his clothes already on, immediately attended. Jones did not think fit to acquaint the sergeant with his design, though he might have done it with great safety, for the halberdier was himself a man of honour and had killed his man. He would therefore have faithfully kept this secret, or indeed any other which no reward was published for discovering. But as Jones knew not these virtues in so short an acquaintance, his caution was perhaps prudent and commendable enough.

He began therefore by acquainting the sergeant that now he was entered into the army, he was ashamed of being without what was perhaps the most necessary implement of a soldier: namely, a sword; adding that he should be infinitely obliged to him if he could procure one. "For which," says he, "I will give you any reasonable price; nor do I insist upon its being silver-hilted, only a good blade, and such as may become a soldier's thigh."

The sergeant, who well knew what had happened and had heard that Jones was in a very dangerous condition, immediately concluded from such a message, at such a time of night, and from a man in such a situation, that he was light-headed. Now, as he had his wit (to use that word in its common signification) always ready, he bethought himself of making his advantage of this humour in the sick man. "Sir," says he, "I believe I can fit you. I have a most excellent piece of stuff by me. It is not indeed silver-hilted, which, as you say, doth not become a soldier; but the handle is decent enough and the blade one of the best in Europe. It is a blade that—a blade that—in short, I will fetch it you this instant, and you shall see it and handle it. I am glad to see your honour so well, all my heart."

Being instantly returned with the sword, he delivered it to Jones, who took it and drew it; and then told the sergeant it would do very well, and bid him name his price.

The sergeant now began to harangue in praise of his goods. He said (nay he swore very heartily) that the blade was taken from a French officer of very high rank, at the Battle of Dettingen. "I took it myself," says he, "from his side after I had knocked him o' the head. The hilt was a golden one. That I sold to one of our fine gentlemen; for there are some of them, an't please your honour, who value the hilt of a sword more than the blade."

Here the other stopped him and begged him to name a price. The sergeant, who thought Jones absolutely out of his senses and very near his end, was afraid lest he should injure his family by asking too litte. However, after a moment's hesitation, he contented himself with naming twenty guineas, and swore he would not sell it for less to his own brother.

"Twenty guineas!" says Jones in the utmost surprise. "Sure

you think I am mad, or that I never saw a sword in my life. Twenty guineas, indeed! I did not imagine you would endeavour to impose upon me. Here, take the sword. No, now I think on't, I will keep it myself and show it your officer in the morning, acquainting him at the same time what a price you asked me for it."

The sergeant, as we have said, had always his wit (*in sensu prædicto*) about him, and now plainly saw that Jones was not in the condition he had apprehended him to be; he now, therefore, counterfeited as great surprise as the other had shown and said, "I am certain, sir, I have not asked you so much out of the way. Besides, you are to consider, it is the only sword I have, and I must run the risk of my officer's displeasure by going without one myself. And truly, putting all this together, I don't think twenty shillings was so much out of the way."

"Twenty shillings!" cries Jones. "Why, you just now asked me twenty guineas." "How!" cries the sergeant. "Sure your honour must have mistaken me, or else I mistook myself—and indeed I am but half awake. Twenty guineas indeed! No wonder your honour flew into such a passion. I say twenty guineas too— No, no, I meant twenty shillings, I assure you. And when your honour comes to consider everything, I hope you will not think that so extravagant a price. It is indeed true you may buy a weapon which looks as well for less money, but——"

Here Jones interrupted him, saying, "I will be so far from making any words with you that I will give you a shilling more than your demand." He then gave him a guinea, bid him return to his bed, and wished him a good march; adding he hoped to overtake them before the division reached Worcester.

The sergeant very civilly took his leave, fully satisfied with his merchandise, and not a little pleased with his dextrous recovery from that false step into which his opinion of the sick man's light-headedness had betrayed him.

As soon as the sergeant was departed, Jones rose from his bed and dressed himself entirely, putting on even his coat, which as its colour was white showed very visibly the streams of blood which had flowed down it; and now, having grasped his new-purchased sword in his hand, he was going to issue forth when the thought of what he was about to undertake laid suddenly hold of him, and he began to reflect that in a few minutes he might possibly deprive a human being of life, or might lose his own. "Very well," said he, "and in what cause do I venture my life? Why, in that of my honour. And who is this human being? A rascal who hath injured and insulted me without provocation. But is not revenge forbidden by heaven? Yes, but it is enjoined by the world. Well, but shall I obey the world in opposition to the express commands of heaven? Shall I incur the divine displeasure rather than be called—ha—coward—scoundrel? I'll think no more; I am resolved, and must fight him."

The clock had now struck twelve, and every one in the house were in their beds except the sentinel who stood to guard Northerton, when Jones, softly opening his door, issued forth in pursuit of his enemy, of whose place of confinement he had received a perfect description from the drawer. It is not easy to conceive a much more tremendous figure than he now exhibited. He had on, as we have said, a light-coloured coat covered with streams of blood. His face, which missed that very blood as well as twenty ounces more drawn from him by the surgeon, was pallid. Round his head was a quantity of bandage, not unlike a turban. In the right hand he carried a sword and in the left a candle, so that the bloody Banquo was not worthy to be compared to him. In fact, I believe a more dreadful apparition was never raised in a churchyard nor in the imagination of any good people met in a winter evening over a Christmas fire in Somersetshire.

When the sentinel first saw our hero approach, his hair began gently to lift up his grenadier's cap, and in the same instant his knees fell to blows with each other. Presently his whole body was seized with worse than an ague fit. He then fired his piece, and fell flat on his face.

Whether fear or courage was the occasion of his firing, or whether he took aim at the object of his terror, I cannot say. If he did, however, he had the good fortune to miss his man.

Jones, seeing the fellow fall, guessed the cause of his fright, at which he could not forbear smiling, not in the least reflecting on the danger from which he had just escaped. He then passed by the fellow, who still continued in the posture in which he fell, and entered the room where Northerton, as he had heard, was confined. Here, in a solitary situation, he found—an empty quart pot standing on the table, on which some beer being spilt, it looked as if the room had lately been inhabited; but at present it was entirely vacant.

Jones then apprehended it might lead to some other apartment, but upon searching all round it, he could perceive no other door than that at which he entered and where the sentinel had been posted. He then proceeded to call Northerton several times by his name, but no one answered; nor did this serve to any other purpose than to confirm the sentinel in his terrors, who was now convinced that the volunteer was dead of his wounds and that his ghost was come in search of the murderer; he now lay in all the agonies of horror, and I wish with all my heart some of those actors who are hereafter to represent a man frighted out of his wits had seen him, that they might be taught to copy nature instead of performing several antic tricks and gestures for the entertainment and applause of the galleries.

Perceiving the bird was flown, at least despairing to find him, and rightly apprehending that the report of the firelock would alarm the whole house, our hero now blew out his candle and gently stole back again to his chamber and to his bed; whither he would not have been able to have gotten undiscovered, had any other person been on the same staircase save only one gentleman, who was confined to his bed by the gout; for before he could reach the door to his chamber, the hall where the sentinel had been posted was half full of people. Some in their shirts, and others not half dressed, all very earnestly inquiring of each other what was the matter.

The soldier was now found lying in the same place and posture in which we just before left him. Several immediately applied themselves to raise him, and some concluded him dead, but they presently saw their mistake; for he not only struggled with those who laid their hands on him but fell a-roaring like a bull. In reality he imagined so many spirits or devils were handling him; for his imagination, being possessed with the horror of an apparition, converted every object he saw or felt into nothing but ghosts and spectres.

At length he was overpowered by numbers, and got upon his legs; when, candles being brought, and seeing two or three of his comrades present, he came a little to himself, but when they asked him what was the matter he answered, "I am a dead man, that's all; I am a dead man. I can't recover it. I have seen him." "What hast thou seen, Jack?" says one of the soldiers. "Why, I have seen the young volunteer that was killed yesterday." He then imprecated the most heavy curses on himself if he had not seen the volunteer, all over blood, vomiting fire out of his mouth and nostrils, pass by him into the chamber where Ensign Northerton was, and then, seizing the ensign by the throat, fly away with him in a clap of thunder.

This relation met with a gracious reception from the audience. All the women present believed it firmly and prayed heaven to defend them from murder. Amongst the men too, many had faith in the story, but others turned it into derision and ridicule, and a sergeant who was present answered very coolly, "Young man, you will hear more of this for going to sleep and dreaming on your post."

The soldier replied, "You may punish me if you please, but I was as broad awake as I am now; and the Devil carry me away, as he hath the ensign, if I did not see the dead man, as I tell you, with eyes as big and as fiery as two large flambeaus."

The commander of the forces and the commander of the house were now both arrived; for the former, being awake at the time and hearing the sentinel fire his piece, thought it his duty to rise immediately, though he had no great apprehensions of any mischief, whereas the apprehensions of the latter were much greater, lest her spoons and tankards should be upon the march without having received any such orders from her.

Our poor sentinel, to whom the sight of this officer was not much more welcome than the apparition, as he thought it, which he had seen before, again related the dreadful story, and with many additions of blood and fire; but he had the misfortune to gain no credit with either of the last-mentioned persons for the officer, though a very religious man, was free from all terrors of this kind; besides, having so lately left Jones in the condition we have seen, he had no suspicion of his being dead. As for the landlady, though not over-religious, she had no kind of aversion to the doctrine of spirits, but there was a circumstance in the tale which she well knew to be false, as we shall inform the reader presently.

But whether Northerton was carried away in thunder or fire, or in whatever other manner he was gone, it was now certain that his body was no longer in custody. Upon this occasion, the lieutenant formed a conclusion not very different from what the sergeant is just mentioned to have made before, and immediately ordered the sentinel to be taken prisoner. So that by a strange reverse of fortune (though not very uncommon in a military life), the guard became the guarded.

15

THE CONCLUSION OF THE FOREGOING ADVENTURE

Besides the suspicion of sleep, the lieutenant harboured another and worse doubt against the poor sentinel, and this was that of treachery; for as he believed not one syllable of the apparition, so he imagined the whole to be an invention formed only to impose upon him, and that the fellow had in reality been bribed by Northerton to let him escape. And this he imagined the rather as the fright appeared to him the more unnatural in one who had the character of as brave and bold a man as any in the regiment, having been in several actions, having received several wounds, and, in a word, having behaved himself always like a good and valiant soldier.

That the reader, therefore, may not conceive the least ill opinion of such a person, we shall not delay a moment in rescuing his character from the imputation of this guilt.

Mr. Northerton, then, as we have before observed, was fully satisfied with the glory which he had obtained from this action. He had, perhaps, seen, or heard, or guessed that envy is apt to attend fame. Not that I would here insinuate that he was heathenishly inclined to believe in or to worship the goddess Nemesis; for in fact I am convinced he never heard of her name. He was, besides, of an active disposition, and had a great antipathy to those close winter quarters in the castle of Gloucester, for which a justice of peace might possibly give him a billet. Nor was he, moreover, free from some uneasy meditations on a certain wooden edifice, which I forbear to name, in conformity to the opinion of mankind, who, I think, rather ought to honour than to be ashamed of this building, as it is, or at least might be made, of more benefit to society than almost any other public erection. In a word, to hint at no more reasons for his conduct, Mr. Northerton was desirous of departing that evening, and nothing remained for him but to contrive the *quomodo*, which appeared to be a matter of some difficulty.

Now, this young gentleman, though somewhat crooked in his morals, was perfectly straight in his person, which was extremely strong and well made. His face too was accounted handsome by the generality of women, for it was broad and ruddy with tolerably good teeth. Such charms did not fail making an impression on my landlady, who had no little relish for this kind of beauty. She had, indeed, a real compassion for the young man, and hearing from the surgeon that affairs were like to go ill with the volunteer, she suspected they might hereafter wear no benign aspect with the ensign. Having obtained, therefore, leave to make him a visit, and finding him in a very melancholy mood, which she considerably heightened by telling him that there were scarce any hopes of the volunteer's life, she proceeded to throw forth some hints, which the other readily and eagerly taking up, they soon came to a right understanding; and it was at length agreed that the ensign should at a certain signal ascend the chimney, which communicating very soon with that of the kitchen, he might there again let himself down, for which she would give him an opportunity, by keeping the coast clear.

But lest our readers of a different complexion should take this occasion of too hastily condemning all compassion as a folly and pernicious to society, we think proper to mention another particular, which might possibly have some little share in this action. The ensign happened to be at this time possessed of the sum of fifty pounds, which did indeed belong to the whole company; for the captain, having quarrelled with his lieutenant, had entrusted the payment of his company to the ensign. This money, however, he thought proper to deposit in my landlady's hand, possibly by way of bail or security that he would hereafter appear and answer to the charge against him; but whatever were the conditions, certain it is, that she had the money and the ensign his liberty.

The reader may perhaps expect, from the compassionate temper of this good woman, that when she saw the poor sentinel taken prisoner for a fact of which she knew him innocent, she should immediately have interposed in his behalf; but whether it was that she had already exhausted all her compassion in the above-mentioned instance, or that the features of this fellow, though not very different from those of the ensign, could not raise it, I will not determine; but far from being an advocate for the present prisoner, she urged his guilt to his officer, declaring with uplifted eyes and hands that she would not have had any concern in the escape of a murderer for all the world.

Everything was now once more quiet, and most of the company returned again to their beds; but the landlady, either from the natural activity of her disposition or from her fear for her plate, having no propensity to sleep, prevailed with the officers, as they were to march within little more than an hour, to spend that time with her over a bowl of punch.

Jones had lain awake all this while and had heard great part of the hurry and bustle that had passed, of which he had now some curiosity to know the particulars. He therefore applied to his bell, which he rung at least twenty times without any effect; for my landllady was in such high mirth with her company that no clapper could be heard there but her own, and the drawer and chambermaid, who were sitting together in the kitchen (for neither durst he sit up, nor she lie, in bed alone), the more they heard the bell ring the more they were frightened and, as it were, nailed down in their places.

At last, at a lucky interval of chat, the sound reached the ears of our good landlady, who presently sent forth her summons, which both her servants instantly obeyed. "Joo," says the mistress, "don't you hear the gentleman's bell ring? Why don't you go up?" "It is not my business," answered the drawer, "to wait upon the chambers. It is Betty Chambermaid's!" "If you come to that," answered the maid, "it is not my business to wait upon gentlemen. I have done it, indeed, sometimes, but the Devil fetch me if ever I do again, since you make your preambles about it." The bell still ringing violently, their mistress fell into a passion and swore if the drawer did not go up immediately, she would turn him away that very morning. "If you do, madam," says he, "I can't help it. I won't do another servant's business." She then applied herself to the maid and endeavoured to prevail by gentle means, but all in vain; Betty was as inflexible as Joo. Both insisted it was not their business and they would not do it.

The lieutenant then fell a-laughing and said, "Come, I will put an end to this contention"; and then, turning to the servants, commended them for their resolution in neither giving up the point, but added he was sure if one would consent to go, the other would. To which proposal they both agreed in an instant, and accordingly went up very lovingly and close together. When they were gone, the lieutenant appeased the wrath of the landlady by satisfying her why they were both so unwilling to go alone.

They returned soon after, and acquainted their mistress

that the sick gentleman was so far from being dead that he spoke as heartily as if he was well; and that he gave his service to the captain, and should be very glad of the favour of seeing him before he marched.

The good lieutenant immediately complied with his desires and, sitting down by his bedside, acquainted him with the scene which had happened below, concluding with his intentions of making an example of the sentinel.

Upon this, Jones related to him the whole truth, and earnestly begged him not to punish the poor soldier, "who, I am confident," says he, "is as innocent of the ensign's escape as he is of forging any lie or of endeavoring to impose on you."

The lieutenant hesitated a few moments and then answered, "Why, as you have cleared the fellow of one part of the charge, so it will be impossible to prove the other, because he was not the only sentinel. But I have a good mind to punish the rascal for being a coward. Yet who knows what effect the terror of such an apprehension may have; and to say the truth, he hath always behaved well against an enemy. Come, it is a good thing to see any sign of religion in these fellows, so I promise you he shall be set at liberty when we march. But hark, the general beats. My dear boy, give me another buss. Don't discompose nor hurry yourself; but remember the Christian doctrine of patience, and I warrant you will soon be able to do yourself justice and to take an honourable revenge on the fellow who hath injured you." The lieutenant then departed, and Jones endeavoured to compose himself to rest.

BOOK VIII

CONTAINING ABOVE TWO DAYS

1

A WONDERFUL LONG CHAPTER CONCERNING THE MARVELLOUS, BEING MUCH THE LONGEST OF ALL OF OUR INTRODUCTORY CHAPTERS

As we are now entering upon a book in which the course of our history will oblige us to relate some matters of a more strange and surprising kind than any which have hitherto occurred, it may not be amiss in the prolegomenous, or introductory, chapter to say something of that species of writing which is called the marvellous. To this we shall, as well for the sake of ourselves as of others, endeavour to set some certain bounds, and indeed nothing can be more necessary, as critics* of different complexions are here apt to run into very different extremes; for while some are with M. Dacier ready to allow that the same thing which is impossible may be yet probable,† others have so little historic or poetic faith that they believe nothing to be either possible or probable the like to which hath not occurred to their own observation.

First, then, I think, it may very reasonably be required of every writer that he keeps within the bounds of possibility, and still remembers that what it is not possible for man to perform, it is scarce possible for man to believe he did perform. This conviction, perhaps, gave birth to many stories of the ancient heathen deities (for most of them are of poetical original). The poet, being desirous to indulge a wanton and extravagant imagination, took refuge in that power, of the

---

* By this word, here and in most other parts of our work, we mean every reader in the world.

† It is happy for M. Dacier that he was not an Irishman.

335

extent of which his readers were no judges, or rather which they imagined to be infinite, and consequently they could not be shocked at any prodigies related of it. This hath been strongly urged in defence of Homer's miracles, and it is, perhaps, a defence; not, as Mr. Pope would have it, because Ulysses told a set of foolish lies to the Phaeacians, who were a very dull nation, but because the poet himself wrote to heathens, to whom poetical fables were articles of faith. For my own part, I must confess, so compassionate is my temper, I wish Polypheme had confined himself to his milk diet and preserved his eye; nor could Ulysses be much more concerned than myself when his companions were turned into swine by Circe, who showed, I think, afterwards, too much regard for man's flesh to be supposed capable of converting it into bacon. I wish, likewise, with all my heart that Homer could have known the rule prescribed by Horace, to introduce supernatural agents as seldom as possible. We should not then have seen his gods coming on trivial errands, and often behaving themselves so as not only to forfeit all title to respect but to become the objects of scorn and derision—a conduct which must have shocked the credulity of a pious and sagacious heathen and which could never have been defended unless by agreeing with a supposition to which I have been sometimes almost inclined: that this most glorious poet, as he certainly was, had an intent to burlesque the superstitious faith of his own age and country.

But I have rested too long on a doctrine which can be of no use to a Christian writer; for as he cannot introduce into his works any of that heavenly host which make a part of his creed, so is it horrid puerility to search the heathen theology for any of those deities who have been long since dethroned from their immortality. Lord Shaftesbury observes that nothing is more cold than the invocation of a muse by a modern; he might have added that nothing can be more absurd. A modern may with much more elegance invoke a ballad, as some have thought Homer did, or a mug of ale with the author of *Hudibras*, which latter may perhaps have inspired much more poetry as well as prose than all the liquors of Hippocrene or Helicon.

The only supernatural agents which can in any manner be allowed to us moderns are ghosts, but of these I would advise an author to be extremely sparing. These are indeed like arsenic and other dangerous drugs in physic, to be used with the utmost caution; nor would I advise the introduction of them at all in those works or by those authors to which, or to whom, a horse-laugh in the reader would be any great prejudice or mortification.

As for elves and fairies and other such mummery, I purposely omit the mention of them, as I should be very unwilling to confine within any bounds those surprising imaginations, for whose vast capacity the limits of human nature are too narrow, whose works are to be considered as a new creation, and who have consequently just right to do what they will with their own.

Man, therefore, is the highest subject (unless on very extraordinary occasions indeed) which presents itself to the pen of our historian or of our poet; and in relating his actions, great care is to be taken that we do not exceed the capacity of the agent we describe.

Nor is possibility alone sufficient to justify us; we must keep likewise within the rules of probability. It is, I think, the opinion of Aristotle, or if not, it is the opinion of some wise man whose authority will be as weighty when it is as old, that it is no excuse for a poet who relates what is incredible that the thing related is really matter of fact. This may perhaps be allowed true with regard to poetry, but it may be thought impracticable to extend it to the historian; for he is obliged to record matters as he finds them, though they may be of so extraordinary a nature as will require no small degree of historical faith to swallow them. Such was the successless armament of Xerxes described by Herodotus, or the successful expedition of Alexander related by Arrian. Such of later years was the victory of Agincourt obtained by Harry the Fifth, or that of Narva won by Charles the Twelfth of Sweden. All of which instances, the more we reflect them, appear still the more astonishing.

Such facts, however, as they occur in the thread of the story, nay, indeed, as they constitute the essential parts of it, the historian is not only justifiable in recording as they really happened but indeed would be unpardonable should he omit or alter them. But there are other facts not of such consequence nor so necessary, which, though ever so well attested, may nevertheless be sacrificed to oblivion in complaisance to the scepticism of a reader. Such is that memorable story of the ghost of George Villiers, which might with more propriety have been made a present of to Dr. Drelincourt, to have kept the ghost of Mrs. Veale company at the head of his *Discourse upon Death,* than have been introduced into so solemn a work as the *History of the Rebellion*.

To say the truth, if the historian will confine himself to what really happened and utterly reject any circumstance which, though never so well attested, he must be well assured is false, he will sometimes fall into the marvellous, but never into the incredible. He will often raise the wonder and surprise of his reader, but never that incredulous hatred mentioned by Horace. It is by falling into fiction, therefore, that we generally offend against this rule of deserting probability, which the historian seldom if ever quits till he forsakes his character and commences a writer of romance. In this, however, those historians who relate public transactions have the advantage of us who confine ourselves to scenes of private life. The credit of the former is by common notoriety supported for a long time; and public records, with the concurrent testimony of many authors, bear evidence to their truth in future ages. Thus a Trajan and an Antoninus, a Nero and a Caligula, have all met with the belief of posterity; and no one doubts but that men so very good and so very bad were once the masters of mankind.

But we who deal in private characters, who search into the most retired recesses and draw forth examples of virtue and vice from holes and corners of the world, are in a more dangerous situation. As we have no public notoriety, no concurrent testimony, no records to support and corroborate what we deliver, it becomes us not only to keep within the limits of possibility but of probability too; and this more especially in painting what is greatly good and amiable. Knavery and folly, though never so exorbitant, will more easily meet with assent, for ill nature adds great support and strength to faith.

Thus we may, perhaps, with little danger relate the history of a Fisher, who, having long owed his bread to the generosity of Mr. Derby and having that very morning received a considerable bounty from his hands, in order to possess himself of what remained in his friend's scrutoire, concealed himself in a public office of the Temple through which there was a passage into Mr. Derby's chambers. Here he overheard Mr. Derby for many hours solacing himself at an entertainment which he that evening gave his friends, and to which Fisher had been invited. During all this time, no tender, no grateful reflections arose to restrain his purpose, but when the poor gentleman had let his company out through the office, Fisher came suddenly from his lurking-place and, walking softly behind his friend into his chamber, discharged a pistol-ball into his head. This may be believed when the bones of Fisher are as rotten as his heart. Nay, perhaps it will be credited that the villain went two days afterwards with some young ladies to the play of *Hamlet,* and with an unaltered countenance heard one of the ladies, who little suspected how near she was to the person, cry out, "Good God! If the man that murdered Mr. Derby was now present!" Manifesting in this a more feared and callous conscience than even Nero himself, of whom we are told by Suetonius that the consciousness of his guilt, after the death of his mother, became immediately intolerable and so continued; nor could all the congratulations of the soldiers, of the senate, and the people allay the horrors of his conscience.

But now, on the other hand, should I tell my reader that I had known a man whose penetrating genius had enabled him to raise a large fortune in a way where no beginning was chalked out to him; that he had done this with the most perfect preservation of his integrity, and not only without the least injustice or injury to any one individual person but with the highest advantage to trade and a vast increase of the public revenue; that he had expended one part of the income of this fortune in discovering a taste superior to most by works where the highest dignity was united with the purest simplicity, and another part in displaying a degree of goodness superior to all men by acts of charity to objects whose only recommendations were their merits or their wants; that he was most industrious in searching after merit in distress, most eager to relieve it, and then as careful (perhaps too careful) to conceal what he had done; that his house, his furniture, his gardens, his table, his private hospitality, and his public beneficence all denoted the mind from which they flowed, and were all intrinsically rich and noble without tinsel or external ostentation; that he filled every relation in life with the most adequate virtue; that he was most piously religious to his Creator, most zealously loyal to his sovereign, a most tender husband to his wife, a kind relation, a munificent patron, a warm and firm friend, a knowing and a cheerful companion, indulgent to his servants, hospitable to his neighbours, charitable to the poor, and benevolent to all mankind. Should I add to these epithets of wise, brave, elegant, and indeed every other amiable epithet in our language, I might surely say,

> —*Quis credet? nemo Hercule! nemo;*
> *Vel duo, vel nemo.*

And yet I know a man who is all I have here described. But a single instance (and I really know not such another) is not sufficient to justify us, while we are writing to thousands who never heard of the person nor of anything like him. Such *rarae aves* should be remitted to the epitaph writer or to some poet who may condescend to hitch him in a distich or to slide him into a rhyme with an air of carelessness and neglect, without giving any offence to the reader.

In the last place, the actions should be such as may not only be within the compass of human agency and which human agents may probably be supposed to do, but they should be likely for the very actors and characters themselves to have performed; for what may be only wonderful and surprising in one man may become improbable or indeed impossible when related of another.

This last requisite is what the dramatic critics call conservation of character, and it requires a very extraordinary degree of judgement and a most exact knowledge of human nature.

It is admirably remarked by a most excellent writer that zeal can no more hurry a man to act in direct opposition to itself than a rapid stream can carry a boat against its own current. I will venture to say that for a man to act in direct contradiction to the dictates of Nature is, if not impossible, as improbable and as miraculous as anything which can well be conceived. Should the best parts of the story of M. Antoninus be ascribed to Nero or should the worst incidents of Nero's life be imputed to Antoninus, what would be more shocking to belief than either instance; whereas both these being related of their proper agent constitute the truly marvellous.

Our modern authors of comedy have fallen almost universally into the error here hinted at: their heroes generally are notorious rogues and their heroines abandoned jades during the first four acts; but in the fifth, the former become very worthy gentlemen and the latter, women of virtue and discretion; nor is the writer often so kind as to give himself the least trouble to reconcile or account for this monstrous change and incongruity. There is, indeed, no other reason to be assigned for it than because the play is drawing to a conclusion; as if it was no less natural in a rogue to repent in the last act of a play than in the last of his life; which we perceive to be generally the case at Tyburn, a place which might, indeed, close the scene of some comedies with much propriety, as the heroes in these are most commonly eminent for those very talents which not only bring men to the gallows but enable them to make an heroic figure when they are there.

Within these few restrictions, I think, every writer may be permitted to deal as much in the wonderful as he pleases; nay, the more he can surprise the reader, if he thus keeps within the rules of credibility, the more he will engage his attention and the more he will charm him. As a genius of the highest rank observes in his fifth chapter of the *Bathos*, "The great art of all poetry is to mix truth with fiction, in order to join the credible with the surprising."

For though every good author will confine himself within the bounds of probability, it is by no means necessary that his characters or his incidents should be trite, common, or vulgar; such as happen in every street, or in every house, or which may be met with in the home articles of a newspaper. Nor must he be inhibited from showing many persons and things which may possibly have never fallen within the knowledge of great part of his readers. If the writer strictly observes the rules above mentioned, he hath discharged his part and is then entitled to some faith from his reader, who is indeed guilty of critical infidelity if he disbelieves him. For want of a portion of such faith, I remember the character of a young lady of quality which was condemned on the stage for being unnatural by the unanimous voice of a very large assembly of clerks and apprentices, though it had had the previous suffrages of many ladies of the first rank, one of whom, very eminent for her understanding, declared it was the picture of half the young people of her acquaintance.

2

IN WHICH THE LANDLADY PAYS A VISIT TO MR. JONES

When Jones had taken leave of his friend the lieutenant, he endeavoured to close his eyes, but all in vain; his spirits were too lively and wakeful to be lulled to sleep. So having amused, or rather tormented, himself with the thoughts of his Sophia till it was open daylight, he called for some tea, upon which occasion my landlady herself vouchsafed to pay him a visit.

This was indeed the first time she had seen him, or at least had taken any notice of him, but as the lieutenant had assured her that he was certainly some young gentleman of fashion, she now determined to show him all the respect in her power; for to speak truly, this was one of those houses where gentlemen, to use the language of advertisements, meet with civil treatment for their money.

She had no sooner begun to make his tea than she likewise began to discourse. "La, sir," said she, "I think it is a great pity that such a pretty young gentleman should undervalue himself so as to go about with these soldier fellows. They call themselves gentlemen, I warrant you; but, as my first husband used to say, they should remember it is we that pay them. And to be sure, it is very hard upon us to be obliged to pay them and to keep 'em too, as we publicans are. I had twenty of 'um last night, besides officers; nay, for matter o' that, I had rather have the soldiers than the officers; for nothing is ever good enough for those sparks, and I am sure, if you was to see the bills; la, sir, it is nothing. I have had less trouble, I warrant you, with a good squire's family, where we take forty or fifty shillings of a night, besides horses. And yet I warrants me, there is narrow a one of all those officer fellows but looks upon himself to be as good as arrow a squire of £500 a year. To be sure, it doth me good to hear their men run about after 'um, crying your honour, and your honour. Marry come up with such honour, and an ordinary at a shilling a head. Then there's such swearing among 'um, to be sure, it frightens me out o' my wits; I thinks nothing can ever prosper with such wicked people. And here one of 'um has

342

used you in so barbarous a manner. I thought indeed how well the rest would secure him; they all hang together, for if you had been in danger of death, which I am glad to see you are not, it would have been all as one to such wicked people. They would have let the murderer go. Laud have mercy upon 'um; I would not have such a sin to answer for, for the whole world. But though you are likely with the blessing to recover, there is laa for him yet; and if you will employ Layer Small, I darest be sworn he'll make the fellow fly the country for him; though perhaps he'll have fled the country before, for it is here to-day and gone tomorrow with such chaps. I hope, however, you will learn more wit for the future and return back to your friends; I warrant they are all miserable for your loss, and if they was but to know what had happened. La, my seeming! I would not for the world they should. Come, come, we know very well what all the matter is, but if one won't, another will; so pretty a gentleman need never want a lady. I am sure if I was as you, I would see the finest she that ever wore a head hanged before I would go for a soldier for her. Nay, don't blush so (for indeed he did to a violent degree); why you thought, sir, I knew nothing of the matter, I warrant you, about Madam Sophia." "How," says Jones, starting up, "do you know my Sophia?" "Do I! Ay marry," cries the landlady, "many's the time hath she lain in this house." "With her aunt, I suppose," says Jones. "Why, there it is now," cries the landlady. "Ay, ay, ay, I know the old lady very well. And a sweet young creature is Madam Sophia, that's the truth on't." "A sweet creature!" cries Jones. "O heavens!

> "Angels are painted fair to look like her.
> There's in her all that we believe of heaven,
> Amazing brightness, purity and truth,
> Eternal joy, and everlasting love.

"And could I ever have imagined that you had known my Sophia!" "I wish," says the landlady, "you knew half so much of her. What would you have given to have sat by her bedside? What a delicious neck she hath! Her lovely limbs have stretched themselves in that very bed you now lie in." "Here!" cries Jones. "Hath Sophia ever lain here?" "Ay, ay, here; there, in that very bed," says the landlady, "where I wish you had her this moment; and she may wish so too, for anything I know to the contrary, for she hath mentioned your name to me." "Ha," cries he, "did she ever mention her poor Jones? You flatter me now; I can never believe so much." "Why, then," answered she, "as I hope to be saved, and may the Devil fetch me if I speak a syllable more than the truth. I have heard her mention Mr. Jones, but in a civil and modest way, I confess; yet I could perceive she thought a great deal more than she said." "Oh, my dear woman," cries Jones, "her thoughts of me I shall never be worthy of. Oh, she is all gentleness, kindness, goodness. Why was such a rascal as I born ever to give her soft bosom a moment's uneasiness? Why am I cursed? I, who would undergo all the plagues and miseries which any demon ever invented for mankind, to procure her any good; nay, torture itself could not be misery to me did I but know that she was happy." "Why, look you there, now," says the landlady, "I told her you was a constant lover." "But pray, madam, tell me when or where you knew anything of me; for I never was here before, nor do I remember ever to have seen you." "Nor is it possible you should," answered she, "for you was a little thing when I had you in my lap at the squire's." "How! The squire's," says Jones. "What, do you know the great and good Mr. Allworthy then?" "Yes, marry do I," says she. "Who in this country doth not?" "The fame of his goodness indeed," answered Jones, "must have extended farther than this, but heaven only can know him, can know that benevolence which it copied from itself and sent upon earth as its own pattern. Mankind are as ignorant of such divine goodness as they are unworthy of it, but none so unworthy of it as myself. I, who was raised by him to such a height, taken in, as you must well know, a poor base-born child, adopted by him and treated as his own son, to dare by my follies to disoblige him, to draw his vengeance upon me. Yes, I deserve it all; for I will never be so ungrateful as even to think he hath done an act of injustice by me. No, I deserve to be turned out-of-doors, as I am. And now, madam," says he, "I believe you will not blame me for turning soldier, especially with such a fortune as this in my pocket." At which words he shook a purse, which had but very little in it and which still appeared to the landlady to have less.

My good landlady was (according to vulgar phrase) struck all of a heap by this relation. She answered coldly that to be sure people were the best judges what was most proper for their circumstances. "But hark," says she, "I think I hear somebody call. Coming! Coming! The Devil's in all our volk; nobody hath any ears. I must go downstairs; if you want any more breakfast, the maid will come up. Coming!" At which words, without taking any leave, she flung out of the room; for the lower sort of people are very tenacious of respect, and though they are contented to give this gratis to persons of quality, yet they never confer it on those of their own order without taking care to be well paid for their pains.

3

IN WHICH THE SURGEON MAKES HIS SECOND APPEARANCE

Before we proceed any farther, that the reader may not be mistaken in imagining the landlady knew more than she did nor surprised that she knew so much, it may be necessary to inform him that the lieutenant had acquainted her that the name of Sophia had been the occasion of the quarrel; and as for the rest of her knowledge, the sagacious reader will observe how she came by it in the preceding scene. Great curiosity was indeed mixed with her virtues, and she never willingly suffered any one to depart from her house without inquiring as much as possible into their names, families, and fortunes.

She was no sooner gone than Jones, instead of animadverting on her behaviour, reflected that he was in the same bed which he was informed had held his dear Sophia. This occasioned a thousand fond and tender thoughts, which we would dwell longer upon did we not consider that such kind of lovers will make a very inconsiderable part of our readers.

In this situation the surgeon found him when he came to dress his wound. The doctor, perceiving upon examination that his pulse was disordered, and hearing that he had not slept, declared that he was in great danger; for he apprehended a fever was coming on, which he would have prevented by bleeding, but Jones would not submit, declaring he would lose no more blood, and, "Doctor," says he, "if you will be so kind only to dress my head, I have no doubt of being well in a day or two."

"I wish," answered the surgeon, "I could assure your being

well in a month or two. Well, indeed! No, no. People are not so soon well of such contusions; but, sir, I am not at this time of day to be instructed in my operations by a patient, and I insist on making a revulsion before I dress you."

Jones persisted obstinately in his refusal and the doctor at last yielded, telling him at the same time that he would not be answerable for the ill consequence and hoped he would do him the justice to acknowledge that he had given him a contrary advice, which the patient promised he would.

The doctor retired into the kitchen, where, addressing himself to the landlady, he complained bitterly of the undutiful behaviour of his patient, who would not be blooded though he was in a fever.

"It is an eating fever, then," says the landlady; "for he hath devoured two swinging buttered toasts this morning for breakfast."

"Very likely," says the doctor. "I have known people eat in a fever, and it is very easily accounted for, because the acidity occasioned by the febrile matter may stimulate the nerves of the diaphragm and thereby occasion a craving which will not be easily distinguishable from a natural appetite; but the aliment will not be concreted nor assimilated into chyle, and so will corrode the vascular orifices, and thus will aggravate the febrific symptoms. Indeed I think the gentleman in a very dangerous way, and if he is not blooded, I am afraid will die."

"Every man must die some time or other," answered the good woman. "It is no business of mine. I hope, doctor, you would not have me hold him while you bleed him. But, harkee, a word in your ear: I would advise you before you proceed too far to take care who is to be your paymaster."

"Paymaster!" said the doctor, staring. "Why, I've a gentleman under my hands, have I not?"

"I imagined so as well as you," said the landlady. "But as my first husband used to say, everything is not what it looks to be. He is an arrant scrub, I assure you. However, take no notice that I mentioned anything to you of the matter, but I think people in business oft always to let one another know such things."

"And have I suffered such a fellow as this," cries the doctor, in a passion, "to instruct me? Shall I hear my practice insulted by one who will not pay me! I am glad I have made this discovery in time. I will see now whether he will be blooded or no." He then immediately went upstairs and,

346

flinging open the door of the chamber with much violence, awakened poor Jones from a very sound nap into which he was fallen and, what was still worse, from a delicious dream concerning Sophia.

"Will you be blooded or no?" cries the doctor in a rage. "I have told you my resolution already," answered Jones, "and I wish with all my heart you had taken my answer; for you have awakened me out of the sweetest sleep which I ever had in my life."

"Ay, ay," cries the doctor, "many a man hath dozed away his life. Sleep is not always good, no more than food; but remember I demand of you for the last time, will you be blooded?" "I answer you for the last time," said Jones; "I will not." "Then I wash my hands of you," cries the doctor, "and I desire you to pay me for the trouble I have had already. Two journeys at 5s. each, two dressings at 5s. more, and half a crown for phlebotomy." "I hope," said Jones, "you don't intend to leave me in this condition." "Indeed but I shall," said the other. "Then," said Jones, "you have used me rascally, and I will not pay you a farthing." "Very well," cries the doctor, "the first loss is the best. What a pox did my landlady mean by sending for me to such vagabonds?" At which words he flung out of the room, and his patient, turning himself about, soon recovered his sleep, but his dream was unfortunately gone.

4

IN WHICH IS INTRODUCED ONE OF THE PLEASANTEST BARBERS THAT WAS EVER RECORDED IN HISTORY, THE BARBER OF BAGHDAD NOR HE IN *Don Quixote* NOT EXCEPTED

The clock had now struck five when Jones awakened from a nap of seven hours, so much refreshed and in such perfect health and spirits that he resolved to get up and dress himself; for which purpose he unlocked his portmanteau and took out clean linen and a suit of clothes; but first he slipped on a frock and went down into the kitchen to bespeak something that might pacify certain tumults he found rising within his stomach.

Meeting the landlady, he accosted her with great civility and asked what he could have for dinner. "For dinner!" says she. "It is an odd time a day to think about dinner.

There is nothing dressed in the house and the fire is almost out." "Well, but," says he, "I must have something to eat, and it is almost indifferent to me what, for to tell you the truth, I never was more hungry in my life." "Then," says she, "I believe there is a piece of cold buttock and carrot which will fit you." "Nothing better," answered Jones, "but I should be obliged to you if you would let it be fried." To which the landlady consented and said, smiling, she was glad to see him so well recovered; for the sweetness of our hero's temper was almost irresistible; besides, she was really no ill-humoured woman at the bottom, but she loved money so much that she hated everything which had the semblance of poverty.

Jones now returned in order to dress himself while his dinner was preparing, and was, according to his orders, attended by the barber.

This barber, who went by the name of Little Benjamin, was a fellow of great oddity and humour, which had frequently led him into small inconveniences such as slaps in the face, kicks in the breech, broken bones, &c. For every one doth not understand a jest, and those who do are often displeased with being themselves the subjects of it. This vice was, however, incurable in him; and though he had often smarted for it, yet if ever he conceived a joke, he was certain to be delivered of it, without the least respect of persons, time, or place.

He had a great many other particularities in his character, which I shall not mention, as the reader will himself very easily perceive them on his farther acquaintance with this extraordinary person.

Jones, being impatient to be dressed, for a reason which may be easily imagined, thought the shaver was very tedious in preparing his suds and begged him to make haste, to which the other answered with much gravity, for he never discomposed his muscles on any account, "*Festina lentè* is a proverb which I learnt long before I ever touched a razor." "I find, friend, you are a scholar," replied Jones. "A poor one," said the barber; "*non omnia possumus omnes.*" "Again!" said Jones. "I fancy you are good at capping verses." "Excuse me, sir," said the barber, "*non tanto me dignor honore.*" And then, proceeding to his operation, "Sir," said he, "since I have dealt in suds I could never discover more than two reasons for shaving: the one is to get a beard and the other to get rid of one. I conjecture, sir, it may not be long since you shaved from the former of these motives. Upon my word you have had good success, for one may say of your beard that it is *tondenti gravior*." "I conjecture," says Jones, "that thou art a very comical fellow." "You mistake me widely, sir," said the barber; "I am too much addicted to the study of philosophy; *hinc illæ lacrymæ*, sir, that's my misfortune. Too much learning hath been my ruin." "Indeed," says Jones, "I confess, friend, you have more learning than generally belongs to your trade, but I can't see how it can have injured you." "Alas, sir," answered the shaver, "my father disinherited me for it. He was a dancing-master; and because I could read before I could dance, he took an aversion to me and left every farthing among his other children. Will you please to have your temples— Oh la, I ask your pardon, I fancy there is *hiatus in manuscriptis*. I heard you was going to the wars, but I find it was a mistake." "Why do you conclude so?" says Jones. "Sure, sir," answered the barber, "you are too wise a man to carry a broken head thither, for that would be carrying coals to Newcastle."

"Upon my word," cries Jones, "thou art a very odd fellow, and I like thy humour extremely; I shall be very glad if thou wilt come to me after dinner and drink a glass with me; I long to be better acquainted with thee."

"Oh, dear sir," said the barber, "I can do you twenty times as great a favour if you will accept of it." "What is that, my friend?" cries Jones. "Why, I will drink a bottle with you if you please; for I dearly love good nature, and as you have found me out to be a comical fellow, so I have no skill in physiognomy if you are not one of the best-natured gentlemen in the universe." Jones now walked downstairs neatly dressed, and perhaps the famed Adonis was not a lovelier figure; and yet he had no charms for my landlady, for as that good woman did not resemble Venus at all in her person, so neither did she in her taste. Happy had it been for Nanny the chambermaid if she had seen with the eyes of her mistress; for that poor girl fell so violently in love with Jones in five minutes that her passion afterwards cost her many a sigh. This Nancy was extremely pretty and altogether as coy, for she had refused a drawer and one or two young farmers in the neighbourhood, but the bright eyes of our hero thawed all her ice in a moment.

When Jones returned to the kitchen, his cloth was not yet laid; nor, indeed, was there any occasion it should, his dinner remaining in *statu quo*, as did the fire which was to dress it. This disappointment might have put many a philosophical temper into a passion, but it had no such effect on Jones. He only gave the landlady a gentle rebuke, saying since it was so difficult to get it heated, he would eat the beef cold. But now the good woman, whether moved by compassion, or by shame, or by whatever other motive I cannot tell, first gave her servants a round scold for disobeying the orders which she had never given, and then, bidding the drawer lay a napkin in the Sun, she set about the matter in good earnest and soon accomplished it.

This Sun, into which Jones was now conducted, was truly named as *lucus a non lucendo,* for it was an apartment into which the sun had scarce ever looked. It was indeed the worst room in the house, and happy was it for Jones that it was so. However, he was now too hungry to find any fault, but, having once satisfied his appetite, he ordered the drawer to carry a bottle of wine into a better room and expressed some resentment at having been shown into a dungeon.

The drawer having obeyed his commands, he was after some time attended by the barber, who would not indeed have suffered him to wait so long for his company had he not been listening in the kitchen to the landlady, who was entertaining a circle that she had gathered round her with the history of poor Jones, part of which she had extracted from his own lips and the other part was her own ingenious composition; for she said he was a poor parish boy taken into the house of Squire Allworthy, where he was bred up as an apprentice and now turned out-of-doors for his misdeeds, particularly for making love to his young mistress and probably for robbing the house; for how else should he come by the little money he hath? "And this," says she, "is your gentleman, forsooth." "A servant of Squire Allworthy!" says the barber. "What's his name?" "Why, he told me his name was Jones," says she. "Perhaps he goes by a wrong name. Nay, and he told me, too, that the squire had maintained him as his own son thof he had quarrelled with him now." "And if his name be Jones, he told you the truth," said the barber, "for I have relations who live in that country; nay, and some people say he is his son." "Why doth he not go by the name of his father?" "I can't tell that," said the barber; "many people's sons don't go by the name of their father." "Nay," said the landlady, "if I thought he was a gentleman's son, thof he was a by-blow, I should behave to him in another-guess manner; for many of these by-blows come to be great men and, as my poor first husband used to say, never affront any customer that's a gentleman."

5

A DIALOGUE BETWEEN MR. JONES AND THE BARBER

This conversation passed partly while Jones was at dinner in his dungeon and partly while he was expecting the barber in the parlour. And as soon as it was ended, Mr. Benjamin, as we have said, attended him, and was very kindly desired to sit down. Jones, then filling out a glass of wine, drank his health by the appellation of *doctissime tonsorum.* "*Ago tibi gratias, domine,*" said the barber; and then, looking very steadfastly at Jones, he said with great gravity and with a seeming surprise, as if he recollected a face he had seen before, "Sir, may I crave the favour to know if your name is not Jones?" To which the other answered that it was. "*Proh deum atque hominum fidem,*" says the barber; "how strangely things come to pass. Mr. Jones, I am your most obedient servant. I find you do not know me, which indeed is no wonder, since you never saw me but once and then you was very young. Pray, sir, how doth the good Squire Allworthy? How doth *ille optimus omnium patronus?*" "I find," said Jones, "you do indeed know me, but I have not the like happiness of recollecting you." "I do not wonder at that," cries Benjamin, "but I am surprised I did not know you sooner, for you are not in the least altered. And pray, sir, may I without offence inquire whither you are travelling this way?" "Fill the glass, Mr. Barber," said Jones, "and ask no more questions." "Nay, sir," answered Benjamin, "I would not be troublesome; and I hope you don't think me a man of an impertinent curiosity, for that is a vice which nobody can lay to my charge; but I ask pardon, for when a gentleman of your figure travels without his servants, we may suppose him to be, as we say, in *casu incognito,* and perhaps I ought not to have mentioned your name." "I own," says Jones, "I did not expect to have been so well known in this country as I find I am, yet for particular reasons I shall be obliged to you if you will not mention my name to any other person till I am gone from hence." "*Pauca verba,*" answered the barber; "and I wish no other here knew you but myself, for some people have tongues, but I promise you I can keep a secret. My enemies will allow me that virtue." "And yet that is not the characteristic of your profession, Mr. Barber," answered Jones. "Alas, sir," replied Benjamin, *"Non si male nunc et olim sic erit*. I was not born nor bred a barber, I assure you. I have spent most of my time among gentlemen, and though I say it, I understand something of gentility. And if you had thought me as worthy of your confidence as you had some other people, I should have shown you I could have kept a secret better. I should not have degraded your name in a public kitchen, for indeed, sir, some people have not used you well; for besides making a public proclamation of what you told them of a quarrel between yourself and Squire Allworthy, they added lies of their own, things which I knew to be lies." "You surprise me greatly," cries Jones. "Upon my word, sir," answered Benjamin, "I tell the truth, and I need not tell you my landlady was the person. I am sure it moved me to hear the story and I hope it is all false, for I have a great respect for you; I do assure you I have and have had ever since the good nature you showed to Black George, which was talked of all over the country, and I received more than one letter about it. Indeed it made you beloved by everybody. You will pardon me, therefore, for it was real concern at what I heard made me ask any questions; for I have no impertinent curiosity about me, but I love good nature, and thence became *amoris abundantia erga te."*

Every profession of friendship easily gains credit with the miserable; it is no wonder, therefore, if Jones, who besides his being miserable was extremely open-hearted, very readily believed all the professions of Benjamin and received him into his bosom. The scraps of Latin, some of which Benjamin applied properly enough, though it did not savour of profound literature seemed yet to indicate something superior to a common barber, and so indeed did his whole behaviour. Jones therefore believed the truth of what he said as to his original and education, and at length after much entreaty he said, "Since you have heard, my friend, so much of my affairs and seem so desirous to know the truth, if you will have patience to hear it, I will inform you of the whole." "Patience," cries Benjamin, "that I will, if the chapter was never so long, and I am very much obliged to you for the honour you do me."

Jones now began and related the whole history, forgetting only a circumstance or two: namely, everything which passed on that day in which he had fought with Thwackum, and ended with his resolution to go to sea till the rebellion in the North had made him change his purpose and had brought him to the place where he then was.

Little Benjamin, who had been all attention, never once interrupted the narrative; but when it was ended, he could not help observing that there must be surely something more invented by his enemies and told Mr. Allworthy against him, or so good a man would never have dismissed one he had loved so tenderly in such a manner. To which Jones answered he doubted not but such villainous arts had been made use of to destroy him.

And surely, it was scarce possible for anyone to have avoided making the same remark with the barber, who had not, indeed, heard from Jones one single circumstance upon which he was condemned; for his actions were not now placed in those injurious lights in which they had been misrepresented to Allworthy, nor could he mention those many false accusations which had been from time to time preferred against him to Allworthy, for with none of these he was himself acquainted. He had likewise, as we have observed, omitted many material facts in his present relation. Upon the whole, indeed, everything now appeared in such favourable colours to Jones that malice itself would have found it no easy matter to fix any blame upon him.

Not that Jones desired to conceal or to disguise the truth; nay, he would have been more unwilling to have suffered any censure to fall on Mr. Allworthy for punishing him than on his own actions for deserving it; but in reality, so it happened, and so it always will happen; for let a man be never so honest, the account of his own conduct will in spite of himself be so very favourable that his vices will come purified through his lips, and like foul liquors well strained will leave all their foulness behind. For though the facts themselves may appear, yet so different will be the motives, circumstances, and consequences when a man tells his own story and when the enemy tells it that we scarce can recognize the facts to be one and the same.

Though the barber had drank down his story with greedy ears, he was not yet satisfied. There was a circumstance behind, which his curiosity, cold as it was, most eagerly longed for. Jones had mentioned the fact of his amour and of his

353

being the rival of Blifil, but had cautiously concealed the name of the young lady. The barber, therefore, after some hesitation and many hums and ha's, at last begged leave to crave the name of the lady who appeared to be the principal cause of all this mischief. Jones paused a moment and then said, "Since I have trusted you with so much, and since, I am afraid, her name is become too public already on this occasion, I will not conceal it from you. Her name is Sophia Western."

"*Proh deum atque hominum fidem!* Squire Western hath a daughter grown a woman!" "Ay, and such a woman," cries Jones, "that the world cannot match. No eye ever saw anything so beautiful; but that is her least excellence. Such sense! Such goodness! Oh, I could praise her forever and yet should omit half her virtues." "Mr. Western a daughter grown up!" cries the barber. "I remember the father a boy; well, *tempus edax rerum.*"

The wine being now at an end, the barber pressed very eagerly to be his bottle, but Jones absolutely refused, saying he had already drank more than he ought, and that he now chose to retire to his room, where he wished he could procure himself a book. "A book!" cries Benjamin. "What book would you have? Latin or English? I have some curious books in both languages. Such as *Erasmi Colloquia, Ovid de Tristibus, Gradus ad Parnassum;* and in English I have several of the best books, though some of them are a little torn; but I have a great part of Stowe's *Chronicle,* the sixth volume of Pope's *Homer,* the third volume of *The Spectator,* the second volume of Echard's *Roman History, The Craftsman, Robinson Crusoe,* Thomas à Kempis, and two volumes of Tom Brown's *Works.*"

"Those last," cries Jones, "are books I never saw, so if you please, lend me one of those volumes." The barber assured him he would be highly entertained, for he looked upon the author to have been one of the greatest wits that ever the nation produced. He then stepped to his house, which was hard by, and immediately returned; after which, the barber having received very strict injunctions of secrecy from Jones and having sworn inviolably to maintain it, they separated; the barber went home and Jones retired to his chamber.

IN WHICH MORE OF THE TALENTS OF MR. BENJAMIN WILL
APPEAR, AS WELL AS WHO THIS EXTRAORDINARY PERSON WAS

In the morning Jones grew a little uneasy at the desertion of his surgeon, as he apprehended some inconvenience or even danger might attend the not dressing his wound; he inquired, therefore, of the drawer what other surgeons were to be met with in that neighbourhood. The drawer told him there was one not far off, but he had known him often refuse to be concerned after another had been sent for before him. "But, sir," says he, "if you will take my advice, there is not a man in the kingdom can do your business better than the barber who was with you last night. We look upon him to be one of the ablest men at a cut in all this neighbourhood. For though he hath not been here above three months, he hath done several great cures."

The drawer was presently dispatched for Little Benjamin, who, being acquainted in what capacity he was wanted, prepared himself accordingly and attended, but with so different an air and aspect from that which he wore when his basin was under his arm that he could scarce be known to be the same person.

"So, Tonsor," says Jones, "I find you have more trades than one; how came you not to inform me of this last night?" "A surgeon," answered Benjamin with great gravity, "is a profession, not a trade. The reason why I did not acquaint you last night that I professed this art was that I then concluded you was under the hands of another gentleman, and I never love to interfere with my brethren in their business. *Ars omnibus communis;* but now, sir, if you please, I will inspect your head, and when I see into your skull, I will give my opinion of your case."

Jones had no great faith in this new professor; however, he suffered him to open the bandage and to look at his wound, which as soon as he had done, Benjamin began to groan and shake his head violently. Upon which Jones in a peevish manner bid him not to play the fool but to tell him in what condition he found him. "Shall I answer you as a surgeon or a friend?" said Benjamin. "As a friend, and seriously," said Jones. "Why, then, upon my soul," cries Benjamin, "it would require a great deal of art to keep you from being well after a very few dressings, and if you will suffer me to apply some salve of mine, I will answer for the success." Jones gave his consent and the plaister was applied accordingly.

"There, sir," cries Benjamin; "now I will, if you please, resume my former self; but a man is obliged to keep up some dignity in his countenance whilst he is performing these operations or the world will not submit to be handled by him. You can't imagine, sir, of how much consequence a grave aspect is to a grave character. A barber may make you laugh, but a surgeon ought rather to make you cry."

"Mr. Barber, or Mr. Surgeon, or Mr. Barber-surgeon," said Jones. "Oh, dear sir," answered Benjamin, interrupting him, *"Infandum, regina, jubes renovare dolorem.* You recall to my mind that cruel separation of the united fraternities, so much to the prejudice of both bodies, as all separations must be, according to the old adage, *vis unita fortior,* which, to be sure, there are not wanting some of one or of the other fraternity who are able to construe. What a blow was this to me, who unite both in my own person." "Well, by whatever name you please to be called," continued Jones, "you certainly are one of the oddest, most comical fellows I ever met with, and must have something very surprising in your story, which you must confess I have a right to hear." "I do confess it," answered Benjamin, "and will very readily acquaint you with it when you have sufficient leisure, for I promise you it will require a good deal of time." Jones told him he could never be more at leisure than at present. "Well, then," said Benjamin, "I will obey you; but first I will fasten the door, that none may interrupt us." He did so and then, advancing with a solemn air to Jones, said, "I must begin by telling you, sir, that you yourself have been the greatest enemy I ever had." Jones was a little startled at this sudden declaration. "I your enemy, sir!" says he with much amazement and some sternness in his look. "Nay, be not angry," said Benjamin, "for I promise you I am not. You are perfectly innocent of having intended me any wrong, for you was then an infant; but I shall, I believe, unriddle all this the moment I mention my name. Did you never hear, sir, of one Partridge, who had the honour of being reputed your father and the misfortune of being ruined by that honour?" "I have indeed heard of that Partridge," says Jones, "and have always believed myself to be his son." "Well, sir," answered Benjamin, "I am that Partridge, but I here absolve you from all filial duty, for I do assure you, you are no son of mine." "How!" replied Jones. "And is it possible that a false suspicion should have drawn all the ill consequences upon you with which I am too well acquainted?" "It is possible," cries Benjamin, "for it is so; but though it is natural enough for men to hate even the innocent causes of their sufferings, yet I am of a different temper. I have loved you ever since I heard of your behaviour to Black George, as I told you, and I am convinced from this extraordinary meeting that you are born to make me amends for all I have suffered on that account. Besides, I dreamt the night before I saw you that I stumbled over a stool without hurting myself, which plainly showed me something good was towards me; and last night I dreamt again, that I rode behind you on a milk-white mare, which is a very excellent dream and betokens much good fortune, which I am resolved to pursue unless you have the cruelty to deny me."

"I should be very glad, Mr. Partridge," answered Jones, "to have it in my power to make you amends for your sufferings on my account, though at present I see no likelihood of it; however, I assure you I will deny you nothing which is in my power to grant."

"It is in your power sure enough," replied Benjamin, "for I desire nothing more than leave to attend you in this expedition. Nay, I have so entirely set my heart upon it that if you should refuse me, you will kill both a barber and a surgeon in one breath."

Jones answered, smiling, that he should be very sorry to be the occasion of so much mischief to the public. He then advanced many prudential reasons in order to dissuade Benjamin (whom we shall hereafter call Partridge) from his purpose; but all were in vain. Partridge relied strongly on his dream of the milk-white mare. "Besides, sir," says he, "I promise you I have as good an inclination to the cause as any man can possibly have, and go I will, whether you admit me to go in your company or not."

Jones, who was as much pleased with Partridge as Partridge could be with him, and who had not consulted his own inclination but the good of the other in desiring him to stay behind, when he found his friend so resolute, at last gave his consent; but then, recollecting himself, he said, "Perhaps, Mr. Partridge, you think I shall be able to support you, but I really am not"; and then, taking out his purse, he told out nine guineas, which he declared were his whole fortune.

Partridge answered that his dependence was only on his future favour, for he was thoroughly convinced he would shortly have enough in his power. "At present, sir," said he, "I believe I am rather the richer man of the two, but all I have is at your service and at your disposal. I insist upon your taking the whole, and I beg only to attend you in the quality of your servant, *Nil desperandum est Teucro duce et auspice Teucro";* but to this generous proposal concerning the money Jones would by no means submit.

It was resolved to set out the next morning, when a difficulty arose concerning the baggage, for the portmanteau of Mr. Jones was too large to be carried without a horse.

"If I may presume to give my advice," says Patridge, "this portmanteau, with everything in it except a few shirts, should be left behind. Those I shall be easily able to carry for you, and the rest of your clothes will remain very safely locked up in my house."

This method was no sooner proposed than agreed to, and then the barber departed in order to prepare everything for his intended expedition.

7

CONTAINING BETTER REASONS THAN ANY WHICH HAVE YET APPEARED FOR THE CONDUCT OF PARTRIDGE, AN APOLOGY FOR THE WEAKNESS OF JONES, AND SOME FARTHER ANECDOTES CONCERNING MY LANDLADY

Though Partridge was one of the most superstitious of men, he would hardly, perhaps, have desired to accompany Jones on his expedition merely from the omens of the joint-stool and white mare if his prospect had been no better than to have shared the plunder gained in the field of battle. In fact, when Partridge came to ruminate on the relation he had heard from Jones, he could not reconcile to himself that Mr. Allworthy should turn his son (for so he most firmly believed him to be) out-of-doors for any reason which he had heard assigned. He concluded, therefore, that the whole was a fiction, and that Jones, of whom he had often from his correspondents heard the wildest character, had in reality run away from his father. It came into his head, therefore, that if he could prevail with the young gentleman to return back to his father, he should by that means render a service to Allworthy which would obliterate all his former anger; nay, indeed, he conceived that very anger was counterfeited and that Allworthy had sacrificed him to his own reputation. And this suspicion, indeed, he well accounted for from the tender behaviour of that excellent man to the foundling child; from his great severity to Partridge, who, knowing himself to be innocent, could not conceive that any other should think him guilty; lastly, from the allowance which he had privately received long after the annuity had been publicly taken from him, and which he looked upon as a kind of smart-money, or rather by way of atonement for injustice; for it is very uncommon, I believe, for men to ascribe the benefactions they receive to pure charity when they can possibly impute them to any other motive. If he could by any means, therefore, persuade the young gentleman to return home, he doubted not but that he should again be received into the favour of Allworthy and well rewarded for his pains; nay, and should be again restored to his native country, a restoration which Ulysses himself never wished more heartily than poor Partridge.

As for Jones, he was well satisfied with the truth of what the other had asserted, and believed that Partridge had no other inducements but love to him and zeal for the cause, a blameable want of caution and diffidence in the veracity of others, in which he was highly worthy of censure. To say the truth, there are but two ways by which men become possessed of this excellent quality: the one is from long experience and the other is from nature; which last, I presume, is often meant by genius, or great natural parts, and it is infinitely the better of the two, not only as we are masters of it much earlier in life but as it is much more infallible and conclusive; for a man who hath been imposed upon by ever so many may still hope to find others more honest, whereas he who receives certain necessary admonitions from within that this is impossible must have very little understanding, indeed, if he ever renders himself liable to be once deceived. As Jones had not this gift from nature, he was too young to have gained it by experience; for at the diffident wisdom which is to be acquired this way we seldom arrive till very late in life, which is perhaps the reason why some old men are apt to despise the understandings of all those who are a little younger than themselves.

Jones spent most part of the day in the company of a new acquaintance. This was no other than the landlord of the house, or rather the husband of the landlady. He had but lately made his descent downstairs after a long fit of the gout, in which distemper he was generally confined to his room during one-half of the year, and during the rest, he walked about the house, smoked his pipe, and drank his bottle with his friends, without concerning himself in the least with any kind of business. He had been bred, as they call it, a gentleman; that is, bred up to do nothing, and had spent a very small fortune, which he inherited from an industrious farmer, his uncle, in hunting, horse-racing, and cock-fighting, and had been married by my landlady for certain purposes which he had long since desisted from answering, for which she hated him heartily. But as he was a surly kind of fellow, so she contented herself with frequently upbraiding him by disadvantageous comparisons with her first husband, whose praise she had eternally in her mouth; and as she was for the most part mistress of the profit, so she was satisfied to take upon herself the care and government of the family, and, after a long successless struggle, to suffer her husband to be master of himself.

In the evening, when Jones retired to his room, a small dispute arose between this fond couple concerning him. "What," says the wife, "you have been tippling with the gentleman, I see!" "Yes," answered the husband, "we have cracked a bottle together, and a very gentleman-like man he is, and hath a very pretty notion of horse-flesh. Indeed, he is young and hath not seen much of the world, for I believe he hath been at very few horse-races." "Oho! He is one of your order, is he?" replies the landlady. "He must be a gentleman, to be sure, if he is a horse-racer. The Devil fetch such gentry; I am sure I wish I had never seen any of them. I have reason to love horse-racers, truly." "That you have," says the husband, "for I was one, you know." "Yes," answered she, "you are a pure one indeed. As my first husband used to say, I may put all the good I have ever got by you in my eyes and see never the worse." "D——n your first husband," cries he. "Don't d——n a better man than yourself," answered the wife. "If he had been alive, you durst not have done it." "Then you think," says he, "I have not so much courage as yourself, for you have d——ned him often in my hearing." "If I did," says she, "I have repented of it many's the good time and oft. And if he was so good to forgive me a word spoken in haste or so, it doth not become such a one as you to twitter me. He was a husband to me, he was; and if ever I did make use of an ill word or so in a passion, I never called him rascal; I should have told a lie if I had called him rascal." Much more she said, but not in his hearing, for, having lighted his pipe, he staggered off as fast as he could. We shall therefore transcribe no more of her speech, as it approached still nearer and nearer to a subject too indelicate to find any place in this history.

Early in the morning Partridge appeared at the bedside of Jones, ready equipped for the journey, with his knapsack at his back. This was his own workmanship, for besides his other trades, he was no indifferent tailor. He had already put up his whole stock of linen in it, consisting of four shirts, to which he now added eight for Mr. Jones; and then, packing up the portmanteau, he was departing with it towards his own house, but was stopped in his way by the landlady, who refused to suffer any removals till after the payment of the reckoning.

The landlady was, as we have said, absolute governess in these regions; it was therefore necessary to comply with her rules, so the bill was presently writ out, which amounted to a much larger sum than might have been expected from the entertainment which Jones had met with. But here we are obliged to disclose some maxims, which publicans hold to be the grand mysteries of their trade. The first is, if they have anything good in their house (which indeed very seldom happens), to produce it only to persons who travel with great equipages; secondly, to charge the same for the very worst provisions as if they were the best; and lastly, if any of their guests call but for little, to make them pay a double price for everything they have, so that the amount by the head may be much the same.

The bill being made and discharged, Jones set forward with Partridge carrying his knapsack; nor did the landlady condescend to wish him a good journey, for this was, it seems, an inn frequented by people of fashion, and I know not whence it is, but all those who get their livelihood by people of fashion contract as much insolence to the rest of mankind as if they really belonged to that rank themselves.

JONES ARRIVES AT GLOUCESTER AND GOES TO THE BELL; THE CHARACTER OF THAT HOUSE AND OF A PETTIFOGGER WHICH HE THERE MEETS WITH

Mr. Jones and Partridge, or Little Benjamin (which epithet of Little was perhaps given him ironically, he being in reality near six feet high), having left their last quarters in the manner before described, travelled on to Gloucester without meeting any adventure worth relating.

Being arrived here, they chose for their house of entertainment the sign of the Bell, an excellent house indeed, and which I do most seriously recommend to every reader who shall visit this ancient city. The master of it is brother to the great preacher Whitefield, but is absolutely untainted with the pernicious principles of Methodism or of any other heretical sect. He is indeed a very honest, plain man and, in my opinion, not likely to create any disturbance either in Church or State. His wife hath, I believe, had much pretension to beauty, and is still a very fine woman. Her person and deportment might have made a shining figure in the politest assemblies, but though she must be conscious of this and many other perfections, she seems perfectly contented with, and resigned to, that state of life to which she is called, and this resignation is entirely owing to the prudence and wisdom of her temper; for she is at present as free from any Methodistical notions as her husband. I say at present; for she freely confesses that her brother's documents made at first some impression upon her, and that she had put herself to the expense of a long hood in order to attend the extraordinary emotions of the spirit, but having found during an experiment of three weeks no emotions, she says, worth a farthing, she very wisely laid by her hood and abandoned the sect. To be concise, she is a very friendly, good-natured woman, and so industrious to oblige that the guests must be of a very morose disposition who are not extremely well satisfied in her house.

Mrs. Whitefield happened to be in the yard when Jones and his attendant marched in. Her sagacity soon discovered in the air of our hero something which distinguished him from the vulgar. She ordered her servants, therefore, immediately to show him into a room, and presently afterwards invited him to dinner with herself, which invitation he very thankfully accepted; for indeed much less agreeable company than that of Mrs. Whitefield and a much worse entertainment than she had provided would have been welcome after so long fasting and so long a walk.

Besides Mr. Jones and the good governess of the mansion, there sat down at table an attorney of Salisbury; indeed, the very same who had brought the news of Mrs. Blifil's death to Mr. Allworthy, and whose name, which, I think, we did not before mention, was Dowling; there was likewise present another person, who styled himself a lawyer and who lived somewhere near Lidlinch, in Somersetshire. This fellow, I say, styled himself a lawyer but was indeed a most vile pettifogger, without sense or knowledge of any kind, one of those who may be termed train-bearers to the law, a sort of supernumeraries in the profession, who are the hackneys of attorneys and will ride more miles for half a crown than a post-boy.

During the time of dinner the Somersetshire lawyer recollected the face of Jones, which he had seen at Mr. Allworthy's, for he had often visited in that gentleman's kitchen. He therefore took occasion to inquire after the good family there with that familiarity which would have become an intimate friend or acquaintance of Mr. Allworthy, and indeed he did all in his power to insinuate himself to be such, though he had never had the honour of speaking to any person in that family higher than the butler. Jones answered all his questions with much civility, though he never remembered to have seen the pettifogger before, and though he concluded from the outward appearance and behaviour of the man that he usurped a freedom with his betters to which he was by no means entitled.

As the conversation of fellows of this kind is of all others the most detestable to men of any sense, the cloth was no sooner removed than Mr. Jones withdrew, and a little barbarously left poor Mrs. Whitefield to do a penance which I have often heard Mr. Timothy Harris and other publicans of good taste lament as the severest lot annexed to their calling: namely, that of being obliged to keep company with their guests.

Jones had no sooner quitted the room than the pettifogger, in a whispering tone, asked Mrs. Whitefield if she knew who that fine spark was. She answered she had never seen the gentleman before. "The gentleman, indeed!" replied the petti-fogger; "a pretty gentleman truly! Why, he's the bastard of a fellow who was hanged for horse-stealing. He was dropped at Squire Allworthy's door, where one of the servants found him in a box so full of rain-water that he would certainly have been drowned had he not been reserved for another fate." "Ay, ay, you need not mention it, I protest; we understand what that fate is very well," cries Dowling, with a most facetious grin. "Well," continued the other, "the squire ordered him to be taken in, for he is a timorsome man, everybody knows, and was afraid of drawing himself into a scrape; and there the bastard was bred up and fed and clothified all to the world like any gentleman; and there he got one of the servant-maids with child and persuaded her to swear it to the squire himself; and afterwards he broke the arm of one Mr. Thwackum, a clergyman, only because he reprimanded him for following whores; and afterwards he snapped a pistol at Mr. Blifil behind his back; and once, when Squire Allworthy was sick, he got a drum and beat it all over the house to prevent him from sleeping; and twenty other pranks he hath played, for all of which about four or five days ago, just before I left the country, the squire stripped him stark naked and turned him out-of-doors."

"And very justly too, I protest," cries Dowling. "I would turn my own son out-of-doors if he was guilty of half as much. And pray what is the name of this pretty gentleman?"

"The name o' un!" answered Pettifogger. "Why, he is called Thomas Jones."

"Jones!" answered Dowling, a little eagerly. "What, Mr. Jones that lived at Mr. Allworthy's? Was that the gentleman that dined with us?" "The very same," said the other. "I have heard of the gentleman," cries Dowling, "often, but I never heard any ill character of him." "And I am sure," says Mrs. Whitefield, "if half what this gentleman hath said be true, Mr. Jones hath the most deceitful countenance I ever saw, for sure his looks promise something very different; and I must say, for the little I have seen of him he is as civil a well-bred man as you would wish to converse with."

Pettifogger, calling to mind that he had not been sworn, as he usually was before he gave his evidence, now bound what he had declared with so many oaths and imprecations that the landlady's ears were shocked, and she put a stop to his swearing by assuring him of her belief. Upon which he said, "I hope, madam, you imagine I would scorn to tell such things of any man unless I knew them to be true. What interest have I in taking away the reputation of a man who never injured me? I promise you every syllable of what I have said is fact and the whole country knows it."

As Mrs. Whitefield had no reason to suspect that the pettifogger had any motive or temptation to abuse Jones, the reader cannot blame her for believing what he so confidently affirmed with many oaths. She accordingly gave up her skill in physiognomy and henceforwards conceived so ill an opinion of her guest that she heartily wished him out of her house.

This dislike was now farther increased by a report which Mr. Whitefield made from the kitchen, where Partridge had informed the company that though he carried the knapsack and contented himself with staying among servants while Tom Jones (as he called him) was regaling in the parlour, he was not his servant, but only a friend and companion, and as good a gentleman as Mr. Jones himself.

Dowling sat all this while silent, biting his fingers, making faces, grinning, and looking wonderfully arch; at last he opened his lips and protested that the gentleman looked like another sort of man. He then called for his bill with the utmost haste, declared he must be at Hereford that evening, lamented his great hurry of business, and wished he could divide himself into twenty pieces in order to be at once in twenty places.

The pettifogger now likewise departed, and then Jones desired the favour of Mrs. Whitefield's company to drink tea with him, but she refused, and with a manner so different from that with which she had received him at dinner that it a little surprised him. And now he soon perceived her behaviour totally changed; for instead of that natural affability which we have before celebrated, she wore a constrained severity on her countenance, which was so disagreeable to Mr. Jones that he resolved, however late, to quit the house that evening.

He did indeed account somewhat unfairly for this sudden change; for besides some hard and unjust surmises concerning female fickleness and mutability, he began to suspect that he owed this want of civility to his want of horses, a sort of animals which, as they dirty no sheets, are thought in inns to pay better for their beds than their riders and are therefore considered as the more desirable company; but Mrs. Whitefield, to do her justice, had a much more liberal way of thinking. She was perfectly well bred and could be very civil to a gentleman though he walked on foot; in reality, she looked on our hero as a sorry scoundrel, and therefore treated him as such, for which not even Jones himself, had he known as much as the reader, could have blamed her; nay, on the contrary, he must have approved her conduct and have esteemed her the more for the disrespect shown towards himself. This is indeed a most aggravating circumstance which attends unjustly depriving men of their reputation; for a man who is conscious of having an ill character cannot justly be angry with those who neglect and slight him, but ought rather to despise such as affect his conversation unless where a perfect intimacy must have convinced them that their friend's character hath been falsely and injuriously aspersed.

This was not, however, the case of Jones; for as he was a perfect stranger to the truth, so he was with good reason offended at the treatment he received. He therefore paid his reckoning and departed, highly against the will of Mr. Partridge, who, having remonstrated much against it to no purpose, at last condescended to take up his knapsack and to attend his friend.

9

CONTAINING SEVERAL DIALOGUES BETWEEN JONES AND PARTRIDGE, CONCERNING LOVE, COLD, HUNGER, AND OTHER MATTERS; WITH THE LUCKY AND NARROW ESCAPE OF PARTRIDGE AS HE WAS ON THE VERY BRINK OF MAKING A FATAL DISCOVERY TO HIS FRIEND

The shadows began now to descend larger from the high mountains; the feathered creation had betaken themselves to their rest. Now the highest order of mortals were sitting down to their dinners and the lowest order to their suppers. In a word, the clock struck five just as Mr. Jones took his leave of Gloucester, an hour at which (as it was now midwinter) the dirty fingers of Night would have drawn her sable curtain over the universe had not the Moon forbid her; who now, with a face as broad and as red as those of some jolly mortals who, like her, turn night into day, began to rise from her bed, where she had slumbered away the day in order to sit up all night. Jones had not travelled far before he paid his compliments to that beautiful planet, and, turning to his companion, asked him if he had ever beheld so delicious an evening. Partridge making no ready answer to his question, he proceeded to comment on the beauty of the moon and repeated some passages from Milton, who hath certainly excelled all other poets in his description of the heavenly luminaries. He then told Partridge the story from *The Spectator* of two lovers who had agreed to entertain themselves when they were at a great distance from each other, by repairing at a certain fixed hour to look at the moon, thus pleasing themselves with the thought that they were both employed in contemplating the same object at the same time. "Those lovers," added he, "must have had souls truly capable of feeling all the tenderness of the sublimest of all human passions." "Very probably," cries Partridge; "but I envy them more if they had bodies incapable of feeling cold; for I am almost frozen to death and am very much afraid I shall lose a piece of my nose before we get to another house of entertainment. Nay, truly, we may well expect some judgement should happen to us for our folly in running away so by night from one of the most excellent inns I ever set my foot into. I am sure I never saw more good things in my life, and the greatest lord in the land cannot live better in his own house than he may there. And to forsake such a house and go a-rambling about the country, the Lord knows whither, *per devia rura viarum*—I say nothing for my part, but some people might not have charity enough to conclude we were in our sober senses." "Fie upon it, Mr. Partridge," says Jones. "Have a better heart; consider you are going to face an enemy, and are you afraid of facing a little cold? I wish, indeed, we had a guide to advise which of these roads we should take." "May I be so bold," says Partridge, "to offer my advice? *Interdum stultus opportuna loquitur.*" "Why, which of them," cries Jones, "would you recommend?" "Truly, neither of them," answered Partridge. "The only road we can be certain of finding is the road we came. A good hearty pace will bring us back to Gloucester in an hour, but if we go forward, the Lord Harry knows when we shall arrive at any place; for I see at least fifty miles before me and no house in all the way." "You see, indeed, a very fair prospect," says Jones, "which receives great additional beauty from the extreme lustre of the moon. However, I will keep the left-hand track, as that seems to lead directly to those hills which we were informed lie not far from Worcester. And here, if you are inclined to quit me, you may, and return back again; but for my part, I am resolved to go forward."

"It is unkind in you, sir," says Partridge, "to suspect me of any such intention. What I have advised hath been as much on your account as on my own; but since you are determined to go on, I am as much determined to follow. *I præ, sequar te.*"

They now travelled some miles without speaking to each other, during which suspense of discourse Jones often sighed and Benjamin groaned as bitterly, though from a very different reason. At length Jones made a full stop and, turning about, cries, "Who knows, Partridge, but the loveliest creature in the universe may have her eyes now fixed on that very moon which I behold at this instant!" "Very likely, sir," answered Partridge; "and if my eyes were fixed on a good sirloin of roast beef, the Devil might take the moon and her horns into the bargain." "Did ever tramontane make such an answer?" cries Jones. "Prithee, Partridge, wast thou never susceptible of love in thy life, or hath time worn away all the traces of it from thy memory?" "Alack-a-day," cries Partridge. "Well would it have been for me if I had never known what love was. *Infandum, regina, jubes renovare dolorem.* I am sure I have tasted all the tenderness and sublimities and bitternesses of the passion." "Was your mistress unkind, then?" says Jones. "Very unkind indeed, sir," answered Partridge, "for she married me and made one of the most confounded wives in the world. However, heaven be praised, she's gone; and if I believed she was in the moon, according to a book I once read, which teaches that to be the receptacle of departed spirits, I would never look at it for fear of seeing her; but I wish, sir, that the moon was a looking-glass, for your sake, and that Miss Sophia Western was now placed before it." "My dear Partridge," cries Jones, "what a thought was there! A thought which I am certain could never have entered into any mind but that of a lover. Oh, Partridge, could I hope once again to see that face; but, alas, all those golden dreams are vanished forever, and my only refuge from future misery is to forget the object of all my former happiness." "And do you really despair of ever seeing Miss Western again?" answered Partridge. "If you will follow my advice, I will engage you shall not only see her but have her in your arms." "Ha! Do not awaken a thought of that nature," cries Jones. "I have struggled sufficiently to conquer all such wishes already." "Nay," answered Partridge, "if you do not wish to have your mistress in your arms, you are a most extraordinary lover indeed." "Well, well," says Jones, "let us avoid this subject, but pray what is your advice?" "To give it you in the military phrase, then," says Partridge, "as we are soldiers: 'To the right about.'" Let us return the way we came; we may yet reach Gloucester to-night, though late, whereas if we proceed, we are likely for aught I see to ramble about forever without coming either to house or home." "I have already told you my resolution is to go on," answered Jones, "but I would have you go back. I am obliged to you for your company hither, and I beg you to accept a guinea as a small instance of my gratitude. Nay, it would be cruel in me to suffer you go any farther; for, to deal plainly with you, my chief end and desire is a glorious death in the service of my king and country." "As for your money," replied Partridge, "I beg, sir, you will put it up; I will receive none of you at this time, for at present I am, I believe, the richer man of the two. And as your resolution is to go on, so mine is to follow you if you do. Nay, now my presence appears absolutely necessary to take care of you since your intentions are so desperate; for I promise you my views are much more prudent: as you are resolved to fall in battle if you can, so I am resolved as firmly to come to no hurt if I can help it. And indeed I have the comfort to think there will be but little danger; for a popish priest told me the other day the business would soon be over and, he believed, without a battle." "A popish priest," cries Jones, "I have heard, is not always to be believed when he speaks in behalf of his religion." "Yes, but so far," answered the other, "from speaking in behalf of his religion, he assured me the Catholics did not expect to be any gainers by the change; for that Prince Charles was as good a Protestant as any in England and that nothing but regard to right made him and the rest of the popish party to be Jacobites." "I believe him to be as much a Protestant as I believe he hath any right," says Jones, "and I make no doubt of our success, but not without a battle. So that I am not so sanguine as your friend the popish priest." "Nay, to be sure, sir," answered Partridge, "all the prophecies I have ever read speak of a great deal of blood to be spilt in the quarrel, and the miller with three thumbs, who is now alive, is to hold the horses of three kings up to his knees in blood. Lord have mercy upon us all and send better times!" "With what stuff and nonsense hast thou filled thy head?" answered Jones. "This too, I suppose, comes from the popish priest. Monsters and prodigies are the proper arguments to support monstrous and absurd doctrines. The cause of King George is the cause of liberty and true religion. In other words, it is the cause of common sense, my boy, and I warrant you will succeed, though Briareus himself was to rise again with his hundred thumbs and to turn miller." Partridge made no reply to this. He was indeed cast into the utmost confusion by this declaration of Jones. For to inform the reader of a secret which we had no proper opportunity of revealing before, Partridge was in truth a Jacobite, and had concluded that Jones was of the same party and was now proceeding to join the rebels—an opinion which was not without foundation. For the tall, long-sided dame mentioned by Hudibras, that many-eyed, many-tongued, many-mouthed, many-eared monster of Virgil, had related the story of the quarrel between Jones and the officer with her usual regard to truth. She had indeed changed the name of Sophia into that of the Pretender, and had reported that drinking his health was the cause for which Jones was knocked down. This Partridge had heard and most firmly believed. 'Tis no wonder, therefore, that he had thence entertained the above-mentioned opinion of Jones, and which he had almost discovered to him before he found out his own mistake. And at this the reader will be less inclined to wonder if he pleases to recollect the doubtful phrase in which Jones first communicated his resolution to Mr. Partridge; and indeed, had the words been less ambiguous, Partridge might very well have construed them as he did, being persuaded as he was that the whole nation were of the same inclination in their hearts; nor did it stagger him that Jones had travelled in the company of soldiers, for he had the same opinion of the army which he had of the rest of the people.

But however well affected he might be to James or Charles, he was still more attached to Little Benjamin than to either; for which reason he no sooner discovered the principles of his fellow-traveller than he thought proper to conceal and outwardly to give up his own to the man on whom he depended for the making of his fortune, since he by no means believed the affairs of Jones to be so desperate as they really were with Mr. Allworthy; for as he had kept a constant correspondence with some of his neighbours since he left that country, he had heard much, indeed more than was true, of the great affection Mr. Allworthy bore this young man, who, as Partridge had been instructed, was to be that gentleman's heir, and whom, as we have said, he did not in the least doubt to be his son.

He imagined, therefore, that whatever quarrel was between them, it would be certainly made up at the return of Mr. Jones, an event from which he promised great advantages if he could take this opportunity of ingratiating himself with that young gentleman; and if he could by any means be instrumental in procuring his return, he doubted not, as we have before said, but it would as highly advance him in the favour of Mr. Allworthy.

We have already observed that he was a very good-natured fellow, and he hath himself declared the violent attachment he had to the person and character of Jones; but possibly the views which I have just before mentioned might likewise have some little share in prompting him to undertake this expedition, at least in urging him to continue it after he had discovered that his master and himself, like some prudent fathers and sons, though they travelled together in great friendship, had embraced opposite parties. I am led into this conjecture by having remarked that though love, friendship, esteem, and such like have very powerful operations in the human mind, interest, however, is an ingredient seldom omitted by wise men when they would work others to their own purposes. This is indeed a most excellent medicine and, like Ward's pill, flies at once to the particular part of the body on which you desire to operate, whether it be the tongue, the hand, or any other member, where it scarce ever fails of immediately producing the desired effect.

10

IN WHICH OUR TRAVELLERS MEET WITH A VERY EXTRAORDINARY ADVENTURE

Just as Jones and his friend came to the end of their dialogue in the preceeding chapter, they arrived at the bottom of a very steep hill. Here Jones stopped short and, directing his eyes upwards, stood for a while silent. At length he called to his companion and said, "Partridge, I wish I was at the top of this hill; it must certainly afford a most charming prospect, especially by this light; for the solemn gloom which the moon casts on all objects is beyond expression beautiful, especially to an imagination which is desirous of cultivating melancholy ideas." "Very probably," answered Partridge; "but if the top of the hill be properest to produce melancholy thoughts, I suppose the bottom is the likeliest to produce merry ones, and these I take to be much the better of the two. I protest you have made my blood run cold with the very mentioning of the top of that mountain, which seems to me to be one of the highest in the world. No, no, if we look for anything, let it be for a place underground to screen ourselves from the frost." "Do so," said Jones, "let it be but within hearing of this place, and I will halloo to you at my return back." "Surely, sir, you are not mad," said Partridge. "Indeed I am," answered Jones, "if ascending this hill be madness; but as you complain so much of the cold already, I would have you stay below. I will certainly return to you within an hour." "Pardon me, sir," cries Partridge, "I have determined to follow you wherever you go." Indeed he was now afraid to stay behind; for though he was coward enough in all respects, yet his chief fear was that of ghosts, with which the present time of night and the wildness of the place extremely well suited.

At this instant Partridge espied a glimmering light through some trees, which seemed very near to them. He immediately cried out in a rapture, "Oh, sir! Heaven hath at last heard my prayers and hath brought us to a house; perhaps it may be an inn. Let me beseech you, sir, if you have any compassion either for me or yourself, do not despise the goodness of Providence, but let us go directly to yon light. Whether it be a public-house or no, I am sure if they be Christians that dwell there, they will not refuse a little house-room to persons in our miserable condition." Jones at length yielded to the earnest supplications of Partridge, and both together made directly towards the place whence the light issued.

They soon arrived at the door of this house or cottage, for it might be called either without much impropriety. Here Jones knocked several times without receiving any answer from within, at which Partridge, whose head was full of nothing but of ghosts, devils, witches, and such like, began to tremble, crying, "Lord have mercy upon us; sure the people must be all dead. I can see no light neither now, and yet I am certain I saw a candle burning but a moment before. Well! I have heard of such things." "What hast thou heard of?" said Jones. "The people are either fast asleep or, probably, as this is a lonely place, are afraid to open their door." He then began to vociferate pretty loudly, and at last an old woman, opening an upper casement, asked who they were and what they wanted. Jones answered they were travellers who had lost their way and, having seen a light in the window, had been led hither in hopes of finding some fire to warm themselves. "Whoever you are," cries the woman, "you have no business here, nor shall I open the door to anybody at this time of night." Partridge, whom the sound of a human voice had recovered from his fright, fell to the most earnest supplications to be admitted for a few minutes to the fire, saying he was almost dead with the cold, to which fear had indeed contributed equally with the frost. He assured her that the gentleman who spoke to her was one of the greatest squires in the country, and made use of every argument save one, which Jones afterwards effectually added, and this was the promise of half a crown, a bribe too great to be resisted by such a person, especially as the genteel appearance of Jones, which the light of the moon plainly discovered to her, together with his affable behaviour, had entirely subdued those apprehensions of thieves which she had at first conceived. She agreed, therefore, at last to let them in, where Partridge to his infinite joy found a good fire ready for his reception.

The poor fellow, however, had no sooner warmed himself than those thoughts which were always uppermost in his mind began a little to disturb his brain. There was no article of his creed in which he had a stronger faith than he had in witchcraft, nor can the reader conceive a figure more adapted to inspire this idea than the old woman who now stood before him. She answered exactly to that picture drawn by Otway in his *Orphan*. Indeed, if this woman had lived in the reign of James the First, her appearance alone would have hanged her almost without any evidence.

Many circumstances likewise conspired to confirm Partridge in his opinion: her living, as he then imagined, by herself in so lonely a place, and in a house the outside of which seemed much too good for her, but where the inside was furnished in the most neat and elegant manner. To say the truth, Jones himself was not a little surprised at what he saw; for besides the extraordinary neatness of the room, it was adorned with a great number of knick-knacks and curiosities, which might have engaged the attention of a virtuoso.

While Jones was admiring these things and Partridge sat trembling with the firm belief that he was in the house of a witch, the old woman said, "I hope, gentlemen, you will make what haste you can, for I expect my master presently and I would not for double the money he should find you here." "Then you have a master," cried Jones; "indeed, you will excuse me, good woman, but I was surprised to see all those fine things in your house." "Ah, sir," said she, "if the twentieth part of these things were mine, I should think myself a rich woman, but pray, sir, do not stay much longer, for I look for him in every minute." "Why, sure he would not be angry with you," said Jones, "for doing a common act of charity." "Alack-a-day, sir," said she, "he is a strange man, not at all like other people. He keeps no company with anybody and seldom walks out but by night, for he doth not care to be seen; and all the country-people are as much afraid of meeting him, for his dress is enough to frighten those who are not used to it. They call him the Man of the Hill (for there he walks by night), and the country-people are not, I believe, more afraid of the Devil himself. He would be terribly angry if he found you here." "Pray, sir," says Partridge, "don't let us offend the gentleman; I am ready to walk and was never warmer in my life. Do pray, sir, let us go—here are pistols over the chimney; who knows whether they be charged or no, or what he may do with them?" "Fear nothing, Partridge," cries Jones; "I will secure thee from danger." "Nay, for matter o' that, he never doth any mischief," said the woman, "but to be sure, it is necessary he should keep some arms for his own safety; for his house hath been beset more than once, and it is not many nights ago that we thought we heard thieves about it; for my own part, I have often wondered that he is not murdered by some villain or other as he walks out by himself at such hours, but then, as I said, the people are afraid of him, and besides, they think, I suppose, he hath nothing about him worth taking." "I should imagine by this collection of rarities," cries Jones, "that your master had been a traveller." "Yes, sir," answered she, "he hath been a very great one; there be few gentlemen that know more of all matters than he. I fancy he hath been crossed in love, or whatever it is I know not, but I have lived with him above these thirty years, and in all that time he hath hardly spoke to six living people." She then again solicited their departure, in which she was backed by Partridge, but Jones purposely protracted the time, for his curiosity was greatly raised to see this extraordinary person. Though the old woman, therefore, concluded every one of her answers with desiring him to be gone and Partridge proceeded so far as to pull him by the sleeve, he still continued to invent new questions till the old woman, with an affrighted countenance, declared she heard her master's signal; and at the same instant, more than one voice was heard without the door, crying, "D—n your blood, show us your money this instant. Your money, you villain, or we will blow your brains about your ears."

"Oh, good heaven!" cries the old woman. "Some villains, to be sure, have attacked my master. Oh la, what shall I do? What shall I do?" "How!" cries Jones. "How! Are these pistols loaded?" "Oh, good sir, there is nothing in them indeed. Oh, pray don't murder us, gentlemen" (for in reality she now had the same opinion of those within as she had of those without). Jones made her no answer; but snatching an old broadsword which hung in the room, he instantly sallied out, where he found the old gentleman struggling with two ruffians and begging for mercy. Jones asked no questions, but fell so briskly to work with his broadsword that the fellows immediately quitted their hold and, without offering to attack our hero, betook themselves to their heels and made their escape; for he did not attempt to pursue them, being contented with having delivered the old gentleman, and indeed he concluded he had pretty well done their business; for both of them, as they ran off, cried out with bitter oaths that they were dead men.

Jones presently ran to lift up the old gentleman, who had been thrown down in the scuffle, expressing at the same time great concern lest he should have received any harm from the villains. The old man stared a moment at Jones and then cried, "No, sir, no; I have very little harm, I thank you. Lord have mercy upon me." "I see, sir," said Jones, "you are not free from apprehensions, even of those who have had the happiness to be your deliverers; nor can I blame any suspicions which you may have, but indeed, you have no real occasion for any; here are none but your friends present. Having missed our way this cold night, we took the liberty of warming ourselves at your fire, whence we were just departing when we heard you call for assistance, which I must say Providence alone seems to have sent you." "Providence indeed," cries the old gentleman, "if it be so." "So it is, I assure you," cries Jones. "Here is your own sword, sir. I have used it in your defence and I now return it into your own hand." The old man, having received the sword, which was stained with the blood of his enemies, looked steadfastly at Jones during some moments and then with a sigh cried out, "You will pardon me, young gentleman, I was not always of a suspicious temper, nor am I a friend to ingratitude." "Be thankful, then," cries Jones, "to that Providence to which you owe your deliverance; as to my part, I have only discharged the common duties of humanity and what I would have done for any fellow-creature in your situation." "Let me look at you a little longer," cries the old gentleman. "You are a human creature, then? Well, perhaps you are. Come, pray walk into my little hut. You have been my deliverer indeed."

The old woman was distracted between the fears which she had of her master and for him, and Partridge was, if possible, in a greater fright. The former of these, however, when she heard her master speak kindly to Jones and perceived what had happened, came again to herself; but Partridge no sooner saw the gentleman than the strangeness of his dress infused greater terrors into that poor fellow than he had before felt either from the strange description which he had heard or from the uproar which had happened at the door.

To say the truth, it was an appearance which might have affected a more constant mind than that of Mr. Partridge. This person was of the tallest size, with a long beard as white as snow. His body was clothed with the skin of an ass, made something into the form of a coat. He wore likewise boots on his legs and a cap on his head, both composed of the skin of some other animals.

As soon as the old gentleman came into his house, the old woman began her congratulations on his happy escape from the ruffians. "Yes," cried he, "I have escaped indeed, thanks to my preserver." "Oh, the blessing on him," answered she; "he is a good gentleman, I warrant him. I was afraid your worship would have been angry with me for letting him in, and to be certain, I should not have done it had I not seen by the moonlight that he was a gentleman, and almost frozen to death. And to be certain, it must have been some good angel that sent him hither and tempted me to do it."

"I am afraid, sir," said the old gentleman to Jones, "that I have nothing in this house which you can either eat or drink unless you will accept a dram of brandy, of which I can give you some most excellent and which I have had by me these thirty years." Jones declined this offer in a very civil and proper speech, and then the other asked him whither he was travelling when he missed his way, saying, "I must own myself surprised to see such a person as you appear to be journeying on foot at this time of night. I suppose, sir, you are a gentleman of these parts, for you do not look like one who is used to travel far without horses."

"Appearances," cried Jones, "are often deceitful; men sometimes look like what they are not. I assure you I am not of this country, and whither I am travelling, in reality, I scarce know myself."

"Whoever you are or whithersoever you are going," answered the old man, "I have obligations to you which I can never return."

"I once more," replied Jones, "affirm that you have none, for there can be no merit in having hazarded that in your service on which I set no value. And nothing is so contemptible in my eyes as life."

"I am sorry, young gentleman," answered the stranger, "that you have any reason to be so unhappy at your years."

"Indeed I am, sir," answered Jones, "the most unhappy of mankind." "Perhaps you have had a friend or a mistress," replied the other. "How could you," cries Jones, "mention two words sufficient to drive me to distraction?" "Either of them are enough to drive any man to distraction," answered the old man. "I inquire no farther, sir. Perhaps my curiosity hath led me too far already."

"Indeed, sir," cries Jones, "I cannot censure a passion which I feel at this instant in the highest degree. You will pardon me when I assure you that everything which I have seen or heard since I first entered this house hath conspired to raise the greatest curiosity in me. Something very extraordinary must have determined you to this course of life, and I have reason to fear your own history is not without misfortunes."

Here the old gentleman again sighed and remained silent for some minutes; at last, looking earnestly on Jones, he said, "I have read that a good countenance is a letter of recommendation; if so, none ever can be more strongly recommended than yourself. If I did not feel some yearnings towards you from another consideration, I must be the most ungrateful monster upon earth, and I am really concerned it is no otherwise in my power than by words to convince you of my gratitude."

Jones after a moment's hesitation answered that it was in his power by words to gratify him extremely. "I have confessed a curiosity," said he, "sir; need I say how much obliged I should be to you if you would condescend to gratify it? Will you suffer me therefore to beg, unless any consideration restrains you, that you would be pleased to acquaint me what motives have induced you thus to withdraw from the society of mankind and to betake yourself to a course of life to which it sufficiently appears you was not born?"

"I scarce think myself at liberty to refuse you anything after what hath happened," replied the old man. "If you desire therefore to hear the story of an unhappy man, I will relate it to you. Indeed you judge rightly in thinking there is commonly something extraordinary in the fortunes of those who fly from society; for however it may seem a paradox, or even a contradiction, certain it is, that great philanthropy chiefly inclines us to avoid and detest mankind, not on account so much of their private and selfish vices, but for those of a relative kind, such as envy, malice, treachery, cruelty, with every other species of malevolence. These are the vices which true philanthropy abhors, and which rather than see and converse with she avoids society itself. However, without a compliment to you, you do not appear to me one of those whom I should shun or detest; nay, I must say, in what little hath dropped from you there appears some parity in our fortunes; I hope, however, yours will conclude more successfully."

Here some compliments passed between our hero and his host, and then the latter was going to begin his history when Partridge interrupted him. His apprehensions had now pretty well left him, but some effects of his terrors remained; he therefore reminded the gentleman of that excellent brandy which he had mentioned. This was presently brought, and Partridge swallowed a large bumper.

The gentleman then, without any farther preface, began as you may read in the next chapter.

IN WHICH THE MAN OF THE HILL BEGINS TO RELATE HIS HISTORY

"I was born in a village of Somersetshire called Mark, in the year 1657; my father was one of those whom they call gentlemen-farmers. He had a little estate of about £300 a year of his own and rented another estate of near the same value. He was prudent and industrious, and so good a husbandman that he might have led a very easy and comfortable life had not an arrant vixen of a wife soured his domestic quiet. But though this circumstance perhaps made him miserable, it did not make him poor; for he confined her almost entirely at home and rather chose to bear eternal upbraidings in his own house than to injure his fortune by indulging her in the extravagancies she desired abroad.

"By this Xantippe——" "So was the wife of Socrates called," said Partridge "——by this Xantippe he had two sons, of which I was the younger. He designed to give us both good educations, but my elder brother, who unhappily for him was the favourite of my mother, utterly neglected his learning, insomuch that after having been five or six years at school with little or no improvement, my father, being told by his master that it would be to no purpose to keep him longer there, at last complied with my mother in taking him home from the hands of that tyrant, as she called his master, though indeed he gave the lad much less correction than his idleness deserved, but much more, it seems, than the young gentleman liked, who constantly complained to his mother of his severe treatment and she as constantly gave him a hearing."

"Yes, yes," cries Partridge, "I have seen such mothers; I have been abused myself by them and very unjustly; such parents deserve correction as much as their children."

Jones chid the pedagogue for his interruption, and then the stranger proceeded. "My brother now, at the age of fifteen, bid adieu to all learning and to everything else but to his dog and gun, with which latter he became so expert that, though perhaps you may think it incredible, he could not only hit a standing mark with great certainty but hath actually shot a crow as it was flying in the air. He was likewise excellent at finding a hare sitting, and was soon reputed one of the best sportsmen in the country—a reputation which both he and his mother enjoyed as much as if he had been thought the finest scholar.

"The situation of my brother made me at first think my lot the harder in being continued at school, but I soon changed my opinion; for as I advanced pretty fast in learning, my labours became easy and my exercise so delightful that holidays were my most unpleasant time; for my mother, who never loved me, now apprehending that I had the greater share of my father's affection and finding, or at least thinking, that I was more taken notice of by some gentlemen of learning and particularly by the parson of the parish than my brother, she now hated my sight and made home so disagreeable to me that what is called by schoolboys Black Monday was to me the whitest in the whole year.

"Having at length gone through the school at Taunton, I was thence removed to Exeter College in Oxford, where I remained four years; at the end of which an accident happened that put a final end to my studies, and whence I may truly date the rise of all which happened to me afterwards in life.

"There was at the same college with myself one Sir George Gresham, a young fellow who was entitled to a very considerable fortune, which he was not, by the will of his father, to come into full possession of till he arrived at the age of twenty-five. However, the liberality of his guardians gave him little cause to regret the abundant caution of his father; for they allowed him five hundred pound a year while he remained at the University, where he kept his horses and his whore, and lived as wicked and as profligate a life as he could have done had he been never so entirely master of his fortune; for besides the five hundred a year which he received from his guardians, he found means to spend a thousand more. He was above the age of twenty-one and had no difficulty of gaining what credit he pleased.

"This young fellow, among many other tolerably bad qualities, had one very diabolical. He had a great delight in destroying and ruining the youth of inferior fortune by drawing them into expenses which they could not afford so well as himself, and the better and worthier and soberer any young man was, the greater pleasure and triumph had he in his destruction, thus acting the character which is recorded of the Devil, and going about seeking whom he might devour.

"It was my misfortune to fall into an acquaintance and intimacy with this gentleman. My reputation of diligence in my studies made me a desirable object of his mischievous intention, and my own inclination made it sufficiently easy for him to effect his purpose; for though I had applied myself with much industry to books, in which I took great delight, there were other pleasures in which I was capable of taking much greater, for I was high-mettled, had a violent flow of animal spirits, was a little ambitious, and extremely amorous.

"I had not long contracted an intimacy with Sir George before I became a partaker of all his pleasures, and when I was once entered on that scene, neither my inclination nor my spirit would suffer me to play an under part. I was second to none of the company in any acts of debauchery; nay, I soon distinguished myself so notably in all riots and disorders that my name generally stood first in the roll of delinquents, and instead of being lamented as the unfortunate pupil of Sir George, I was now accused as the person who had misled and debauched that hopeful young gentleman, for though he was the ringleader and promoter of all the mischief, he was never so considered. I fell at last under the censure of the Vice-Chancellor and very narrowly escaped expulsion.

"You will easily believe, sir, that such a life as I am now describing must be incompatible with my further progress in learning, and that in proportion as I addicted myself more and more to loose pleasure I must grow more and more remiss in application to my studies. This was truly the consequence, but this was not all. My expenses now greatly exceeded not only my former income but those additions which I extorted from my poor generous father, by pretences of sums being necessary for preparing for my approaching degree of Bachelor of Arts. These demands, however, grew at last so frequent and exorbitant that my father by slow degrees opened his ears to the accounts which he received from many quarters of my present behaviour, and which my mother failed not to echo very faithfully and loudly, adding, 'Ay, this is the fine gentleman, the scholar who doth so much honour to his family and is to be the making of it. I thought what all his learning would come to. He is to be the ruin of us all, I find, after his elder brother hath been denied necessaries for his sake, to perfect his education, forsooth, for which he was to pay us such interest. I thought what the interest would come to'; with much more of the same kind; but I have, I believe, satisfied you with this taste.

"My father, therefore, began now to return remonstrances instead of money to my demands, which brought my affairs perhaps a little sooner to a crisis; but had he remitted me his whole income, you will imagine it could have sufficed a very short time to support one who kept pace with the expenses of Sir George Gresham.

"It is more than possible that the distress I was now in for money, and the impracticability of going on in this manner, might have restored me at once to my senses and to my studies had I opened my eyes before I became involved in debts from which I saw no hopes of ever extricating myself. This was indeed the great art of Sir George, and by which he accomplished the ruin of many, whom he afterwards laughed at as fools and coxcombs for vying, as he called it, with a man of his fortune. To bring this about he would now and then advance a little money himself, in order to support the credit of the unfortunate youth with other people, till by means of that very credit he was irretrievably undone.

"My mind being, by these means, grown as desperate as my fortune, there was scarce a wickedness which I did not meditate in order for my relief. Self-murder itself became the subject of my serious deliberation, and I had certainly resolved on it had not a more shameful, though perhaps less sinful, thought expelled it from my head." Here he hesitated a moment and then cried out, "I protest, so many years have not washed away the shame of this act, and I shall blush while I relate it." Jones desired him to pass over anything that might give him pain in the relation, but Partridge eagerly cried out, "Oh, pray, sir, let us hear this; I had rather hear this than all the rest; as I hoped to be saved, I will never mention a word of it." Jones was going to rebuke him, but the stranger prevented it by proceeding thus: "I had a chum, a very prudent, frugal young lad, who, though he had no very large allowance, had by his parsimony heaped up upwards of forty guineas, which I knew he kept in his escritoire. I took, therefore, an opportunity of purloining his key from his breeches-pocket while he was asleep, and thus made myself master of all his riches. After which

I again conveyed his key to his pocket and, counterfeiting sleep, though I never once closed my eyes, lay in bed till after he arose and went to prayers, an exercise to which I had long been unaccustomed.

"Timorous thieves by extreme caution often subject themselves to discoveries, which those of a bolder kind escape. Thus it happened to me; for had I boldly broken open his escritoire, I had, perhaps, escaped even his suspicion, but as it was plain that the person who robbed him had possessed himself of his key, he had no doubt when he first missed his money but that his chum was certainly the thief. Now, as he was of a fearful disposition and much my inferior in strength and, I believe, in courage, he did not dare to confront me with my guilt for fear of worse bodily consequences which might happen to him. He repaired therefore immediately to the Vice-Chancellor and, upon swearing to the robbery and to the circumstances of it, very easily obtained a warrant against one who had now so bad a character through the whole University.

"Luckily for me, I lay out of the college the next evening; for that day I attended a young lady in a chaise to Whitney, where we stayed all night, and in our return the next morning to Oxford, I met one of my cronies, who acquainted me with sufficient news concerning myself to make me turn my horse another way."

"Pray, sir, did he mention anything of the warrant?" said Partridge. But Jones begged the gentleman to proceed without regarding any impertinent questions, which he did as follows:

"Having now abandoned all thoughts of returning to Oxford, the next thing which offered itself was a journey to London. I imparted this intention to my female companion, who at first remonstrated against it, but upon producing my wealth, she immediately consented. We then struck across the country into the great Cirencester Road, and made such haste that we spent the next evening (save one) in London.

"When you consider the place where I now was and the company with whom I was, you will, I fancy, conceive that a very short time brought me to an end of that sum of which I had so iniquitously possessed myself.

"I was now reduced to a much higher degree of distress than before; the necessaries of life began to be numbered among my wants, and what made my case still the more grievous was that my paramour, of whom I was now grown immoderately fond, shared the same distresses with myself. To see a woman you love in distress, to be unable to relieve her, and at the same time to reflect that you have brought her into this situation is, perhaps, a curse of which no imagination can represent the horrors to those who have not felt it." "I believe it from my soul," cries Jones, "and I pity you from the bottom of my heart." He then took two or three disorderly turns about the room, and at last begged pardon and flung himself into his chair, crying, "I thank heaven I have escaped that."

"This circumstance," continued the gentleman, "so severely aggravated the horrors of my present situation that they became absolutely intolerable. I could with less pain endure the raging of my own natural unsatisfied appetites, even hunger or thirst, than I could submit to leave ungratified the most whimsical desires of a woman on whom I so extravagantly doted that though I knew she had been the mistress of half my acquaintance, I firmly intended to marry her. But the good creature was unwilling to consent to an action which the world might think so much to my disadvantage. And as, possibly, she compassionated the daily anxieties which she must have perceived me suffer on her account, she resolved to put an end to my distress. She soon, indeed, found means to relieve me from my troublesome and perplexed situation; for while I was distracted with various inventions to supply her with pleasures she very kindly— betrayed me to one of her former lovers at Oxford, by whose care and diligence I was immediately apprehended and committed to gaol.

"Here I first began seriously to reflect on the miscarriages of my former life, on the errors I had been guilty of, on the misfortunes which I had brought on myself, and on the grief which I must have occasioned to one of the best of fathers. When I added to all these the perfidy of my mistress, such was the horror of my mind that life, instead of being longer desirable, grew the object of my abhorrence, and I could have gladly embraced death as my dearest friend if it had offered itself to my choice unattended by shame.

"The time of the assizes soon came, and I was removed by *habeas corpus* to Oxford, where I expected certain conviction and condemnation; but to my great surprise none appeared against me, and I was at the end of the sessions discharged for want of prosecution. In short, my chum had left Oxford and, whether from indolence or from what other motive I am ignorant, had declined concerning himself any farther in the affair."

"Perhaps," cries Partridge, "he did not care to have your blood upon his hands, and he was in the right on't. If any person was to be hanged upon my evidence, I should never be able to lie alone afterwards for fear of seeing his ghost."

"I shall shortly doubt, Partridge," says Jones, "whether thou art more brave or wise." "You may laugh at me, sir, if you please," answered Partridge, "but if you will hear a very short story which I can tell, and which is most certainly true, perhaps you may change your opinion. In the parish where I was born——" Here Jones would have silenced him; but the stranger interceded, that he might be permitted to tell his story and in the meantime promised to recollect the remainder of his own.

Partridge then proceeded thus: "In the parish where I was born, there lived a farmer whose name was Bridle, and he had a son named Francis, a good hopeful young fellow; I was at the grammar-school with him, where I remember he was got into Ovid's *Epistles,* and he could construe you three lines together sometimes without looking into a dictionary. Besides all this, he was a very good lad, never missed church o' Sundays, and was reckoned one of the best psalm-singers in the whole parish. He would indeed now and then take a cup too much, and that was the only fault he had." "Well, but come to the ghost," cries Jones. "Never fear, sir, I shall come to him soon enough," answered Partridge. "You must know, then, that Farmer Bridle lost a mare, a sorrel one to the best of my remembrance; and so it fell out that this young Francis shortly afterward being at a fair at Hindon, and as I think it was on—I can't remember the day—and being as he was, what should he happen to meet but a man upon his father's mare. Frank called out presently, 'Stop thief,' and it being in the middle of the fair, it was impossible, you know, for the man to make his escape. So they apprehended him and carried him before the justice; I remember it was Justice Willoughby, of Noyle, a very worthy good gentleman, and he committed him to prison and bound Frank in a recognizance, I think they call it; a hard word compounded of *re* and *cognosco*, but it differs in its meaning from the use of the simple, as many other compounds do. Well, at last down came my Lord

Justice Page to hold the assizes, and so the fellow was had up, and Frank was had up for a witness. To be sure, I shall never forget the face of the judge when he begun to ask him what he had to say against the prisoner. He made poor Frank tremble and shake in his shoes. 'Well, you fellow,' says my lord, 'what have you to say? Don't stand humming and hawing, but speak out'; but, however, he soon turned altogether as civil to Frank and began to thunder at the fellow, and when he asked him if he had anything to say for himself, the fellow said he had found the horse. 'Ay,' answered the judge, 'thou art a lucky fellow; I have travelled the circuit these forty years and never found a horse in my life; but I'll tell thee what, friend, thou wast more lucky than thou didst know of, for thou didst not only find a horse but a halter too, I promise thee.' To be sure I shall never forget the word. Upon which everybody fell a-laughing, as how could they help it? Nay, and twenty other jests he made which I can't remember now. There was something about his skill in horse-flesh which made all the folks laugh. To be certain the judge must have been a very brave man as well as a man of much learning. It is indeed charming sport to hear trials upon life and death. One thing I own I thought a little hard: that the prisoner's counsel was not suffered to speak for him, though he desired only to be heard one very short word, but my lord would not hearken to him, though he suffered a counsellor to talk against him for above half an hour. I thought it hard, I own, that there should be so many of them: my lord, and the court, and the jury, and the counsellors, and the witnesses all upon one poor man; and he too in chains. Well, the fellow was hanged, as to be sure it could be no otherwise, and poor Frank could never be easy about it. He never was in the dark alone but he fancied he saw the fellow's spirit." "Well, and this is thy story?" cries Jones. "No, no," answered Partridge. "O Lord, have mercy upon me. I am just now coming to the matter; for one night, coming from the ale-house in a long narrow dark lane, there he ran directly up against him, and the spirit was all in white, and fell upon Frank, and Frank, who is a sturdy lad, fell upon the spirit again, and there they had a tussle together, and poor Frank was dreadfully beat; indeed, he made a shift at last to crawl home, but what with the beating and what with the fright, he lay ill above a fortnight, and all this is most certainly true, and the whole parish will bear witness to it."

The stranger smiled at this story and Jones burst into a loud fit of laughter, upon which Partridge cried, "Ay, you may laugh, sir, and so did some others, particularly a squire, who is thought to be no better than an atheist; who, forsooth, because there was a calf with a white face found dead in the same lane the next morning, would fain have it that the battle was between Frank and that, as if a calf would set upon a man. Besides, Frank told me he knew it to be a spirit and could swear to him in any court in Christendom, and he had not drank above a quart or two, or such a matter of liquor, at the time. Lud have mercy upon us and keep us all from dipping our hands in blood, I say."

"Well, sir," said Jones to the stranger, "Mr. Partridge hath finished his story and, I hope, will give you no future interruption if you will be so kind to proceed." He then resumed his narration; but as he hath taken breath for a while, we think proper to give it to our reader, and shall therefore put an end to this chapter.

12

IN WHICH THE MAN OF THE HILL CONTINUES HIS HISTORY

"I had now regained my liberty," said the stranger, "but I had lost my reputation; for there is a wide difference between the case of a man who is barely acquitted of a crime in a court of justice and of him who is acquitted in his own heart and in the opinion of the people. I was conscious of my guilt and ashamed to look any one in the face, so resolved to leave Oxford the next morning before the daylight discovered me to the eyes of any beholders.

"When I had got clear of the city, it first entered into my head to return home to my father and endeavour to obtain his forgiveness, but as I had no reason to doubt his knowledge of all which had passed, and as I was well assured of his great aversion to all acts of dishonesty, I could entertain no hopes of being received by him, especially since I was too certain of all the good offices in the power of my mother; nay, had my father's pardon been as sure as I conceived his resentment to be, I yet question whether I could have had the assurance to behold him, or whether I could upon any terms have submitted to live and converse with those who, I was convinced, knew me to have been guilty of so base an action.

"I hastened, therefore, back to London, the best retirement of either grief or shame, unless for persons of a very public character; for here you have the advantage of solitude without its disadvantage, since you may be alone and in company at the same time; and while you walk or sit unobserved, noise, hurry, and a constant succession of objects entertain the mind and prevent the spirits from preying on themselves, or rather on grief or shame, which are the most unwholesome diet in the world, and on which (though there are many who never taste either but in public) there are some who can feed very plentifully and very fatally when alone.

"But as there is scarce any human good without its concomitant evil, so there are people who find an inconvenience in this unobserving temper of mankind: I mean persons who have no money; for as you are not put out of countenance, so neither are you clothed or fed by those who do not know you. And a man may be as easily starved in Leadenhall Market as in the deserts of Arabia.

"It was at present my fortune to be destitute of that great evil, as it is apprehended to be by several writers who, I suppose, were overburdened with it: namely, money." "With submission, sir," said Patridge, "I do not remember any writers who have called it *malorum*, but *irritamenta malorum. Effodiuntur opes irritamenta malorum.*" "Well, sir," continued the stranger, "whether it be an evil or only the cause of evil, I was entirely void of it and at the same time of friends and, as I thought, of acquaintance, when one evening, as I was passing through the Inner Temple, very hungry and very miserable, I heard a voice on a sudden hailing me with great familiarity by my Christian name; and upon my turning about, I presently recollected the person who so saluted me to have been my fellow-collegiate, one who had left the University above a year, and long before any of my misfortunes had befallen me. This gentleman, whose name was Watson, shook me heartily by the hand and, expressing great joy at meeting me, proposed our immediately drinking a bottle together. I first declined the proposal and pretended business, but as he was very earnest and pressing, hunger at last overcame my pride and I fairly confessed to him I had no money in my pocket, yet not without framing a lie for an excuse, and imputing it to my having changed my breeches that morning. Mr. Watson answered, 'I thought, Jack, you and I had been too old acquaintance for you to mention such a matter.' He then took me by the arm and was pulling me along, but I gave him very little trouble, for my own inclinations pulled me much stronger than he could do.

"We then went into the Friars, which you know is the scene of all mirth and jollity. Here, when we arrived at the tavern, Mr. Watson applied himself to the drawer only, without taking the least notice of the cook, for he had no suspicion but that I had dined long since. However, as the case was really otherwise, I forged another falsehood and told my companion I had been at the further end of the city on business of consequence, and had snapped up a mutton-chop in haste, so that I was again hungry and wished he would add a beef-steak to his bottle." "Some people," cries Partridge, "ought to have good memories, or did you find just money enough in your breeches to pay for the mutton-chop?" "Your observation is right," answered the stranger, "and I believe such blunders are inseparable from all dealing in untruth. But to proceed: I began now to feel myself extremely happy. The meat and wine soon revived my spirits to a high pitch, and I enjoyed much pleasure in the conversation of my old acquaintance, the rather as I thought him entirely ignorant of what had happened at the University since his leaving it.

"But he did not suffer me to remain long in this agreeable delusion; for taking a bumper in one hand and holding me by the other, 'Here, my boy,' cries he, 'here's wishing you joy of your being so honourably acquitted of that affair laid to your charge.' I was thunderstruck with confusion at those words, which Watson observing proceeded thus: 'Nay, never be ashamed, man; thou hast been acquitted and no one now dares call thee guilty; but prithee do tell me, who am thy friend, I hope thou didst really rob him; for rat me if it was not a meritorious action to strip such a sneaking pitiful rascal, and instead of the two hundred guineas I wish you had taken as many thousand. Come, come, boy, don't be shy of confessing to me; you are not now brought before one of the pimps. D—n me if I don't honour you for it; for, as I hope for salvation, I would have made no manner of scruple of doing the same thing.'

"This declaration a little relieved my abashment, and as wine had now somewhat opened my heart, I very freely acknowledged the robbery, but acquainted him that he had been misinformed as to the sum taken, which was little more than a fifth part of what he had mentioned.

" 'I am sorry for it with all my heart,' quoth he, 'and I wish thee better success another time. Though if you will take my advice, you shall have no occasion to run any such risk. Here,' said he, taking some dice out of his pocket, 'here's the stuff. Here are the implements; here are the little doctors which cure the distempers of the purse. Follow but my counsel and I will show you a way to empty the pockets of a queer cull without any danger of the nubbing cheat.' "

"Nubbing cheat!" cries Partridge. "Pray, sir, what is that?"

"Why that, sir," says the stranger, "is a cant phrase for the gallows; for as gamesters differ little from highwaymen in their morals, so do they very much resemble them in their language.

"We had now each drank our bottle when Mr. Watson said the board was sitting and that he must attend, earnestly pressing me at the same time to go with him and try my fortune. I answered he knew that was at present out of my power, as I had informed him of the emptiness of my pocket. To say the truth, I doubted not from his many strong expressions of friendship but that he would offer to lend me a small sum for that purpose, but he answered, 'Never mind that, man; e'en boldly run a levant' " (Partridge was going to inquire the meaning of that word, but Jones stopped his mouth), " 'but be circumspect as to the man. I will tip you the proper person, which may be necessary, as you do not know the town nor can distinguish a rum cull from a queer one.'

"The bill was now brought, when Watson paid his share and was departing. I reminded him, not without blushing, of my having no money. He answered, 'That signifies nothing, score it behind the door, or make a bold brush and take no notice or—stay,' says he, 'I will go downstairs first, and then do you take up my money and score the whole reckoning at the bar, and I will wait for you at the corner.' I expressed some dislike at this and hinted my expectations that he would have deposited the whole, but he swore he had not another sixpence in his pocket.

"He then went down, and I was prevailed on to take up the money and follow him, which I did close enough to hear him tell the drawer the reckoning was upon the table. The drawer passed by me upstairs, but I made such haste into the street that I heard nothing of his disappointment, nor did

390

I mention a syllable at the bar, according to my instructions.

"We now went directly to the gaming-table, where Mr. Watson to my surprise pulled out a large sum of money and placed it before him, as did many others; all of them, no doubt, considering their own heaps as so many decoy birds, which were to entice and draw over the heaps of their neighbours.

"Here it would be tedious to relate all the freaks which Fortune, or rather the dice, played in this her temple. Mountains of gold were in a few moments reduced to nothing at one part of the table, and rose as suddenly in another. The rich grew in a moment poor and the poor as suddenly became rich, so that it seemed a philosopher could nowhere have so well instructed his pupils in the contempt of riches, at least he could nowhere have better inculcated the uncertainty of their duration.

"For my own part, after having considerably improved my small estate, I at last entirely demolished it. Mr. Watson too, after much variety of luck, rose from the table in some heat and declared he had lost a cool hundred and would play no longer. Then, coming up to me, he asked me to return with him to the tavern, but I positively refused, saying I would not bring myself a second time into such a dilemma, and especially as he had lost all his money and was now in my own condition. 'Pooh,' says he, 'I have just borrowed a couple of guineas of a friend, and one of them is at your service.' He immediately put one of them into my hand and I no longer resisted his inclination.

"I was at first a little shocked at returning to the same house whence we had departed in so unhandsome a manner, but when the drawer, with a very civil address, told us he believed we had forgot to pay our reckoning, I became perfectly easy and very readily gave him a guinea, bid him pay himself, and acquiesced in the unjust charge which had been laid on my memory.

"Mr. Watson now bespoke the most extravagant supper he could well think of, and though he had contented himself with simple claret before, nothing now but the most precious burgundy would serve his purpose.

"Our company was soon increased by the addition of several gentlemen from the gaming-table, most of whom, as I afterwards found, came not to the tavern to drink but in the way of business; for the true gamesters pretended to be ill and refused their glass, while they plied heartily two young fellows who were to be afterwards pillaged, as indeed they were without mercy. Of this plunder I had the good fortune to be a sharer, though I was not yet let into the secret.

"There was one remarkable accident attended this tavern play; for the money by degrees totally disappeared, so that though at the beginning the table was half covered with gold, yet before the play ended, which it did not till the next day, being Sunday, at noon, there was scarce a single guinea to be seen on the table; and this was the stranger as every person present except myself declared he had lost, and what was become of the money, unless the Devil himself carried it away, is difficult to determine."

"Most certainly he did," says Partridge, "for evil spirits can carry away anything without being seen, though there were never so many folk in the room; and I should not have been surprised if he had carried away all the company of a set of wicked wretches, who were at play in sermon-time. And I could tell you a true story, if I would, where the Devil took a man out of bed from another man's wife and carried him away through the keyhole of the door. I've seen the very house where it was done, and nobody hath lived in it these thirty years."

Though Jones was a little offended by the impertinence of Partridge, he could not, however, avoid smiling at his simplicity. The stranger did the same and then proceeded with his story, as will be seen in the next chapter.

13

IN WHICH THE FOREGOING STORY IS FARTHER CONTINUED

"My fellow-collegiate had now entered me in a new scene of life. I soon became acquainted with the whole fraternity of sharpers and was let into their secrets. I mean into the knowledge of those gross cheats which are proper to impose on the raw and unexperienced; for there are some tricks of a finer kind, which are only known to a few of the gang, who are at the head of their profession; a degree of honour beyond my expectation, for drink, to which I was immoderately addicted, and the natural warmth of my passions prevented me from arriving at any great success in an art which requires as much coolness as the most austere school of philosophy.

"Mr. Watson, with whom I now lived in the closest amity, had unluckily the former failing to a very great excess, so that instead of making a fortune by his profession, as some others did, he was alternately rich and poor, and was often obliged to surrender to his cooler friends over a bottle which they never tasted that plunder that he had taken from culls at the public table.

"However, we both made a shift to pick up an uncomfortable livelihood, and for two years I continued of the calling, during which time I tasted all the varieties of fortune, sometimes flourishing in affluence and at others being obliged to struggle with almost incredible difficulties; to-day wallowing in luxury and to-morrow reduced to the coarsest and most homely fare; my fine clothes being often on my back in the evening and at the pawnshop the next morning.

"One night, as I was returning penniless from the gaming-table, I observed a very great disturbance and a large mob gathered in the street. As I was in no danger from pickpockets, I ventured into the crowd, where upon inquiry I found that a man had been robbed and very ill used by some ruffians. The wounded man appeared very bloody and seemed scarce able to support himself on his legs. As I had not, therefore, been deprived of my humanity by my present life and conversation, though they had left me very little of either honesty or shame, I immediately offered my assistance to the unhappy person, who thankfully accepted it and, putting himself under my conduct, begged me to convey him to some tavern, where he might send for a surgeon, being, as he said, faint with loss of blood. He seemed indeed highly pleased at finding one who appeared in the dress of a gentleman; for as to all the rest of the company present, their outside was such that he could not wisely place any confidence in them.

"I took the poor man by the arm and led him to the tavern where we kept our rendezvous, as it happened to be the nearest at hand. A surgeon, happening luckily to be in the house, immediately attended and applied himself to dressing his wounds, which I had the pleasure to hear were not likely to be mortal.

"The surgeon, having very expeditiously and dextrously finished his business, began to inquire in what part of the town the wounded man lodged, who answered that he was come to town that very morning, that his horse was at an inn in Piccadilly, and that he had no other lodging and very little or no acquaintance in town.

"This surgeon, whose name I have forgot, though I remember it began with an *R*, had the first character in his profession and was sergeant-surgeon to the king. He had, moreover, many good qualities and was a very generous, good-natured man, and ready to do any service to his fellow-creatures. He offered his patient the use of his chariot to carry him to his inn and at the same time whispered in his ear that if he wanted any money, he would furnish him.

"The poor man was not now capable of returning thanks for this generous offer; for having had his eyes for some time steadfastly on me, he threw himself back in his chair, crying, 'Oh, my son! My son!' and then fainted away.

"Many of the people present imagined this accident had happened through his loss of blood, but I, who at the same time began to recollect the features of my father, was now confirmed in my suspicion and satisfied that it was he himself who appeared before me. I presently ran to him, raised him in my arms, and kissed his cold lips with the utmost eagerness. Here I must draw a curtain over a scene which I cannot describe; for though I did not lose my being, as my father for a while did, my senses were, however, so overpowered with affright and surprise that I am a stranger to what passed during some minutes, and, indeed, till my father had again recovered from his swoon and I found myself in his arms, both tenderly embracing each other while the tears trickled apace down the cheeks of each of us.

"Most of those present seemed affected by this scene, which we, who might be considered as the actors in it, were desirous of removing from the eyes of all spectators as fast as we could; my father therefore accepted the kind offer of the surgeon's chariot, and I attended him in it to his inn.

"When we were alone together, he gently upbraided me with having neglected to write to him during so long a time, but entirely omitted the mention of that crime which had occasioned it. He then informed me of my mother's death and insisted on my returning home with him, saying that he had long suffered the greatest anxiety on my account, that he knew not whether he had most feared my death or wished it, since he had so many more dreadful apprehensions for me. At last he said a neighbouring gentleman, who had just recovered a son from the same place, informed him where I was, and that to reclaim me from this course of life was the sole cause of his journey to London. He thanked heaven he had succeeded so far as to find me out by means of an accident which had like to have proved fatal to him, and had the pleasure to think he partly owed his preservation to my humanity, with which he professed himself to be more delighted than he should have been with my filial piety if I had known that the object of all my care was my own father.

"Vice had not so depraved my heart as to excite in it an insensibility of so much paternal affection, though so unworthily bestowed. I presently promised to obey his commands in my return home with him as soon as he was able to travel, which indeed he was in a very few days by the assistance of that excellent surgeon who had undertaken his cure.

"The day preceding my father's journey (before which time I scarce ever left him) I went to take my leave of some of my most intimate acquaintance, particularly of Mr. Watson, who dissuaded me from burying myself, as he called it, out of a simple compliance with the fond desires of a foolish old fellow. Such solicitations, however, had no effect, and I once more saw my own home. My father now greatly solicited me to think of marriage, but my inclinations were utterly averse to any such thoughts. I had tasted of love already, and perhaps you know the extravagant excesses of that most tender and most violent passion." Here the old gentleman paused and looked earnestly at Jones, whose countenance within a minute's space displayed the extremities of both red and white. Upon which the old man without making any observations renewed his narrative.

"Being now provided with all the necessities of life, I betook myself once again to study, and that with a more inordinate application than I had ever done formerly. The books which now employed my time solely were those, as well ancient as modern, which treat of true philosophy, a word which is by many thought to be the subject only of farce and ridicule. I now read over the works of Aristotle and Plato with the rest of those inestimable treasures which ancient Greece hath bequeathed to the world.

"These authors, though they instructed me in no science by which men may promise to themselves to acquire the least riches or worldly power, taught me, however, the art of despising the highest acquisitions of both. They elevate the mind, and steel and harden it against the capricious invasions of fortune. They not only instruct in the knowledge of Wisdom but confirm men in her habits and demonstrate plainly that this must be our guide if we propose ever to arrive at the greatest worldly happiness, or to defend ourselves with any tolerable security against the misery which everywhere surrounds and invests us.

"To this I added another study, compared to which all the philosophy taught by the wisest heathens is little better than a dream, and is indeed as full of vanity as the silliest jester ever pleased to represent it. This is that divine wisdom which is alone to be found in the Holy Scriptures, for they impart to us the knowledge and assurance of things much more worthy our attention than all which this world can offer to our acceptance; of things which heaven itself hath condescended to reveal to us, and to the smallest knowledge of which the highest human wit unassisted could never ascend. I began now to think all the time I had spent with the best heathen writers was little more than labour lost; for however pleasant and delightful their lessons may be or however adequate to the right regulation of our conduct with respect to this world only, yet when compared with the glory revealed in Scripture, their highest documents will appear as trifling and of as little consequence as the rules by which children regulate their childish little games and pastime. True it is, that philosophy makes us wiser, but Christianity makes us better men. Philosophy elevates and steels the mind; Christianity softens and sweetens it. The former makes us the objects of human admiration; the latter of divine love. That ensures us a temporal, but this an eternal, happiness. But I am afraid I tire you with my rhapsody."

"Not at all," cries Partridge. "Lud forbid we should be tired with good things."

"I had spent," continued the stranger, "about four years in the most delightful manner to myself, totally given up to contemplation and entirely unembarrassed with the affairs of the world, when I lost the best of fathers, and one whom I so sincerely loved that my grief at his loss exceeds all description. I now abandoned my books and gave myself up for a whole month to the effects of melancholy and despair. Time, however, the best physician of the mind, at length brought me relief." "Ay, ay; *tempus edax rerum*," said Partridge. "I then," continued the stranger, "betook myself again to my former studies, which I may say perfected my cure; for philosophy and religion may be called the exercises of the mind, and when this is disordered they are as wholesome as exercise can be to a distempered body. They do indeed produce similar effects with exercise, for they strengthen and confirm the mind till man becomes, in the noble strain of Horace,

> "Fortis, et in seipso totus teres atque rotundus,
> Externi ne quid valeat per læve morari;
> In quem manca ruit semper Fortuna." *

Here Jones smiled at some conceit which intruded itself into his imagination, but the stranger, I believe, perceived it not and proceeded thus:

"My circumstances were now greatly altered by the death of that best of men; for my brother, who was now become master of the house, differed so widely from me in his inclinations, and our pursuits in life had been so very various, that we were the worst of company to each other; but what made our living together still more disagreeable was the little harmony which could subsist between the few who resorted to me and the numerous train of sportsmen who often attended my brother from the field to the table; for such fellows, besides the noise and nonsense with which they persecute the ears of sober men, endeavor always to attack them with affronts and contempt. This was so much the case that neither I myself nor my friends could ever sit down to a meal with them where we were not treated with derision because we were unacquainted with the phrases of sportsmen. For men of true learning and almost universal knowledge always compassionate the ignorance of others, but fellows who excel in some little, low, contemptible art are always certain to despise those who are unacquainted with that art.

"In short, we soon separated and I went by the advice of a physician to drink the Bath waters; for my violent affliction added to a sedentary life had thrown me into a kind of paralytic disorder, for which those waters are accounted an almost certain cure. The second day after my arrival, as I was walking by the river, the sun shone so intensely hot (though it was early in the year) that I retired to the shelter of some willows and sat down by the riverside. Here I had

---

* Firm in himself, who on himself relies,
Polished and round, who runs his proper course,
And breaks misfortunes with superior force.
                                        MR. FRANCIS.

not been seated long before I heard a person on the other side the willows sighing and bemoaning himself bitterly. On a sudden, having uttered a most impious oath, he cried, 'I am resolved to bear it no longer,' and directly threw himself into the water. I immediately started and ran towards the place, calling at the same time as loudly as I could for assistance. An angler happened luckily to be a-fishing a little below me, though some very high sedge had hid him from my sight. He immediately came up, and both of us together, not without some hazard of our lives, drew the body to the shore. At first we perceived no sign of life remaining, but having held the body up by the heels (for we soon had assistance enough), it discharged a vast quantity of water at the mouth and at length began to discover some symptoms of breathing, and a little afterwards to move both its hands and its legs.

"An apothecary, who happened to be present among others, advised that the body, which seemed now to have pretty well emptied itself of water and which began to have many convulsive motions, should be directly taken up and carried into a warm bed. This was accordingly performed, the apothecary and myself attending.

"As we were going towards an inn (for we knew not the man's lodgings), luckily a woman met us, who after some violent screaming told us that the gentleman lodged at her house.

"When I had seen the man safely deposited there, I left him to the care of the apothecary, who, I suppose, used all the right methods with him, for the next morning I heard he had perfectly recovered his senses.

"I then went to visit him, intending to search out as well as I could the cause of his having attempted so desperate an act, and to prevent as far as I was able his pursuing such wicked intentions for the future. I was no sooner admitted into his chamber than we both instantly knew each other, for who should this person be but my good friend Mr. Watson! Here I will not trouble you with what passed at our first interview, for I would avoid prolixity as much as possible." "Pray let us hear all," cries Partridge. "I want mightily to know what brought him to Bath."

"You shall hear everything material," answered the stranger, and then proceeded to relate what we shall proceed to write after we have given a short breathing-time to both ourselves and the reader.

14

IN WHICH THE MAN OF THE HILL CONCLUDES HIS HISTORY

"Mr. Watson," continued the stranger, "very freely acquainted me that the unhappy situation of his circumstances, occasioned by a tide of ill luck, had in a manner forced him to a resolution of destroying himself.

"I now began to argue very seriously with him in opposition to this heathenish or, indeed, diabolical practice, and said everything which occurred to me on the subject, but to my great concern, it seemed to have very little effect on him. He seemed not at all to repent of what he had done and gave me reason to fear he would soon make a second attempt of the like horrible kind.

"When I had finished my discourse, instead of endeavouring to answer my arguments he looked me steadfastly in the face and with a smile said, 'You are strangely altered, my good friend, since I remember you. I question whether any of our bishops could make a better argument against suicide than you have entertained me with, but unless you can find somebody who will lend me a cool hundred, I must either hang or drown or starve, and in my opinion the last death is the most terrible of the three.'

"I answered him very gravely that I was indeed altered since I had seen him last; that I had found leisure to look into my follies, and to repent of them. I then advised him to pursue the same steps, and at last concluded with an assurance that I myself would lend him a hundred pound if it would be of any service to his affairs, and he would not put it into the power of a die to deprive him of it.

"Mr. Watson, who seemed almost composed in slumber by the former part of my discourse, was roused by the latter. He seized my hand eagerly, gave me a thousand thanks, and declared I was a friend indeed; adding that he hoped I had a better opinion of him than to imagine he had profited so little by experience as to put any confidence in those damned dice, which had so often deceived him. 'No, no,' cries he. 'Let me but once handsomely be set up again, and if ever Fortune makes a broken merchant of me afterwards, I will forgive her.'

"I very well understood the language of *setting up* and *broken merchant*. I therefore said to him with a very grave face, 'Mr. Watson, you must endeavour to find out some business or employment by which you may procure yourself a livelihood, and I promise you, could I see any probability of being repaid hereafter, I would advance a much larger sum than what you have mentioned to equip you in any fair and honourable calling; but as to gaming, besides the baseness and wickedness of making it a profession, you are really to my own knowledge unfit for it, and it will end in your certain ruin.'

"'Why, now, that's strange,' answered he. 'Neither you nor any of my friends would ever allow me to know anything of the matter, and yet, I believe, I am as good a hand at every game as any of you all, and I heartily wish I was to play with you only for your whole fortune; I should desire no better sport and I would let you name your game into the bargain; but come, my dear boy, have you the hundred in your pocket?'

"I answered I had only a bill for £50, which I delivered him, and promised to bring him the rest the next morning; and after giving him a little more advice, took my leave.

"I was indeed better than my word, for I returned to him that very afternoon. When I entered the room, I found Mr. Watson sitting up in his bed at cards with a notorious gamester. This sight, you will imagine, shocked me not a little, to which I may add the mortification of seeing my bill delivered by Mr. Watson to his antagonist and thirty guineas only given in exchange for it.

"The other gamester presently quitted the room, and then Watson declared he was ashamed to see me. 'But,' says he, 'I find luck runs so damnably against me that I will resolve to leave off play forever. I have thought of the kind proposal you made me ever since, and I promise you there shall be no fault in me if I do not put it in execution.'

"Though I had no great faith in his promises, I produced him the remainder of the hundred in consequence of my own, for which he gave me a note, and which note was all I ever expected to see in return for my money.

"We were prevented from any further discourse at present by the arrival of the apothecary, who with much joy in his countenance and without even asking his patient how he did proclaimed there was great news arrived in a letter to himself, which he said would shortly be public: that the Duke of Monmouth was landed in the west with a vast army of Dutch, and that another vast fleet hovered over the coast of Norfolk and was to make a descent there in order to favour the Duke's enterprise with a diversion on that side.

"This apothecary was one of the greatest politicians of his time. He was more delighted with the most paltry packet than with the best patient, and the highest joy he was capable of he received from having a piece of news in his possession an hour or two sooner than any other person in the town. His advices, however, were seldom authentic, for he would swallow almost anything as a truth, a humour which many made use of to impose upon him.

"Thus it happened with what he at present communicated; for it was known within a short time afterwards that the Duke was really landed, but that his army consisted only of a few attendants, and as to the diversion in Norfolk, it was entirely false.

"The apothecary stayed no longer in the room than while he acquainted us with his news, and then, without saying a syllable to his patient on any other subject, departed to spread his advices all over the town.

"Events of this nature in the public are generally apt to eclipse all private concerns. Our discourse, therefore, now became entirely political. For my own part, I had been for some time very seriously affected with the danger to which the Protestant religion was so visibly exposed, that nothing but the immediate interposition of Providence seemed capable of preserving it; for King James had indeed declared war against the Protestant cause. He had brought known papists into the army and attempted to bring them into the Church and into the University. Popish priests swarmed through the nation, appeared publicly in their habits, and boasted that they should shortly walk in procession through the streets. Our own clergy were forbid to preach against popery, and bishops were ordered to supend those who did; and to do the business at once an illegal ecclesiastical commission was erected, little inferior to an inquisition, of which, probably, it was intended to be the ringleader. Thus, as our duty to the king can never be called more than our second duty, he had discharged us from this by making it incompatible with our preserving the first, which is surely to heaven. Besides this, he had dissolved his subjects from their allegiance by breaking his Coronation Oath, to which their allegiance is annexed; for he had imprisoned bishops because they would not give up their religion, and turned out judges because they would not absolutely surrender the law into his hands; nay, he seized this himself, and when he claimed a dispensing power, he declared himself, in fact, as absolute as any tyrant ever was or can be. I have recapitulated these matters in full lest some of them should have been omitted in history; and I think nothing less than such provocations as I have here mentioned, nothing less than certain and imminent danger to their religion and liberties, can justify or even mitigate the dreadful sin of rebellion in any people."

"I promise you, sir," says Jones, "all these facts, and more, I have read in history, but I will tell you a fact which is not yet recorded and of which I suppose you are ignorant. There is actually now a rebellion on foot in this kingdom in favour of the son of that very King James, a professed papist, more bigoted, if possible, than his father, and this carried on by Protestants against a king who hath never in *one single instance* made the least invasion on our liberties."

"Prodigious indeed!" answered the stranger. "You tell me what would be incredible of a nation which did not deserve the character that Virgil gives of a woman, *varium et mutabile semper*. Surely this is to be unworthy of the care which Providence seems to have taken of us in the preservation of our religion against the powerful designs and constant machinations of Popery, a preservation so strange and unaccountable that I almost think we may appeal to it as to a miracle for the proof of its holiness. Prodigious indeed! A Protestant rebellion in favour of a popish prince! The folly of mankind is as wonderful as their knavery— But to conclude my story: I resolved to take arms in defence of my country, of my religion, and my liberty, and Mr. Watson joined in the same resolution. We soon provided ourselves with all necessaries and joined the Duke at Bridgewater.

"The unfortunate event of this enterprise you are perhaps better acquainted with than myself. I escaped together with Mr. Watson from the battle at Sedgemore, in which action I received a slight wound. We rode near forty miles together on the Exeter Road and then, abandoning our horses, scrambled as well as we could through the fields and byroads till we arrived at a little wild hut on a common, where a poor old woman took all the care of us she could and dressed my wound with salve, which quickly healed it."

"Pray, sir, where was the wound?" says Partridge. The stranger satisfied him it was in his arm, and then continued his narrative. "Here, sir," said he, "Mr. Watson left me the next morning in order, as he pretended, to get us some provision from the town of Cullumpton, but— Can I relate it? Or can you believe it? This Mr. Watson, this friend, this base, barbarous, treacherous villain, betrayed me to a party of horse belonging to King James and, at his return, delivered me into their hands.

"The soldiers, being six in number, had now seized me and were conducting me to Taunton Gaol, but neither my present situation nor the apprehensions of what might happen to me were half so irksome to my mind as the company of my false friend, who, having surrendered himself, was likewise considered as a prisoner, though he was better treated, as being to make his peace at my expense. He at first endeavoured to excuse his treachery, but when he received nothing but scorn and upbraiding from me, he soon changed his note, abused me as the most atrocious and malicious rebel, and laid all his own guilt to my charge, who, as he declared, had solicited and even threatened him to take up arms against his gracious, as well as lawful, sovereign.

"This false evidence (for in reality he had been much the forwarder of the two) stung me to the quick and raised an indignation scarce conceivable by those who have not felt it. However, Fortune at length took pity on me; for as we were got a little beyond Wellington, in a narrow lane, my guards received a false alarm that near fifty of the enemy were at hand, upon which they shifted for themselves and left me and my betrayer to do the same. That villain immediately ran from me, and I am glad he did or I should have certainly endeavoured though I had no arms to have executed vengeance on his baseness.

"I was now once more at liberty, and immediately withdrawing from the highway into the fields, I travelled on, scarce knowing which way I went, and making it my chief care to avoid all public roads and all towns, nay, even the most homely houses, for I imagined every human creature whom I saw desirous of betraying me.

"At last, after rambling several days about the country, during which the field afforded me the same bed and the same food which Nature bestows on our savage brothers of the Creation, I at length arrived in this place, where the solitude and wildness of the country invited me to fix my abode. The first person with whom I took up my habitation was the mother of this old woman, with whom I remained concealed till the news of the Glorious Revolution put an end to all my apprehensions of danger and gave me an opportunity of once more visiting my own home and of inquiring a little into my affairs, which I soon settled as agreeably to my brother as to myself, having resigned everything to him, for which he paid me the sum of a thousand pound and settled on me an annuity for life.

"His behaviour in this last instance, as in all others, was selfish and ungenerous. I could not look on him as my friend, nor, indeed, did he desire that I should, so I presently took my leave of him as well as of my other acquaintance; and from that day to this, my history is little better than a blank."

"And is it possible, sir," said Jones, "that you can have resided here from that day to this?" "Oh, no, sir," answered the gentleman; "I have been a great traveller, and there are few parts of Europe with which I am not acquainted." "I have not, sir," cried Jones, "the assurance to ask it of you now. Indeed it would be cruel after so much breath as you have already spent. But you will give me leave to wish for some further opportunity of hearing the excellent observations which a man of your sense and knowledge of the world must have made in so long a course of travels." "Indeed, young gentleman," answered the stranger, "I will endeavour to satisfy your curiosity on this head likewise as far as I am able." Jones attempted fresh apologies, but was prevented, and while he and Partridge sat with greedy and impatient ears the stranger proceeded as in the next chapter.

15

A BRIEF HISTORY OF EUROPE, AND A CURIOUS DISCOURSE
BETWEEN MR. JONES AND THE MAN OF THE HILL

"In Italy the landlords are very silent. In France they are more talkative, but yet civil. In Germany and Holland they are generally very impertinent. And as for their honesty, I believe it is pretty equal in all those countries. The *valets à louage* are sure to lose no opportunity of cheating you; and as for the postilions, I think they are pretty much alike all the world over. These, sir, are the observations on men which I made in my travels. My design when I went abroad was to divert myself by seeing the great variety with which God hath been pleased to enrich the several parts of this globe—a variety which, as it must give great pleasure to a contemplative beholder, so doth it greatly display the vast powers of its omnipotent Author. Indeed, to say the truth, there is but one work in His whole creation that doth Him any dishonour, and with that I have long since avoided holding any conversation."

"You will pardon me," cries Jones, "but I have always imagined that there is in this very work you mention as great variety as in all the rest; for besides the difference of inclination, customs and climates have, I am told, introduced the utmost diversity into human nature." "Very little indeed," answered the other; "those who travel in order to acquaint themselves with the different manners of men might spare themselves much pains by going to a carnival at Venice, for here they will see at once all which they can discover in the several courts of Europe: the same hypocrisy, the same fraud, in short, the same follies and vices dressed in different habits. In Spain these are equipped with much gravity, and in Italy with vast splendour. In France a knave is dressed like a fop, and in the northern countries like a sloven. But human nature is everywhere the same, everywhere the object of detestation and avoidance.

"Thus, sir, I have ended the history of my life; for as to all that series of years in which I have retired here, they afford no variety to entertain you and may almost be considered as one day."

Jones thanked the stranger for the trouble he had taken in relating his story, and then expressed some wonder how he could possibly endure a life of such solitude, "in which," says he, "you may well complain of the want of variety. Indeed I am astonished how you have filled up, or rather killed, so much of your time."

"I am not at all surprised," answered the other, "that to one whose affections and thoughts are fixed on the world, my hours shall appear to have wanted employment in this place; but there is one single act for which the whole life of man is infinitely short. What time can suffice for the contemplation and worship of that glorious, immortal, and eternal Being, among the works of whose stupendous creation not only this vast globe but even those numberless luminaries which we may here behold spangling all the sky, though they should many of them be suns lighting different systems of worlds, may possibly appear but as a few atoms opposed to the whole earth which we inhabit? Can a man who by divine meditations is admitted, as it were, into the conversation of this ineffable, incomprehensible majesty think days or years or ages too long for the continuance of so ravishing an honour? Shall the trifling amusements, the palling pleasures, the silly business of the world, roll away our hours too swiftly from us, and shall the pace of time seem sluggish to a mind exercised in studies so high, so important, and so glorious! And as no time is sufficient, so neither is any place improper for this great concern. On what object can we cast our eyes which may not inspire us with ideas of His power, of His wisdom, and of His goodness? It is not necessary that the rising sun should dart his fiery glories over the eastern horizon, nor that the boisterous winds should rush from their caverns and shake the lofty forest, nor that the opening clouds should pour their deluges on the plains: it is not necessary, I say, that any of these should proclaim His majesty; there is not an insect, not a vegetable, of so low an order in the Creation but it is honoured with bearing marks of the attributes of its great Creator, marks not only of His power but of His wisdom and goodness. Man alone, the king of this globe, the last and greatest work of the Supreme Being below the sun, man alone hath basely dishonoured his own nature, and by dishonesty, cruelty, ingratitude, and accursed treachery hath called his Maker's goodness in question by puzzling us to account how a benevolent Being should form so imperfect and so vile an animal. Yet this is the Being from whose conversation you think, I suppose, that I have been unfortunately restrained, and without whose blessed society life in your opinion must be tedious and insipid."

"In the former part of what you said," replied Jones, "I most heartily and readily concur; but I believe as well as hope that the abhorrence which you express for mankind in the conclusion is much too general. Indeed you here fall into an error which, in my little experience, I have observed to be a very common one, by taking the character of mankind from the worst and basest among them, whereas indeed, as an excellent writer observes, nothing should be esteemed as characteristical of a species but what is to be found among the best and most perfect individuals of that species. This error, I believe, is generally committed by those who, from want of proper caution in the choice of their friends and acquaintance, have suffered injuries from bad and worthless men, two or three instances of which are very unjustly charged on all the human race."

"I think I had experience enough of them," answered the other. "My first mistress and my first friend betrayed me in the basest manner, and in matters which threatened to be of the worst consequences, even to bring me to a shameful death."

"But you will pardon me," cries Jones, "if I desire you to reflect who this mistress and who that friend was. What better, my good sir, could be expected in love derived from the stews or in friendship first produced and nourished at the gaming-table! To take the characters of women from the former instance or of men from the latter would be as unjust as to assert that air is a nauseous and unwholesome element because we find it so in a jakes. I have lived but a short time in the world and yet have known men worthy of the highest friendship and women of the highest love."

"It is possible," answered the stranger; "but you have lived, you confess, a very short time only in the world; I was somewhat older than you when I was of the same opinion."

"You might have remained so still," replies Jones, "if you had not been unfortunate, I will venture to say incautious, in the placing your affections. If there was indeed much more wickedness in the world than there is, it would not prove such general assertions against human nature, since much of this arrives by mere accident, and many a man who commits evil is not totally bad and corrupt in his heart. In truth, none seem to have any title to assert human nature to be necessarily and universally evil but those whose own minds afford them one instance of this natural depravity, which is not, I am convinced, your case."

"And such," said the stranger, "will be always the most backward to assert any such thing. Knaves will no more endeavour to persuade us of the baseness of mankind than a highwayman will inform you that there are thieves on the road. This would indeed be a method to put you on your guard and to defeat their own purposes; for which reason though knaves, as I remember, are very apt to abuse particular persons, yet they never cast any reflection on human nature in general." The old gentleman spoke this so warmly that as Jones despaired of making a convert and was unwilling to offend, he returned no answer.

The day now began to send forth its first streams of light, when Jones made an apology to the stranger for his having stayed so long and perhaps having detained him from his rest. The stranger answered he never wanted rest less than at present, for that day and night were indifferent seasons to him, and that he commonly made use of the former for the time of his repose and of the latter for his walks and lucubrations. "However," said he, "it is now a most lovely morning, and if you can bear any longer to be without your own rest or food, I will gladly entertain you with the sight of some very fine prospects, which I believe you have not yet seen."

Jones very readily embraced this offer and they immediately set forward together from the cottage. As for Partridge, he had fallen into a profound repose just as the stranger had finished his story; for his curiosity was satisfied and the subsequent discourse was not forcible enough in its operation to conjure down the charms of sleep. Jones therefore left him to enjoy his nap, and as the reader may perhaps be at this season glad of the same favour, we will here put an end to the eighth book of our history.

BOOK IX

1

OF THOSE WHO LAWFULLY MAY, AND OF THOSE WHO MAY NOT, WRITE SUCH HISTORIES AS THIS

Among other good uses for which I have thought proper to institute these several introductory chapters, I have considered them as a kind of mark or stamp which may hereafter enable a very indifferent reader to distinguish what is true and genuine in this historic kind of writing from what is false and counterfeit. Indeed it seems likely that some such mark may shortly become necessary, since the favourable reception which two or three authors have lately procured for their works of this nature from the public will probably serve as an encouragement to many others to undertake the like. Thus a swarm of foolish novels and monstrous romances will be produced, either to the great impoverishing of booksellers or to the great loss of time and depravation of morals in the reader; nay, often to the spreading of scandal and calumny and to the prejudice of the characters of many worthy and honest people.

I question not but the ingenious author of *The Spectator* was principally induced to prefix Greek and Latin mottos to every paper from the same consideration of guarding against the pursuit of those scribblers who, having no talents of a writer but what is taught by the writing-master, are yet nowise afraid nor ashamed to assume the same titles with the greatest genius than their good brother in the fable was of braying in the lion's skin.

By the device, therefore, of his motto, it became impracticable for any man to presume to imitate the *Spectators* without understanding at least one sentence in the learned languages. In the same manner I have now secured myself from the imitation of those who are utterly incapable of any degree of reflection and whose learning is not equal to an essay.

I would not be here understood to insinuate that the greatest merit of such historical productions can ever lie in these introductory chapters, but, in fact, those parts which contain mere narrative only, afford much more encouragement to the pen of an imitator than those which are composed of observation and reflection. Here I mean such imitators as Rowe was of Shakespeare, or as Horace hints some of the Romans were of Cato, by bare feet and sour faces.

To invent good stories and to tell them well are possibly very rare talents, and yet I have observed few persons who have scrupled to aim at both; and if we examine the romances and novels with which the world abounds, I think we may fairly conclude that most of the authors would not have attempted to show their teeth (if the expression may be allowed me) in any other way of writing, nor could indeed have strung together a dozen sentences on any other subject whatever. *Scribimus indocti doctique passim** may be more truly said of the historian and biographer than of any other species of writing; for all the arts and sciences (even criticism itself) require some little degree of learning and knowledge. Poetry indeed may perhaps be thought an exception, but then it demands numbers, or something like numbers, whereas to the composition of novels and romances nothing is necessary but paper, pens, and ink, with the manual capacity of using them. This, I conceive, their productions show to be the opinion of the authors themselves, and this must be the opinion of their readers if indeed, there be any such.

Hence we are to derive that universal contempt which the world, who always denominate the whole from the majority, have cast on all historical writers who do not draw their materials from records. And it is the apprehension of this contempt that hath made us so cautiously avoid the

---

* ——Each desperate blockhead dares to write;
Verse is the trade of every living wight.
FRANCIS.

term *romance*, a name with which we might otherwise have been well enough contented. Though as we have good authority for all our characters, no less indeed than the vast authentic book of nature, as is elsewhere hinted, our labours have sufficient title to the name of history. Certainly they deserve some distinction from those works which one of the wittiest of men regarded only as proceeding from a *pruritus* or, indeed, rather from a looseness of the brain.

But besides the dishonour which is thus cast on one of the most useful as well as entertaining of all kinds of writing, there is just reason to apprehend that by encouraging such authors we shall propagate much dishonour of another kind—I mean to the characters of many good and valuable members of society, for the dullest writers, no more than the dullest companions, are always inoffensive. They have both enough of language to be indecent and abusive. And surely if the opinion just above cited be true, we cannot wonder that works so nastily derived should be nasty themselves or have a tendency to make others so.

To prevent, therefore, for the future such intemperate abuses of leisure, of letters, and of the liberty of the press, especially as the world seems at present to be more than usually threatened with them, I shall here venture to mention some qualifications, every one of which are in a pretty high degree necessary to this order of historians.

The first is genius, without a rich vein of which no study, says Horace, can avail us. By genius I would understand that power, or rather powers of the mind, which are capable of penetrating into all things within our reach and knowledge and of distinguishing their essential differences. These are no other than invention and judgement, and they are both called by the collective name of genius, as they are of those gifts of nature which we bring with us into the world. Concerning each of which, many seem to have fallen into very great errors; for by invention, I believe, is generally understood a creative faculty, which would indeed prove most romance-writers to have the highest pretensions to it, whereas by invention is really meant no more (and so the word signifies) than discovery, or finding out; or to explain it at large, a quick and sagacious penetration into the true essence of all the objects of our contemplation. This, I think, can rarely exist without the concomitancy of judgement; for how we can be said to have discovered the true essence of two things without discerning their difference seems to me hard to conceive. Now, this last is the undisputed province of judgement, and yet some few men of wit have agreed with all the dull fellows in the world in representing these two to have been seldom or never the property of one and the same person.

But though they should be so, they are not sufficient for our purpose without a good share of learning; for which I could again cite the authority of Horace and of many others if any was necessary to prove that tools are of no service to a workman when they are sharpened by art, or when he wants rules to direct him in his work, or hath no matter to work upon. All these uses are supplied by learning; for nature can only furnish us with capacity or, as I have chose to illustrate it, with the tools of our profession; learning must fit them for use, must direct them in it, and, lastly, must contribute part at least of the materials. A competent knowledge of history and of the *belles-lettres* is here absolutely necessary; and without this share of knowledge at least, to affect the character of an historian is as vain as to endeavour at building a house without timber or mortar, or brick or stone. Homer and Milton, who though they added the ornament of numbers to their works were both historians of our order, were masters of all the learning of their times.

Again, there is another sort of knowledge beyond the power of learning to bestow, and this is to be had by conversation. So necessary is this to the understanding the characters of men that none are more ignorant of them than those learned pedants whose lives have been entirely consumed in colleges and among books; for however exquisitely human nature may have been described by writers, the true practical system can only be learnt in the world. Indeed the like happens in every other kind of knowledge. Neither physic nor law are to be practically known from books. Nay, the farmer, the planter, the gardener, must perfect by experience what he hath acquired the rudiments of by reading. How accurately soever the ingenious Mr. Miller may have described the plant, he himself would advise his disciple to see it in the garden. As we must perceive that after the nicest strokes of a Shakespeare or a Jonson, of a Wycherly or an Otway, some touches of nature will escape the reader which the judicious action of a Garrick, of a Cibber, or a Clive* can convey to him, so on the real stage the character shows himself in a stronger and bolder light than he can be described. And if this be the case in those fine and nervous descriptions which great authors themselves have taken from life, how much more strongly will it hold when the writer himself takes his lines not from nature but from books! Such characters are only the faint copy of a copy and can have neither the justness nor spirit of an original.

Now, this conversation in our historian must be universal, that is, with all ranks and degrees of men; for the knowledge of what is called high life will not instruct him in low, nor, è converso, will his being acquainted with the inferior part of mankind teach him the manners of the superior. And though it may be thought that the knowledge of either may sufficiently enable him to describe at least that in which he hath been conversant, yet he will even here fall greatly short of perfection, for the follies of either rank do in reality illustrate each other. For instance, the affectation of high life appears more glaring and ridiculous from the simplicity of the low, and again, the rudeness and barbarity of this latter strikes with much stronger ideas of absurdity when contrasted with and opposed to the politeness which controls the former. Besides, to say the truth, the manners of our historian will be improved by both these conversations; for in the one he will easily find examples of plainness, honesty, and sincerity; in the other, of refinement, elegance, and a liberality of spirit, which last quality I myself have scarce ever seen in men of low birth and education.

Nor will all the qualities I have hitherto given my historian avail him unless he have what is generally meant by a good heart and be capable of feeling. The author who will make me weep, says Horace, must first weep himself. In reality, no man can paint a distress well which he doth not feel while he is painting it, nor do I doubt but that the most pathetic and affecting scenes have been writ with tears. In the same manner it is with the ridiculous. I am convinced I never make my reader laugh heartily but where I

* There is a peculiar propriety in mentioning this great actor and these two most justly celebrated actresses in this place, as they have all formed themselves on the study of nature only, and not on the imitation of their predecessors. Hence they have been able to excel all who have gone before them—a degree of merit which the servile herd of imitators can never possibly arrive at.

have laughed before him; unless it should happen at any time that instead of laughing with me, he should be inclined to laugh at me. Perhaps this may have been the case at some passages in this chapter, from which apprehension I will here put an end to it.

2

CONTAINING A VERY SURPRISING ADVENTURE INDEED, WHICH MR. JONES MET WITH IN HIS WALK WITH THE MAN OF THE HILL

Aurora now first opened her casement, *Anglice* the day began to break, when Jones walked forth in company with the stranger and mounted Mazard Hill, of which they had no sooner gained the summit than one of the most noble prospects in the world presented itself to their view, and which we would likewise present to the reader, but for two reasons. *First,* we despair of making those who have seen this prospect admire our description. *Secondly,* we very much doubt whether those who have not seen it would understand it.

Jones stood for some minutes fixed in one posture and directing his eyes towards the south; upon which the old gentleman asked what he was looking at with so much attention. "Alas, sir," answered he with a sigh, "I was endeavouring to trace out my own journey hither. Good heavens! What a distance is Gloucester from us! What a vast tract of land must be between me and my own home." "Ay, ay, young gentleman," cries the other, "and, by your sighing, from what you love better than your own home, or I am mistaken. I perceive now the object of your contemplation is not within your sight, and yet I fancy you have a pleasure in looking that way." Jones answered with a smile, "I find, old friend, you have not yet forgot the sensations of your youth. I own my thoughts were employed as you have guessed."

They now walked to that part of the hill which looks to the north-west and which hangs over a vast and extensive wood. Here they were no sooner arrived than they heard at a distance the most violent screams of a woman, proceeding from the wood below them. Jones listened a moment and then, without saying a word to his companion (for indeed the occasion seemed sufficiently pressing), ran, or rather slid, down the hill, and without the least apprehension or concern for his own safety made directly to the thicket whence the sound had issued.

He had not entered far into the wood before he beheld a most shocking sight indeed, a woman stripped half naked under the hands of a ruffian, who had put his garter round her neck and was endeavouring to draw her up to a tree. Jones asked no questions at this interval, but fell instantly upon the villain and made such good use of his trusty oaken stick that he laid him sprawling on the ground before he could defend himself, indeed, almost before he knew he was attacked; nor did he cease the prosecution of his blows till the woman herself begged him to forbear, saying she believed he had sufficiently done his business.

The poor wretch then fell upon her knees to Jones and gave him a thousand thanks for her deliverance; he presently lifted her up and told her he was highly pleased with the extraordinary accident which had sent him thither for her relief, where it was so improbable she should find any, adding that heaven seemed to have designed him as the happy instrument of her protection. "Nay," answered she, "I could almost conceive you to be some good angel, and to say the truth, you look more like an angel than a man, in my eye." Indeed he was a charming figure, and if a very fine person and a most comely set of features adorned with youth, health, strength, freshness, spirit, and good nature can make a man resemble an angel, he certainly had that resemblance.

The redeemed captive had not altogether so much of the human-angelic species: she seemed to be at least of the middle age, nor had her face much appearance of beauty; but her clothes being torn from all the upper part of her body, her breasts, which were well formed and extremely white, attracted the eyes of her deliverer, and for a few moments they stood silent and gazing at each other till the ruffian on the ground beginning to move, Jones took the garter which had been intended for another purpose and bound both his hands behind him. And now, on contemplating his face, he discovered, greatly to his surprise and perhaps not a little to his satisfaction, this very person to be no other than Ensign Northerton. Nor had the ensign forgotten his former antagonist, whom he knew the moment he came to himself.

His surprise was equal to that of Jones, but I conceive his pleasure was rather less on this occasion.

Jones helped Northerton upon his legs, and then, looking him steadfastly in the face, "I fancy, sir," said he, "you did not expect to meet me any more in this world, and I confess I had as little expectation to find you here. However, Fortune, I see, hath brought us once more together and hath given me satisfaction for the injury I have received, even without my own knowledge."

"It is very much like a man of honour indeed," answered Northerton, "to take satisfaction by knocking a man down behind his back. Neither am I capable of giving you satisfaction here, as I have no sword; but if you dare behave like a gentleman, let us go where I can furnish myself with one and I will do by you as a man of honour ought."

"Doth it become such a villain as you are," cries Jones, "to contaminate the name of honour by assuming it? But I shall waste no time in discourse with you. Justice requires satisfaction of you now and shall have it." Then, turning to the woman, he asked her if she was near her home or, if not, whether she was acquainted with any house in the neighbourhood where she might procure herself some decent clothes in order to proceed to a justice of the peace.

She answered she was an entire stranger in that part of the world. Jones then, recollecting himself, said he had a friend near who would direct them; indeed, he wondered at his not following, but in fact the good Man of the Hill, when our hero departed, sat himself down on the brow, where, though he had a gun in his hand, he with great patience and unconcern had attended the issue.

Jones then stepping without the wood perceived the old man sitting as we have just described him; he presently exerted his utmost agility and with surprising expedition ascended the hill.

The old man advised him to carry the woman to Upton, which, he said, was the nearest town, and there he would be sure of furnishing her with all manner of conveniencies. Jones, having received his direction to the place, took his leave of the Man of the Hill and, desiring him to direct Partridge the same way, returned hastily to the wood.

Our hero, at his departure to make this inquiry of his friend, had considered that as the ruffian's hands were tied behind him, he was incapable of executing any wicked purposes on the poor woman. Besides, he knew he should not be beyond the reach of her voice and could return soon enough to prevent any mischief. He had, moreover, declared to the villain that if he attempted the least insult, he would be himself immediately the executioner of vengeance on him. But Jones unluckily forgot that though the hands of Northerton were tied, his legs were at liberty; nor did he lay the least injunction on the prisoner that he should not make what use of these he pleased. Northerton, therefore, having given no parole of that kind, thought he might without any breach of honour depart, not being obliged, as he imagined, by any rules to wait for a formal discharge. He therefore took up his legs, which were at liberty, and walked off through the wood, which favoured his retreat; nor did the woman, whose eyes were perhaps rather turned towards her deliverer, once think of his escape or give herself any concern or trouble to prevent it.

Jones, therefore, at his return found the woman alone. He would have spent some time in searching for Northerton, but she would not permit him, earnestly entreating that he would accompany her to the town whither they had been directed. "As to the fellow's escape," said she, "it gives me no uneasiness, for philosophy and Christianity both preach up forgiveness of injuries. But for you, sir, I am concerned at the trouble I give you; nay, indeed, my nakedness may well make me ashamed to look you in the face, and if it was not for the sake of your protection, I should wish to go alone."

Jones offered her his coat but, I know not for what reason, she absolutely refused the most earnest solicitations to accept it. He then begged her to forget both the causes of her confusion. "With regard to the former," says he, "I have done no more than my duty in protecting you, and as for the latter, I will entirely remove it by walking before you all the way; for I would not have my eyes offend you and I could not answer for my power of resisting the attractive charms of so much beauty."

Thus our hero and the redeemed lady walked in the same manner as Orpheus and Eurydice marched heretofore, but though I cannot believe that Jones was designedly tempted by his fair one to look behind him, yet as she frequently wanted his assistance to help her over styles and had, besides, many trips and other accidents, he was often obliged to turn about. However, he had better fortune than what attended poor Orpheus, for his brought his companion, or rather follower, safe into the famous town of Upton.

3

THE ARRIVAL OF MR. JONES WITH HIS LADY AT THE INN;
WITH A VERY FULL DESCRIPTION OF THE BATTLE OF UPTON

Though the reader, we doubt not, is very eager to know who this lady was and how she fell into the hands of Mr. Northerton, we must beg him to suspend his curiosity for a short time, as we are obliged for some very good reasons, which hereafter perhaps he may guess, to delay his satisfaction a little longer.

Mr. Jones and his fair companion no sooner entered the town than they went directly to that inn which in their eyes presented the fairest appearance to the street. Here Jones, having ordered a servant to show a room above-stairs, was ascending when the dishevelled fair, hastily following, was laid hold on by the master of the house, who cried, "Heyday, where is that beggar wench going? Stay below-stairs, I desire you"; but Jones at that instant thundered from above, "Let the lady come up," in so authoritative a voice that the good man instantly withdrew his hands and the lady made the best of her way to the chamber.

Here Jones wished her joy of her safe arrival and then departed, in order, as he promised, to send the landlady up with some clothes. The poor woman thanked him heartily for all his kindness, and said she hoped she should see him again soon to thank him a thousand times more. During this short conversation, she covered her white bosom as well as she could possibly with her arms; for Jones could not avoid stealing a sly peep or two, though he took all imaginable care to avoid giving any offence.

Our travellers had happened to take up their residence at a house of exceeding good repute, whither Irish ladies of strict virtue and many northern lasses of the same predicament were accustomed to resort in their way to Bath. The landlady therefore would by no means have admitted any conversation of a disreputable kind to pass under her roof. Indeed, so foul and contagious are all such proceedings that they contaminate the very innocent scenes where they are committed, and give the name of a bad house, or of a house of ill repute, to all those where they are suffered to be carried on.

Not that I would intimate that such strict chastity as was preserved in the temple of Vesta can possibly be maintained at a public inn. My good landlady did not hope for such a blessing, nor would any of the ladies I have spoken of, or indeed, any others of the most rigid note have expected or insisted on any such thing. But to exclude all vulgar concubinage, and to drive all whores in rags from within the walls, is within the power of every one. This my landlady very strictly adhered to, and this her virtuous guests, who did not travel in rags, would very reasonably have expected of her.

Now, it required no very blameable degree of suspicion to imagine that Mr. Jones and his ragged companion had certain purposes in their intention which, though tolerated in some Christian countries, connived at in others, and practised in all, are, however, as expressly forbidden as murder or any other horrid vice by that religion which is universally believed in those countries. The landlady, therefore, had no sooner received an intimation of the entrance of the above-said persons than she began to meditate the most expeditious means for their expulsion. In order to this she had provided herself with a long and deadly instrument, with which in times of peace the chambermaid was wont to demolish the labours of the industrious spider. In vulgar phrase, she had taken up the broomstick and was just about to sally from the kitchen when Jones accosted her with a demand of a gown and other vestments to cover the half-naked woman above-stairs.

Nothing can be more provoking to the human temper nor more dangerous to that cardinal virtue, patience, than solicitations of extraordinary offices of kindness on behalf of those very persons with whom we are highly incensed. For this reason Shakespeare hath artfully introduced his Desdemona soliciting favours for Cassio of her husband as the means of enflaming not only his jealousy but his rage to the highest pitch of madness; and we find the unfortunate Moor less able to command his passion on this occasion than even when he beheld his valued present to his wife in the hands of his supposed rival. In fact, we regard these efforts as insults on our understanding, and to such the pride of man is very difficultly brought to submit.

My landlady, though a very good-tempered woman, had,

I suppose, some of this pride in her composition; for Jones had scarce ended his request when she fell upon him with a certain weapon which, though it be neither long, nor sharp, nor hard, nor indeed threatens from its appearance with either death or wound, hath been, however, held in great dread and abhorrence by many wise men; nay, by many brave ones, insomuch that some who have dared to look into the mouth of a loaded cannon have not dared to look into a mouth where this weapon was brandished, and rather than run the hazard of its execution have contented themselves with making a most pitiful and sneaking figure in the eyes of all their acquaintance.

To confess the truth, I am afraid Mr. Jones was one of these; for though he was attacked and violently belaboured with the aforesaid weapon, he could not be provoked to make any resistance, but in a most cowardly manner applied with many entreaties to his antagonist to desist from pursuing her blows; in plain English, he only begged her with the utmost earnestness to hear him, but before he could obtain his request, my landlord himself entered into the fray and embraced that side of the cause which seemed to stand very little in need of assistance.

There are a sort of heroes who are supposed to be determined in their choosing or avoiding a conflict by the character and behaviour of the person whom they are to engage. These are said to know their man, and Jones, I believe, knew his woman; for though he had been so submissive to her, he was no sooner attacked by her husband than he demonstrated an immediate spirit of resentment and enjoined him silence under a very severe penalty, no less than that, I think, of being converted into fuel for his own fire.

The husband, with great indignation, but with a mixture of pity, answered, "You must pray first to be made able; I believe I am a better man than yourself, ay, every way, that I am"; and presently proceeded to discharge half a dozen "whores" at the lady above-stairs, the last of which had scarce issued from his lips when a swinging blow from the cudgel that Jones carried in his hand assaulted him over the shoulders.

It is a question whether the landlord or the landlady was the most expeditious in returning this blow. My landlord, whose hands were empty, fell to with his fist, and the good wife, uplifting her broom and aiming at the head of Jones, had probably put an immediate end to the fray and to Jones likewise had not the descent of this broom been prevented —not by the miraculous intervention of any heathen deity, but by a very natural though fortunate accident: viz., by the arrival of Partridge, who entered the house at that instant (for fear had caused him to run every step from the hill) and who, seeing the danger which threatened his master, or companion (which you choose to call him), prevented so sad a catastrophe by catching hold of the landlady's arm as it was brandished aloft in the air.

The landlady soon perceived the impediment which prevented her blow, and being unable to rescue her arm from the hands of Partridge, she let fall the broom; and then, leaving Jones to the discipline of her husband, she fell with the utmost fury on that poor fellow, who had already given some intimation of himself by crying, "Zounds! Do you intend to kill my friend?"

Partridge, though not much addicted to battle, would not, however, stand still when his friend was attacked, nor was he much displeased with that part of the combat which fell to his share; he therefore returned my landlady's blows as soon as he received them; and now the fight was obstinately maintained on all parts, and it seemed doubtful to which side Fortune would incline, when the naked lady, who had listened at the top of the stairs to the dialogue which preceded the engagement, descended suddenly from above and, without weighing the unfair inequality of two to one, fell upon the poor woman, who was boxing with Partridge; nor did that great champion desist, but rather redoubled his fury when he found fresh succours were arrived to his assistance.

Victory must now have fallen to the side of the travellers (for the bravest troops must yield to numbers) had not Susan the chambermaid come luckily to support her mistress. This Susan was as two-handed a wench (according to the phrase) as any in the country, and would, I believe, have beat the famed Thalestris herself or any of her subject Amazons, for her form was robust and manlike, and every way made for such encounters. As her hands and arms were formed to give blows with great mischief to an enemy, so was her face as well contrived to receive blows without any great injury to herself, her nose being already flat to her face; her lips were so large that no swelling could be perceived in them, and, moreover, they were so hard that a fist could hardly make any impression on them. Lastly, her cheek-bones stood out as if nature had intended them for two bastions to defend her eyes in those encounters for which she seemed so well calculated and to which she was most wonderfully well inclined.

This fair creature, entering the field of battle, immediately filed to that wing where her mistress maintained so unequal a fight with one of either sex. Here she presently challenged Partridge to single combat. He accepted the challenge, and a most desperate fight began between them.

Now the dogs of war, being let loose, began to lick their bloody lips; now Victory with golden wings hung hovering in the air. Now Fortune, taking her scales from her shelf, began to weigh the fates of Tom Jones, his female companion, and Partridge against the landlord, his wife, and maid; all which hung in exact balance before her when a good-natured accident put suddenly an end to the bloody fray, with which half of the combatants had already sufficiently feasted. This accident was the arrival of a coach and four, upon which my landlord and landlady immediately desisted from fighting and at their entreaty obtained the same favour of their antagonists; but Susan was not so kind to Partridge, for that Amazonian fair, having overthrown and bestrid her enemy, was now cuffing him lustily with both her hands, without any regard to his request of a cessation of arms or to those loud exclamations of murder which he roared forth.

No sooner, however, had Jones quitted the landlord than he flew to the rescue of his defeated companion, from whom he with much difficulty drew off the enraged chambermaid; but Partridge was not immediately sensible of his deliverance, for he still lay flat on the floor, guarding his face with his hands, nor did he cease roaring till Jones had forced him to look up and to perceive that the battle was at an end.

The landlord, who had no visible hurt, and the landlady, hiding her well-scratched face with her handkerchief, ran both hastily to the door to attend the coach, from which a young lady and her maid now alighted. These the landlady presently ushered into that room where Mr. Jones had at first deposited his fair prize, as it was the best apartment in the house. Hither they were obliged to pass through the field of battle, which they did with the utmost haste, covering their faces with their handkerchiefs as desirous to avoid the notice of any one. Indeed, their caution was quite unnecessary; for the poor unfortunate Helen, the fatal cause of all the bloodshed, was entirely taken up in endeavouring to conceal her own face, and Jones was no less occupied in rescuing Partridge from the fury of Susan, which being happily effected, the poor fellow immediately departed to the pump to wash his face and to stop that bloody torrent which Susan had plentifully set a-flowing from his nostrils.

4

IN WHICH THE ARRIVAL OF A MAN-OF-WAR PUTS A FINAL
END TO HOSTILITIES, AND CAUSES THE CONCLUSION OF A
FIRM AND LASTING PEACE BETWEEN ALL PARTIES

A sergeant and a file of musketeers with a deserter in their custody arrived about this time. The sergeant presently inquired for the principal magistrate of the town, and was informed by my landlord that he himself was vested in that office. He then demanded his billets, together with a mug of beer, and, complaining it was cold, spread himself before the kitchen fire.

Mr. Jones was at this time comforting the poor distressed lady, who sat down at a table in the kitchen, and leaning her head upon her arm, was bemoaning her misfortunes; but lest my fair readers should be in pain concerning a particular circumstance, I think proper here to acquaint them that before she had quitted the room above-stairs she had so well covered herself with a pillow-bere which she there found that her regard to decency was not in the least violated by the presence of so many men as were now in the room.

One of the soldiers now went up to the sergeant and whispered something in his ear; upon which he steadfastly fixed his eyes on the lady, and having looked at her for near a minute, he came up to her, saying, "I ask pardon, madam, but I am certain I am not deceived; you can be no other person than Captain Waters' lady."

The poor woman, who in her present distress had very little regarded the face of any person present, no sooner looked at the sergeant than she presently recollected him and, calling him by his name, answered that she was indeed the unhappy person he imagined her to be, but added, "I wonder any one should know me in this disguise." To which the sergeant replied he was very much surprised to see her ladyship in such a dress, and was afraid some accident had happened to her. "An accident hath happened to me, indeed," says she, "and I am highly obliged to this gentleman" (pointing to Jones) "that it was not a fatal one or that I am now living to mention it." "Whatever the gentleman hath done," cries the sergeant, "I am sure the captain will make him amends for it; and if I can be of any service, your ladyship may command me, and I shall think myself very happy to have it in my power to serve your ladyship; and so, indeed, may any one, for I know the captain will well reward them for it."

The landlady, who heard from the stairs all that passed between the sergeant and Mrs. Waters, came hastily down and, running directly up to her, began to ask pardon for the offences she had committed, begging that all might be imputed to ignorance of her quality; for, "Lud, madam," says she, "how should I have imagined that a lady of your fashion would appear in such a dress? I am sure, madam, if I had once suspected that your ladyship was your ladyship, I would sooner have burnt my tongue out than have said what I have said; and I hope your ladyship will accept of a gown till you can get your own clothes."

"Prithee woman," says Mrs. Waters, "cease your impertinence; how can you imagine I should concern myself about anything which comes from the lips of such low creatures as yourself. But I am surprised at your assurance in thinking after what is past that I will condescend to put on any of your dirty things. I would have you know, creature, I have a spirit above that."

Here Jones interfered and begged Mrs. Waters to forgive the landlady and to accept her gown; "for I must confess," cries he, "our appearance was a little suspicious when first we came in, and I am well assured all this good woman did was, as she professed, out of regard to the reputation of her house."

"Yes, upon my truly was it," says she; "the gentleman speaks very much like a gentleman, and I see very plainly is so; and to be certain, the house is well known to be a house of as good reputation as any on the road and, though I say it, is frequented by gentry of the best quality, both Irish and English. I defy anybody to say black is my eye, for that matter. And as I was saying, if I had known your ladyship to be your ladyship, I would as soon have burnt my fingers as have affronted your ladyship, but truly, where gentry come and spend their money, I am not willing that they should be scandalized by a set of poor shabby vermin that wherever they go leave more lice than money behind them; such folks never raise my compassion, for to be certain, it is foolish to have any for them, and if our justices did as they ought, they would be all whipped out of the kingdom; for to be certain, it is what is most fitting for them. But as for your ladyship, I am heartily sorry your ladyship hath had a misfortune, and if your ladyship will do me the honour to wear my clothes till you can get some of your ladyship's own, to be certain, the best I have is at your ladyship's service."

Whether cold, shame, or the persuasions of Mr. Jones prevailed most with Mrs. Waters I will not determine, but she suffered herself to be pacified by this speech of my landlady and retired with that good woman in order to apparel herself in a decent manner.

My landlord was likewise beginning his oration to Jones, but was presently interrupted by that generous youth, who shook him heartily by the hand and assured him of entire forgiveness, saying, "If you are satisfied, my worthy friend, I promise you I am"; and indeed, in one sense the landlord had the better reason to be satisfied, for he had received a bellyful of drubbing, whereas Jones had scarce felt a single blow.

Partridge, who had been all this time washing his bloody nose at the pump, returned into the kitchen at the instant when his master and the landlord were shaking hands with each other. As he was of a peaceable disposition, he was pleased with those symptoms of reconciliation, and though his face bore some marks of Susan's fist, and many more of her nails, he rather chose to be contented with his fortune in the last battle than to endeavour at bettering it in another.

The heroic Susan was likewise well contented with her victory, though it had cost her a black eye, which Partridge had given her at the first onset. Between these two, therefore, a league was struck, and those hands which had been the instruments of war became now the mediators of peace.

Matters were thus restored to a perfect calm, at which the sergeant, though it may seem so contrary to the principles of his profession, testified his approbation. "Why, now, that's friendly," said he; "d—n me, I hate to see two people bear ill will to one another after they have had a tussle. The only way when friends quarrel is to see it out fairly in a friendly manner, as a man may call it, either with fist, or sword, or pistol, according as they like, and then let it be all over; for my own part, d—n me if ever I love my friend better than when I am fighting with him. To bear malice is more like a Frenchman than an Englishman."

He then proposed a libation as a necessary part of the ceremony at all treaties of this kind. Perhaps the reader may here conclude that he was well versed in ancient history, but this, though highly probable, as he cited no authority to support the custom, I will not affirm with any confidence. Most likely indeed it is that he founded his opinion on very good authority, since he confirmed it with many violent oaths.

Jones no sooner heard the proposal than, immediately agreeing with the learned sergeant, he ordered a bowl, or rather a large mug, filled with the liquor used on these occasions to be brought in, and then began the ceremony himself. He placed his right hand in that of the landlord and, seizing the bowl with his left, uttered the usual words, and then made his libation. After which the same was observed by all present. Indeed there is very little need of being particular in describing the whole form, as it differed so little from those libations of which so much is recorded in ancient authors and their modern transcribers. The principal difference lay in two instances: for first, the present company poured the liquor only down their throats, and secondly, the sergeant, who officiated as priest, drank the last; but he preserved, I believe, the ancient form in swallowing much the largest draught of the whole company, and in being the only person present who contributed nothing towards the libation besides his good offices in assisting at the performance.

The good people now ranged themselves round the kitchen fire, where good humour seemed to maintain an absolute dominion, and Partridge not only forgot his shameful defeat but converted hunger into thirst, and soon became extremely facetious. We must, however, quit this agreeable assembly for a while and attend Mr. Jones to Mrs. Waters' apartment, where the dinner which he had bespoke was now on the table. Indeed it took no long time in preparing, having been all dressed three days before, and required nothing more from the cook than to warm it over again.

AN APOLOGY FOR ALL HEROES WHO HAVE GOOD STOMACHS, WITH A DESCRIPTION OF A BATTLE OF THE AMOROUS KIND

Heroes, notwithstanding the high ideas which by the means of flatterers they may entertain of themselves or the world may conceive of them, have certainly more of mortal than divine about them. However elevated their minds may be, their bodies at least (which is much the major part of most) are liable to the worst infirmities and subject to the vilest offices of human nature. Among these latter the act of eating, which hath by several wise men been considered as extremely mean and derogatory from the philosophic dignity, must be in some measure performed by the greatest prince, hero, or philosopher upon earth; nay, sometimes Nature hath been so frolicsome as to exact of these dignified characters a much more exorbitant share of this office than she hath obliged those of the lowest order to perform.

To say the truth, as no known inhabitant of this globe is really more than man, so none need be ashamed of submitting to what the necessities of man demand; but when those great personages I have just mentioned condescend to aim at confining such low offices to themselves, as when by hoarding or destroying they seem desirous to prevent any others from eating, they then surely become very low and despicable.

Now, after this short preface, we think it no disparagement to our hero to mention the immoderate ardour with which he laid about him at this season. Indeed it may be doubted whether Ulysses, who by the way seems to have had the best stomach of all the heroes in that eating poem of the *Odyssey*, ever made a better meal. Three pounds at least of that flesh which formerly had contributed to the composition of an ox was now honoured with becoming part of the individual Mr. Jones.

This particular we thought ourselves obliged to mention, as it may account for our hero's temporary neglect of his fair companion, who eat but very little, and was, indeed, employed in considerations of a very different nature, which passed unobserved by Jones till he had entirely satisfied that appetite which a fast of twenty-four hours had procured him; but his dinner was no sooner ended than his attention to other matters revived; with these matters, therefore, we shall now proceed to acquaint the reader.

Mr. Jones, of whose personal accomplishments we have hitherto said very little, was in reality one of the handsomest young fellows in the world. His face, besides being the picture of health, had in it the most apparent marks of sweetness and good nature. These qualities were indeed so characteristical in his countenance that while the spirit and sensibility in his eyes, though they must have been perceived by an accurate observer, might have escaped the notice of the less discerning, so strongly was this good nature painted in his look that it was remarked by almost every one who saw him.

It was, perhaps, as much owing to this as to a very fine complexion that his face had a delicacy in it almost inexpressible, and which might have given him an air rather too effeminate had it not been joined to a most masculine person and mien; which latter had as much in them of the Hercules as the former had of the Adonis. He was, besides, active, genteel, gay, and good-humoured, and had a flow of animal spirits which enlivened every conversation where he was present.

When the reader hath duly reflected on these many charms which all centered in our hero, and considers at the same time the fresh obligations which Mrs. Waters had to him, it will be a mark of more prudery than candour to entertain a bad opinion of her because she conceived a very good opinion of him.

But whatever censures may be passed upon her, it is my business to relate matters of fact with veracity. Mrs. Waters had, in truth, not only a good opinion of our hero but a very great affection for him. To speak out boldly at once, she was in love, according to the present universally received sense of that phrase, by which love is applied indiscriminately to the desirable objects of all our passions, appetites, and senses, and is understood to be that preference which we give to one kind of food rather than to another.

But though the love to these several objects may possibly be one and the same in all cases, its operations, however, must be allowed to be different; for how much soever we may be in love with an excellent sirloin of beef or bottle of burgundy, with a damask rose or Cremona fiddle, yet do we never smile, nor ogle, nor dress, nor flatter, nor endeavour by any other arts or tricks to gain the affection of the said beef, &c. Sigh indeed we sometimes may, but it is generally in the absence, not in the presence, of the beloved object. For otherwise we might possibly complain of their ingratitude and deafness with the same reason as Pasiphaë doth of her bull, whom she endeavoured to engage by all the coquetry practised with good success in the drawing-room on the much more sensible as well as tender hearts of the fine gentlemen there.

The contrary happens in that love which operates between persons of the same species but of different sexes. Here we are no sooner in love than it becomes our principal care to engage the affection of the object beloved. For what other purpose indeed are our youth instructed in all the arts of rendering themselves agreeable? If it was not with a view to this love, I question whether any of those trades which deal in setting off and adorning the human person would procure a livelihood. Nay, those great polishers of our manners, who are by some thought to teach what principally distinguishes us from the brute creation, even dancing-masters themselves, might possibly find no place in society. In short, all the graces which young ladies and young gentlemen too learn from others, and the many improvements which by the help of a looking-glass they add of their own, are in reality those very *spicula et faces amoris* so often mentioned by Ovid, or, as they are sometimes called in our own language, "the whole artillery of love."

Now, Mrs. Waters and our hero had no sooner sat down together than the former began to play this artillery upon the latter. But here, as we are about to attempt a description hitherto unassayed either in prose or verse, we think proper to invoke the assistance of certain aerial beings, who will, we doubt not, come kindly to our aid on this occasion.

"Say then, you Graces, you that inhabit the heavenly mansions of Seraphina's countenance—for you are truly divine, are always in her presence, and well know all the arts of charming—say what were the weapons now used to captivate the heart of Mr. Jones."

"First, from two lovely blue eyes, whose bright orbs flashed lightning at their discharge, flew forth two pointed ogles, but, happily for our hero, hit only a vast piece of beef which he was then conveying into his plate and harmless spent their force. The fair warrior perceived their miscarriage, and immediately from her fair bosom drew forth a deadly sigh—a sigh which none could have heard unmoved and which was sufficient at once to have swept off a dozen beaux; so soft, so sweet, so tender that the insinuating air must have found its subtle way to the heart of our hero had it not luckily been driven from his ears by the coarse bubbling of some bottled ale, which at that time he was pouring forth. Many other weapons did she assay; but the God of Eating (if there be any such deity, for I do not confidently assert it) preserved his votary; or perhaps it may not be *dignus vindice nodus,* and the present security of Jones may be accounted for by natural means; for as love frequently preserves from the attacks of hunger, so may hunger possibly in some cases defend us against love.

"The fair one, enraged at her frequent disappointments, determined on a short cessation of arms; which interval she employed in making ready every engine of amorous warfare for the renewing of the attack when dinner should be over.

"No sooner, then, was the cloth removed than she again began her operations. First, having planted her right eye sideways against Mr. Jones, she shot from its corner a most penetrating glance, which, though great part of its force was spent before it reached our hero, did not vent itself absolutely without effect. This the fair one perceiving hastily withdrew her eyes, and levelled them downwards as if she was concerned for what she had done; though by this means she designed only to draw him from his guard and, indeed, to open his eyes, through which she intended to surprise his heart. And now, gently lifting up those two bright orbs which had already begun to make an impression on poor Jones, she discharged a volley of small charms at once from her whole countenance in a smile. Not a smile of mirth, nor of joy; but a smile of affection, which most ladies have always ready at their command and which serves them to show at once their good humour, their pretty dimples, and their white teeth.

"This smile our hero received full in his eyes, and was immediately staggered with its force. He then began to see the designs of the enemy and, indeed, to feel their success. A parley now was set on foot between the parties, during which the artful fair so slyly and imperceptibly carried on her attack that she had almost subdued the heart of our hero before she again repaired to acts of hostility. To confess the truth, I am afraid Mr. Jones maintained a kind of Dutch defence, and treacherously delivered up the garrison without duly weighing his allegiance to the fair Sophia. In short, no sooner had the amorous parley ended and the lady had unmasked the royal battery, by carelessly letting her handkerchief drop from her neck, than the heart of Mr. Jones was entirely taken, and the fair conqueror enjoyed the usual fruits of her victory."

Here the Graces think proper to end their description, and here we think proper to end the chapter.

6

While our lovers were entertaining themselves in the manner which is partly described in the foregoing chapter, they were likewise furnishing out an entertainment for their good friends in the kitchen. And this in a double sense: by affording them matter for their conversation and, at the same time, drink to enliven their spirits.

There were now assembled round the kitchen fire, besides my landlord and landlady, who occasionally went backward and forward, Mr. Partridge, the sergeant, and the coachman who drove the young lady and her maid.

Partridge having acquainted the company with what he had learned from the Man of the Hill concerning the situation in which Mrs. Waters had been found by Jones, the sergeant proceeded to that part of her history which was known to him. He said she was the wife of Mr. Waters, who was a captain in their regiment, and had often been with him at quarters. "Some folks," says he, "used indeed to doubt whether they were lawfully married in a church or no. But, for my part, that's no business of mine; I must own, if I was put to my corporal oath, I believe she is little better than one of us, and I fancy the captain may go to heaven when the sun shines upon a rainy day. But if he does, that is neither here nor there, for he won't want company. And the lady, to give the Devil his due, is a very good sort of lady and loves the cloth, and is always desirous to do strict justice to it; for she hath begged off many a poor soldier, and by her goodwill would never have

any of them punished. But yet, to be sure, Ensign Northerton and she were well acquainted together at our last
quarters; that is the very right and truth of the matter.
But the captain, he knows nothing about it, and as long
as there is enough for him too, what does it signify? He
loves her not a bit the worse, and I am certain would
run any man through the body that was to abuse her;
therefore, I don't abuse her, for my part. I only repeat
what other folks say, and to be certain, what everybody
says there must be some truth in." "Ay, ay, a great deal of
truth, I warrant you," cries Partridge. *"Veritas odium parit."*
"All a parcel of scandalous stuff," answered the mistress
of the house. "I am sure, now she is dressed, she looks
like a very good sort of lady, and she behaves herself like
one, for she gave me a guinea for the use of my clothes."
"A very good lady indeed," cried the landlord; "and if
you had not been a little too hasty, you would not have
quarrelled with her as you did at first." "You need mention that with my truly," answered she; "if it had not been
for your nonsense, nothing had happened. You must be
meddling with what did not belong to you and throw in
your fool's discourse." "Well, well," answered he, "what's
past cannot be mended, so there's an end of the matter."
"Yes," cries she, "for this once; but will it be mended ever
the more hereafter? This is not the first time I have suffered for your numskull's pate. I wish you would always
hold your tongue in the house and meddle only in matters
without doors which concern you. Don't you remember
what happened about seven years ago?" "Nay, my dear,"
returned he, "don't rip up old stories. Come, come, all's
well, and I am sorry for what I have done." The landlady
was going to reply, but was prevented by the peace-making
sergeant, sorely to the displeasure of Partridge, who was a
great lover of what is called fun and a great promoter of
those harmless quarrels which tend rather to the production
of comical than tragical incidents.

The sergeant asked Partridge whither he and his master
were travelling. "None of your magisters," answered Partridge; "I am no man's servant, I assure you; for though
I have had misfortunes in the world, I write gentleman
after my name, and as poor and simple as I may appear
now, I have taught grammar-school in my time. *Sed hei
mihi! non sum quod fui.*" "No offence, I hope, sir," said
the sergeant. "Where, then, if I may venture to be so bold,

may you and your friend be travelling?" "You have now denominated us right," says Partridge: "*Amici sumus*. And I promise you my friend is one of the greatest gentlemen in the kingdom" (at which words both landlord and landlady pricked up their ears). "He is the heir of Squire Allworthy." "What, the squire who doth so much good all over the country!" cries my landlady. "Even he," answered Partridge. "Then I warrant," says she, "he'll have a swinging great estate hereafter." "Most certainly," answered Partridge. "Well," replied the landlady, "I thought the first moment I saw him he looked like a good sort of gentleman, but my husband here, to be sure, is wiser than anybody." "I own, my dear," cries he. "it was a mistake." "A mistake indeed!" answered she. "But when did you ever know me to make such mistakes?" "But how comes it, sir," cries the landlord, "that such a great gentleman walks about the country afoot?" "I don't know," returned Partridge; "great gentlemen have humours sometimes. He hath now a dozen horses and servants at Gloucester, and nothing would serve him but last night, it being very hot weather, he must cool himself with a walk to yon high hill, whither I likewise walked with him to bear him company; but if ever you catch me there again—for I was never so frightened in all my life. He met with the strangest man there." "I'll be hanged," cries the landlord, "if it was not the Man of the Hill, as they call him, if indeed he be a man; but I know several people who believe it is the Devil that lives there." "Nay, nay, like enough," says Partridge, "and now you put me in the head of it, I verily and sincerely believe it was the Devil, though I could not perceive his cloven foot, but perhaps he might have the power given him to hide that, since evil spirits can appear in what shapes they please." "And pray, sir," says the sergeant, "no offence I hope; but pray what sort of a gentleman is the Devil? For I have heard some of our officers say there is no such person, and that it is only a trick of the parsons to prevent their being broke; for if it was publicly known that there was no Devil, the parsons would be of no more use than we are in time of peace." "Those officers," says Partridge, "are very great scholars, I suppose." "Not much of schollards neither," answered the sergeant; "they have not half your learning, sir, I believe; and to be sure, I thought there must be a Devil, notwithstanding what they said, though one of them was a captain; for methought, thinks I to myself, if there be no Devil, how can wicked people be sent to him, and I have read all that upon a book." "Some of your officers," quoth the landlord, "will find there is a Devil, to their shame, I believe. I don't question but he'll pay off some old scores upon my account. Here was one quartered upon me half a year, who had the conscience to take up one of my best beds, though he hardly spent a shilling a day in the house, and suffered his men to roast cabbages at the kitchen fire because I would not give them a dinner on a Sunday. Every good Christian must desire there should be a Devil for the punishment of such wretches." Harkee, landlord," said the sergeant, "don't abuse the cloth, for I won't take it." "D—n the cloth," answered the landlord; "I have suffered enough by them." "Bear witness, gentlemen," says the sergeant; "he curses the king, and that's high treason." "I curse the king! You villain," said the landlord. "Yes you did," cries the sergeant, "you cursed the cloth, and that's cursing the king. It's all one and the same, for every man who curses the cloth would curse the king if he durst; so for matter o' that, it's all one and the same thing." "Excuse me there, Mr. Sergeant," quoth Partridge, "that's a *non sequitur*." "None of your outlandish linguo," answered the sergeant, leaping from his seat; "I will not sit still and hear the cloth abused." "You mistake me, friend," cries Partridge, "I did not mean to abuse the cloth; I only said your conclusion was a *non sequitur*.* " "You are another," cries the sergeant, "an you come to that. No more a *sequitur* than yourself. You are a pack of rascals, and I'll prove it, for I will fight the best man of you all for twenty pound." This challenge effectually silenced Partridge, whose stomach for drubbing did not so soon return after the hearty meal which he had lately been treated with, but the coachman, whose bones were less sore and whose appetite for fighting was somewhat sharper, did not so easily brook the affront, of which he conceived some part at least fell to his share. He started therefore from his seat and, advancing to the sergeant, swore he looked on himself to be as good a man as any in the army, and offered to box for a guinea. The military man accepted the combat but refused the wager; upon which both immediately stripped and engaged till the driver of horses was

* This word, which the sergeant unhappily mistook for an affront, is a term in logic and means that the conclusion doth not follow from the premises.

so well mauled by the leader of men that he was obliged to exhaust his small remainder of breath in begging for quarter.

The young lady was now desirous to depart and had given orders for her coach to be prepared; but all in vain, for the coachman was disabled from performing his office for that evening. An ancient heathen would perhaps have imputed this disability to the God of Drink no less than to the God of War; for in reality both the combatants had sacrificed as well to the former deity as to the latter. To speak plainly, they were both dead drunk; nor was Partridge in a much better situation. As for my landlord, drinking was his trade, and the liquor had no more effect on him than it had on any other vessel in his house.

The mistress of the inn, being summoned to attend Mr. Jones and his companion at their tea, gave a full relation of the latter part of the foregoing scene, and at the same time expressed great concern for the young lady, who, she said, was under the utmost uneasiness at being prevented from pursuing her journey. "She is a sweet, pretty creature," added she, "and I am certain I have seen her face before. I fancy she is in love and running away from her friends. Who knows but some young gentleman or other may be expecting her with a heart as heavy as her own."

Jones fetched a hearty sigh at those words, of which, though Mrs. Waters observed it, she took no notice while the landlady continued in the room, but after the departure of that good woman, she could not forbear giving our hero certain hints of her suspecting some very dangerous rival in his affections. The awkward behaviour of Mr. Jones on this occasion convinced her of the truth without his giving her a direct answer to any of her questions, but she was not nice enough in her amours to be greatly concerned at the discovery. The beauty of Jones highly charmed her eye, but as she could not see his heart, she gave herself no concern about it. She could feast heartily at the table of love without reflecting that some other already had been, or hereafter might be, feasted with the same repast. A sentiment which, if it deals but little in refinement deals, however, much in substance, and is less capricious and perhaps less ill-natured and selfish than the desires of those females who can be contented enough to abstain from the possession of their lovers provided they are sufficiently satisfied that no one else possesses them.

CONTAINING A FULLER ACCOUNT OF MRS. WATERS, AND BY WHAT MEANS SHE CAME INTO THAT DISTRESSFUL SITUATION FROM WHICH SHE WAS RESCUED BY JONES

Though Nature hath by no means mixed up an equal share either of curiosity or vanity in every human composition, there is perhaps no individual to whom she hath not allotted such a proportion of both as requires much art, and pains too, to subdue and keep under—a conquest, however, absolutely necessary to every one who would in any degree deserve the characters of wisdom or good breeding.

As Jones, therefore, might very justly be called a well-bred man, he had stifled all that curiosity which the extraordinary manner in which he had found Mrs. Waters must be supposed to have occasioned. He had, indeed, at first thrown out some few hints to the lady, but when he perceived her industriously avoiding any explanation, he was contented to remain in ignorance, the rather as he was not without suspicion that there were some circumstances which must have raised her blushes had she related the whole truth.

Now, since it is possible that some of our readers may not so easily acquiesce under the same ignorance, and as we are very desirous to satisfy them all, we have taken uncommon pains to inform ourselves of the real fact, with the relation of which we shall conclude this book.

This lady, then, had lived some years with one Captain Waters, who was a captain in the same regiment to which Mr. Northerton belonged. She passed for that gentleman's wife and went by his name, and yet, as the sergeant said, there were some doubts concerning the reality of their marriage, which we shall not at present take upon us to resolve.

Mrs. Waters, I am sorry to say it, had for some time contracted an intimacy with the above-mentioned ensign, which did no great credit to her reputation. That she had a remarkable fondness for that young fellow is most certain, but whether she indulged this to any very criminal lengths is not so extremely clear unless we will suppose that women never grant every favour to a man but one without granting him that one also.

The division of the regiment to which Captain Waters belonged had two days preceded the march of that company to which Mr. Northerton was the ensign, so that the former had reached Worcester the very day after the unfortunate rencounter between Jones and Northerton, which we have before recorded.

Now, it had been agreed between Mrs. Waters and the captain that she would accompany him in his march as far as Worcester, where they were to take their leave of each other, and she was thence to return to Bath, where she was to stay till the end of the winter's campaign against the rebels.

With this agreement Mr. Northerton was made acquainted. To say the truth, the lady had made him an assignation at this very place and promised to stay at Worcester till his division came thither, with what view and for what purpose must be left to the reader's divination; for though we are obliged to relate facts, we are not obliged to do a violence to our nature by any comments to the disadvantage of the loveliest part of the Creation.

Northerton no sooner obtained a release from his captivity, as we have seen, than he hasted away to overtake Mrs. Waters, which as he was a very active nimble fellow he did at the last-mentioned city, some few hours after Captain Waters had left her. At his first arrival he made no scruple of acquainting her with the unfortunate accident, which he made appear very unfortunate indeed; for he totally extracted every particle of what could be called fault, at least in a court of honour, though he left some circumstances which might be questionable in a court of law.

Women, to their glory be it spoken, are more generally capable of that violent and apparently disinterested passion of love, which seeks only the good of its object, than men. Mrs. Waters, therefore, was no sooner apprised of the danger to which her lover was exposed than she lost every consideration besides that of his safety, and this being a matter equally agreeable to the gentleman, it became the immediate subject of debate between them.

After much consultation on this matter, it was at length agreed that the ensign should go across the country to Hereford, whence he might find some conveyance to one of the seaports in Wales, and thence might make his escape abroad. In all which expedition Mrs. Waters declared she would bear him company, and for which she was able to furnish him with money, a very material article to Mr. Northerton, she having then in her pocket three bank-notes to the amount of £90, besides some cash and a diamond ring of pretty considerable value on her finger. All which she with the utmost confidence revealed to this wicked man, little suspecting she should by these means inspire him with a design of robbing her. Now, as they must by taking horses from Worcester have furnished any pursuers with the means of hereafter discovering their route, the ensign proposed, and the lady presently agreed, to make their first stage on foot, for which purpose the hardness of the frost was very seasonable.

The main part of the lady's baggage was already at Bath, and she had nothing with her at present besides a very small quantity of linen, which the gallant undertook to carry in his own pockets. All things, therefore, being settled in the evening, they arose early the next morning and at five o'clock departed from Worcester, it being then above two hours before day. But the moon, which was then at the full, gave them all the light she was capable of affording.

Mrs. Waters was not of that delicate race of women who are obliged to the invention of vehicles for the capacity of removing themselves from one place to another, and with whom consequently a coach is reckoned among the necessaries of life. Her limbs were indeed full of strength and agility, and as her mind was no less animated with spirit, she was perfectly able to keep pace with her nimble lover.

Having travelled on for some miles in a high road, which Northerton said he was informed led to Hereford, they came at the break of day to the side of a large wood, where he suddenly stopped and, affecting to meditate a moment with himself, expressed some apprehensions from travelling any longer in so public a way. Upon which he easily persuaded his fair companion to strike with him into a path which seemed to lead directly through the wood, and which at length brought them both to the bottom of Mazard Hill.

Whether the execrable scheme which he now attempted to execute was the effect of previous deliberation or whether it now first came into his head, I cannot determine. But being arrived in this lonely place, where it was very improbable he should meet with any interruption, he suddenly slipped his garter from his leg and, laying violent hands on the poor woman, endeavoured to perpetrate that dreadful and detestable fact which we have before commemorated, and which the providential appearance of Jones did so fortunately prevent.

Happy was it for Mrs. Waters that she was not of the weakest order of females; for no sooner did she perceive by his tying a knot in his garter and by his declarations what his hellish intentions were than she stood stoutly to her defence, and so strongly struggled with her enemy, screaming all the while for assistance, that she delayed the execution of the villain's purpose several minutes, by which means Mr. Jones came to her relief, at the very instant when her strength failed and she was totally overpowered, and delivered her from the ruffian's hands with no other loss than that of her clothes, which were torn from her back, and of the diamond ring, which during the contention either dropped from her finger or was wrenched from it by Northerton.

Thus, reader, we have given thee the fruits of a very painful inquiry, which for thy satisfaction we have made into this matter. And here we have opened to thee a scene of folly, as well as villainy, which we could scarce have believed a human creature capable of being guilty of had we not remembered that this fellow was at that time firmly persuaded that he had already committed a murder and had forfeited his life to the law. As he concluded, therefore, that his only safety lay in flight, he thought the possessing himself of this poor woman's money and ring would make him amends for the additional burden he was to lay on his conscience.

And here, reader, we must strictly caution thee that thou dost not take any occasion from the misbehaviour of such a wretch as this to reflect on so worthy and honourable a body of men as are the officers of our army in general. Thou wilt be pleased to consider that this fellow, as we have already informed thee, had neither the birth nor education of a gentleman, nor was a proper person to be enrolled among the number of such. If, therefore, his baseness can justly reflect on any besides himself, it must be only on those who gave him his commission.

BOOK X

In Which the History Goes Forward About Twelve Hours

1

CONTAINING INSTRUCTIONS VERY NECESSARY TO BE PERUSED BY MODERN CRITICS

Reader, it is impossible we should know what sort of person thou wilt be, for, perhaps, thou may'st be as learned in human nature as Shakespeare himself was, and, perhaps, thou may'st be no wiser than some of his editors. Now, lest this latter should be the case, we think proper before we go any farther together to give thee a few wholesome admonitions, that thou may'st not as grossly misunderstand and misrepresent us as some of the said editors have misunderstood and misrepresented their author.

First, then, we warn thee not too hastily to condemn any of the incidents in this our history as impertinent and foreign to our main design because thou dost not immediately conceive in what manner such incident may conduce to that design. This work may, indeed, be considered as a great creation of our own, and for a little reptile of a critic to presume to find fault with any of its parts without knowing the manner in which the whole is connected, and before he comes to the final catastrophe, is a most presumptuous absurdity. The allusion and metaphor we have here made use of we must acknowledge to be infinitely too great for our occasion, but there is, indeed, no other which is at all adequate to express the difference between an author of the first rate and a critic of the lowest.

Another caution we would give thee, my good reptile, is that thou dost not find out too near a resemblance between certain characters here introduced, as, for instance, between the landlady who appears in the seventh book and her in the ninth. Thou art to know, friend, that there are certain characteristics in which most individuals of every profession and occupation agree. To be able to preserve these characteristics and at the same time to diversify their operations is one talent of a good writer. Again, to mark the nice distinction between two persons actuated by the same vice or folly is another; and as this last talent is found in very few writers, so is the true discernment of it found in as few readers, though, I believe, the observation of this forms a very principal pleasure in those who are capable of the discovery; every person, for instance, can distinguish between Sir Epicure Mammon and Sir Fopling Flutter, but to note the difference between Sir Fopling Flutter and Sir Courtly Nice requires a more exquisite judgement, for want of which, vulgar spectators of plays very often do great injustice in the theatre, where I have sometimes known a poet in danger of being convicted as a thief upon much worse evidence than the resemblance of hands hath been held to be in the law. In reality, I apprehend every amorous widow on the stage would run the hazard of being condemned as a servile imitation of Dido but that happily very few of our playhouse critics understand enough of Latin to read Virgil.

In the next place, we must admonish thee, my worthy friend (for, perhaps, thy heart may be better than thy head), not to condemn a character as a bad one because it is not perfectly a good one. If thou dost delight in these models of perfection, there are books enow written to gratify thy taste; but as we have not in the course of our conversation ever happened to meet with any such person, we have not chosen to introduce any such here. To say the truth, I a little question whether mere man ever arrived at this consummate degree of excellence, as well as whether there hath ever existed a monster bad enough to verify that

> ——nulla virtute redemptum
> A vitiis——*

in Juvenal; nor do I, indeed, conceive the good purposes served by inserting characters of such angelic perfection or such diabolical depravity in any work of invention, since

* Whose vices are not allayed with a single virtue.

from contemplating either, the mind of man is more likely to be overwhelmed with sorrow and shame than to draw any good uses from such patterns; for in the former instance he may be both concerned and ashamed to see a pattern of excellence in his nature which he may reasonably despair of ever arriving at, and in contemplating the latter, he may be no less affected with those uneasy sensations at seeing the nature of which he is a partaker degraded into so odious and detestable a creature.

In fact, if there be enough of goodness in a character to engage the admiration and affection of a well-disposed mind, though there should appear some of those little blemishes, *quas humana parum cavit natura,* they will raise our compassion rather than our abhorrence. Indeed, nothing can be of more moral use than the imperfections which are seen in examples of this kind, since such form a kind of surprise more apt to affect and dwell upon our minds than the faults of very vicious and wicked persons. The foibles and vices of men, in whom there is great mixture of good, become more glaring objects from the virtues which contrast them and show their deformity; and when we find such vices attended with their evil consequence to our favourite characters, we are not only taught to shun them for our own sake but to hate them for the mischiefs they have already brought on those we love.

And now, my friend, having given you these few admonitions, we will, if you please, once more set forward with our history.

2

Now the little trembling hare, whom the dread of all her numerous enemies, and chiefly of that cunning, cruel, carnivorous animal, man, had confined all the day to her lurking-place, sports wantonly o'er the lawns; now on some hollow tree the owl, shrill chorister of the night, hoots forth notes which might charm the ears of some modern connoisseurs in music; now in the imagination of the half-drunk clown, as he staggers through the churchyard, or rather charnel-yard, to his home, fear paints the bloody hob-goblin; now thieves and ruffians are awake and honest watchmen fast asleep: in plain English, it was now midnight, and the company at the inn, as well those who have been already mentioned in this history, as some others who arrived in the evening, were all in bed. Susan Chambermaid was now only stirring, she being obliged to wash the kitchen before she retired to the arms of the fond, expecting ostler.

In this posture were affairs at the inn when a gentleman arrived there post. He immediately alighted from his horse and, coming up to Susan, inquired of her in a very abrupt and confused manner, being almost out of breath with eagerness, whether there was any lady in the house. The hour of night and the behaviour of the man, who stared very wildly all the time, a little surprised Susan, so that she hesitated before she made any answer; upon which the gentleman with redoubled eagerness begged her to give him a true information, saying he had lost his wife and was come in pursuit of her. "Upon my shoul," cries he, "I have been near catching her already in two or three places if I had not found her gone just as I came up with her. If she be in the house, do carry me up in the dark and show her to me; and if she be gone away before me, do tell me which way I shall go after her to meet her, and upon my shoul, I will make you the richest poor woman in the nation." He then pulled out a handful of guineas, a sight which would have bribed persons of much greater consequence than this poor wench to much worse purposes.

Susan, from the account she had received of Mrs. Waters, made not the least doubt but that she was the very identical stray whom the right owner pursued. As she concluded, therefore, with great appearance of reason, that she never could get money in an honester way than by restoring a wife to her husband, she made no scruple of assuring the gentleman that the lady he wanted was then in the house, and was presently afterward prevailed upon (by very liberal promises and some earnest paid into her hands) to conduct him to the bedchamber of Mrs. Waters.

It hath been a custom long established in the polite world, and that upon very solid and substantial reasons, that a husband shall never enter his wife's apartment without first knocking at the door. The many excellent uses of this custom need scarce be hinted to a reader who hath any knowledge of the world, for by this means the lady hath time to adjust herself or to remove any disagreeable object out of the way; for there are some situations in which nice and delicate women would not be discovered by their husbands.

To say the truth, there are several ceremonies instituted among the polished part of mankind which, though they may to coarser judgements appear as matters of mere form, are found to have much of substance in them by the more discerning; and lucky would it have been had the custom above mentioned been observed by our gentleman in the present instance. Knock, indeed, he did at the door, but not with one of those gentle raps which is usual on such occasions. On the contrary, when he found the door locked, he flew at it with such violence that the lock immediately gave way, the door burst open, and he fell headlong into the room.

He had no sooner recovered his legs than forth from the bed upon his legs likewise appeared—with shame and sorrow are we obliged to proceed—our hero himself, who with a menacing voice demanded of the gentleman who he was, and what he meant by daring to burst open his chamber in that outrageous manner.

The gentleman at first thought he had committed a mistake and was going to ask pardon and retreat when, on a sudden, as the moon shone very bright, he cast his eyes on stays, gowns, petticoats, caps, ribbons, stockings, garters, shoes, clogs, &c., all which lay in a disordered manner on the floor. All these operating on the natural jealousy of his temper so enraged him that he lost all power of speech, and without returning any answer to Jones, he endeavoured to approach the bed.

Jones immediately interposing, a fierce contention arose, which soon proceeded to blows on both sides. And now Mrs. Waters (for we must confess she was in the same bed), being, I suppose, awakened from her sleep, and seeing two men fighting in her bedchamber, began to scream in the most violent manner, crying out, "Murder! Robbery!" and more frequently, "Rape!" which last some, perhaps, may wonder she should mention, who do not consider that these words of exclamation are used by ladies in a fright, as fa, la, la, ra, da, &c., are in music, only as the vehicles of sound and without any fixed ideas.

Next to the lady's chamber was deposited the body of an Irish gentleman who arrived too late at the inn to have been mentioned before. This gentleman was one of those whom the Irish call a calabalaro, or cavalier. He was a younger brother of a good family, and having no fortune at home, was obliged to look abroad in order to get one; for which purpose he was proceeding to the Bath to try his luck with cards and the women.

This young fellow lay in bed reading one of Mrs. Behn's novels; for he had been instructed by a friend that he would find no more effectual method of recommending himself to the ladies than the improving his understanding and filling his mind with good literature. He no sooner, therefore, heard the violent uproar in the next room than he leaped from his bolster, and taking his sword in one hand and the candle which burned by him in the other, he went directly to Mrs. Waters's chamber.

If the sight of another man in his shirt at first added some shock to the decency of the lady, it made her presently amends by considerably abating her fears; for no sooner had the calabalaro entered the room than he cried out, "Mr. Fitzpatrick, what the devil is the *maning* of this?" Upon which the other immediately answered, "Oh, Mr. Maclachlan, I am rejoiced you are here. This villain hath debauched my wife, and is got into bed with her." "What wife?" cries Maclachlan. "Do not I know Mrs. Fitzpatrick very well, and don't I see that the lady whom the gentleman who stands here in his shirt is lying in bed with is none of her?"

Fitzpatrick, now perceiving as well by the glimpse he had of the lady as by her voice, which might have been distinguished at a greater distance than he now stood from her, that he had made a very unfortunate mistake, began to ask many pardons of the lady; and then, turning to Jones, he said, "I would have you take notice I do not ask your pardon, for you have *bate* me; for which I am resolved to have your blood in the morning."

Jones treated this menace with much contempt, and Mr. Maclachlan answered, "Indeed, Mr. Fitzpatrick, you may be ashamed of your own self to disturb people at this time of night; if all the people in the inn were not asleep, you would have awakened them as you have me. The gentleman has served you very rightly. Upon my conscience, though I have no wife, if you had treated her so, I would have cut your throat."

Jones was so confounded with his fears for his lady's reputation that he knew neither what to say or do, but the invention of women is, as hath been observed, much readier

445

than that of men. She recollected that there was a communication between her chamber and that of Mr. Jones; relying, therefore, on his honour and her own assurance, she answered, "I know not what you mean, villains! I am wife to none of you. Help! Rape! Murder! Rape!" And now, the landlady coming into the room, Mrs. Waters fell upon her with the utmost virulence, saying she thought herself in a sober inn and not in a bawdy-house, but that a set of villains had broke into her room with an intent upon her honour if not upon her life; and both, she said, were equally dear to her.

The landlady now began to roar as loudly as the poor woman in bed had done before. She cried she was undone, and that the reputation of her house, which was never blown upon before, was utterly destroyed. Then, turning to the men, she cried, "What in the devil's name is the reason of all this disturbance in the lady's room?" Fitzpatrick, hanging down his head, repeated that he had committed a mistake, for which he heartily asked pardon, and then retired with his countryman. Jones, who was too ingenious to have missed the hint given him by his fair one, boldly asserted that he had run to her assistance upon hearing the door broke open, with what design he could not conceive, unless of robbing the lady; which if they intended, he said, he had had the good fortune to prevent. "I never had a robbery committed in my house since I have kept it," cries the landlady; "I would have you to know, sir, I harbour no highwaymen here; I scorn the word, thof I say it. None but honest, good gentle-folks are welcome to my house, and I thank good luck I have always had enow of such customers; indeed, as many as I could entertain. Here hath been my Lord——"; and then she repeated over a catalogue of names and titles, many of which we might, perhaps, be guilty of a breach of privilege by inserting.

Jones, after much patience, at length interrupted her, by making an apology to Mrs. Waters for having appeared before her in his shirt, assuring her that nothing but a concern for her safety could have prevailed on him to do it. The reader may inform himself of her answer and, indeed, of her whole behaviour to the end of the scene by considering the situation which she affected, being that of a modest lady who was awakened out of her sleep by three strange men in her chamber. This was the part which she undertook to perform, and indeed she executed it so well that none of our theatrical actresses could exceed her in any of their performances, either on or off the stage.

And hence, I think, we may very fairly draw an argument to prove how extremely natural virtue is to the fair sex; for though there is not, perhaps, one in ten thousand who is capable of making a good actress, and even among these we rarely see two who are equally able to 'personate the same character, yet this of virtue they can all admirably well put on; and as well those individuals who have it not as those who possess it can all act it to the utmost degree of perfection.

When the men were all departed, Mrs. Waters, recovering from her fear, recovered likewise from her anger, and spoke in much gentler accents to the landlady, who did not so readily quit her concern for the reputation of the house, in favour of which she began again to number the many great persons who had slept under her roof; but the lady stopped her short and, having absolutely acquitted her of having had any share in the past disturbance, begged to be left to her repose, which, she said, she hoped to enjoy unmolested during the remainder of the night. Upon which the landlady, after much civility and many curtsies, took her leave.

3

A DIALOGUE BETWEEN THE LANDLADY AND SUSAN THE CHAMBERMAID, PROPER TO BE READ BY ALL INNKEEPERS AND THEIR SERVANTS; WITH THE ARRIVAL AND AFFABLE BEHAVIOUR OF A BEAUTIFUL YOUNG LADY, WHICH MAY TEACH PERSONS OF CONDITION HOW THEY MAY ACQUIRE THE LOVE OF THE WHOLE WORLD

The landlady, remembering that Susan had been the only person out of bed when the door was burst open, resorted presently to her to inquire into the first occasion of the disturbance, as well as who the strange gentleman was and when and how he arrived.

Susan related the whole story which the reader knows already, varying the truth only in some circumstances as she saw convenient and totally concealing the money which she had received. But whereas her mistress had in the preface to her inquiry spoken much in compassion for the fright which the lady had been in concerning any intended depredations on her virtue, Susan could not help endeavouring to quiet the concern which her mistress seemed to be under on that account, by swearing heartily she saw Jones leap out from her bed.

The landlady fell into a violent rage at these words. "A likely story, truly," cried she, "that a woman should cry out and endeavour to expose herself if that was the case! I desire to know what better proof any lady can give of her virtue than her crying out, which, I believe, twenty people can witness for her she did. I beg, madam, you would spread no such scandal of any of my guests; for it will not only reflect on them but upon the house, and I am sure no vagabonds nor wicked beggarly people come here."

"Well," says Susan, "then I must not believe my own eyes." "No, indeed, must you not always," answered her mistress. "I would not have believed my own eyes against such good gentlefolks. I have not had a better supper ordered this half-year than they ordered last night, and so easy and good-humoured were they that they found no fault with my Worcestershire perry, which I sold them for champagne; and, to be sure, it is as well tasted and as wholesome as the best champagne in the kingdom—otherwise I would scorn to give it 'em—and they drank me two bottles. No, no, I will never believe any harm of such sober good sort of people."

Susan being thus silenced, her mistress proceeded to other matters. "And so you tell me," continued she, "that the strange gentleman came post, and there is a footman without with the horses; why, then, he is certainly some of your great gentlefolks too. Why did not you ask him whether he'd have any supper? I think he is in the other gentleman's room; go up and ask whether he called. Perhaps he'll order something when he finds anybody stirring in the house to dress it. Now, don't commit any of your usual blunders by telling him the fire's out and the fowl's alive. And if he should order mutton, don't blab out that we have none. The butcher, I know, killed a sheep just before I went to bed, and he never refuses to cut it up warm when I desire it. Go, remember there's all sorts of mutton and fowls; go, open the door, with 'Gentlemen, d'ye call?' and if they say nothing, ask what his honour will be pleased to have for supper. Don't forget his honour. Go; if you don't mind all these matters better, you'll never come to anything."

Susan departed, and soon returned with an account that the two gentlemen were got both into the same bed. "Two gentlemen," says the landlady, "in the same bed! That's impossible; they are two arrant scrubs, I warrant them, and

I believe young Squire Allworthy guessed right that the fellow intended to rob her ladyship; for if he had broke open the lady's door with any of the wicked designs of a gentleman, he would never have sneaked away to another room to save the expense of a supper and a bed to himself. They are certainly thieves, and their searching after a wife is nothing but a pretence."

In these censures my landlady did Mr. Fitzpatrick great injustice; for he was really born a gentleman, though not worth a groat, and though, perhaps, he had some few blemishes in his heart as well as in his head, yet being a sneaking or a niggardly fellow was not one of them. In reality he was so generous a man that whereas he had received a very handsome fortune with his wife, he had now spent every penny of it except some little pittance which was settled upon her; and in order to possess himself of this, he had used her with such cruelty that together with his jealousy, which was of the bitterest kind, it had forced the poor woman to run away from him.

This gentleman, then, being well tired with his long journey from Chester in one day, with which, and some good dry blows he had received in the scuffle, his bones were so sore that, added to the soreness of his mind, it had quite deprived him of any appetite for eating; and being now so violently disappointed in the woman whom at the maid's instance he had mistaken for his wife, it never once entered into his head that she might nevertheless be in the house though he had erred in the first person he had attacked. He therefore yielded to the dissuasions of his friend from searching any farther after her that night and accepted the kind offer of part of his bed.

The footman and post-boy were in a different disposition. They were more ready to order than the landlady was to provide; however, after being pretty well satisfied by them of the real truth of the case, and that Mr. Fitzpatrick was no thief, she was at length prevailed on to set some cold meat before them, which they were devouring with great greediness when Partridge came into the kitchen. He had been first awaked by the hurry which we have before seen, and while he was endeavouring to compose himself again on his pillow a screech-owl had given him such a serenade at his window that he leaped in a most horrible affright from his bed and, huddling on his clothes with great expedition, ran down to the protection of the company, whom he heard talking below in the kitchen.

His arrival detained my landlady from returning to her rest, for she was just about to leave the other two guests to the care of Susan, but the friend of young Squire Allworthy was not to be so neglected, especially as he called for a pint of wine to be mulled. She immediately obeyed by putting the same quantity of perry to the fire; for this readily answered to the name of every kind of wine.

The Irish footman was retired to bed and the post-boy was going to follow, but Partridge invited him to stay and partake of his wine, which the lad very thankfully accepted. The schoolmaster was indeed afraid to return to bed by himself, and as he did not know how soon he might lose the company of my landlady, he was resolved to secure that of the boy, in whose presence he apprehended no danger from the Devil or any of his adherents.

And now arrived another post-boy at the gate; upon which Susan, being ordered out, returned, introducing two young women in riding-habits, one of which was so very richly laced that Partridge and the post-boy instantly started from their chairs, and my landlady fell to her curtsies and her "ladyships" with great eagerness.

The lady in the rich habit said with a smile of great condescension, "If you will give me leave, madam, I will warm myself a few minutes at your kitchen fire, for it is really very cold; but I must insist on disturbing no one from their seats." This was spoken on account of Partridge, who had retreated to the other end of the room, struck with the utmost awe and astonishment at the splendour of the lady's dress. Indeed she had a much better title to respect than this, for she was one of the most beautiful creatures in the world.

The lady earnestly desired Partridge to return to his seat, but could not prevail. She then pulled off her gloves and displayed two hands, which had every property of snow in them except that of melting, to the fire. Her companion, who was indeed her maid, likewise pulled off her gloves and discovered what bore an exact resemblance in cold and colour to a piece of frozen beef.

"I wish, madam," quoth the latter, "your ladyship would not think of going any farther to-night. I am terribly afraid your ladyship will not be able to bear the fatigue."

"Why, sure," cries the landlady, "her ladyship's honour

can never intend it. Oh, bless me, farther to-night indeed! Let me beseech your ladyship not to think on't. But to be sure, your ladyship can't. What will your honour be pleased to have for supper? I have mutton of all kinds and some nice chicken."

"I think, madam," said the lady, "it would be rather breakfast than supper; but I can't eat anything, and if I stay, shall only lie down for an hour or two. However, if you please, madam, you may get me a little sack-whey, made very small and thin."

"Yes, madam," cries the mistress of the house, "I have some excellent white wine." "You have no sack, then?" says the lady. "Yes, an't please your honour, I have; I may challenge the country for that— But let me beg your ladyship to eat something."

"Upon my word, I can't eat a morsel," answered the lady, "and I shall be much obliged to you if you will please to get my apartment ready as soon as possible; for I am resolved to be on horse-back again in three hours."

"Why, Susan," cries the landlady, "is there a fire lit yet in the Wild Goose? I am sorry, madam, all my best rooms are full. Several people of the first quality are now in bed. Here's a great young squire, and many other great gentlefolks of quality."

Susan answered that the Irish gentlemen were got into the Wild Goose.

"Was ever anything like it!" says the mistress. "Why the devil would you not keep some of the best rooms for the quality when you know scarce a day passes without some calling here? If they be gentlemen, I am certain when they know it is for her ladyship, they will get up again."

"Not upon my account," says the lady; "I will have no person disturbed for me. If you have a room that is commonly decent, it will serve me very well though it be never so plain. I beg, madam, you will not give yourself so much trouble on my account." "Oh, madam," cries the other, "I have several very good rooms for that matter, but none good enough for your honour's ladyship. However, as you are so condescending to take up with the best I have, do, Susan, get a fire in the Rose this minute. Will your ladyship be pleased to go up now or stay till the fire is lighted?" "I think I have sufficiently warmed myself," answered the lady, "so if you please, I will go now; I am afraid I have kept people, and particularly that gentleman" (meaning

Partridge) "too long in the cold already. Indeed I cannot bear to think of keeping any person from the fire this dreadful weather." She then departed with her maid, the landlady marching with two lighted candles before her.

When that good woman returned, the conversation in the kitchen was all upon the charms of the young lady. There is, indeed, in perfect beauty a power which none almost can withstand, for my landlady, though she was not pleased at the negative given to the supper, declared she had never seen so lovely a creature. Partridge ran out into the most extravagant encomiums on her face, though he could not refrain from paying some compliments to the gold lace on her habit; the post-boy sung forth the praises of her goodness, which were likewise echoed by the other post-boy, who was now come in. "She's a true good lady, I warrant her," says he; "for she hath mercy upon dumb creatures; for she asked me every now and tan upon the journey if I did not think she should hurt the horses by riding too fast, and when she came in, she charged me to give them as much corn as ever they would eat."

Such charms are there in affability and so sure is it to attract the praises of all kinds of people. It may indeed be compared to the celebrated Mrs. Hussey.* It is equally sure to set off every female perfection to the highest advantage, and to palliate and conceal every defect—a short reflection which we could not forbear making in this place, where my reader hath seen the loveliness of an affable deportment; and truth will now oblige us to contrast it by showing the reverse.

4

CONTAINING INFALLIBLE NOSTRUMS FOR PROCURING UNIVERSAL DISESTEEM AND HATRED

The lady had no sooner laid herself on her pillow than the waiting-woman returned to the kitchen to regale with some of those dainties which her mistress had refused.

The company, at her entrance, showed her the same respect which they had before paid to her mistress by rising, but she forgot to imitate her by desiring them to sit down

* A celebrated mantua-maker in the Strand, famous for setting off the shapes of women.

again. Indeed it was scarce possible they should have done so, for she placed her chair in such a posture as almost to occupy the whole fire. She then ordered a chicken to be broiled that instant, declaring if it was not ready in a quarter of an hour, she would not stay for it. Now, though the said chicken was then at roost in the stable and required the several ceremonies of catching, killing, and picking before it was brought to the gridiron, my landlady would nevertheless have undertaken to do all within the time, but the guest, being unfortunately admitted behind the scenes, must have been witness to the *fourberie;* the poor woman was therefore obliged to confess that she had none in the house, "But, madam," said she, "I can get any kind of mutton in an instant from the butcher's."

"Do you think, then," answered the waiting-gentlewoman, "that I have the stomach of a horse to eat mutton at this time of night? Sure you people that keep inns imagine your betters are like yourselves. Indeed I expected to get nothing at this wretched place. I wonder my lady would stop at it. I suppose none but tradesmen and graziers ever call here." The landlady fired at this indignity offered to her house; however, she suppressed her temper and contented herself with saying very good quality frequented it, she thanked heaven! "Don't tell me," cries the other, "of quality! I believe I know more of people of quality than such as you. But, prithee, without troubling me with any of your impertinence, do tell me what I can have for supper, for though I cannot eat horse-flesh, I am really hungry." "Why, truly, madam," answered the landlady, "you could not have taken me again at such a disadvantage; for I must confess I have nothing in the house unless a cold piece of beef, which, indeed, a gentleman's footman and the post-boy have almost cleared to the bone." "Woman," said Mrs. Abigail (so for shortness we will call her), "I entreat you not to make me sick. If I had fasted a month, I could not eat what had been touched by the fingers of such fellows. Is there nothing neat or decent to be had in this horrid place?" "What think you of some eggs and bacon, madam?" said the landlady. "Are your eggs new laid? Are you certain they were laid to-day? And let me have the bacon cut very nice and thin, for I can't endure anything that's gross. Prithee try if you can do a little tolerably for once, and don't think you have a farmer's wife or some of those creatures in the house." The landlady begun then to handle her knife, but the other stopped her, saying, "Good woman, I must insist upon your first washing your hands; for I am extremely nice and have been always used from my cradle to have everything in the most elegant manner."

The landlady, who governed herself with much difficulty, began now the necessary preparations; for as to Susan, she was utterly rejected, and with such disdain that the poor wench was as hard put to it to restrain her hands from violence as her mistress had been to hold her tongue. This indeed Susan did not entirely; for though she literally kept it within her teeth, yet there it muttered many "marry-come-ups, as good flesh and blood as yourself," with other such indignant phrases.

While the supper was preparing, Mrs. Abigail began to lament she had not ordered a fire in the parlour, but she said that was now too late. "However," said she, "I have novelty to recommend a kitchen, for I do not believe I ever eat in one before." Then, turning to the post-boys, she asked them why they were not in the stable with their horses. "If I must eat my hard fare here, madam," cries she to the landlady, "I beg the kitchen may be kept clear, that I may not be surrounded with all the blackguards in town; as for you, sir," says she to Partridge, "you look somewhat like a gentleman, and may sit still if you please; I don't desire to disturb anybody but mob."

"Yes, yes, madam," cries Partridge, "I am a gentleman, I do assure you, and I am not so easily to be disturbed. *Non semper vox causalis est verbo nominativus.*" This Latin she took to be some affront and answered, "You may be a gentleman, sir, but you don't show yourself as one to talk Latin to a woman." Partridge made a gentle reply and concluded with more Latin; upon which she tossed up her nose and contented herself by abusing him with the name of a great scholar.

The supper being now on the table, Mrs. Abigail eat very heartily for so delicate a person; and while a second course of the same was by her order preparing she said, "And so, madam, you tell me your house is frequented by people of great quality?"

The landlady answered in the affirmative, saying there were a great many very good quality and gentlefolks in it now. "There's young Squire Allworthy, as that gentleman there knows."

"And pray who is this young gentleman of quality, this young Squire Allworthy?" said Abigail.

"Who should he be," answered Partridge, "but the son and heir of the great Squire Allworthy of Somersetshire."

"Upon my word," said she, "you tell me strange news; for I know Mr. Allworthy of Somersetshire very well and I know he hath no son alive."

The landlady pricked up her ears at this, and Partridge looked a little confounded. However, after a short hesitation he answered, "Indeed, madam, it is true, everybody doth not know him to be Squire Allworthy's son, for he was never married to his mother, but his son he certainly is, and will be his heir too, as certainly as his name is Jones." At that word, Abigail let drop the bacon which she was conveying to her mouth and cried out, "You surprise me, sir. Is it possible Mr. Jones should be now in the house?" *"Quare non?"* answered Partridge. "It is possible, and it is certain."

Abigail now made haste to finish the remainder of her meal and then repaired back to her mistress, when the conversation passed which may be read in the next chapter.

5

SHOWING WHO THE AMIABLE LADY AND HER UNAMIABLE MAID WERE

As in the month of June the damask rose which chance hath planted among the lilies with their candid hue mixes his vermilion; or as some playsome heifer in the pleasant month of May diffuses her odiferous breath over the flowery meadows; or as in the blooming month of April the gentle, constant dove, perched on some fair bough, sits meditating her mate, so looking a hundred charms and breathing as many sweets, her thoughts being fixed on her Tommy, with a heart as good and innocent as her face was beautiful, Sophia (for it was she herself) lay reclining her lovely head on her hand when her maid entered the room and, running directly to the bed, cried, "Madam—madam—who doth your ladyship think is in the house?" Sophia, starting up, cried, "I hope my father hath not overtaken us." "No, madam, it is one worth a hundred fathers; Mr. Jones himself is here at this very instant." "Mr. Jones!" says Sophia. "It is impossible; I cannot be so fortunate." Her maid averred the fact, and was presently detached by her mistress to order him to be called, for she said she was resolved to see him immediately.

Mrs. Honour had no sooner left the kitchen in the manner we have before seen than the landlady fell severely upon her. The poor woman had, indeed, been loading her heart with foul language for some time, and now it scoured out of her mouth as filth doth from a mud-cart when the board which confines it is removed. Partridge likewise shovelled in his share of calumny, and (what may surprise the reader) not only bespattered the maid but attempted to sully the lily-white character of Sophia herself. "Never a barrel the better herring," cries he. "*Noscitur à socio* is a true saying. It must be confessed indeed that the lady in the fine garments is the civiller of the two, but I warrant neither of them are a bit better than they should be. A couple of Bath trulls, I'll answer for them; your quality don't ride about at this time o' night without servants." " 'Sbodlikins, and that's true," cries the landlady; "you have certainly hit upon the very matter, for quality don't come into a house without bespeaking a supper whether they eat any or no."

While they were thus discoursing Mrs. Honour returned and discharged her commission by bidding the landlady immediately wake Mr. Jones and tell him a lady wanted to speak with him. The landlady referred her to Partridge, saying he was the squire's friend, but, for her part, she never called men-folks, especially gentlemen, and then walked sullenly out of the kitchen. Honour applied herself to Partridge, but he refused; "for my friend," cries he, "went to bed very late, and he would be very angry to be disturbed so soon." Mrs. Honour insisted still to have him called, saying she was sure, instead of being angry, that he would be to the highest degree delighted when he knew the occasion. "Another time, perhaps, he might," cries Partridge, "but *non omnia possumus omnes*. One woman is enough at once for a reasonable man." "What do you mean by one woman, fellow?" cries Honour. "None of your fellow," answered Partridge. He then proceeded to inform her plainly that Jones was in bed with a wench, and made use of an expression too indelicate to be here inserted, which so enraged Mrs. Honour that she called him jackanapes and returned in a violent hurry to her mistress, whom she acquainted with the success of her errand and with the account she had received; which if possible she exaggerated, being as angry with Jones as if he had pronounced all the words that came from the mouth of Partridge. She discharged a torrent of abuse on the master, and advised her mistress to quit all thoughts of a man who had never shown himself deserving of her. She then ripped up the story of Molly Seagrim and gave the most malicious turn to his formerly quitting Sophia herself, which, I must confess, the present incident not a little countenanced.

The spirits of Sophia were too much dissipated by concern to enable her to stop the torrent of her maid. At last, however, she interrupted her, saying, "I never can believe this; some villain hath belied him. You say you had it from his friend, but surely it is not the office of a friend to betray such secrets." "I suppose," cries Honour, "the fellow is his pimp, for I never saw so ill-looked a villain. Besides, such profligate rakes as Mr. Jones are never ashamed of these matters."

To say the truth, this behaviour of Partridge was a little inexcusable, but he had not slept off the effect of the dose which he swallowed the evening before, which had in the morning received the addition of above a pint of wine, or indeed, rather of malt spirits, for the perry was by no means pure. Now that part of his head which nature designed for the reservoir of drink being very shallow, a small quantity of liquor overflowed it and opened the sluices of his heart, so that all the secrets there deposited run out. These sluices were indeed naturally very ill-secured. To give the best-natured turn we can to his disposition, he was a very honest man; for as he was the most inquisitive of mortals and eternally prying into the secrets of others, so he very faithfully paid them by communicating in return everything within his knowledge.

While Sophia, tormented with anxiety, knew not what to believe nor what resolution to take, Susan arrived with the sack-whey. Mrs. Honour immediately advised her mistress in a whisper to pump this wench, who probably could inform her of the truth. Sophia approved it and began as follows: "Come hither, child; now answer me truly what I am going to ask you and I promise you I will very well reward you. Is there a young gentleman in this house, a handsome young gentleman that—" Here Sophia blushed and was confounded. "A young gentleman," cries Honour, "that came hither in company with that saucy rascal who is now in the kitchen?" Susan answered there was. "Do you know anything of any lady?" continues Sophia. "Any lady? I don't ask you whether she is handsome or no; perhaps she is not, that's nothing to the purpose, but do you know of any lady?" "La, madam," cries Honour, "you will make a very bad examiner. Harkee, child," says she, "is not that very young gentleman now in bed with some nasty trull or other?" Here Susan smiled and was silent. "Answer the question, child," says Sophia, "and here's a guinea for you." "A guinea, madam!" cries Susan. "La, what's a guinea? If my mistress should know it, I shall certainly lose my place that very instant." "Here's another for you," says Sophia, "and I promise you faithfully your mistress shall never know it." Susan, after a very short hesitation, took the money and told the whole story, concluding with saying, "If you have a great curiosity, madam, I can steal softly into his room and see whether he be in his own bed or no." She accordingly did this, by Sophia's desire, and returned with an answer in the negative.

Sophia now trembled and turned pale. Mrs. Honour begged her to be comforted and not to think any more of so worthless a fellow. "Why there," says Susan; "I hope, madam, your ladyship won't be offended, but pray, madam, is not your ladyship's name Madam Sophia Western?" "How is it possible you should know me?" answered Sophia. "Why, that man that the gentlewoman spoke of, who is in the kitchen, told about you last night. But I hope your ladyship is not angry with me." "Indeed, child," said she, "I am not; pray tell me all and I promise I'll reward you." "Why, madam," continued Susan, "that man told us all in the kitchen that Madam Sophia Western—indeed I don't know how to bring it out." Here she stopped till, having received encouragement from Sophia and being vehemently pressed by Mrs. Honour, she proceeded thus: "He told us, madam, though to be sure it is all a lie, that your ladyship was dying for love of the young squire and that he was going to the wars to get rid of you. I thought to myself then he was a false-hearted wretch, but now to see such a fine, rich, beautiful lady as you be forsaken for such an ordinary woman; for to be sure, so she is, and another man's wife into the bargain. It is such a strange, unnatural thing, in a manner."

Sophia gave her a third guinea and, telling her she would certainly be her friend if she mentioned nothing of what had passed nor informed any one who she was, dismissed the girl with orders to the post-boy to get the horses ready immediately.

Being now left alone with her maid, she told her trusty waiting-woman that she never was more easy than at present. "I am now convinced," said she, "he is not only a villain but a low, despicable wretch. I can forgive all rather than his exposing my name in so barbarous a manner. That renders him the object of my contempt. Yes, Honour, I am now easy. I am indeed. I am very easy"; and then she burst into a violent flood of tears.

After a short interval spent chiefly by Sophia in crying and assuring her maid that she was perfectly easy, Susan arrived with an account that the horses were ready, when a very extraordinary thought suggested itself to our young heroine, by which Mr. Jones would be acquainted with her having been at the inn in a way which, if any sparks of affection for her remained in him, would be some punishment at least for his faults.

The reader will be pleased to remember a little muff, which hath had the honour of being more than once remembered already in this history. This muff, ever since the departure of Mr. Jones, had been the constant companion of Sophia by day and her bedfellow by night, and this muff she had at this very instant upon her arm, whence she took it off with great indignation, and having writ her name with her pencil upon a piece of paper, which she pinned to it, she bribed the maid to convey it into the empty bed of Mr. Jones; in which, if he did not find it, she charged her to take some method of conveying it before his eyes in the morning.

Then, having paid for what Mrs. Honour had eaten, in which bill was included an account for what she herself might have eaten, she mounted her horse and, once more assuring her companion that she was perfectly easy, continued her journey.

6

CONTAINING, AMONG OTHER THINGS, THE INGENUITY OF PAR-TRIDGE, THE MADNESS OF JONES, AND THE FOLLY OF FITZPATRICK

It was now past five in the morning, and other company began to rise and come to the kitchen, among whom were the sergeant and the coachman, who, being thoroughly reconciled, made a libation, or in the English phrase, drank a hearty cup together.

In this drinking nothing more remarkable happened than the behaviour of Partridge, who when the sergeant drank a health to King George repeated only the word *King;* nor could he be brought to utter more, for though he was going to fight against his own cause, yet he could not be prevailed upon to drink against it.

Mr. Jones, being now returned to his own bed (but from whence he returned we must beg to be excused from relating), summoned Partridge from this agreeable company, who after a ceremonious preface, having obtained leave to offer his advice, delivered himself as follows:

"It is, sir, an old saying and a true one that a wise man may sometimes learn counsel from a fool; I wish, therefore, I might be so bold as to offer you my advice, which is to return home again and leave these *horrida bella,* these bloody wars, to fellows who are contented to swallow gunpowder because they have nothing else to eat. Now, everybody knows your honour wants for nothing at home; when that's the case, why should any man travel abroad?"

"Partridge," cries Jones, "thou art certainly a coward; I wish therefore thou wouldst return home thyself and trouble me no more."

"I ask your honour's pardon," cries Partridge; "I spoke on your account more than my own; for as to me, heaven knows my circumstances are bad enough, and I am so far from being afraid that I value a pistol or a blunderbuss or any such thing no more than a pop-gun. Every man must die once, and what signifies the manner how? Besides, perhaps I may come off with the loss only of an arm or a leg. I assure you, sir, I was never less afraid in my life, and so if your honour is resolved to go on, I am resolved to follow you. But, in that case, I wish I might give my opinion. To be sure it is a scandalous way of travelling for a great gentleman like you to walk afoot. Now here are two or three good horses in the stable, which the landlord will certainly make no scruple of trusting you with, but if he should, I can easily contrive to take them; and let the worst come to the worst, the king would certainly pardon you, as you are going to fight in his cause."

Now, as the honesty of Partridge was equal to his understanding, and both dealt only in small matters, he would never have attempted a roguery of this kind had he not imagined it altogether safe, for he was one of those who have more consideration of the gallows than of the fitness of things; but in reality he thought he might have committed this felony without any danger, for besides that he doubted not but the name of Mr. Allworthy would sufficiently quiet the landlord, he conceived they should be altogether safe whatever turn affairs might take, as Jones, he imagined, would have friends enough on one side, and as his friends would as well secure him on the other.

When Mr. Jones found that Partridge was in earnest in this proposal, he very severely rebuked him, and that in such bitter terms that the other attempted to laugh it off, and presently turned the discourse to other matters, saying he believed they were then in a bawdy-house and that he had with much ado prevented two wenches from disturbing his honour in the middle of the night. "Hey-day!" says he. "I believe they got into your chamber whether I would or no, for here lies the muff of one of them on the ground." Indeed, as Jones returned to his bed in the dark he had never perceived the muff on the quilt, and in leaping into his bed, he had tumbled it on the floor. This Partridge now took up, and was going to put into his pocket when Jones desired to see it. The muff was so very remarkable that our hero might possibly have recollected it without the information annexed. But his memory was not put to that hard office, for at the same instant he saw and read the words *Sophia Western* upon the paper which was pinned to it. His looks now grew frantic in a moment and he eagerly cried out, "Oh, heavens, how came this muff here!" "I know no more than your honour," cried Partridge, "but I saw it upon the arm of one of the women who would have disturbed you if I would have suffered them." "Where are they?" cries Jones, jumping out of bed and laying hold of his clothes. "Many miles off, I believe, by this time," said Partridge. And now Jones, upon further inquiry, was sufficiently assured that the bearer of this muff was no other than the lovely Sophia herself.

The behaviour of Jones on this occasion, his thoughts, his looks, his words, his actions, were such as beggar all description. After many bitter execrations on Partridge and not fewer on himself, he ordered the poor fellow, who was frightened out of his wits, to run down and hire him horses at any rate, and a very few minutes afterwards, having shuffled on his clothes, he hastened downstairs to execute the orders himself which he had just before given.

But before we proceed to what passed on his arrival in the kitchen, it will be necessary to recur to what had there happened since Partridge had first left it on his master's summons.

The sergeant was just marched off with his party when the two Irish gentlemen arose and came downstairs, both complaining that they had been so often waked by the noises in the inn that they had never once been able to close their eyes all night.

The coach, which had brought the young lady and her maid and which, perhaps, the reader may have hitherto concluded was her own, was indeed a returned coach belonging to Mr. King of Bath, one of the worthiest and honestest men that ever dealt in horse-flesh, and whose coaches we heartily recommend to all our readers who travel that road. By which means they may, perhaps, have the pleasure of riding in the very coach and being driven by the very coachman that is recorded in this history.

The coachman, having but two passengers, and hearing Mr. Maclachlan was going to Bath, offered to carry him thither at a very moderate price. He was induced to this by the report of the ostler, who said that the horse which Mr. Maclachlan had hired from Worcester would be much more pleased with returning to his friends there than to prosecute a long journey, for that the said horse was rather a two-legged than a four-legged animal.

Mr. Maclachlan immediately closed with the proposal of the coachman and at the same time persuaded his friend Fitzpatrick to accept of the fourth place in the coach. This conveyance the soreness of his bones made more agreeable to him than a horse, and being well assured of meeting with his wife at Bath, he thought a little delay would be of no consequence.

Maclachlan, who was much the sharper man of the two, no sooner heard that this lady came from Chester, with the other circumstances which he learned from the ostler, than it came into his head that she might possibly be his friend's wife, and presently acquainted him with this suspicion, which had never once occurred to Fitzpatrick himself. To say the truth, he was one of those compositions which Nature makes up in too great a hurry and forgets to put any brains in their head.

Now, it happens to this sort of men as to bad hounds, who never hit off a fault themselves, but no sooner doth a dog of sagacity open his mouth than they immediately do the same and without the guide of any scent run directly forwards as fast as they are able. In the same manner, the very moment Mr. Maclachlan had mentioned his apprehension, Mr. Fitzpatrick instantly concurred and flew directly upstairs to surprise his wife before he knew where she was; and unluckily (as Fortune loves to play tricks with those gentlemen who put themselves entirely under her conduct) ran his head against several doors and posts to no purpose. Much kinder was she to me when she suggested that simile of the hounds just before inserted, since the poor wife may on these occasions be so justly compared to a hunted hare. Like that little wretched animal, she pricks up her ears to listen after the voice of her pursuer; like her, flies away trembling when she hears it; and like her, is generally overtaken and destroyed in the end.

This was not, however, the case at present; for after a long fruitless search Mr. Fitzpatrick returned to the kitchen, where, as if this had been a real chase, entered a gentleman hallooing as hunters do when the hounds are at a fault. He was just alighted from his horse and had many attendants at his heels.

Here, reader, it may be necessary to acquaint thee with some matters which, if thou dost know already, thou art wiser than I take thee to be. And this information thou shalt receive in the next chapter.

7

IN WHICH ARE CONCLUDED THE ADVENTURES THAT HAPPENED AT THE INN AT UPTON

In the first place, then, this gentleman just arrived was no other person than Squire Western himself, who was come hither in pursuit of his daughter; and had he fortunately been two hours earlier, he had not only found her but his niece into the bargain; for such was the wife of Mr. Fitzpatrick, who had run away with her five years before out of the custody of that sage lady Madam Western.

Now, this lady had departed from the inn much about at the same time with Sophia; for having been waked by the voice of her husband, she had sent up for the landlady and, being by her apprised of the matter, had bribed the good woman at an extravagant price to furnish her with horses for her escape. Such prevalence had money in this family; and though the mistress would have turned away her maid for a corrupt hussy if she had known as much as the reader, yet she was no more proof against corruption herself than poor Susan had been.

Mr. Western and his nephew were not known to one another, nor indeed would the former have taken any notice of the latter if he had known him; for this being a stolen match and consequently an unnatural one, in the opinion of the good squire, he had from the time of her committing it abandoned the poor young creature, who was then no more than eighteen, as a monster, and had never since suffered her to be named in his presence.

The kitchen was now a scene of universal confusion, Western inquiring after his daughter and Fitzpatrick as eagerly after his wife, when Jones entered the room, unfortunately having Sophia's muff in his hand.

As soon as Western saw Jones, he set up the same holla as is used by sportsmen when their game is in view. He then immediately run up and laid hold of Jones, crying, "We have got the dog fox, I warrant the bitch is not far off." The jargon which followed for some minutes, where many spoke different things at the same time, as it would be very difficult to describe, so would it be no less unpleasant to read.

Jones having at length shaken Mr. Western off, and some of the company having interfered between them, our hero protested his innocence as to knowing anything of the lady, when Parson Supple stepped up and said, "It is folly to deny it, for why, the marks of guilt are in thy hands. I will myself asseverate and bind it by an oath that the muff thou bearest in thy hand belongeth unto Madam Sophia, for I have frequently observed her of later days to bear it about her." "My daughter's muff!" cries the squire in a rage. "Hath he got my daughter's muff! Bear witness the goods are found upon him. I'll have him before a justice of peace this instant. Where is my daughter, villain?" "Sir," said Jones, "I beg you would be pacified. The muff, I acknowledge, is the young lady's, but, upon my honour, I have never seen her." At these words Western lost all patience and grew inarticulate with rage.

Some of the servants had acquainted Fitzpatrick who Mr.

Western was. The good Irishman, therefore, thinking he had now an opportunity to do an act of service to his uncle and by that means might possibly obtain his favour, stepped up to Jones and cried out, "Upon my conscience, sir, you may be ashamed of denying your having seen the gentleman's daughter before my face, when you know I found you there upon the bed together." Then, turning to Western, he offered to conduct him immediately to the room where his daughter was; which offer being accepted, he, the squire, the parson, and some others ascended directly to Mrs. Waters' chamber, which they entered with no less violence than Mr. Fitzpatrick had done before.

The poor lady started from her sleep with as much amazement as terror, and beheld at her bedside a figure which might very well be supposed to have escaped out of Bedlam. Such wildness and confusion were in the looks of Mr. Western, who no sooner saw the lady than he started back, showing sufficiently by his manner before he spoke that this was not the person sought after.

So much more tenderly do women value their reputation than their persons that though the latter seemed now in more danger than before, yet as the former was secure, the lady screamed not with such violence as she had done on the other occasion. However, she no sooner found herself alone than she abandoned all thoughts of further repose, and as she had sufficient reason to be dissatisfied with her present lodging, she dressed herself with all possible expedition.

Mr. Western now proceeded to search the whole house, but to as little purpose as he had disturbed poor Mrs. Waters. He then returned disconsolate into the kitchen, where he found Jones in the custody of his servants.

This violent uproar had raised all the people in the house, though it was yet scarcely daylight. Among these was a grave gentleman, who had the honour to be in the commission of the peace for the county of Worcester. Of which Mr. Western was no sooner informed than he offered to lay his complaint before him. The justice declined executing his office, as, he said, he had no clerk present, nor no book about justice business; and that he could not carry all the law in his head about stealing away daughters and such sort of things.

Here Mr. Fitzpatrick offered to lend him his assistance, informing the company that he had been himself bred to the law. (And indeed he had served three years as clerk to an attorney in the north of Ireland when, choosing a genteeler walk in life, he quitted his master, came over to England, and set up that business which requires no apprenticeship: namely, that of a gentleman, in which he had succeeded as hath been already partly mentioned.)

Mr. Fitzpatrick declared that the law concerning daughters was out of the present case; that stealing a muff was undoubtedly felony, and the goods being found upon the person were sufficient evidence of the fact.

The magistrate, upon the encouragement of so learned a coadjutor and upon the violent intercession of the squire, was at length prevailed upon to seat himself in the chair of Justice, where being placed, upon viewing the muff, which Jones still held in his hand, and upon the parson's swearing it to be the property of Mr. Western, he desired Mr. Fitzpatrick to draw up a commitment, which he said he would sign.

Jones now desired to be heard, which was at last with difficulty granted him. He then produced the evidence of Mr. Partridge as to the finding it; but what was still more, Susan deposed that Sophia herself had delivered the muff to her and had ordered her to convey it into the chamber where Mr. Jones had found it.

Whether a natural love of justice or the extraordinary comeliness of Jones had wrought on Susan to make the discovery, I will not determine, but such were the effects of her evidence that the magistrate, throwing himself back in his chair, declared that the matter was now altogether as clear on the side of the prisoner as it had before been against him; with which the parson concurred, saying the Lord forbid he should be instrumental in committing an innocent person to durance. The justice then arose, acquitted the prisoner, and broke up the court.

Mr. Western now gave every one present a hearty curse and, immediately ordering his horses, departed in pursuit of his daughter without taking the least notice of his nephew, Fitzpatrick, or returning any answer to his claim of kindred, notwithstanding all the obligations he had just received from that gentleman. In the violence, moreover, of his hurry and of his passion, he luckily forgot to demand the muff of Jones; I say luckily, for he would have died on the spot rather than have parted with it.

Jones likewise, with his friend Partridge, set forward the moment he had paid his reckoning in quest of his lovely

Sophia, whom he now resolved never more to abandon the pursuit of. Nor could he bring himself even to take leave of Mrs. Waters, of whom he detested the very thoughts, as she had been, though not designedly, the occasion of his missing the happiest interview with Sophia, to whom he now vowed eternal constancy.

As for Mrs. Waters, she took the opportunity of the coach which was going to Bath, for which place she set out in company with the two Irish gentlemen, the landlady kindly lending her her clothes; in return for which she was contented only to receive about double their value as a recompense for the loan. Upon the road she was perfectly reconciled to Mr. Fitzpatrick, who was a very handsome fellow, and indeed did all she could to console him in the absence of his wife.

Thus ended the many odd adventures which Mr. Jones encountered at his inn at Upton, where they talk to this day of the beauty and lovely behaviour of the charming Sophia, by the name of the Somersetshire angel.

8

IN WHICH THE HISTORY GOES BACKWARD

Before we proceed any farther in our history, it may be proper to look a little back in order to account for the extraordinary appearance of Sophia and her father at the inn at Upton.

The reader may be pleased to remember that in the ninth chapter of the seventh book of our history we left Sophia, after a long debate between love and duty, deciding the cause as it usually, I believe, happens, in favour of the former.

This debate had arisen, as we have there shown, from a visit which her father had just before made her in order to force her consent to a marriage with Blifil, and which he had understood to be fully implied in her acknowledgement *that she neither must nor could refuse any absolute command of his*.

Now, from this visit the squire retired to his evening potation, overjoyed at the success he had had with his daughter; and as he was of a social disposition and willing to have partakers in his happiness, the beer was ordered to flow very liberally into the kitchen, so that before eleven in the evening, there was not a single person sober in the house except only Mrs. Western herself and the charming Sophia.

Early in the morning a messenger was dispatched to summon Mr. Blifil; for though the squire imagined that young gentleman had been much less acquainted than he really was with the former aversion of his daughter, as he had not, however, yet received her consent, he longed impatiently to communicate it to him, not doubting but that the intended bride herself would confirm it with her lips. As to the wedding, it had the evening before been fixed by the male parties to be celebrated on the next morning save one.

Breakfast was now set forth in the parlour, where Mr. Blifil attended and where the squire and his sister likewise were assembled; and now Sophia was ordered to be called.

O Shakespeare, had I thy pen! O Hogarth, had I thy pencil! Then would I draw the picture of the poor serving-man, who with pale countenance, staring eyes, chattering teeth, faltering tongue, and trembling limbs

(E'en such a man, so faint, so spiritless,
So dull, so dead in look, so woe-begone,
Drew Priam's curtains in the dead of night,
And would have told him half his Troy was burned)

entered the room and declared—*that Madam Sophia was not to be found*.

"Not to be found!" cries the squire, starting from his chair. "Zounds and d—nation! Blood and fury! Where, when, how, what—not to be found! Where?"

"La, brother," said Mrs. Western with true political coldness, "you are always throwing yourself into such violent passions for nothing. My niece, I suppose, is only walked out into the garden. I protest you are grown so unreasonable that it is impossible to live in the house with you."

"Nay, nay," answered the squire, returning as suddenly to himself as he had gone from himself; "if that be all the matter, it signifies not much, but, upon my soul, my mind misgave me when the fellow said she was not to be found." He then gave orders for the bell to be rung in the garden, and sat himself contentedly down.

No two things could be more the reverse of each other than were the brother and sister in most instances, particularly in this: that as the brother never foresaw anything at a distance, but was most sagacious in immediately seeing everything the moment it had happened, so the sister eternally foresaw at a distance, but was not so quick-sighted to objects before her eyes. Of both these the reader may have observed examples, and indeed both their several talents were excessive; for as the sister often foresaw what never came to pass, so the brother often saw much more than was actually the truth.

This was not, however, the case at present. The same report was brought from the garden as before had been brought from the chamber: that Madam Sophia was not to be found.

The squire himself now sallied forth, and begun to roar forth the name of Sophia as loudly and in as hoarse a voice as whilom did Hercules that of Hylas; and as the poet tells us that the whole shore echoed back the name of that beautiful youth, so did the house, the garden, and all the neighbouring fields resound nothing but the name of Sophia, in the hoarse voices of the men and in the shrill pipes of the women; while Echo seemed so pleased to repeat the beloved sound that if there is really such a person, I believe Ovid hath belied her sex.

Nothing reigned for a long time but confusion till at last the squire, having sufficiently spent his breath, returned to the parlour, where he found Mrs. Western and Mr. Blifil, and threw himself with the utmost dejection in his countenance into a great chair.

Here Mrs. Western began to apply the following consolation:

"Brother, I am sorry for what hath happened, and that my niece should have behaved herself in a manner so unbecoming her family, but it is all your own doings and you have nobody to thank but yourself. You know she hath been educated always in a manner directly contrary to my advice, and now you see the consequence. Have I not a thousand times argued with you about giving my niece her own will? But you know I never could prevail upon you; and when I had taken so much pains to eradicate her headstrong opinions and to rectify your errors in policy, you know she was taken out of my hands, so that I have nothing to answer for. Had I been trusted entirely with the care of her education, no such accident as this had ever befallen you; so that you must comfort yourself by thinking it was all your own doing, and, indeed, what else could be expected from such indulgence?"

"Zounds, sister," answered he, "you are enough to make one mad. Have I indulged her? Have I given her her will? It was no longer ago than last night that I threatened if she disobeyed me to confine her to her chamber upon bread and water as long as she lived. You would provoke the patience of Job."

"Did ever mortal hear the like?" replied she. "Brother, if I had not the patience of fifty Jobs, you would make me forget all decency and decorum. Why would you interfere? Did I not beg you, did I not entreat you, to leave the whole conduct to me? You have defeated all the operations of the campaign by one false step. Would any man in his senses have provoked a daughter by such threats as these? How often have I told you that English women are not to be treated like Ciracessian * slaves. We have the protection of the world; we are to be won by gentle means only, and not to be hectored and bullied and beat into compliance. I thank heaven no Salic Law governs here. Brother, you have a roughness in your manner which no woman but myself would bear. I do not wonder my niece was frightened and terrified into taking this measure, and to speak honestly, I think my niece will be justified to the world for what she hath done. I repeat it to you again, brother: you must comfort yourself by remembering that it is all your own fault. How often have I advised——" Here Western rose hastily from his chair and, venting two or three horrid imprecations, ran out of the room.

When he was departed, his sister expressed more bitterness (if possible) against him than she had done while he was present; for the truth of which she appealed to Mr. Blifil, who with great complaisance acquiesced entirely in all she said, but excused all the faults of Mr. Western, "as they must be considered," he said, "to have proceeded from the too inordinate fondness of a father, which must be allowed the name of an amiable weakness." "So much the more inexcusable," answered the lady; "for whom doth he ruin by his fondness but his own child?" To which Blifil immediately agreed.

Mrs. Western then began to express great confusion on the account of Mr. Blifil, and of the usage which he had received

* Possibly Circassian.

from a family to which he intended so much honour. On this subject she treated the folly of her niece with great severity, but concluded with throwing the whole on her brother, who, she said, was inexcusable to have proceeded so far without better assurances of his daughter's consent; "but he was," says she, "always of a violent, headstrong temper; and I can scarce forgive myself for all the advice I have thrown away upon him."

After much of this kind of conversation, which perhaps would not greatly entertain the reader was it here particularly related, Mr. Blifil took his leave and returned home, not highly pleased with his disappointment; which, however, the philosophy which he had acquired from Square and the religion infused into him by Thwackum, together with somewhat else, taught him to bear rather better than more passionate lovers bear these kinds of evils.

9

THE ESCAPE OF SOPHIA

It is now time to look after Sophia, whom the reader, if he loves her half so well as I do, will rejoice to find escaped from the clutches of her passionate father and from those of her dispassionate lover.

Twelve times did the iron register of time beat on the sonorous bell-metal, summoning the ghosts to rise and walk their nightly round. In plainer language, it was twelve o'clock, and all the family, as we have said, lay buried in drink and sleep except only Mrs. Western, who was deeply engaged in reading a political pamphlet, and except our heroine, who now softly stole downstairs and, having unbarred and unlocked one of the house-doors, sallied forth and hastened to the place of appointment.

Notwithstanding the many pretty arts which ladies sometimes practise to display their fears on every little occasion (almost as many as the other sex uses to conceal theirs), certainly there is a degree of courage which not only becomes a woman but is often necessary to enable her to discharge her duty. It is, indeed, the idea of fierceness, and not of bravery, which destroys the female character; for who can read the story of the justly celebrated Arria without conceiving as high an opinion of her gentleness and tenderness as of her fortitude? At the same time, perhaps, many a woman who shrieks at a mouse or a rat may be capable of poisoning a husband or, what is worse, of driving him to poison himself.

Sophia, with all the gentleness which a woman can have, had all the spirit which she ought to have. When, therefore, she came to the place of appointment, and instead of meeting her maid, as was agreed, saw a man ride directly up to her, she neither screamed out nor fainted away; not that her pulse then beat with its usual regularity, for she was at first under some surprise and apprehension; but these were relieved almost as soon as raised when the man, pulling off his hat, asked her in a very submissive manner if her ladyship did not expect to meet another lady; and then proceeded to inform her that he was sent to conduct her to that lady.

Sophia could have no possible suspicion of any falsehood in this account; she therefore mounted resolutely behind the fellow, who conveyed her safe to a town about five miles distant, where she had the satisfaction of finding the good Mrs. Honour; for as the soul of the waiting-woman was wrapped up in those very habiliments which used to enwrap her body, she could by no means bring herself to trust them out of her sight. Upon these, therefore, she kept guard in person, while she detached the aforesaid fellow after her mistress, having given him all proper instructions.

They now debated what course to take in order to avoid the pursuit of Mr. Western, who, they knew, would send after them in a few hours. The London Road had such charms for Honour that she was desirous of going on directly, alleging that as Sophia could not be missed till eight or nine the next morning, her pursuers would not be able to overtake her even though they knew which way she had gone. But Sophia had too much at stake to venture anything to chance, nor did she dare trust too much to her tender limbs in a contest which was to be decided only by swiftness. She resolved, therefore, to travel across the country for at least twenty or thirty miles, and then to take the direct road to London. So, having hired her horses to go twenty miles one way when she intended to go twenty miles the other, she set forward with the same guide behind whom she had ridden from her father's house, the guide having now taken up behind him in the room of Sophia a much heavier, as well as much less lovely, burden, being, indeed, a huge portmanteau well stuffed with those outside ornaments by means of which the fair Honour hoped to gain many conquests and, finally, to make her fortune in London City.

When they had gone about two hundred paces from the inn, on the London Road, Sophia rode up to the guide, and with a voice much fuller of honey than was ever that of Plato, though his mouth is supposed to have been a beehive, begged him to take the first turning which led towards Bristol.

Reader, I am not superstitious nor any great believer in modern miracles. I do not, therefore, deliver the following as a certain truth, for indeed I can scarce credit it myself; but the fidelity of an historian obliges me to relate what hath been confidently asserted. The horse, then, on which the guide rode, is reported to have been so charmed by Sophia's voice that he made a full stop and expressed an unwillingness to proceed any farther.

Perhaps, however, the fact may be true and less miraculous than it hath been represented, since the natural cause seems adequate to the effect; for as the guide at that moment desisted from a constant application of his armed right heel (for like Hudibras he wore but one spur), it is more than possible that this omission alone might occasion the beast to stop, especially as this was very frequent with him at other times.

But if the voice of Sophia had really an effect on the horse, it had very little on the rider. He answered somewhat surlily that measter had ordered him to go a different way, and that he should lose his place if he went any other than that he was ordered.

Sophia, finding all her persuasions had no effect, began now to add irresistible charms to her voice, charms which, according to the proverb, makes the old mare trot instead of standing still; charms to which modern ages have attributed all that irresistible force which the ancients imputed to perfect oratory. In a word, she promised she would reward him to his utmost expectation.

The lad was not totally deaf to these promises, but he disliked their being indefinite. For though perhaps he had never heard that word, yet that in fact was his objection. He said gentlevolks did not consider the case of poor volks; that he had like to have been turned away the other day for riding about the country with a gentleman from Squire Allworthy's, who did not reward him as he should have done.

"With whom?" says Sophia eagerly. "With a gentleman from Squire Allworthy's," repeated the lad; "the squire's son, I think they call 'un." "Whither? Which way did he go?" says Sophia. "Why, a little o' one side o' Bristol, about twenty miles off," answered the lad. "Guide me," says Sophia, "to the same place, and I'll give thee a guinea, or two if one is not sufficient." "To be certain," said the boy, "it is honestly worth two when your ladyship considers what a risk I run, but, however, if your ladyship will promise me the two guineas, I'll e'en venture; to be certain, it is a sinful thing to ride about my master's horses, but one comfort is, I can only be turned away, and two guineas will partly make me amends."

The bargain being thus struck, the lad turned aside into the Bristol Road, and Sophia set forward in pursuit of Jones, highly contrary to the remonstrances of Mrs. Honour, who had much more desire to see London than to see Mr. Jones; for indeed she was not his friend with her mistress, as he had been guilty of some neglect in certain pecuniary civilities which are by custom due to the waiting-gentlewomen in all love affairs, and more especially in those of a clandestine kind. This we impute rather to the carelessness of his temper than to any want of generosity, but perhaps she derived it from the latter motive. Certain it is, that she hated him very bitterly on that account and resolved to take every opportunity of injuring him with her mistress. It was, therefore, highly unlucky for her that she had gone to the very same town and inn whence Jones had started, and still more unlucky was she in having stumbled on the same guide and on this accidental discovery which Sophia had made.

Our travellers arrived at Hambrook * at the break of day, where Honour was against her will charged to inquire the route which Mr. Jones had taken. Of this, indeed, the guide himself could have informed them, but Sophia, I know not for what reason, never asked him the question.

When Mrs. Honour had made her report from the landlord, Sophia with much difficulty procured some indifferent horses, which brought her to the inn where Jones had been confined rather by the misfortune of meeting with a surgeon than by having met with a broken head.

* This was the village where Jones met the Quaker.

Here Honour, being again charged with a commission of inquiry, had no sooner applied herself to the landlady and had described the person of Mr. Jones than that sagacious woman began, in the vulgar phrase, to smell a rat. When Sophia therefore entered the room, instead of answering the maid, the landlady, addressing herself to the mistress, began the following speech: "Good lackaday! Why, there now, who would have thought it! I protest the loveliest couple that ever eye beheld. I' fackins, madam, it is no wonder the squire run on so about your ladyship. He told me, indeed, you was the finest lady in the world, and to be sure, so you be. Mercy on him, poor heart; I bepitied him, so I did, when he used to hug his pillow and call it his dear Madam Sophia. I did all I could to dissuade him from going to the wars; I told him there were men enow that were good for nothing else but to be killed, that had not the love of such fine ladies." "Sure," says Sophia, "the good woman is distracted." "No, no," cries the landlady, "I am not distracted. What, doth your ladyship think I don't know, then? I assure you he told me all." "What saucy fellow," cries Honour, "told you anything of my lady?" "No saucy fellow," answered the landlady, "but the young gentleman you inquired after, and a very pretty young gentleman he is, and he loves Madam Sophia Western to the bottom of his soul." "He love my lady! I'd have you to know, woman, she is meat for his master." "Nay, Honour," said Sophia, interrupting her, "don't be angry with the good woman; she intends no harm." "No, marry don't I," answered the landlady, emboldened by the soft accents of Sophia; and then launched into a long narrative too tedious to be here set down, in which some passages dropped that gave a little offence to Sophia and much more to her waiting-woman, who hence took occasion to abuse poor Jones to her mistress the moment they were alone together, saying that he must be a very pitiful fellow, and could have no love for a lady whose name he would thus prostitute in an ale-house.

Sophia did not see his behaviour in so very disadvantageous a light, and was perhaps more pleased with the violent raptures of his love (which the landlady exaggerated as much as she had done every other circumstance) than she was offended with the rest; and, indeed, she imputed the whole to the extravagance, or rather ebullience, of his passion and to the openness of his heart.

This incident, however, being afterwards revived in her

mind and placed in the most odious colours by Honour, served to heighten and give credit to those unlucky occurrences at Upton, and assisted the waiting-woman in her endeavours to make her mistress depart from that inn without seeing Jones.

The landlady, finding Sophia intended to stay no longer than till her horses were ready, and that without either eating or drinking, soon withdrew, when Honour began to take her mistress to task (for indeed she used great freedom), and after a long harangue, in which she reminded her of her intention to go to London and gave frequent hints of the impropriety of pursuing a young fellow, she at last concluded with this serious exhortation: "For heaven's sake, madam, consider what you are about and whither you are going."

This advice to a lady who had already rode near forty miles, and in no very agreeable season, may seem foolish enough. It may be supposed she had well considered and resolved this already; nay, Mrs. Honour by the hints she threw out seemed to think so; and this I doubt not is the opinion of many readers, who have, I make no doubt, been long since well convinced of the purpose of our heroine and have heartily condemned her for it as a wanton baggage.

But in reality this was not the case. Sophia had been lately so distracted between hope and fear, her duty and love to her father, her hatred to Blifil, her compassion, and (why should we not confess the truth) her love for Jones—which last the behaviour of her father, of her aunt, of every one else, and more particularly of Jones himself, had blown into a flame—that her mind was in that confused state which may be truly said to make us ignorant of what we do or whither we go, or rather, indeed, indifferent as to the consequence of either.

The prudent and sage advice of her maid produced, however, some cool reflection; and she at length determined to go to Gloucester and thence to proceed directly to London.

But, unluckily, a few miles before she entered that town, she met the hack-attorney who, as is before mentioned, had dined there with Mr. Jones. This fellow, being well known to Mrs. Honour, stopped and spoke to her, of which Sophia at that time took little notice more than to inquire who he was.

But having had a more particular account from Honour of this man afterwards at Gloucester, and hearing of the great expedition he usually made in travelling, for which (as hath been before observed) he was particularly famous; recollecting likewise that she had overheard Mrs. Honour inform him that they were going to Gloucester, she began to fear lest her father might by this fellow's means be able to trace her to that city; wherefore, if she should there strike into the London Road, she apprehended he would certainly be able to overtake her. She therefore altered her resolution, and having hired horses to go a week's journey a way which she did not intend to travel, she again set forward after a light refreshment, contrary to the desire and earnest entreaties of her maid and to the no less vehement remonstrances of Mrs. Whitefield, who from good breeding or, perhaps, from good nature (for the poor young lady appeared fatigued) pressed her very heartily to stay that evening at Gloucester.

Having refreshed herself only with some tea, and with lying about two hours on the bed while her horses were getting ready, she resolutely left Mrs. Whitefield's about eleven at night and, striking directly into the Worcester Road, within less than four hours arrived at that very inn where we last saw her.

Having thus traced our heroine very particularly back from her departure till her arrival at Upton, we shall in a very few words bring her father to the same place; who, having received the first scent from the post-boy who conducted his daughter to Hambrook, very easily traced her afterwards to Gloucester, whence he pursued her to Upton, as he had learned Mr. Jones had taken that route (for Partridge, to use the squire's expression, left everywhere a strong scent behind him), and he doubted not in the least but Sophia travelled or, as he phrased it, ran the same way. He used indeed a very coarse expression, which need not be here inserted as fox-hunters, who alone would understand it, will easily suggest it to themselves.

BOOK XI

1

A CRUST FOR THE CRITICS

In our last initial chapter we may be supposed to have treated that formidable set of men who are called critics with more freedom than becomes us, since they exact, and indeed generally receive, great condescension from authors. We shall in this, therefore, give the reasons of our conduct to this august body, and here we shall perhaps place them in a light in which they have not hitherto been seen.

This word *critic* is of Greek derivation, and signifies judgement. Hence I presume some persons who have not understood the original, and have seen the English translation of the primitive, have concluded that it meant judgement in the legal sense, in which it is frequently used as equivalent to condemnation.

I am the rather inclined to be of that opinion as the greatest number of critics hath of late years been found amongst the lawyers. Many of these gentlemen, from despair, perhaps, of ever rising to the Bench in Westminster Hall, have placed themselves on the benches at the playhouse, where they have exerted their judicial capacity and have given judgement, i.e., condemned without mercy.

The gentlemen would perhaps be well enough pleased if we were to leave them thus compared to one of the most important and honourable offices in the commonwealth, and if we intended to apply to their favour, we would do so; but as we design to deal very sincerely, and plainly too, with them, we must remind them of another officer of justice of a much lower rank, to whom, as they not only pronounce but execute their own judgement, they bear likewise some remote resemblance.

But in reality there is another light in which these modern critics may with great justice and propriety be seen, and this is that of a common slanderer. If a person who pries into the characters of others with no other design but to discover their faults and to publish them to the world deserves the title of a slanderer of the reputations of men, why should not a critic, who reads with the same malevolent view, be as properly styled the slanderer of the reputation of books?

Vice hath not, I believe, a more abject slave; society produces not a more odious vermin; nor can the Devil receive a guest more worthy of him, nor possibly more welcome to him, than a slanderer. The world, I am afraid, regards not this monster with half the abhorrence which he deserves, and I am more afraid to assign the reason of this criminal lenity shown towards him; yet it is certain that the thief looks innocent in the comparison; nay, the murderer himself can seldom stand in competition with his guilt, for slander is a more cruel weapon than a sword, as the wounds which the former gives are always incurable. One method, indeed, there is of killing, and that the basest and most execrable of all, which bears an exact analogy to the vice here disclaimed against, and that is poison. A means of revenge so base and yet so horrible that it was once wisely distinguished by our laws from all other murders in the peculiar severity of the punishment.

Besides the dreadful mischiefs done by slander and the baseness of the means by which they are effected, there are other circumstances that highly aggravate its atrocious quality; for it often proceeds from no provocation and seldom promises itself any reward, unless some black and infernal mind may propose a reward in the thoughts of having procured the ruin and misery of another.

Shakespeare hath nobly touched this vice when he says,

Who steals my purse steals trash; 'tis something, nothing;
'Twas mine, 'tis his, and has been slave to thousands:
But he that filches from me my good name
Robs me of that *which not enriches him,*
And makes me poor indeed.

With all this my good reader will doubtless agree, but

much of it will probably seem too severe when applied to the slanderer of books. But let it here be considered that both proceed from the same wicked disposition of mind and are alike void of the excuse of temptation. Nor shall we conclude the injury done this way to be very slight when we consider a book as the author's offspring and, indeed, as the child of his brain.

The reader who hath suffered his Muse to continue hitherto in a virgin state can have but a very inadequate idea of this kind of paternal fondness. To such we may parody the tender exclamation of Macduff: *Alas! Thou hast written no book*. But the author whose Muse hath brought forth will feel the pathetic strain, perhaps will accompany me with tears (especially if his darling be already no more), while I mention the uneasiness with which the big Muse bears about her burden, the painful labour with which she produces it, and lastly, the care, the fondness, with which the tender father nourishes his favourite till it be brought to maturity and produced into the world.

Nor is there any paternal fondness which seems less to savour of absolute instinct, and which may so well be reconciled to worldly wisdom, as this. These children may most truly be called the riches of their father, and many of them have with true filial piety fed their parent in his old age; so that not only the affection but the interest of the author may be highly injured by these slanderers, whose poisonous breath brings his book to an untimely end.

Lastly, the slander of a book is, in truth, the slander of the author; for as no one can call another bastard without calling the mother a whore, so neither can any one give the names of sad stuff, horrid nonsense, &c., to a book without calling the author a blockhead, which though in a moral sense it is a preferable appellation to that of villain is, perhaps, rather more injurious to his worldly interest.

Now, however ludicrous all this may appear to some, others, I doubt not, will feel and acknowledge the truth of it; nay, may perhaps think I have not treated the subject with decent solemnity; but surely a man may speak truth with a smiling countenance. In reality, to depreciate a book maliciously, or even wantonly, is at least a very ill-natured office, and a morose, snarling critic may, I believe, be suspected to be a bad man.

I will therefore endeavour in the remaining part of this chapter to explain the marks of this character and to show what criticism I here intend to obviate; for I can never be understood, unless by the very persons here meant, to insinuate that there are no proper judges of writing, or to endeavour to exclude from the commonwealth of literature any of those noble critics to whose labours the learned world are so greatly indebted. Such were Aristotle, Horace, and Longinus among the ancients, Dacier and Bossu among the French, and some perhaps among us who have certainly been duly authorized to execute at least a judicial authority *in foro literario*.

But without ascertaining all the proper qualifications of a critic, which I have touched on elsewhere, I think I may very boldly object to the censures of any one passed upon works which he hath not himself read. Such censurers as these, whether they speak from their own guess or suspicion or from the report and opinion of others, may properly be said to slander the reputation of the book they condemn.

Such may likewise be suspected of deserving this character who without assigning any particular faults condemn the whole in general defamatory terms, such as vile, dull, da—d stuff, &c., and particularly by the use of the monosyllable *low,* a word which becomes the mouth of no critic who is not RIGHT HONOURABLE.

Again, though there may be some faults justly assigned in the work, yet if those are not in the most essential parts, or if they are compensated by greater beauties, it will savour rather of the malice of a slanderer than of the judgement of a true critic to pass a severe sentence upon the whole merely on account of some vicious part. This is directly contrary to the sentiments of Horace:

> *Verum ubi plura nitent in carmine, non ego paucis*
> *Offendor maculis, quas aut incuria fudit,*
> *Aut humana parum cavit natura——*

> But where the beauties more in number shine,
> I am not angry when a casual line
> (That with some trivial faults unequal flows)
> A careless hand or human frailty shows.
>
> MR. FRANCIS.

For as Martial says, *Aliter non fit, avite, liber.* "No book can be otherwise composed." All beauty of character, as well as of countenance, and, indeed, of everything human, is to

481

be tried in this manner. Cruel indeed would it be if such a work as this history, which hath employed some thousands of hours in the composing, should be liable to be condemned because some particular chapter or perhaps chapters may be obnoxious to very just and sensible objections. And yet nothing is more common than the most rigorous sentence upon books supported by such objections, which if they were rightly taken (and that they are not always) do by no means go to the merit of the whole. In the theatre especially, a single expression which doth not coincide with the taste of the audience or with any individual critic of that audience is sure to be hissed; and one scene which should be disapproved would hazard the whole piece. To write within such severe rules as these is as impossible as to live up to some splenetic opinions, and if we judge according to the sentiments of some critics and of some Christians, no author will be saved in this world, and no man in the next.

2

THE ADVENTURES WHICH SOPHIA MET WITH AFTER HER LEAVING UPTON

Our history, just before it was obliged to turn about and travel backwards, had mentioned the departure of Sophia and her maid from the inn; we shall now, therefore, pursue the steps of that lovely creature and leave her unworthy lover a little longer to bemoan his ill luck, or rather his ill conduct.

Sophia having directed her guide to travel through by-roads across the country, they now passed the Severn, and had scarce got a mile from the inn when the young lady, looking behind her, saw several horses coming after on full speed. This greatly alarmed her fears and she called to the guide to put on as fast as possible.

He immediately obeyed her, and away they rode a full gallop. But the faster they went, the faster were they followed, and as the horses behind were somewhat swifter than those before, so the former were at length overtaken. A happy circumstance for poor Sophia, whose fears joined to her fatigue had almost overpowered her spirits; but she was now instantly relieved by a female voice that greeted her in the softest manner and with the utmost civility. This greeting,

Sophia, as soon as she could recover her breath, with like civility and with the highest satisfaction to herself, returned.

The travellers who joined Sophia, and who had given her such terror, consisted like her own company of two females and a guide. The two parties proceeded three full miles together before any one offered again to open their mouths, when our heroine, having pretty well got the better of her fear (but yet being somewhat surprised that the other still continued to attend her, as she pursued no great road and had already passed through several turnings), accosted the strange lady in a most obliging tone, and said she was very happy to find they were both travelling the same way. The other, who like a ghost only wanted to be spoke to, readily answered that the happiness was entirely hers; that she was a perfect stranger in that country, and was so overjoyed at meeting a companion of her own sex that she had perhaps been guilty of an impertinence, which required great apology, in keeping pace with her. More civilities passed between these two ladies, for Mrs. Honour had now given place to the fine habit of the stranger and had fallen into the rear. But though Sophia had great curiosity to know why the other lady continued to travel on through the same by-roads with herself, nay, though this gave her some uneasiness, yet fear or modesty or some other consideration restrained her from asking the question.

The strange lady now laboured under a difficulty which appears almost below the dignity of history to mention. Her bonnet had been blown from her head not less than five times within the last mile, nor could she come at any ribbon or handkerchief to tie it under her chin. When Sophia was informed of this, she immediately supplied her with a handkerchief for this purpose, which while she was pulling from her pocket she, perhaps, too much neglected the management of her horse, for the beast, now unluckily making a false step, fell upon his forelegs and threw his fair rider from his back.

Though Sophia came head foremost to the ground, she happily received not the least damage, and the same circumstances which had perhaps contributed to her fall now preserved her from confusion; for the lane which they were then passing was narrow and very much overgrown with trees, so that the moon could here afford very little light, and was, moreover, at present so obscured in a cloud that it was almost perfectly dark. By these means the young lady's modesty, which was extremely delicate, escaped as free from injury as her limbs and she was once more reinstated in her saddle, having received no other harm than a little fright by her fall.

Daylight at length appeared in its full lustre; and now the two ladies, who were riding over a common side by side, looking steadfastly at each other, at the same moment both their eyes became fixed; both their horses stopped, and both speaking together, with equal joy pronounced, the one the name of Sophia, the other that of Harriet.

This unexpected encounter surprised the ladies much more than I believe it will the sagacious reader, who must have imagined that the strange lady could be no other than Mrs. Fitzpatrick, the cousin of Miss Western, whom we before mentioned to have sallied from the inn a few minutes after her.

So great was the surprise and joy which these two cousins conceived at this meeting (for they had formerly been most intimate acquaintance and friends and had long lived together with their aunt Western) that it is impossible to recount half the congratulations which passed between them before either asked a very natural question of the other: namely, whither she was going.

This at last, however, came first from Mrs. Fitzpatrick, but easy and natural as the question may seem, Sophia found it difficult to give it a very ready and certain answer. She begged her cousin, therefore, to suspend all curiosity till they arrived at some inn, "which I suppose," says she, "can hardly be far distant; and believe me, Harriet, I suspend as much curiosity on my side, for indeed I believe our astonishment is pretty equal."

The conversation which passed between these ladies on the road was, I apprehend, little worth relating; and less certainly was that between the two waiting-women, for they likewise began to pay their compliments to each other. As for the guides, they were debarred from the pleasure of discourse, the one being placed in the van and the other obliged to bring up the rear.

In this posture they travelled many hours till they came into a wide and well-beaten road, which, as they turned to the right, soon brought them to a very fair promising inn, where they all alighted; but so fatigued was Sophia that as she had sat her horse during the last five or six miles with great difficulty, so was she now incapable of dismounting from him without assistance. This the landlord, who had hold of her horse, presently perceiving, offered to lift her in his arms from her saddle; and she too readily accepted the tender of his service. Indeed Fortune seems to have resolved to put Sophia to the blush that day, and the second malicious attempt succeeded better than the first; for my landlord had no sooner received the young lady in his arms than his feet, which the gout had lately very severely handled, gave way, and down he tumbled; but at the same time, with no less dexterity than gallantry, contrived to throw himself under his charming burden, so that he alone received any bruise from the fall; for the greatest injury which happened to Sophia was a violent shock given to her modesty by an immoderate grin which, at her rising from the ground, she observed in the countenances of most of the bystanders. This made her suspect what had really happened, and what we shall not here relate for the indulgence of those readers who are capable of laughing at the offence given to a young lady's delicacy. Accidents of this kind we have never regarded in a comical light, nor will we scruple to say that he must have a very inadequate idea of the modesty of a beautiful young woman who would wish to sacrifice it to so paltry a satisfaction as can arise from laughter.

This fright and shock, joined to the violent fatigue which both her mind and body had undergone, almost overcame the excellent constitution of Sophia, and she had scarce strength sufficient to totter into the inn, leaning on the arm of her maid. Here she was no sooner seated than she called for a glass of water, but Mrs. Honour very judiciously, in my opinion, changed it into a glass of wine.

Mrs. Fitzpatrick, hearing from Mrs. Honour that Sophia had not been in bed during the two last nights, and observing her to look very pale and wan with her fatigue, earnestly entreated her to refresh herself with some sleep. She was yet a stranger to her history or her apprehension, but had she known both, she would have given the same advice; for rest was visibly necessary for her, and their long journey through by-roads so entirely removed all danger of pursuit that she was herself perfectly easy on that account.

Sophia was easily prevailed on to follow the counsel of her friend, which was heartily seconded by her maid. Mrs. Fitzpatrick likewise offered to bear her cousin company, which Sophia with much complaisance accepted.

The mistress was no sooner in bed than the maid prepared to follow her example. She began to make many apologies to her sister Abigail for leaving her alone in so horrid a place as an inn, but the other stopped her short, being as well inclined to a nap as herself, and desired the honour of being her bedfellow. Sophia's maid agreed to give her a share of her bed, but put in her claim to all the honour. So, after many courtesies and compliments, to bed together went the waiting-women, as their mistresses had done before them.

It was usual with my landlord (as indeed it is with the whole fraternity) to inquire particularly of all coachmen, footmen, post-boys, and others into the names of all his guests, what their estate was, and where it lay. It cannot therefore be wondered at that the many particular circumstances which attended our travellers, and especially their retiring all to sleep at so extraordinary and unusual an hour as ten in the morning, should excite his curiosity. As soon, therefore, as the guides entered the kitchen, he began to examine who the ladies were and whence they came, but the guides, though they faithfully related all they knew, gave him very little satisfaction. On the contrary, they rather inflamed his curiosity than extinguished it.

This landlord had the character among all his neighbours of being a very sagacious fellow. He was thought to see farther and deeper into things than any man in the parish, the parson himself not excepted. Perhaps his look had contributed not a little to procure him this reputation; for there was in this something wonderfully wise and significant, especially when he had a pipe in his mouth, which, indeed, he seldom was without. His behaviour, likewise, greatly assisted in promoting the opinion of his wisdom. In his deportment he was solemn, if not sullen; and when he spoke, which was seldom, he always delivered himself in a slow voice; and though his sentences were short, they were still interrupted with many hums and ha's, ay, ays, and other expletives, so that though he accompanied his words with certain explanatory gestures, such as shaking or nodding the head, or pointing with his forefinger, he generally left his hearers to understand more than he expressed; nay, he commonly gave them a hint that he knew much more than he thought proper to disclose. This last circumstance alone may, indeed, very well account for his character of wisdom, since men are strangely inclined to worship what they do not understand—a grand secret, upon which several imposers on mankind have totally relied for the success of their frauds.

This politic person, now taking his wife aside, asked her what she thought of the ladies lately arrived. "Think of them!" said the wife; "why, what should I think of them?" "I know," answered he, "what I think. The guides tell strange stories. One pretends to be come from Gloucester and the other from Upton; and neither of them, for what I can find, can tell whither they are going. But what people ever travel across the country from Upton hither, especially to London? And one of the maidservants, before she alighted from her horse, asked if this was not the London Road. Now I have put all these circumstances together, and whom do you think I have found them out to be?" "Nay," answered she, "you know I never pretend to guess at your discoveries." "It is a good girl," replied he, chucking her under the chin; "I must own you have always submitted to my knowledge of these matters. Why, then, depend upon it—mind what I say—depend upon it, they are certainly some of the rebel ladies, who, they say, travel with the Young Chevalier, and have taken a roundabout way to escape the Duke's army."

"Husband," quoth the wife, "you have certainly hit it; for one of them is dressed as fine as any princess, and to be sure, she looks for all the world like one. But yet, when I consider one thing——" "When you consider," cries the landlord contemptuously. "Come, pray let's hear what you consider." "Why, it is," answered the wife, "that she is too humble to be any very great lady; for while our Betty was warming the bed she called her nothing but child and my dear and sweetheart; and when Betty offered to pull off her shoes and stockings, she would not suffer her, saying she would not give her the trouble."

"Pugh!" answered the husband. "This is nothing. Dost think, because you have seen some great ladies rude and uncivil to persons below them, that none of them know how to behave themselves when they come before their inferiors? I think I know people of fashion when I see them. I think I do. Did not she call for a glass of water when she came in? Another sort of women would have called for a dram; you know they would. If she be not a woman of very great quality, sell me for a fool; and, I believe, those who buy me will have a bad bargain. Now, would a woman of her quality travel without a footman unless upon some such extraordinary occasion?" "Nay, to be sure, husband," cries she, "you know these matters better than I or most folk." "I think I do know something," said he. "To be sure," answered the wife, "the poor little heart looked so piteous when she sat down in the chair, I protest I could not help having a compassion for her, almost as much as if she had been a poor body. But what's to be done, husband? If an she be a rebel, I suppose you intend to betray her up to the court. Well, she's a sweet-tempered, good-humoured lady, be she what she will, and I shall hardly refrain from crying when I hear she is hanged or beheaded." "Pooh!" answered the husband. "But as to what's to be done, it is not so easy a matter to determine. I hope before she goes away we shall have the news of a battle; for if the Chevalier should get the better, she may gain us interest at court and make our fortunes without betraying her." "Why, that's true," replied the wife; "and I heartily hope she will have it in her power. Certainly she's a sweet good lady; it would go horribly against me to have her come to any harm." "Pooh," cries the landlord. "Women are always so tender-hearted. Why, you would not harbour rebels, would you?" "No, certainly," answered the wife; "and as for betraying her, come what will on't, nobody can blame us. It is what anybody would do in our case."

While our politic landlord, who had not, we see, undeservedly the reputation of great wisdom among his neighbours, was engaged in debating this matter with himself (for he paid little attention to the opinion of his wife) news arrived that the rebels had given the Duke the slip and had got a day's march towards London; and soon after arrived a famous Jacobite squire, who with great joy in his countenance shook the landlord by the hand, saying, "All's our own, boy; ten thousand honest Frenchmen are landed in Suffolk. Old England forever! Ten thousand French, my brave lad! I am going to tap away directly."

This news determined the opinion of the wise man, and he resolved to make his court to the young lady when she arose, for he had now (he said) discovered that she was no other than Madam Jenny Cameron herself.

3

A VERY SHORT CHAPTER, IN WHICH, HOWEVER, IS A SUN, A MOON, A STAR, AND AN ANGEL

The sun (for he keeps very good hours at this time of the year) had been some time retired to rest when Sophia arose greatly refreshed by her sleep, which, short as it was, nothing but her extreme fatigue could have occasioned; for though she had told her maid and, perhaps, herself too that she was perfectly easy when she left Upton, yet it is certain her mind was a little affected with that malady which is attended with all the restless symptoms of a fever and is, perhaps, the very distemper which physicians mean (if they mean anything) by the fever on the spirits.

Mrs. Fitzpatrick likewise left her bed at the same time and, having summoned her maid, immediately dressed herself. She was really a very pretty woman and, had she been in any other company but that of Sophia, might have been thought beautiful, but when Mrs. Honour of her own accord attended (for her mistress would not suffer her to be waked) and had equipped our heroine, the charms of Mrs. Fitzpatrick, who had performed the office of the morning star and had preceded greater glories, shared the fate of that star and were totally eclipsed the moment those glories shone forth.

Perhaps Sophia never looked more beautiful than she did at this instant. We ought not therefore to condemn the maid of the inn for her hyperbole, who when she descended after having lighted the fire declared, and ratified it with an oath, that if ever there was an angel upon earth, she was now above-stairs.

Sophia had acquainted her cousin with her design to go to London, and Mrs. Fitzpatrick had agreed to accompany her; for the arrival of her husband at Upton had put an end to her design of going to Bath or to her aunt Western. They had therefore no sooner finished their tea than Sophia proposed to set out, the moon then shining extremely bright, and as for the frost, she defied it; nor had she any of those apprehensions which many young ladies would have felt at travelling by night, for she had, as we have before observed, some little degree of natural courage, and this her present sensations, which bordered somewhat on despair, greatly increased. Besides, as she had already travelled twice with safety by the light of the moon, she was the better emboldened to trust to it a third time.

The disposition of Mrs. Fitzpatrick was more timorous; for though the greater terrors had conquered the less, and the presence of her husband had driven her away at so unseasonable an hour from Upton, yet being now arrived at a place where she thought herself safe from his pursuit, these lesser terrors of I'know not what operated so strongly that she earnestly entreated her cousin to stay till the next morning and not expose herself to the dangers of travelling by night.

Sophia, who was yielding to an excess, when she could neither laugh nor reason her cousin out of these apprehensions, at last gave way to them. Perhaps, indeed, had she known of her father's arrival at Upton, it might have been more difficult to have persuaded her, for as to Jones, she had, I am afraid, no great horror at the thoughts of being overtaken by him; nay, to confess the truth, I believe she rather wished than feared it, though I might honestly enough have concealed this wish from the reader, as it was one of those secret, spontaneous emotions of the soul to which the reason is often a stranger.

When our young ladies had determined to remain all that evening in their inn, they were attended by the landlady, who desired to know what their ladyships would be pleased to eat. Such charms were there in the voice, in the manner, and in the affable deportment of Sophia that she ravished the landlady to the highest degree, and that good woman, concluding that she had attended Jenny Cameron, became in a moment a staunch Jacobite and wished heartily well to the Young Pretender's cause from the great sweetness and affability with which she had been treated by his supposed mistress.

The two cousins began now to impart to each other their reciprocal curiosity to know what extraordinary accidents on both sides occasioned this so strange and unexpected meeting. At last Mrs. Fitzpatrick, having obtained of Sophia a promise of communicating likewise in her turn, began to relate what the reader, if he is desirous to know her history, may read in the ensuing chapter.

4

THE HISTORY OF MRS. FITZPATRICK

Mrs. Fitzpatrick, after a silence of a few moments, fetching a deep sigh, thus began:

"It is natural to the unhappy to feel a secret concern in recollecting those periods of their lives which have been most delightful to them. The remembrance of past pleasures affects us with a kind of tender grief, like what we suffer for departed friends, and the ideas of both may be said to haunt our imaginations.

"For this reason, I never reflect without sorrow on those days (the happiest far of my life) which we spent together when both were under the care of my aunt Western. Alas, why are Miss Graveairs and Miss Giddy no more. You remember, I am sure, when we knew each other by no other names. Indeed you gave the latter appellation with too just cause. I have since experienced how much I deserved it. You, my Sophia, was always my superior in everything, and I heartily hope you will be so in your fortune. I shall never forget the wise and matronly advice you once gave me when I lamented being disappointed of a ball, though you could not be then fourteen years old. Oh, my Sophy, how blest must have been my situation when I could think such a disappointment a misfortune, and when indeed it was the greatest I had ever known."

"And yet, my dear Harriet," answered Sophia, "it was then a serious matter with you. Comfort yourself therefore with thinking that whatever you now lament may hereafter appear as trifling and contemptible as a ball would at this time."

"Alas, my Sophia," replied the other lady, "you yourself will think otherwise of my present situation; for greatly must that tender heart be altered if my misfortunes do not draw many a sigh, nay, many a tear, from you. The knowledge of this should perhaps deter me from relating what I am convinced will so much affect you." Here Mrs. Fitzpatrick stopped, till at the repeated entreaties of Sophia, she thus proceeded:

"Though you must have heard much of my marriage, yet

as matters may probably have been misrepresented, I will set out from the very commencement of my unfortunate acquaintance with my present husband, which was at Bath, soon after you left my aunt and returned home to your father.

"Among the gay young fellows who were at this season at Bath, Mr. Fitzpatrick was one. He was handsome, *dégagé*, extremely gallant, and in his dress exceeded most others. In short, my dear, if you was unluckily to see him now, I could describe him no better than by telling you he was the very reverse of everything which he is; for he hath rusticated himself so long that he is become an absolute wild Irishman. But to proceed in my story: The qualifications which he then possessed so well recommended him that though the people of quality at this time lived separate from the rest of the company and excluded them from all their parties, Mr. Fitzpatrick found means to gain admittance. It was perhaps no easy matter to avoid him, for he required very little or no invitation, and as being handsome and genteel, he found it no difficult matter to ingratiate himself with the ladies; so, he having frequently drawn his sword, the men did not care publicly to affront him. Had it not been for some such reason, I believe he would have been soon expelled by his own sex; for surely he had no strict title to be preferred to the English gentry, nor did they seem inclined to show him any extraordinary favour. They all abused him behind his back, which might probably proceed from envy, for he was well received and very particularly distinguished by the women.

"My aunt, though no person of quality herself, as she had always lived about the court, was enrolled in that party; for by whatever means you get into the polite circle, when you are once there, it is sufficient merit for you that you are there. This observation, young as you was, you could scarce avoid making from my aunt, who was free or reserved with all people just as they had more or less of this merit.

"And this merit, I believe, it was which principally recommended Mr. Fitzpatrick to her favour, in which he so well succeeded that he was always one of her private parties. Nor was he backward in returning such distinction; for he soon grew so very particular in his behaviour to her that the scandal club first began to take notice of it, and the better-disposed persons made a match between them.

For my own part, I confess, I made no doubt but that his designs were strictly honourable, as the phrase is: that is, to rob a lady of her fortune by way of marriage. My aunt was, I conceived, neither young enough nor handsome enough to attract much wicked inclination, but she had matrimonial charms in great abundance.

"I was the more confirmed in this opinion from the extraordinary respect which he showed to myself from the first moment of our acquaintance. This I understood as an attempt to lessen if possible that disinclination which my interest might be supposed to give me towards the match, and I know not but in some measure it had that effect; for as I was well contented with my own fortune, and of all people the least a slave to interested views, so I could not be violently the enemy of a man with whose behaviour to me I was greatly pleased, and the more so as I was the only object of such respect, for he behaved at the same time to many women of quality without any respect at all.

"Agreeable as this was to me, he soon changed it into another kind of behaviour, which was perhaps more so. He now put on much softness and tenderness, and languished and sighed abundantly. At times indeed, whether from art or nature I will not determine, he gave his usual loose to gaiety and mirth, but this was always in general company and with other women; for even in a country dance, when he was not my partner, he became grave and put on the softest look imaginable the moment he approached me. Indeed, he was in all things so very particular towards me that I must have been blind not to have discovered it. And, and, and——" "And you was more pleased still, my dear Harriet," cries Sophia; "you need not be ashamed," added she, sighing, "for sure there are irresistible charms in tenderness, which too many men are able to affect." "True," answered her cousin. "Men who in all other instances want common sense are very Machiavels in the art of loving. I wish I did not know an instance. Well, scandal now began to be as busy with me as it had before been with my aunt, and some good ladies did not scruple to affirm that Mr. Fitzpatrick had an intrigue with us both.

"But what may seem astonishing, my aunt never saw, nor in the least seemed to suspect, that which was visible enough, I believe, from both our behaviours. One would indeed think that love quite puts out the eyes of an old woman. In fact, they so greedily swallow the addresses which are made to them that like an outrageous glutton they are not at leisure to observe what passes amongst others at the same table. This I have observed in more cases than my own; and this was so strongly verified by my aunt that though she often found us together at her return from the Pump, the least canting word of his, pretending impatience at her absence, effectually smothered all suspicion. One artifice succeeded with her to admiration. This was his treating me like a little child and never calling me by any other name in her presence but that of pretty miss. This indeed did him some disservice with your humble servant, but I soon saw through it, especially as in her absence he behaved to me, as I have said, in a different manner. However, if I was not greatly disobliged by a conduct of which I had discovered the design, I smarted very severely for it; for my aunt really conceived me to be what her lover (as she thought him) called me, and treated me in all respects as a perfect infant. To say the truth, I wonder she had not insisted on my again wearing leading-strings.

"At last, my lover (for so he was) thought proper in a most solemn manner to disclose a secret which I had known long before. He now placed all the love which he had pretended to my aunt to my account. He lamented the encouragement she had given him in very pathetic terms, and made a high merit of the tedious hours in which he had undergone her conversation. What shall I tell you, my dear Sophia? Then I will confess the truth. I was pleased with my man. I was pleased with my conquest. To rival my aunt delighted me; to rival so many other women charmed me. In short, I am afraid I did not behave as I should do, even upon the very first declaration. I wish I did not almost give him positive encouragement before we parted.

"The Bath now talked loudly, I might almost say roared, against me. Several young women affected to shun my acquaintance, not so much, perhaps, from any real suspicion, as from a desire of banishing me from a company in which I too much engrossed their favourite man. And here I cannot omit expressing my gratitude to the kindness intended me by Mr. Nash, who took me one day aside and gave me advice which, if I had followed, I had been a happy woman. 'Child,' says he, 'I am sorry to see the familiarity which subsists between you and a fellow who is altogether unworthy of you, and I am afraid will prove your ruin. As for your old stinking aunt, if it was to be no injury to you and my pretty Sophy Western' (I assure you I repeat his words), 'I should be heartily glad that the fellow was in possession of all that belongs to her. I never advise old women; for if they take it into their heads to go to the devil, it is no more possible than worth-while to keep them from him. Innocence and youth and beauty are worthy a better fate, and I would save them from his clutches. Let me advise you therefore, dear child; never suffer this fellow to be particular with you again.' Many more things he said to me, which I have now forgotten, and indeed I attended very little to them at that time, for inclination contradicted all he said; and besides, I could not be persuaded that women of quality would condescend to familiarity with such a person as he described.

"But I am afraid, my dear, I shall tire you with a detail of so many minute circumstances. To be concise, therefore, imagine me married; imagine me with my husband at the feet of my aunt; and then imagine the maddest woman in Bedlam in a raving fit, and your imagination will suggest to you no more than what really happened.

"The very next day my aunt left the place, partly to avoid seeing Mr. Fitzpatrick or myself and as much, perhaps, to avoid seeing any one else; for though I am told she hath since denied everything stoutly, I believe she was then a little confounded at her disappointment. Since that time I have written to her many letters, but never could obtain an answer, which I must own sits somewhat the heavier as she herself was, though undesignedly, the occasion of all my sufferings; for had it not been under the colour of paying his addresses to her, Mr. Fitzpatrick would never have found sufficient opportunities to have engaged my heart, which in other circumstances I still flatter myself would not have been an easy conquest to such a person. Indeed, I believe I should not have erred so grossly in my choice if I had relied on my own judgement, but I trusted totally to the opinion of others and very foolishly took the merit of a man for granted whom I saw so universally well received by the women. What is the reason, my dear, that we who have understandings equal to the wisest and greatest of the other sex so often make choice of the silliest fellows for companions and favourites? It raises my indignation to the highest pitch to reflect on the numbers of women of sense who have been undone by fools." Here she paused a moment; but Sophia making no answer, she proceeded as in the next chapter.

5

IN WHICH THE HISTORY OF MRS. FITZPATRICK IS CONTINUED

"We remained at Bath no longer than a fortnight after our wedding; for as to any reconciliation with my aunt, there were no hopes, and of my fortune, not one farthing could be touched till I was at age, of which I now wanted more than two years. My husband, therefore, was resolved to set out for Ireland, against which I remonstrated very earnestly, and insisted on a promise, which he had made me before our marriage, that I should never take this journey against my consent; and indeed I never intended to consent to it, nor will anybody, I believe, blame me for that resolution; but this, however, I never mentioned to my husband, and petitioned only for the reprieve of a month, but he had fixed the day and to that day he obstinately adhered.

"The evening before our departure, as we were disputing this point with great eagerness on both sides, he started suddenly from his chair and left me abruptly, saying he was going to the rooms. He was hardly out of the house when I saw a paper lying on the floor, which, I suppose, he had carelessly pulled from his pocket together with his handkerchief. This paper I took up, and finding it to be a letter, I made no scruple to open and read it; and indeed I read it so often that I can repeat it to you almost word for word. This, then, was the letter:

'To Mr. Brian Fitzpatrick.

'Sir,

'Yours received, and am surprised you should use me in this manner, as have never seen any of your cash unless for one linsey-woolsey coat, and your bill now is upwards of £150. Consider, sir, how often you have fobbed me off with your being shortly to be married to this lady and t'other lady, but I can neither live on hopes or promises, nor will my woollen-draper take any such in payment. You tell me you are secure of having either the aunt or the niece, and that you might have married the aunt before this, whose jointure you say is immense, but that you prefer the niece on account of her ready money. Pray, sir, take a fool's advice for once, and marry the first you can get. You will pardon my offering my advice, as you know I sincerely wish you well. Shall draw on you per next post in favour of Messieurs John Drugget and Company, at fourteen days, which doubt not your honouring, and am,

Sir,

Your humble servant,

SAM. COSGRAVE.'

"This was the letter, word for word. Guess, my dear girl, guess how this letter affected me. 'You prefer the niece on account of her ready money!' If every one of these words had been a dagger, I could with pleasure have stabbed them into his heart, but I will not recount my frantic behaviour on the occasion. I had pretty well spent my tears before his return home, but sufficient remains of them appeared in my swollen eyes. He threw himself sullenly into his chair and for a long time we were both silent. At length, in a haughty tone he said, 'I hope, madam, your servants have packed up all your things, for the coach will be ready by six in the morning.' My patience was totally subdued by this provocation, and I answered, 'No, sir, there is a letter still remains unpacked'; and then, throwing it on the table, I fell to upbraiding him with the most bitter language I could invent.

"Whether guilt, or shame, or prudence restrained him, I cannot say, but though he is the most passionate of men, he exerted no rage on this occasion. He endeavoured on the contrary to pacify me by the most gentle means. He swore the phrase in the letter to which I principally objected was not his, nor had he ever written any such. He owned, indeed, the having mentioned his marriage and that preference which he had given to myself, but denied with many oaths the having assigned any such reason. And he excused the having mentioned any such matter at all on account of the straits he was in for money, arising, he said, from his having too long neglected his estate in Ireland. And this, he said, which he could not bear to discover to me, was the only reason of his having so strenuously insisted on our journey. He then used several very

497

endearing expressions, and concluded by a very fond caress and many violent protestations of love.

"There was one circumstance which, though he did not appeal to it, had much weight with me in his favour, and that was the word *jointure* in the tailor's letter, whereas my aunt never had been married, and this Mr. Fitzpatrick well knew. As I imagined therefore that the fellow must have inserted this of his own head or from hearsay, I persuaded myself he might have ventured likewise on that odious line on no better authority. What reasoning was this, my dear? Was I not an advocate rather than a judge? But why do I mention such a circumstance as this, or appeal to it for the justification of my forgiveness! In short, had he been guilty of twenty times as much, half the tenderness and fondness which he used would have prevailed on me to have forgiven him. I now made no farther objections to our setting out, which we did the next morning, and in a little more than a week arrived at the seat of Mr. Fitzpatrick.

"Your curiosity will excuse me from relating any occurrences which passed during our journey; for it would indeed be highly disagreeable to travel it over again and no less so to you to travel it over with me.

"This seat, then, is an ancient mansion-house; if I was in one of those merry humours in which you have so often seen me, I could describe it to you ridiculously enough. It looked as if it had been formerly inhabited by a gentleman. Here was room enough, and not the less room on account of the furniture; for indeed there was very little in it. An old woman, who seemed coeval with the building and greatly resembled her whom Chamont mentions in the *Orphan*, received us at the gate, and in a howl scarce human, and to me unintelligible, welcomed her master home. In short, the whole scene was so gloomy and melancholy that it threw my spirits into the lowest dejection, which my husband discerning, instead of relieving, increased by two or three malicious observations. 'There are good houses, madam,' says he, 'as you find, in other places besides England, but perhaps you had rather be in a dirty lodgings at Bath.'

"Happy, my dear, is the woman who in any state of life hath a cheerful good-natured companion to support and comfort her; but why do I reflect on happy situations only to aggravate my own misery! My companion, far from clearing up the gloom of solitude, soon convinced me that I must have been wretched with him in any place and in any condition. In a word, he was a surly fellow, a character you have perhaps never seen; for indeed no woman ever sees it exemplified but in a father, a brother, or a husband, and though you have a father, he is not of that character. This surly fellow had formerly appeared to me the very reverse, and so he did still to every other person. Good heaven! How is it possible for a man to maintain a constant lie in his appearance abroad and in company, and to content himself with showing disagreeable truth only at home? Here, my dear, they make themselves amends for the uneasy restraint which they put on their tempers in the world; for I have observed the more merry and gay and good-humoured my husband hath at any time been in company, the more sullen and morose he was sure to become at our next private meeting. How shall I describe his barbarity? To my fondness he was cold and insensible. My little comical ways, which you, my Sophy, and which others have called so agreeable, he treated with contempt. In my most serious moments he sung and whistled, and whenever I was thoroughly dejected and miserable, he was angry and abused me; for though he was never pleased with my good humour, nor ascribed it to my satisfaction in him, yet my low spirits always offended him, and those he imputed to my repentance of having (as he said) married an Irishman.

"You will easily conceive, my dear Graveairs (I ask your pardon; I really forgot myself), that when a woman makes an imprudent match in the sense of the world, that is, when she is not an arrant prostitute to pecuniary interest, she must necessarily have some inclination and affection for her man. You will as easily believe that this affection may possibly be lessened; nay, I do assure you, contempt will wholly eradicate it. This contempt I now began to entertain for my husband, whom I now discovered to be—I must use the expression—an arrant blockhead. Perhaps you will wonder I did not make this discovery long before, but women will suggest a thousand excuses to themselves for the folly of those they like; besides, give me leave to tell you, it requires a most penetrating eye to discern a fool through the disguises of gaiety and good breeding.

"It will be easily imagined that when I once despised my husband, as I confess to you I soon did, I must consequently dislike his company; and indeed, I had the happiness of being very little troubled with it, for our house was now most elegantly furnished, our cellars well stocked, and dogs and horses provided in great abundance. As my gentleman therefore entertained his neighbours with great hospitality, so his neighbours resorted to him with great alacrity, and sports and drinking consumed so much of his time that a small part of his conversation, that is to say, of his ill humours, fell to my share.

"Happy would it have been for me if I could as easily have avoided all other disagreeable company, but alas, I was confined to some which constantly tormented me, and the more, as I saw no prospect of being relieved from them. These companions were my own racking thoughts, which plagued and in a manner haunted me night and day. In this situation I passed through a scene the horrors of which can neither be painted nor imagined. Think, my dear; figure, if you can, to yourself what I must have undergone. I became a mother by the man I scorned, hated, and detested. I went through all the agonies and miseries of a lying-in (ten times more painful in such a circumstance than the worst labour can be when one endures it for a man one loves) in a desert, or rather indeed a scene of riot and revel, without a friend, without a companion, or without any of those agreeable circumstances which often alleviate and, perhaps, sometimes more than compensate the sufferings of our sex at this season."

6

IN WHICH THE MISTAKE OF THE LANDLORD THROWS SOPHIA INTO A DREADFUL CONSTERNATION

Mrs. Fitzpatrick was proceeding in her narrative when she was interrupted by the entrance of dinner, greatly to the concern of Sophia; for the misfortunes of her friend had raised her anxiety and left her no appetite but what Mrs. Fitzpatrick was to satisfy by her relation.

The landlord now attended with a plate under his arm, and with the same respect in his countenance and address which he would have put on had the ladies arrived in a coach and six.

The married lady seemed less affected with her own misfortunes than was her cousin, for the former eat very heartily, whereas the latter could hardly swallow a morsel. Sophia likewise showed more concern and sorrow in her countenance than appeared in the other lady, who, having observed these symptoms in her friend, begged her to be comforted, saying, "Perhaps all may yet end better than either you or I expect."

Our landlord thought he had now an opportunity to open his mouth and was resolved not to omit it. "I am sorry, madam," cries he, "that your ladyship can't eat, for to be sure, you must be hungry after so long fasting. I hope your ladyship is not uneasy at anything, for as madam there says, all may end better than anybody expects. A gentleman who was here just now brought excellent news, and perhaps some folks who have given other folks the slip may get to London before they are overtaken; and if they do, I make no doubt but they will find people who will be very ready to receive them."

All persons under the apprehension of danger convert whatever they see and hear into the objects of that apprehension. Sophia, therefore, immediately concluded from the foregoing speech that she was known and pursued by her father. She was now struck with the utmost consternation and for a few minutes deprived of the power of speech, which she no sooner recovered than she desired the landlord to send his servants out of the room, and then addressing herself to him, said, "I perceive, sir, you know who we are, but I beseech you—nay, I am convinced, if you have any compassion or goodness, you will not betray us."

"I betray your ladyship!" quoth the landlord. "No" (and then he swore several very hearty oaths), "I would sooner be cut into ten thousand pieces. I hate all treachery. I! I never betrayed any one in my life yet, and I am sure I shall not begin with so sweet a lady as your ladyship. All the world would very much blame me if I should, since it will be in your ladyship's power so shortly to reward me. My wife can witness for me I knew your ladyship the moment you came into the house; I said it was your honour before I lifted you from your horse, and I shall carry the bruises I got in your ladyship's service to the grave, but what signified that as long as I saved your ladyship. To be sure, some people this morning would have thought of getting a reward, but no such thought ever entered into my head. I would sooner starve than take any reward for betraying your ladyship."

"I promise you, sir," says Sophia, "if it be ever in my

power to reward you, you shall not lose by your generosity."

"Alack-a-day, madam!" answered the landlord, "in your ladyship's power! Heaven put it as much into your will. I am only afraid your honour will forget such a poor man as an innkeeper, but if your ladyship should not, I hope you will remember what reward I refused—refused! That is, I would have refused; and to be sure, it may be called refusing, for I might have had it certainly; and to be sure, you might have been in some houses—but for my part, I would not, methinks, for the world have your ladyship wrong me so much as to imagine I ever thought of betraying you, even before I heard the good news."

"What news, pray?" says Sophia, something eagerly.

"Hath not your ladyship heard it, then?" cries the landlord. "Nay, like enough; for I heard it only a few minutes ago, and if I had never heard it, may the Devil fly away with me this instant if I would have betrayed your honour; no, if I would, may I—" Here he subjoined several dreadful execrations, which Sophia at last interrupted and begged to know what he meant by the news. He was going to answer when Mrs. Honour came running into the room, all pale and breathless, and cried out, "Madam, we are all undone, all ruined; they are come, they are come!" These words almost froze up the blood of Sophia, but Mrs. Fitzpatrick asked Honour who were come. "Who?" answered she. "Why, the French; several hundred thousands of them are landed, and we shall be all murdered and ravished."

As a miser who hath in some well-built city a cottage, value twenty shillings, when at a distance he is alarmed with the news of a fire, turns pale and trembles at his loss, but when he finds the beautiful palaces only are burnt and his own cottage remains safe, he comes instantly to himself and smiles at his good fortune; or as (for we dislike something in the former simile) the tender mother when terrified with the apprehension that her darling boy is drowned is struck senseless and almost dead with consternation, but when she is told that little master is safe and the *Victory* only, with twelve hundred brave men, gone to the bottom, life and sense again return, maternal fondness enjoys the sudden relief from all its fears, and the general benevolence which at another time would have deeply felt the dreadful catastrophe lies fast asleep in her mind—so Sophia, than whom none was more capable of tenderly feeling the general calamity of her country, found such immediate satisfaction from the relief of those terrors she had of being overtaken by her father that the arrival of the French scarce made any impression on her. She gently chid her maid for the fright into which she had thrown her, and said she was glad it was no worse, for that she had feared somebody else was come.

"Ay, ay," quoth the landlord smiling, "her ladyship knows better things; she knows the French are our very best friends and come over hither only for our good. They are the people who are to make old England flourish again. I warrant her honour thought the Duke was coming, and that was enough to put her into a fright. I was going to tell your ladyship the news. Her honour's Majesty, heaven bless him, hath given the Duke the slip, and is marching as fast as he can to London, and ten thousand French are landed to join him on the road."

Sophia was not greatly pleased with this news, nor with the gentleman who related it, but as she still imagined he knew her (for she could not possibly have any suspicion of the real truth), she durst not show any dislike. And now the landlord, having removed the cloth from the table, withdrew, but at his departure frequently repeated his hopes of being remembered hereafter.

The mind of Sophia was not at all easy under the supposition of being known at this house, for she still applied to herself many things which the landlord had addressed to Jenny Cameron; she therefore ordered her maid to pump out of him by what means he had become acquainted with her person, and who had offered him the reward for betraying her; she likewise ordered the horses to be in readiness by four in the morning, at which hour Mrs. Fitzpatrick promised to bear her company, and then, composing herself as well as she could, she desired that lady to continue her story.

7

IN WHICH MRS. FITZPATRICK CONCLUDES HER HISTORY

While Mrs. Honour in pursuance of the commands of her mistress ordered a bowl of punch, and invited my landlord and landlady to partake of it, Mrs. Fitzpatrick thus went on with her relation:

"Most of the officers who were quartered at a town in our neighbourhood were of my husband's acquaintance. Among these was a lieutenant, a very pretty sort of man, and who was married to a woman so agreeable both in her temper and conversation that, from our first knowing each other, which was soon after my lying-in, we were almost inseparable companions, for I had the good fortune to make myself equally agreeable to her.

"The lieutenant, who was neither a sot nor a sportsman, was frequently of our parties; indeed, he was very little with my husband, and no more than good breeding constrained him to be, as he lived almost constantly at our house. My husband often expressed much dissatisfaction at the lieutenant's preferring my company to his; he was very angry with me on that account and gave me many a hearty curse for drawing away his companions, saying I ought to be d—ned for having spoiled one of the prettiest fellows in the world by making a milksop of him.

"You will be mistaken, my dear Sophia, if you imagine that the anger of my husband arose from my depriving him of a companion; for the lieutenant was not a person with whose society a fool could be pleased, and if I should admit the possibility of this, so little right had my husband to place the loss of his companion to me that I am convinced it was my conversation alone which induced him ever to come to the house. No, child, it was envy, the worst and most rancorous kind of envy, the envy of superiority of understanding. The wretch could not bear to see my conversation preferred to his by a man of whom he could not entertain the least jealousy. Oh, my dear Sophy, you are a woman of sense; if you marry a man, as is most probable you will, of less capacity than yourself, make frequent trials of his temper before marriage and see whether he can bear to submit to such a superiority. Promise me, Sophy, you will take this advice, for you will hereafter find its importance." "It is very likely I shall never marry at all," answered Sophia. "I think at least I shall never marry a man in whose understanding I see any defects before marriage, and I promise you I would rather give up my own than see any such afterwards." "Give up your understanding!" replied Mrs. Fitzpatrick. "Oh fie, child, I will not believe so meanly of you. Everything else I might myself be brought to give up, but never this. Nature would not have allotted this superiority to the wife in so many instances if she had intended we should have all surrendered it to the husband. This, indeed, men of sense never expect of us; of which the lieutenant I have just mentioned was one notable example, for though he had a very good understanding, he always acknowledged (as was really true) that his wife had a better. And this, perhaps, was the one reason of the hatred my tyrant bore her.

"Before he would be so governed by a wife, he said, especially such an ugly b— (for indeed she was not a regular beauty, but very agreeable and extremely genteel), he would see all the women upon earth at the Devil, which was a very usual phrase with him. He said he wondered what I could see in her to be so charmed with her company. 'Since this woman,' says he, 'hath come among us, there is an end of your beloved reading, which you pretended to like so much that you could not afford time to return the visits of the ladies in this country'; and I must confess I had been guilty of a little rudeness this way; for the ladies there are at least no better than the mere country-ladies here, and I think I need make no other excuse to you for declining any intimacy with them.

"This correspondence, however, continued a whole year, even all the while the lieutenant was quartered in that town, for which I was contented to pay the tax of being constantly abused in the manner above mentioned by my husband; I mean when he was at home, for he was frequently absent a month at a time at Dublin and once made a journey of two months to London, in all which journeys I thought it a very singular happiness that he never once desired my company; nay, by his frequent censures on men who could not travel, as he phrased it, without a wife tied up to their tail, he sufficiently intimated that had I been never so desirous of accompanying him, my wishes would have been in vain, but heaven knows such wishes were very far from my thoughts.

"At length my friend was removed from me, and I was again left to my solitude, to the tormenting conversation with my own reflections, and to apply to books for my only comfort. I now read almost all day long. How many books do you think I read in three months?" "I can't guess, indeed, cousin," answered Sophia. "Perhaps half a score!" "Half a score! Half a thousand, child," answered the other. "I read a good deal in Daniel's *English History of France;* a great deal in Plutarch's *Lives;* the *Atlantis,* Pope's *Homer,* Dryden's plays, Chillingworth, the Countess D'Aulnois, and Locke's *Human Understanding.*

"During this interval I wrote three very supplicating and, as I thought, moving letters to my aunt, but as I received no answer to any of them, my disdain would not suffer me to continue my application." Here she stopped and, looking earnestly at Sophia, said, "Methinks, my dear, I read something in your eyes which reproaches me of a neglect in another place, where I should have met with a kinder return." "Indeed, dear Harriet," answered Sophia, "your story is an apology for any neglect, but indeed I feel that I have been guilty of a remissness without so good an excuse. Yet pray proceed; for I long, though I tremble, to hear the end."

Thus, then, Mrs. Fitzpatrick resumed her narrative: "My husband now took a second journey to England, where he continued upwards of three months. During the greater part of this time I led a life which nothing but having led a worse could make me think tolerable; for perfect solitude can never be reconciled to a social mind like mine but when it relieves you from the company of those you hate. What added to my wretchedness was the loss of my little infant; not that I pretend to have had for it that extravagant tenderness of which I believe I might have been capable under other circumstances, but I resolved in every instance to discharge the duty of the tenderest mother, and this care prevented me from feeling the weight of that heaviest of all things when it can be at all said to lie heavy on our hands.

"I had spent full ten weeks almost entirely by myself, having seen nobody all that time except my servants and a very few visitors, when a young lady, a relation to my husband, came from a distant part of Ireland to visit me. She had stayed once before a week at my house and then I gave her a pressing invitation to return, for she was a very agreeable woman and had improved good natural parts by a proper education. Indeed, she was to me a most welcome guest.

"A few days after her arrival, perceiving me in very low spirits, without inquiring the cause, which indeed she very well knew, the young lady fell to compassionating my case. She said though politeness had prevented me from complaining of my husband's behaviour to his relations, yet they all were very sensible of it and felt great concern upon that account; but none more than herself; and after some more general discourse on this head, which I own I could not forbear countenancing, at last, after much previous precaution and enjoined concealment, she communicated to me as a profound secret—that my husband kept a mistress.

"You will certainly imagine I heard this news with the utmost insensibility. Upon my word, if you do, your imagination will mislead you. Contempt had not so kept down my anger to my husband, but that hatred rose again on this occasion. What can be the reason of this? Are we so abominably selfish that we can be concerned at others having possession even of what we despise? Or are we not rather abominably vain, and is not this the greatest injury done to our vanity? What think you, Sophia?"

"I don't know, indeed," answered Sophia; "I have never troubled myself with any of these deep contemplations, but I think the lady did very ill in communicating to you such a secret."

"And yet, my dear, this conduct is natural," replied Mrs. Fitzpatrick, "and when you have seen and read as much as myself, you will acknowledge it to be so."

"I am sorry to hear it is natural," returned Sophia; "for I want neither reading nor experience to convince me that it is very dishonourable and very ill-natured; nay, it is surely as ill-bred to tell a husband or wife of the faults of each other as to tell them of their own."

"Well," continued Mrs. Fitzpatrick, "my husband at last returned, and if I am thoroughly acquainted with my own thoughts, I hated him now more than ever; but I despised him rather less, for certainly nothing so much weakens our contempt as an injury done to our pride or our vanity.

"He now assumed a carriage to me so very different from what he had lately worn and so nearly resembling his behaviour the first week of our marriage that had I now had any spark of love remaining, he might, possibly, have rekindled my fondness for him. But though hatred may succeed to contempt and may, perhaps, get the better of it, love, I believe, cannot. The truth is, the passion of love is too restless to remain contented without the gratification which it receives from its object, and one can no more be inclined to love without loving than we can have eyes without seeing. When a husband, therefore, ceases to be the object of this passion, it is most probable some other man—I say, my dear, if your husband grows indifferent to you—if you once come to despise him—I say—that is—if you have the passion of love in you—Lud! I have bewildered myself so—but one is apt in these abstracted considerations to lose the concatenation of ideas, as Mr. Locke says. In short, the truth is—in short, I scarce know what it is; but as I was saying, my husband returned, and his behaviour at first greatly surprised me; but he soon acquainted me with the motive and taught me to account for it. In a word, then, he had spent and lost all the ready money of my fortune, and as he could mortgage his own estate no deeper, he was now desirous to supply himself with cash for his extravagance by selling a little estate of mine, which he could not do without my assistance; and to obtain this favour was the whole and sole motive of all the fondness which he now put on.

"With this I peremptorily refused to comply. I told him, and I told him truly, that had I been possessed of the Indies at our first marriage, he might have commanded it all; for it had been a constant maxim with me that where a woman disposes of her heart she should always deposit her fortune, but as he had been so kind long ago to restore the former into my possession, I was resolved likewise to retain what little remained of the latter.

"I will not describe to you the passion into which these words, and the resolute air in which they were spoken, threw him; nor will I trouble you with the whole scene which succeeded between us. Out came, you may be well assured, the story of the mistress, and out it did come with all the embellishments which anger and disdain could bestow upon it.

"Mr. Fitzpatrick seemed a little thunderstruck with this, and more confused than I had seen him, though his ideas are always confused enough, heaven knows. He did not, however, endeavour to exculpate himself, but took a method which almost equally confounded me. What was this but recrimination! He affected to be jealous; he may, for aught I know, be inclined enough to jealousy in his natural temper; nay, he must have had it from nature or the Devil must have put it into his head, for I defy all the world to cast a just aspersion on my character; nay, the most scandalous tongues have never dared censure my reputation. My fame, I thank heaven, hath been always as spotless as my life, and let falsehood itself accuse that if it dare. No, my dear Graveairs, however provoked, however ill-treated, however injured in my love, I have firmly resolved never to give the least room for censure on this account. And yet, my dear, there are some people so malicious, some tongues so venomous, that no innocence can escape them. The most undesigned word, the most accidental look, the least familiarity, the most innocent freedom, will be misconstrued and magnified into I know not what by some people. But I despise, my dear Graveairs, I despise all such slander. No such malice, I assure you, ever gave me an uneasy moment. No, no, I promise you I am above all that. But where was I? Oh, let me see, I told you my husband was jealous—and of whom, pray? Why, of whom but the lieutenant I mentioned to you before. He was obliged to resort above a year and more back to find any object for this unaccountable passion, if indeed he really felt any such and was not an arrant counterfeit in order to abuse me.

"But I have tired you already with too many particulars. I will now bring my story to a very speedy conclusion. In short, then, after many scenes very unworthy to be repeated, in which my cousin engaged so heartily on my side that Mr. Fitzpatrick at last turned her out-of-doors, when he found I was neither to be soothed nor bullied into compliance, he took a very violent method indeed. Perhaps you will conclude he beat me, but this, though he hath approached very near to it, he never actually did. He confined me to my room, without suffering me to have either pen, ink, paper, or book, and a servant every day made my bed and brought me my food.

"When I had remained a week under this imprisonment, he made me a visit and with the voice of a schoolmaster, or, what is often much the same, of a tyrant, asked me if I would yet comply. I answered very stoutly that I would die first. 'Then so you shall, and be d—ned,' cries he, 'for you shall never go alive out of this room.'

"Here I remained a fortnight longer; and to say the truth, my constancy was almost subdued and I began to think of submission, when one day, in the absence of my husband, who was gone abroad for some short time, by the greatest good fortune in the world an accident happened. I—at a time when I began to give way to the utmost despair—everything would be excusable at such a time—at that very time I received—but it would take up an hour to tell you all particulars—in one word, then (for I will not tire you with circumstances), gold, the common key to all padlocks, opened my door and set me at liberty.

"I now made haste to Dublin, where I immediately procured a passage to England, and was proceeding to Bath in order to throw myself into the protection of my aunt or of your father or of any relation who would afford it me. My husband overtook me last night at the inn where I lay and which you left a few minutes before me, but I had the good luck to escape him and to follow you.

"And thus, my dear, ends my history: a tragical one, I am sure, it is to myself, but perhaps I ought rather to apologize to you for its dullness."

Sophia heaved a deep sigh and answered, "Indeed, Harriet, I pity you from my soul! But what could you expect? Why, why, would you marry an Irishman?"

"Upon my word," replied her cousin, "your censure is unjust. There are among the Irish men of as much worth and honour as any among the English. Nay, to speak the truth, generosity of spirit is rather more common among them. I have known some examples there too of good husbands, and, I believe, these are not very plenty in England. Ask me rather what I could expect when I married a fool, and I will tell you a solemn truth: I did not know him to be so." "Can no man," said Sophia in a very low and altered voice, "do you think, make a bad husband who is not a fool?" "That," answered the other, "is too general a negative, but none, I believe, is so likely as a fool to prove so. Among my acquaintance the silliest fellows are the worst husbands, and I will venture to assert as a fact that a man of sense rarely behaves very ill to a wife who deserves very well."

8

A DREADFUL ALARM IN THE INN, WITH THE ARRIVAL OF AN
UNEXPECTED FRIEND OF MRS. FITZPATRICK

Sophia now, at the desire of her cousin, related—not what follows, but what hath gone before in this history; for which reason the reader will, I suppose, excuse me for not repeating it over again.

One remark, however, I cannot forbear making on her narrative; namely, that she made no more mention of Jones from the beginning to the end than if there had been no such person alive. This I will neither endeavour to account for nor to excuse. Indeed, if this may be called a kind of dishonesty, it seems the more inexcusable from the apparent openness and explicit sincerity of the other lady. But so it was.

Just as Sophia arrived at the conclusion of her story, there arrived in the room where the two ladies were sitting a noise, not unlike in loudness to that of a pack of hounds just let out from their kennel, nor in shrillness to cats when caterwauling, or to screech-owls, or, indeed, more like (for what animal can resemble a human voice) to those sounds which, in the pleasant mansions of that gate which seems to derive its name from a duplicity of tongues, issue from the mouths, and sometimes from the nostrils, of those fair river nymphs ycleped of old the Napaeae, or the Naiads—in the vulgar tongue, translated oyster-wenches; for when, instead of the ancient libations of milk and honey and oil, the rich distillation from the juniper-berry or, perhaps, from malt hath by the early devotion of their votaries been poured forth in great abundance, should any daring tongue with unhallowed license profane, i.e., depreciate the delicate fat Milton oyster, the plaice sound and firm, the flounder as much alive as when in the water, the shrimp as big as a prawn, the fine cod alive but a few hours ago, or any other of the various treasures which those water-deities who fish the sea and rivers have committed to the care of the nymphs, the angry Naiads lift up their immortal voices and the profane wretch is struck deaf for his impiety.

Such was the noise which now burst from one of the rooms below, and soon the thunder, which long had rattled at a distance, began to approach nearer and nearer till, having ascended by degrees upstairs, it at last entered the apartment where the ladies were. In short, to drop all metaphor and figure, Mrs. Honour, having scolded violently belowstairs and continued the same all the way up, came in to her mistress in a most outrageous passion, crying out, "What doth your ladyship think? Would you imagine that this impudent villain, the master of this house, hath had the impudence to tell me, nay, to stand it out to my face, that your ladyship is that nasty, stinking wh—re (Jenny Cameron they call her) that runs about the country with the Pretender? Nay, the lying, saucy villain had the assurance to tell me that your ladyship had owned yourself to be so; but I have clawed the rascal; I have left the marks of my nails in his impudent face. 'My lady!' says I. 'You saucy scoundrel, my lady is meat for no Pretenders. She is a young lady of as good fashion and family and fortune as any in Somersetshire. Did you never hear of the great Squire Western, sirrah? She is his only daughter, she is—and heiress to all his great estate.' My lady to be called a nasty Scotch wh—re by such a varlet—to be sure, I wish I had knocked his brains out with the punch-bowl."

The principal uneasiness with which Sophia was affected on this occasion Honour had herself caused, by having in her passion discovered who she was. However, as this mistake of the landlord sufficiently accounted for those passages which Sophia had before mistaken, she acquired some ease on that account; nor could she upon the whole forbear smiling. This enraged Honour and she cried, "Indeed, madam, I did not think your ladyship would have made a laughing matter of it. To be called whore by such an impudent low rascal. Your ladyship may be angry with me, for aught I know, for taking your part, since proffered service, they say, stinks; but to be sure, I could never bear to hear a lady of mine called whore. Nor will I bear it. I am sure your ladyship is as virtuous a lady as ever sat foot on English ground, and I will claw any villain's eyes out who dares for to offer to presume for to say the least word to the contrary. Nobody ever could say the least ill of the character of any lady that ever I waited upon."

Hinc illæ lachrymæ; in plain truth, Honour had as much love for her mistress as most servants have, that is to say—But besides this, her pride obliged her to support the character of the lady she waited on, for she thought her own was in a very close manner connected with it. In proportion as the character of her mistress was raised, hers likewise, as she conceived, was raised with it; and on the contrary, she thought the one could not be lowered without the other.

On this subject, reader, I must stop a moment to tell thee a story. The famous Nell Gwynn, stepping one day from a house where she had made a short visit into her coach, saw a great mob assembled and her footman all bloody and dirty. The fellow, being asked by his mistress the reason of his being in that condition, answered, "I have been fighting, madam, with an impudent rascal who called your ladyship a wh—re." "You blockhead," replied Mrs. Gwynn, "at this rate you must fight every day of your life; why, you fool, all the world knows it." "Do they?" cries the fellow in a muttering voice after he had shut the coach-door. "They shan't call me a whore's footman for all that."

Thus, the passion of Mrs. Honour appears natural enough even if it were to be no otherwise accounted for, but in reality there was another cause of her anger, for which we must beg leave to remind our reader of a circumstance mentioned in the above simile. There are indeed certain liquors which, being applied to our passions, or to fire, produce effects the very reverse of those produced by water, as they serve to kindle and inflame rather than to extinguish. Among these the generous liquor called punch is one. It was not therefore without reason that the learned Dr. Cheney used to call drinking punch pouring liquid fire down your throat.

Now, Mrs. Honour had unluckily poured so much of this liquid fire down her throat that the smoke of it began to ascend into her pericranium and blinded the eyes of Reason, which is there supposed to keep her residence, while the fire itself from the stomach easily reached the heart and there inflamed the noble passion of pride; so that upon the whole we shall cease to wonder at the violent rage of the waiting-woman, though at first sight we must confess the cause seems inadequate to the effect.

Sophia and her cousin both did all in their power to extinguish these flames which had roared so loudly all over the house. They at length prevailed, or, to carry the metaphor one step farther, the fire, having consumed all the fuel which the language affords, to wit, every reproachful term in it, at last went out of its own accord.

But though tranquillity was restored above-stairs, it was not so below, where my landlady, highly resenting the injury done to the beauty of her husband by the flesh-spades of Mrs. Honour, called aloud for revenge and justice. As to the poor man who had principally suffered in the engagement, he was perfectly quiet. Perhaps the blood which he lost might have cooled his anger; for the enemy had not only applied her nails to his cheeks but likewise her fist to his nostrils, which lamented the blow with tears of blood in great abundance. To this we may add reflections on his mistake; but indeed, nothing so effectually silenced his resentment as the manner in which he now discovered his error; for as to the behaviour of Mrs. Honour, it had the more confirmed him in his opinion, but he was now assured by a person of great figure, and who was attended by a great equipage, that one of the ladies was a woman of fashion and his intimate acquaintance.

By the orders of this person the landlord now ascended and acquainted our fair travellers that a great gentleman below desired to do them the honour of waiting on them. Sophia turned pale and trembled at this message, though the reader will conclude it was too civil, notwithstanding the landlord's blunder, to have come from her father; but fear hath the common fault of a justice of peace and is apt to conclude hastily from every slight circumstance without examining the evidence on both sides.

To ease the reader's curiosity, therefore, rather than his apprehensions, we proceed to inform him that an Irish peer had arrived very late that evening at the inn in his way to London. This nobleman, having sallied from his supper at the hurricane before commemorated, had seen the attendant of Mrs. Fitzpatrick, and upon a short inquiry was informed that her lady, with whom he was very particularly acquainted, was above. This information he had no sooner received than he addressed himself to the landlord, pacified him, and sent him upstairs with compliments rather civiller than those which were delivered.

It may perhaps be wondered at that the waiting-woman herself was not the messenger employed on this occasion, but we are sorry to say she was not at present qualified for that, or indeed for any other office. The rum (for so the landlord chose to call the distillation from malt) had basely taken the advantage of the fatigue which the poor woman had undergone, and had made terrible depredations on her noble faculties at a time when they were very unable to resist the attack.

We shall not describe this tragical scene too fully, but we thought ourselves obliged by that historic integrity which we profess shortly to hint a matter which we would otherwise have been glad to have spared. Many historians, indeed, for want of this integrity or of diligence, to say no worse, often leave the reader to find out these little circumstances in the dark, and sometimes to his great confusion and perplexity.

Sophia was very soon eased of her causeless fright by the entry of the noble peer, who was not only an intimate acquaintance of Mrs. Fitzpatrick but in reality a very particular friend of that lady. To say truth, it was by his assistance that she had been enabled to escape from her husband; for this nobleman had the same gallant disposition with those renowned knights of whom we read in heroic story and had delivered many an imprisoned nymph from durance. He was, indeed, as bitter an enemy to the savage authority too often exercised by husbands and fathers over the young and lovely of the other sex as ever knight-errant was to the barbarous power of enchanters; nay, to say truth,

I have often suspected that those very enchanters with which romance everywhere abounds were in reality no other than the husbands of those days, and matrimony itself was perhaps the enchanted castle in which the nymphs were said to be confined.

This nobleman had an estate in the neighbourhood of Fitzpatrick and had been for some time acquainted with the lady. No sooner, therefore, did he hear of her confinement than he earnestly applied himself to procure her liberty, which he presently effected not by storming the castle, according to the example of ancient heroes, but by corrupting the governor, in conformity with the modern art of war, in which craft is held to be preferable to valour and gold is found to be more irresistible than either lead or steel.

This circumstance, however, as the lady did not think it material enough to relate to her friend, we would not at that time impart it to the reader. We rather chose to leave him awhile under a supposition that she had found or coined or by some very extraordinary, perhaps supernatural, means had possessed herself of the money with which she had bribed her keeper than to interrupt her narrative by giving a hint of what seemed to her of too little importance to be mentioned.

The peer after a short conversation could not forbear expressing some surprise at meeting the lady in that place, nor could he refrain from telling her he imagined she had been gone to Bath. Mrs. Fitzpatrick very freely answered that she had been prevented in her purpose by the arrival of a person she need not mention. "In short," says she, "I was overtaken by my husband (for I need not affect to conceal what the world knows too well already). I had the good fortune to escape in a most surprising manner and am now going to London with this young lady, who is a near relation of mine and who hath escaped from as great a tyrant as my own."

His lordship, concluding that this tyrant was likewise a husband, made a speech full of compliments to both the ladies and as full of invectives against his own sex; nor, indeed, did he avoid some oblique glances at the matrimonial institution itself and at the unjust powers given by it to man over the more sensible and more meritorious part of the species. He ended his oration with an offer of his protection and of his coach and six, which was instantly accepted by Mrs. Fitzpatrick, and at last, upon her persuasions, by Sophia.

Matters being thus adjusted, his lordship took his leave and the ladies retired to rest, where Mrs. Fitzpatrick entertained her cousin with many high encomiums on the character of the noble peer, and enlarged very particularly on his great fondness for his wife, saying she believed he was almost the only person of high rank who was entirely constant to the marriage-bed. "Indeed," added she, "my dear Sophy, that is a very rare virtue amongst men of condition. Never expect it when you marry; for, believe me, if you do, you will certainly be deceived."

A gentle sigh stole from Sophia at these words, which perhaps contributed to form a dream of no very pleasant kind, but as she never revealed this dream to any one, so the reader cannot expect to see it related here.

9

THE MORNING INTRODUCED IN SOME PRETTY WRITING. A STAGE-COACH. THE CIVILITY OF CHAMBERMAIDS. THE HEROIC TEMPER OF SOPHIA. HER GENEROSITY. THE RETURN TO IT. THE DEPARTURE OF THE COMPANY AND THEIR ARRIVAL AT LONDON; WITH SOME REMARKS FOR THE USE OF TRAVELLERS

Those members of the society who are born to furnish the blessings of life now began to light their candles, in order to pursue their daily labours for the use of those who are born to enjoy these blessings. The sturdy hind now attends the levee of his fellow-labourer the ox; the cunning artificer, the diligent mechanic, spring from their hard mattress; and now the bonny housemaid begins to repair the disordered drumroom while the riotous authors of that disorder in broken, interrupted slumbers tumble and toss as if the hardness of down disquieted their repose.

In simple phrase, the clock had no sooner struck seven than the ladies were ready for their journey, and at their desire his lordship and his equipage were prepared to attend them.

And now a matter of some difficulty arose, and this was how his lordship himself should be conveyed; for though in stage-coaches, where passengers are properly considered as so much luggage, the ingenious coachman stows half a dozen with perfect ease into the place of four—for well he contrives that the fat hostess or well-fed alderman may take up no more room than the slim miss or taper master, it being the nature of guts when well squeezed to give way and to lie in a narrow compass—yet in these vehicles which are called for distinction's sake gentlemen's coaches, though they are often larger than the others, this method of packing is never attempted.

His lordship would have put a short end to the difficulty by very gallantly desiring to mount his horse, but Mrs. Fitzpatrick would by no means consent to it. It was therefore concluded that the Abigails should by turns relieve each other on one of his lordship's horses, which was presently equipped with a side-saddle for that purpose.

Everything being settled at the inn, the ladies discharged their former guides and Sophia made a present to the landlord, partly to repair the bruise which he had received under herself and partly on account of what he had suffered under the hands of her enraged waiting-woman. And now Sophia first discovered a loss which gave her some uneasiness, and this was of the hundred-pound bank-bill which her father had given her at their last meeting, and which, within a very inconsiderable trifle, was all the treasure she was at present worth. She searched everywhere, and shook and tumbled all her things to no purpose; the bill was not to be found; and she was at last fully persuaded that she had lost it from her pocket when she had the misfortune of tumbling from her horse in the dark lane, as before recorded—a fact that seemed the more probable as she now recollected some discomposure in her pockets which had happened at that time, and the great difficulty with which she had drawn forth her handkerchief the very instant before her fall in order to relieve the distress of Mrs. Fitzpatrick.

Misfortunes of this kind, whatever inconveniences they may be attended with, are incapable of subduing a mind in which there is any strength without the assistance of avarice. Sophia, therefore, though nothing could be worse timed than this accident at such a season, immediately got the better of her concern, and with her wonted serenity and cheerfulness of countenance returned to her company. His lordship conducted the ladies into the vehicle, as he did likewise Mrs. Honour, who after many civilities and more "dear madams" at last yielded to the well-bred importunities of her sister Abigail and submitted to be complimented with the first ride in the coach; in which, indeed, she would afterwards have been contented to have pursued her whole journey had not her mistress, after several fruitless intimations, at length forced her to take her turn on horse-back.

The coach, now having received its company, began to move forwards, attended by many servants and led by two captains, who had before rode with his lordship and who would have been dismissed from the vehicle upon a much less worthy occasion than was this of accommodating two ladies. In this they acted only as gentlemen, but were ready at any time to have performed the office of a footman, or indeed would have condescended lower for the honour of his lordship's company and for the convenience of his table.

My landlord was so pleased with the present he had received from Sophia that he rather rejoiced in than regretted his bruise or his scratches. The reader will perhaps be curious to know the *quantum* of this present, but we cannot satisfy his curiosity. Whatever it was, it satisfied the landlord for his bodily hurt, but he lamented he had not known before how little the lady valued her money; "for to be sure," says he, "one might have charged every article double, and she would have made no cavil at the reckoning."

His wife, however, was far from drawing this conclusion; whether she really felt any injury done to her husband more than he did himself I will not say; certain it is, she was much less satisfied with the generosity of Sophia. "Indeed," cries she, "my dear, the lady knows better how to dispose of her money than you imagine. She might very well think we should not put up such a business without some satisfaction, and the law would have cost her an infinite deal more than this poor little matter, which I wonder you would take." "You are always so bloodily wise," quoth the husband; "it would have cost her more, would it? Dost fancy I don't know that as well as thee? But would any of that more, or so much, have come into our pockets? Indeed, if son Tom the lawyer had been alive, I could have been glad to have put such a pretty business into his hands. He would have got a good picking out of it, but I have no relation now who is a lawyer, and why should I go to law for the benefit of strangers?" "Nay, to be sure," answered she, "you must know best." "I believe I do," replied he. "I fancy when money is to be got, I can smell it out as well as another. Everybody, let me tell you, would not have talked people out of this. Mind that, I say; everybody would not have cajoled this out of her, mind that." The wife then joined in the applause of her husband's sagacity, and thus ended the short dialogue between them on this occasion.

We will therefore take our leave of these good people and attend his lordship and his fair companions, who made such good expedition that they performed a journey of ninety miles in two days, and on the second evening arrived in London without having encountered any one adventure on the road worthy the dignity of this history to relate. Our pen, therefore, shall imitate the expedition which it describes, and our history shall keep pace with the travellers who are its subject. Good writers will indeed do well to imitate the ingenious traveller in this instance, who always proportions his stay at any place to the beauties, elegancies, and curiosities which it affords. At Eshur, at Stowe, at Wilton, at Eastbury, and at Prior's Park, days are too short for the ravished imagination, while we admire the wondrous power of Art in improving Nature. In some of these, Art chiefly engages our admiration; in others, Nature and Art contend for our applause; but in the last, the former seems to triumph. Here Nature appears in her richest attire, and Art dressed with the modestest simplicity attends her benignant mistress. Here Nature indeed pours forth the choicest treasures which she hath lavished on this world, and here human nature presents you with an object which can be only exceeded in the other.

The same taste, the same imagination, which luxuriously riots in these elegant scenes, can be amused with objects of far inferior note. The woods, the rivers, the lawns of Devon and of Dorset, attract the eye of the ingenious traveller and retard his pace, which delay he afterwards compensates by swiftly scouring over the gloomy heath of Bagshot or that pleasant plain which extends itself westward from Stockbridge, where no other object than one single tree only in sixteen miles presents itself to the view, unless the clouds in compassion to our tired spirits kindly open their variegated mansions to our prospect.

Not so travels the money-meditating tradesman, the sagacious justice, the dignified doctor, the warm-clad grazier, with all the numerous offspring of wealth and dullness. On they jog with equal pace through the verdant meadows or over the barren heath, their horses measuring four miles and a half per hour with the utmost exactness, the eyes of the beast and of his master being alike directed forwards and employed in contemplating the same objects in the same manner. With equal rapture the good rider surveys the proudest boasts of the architect and those fair buildings with which some unknown name hath adorned the rich clothing-town, where heaps of bricks are piled up as a kind of monument to show that heaps of money have been piled there before.

And now, reader, as we are in haste to attend our heroine, we will leave to thy sagacity to apply all this to the Boeotian writers and to those authors who are their opposites. This thou wilt be abundantly able to perform without our aid. Bestir thyself, therefore, on this occasion; for though we will always lend thee proper assistance in difficult places, as we do not, like some others, expect thee to use the arts of divination to discover our meaning, yet we shall not indulge thy laziness where nothing but thy own attention is required; for thou art highly mistaken if thou dost imagine that we intended when we begun this great work to leave thy sagacity nothing to do, or that without sometimes exercising this talent thou wilt be able to travel through our pages with any pleasure or profit to thyself.

10

CONTAINING A HINT OR TWO CONCERNING VIRTUE, AND A FEW MORE CONCERNING SUSPICION

Our company, being arrived at London, were set down at his lordship's house, where while they refreshed themselves after the fatigue of their journey servants were dispatched to provide a lodging for the two ladies, for as her ladyship was not then in town, Mrs. Fitzpatrick would by no means consent to accept a bed in the mansion of the peer.

Some readers will perhaps condemn this extraordinary delicacy, as I may call it, of virtue as too nice and scrupulous, but we must make allowances for her situation, which must be owned to have been very ticklish; and when we consider the malice of censorious tongues, we must allow, if it was a fault, the fault was an excess on the right side, and which every woman who is in the self-same situation will do well to imitate. The most formal appearance of virtue when it is only an appearance may, perhaps, in very abstracted considerations seem to be rather less commendable than virtue itself without this formality, but it will, however, be always more commended; and this, I believe, will be granted by all: that it is necessary, unless in some very particular cases, for every woman to support either the one or the other.

A lodging being prepared, Sophia accompanied her cousin for that evening, but resolved early in the morning to inquire after the lady into whose protection, as we have formerly mentioned, she had determined to throw herself when she quitted her father's house. And this she was the more eager in doing from some observations she had made during her journey in the coach.

Now, as we would by no means fix the odious character of suspicion on Sophia, we are almost afraid to open to our reader the conceits which filled her mind concerning Mrs. Fitzpatrick, of whom she certainly entertained at present some doubts which, as they are very apt to enter into the bosoms of the worst of people, we think proper not to mention more plainly till we have first suggested a word or two to our reader touching suspicion in general.

Of this there have always appeared to me to be two degrees. The first of these I choose to derive from the heart, as the extreme velocity of its discernment seems to denote some previous inward impulse, and the rather as this superlative degree often forms its own objects, sees what is not, and always more than really exists. This is that quick-sighted penetration whose hawk's eyes no symptom of evil can escape; which observes not only upon the actions but upon the words and looks of men; and as it proceeds from the heart of the observer, so it dives into the heart of the observed and there espies evil, as it were, in the first embryo, nay, sometimes before it can be said to be conceived. An admirable faculty if it were infallible, but as this degree of perfection is not even claimed by more than one mortal being, so from the fallibility of such acute discernment have arisen many sad mischiefs and most grievous heart-aches to innocence and virtue. I cannot help, therefore, regarding this vast quick-sightedness into evil as a vicious excess, and as a very pernicious evil in itself. And I am the more inclined to this opinion as I am afraid it always proceeds from a bad heart, for the reasons I have above mentioned, and for one more: namely, because I never knew it the property of a good one. Now, from this degree of suspicion I entirely and absolutely acquit Sophia.

A second degree of this quality seems to arise from the head. This is indeed no other than the faculty of seeing what is before your eyes and of drawing conclusions from what you see. The former of these is unavoidable by those who have any eyes, and the latter is perhaps no less certain and necessary a consequence of our having any brains. This is altogether as bitter an enemy to guilt as the former is to innocence; nor can I see it in an unamiable light, even though through human fallibility it should be sometimes mistaken. For instance, if a husband should accidentally surprise his wife in the lap or in the embraces of some of those pretty young gentlemen who profess the art of cuckoldom, I should not highly, I think, blame him for concluding something more than what he saw from the familiarities which he really had seen, and which we are at least favourable enough to when we call them innocent freedoms. The reader will easily suggest great plenty of instances to himself; I shall add but one more, which, however unchristian it may be thought by some, I cannot help esteeming to be strictly justifiable, and this is a suspicion that a man is capable of doing what he hath done already, and that it is possible for one who hath been a villain once to act the same part again. And to confess the truth, of this degree of suspicion I believe Sophia was guilty. From this degree of suspicion she had, in fact, conceived an opinion that her cousin was really not better than she should be.

The case, it seems, was this: Mrs. Fitzpatrick wisely considered that the virtue of a young lady is in the world in the same situation with a poor hare, which is certain whenever it ventures abroad to meet its enemies, for it can hardly meet any other. No sooner, therefore, was she determined to take the first opportunity of quitting the protection of her husband than she resolved to cast herself under the protection of some other man, and whom could she so properly choose to be her guardian as a person of quality, of fortune, of honour, and who, besides a gallant disposition which inclines men to knight-errantry, that is, to be the champions of ladies in distress, had often declared a violent attachment to herself and had already given her all the instances of it in his power?

But as the law hath foolishly omitted this office of vice-husband, or guardian to an eloped lady, and as malice is apt to denominate him by a more disagreeable appellation, it was concluded that his lordship should perform all such kind offices to the lady in secret and without publicly assuming the character of her protector. Nay, to prevent any other person from seeing him in this light, it was agreed that the lady should proceed directly to Bath, and that his lordship should first go to London and thence should go down to that place by the advice of his physicians.

Now, all this Sophia very plainly understood, not from the lips or behaviour of Mrs. Fitzpatrick but from the peer, who was infinitely less expert at retaining a secret than was the good lady; and perhaps the exact secrecy which Mrs. Fitzpatrick had observed on this head in her narrative served not a little to heighten those suspicions which were now risen in the mind of her cousin.

Sophia very easily found out the lady she sought, for indeed there was not a chairman in town to whom her house was not perfectly well known; and as she received in return of her first message a most pressing invitation, she immediately accepted it. Mrs. Fitzpatrick, indeed, did not desire her cousin to stay with her with more earnestness than civility required. Whether she had discerned and resented the suspicion above mentioned, or from what other motive it arose, I cannot say; but certain it is, she was full as desirous of parting with Sophia as Sophia herself could be of going.

The young lady, when she came to take leave of her cousin, could not avoid giving her a short hint of advice. She begged her for heaven's sake to take care of herself, and to consider in how dangerous a situation she stood, adding she hoped some method would be found of reconciling her to her husband. "You must remember, my dear," says she, "the maxim which my aunt Western hath so often repeated to us both: *that whenever the matrimonial alliance is broke, and war declared between husband and wife, she can hardly make a disadvantageous peace for herself on any conditions.* These are my aunt's very words, and she hath had a great deal of experience in the world." Mrs. Fitzpatrick answered with a contemptuous smile, "Never fear me, child; take care of yourself, for you are younger than me. I will come and visit you in a few days, but, dear Sophy, let me give you one piece of advice: leave the character of Graveairs in the country, for believe me, it will sit very awkwardly upon you in this town."

Thus the two cousins parted, and Sophia repaired directly to Lady Bellaston, where she found a most hearty as well as most polite welcome. The lady had taken a great fancy to her when she had seen her formerly with her aunt Western. She was, indeed, extremely glad to see her, and was no sooner acquainted with the reasons which induced her to leave the squire and fly to London than she highly applauded her sense and resolution; and after expressing the highest satisfaction in the opinion which Sophia had declared she entertained of her ladyship by choosing her house for an asylum, she promised her all the protection which it was in her power to give.

As we have now brought Sophia into safe hands, the reader will, I apprehend, be contented to deposit her there awhile and to look a little after other personages; and particularly poor Jones, whom we have left long enough to do penance for his past offences, which, as is the nature of vice, brought sufficient punishment upon him themselves.

BOOK XII

CONTAINING THE SAME INDIVIDUAL TIME WITH THE FORMER

1

SHOWING WHAT IS TO BE DEEMED PLAGIARISM IN A MODERN AUTHOR, AND WHAT IS TO BE CONSIDERED AS LAWFUL PRIZE

The learned reader must have observed that in the course of this mighty work I have often translated passages out of the best ancient authors, without quoting the original or without taking the least notice of the book from whence they were borrowed.

This conduct in writing is placed in a very proper light by the ingenious Abbé Bannier in his preface to his *Mythology,* a work of great erudition and of equal judgement. "It will be easy," says he, "for the reader to observe that I have frequently had greater regard to him than to my own reputation; for an author certainly pays him a considerable compliment when, for his sake, he suppresses learned quotations that come in his way and which would have cost him but the bare trouble of translating."

To fill up a work with these scraps may, indeed, be considered as a downright cheat on the learned world, who are by such means imposed upon to buy a second time in fragments and by retail what they have already in gross, if not in their memories, upon their shelves; and it is still more cruel upon the illiterate, who are drawn in to pay for what is of no manner of use to them. A writer who intermixes great quantity of Greek and Latin with his works deals by the ladies and fine gentlemen in the same paltry manner with which they are treated by the auctioneers, who often endeavour so to confound and mix up their lots that in order to purchase the commodity you want, you are obliged at the same time to purchase that which will do you no service.

And yet, as there is no conduct so fair and disinterested but that it may be misunderstood by ignorance and mis-represented by malice, I have been sometimes tempted to preserve my own reputation at the expense of my reader, and to transcribe the original or at least to quote chapter and verse whenever I have made use either of the thought or expression of another. I am indeed in some doubt that I have often suffered by the contrary method, and that by suppressing the original author's name, I have been rather suspected of plagiarism than reputed to act from the amiable motive above assigned by that justly celebrated Frenchman.

Now, to obviate all such imputations for the future, I do here confess and justify the fact. The ancients may be considered as a rich common, where every person who hath the smallest tenement in Parnassus hath a free right to fatten his Muse. Or, to place it in a clearer light, we moderns are to the ancients what the poor are to the rich. By the poor, here, I mean that large and venerable body which in English we call the Mob. Now, whoever hath had the honour to be admitted to any degree of intimacy with this mob must well know that it is one of their estab-lished maxims to plunder and pillage their rich neighbours without any reluctance, and that this is held to be neither sin nor shame among them. And so constantly do they abide and act by this maxim that in every parish almost in the kingdom there is a kind of confederacy ever carry-ing on against a certain person of opulence called the squire, whose property is considered as free-booty by all his poor neighbours, who, as they conclude that there is no manner of guilt in such depredations, look upon it as a point of honour and moral obligation to conceal and to preserve each other from punishment on all such occasions.

In like manner are the ancients, such as Homer, Virgil, Horace, Cicero, and the rest, to be esteemed among us writers as so many wealthy squires, from whom we, the poor of Parnassus, claim an immemorial custom of taking whatever we can come at. This liberty I demand and this I am as ready to allow again to my poor neighbours in their turn. All I profess, and all I require of my brethren, is to maintain the same strict honesty among ourselves which the mob show to one another. To steal from one another is indeed highly criminal and indecent; for this may be strictly styled defrauding the poor (sometimes perhaps those who are poorer than ourselves) or, to see it under the most opprobrious colours, robbing the spital.

Since, therefore, upon the strictest examination my own conscience cannot lay any such pitiful theft to my charge, I am contented to plead guilty to the former accusation; nor shall I ever scruple to take to myself any passage which I shall find in an ancient author to my purpose without setting down the name of the author from whence it was taken. Nay, I absolutely claim a property in all such sentiments the moment they are transcribed into my writings, and I expect all readers henceforwards to regard them as purely and entirely my own. This claim, however, I desire to be allowed me only on condition that I preserve strict honesty towards my poor brethren, from whom if ever I borrow any of that little of which they are possessed, I shall never fail to put their mark upon it, that it may be at all times ready to be restored to the right owner.

The omission of this was highly blameable in one Mr. Moore, who, having formerly borrowed some lines of Pope and Company, took the liberty to transcribe six of them into his play of the *Rival Modes*. Mr. Pope, however, very luckily found them in the said play and, laying violent hands on his own property, transferred it back again into his own works; and for a further punishment, imprisoned the said Moore in the loathsome dungeon of the *Dunciad*, where his unhappy memory now remains, and eternally will remain, as a proper punishment for such his unjust dealings in the poetical trade.

2

IN WHICH, THOUGH THE SQUIRE DOTH NOT FIND HIS
DAUGHTER, SOMETHING IS FOUND WHICH PUTS AN END TO
HIS PURSUIT

The history now returns to the inn at Upton, whence we shall first trace the footsteps of Squire Western; for as he will soon arrive at an end of his journey, we shall have then full leisure to attend our hero.

The reader may be pleased to remember that the said squire departed from the inn in great fury, and in that

527

fury he pursued his daughter. The hostler having informed him that she had crossed the Severn, he likewise passed that river with his equipage and rode full speed, vowing the utmost vengeance against poor Sophia if he should but overtake her.

He had not gone far before he arrived at a cross-way. Here he called a short council of war, in which, after hearing different opinions, he at last gave the direction of his pursuit to Fortune and struck directly into the Worcester Road.

In this road he proceeded about two miles, when he began to bemoan himself most bitterly, frequently crying out, "What pity is it! Sure never was so unlucky a dog as myself!" and then burst forth a volley of oaths and execrations.

The parson attempted to administer comfort to him on this occasion. "Sorrow not, sir," says he, "like those without hope. Howbeit we have not yet been able to overtake young madam, we may account it some good fortune that we have hitherto traced her course aright. Peradventure she will soon be fatigued with her journey and will tarry in some inn in order to renovate her corporeal functions, and in that case, in all moral certainty, you will very briefly be *compos voti*."

"Pogh! D—n the slut," answered the squire. "I am lamenting the loss of so fine a morning for hunting. It is confounded hard to lose one of the best scenting days, in all appearance, which hath been this season, and especially after so long a frost."

Whether Fortune, who now and then shows some compassion in wantonest tricks, might not take pity of the squire, and as she had determined not to let him overtake his daughter, might not resolve to make him amends some other way, I will not assert, but he had hardly uttered the words just before commemorated and two or three oaths at their heels when a pack of hounds began to open their melodious throats at a small distance from them, which the squire's horse and his rider both perceiving, both immediately pricked up their ears, and the squire crying, "She's gone, she's gone! Damn me if she is not gone!" instantly clapped spurs to the beast, who little needed it, having, indeed, the same inclination with his master; and now the whole company, crossing into a corn-field, rode directly towards the hounds with much hallooing and hooping, while the poor parson, blessing himself, brought up the rear.

Thus fable reports that the fair Grimalkin, whom Venus at the desire of a passionate lover converted from a cat into a fine woman, no sooner perceived a mouse than, mindful of her former sport and still retaining her pristine nature, she leapt from the bed of her husband to pursue the little animal.

What are we to understand by this? Not that the bride was displeased with the embraces of her amorous bridegroom; for though some have remarked that cats are subject to ingratitude, yet women and cats too will be pleased and purr on certain occasions. The truth is, as the sagacious Sir Roger L'Estrange observes in his deep reflections, that if we shut Nature out at the door, she will come in at the window; and that puss, though a madam, will be a mouser still. In the same manner we are not to arraign the squire of any want of love for his daughter, for in reality he had a great deal; we are only to consider that he was a squire and a sportsman, and then we may apply the fable to him and the judicious reflections likewise.

The hounds ran very hard, as it is called, and the squire pursued over hedge and ditch, with all his usual vociferation and alacrity and with all his usual pleasure; nor did the thoughts of Sophia ever once intrude themselves to allay the satisfaction he enjoyed in the chase, which, he said, was one of the finest he ever saw and which he swore was very well worth going fifty miles for. As the squire forgot his daughter, the servants, we may easily believe, forgot their mistress; and the parson, after having expressed much astonishment in Latin to himself, at length likewise abandoned all farther thoughts of the young lady and, jogging on at a distance behind, began to meditate a portion of doctrine for the ensuing Sunday.

The squire who owned the hounds was highly pleased with the arrival of his brother squire and sportsman; for all men approve merit in their own way, and no man was more expert in the field than Mr. Western, nor did any other better know how to encourage the dogs with his voice and to animate the hunt with his holla.

Sportsmen in the warmth of a chase are too much engaged to attend to any manner of ceremony, nay, even to the offices of humanity; for if any of them meet with an accident by tumbling into a ditch or into a river, the rest pass on regardless and generally leave him to his fate;

during this time, therefore, the two squires, though often close to each other, interchanged not a single word. The Master of the Hunt, however, often saw and approved the great judgement of the stranger in drawing the dogs when they were at a fault, and hence conceived a very high opinion of his understanding, as the number of his attendants inspired no small reverence to his quality. As soon, therefore, as the sport was ended by the death of the little animal which had occasioned it, the two squires met and in all squire-like greeting saluted each other.

The conversation was entertaining enough, and what we may perhaps relate in an appendix or on some other occasion, but as it nowise concerns this history, we cannot prevail on ourselves to give it a place here. It concluded with a second chase, and that with an invitation to dinner. This being accepted was followed by a hearty bout of drinking, which ended in as hearty a nap on the part of Squire Western.

Our squire was by no means a match either for his host or for Parson Supple at his cups that evening; for which the violent fatigue of mind as well as body that he had undergone may very well account without the least derogation from his honour. He was, indeed, according to the vulgar phrase, whistled drunk; for before he had swallowed the third bottle, he became so entirely overpowered that, though he was not carried off to bed till long after, the parson considered him as absent, and having acquainted the other squire with all relating to Sophia, he obtained his promise of seconding those arguments which he intended to urge the next morning for Mr. Western's return.

No sooner, therefore, had the good squire shaken off his evening and began to call for his morning draught, and to summon his horses in order to renew his pursuit, than Mr. Supple began his dissuasives, which the host so strongly seconded that they at length prevailed and Mr. Western agreed to return home, being principally moved by one argument: viz., that he knew not which way to go and might probably be riding farther from his daughter instead of towards her. He then took leave of his brother sportsman and, expressing great joy that the frost was broken (which might perhaps be no small motive to his hastening home), set forwards, or rather backwards, for Somersetshire; but not before he had first dispatched part of his retinue in quest of his daughter, after whom he likewise sent a volley of the most bitter execrations which he could invent.

3

THE DEPARTURE OF JONES FROM UPTON, WITH WHAT PASSED BETWEEN HIM AND PARTRIDGE ON THE ROAD

At length we are once more come to our hero, and to say truth, we have been obliged to part with him so long that considering the condition in which we left him, I apprehend many of our readers have concluded we intended to abandon him forever, he being at present in that situation in which prudent people usually desist from inquiring any farther after their friends lest they should be shocked by hearing such friends had hanged themselves.

But, in reality, if we have not all the virtues, I will boldly say neither have we all the vices of a prudent character, and though it is not easy to conceive circumstances much more miserable than those of poor Jones at present, we shall return to him and attend upon him with the same diligence as if he was wantoning in the brightest beams of Fortune.

Mr. Jones, then, and his companion, Partridge, left the inn a few minutes after the departure of Squire Western and pursued the same road on foot, for the ostler told them that no horses were by any means to be at that time procured at Upton. On they marched with heavy hearts; for though their disquiet proceeded from very different reasons, yet displeased they were both, and if Jones sighed bitterly, Partridge grunted altogether as sadly at every step.

When they came to the cross-roads where the squire had stopped to take council, Jones stopped likewise and, turning to Partridge, asked his opinion which track they should pursue. "Ah, sir," answered Partridge, "I wish your honour would follow my advice." "Why should I not?" replied Jones. "For it is now indifferent to me whither I go or what becomes of me." "My advice, then," said Partridge, "is that you immediately face about and return home; for who that hath such a home to return to as your honour would travel thus about the country like a vagabond? I ask pardon, *sed vox ea sola reperta est.*"

"Alas!" cries Jones. "I have no home to return to; but if

my friend, my father, would receive me, could I bear the country from which Sophia is flown? Cruel Sophia! Cruel! No, let me blame myself. No, let me blame thee. D—nation seize thee, fool, blockhead! Thou hast undone me, and I will tear thy soul from thy body." At which words he laid violent hands on the collar of poor Partridge and shook him more heartily than an ague fit or his own fears had ever done before.

Partridge fell trembling on his knees and begged for mercy, vowing he had meant no harm—when Jones, after staring wildly on him for a moment, quitted his hold and discharged a rage on himself that, had it fallen on the other, would certainly have put an end to his being, which, indeed, the very apprehension of it had almost effected.

We would bestow some pains here in minutely describing all the mad pranks which Jones played on this occasion could we be well assured that the reader would take the same pains in perusing them, but as we are apprehensive that after all the labour which we should employ in painting this scene the said reader would be very apt to skip it entirely over, we have saved ourself that trouble. To say the truth, we have from this reason alone often done great violence to the luxuriance of our genius, and have left many excellent descriptions out of our work which would otherwise have been in it. And this suspicion, to be honest, arises, as is generally the case, from our own wicked heart; for we have ourselves been very often most horridly given to jumping as we have run through the pages of voluminous historians.

Suffice it, then, simply to say that Jones, after having played the part of a madman for many minutes, came by degrees to himself; which no sooner happened than, turning to Partridge, he very earnestly begged his pardon for the attack he had made on him in the violence of his passion, but concluded by desiring him never to mention his return again, for he was resolved never to see that country any more.

Partridge easily forgave and faithfully promised to obey the injunction now laid upon him. And then Jones very briskly cried out, "Since it is absolutely impossible for me to pursue any farther the steps of my angel, I will pursue those of glory. Come on, my brave lad, now for the army. It is a glorious cause, and I would willingly sacrifice my life in it, even though it was worth my preserving." And so saying, he immediately struck into the different road from that which the squire had taken and, by mere chance, pursued the very same through which Sophia had before passed.

Our travellers now marched a full mile without speaking a syllable to each other, though Jones, indeed, muttered many things to himself. As to Partridge, he was profoundly silent, for he was not, perhaps, perfectly recovered from his former fright; besides, he had apprehensions of provoking his friend to a second fit of wrath, especially as he now began to entertain a conceit which may not, perhaps, create any great wonder in the reader. In short, he began now to suspect that Jones was absolutely out of his senses. At length, Jones being weary of soliloquy, addressed himself to his companion and blamed him for his taciturnity; for which the poor man very honestly accounted, from his fear of giving offence. And now this fear being pretty well removed by the most absolute promises of indemnity, Partridge again took the bridle from his tongue, which, perhaps, rejoiced no less at regaining its liberty than a young colt when the bridle is slipped from his neck and he is turned loose into the pastures.

As Partridge was inhibited from that topic which would have first suggested itself, he fell upon that which was next uppermost in his mind: namely, the Man of the Hill. "Certainly, sir," says he, "that could never be a man, who dresses himself and lives after such a strange manner and so unlike other folks. Besides, his diet, as the old woman told me, is chiefly upon herbs, which is fitter food for a horse than a Christian; nay, landlord at Upton says that the neighbours thereabouts have very fearful notions about him. It runs strangely in my head that it must have been some spirit, who, perhaps, might be sent to forewarn us; and who knows but all that matter which he told us, of his going to fight and of his being taken prisoner and of the great danger he was in of being hanged, might be intended as a warning to us, considering what we are going about; besides, I dreamt of nothing all last night but of fighting, and methought the blood ran out of my nose as liquor out of a tap. Indeed, sir, *Infandum, regina, jubes renovare dolorem.*"

"Thy story, Partridge," answered Jones, "is almost as ill applied as thy Latin. Nothing can be more likely to happen than death to men who go into battle. Perhaps we shall both fall in it—and what then?" "What then!" replied Partridge. "Why, then there is an end of us, is there not? When I am gone, all is over with me. What matters the cause to me or who gets the victory if I am killed? I shall never enjoy any advantage from it. What are all the ringing of bells and bonfires to one that is six foot underground? There will be an end of poor Partridge." "And an end of poor Partridge," cries Jones, "there must be one time or other. If you love Latin, I will repeat you some fine lines out of Horace, which would inspire courage into a coward:

> "Dulce et decorum est pro patria mori.
> Mors et fugacem persequitur virum
> Nec parcit imbellis juventæ
> Poplitibus, timidoque tergo."

"I wish you would construe them," cries Partridge; "for Horace is a hard author, and I cannot understand as you repeat them."

"I will repeat you a bad imitation, or rather paraphrase, of my own," said Jones, "for I am but an indifferent poet.

> "Who would not die in his dear country's cause?
> Since, if the base fear his dastard step withdraws,
> From death he cannot fly: One common grave
> Receives at last the coward and the brave."

"That's very certain," cries Partridge. "Ay, sure, mors omnibus communis; but there is a great difference between dying in one's bed a great many years hence like a good Christian, with all our friends crying about us, and being shot to-day or to-morrow like a mad dog, or perhaps hacked in twenty pieces with a sword, and that, too, before we have repented of all our sins. O Lord, have mercy upon us! To be sure, the soldiers are a wicked kind of people. I never loved to have anything to do with them. I never could bring myself hardly to look upon them as Christians. There is nothing but cursing and swearing among them. I wish your honour would repent; I heartily wish you would repent before it is too late, and not think of going among them. Evil communication corrupts good manners. That is my principal reason. For as for that matter, I am no more afraid than another man; not I, as to matter of that. I know all human flesh must die, but yet a man may live many years for all that.

Why, I am a middle-aged man now, and yet I may live a great number of years. I have read of several who have lived to be above a hundred, and some a great deal above a hundred. Not that I hope, I mean that I promise myself, to live to any such age as that neither. But if it be only to eighty or ninety, heaven be praised, that is a great ways off yet; and I am not afraid of dying then, no more than another man: but surely, to tempt death before a man's time is come seems to me downright wickedness and presumption. Besides, if it was to do any good indeed, but let the cause be what it will, what mighty matter of good can two people do? And for my part, I understand nothing of it. I never fired off a gun above ten times in my life, and then it was not charged with bullets. And for the sword, I never learned to fence and know nothing of the matter. And then there are those cannons, which certainly it must be thought the highest presumption to go in the way of, and nobody but a madman—I ask pardon; upon my soul, I meant no harm; I beg I may not throw your honour into another passion."

"Be under no apprehension, Partridge," cries Jones; "I am now so well convinced of thy cowardice that thou couldst not provoke me on any account." "Your honour," answered he, "may call me a coward or anything else you please. If loving to sleep in a whole skin makes a man a coward, *non immunes ab illis malis sumus.* I never read in my grammar that a man can't be a good man without fighting. *Vir bonus est quis? Qui consulta patrum, qui leges juraque servat.* Not a word of fighting; and I am sure the Scripture is so much against it that a man shall never persuade me he is a good Christian while he sheds Christian blood."

4

THE ADVENTURE OF A BEGGAR-MAN

Just as Partridge had uttered that good and pious doctrine with which the last chapter concluded, they arrived at another cross-way, when a lame fellow in rags asked them for alms; upon which Partridge gave him a severe rebuke, saying, "Every parish ought to keep their own poor." Jones then fell a-laughing and asked Partridge if he was not ashamed with so much charity in his mouth to have no charity in his heart.

"Your religion," says he, "serves you only for an excuse for your faults, but is no incentive to your virtue. Can any man who is really a Christian abstain from relieving one of his brethren in such a miserable condition?" And, at the same time putting his hand in his pocket, he gave the poor object a shilling.

"Master," cries the fellow after thanking him, "I have a curious thing here in my pocket, which I found about two miles off, if your worship will please to buy it. I should not venture to pull it out to every one, but as you are so good a gentleman and so kind to the poor, you won't suspect a man of being a thief only because he is poor." He then pulled out a little gilt pocket-book and delivered it into the hands of Jones.

Jones presently opened it and (guess, reader, what he felt) saw in the first page the words *Sophia Western,* written by her own fair hand. He no sooner read the name than he pressed it close to his lips, nor could he avoid falling into some very frantic raptures, notwithstanding his company, but perhaps these very raptures made him forget he was not alone.

While Jones was kissing and mumbling the book as if he had had an excellent brown buttered crust in his mouth, or as if he had really been a book-worm or an author who had nothing to eat but his own works, a piece of paper fell from its leaves to the ground, which Partridge took up and delivered to Jones, who presently perceived it to be a bank-bill. It was, indeed, the very bill which Western had given his daughter the night before her departure, and a Jew would have jumped to purchase it at five shillings less than £100.

The eyes of Partridge sparkled at this news, which Jones now proclaimed aloud, and so did (though with somewhat a different aspect) those of the poor fellow who had found the book, and who (I hope from a principle of honesty) had never opened it; but we should not deal honestly by the reader if we omitted to inform him of a circumstance which may be here a little material: viz., that the fellow could not read.

Jones, who had felt nothing but pure joy and transport from the finding the book, was affected with a mixture of concern at this new discovery; for his imagination instantly suggested to him that the owner of the bill might possibly want it before he should be able to convey it to her. He then acquainted the finder that he knew the lady to whom the book belonged, and would endeavour to find her out as soon as possible and return it her.

The pocket-book was a late present from Mrs. Western to her niece; it had cost five and twenty shillings, having been bought of a celebrated toyman, but the real value of the silver which it contained in its clasp was about 18d., and that price the said toyman, as it was altogether as good as when it first issued from his shop, would now have given for it. A prudent person would, however, have taken proper advantage of the ignorance of this fellow and would not have offered more than a shilling or, perhaps, sixpence for it; nay, some perhaps would have given nothing and left the fellow to his action of trover, which some learned sergeants may doubt whether he could under these circumstances have maintained.

Jones, on the contrary, whose character was on the outside of generosity and may perhaps not very unjustly have been suspected of extravagance, without any hesitation gave a guinea in exchange for the book. The poor man, who had not for a long time before been possessed of so much treasure, gave Mr. Jones a thousand thanks and discovered little less of transport in his muscles than Jones had before shown, when he had first read the name of Sophia Western.

The fellow very readily agreed to attend our travellers to the place where he had found the pocket-book. Together, therefore, they proceeded directly thither, but not so fast as Mr. Jones desired, for his guide unfortunately happened to be lame and could not possibly travel faster than a mile an hour. As this place, therefore, was at above 'three miles' distance, though the fellow had said otherwise, the reader need not be acquainted how long they were in walking it.

Jones opened the book a hundred times during their walk, kissed it as often, talked much to himself and very little to his companions. At all which the guide expressed some signs of astonishment to Partridge, who more than once shook his head and cried, "Poor gentleman! *Orandum est ut sit mens sana in corpore sano.*"

At length they arrived at the very spot where Sophia unhappily dropped the pocket-book and where the fellow had as happily found it. Here Jones offered to take leave of his guide and to improve his pace, but the fellow, in whom that violent surprise and joy which the first receipt of the guinea had occasioned was now considerably abated, and who had now had sufficient time to recollect himself, put on a discontented look and, scratching his head, said he hoped his worship would give him something more. "Your worship," said he, "will, I hope, take it into your consideration that if I had not been honest, I might have kept the whole." And indeed, this the reader must confess to have been true. "If the paper there," said he, "be worth £100, I am sure the finding it deserves more than a guinea. Besides, suppose your worship should never see the lady, nor give it her—and though your worship looks and talks very much like a gentleman, yet I have only your worship's bare word; and certainly, if the right owner ben't to be found, it all belongs to the first finder. I hope your worship will consider all these matters. I am but a poor man and therefore don't desire to have all, but it is but reasonable I should have my share. Your worship looks like a good man and, I hope, will consider my honesty; for I might have kept every farthing and nobody ever the wiser." "I promise thee, upon my honour," cries Jones, "that I know the right owner and will restore it her." "Nay, your worship," answered the fellow, "may do as you please as to that, if you will but give me my share, that is, one-half of the money; your honour may keep the rest yourself if you please"; and concluded with swearing by a very vehement oath that he would never mention a syllable of it to any man living.

"Lookee, friend," cries Jones, "the right owner shall certainly have again all that she lost, and as for any further gratuity, I really cannot give it you at present; but let me know your name and where you live, and it is more than possible you may hereafter have further reason to rejoice at this morning's adventure."

"I don't know what you mean by venture," cries the fellow; "it seems I must venture whether you will return the lady her money or no; but I hope your worship will consider——" "Come, come," said Partridge, "tell his honour your name and where you may be found; I warrant you will never repent having put the money into his hands." The fellow, seeing no hopes of recovering the possession of the pocket-book, at last complied in giving in his name and place of abode, which Jones writ upon a piece of paper with the pencil of Sophia; and then, placing the paper in the same page where she had writ her name, he cried out, "There, friend, you are the happiest man alive; I have joined your name to that of an angel." "I don't know anything about angels," answered the fellow, "but I wish you would give me a little more money or else return me the pocket-book."

Partridge now waxed wroth; he called the poor cripple by several vile and opprobrious names, and was absolutely proceeding to beat him, but Jones would not suffer any such thing; and now, telling the fellow he would certainly find some opportunity of serving him, Mr. Jones departed as fast as his heels would carry him, and Partridge, into whom the thoughts of the hundred pound had infused new spirits, followed his leader, while the man who was obliged to stay behind fell to cursing them both as well as his parents; "for had they," says he, "sent me to charity-school to learn to write and read and cast account, I should have known the value of these matters as well as other people."

5

CONTAINING MORE ADVENTURES WHICH MR. JONES AND HIS COMPANION MET ON THE ROAD

Our travellers now walked so fast that they had very little time or breath for conversation, Jones meditating all the way on Sophia, and Partridge on the bank-bill, which, though it gave him some pleasure, caused him at the same time to repine at Fortune, which in all his walks had never given him such an opportunity of showing his honesty. They had proceeded above three miles when Partridge, being unable any longer to keep up with Jones, called to him and begged him a little to slacken his pace; with this he was the more ready to comply as he had for some time lost the footsteps of the horses, which the thaw had enabled him to trace during several miles, and he was now upon a wide common where were several roads.

He here, therefore, stopped to consider which of these roads he should pursue, when on a sudden they heard the noise of a drum that seemed at no great distance. This sound presently alarmed the fears of Partridge, and he cried out, "Lord have mercy upon us all; they are certainly a-coming!" "Who is coming?" cries Jones; for fear had long since given place to softer ideas in his mind, and since his adventure with the lame man, he had been totally intent on pursuing Sophia without entertaining one thought of an enemy. "Who!" cries Partridge. "Why, the rebels; but why should I call them rebels? They may be very honest gentlemen, for anything I know to the contrary. The devil take him that affronts them, I say. I am sure if they have nothing to say to me, I will have nothing to say to them but in a civil way. For heaven's sake, sir, don't affront them if they should come, and perhaps they may do us no harm; but would it not be the wiser way to creep into some of yonder bushes till they are gone by? What can two unarmed men do perhaps against fifty thousand? Certainly nobody but a madman—I hope your honour is not offended—but certainly no man who hath *mens sana in corpore sano*——" Here Jones interrupted this torrent of eloquence, which fear had inspired, saying that by the drum, he perceived they were near some town. He then made directly towards the place whence the noise proceeded, bidding Partridge take courage, for that he would lead him into no danger, and adding it was impossible the rebels should be so near.

Partridge was a little comforted with this last assurance, and though he would more gladly have gone the contrary way, he followed his leader, his heart beating time—but not after the manner of heroes—to the music of the drum, which ceased not till they had traversed the common and were come into a narrow lane.

And now Partridge, who kept even pace with Jones, discovered something painted flying in the air a very few yards before him, which fancying to be the colours of the enemy, he fell a-bellowing, "Oh, Lord, sir, here they are; there is the crown and coffin. Oh, Lord! I never saw anything so terrible, and we are within gun-shot of them already."

Jones no sooner looked up than he plainly perceived what it was which Partridge had thus mistaken. "Partridge," says he, "I fancy you will be able to engage this whole army yourself; for by the colours, I guess what the drum was which we heard before, and which beats up for recruits to a puppet-show."

"A puppet-show!" answered Partridge with most eager transport. "And is it really no more than that? I love a puppet-show of all the pastimes upon earth. Do, good sir, let us tarry and see it. Besides, I am quite famished to death, for it is now almost dark and I have not eat a morsel since three o'clock in the morning."

They now arrived at an inn, or indeed an ale-house, where Jones was prevailed upon to stop, the rather as he had no longer any assurance of being in the road he desired. They walked both directly into the kitchen, where Jones began to inquire if no ladies had passed that way in the morning and Partridge as eagerly examined into the state of their provisions; and indeed, his inquiry met with the better success, for Jones could not hear news of Sophia, but Partridge to his great satisfaction found good reason to expect very shortly the agreeable sight of an excellent smoking dish of eggs and bacon.

In strong and healthy constitutions love hath a very different effect from what it causes in the puny part of the species. In the latter it generally destroys all that appetite which tends towards the conservation of the individual; but in the former, though it often induces forgetfulness and a neglect of food, as well as of everything else, yet place a good piece of well-powdered buttock before a hungry lover, and he seldom fails very handsomely to play his part. Thus it happened in the present case; for though Jones perhaps wanted a prompter, and might have travelled much farther, had he been alone, with an empty stomach, yet no sooner did he sit down to the bacon and eggs than he fell to as heartily and voraciously as Partridge himself.

Before our travellers had finished their dinner, night came on, and as the moon was now past the full, it was extremely dark. Partridge, therefore, prevailed on Jones to stay and see the puppet-show, which was just going to begin and to which they were very eagerly invited by the master of the said show, who declared that his figures were the finest which the world had ever produced and that they had given great satisfaction to all the quality in every town in England.

The puppet-show was performed with great regularity and decency. It was called the fine and serious part of the *Provoked Husband,* and it was, indeed, a very grave and solemn entertainment, without any low wit or humour or jests; or, to do it no more than justice, without anything which could provoke a laugh. The audience were all highly pleased. A grave matron told the master she would bring her two daughters the next night, as he did not show any stuff, and an attorney's clerk and an exciseman both declared that the characters of Lord and Lady Townley were well preserved and highly in nature. Partridge likewise concurred with this opinion.

The master was so highly elated with these encomiums that he could not refrain from adding some more of his own. He said the present age was not improved in anything so much as in their puppet-shows, which by throwing out Punch and his wife Joan, and such idle trumpery, were at last brought to be a rational entertainment. "I remember," said he, "when I first took to the business, there was a great deal of low stuff that did very well to make folks laugh, but was never calculated to improve the morals of young people, which certainly ought to be principally aimed at in every puppet-show; for why may not good and instructive lessons be conveyed this way as well as any other? My figures are as big as the life, and they represent the life in every particular, and I question not but people rise from my little drama as much improved as they do from the great." "I would by no means degrade the ingenuity of your profession," answered Jones, "but I should have been glad to have seen my old acquaintance Master Punch, for all that; and so far from improving, I think by leaving out him and his merry wife, Joan, you have spoiled your puppet-show."

The dancer of wires conceived an immediate and high contempt for Jones from these words. And with much disdain in his countenance he replied, "Very probably, sir, that may be your opinion; but I have the satisfaction to know the best judges differ from you, and it is impossible to please every taste. I confess, indeed, some of the quality at Bath two or three years ago wanted mightily to bring Punch again upon the stage. I believe I lost some money for not agreeing to it, but let others do as they will, a little matter shall never bribe me to degrade my own profession, nor will I ever willingly consent to the spoiling the decency and regularity of my stage by introducing any such low stuff upon it."

"Right, friend," cries the clerk; "you are very right. Always avoid what is low. There are several of my acquaintance in London who are resolved to drive everything which is low from the stage." "Nothing can be more proper," cries the exciseman, pulling his pipe from his mouth. "I remember," added he, "(for I then lived with my lord) I was in the footman's gallery the night when this play of the *Provoked Husband* was acted first. There was a great deal of low stuff in it about a country-gentleman come up to town to stand for Parliament-man, and there they brought a parcel of his servants upon the stage—his coachman I remember particularly—but the gentlemen in our gallery could not bear anything so low, and they damned it. I observe, friend, you have left all that matter out, and you are to be commended for it."

"Nay, gentlemen," cries Jones, "I can never maintain my opinion against so many; indeed, if the generality of his audience dislike him, the learned gentleman who conducts the show may have done very right in dismissing Punch from his service."

The master of the show then began a second harangue, and said much of the great force of example and how much the inferior part of mankind would be deterred from vice by observing how odious it was in their superiors, when he was unluckily interrupted by an incident which, though perhaps we might have omitted it at another time, we cannot help relating at present, but not in this chapter.

6

FROM WHICH IT MAY BE INFERRED THAT THE BEST THINGS ARE LIABLE TO BE MISUNDERSTOOD AND MISINTERPRETED

A violent uproar now arose in the entry, where my landlady was well cuffing her maid both with her fist and tongue. She had, indeed, missed the wench from her employment, and after a little search had found her on the puppet-show stage in company with the merry-andrew, and in a situation not very proper to be described.

Though Grace (for that was her name) had forfeited all title to modesty, yet had she not impudence enough to deny a fact in which she was actually surprised; she therefore took another turn and attempted to mitigate the offence. "Why do you beat me in this manner, mistress?" cries the wench. "If you don't like my doings, you may turn me away. If I am a w—e" (for the other had liberally bestowed that appellation on her), "my betters are so as well as I. What was the fine lady in the puppet-show just now? I suppose she did not lie all night out from her husband for nothing."

The landlady now burst into the kitchen and fell foul on both her husband and the poor puppet-mover. "Here, husband," says she, "you see the consequence of harbouring these people in your house. If one doth draw a little drink the more for them, one is hardly made amends for the litter they make, and then to have one's house made a bawdy-house of by such lousy vermin. In short, I desire you would be gone to-morrow morning, for I will tolerate no more such doings. It is only the way to teach our servants idleness and nonsense; for to be sure, nothing better can be learned by such idle shows as these. I remember when puppet-shows were made of good Scripture stories, as 'Jephtha's Rash Vow' and such good things, and when wicked people were carried away by the Devil. There was some sense in those matters, but as the parson told us last Sunday, nobody believes in the Devil now-a-days; and here you bring about a parcel of puppets dressed up like lords and ladies only to turn the heads of poor country-wenches, and when their heads are once turned topsy-turvy, no wonder everything else is so."

Virgil, I think, tells us that when the mob are assembled in a riotous and tumultuous manner and all sorts of missile weapons fly about, if a man of gravity and authority appears amongst them, the tumult is presently appeased and the mob, which when collected into one body may be well compared to an ass, erect their long ears at the grave man's discourse.

On the contrary, when a set of grave men and philosophers are disputing, when Wisdom herself may in a manner be considered as present and administering arguments to the disputants, should a tumult arise among the mob, or should one scold, who is herself equal in noise to a mighty mob, appear among the said philosophers, their disputes cease in a moment, Wisdom no longer performs her ministerial office, and the attention of every one is immediately attracted by the scold alone.

Thus, the uproar aforesaid and the arrival of the landlady silenced the mastery of the puppet-show, and put a speedy and final end to that grave and solemn harangue of which we have given the reader a sufficient taste already. Nothing indeed could have happened so very inopportune as this accident; the most wanton malice of Fortune could not have contrived such another stratagem to confound the poor fellow while he was so triumphantly descanting on the good morals inculcated by his exhibitions. His mouth was now as effectually stopped as that of a quack must be if in the midst of a declamation on the great virtues of his pills and powders, the corpse of one of his martyrs should be brought forth and deposited before the stage as a testimony of his skill.

Instead, therefore, of answering my landlady, the puppet-show man ran out to punish his merry-andrew; and now the moon beginning to put forth her silver light, as the poets call it (though she looked at that time more like a piece of copper), Jones called for his reckoning and ordered Partridge, whom my landlady had just awaked from a profound nap, to prepare for his journey; but Partridge having lately carried two points, as my reader hath seen before, was emboldened to attempt a third, which was to prevail with Jones to take up a lodging that evening in the house where he then was. He introduced this with an affected surprise at the intention which Mr. Jones declared of removing, and after urging many excellent arguments against it, he at last insisted strongly that it could be to no manner of purpose whatever; for that unless Jones knew which way the lady was gone, every step he took might very possibly lead him the farther from her; "for you find, sir," said he, "by all the people in the house, that she is not gone this way. How much better, therefore, would it be to stay till the morning, when we may expect to meet with somebody to inquire of?"

This last argument had indeed some effect on Jones, and while he was weighing it the landlord threw all the rhetoric of which he was master into the same scale. "Sure, sir," said he, "your servant gives you most excellent advice, for who would travel by night at this time of the year?" He then began in the usual style to trumpet forth the excellent accommodation which his house afforded, and my landlady likewise opened on the occasion. But not to detain the reader with what is common to every host and hostess, it is sufficient to tell him Jones was at last prevailed on to stay and refresh himself with a few hours' rest, which indeed he very much wanted, for he had hardly shut his eyes since he had left the inn where the accident of the broken head had happened.

As soon as Jones had taken a resolution to proceed no farther that night, he presently retired to rest with his two bedfellows, the pocket-book and the muff, but Partridge, who at several times had refreshed himself with several naps, was more inclined to eating than to sleeping, and more to drinking than to either.

And now, the storm which Grace had raised being at an end and my landlady being again reconciled to the puppet-man, who on his side forgave the indecent reflections which the good woman in her passion had cast on his performances, a face of perfect peace and tranquillity reigned in the kitchen, where there assembled round the fire the landlord and landlady of the house, the master of the puppet-show, the attorney's clerk, the exciseman, and the ingenious Mr. Partridge; in which company passed the agreeable conversation which will be found in the next chapter.

CONTAINING A REMARK OR TWO OF OUR OWN, AND MANY
MORE OF THE GOOD COMPANY ASSEMBLED IN THE KITCHEN

Though the pride of Partridge did not submit to acknowledge
himself a servant, yet he condescended in most particulars to
imitate the manners of that rank. One instance of this was
his greatly magnifying the fortune of his companion, as he
called Jones; such is a general custom with all servants
among strangers, as none of them would willingly be thought
the attendant on a beggar, for the higher the situation of the
master is, the higher consequently is that of the man in his
own opinion; the truth of which observation appears from
the behaviour of all the footmen of the nobility.

But though title and fortune communicate a splendour all
around them, and the footmen of men of quality and of
estate think themselves entitled to a part of that respect which
is paid to the quality and estates of their masters, it is clearly
otherwise with regard to virtue and understanding. These
advantages are strictly personal and swallow themselves all
the respect which is paid to them. To say the truth, this is
so very little that they cannot well afford to let any others
partake with them. As these therefore reflect no honour
on the domestic, so neither is he at all dishonoured by
the most deplorable want of both in his master. Indeed, it
is otherwise in the want of what is called virtue in a mistress,
the consequence of which we have before seen; for in this
dishonour there is a kind of contagion, which, like that of
poverty, communicates itself to all who approach it.

Now, for these reasons we are not to wonder that servants
(I mean among the men only) should have so great regard for the reputation of the wealth of their masters, and
little or none at all for their character in other points; and
that though they would be ashamed to be the footman of a
beggar, they are not so to attend upon a rogue or a blockhead, and do consequently make no scruple to spread the
fame of the iniquities and follies of their said masters as
far as possible, and this often with great humour and merriment. In reality, a footman is often a wit, as well as a beau,
at the expense of the gentleman whose livery he wears.

After Partridge, therefore, had enlarged greatly on the

vast fortune to which Mr. Jones was heir, he very freely communicated an apprehension which he had begun to conceive the day before and for which, as we hinted at that very time, the behaviour of Jones seemed to have furnished a sufficient foundation. In short, he was now pretty well confirmed in an opinion that his master was out of his wits, with which opinion he very bluntly acquainted the good company round the fire.

With this sentiment the puppet-show man immediately coincided. "I own," said he, "the gentleman surprised me very much when he talked so absurdly about puppet-shows. It is, indeed, hardly to be conceived that any man in his senses should be so much mistaken; what you say now accounts very well for all his monstrous notions. Poor gentleman, I am heartily concerned for him; indeed, he hath a strange wildness about his eyes, which I took notice of before, though I did not mention it."

The landlord agreed with this last assertion and likewise claimed the sagacity of having observed it. "And certainly," added he, "it must be so; for no one but a madman would have thought of leaving so good a house to ramble about the country at that time of night."

The exciseman, pulling his pipe from his mouth, said he thought the gentleman looked and talked a little wildly, and then, turning to Partridge, "If he be a madman," says he, "he should not be suffered to travel thus about the country, for possibly he may do some mischief. It is pity he was not secured and sent home to his relations."

Now, some conceits of this kind were likewise lurking in the mind of Partridge; for as he was now persuaded that Jones had run away from Mr. Allworthy, he promised himself the highest rewards if he could by any means convey him back. But fear of Jones, of whose fierceness and strength he had seen and, indeed, felt some instances, had, however, represented any such scheme as impossible to be executed, and had discouraged him from applying himself to form any regular plan for the purpose. But no sooner did he hear the sentiments of the exciseman than he embraced that opportunity of declaring his own and expressed a hearty wish that such a matter could be brought about.

"Could be brought about?" says the exciseman. "Why, there is nothing easier."

"Ah, sir," answered Partridge, "you don't know what a devil of a fellow he is. He can take me up with one hand

and throw me out at window, and he would, too, if he did but imagine——"

"Pogh!" says the exciseman. "I believe I am as good a man as he. Besides, here are five of us."

"I don't know what five," cries the landlady; "my husband shall have nothing to do in it. Nor shall any violent hands be laid upon anybody in my house. The young gentleman is as pretty a young gentleman as ever I saw in my life, and I believe he is no more mad than any of us. What do you tell of his having a wild look with his eyes? They are the prettiest eyes I ever saw, and he hath the prettiest look with them; and a very modest civil young man he is. I am sure I have bepitied him heartily ever since the gentleman there in the corner told us he was crossed in love. Certainly it is enough to make any man, especially such a sweet young gentleman as he is, to look a little otherwise than he did before. Lady indeed! What the devil would the lady have better than such a handsome man with a great estate? I suppose she is one of your quality-folks, one of your Townley ladies that we saw last night in the puppet-show, who don't know what they would be at."

The attorney's clerk likewise declared he would have no concern in the business without the advice of counsel. "Suppose," says he, "an action of false imprisonment should be brought against us; what defence could we make? Who knows what may be sufficient evidence of madness to a jury? But I only speak upon my own account, for it don't look well for a lawyer to be concerned in these matters unless it be as a lawyer. Juries are always less favourable to us than to other people. I don't therefore dissuade you, Mr. Thompson" (to the exciseman), "nor the gentleman, nor anybody else."

The exciseman shook his head at this speech, and the puppet-show man said madness was sometimes a difficult matter for a jury to decide; "for I remember," says he, "I was once present at a trial of madness where twenty witnesses swore that the person was as mad as a March hare, and twenty others that he was as much in his senses as any man in England. And indeed, it was the opinion of most people that it was only a trick of his relations to rob the poor man of his right."

"Very likely!" cries the landlady. "I myself knew a poor gentleman who was kept in a madhouse all his life by his family, and they enjoyed his estate; but it did them no good, for though the law gave it them, it was the right of another."

"Pogh!" cries the clerk with great contempt. "Who hath any right but what the law gives them? If the law gave me the best estate in the country, I should never trouble myself much who had the right."

"If it be so," says Partridge, "*Felix quem faciunt aliena pericula cautum.*"

My landlord, who had been called out by the arrival of a horseman at the gate, now returned into the kitchen and with an affrighted countenance cried out, "What do you think, gentlemen? The rebels have given the Duke the slip and are got almost to London. It is certainly true, for a man on horse-back just now told me so."

"I am glad of it with all my heart," cries Partridge; "then there will be no fighting in these parts."

"I am glad," cries the clerk, "for a better reason, for I would always have right take place."

"Ay, but," answered the landlord, "I have heard some people say this man hath no right."

"I will prove the contrary in a moment," cries the clerk: "if my father dies seized of a right, do you mind me, seized of a right, I say, doth not that right descend to his son? And doth not one right descend as well as another?"

"But how can he have any right to make us papishes?" says the landlord.

"Never fear that," cries Partridge. "As to the matter of right, the gentleman there hath proved it as clear as the sun, and as to the matter of religion, it is quite out of the case. The papists themselves don't expect any such thing. A popish priest whom I know very well and who is a very honest man told me upon his word and honour they had no such design."

"And another priest of my acquaintance," said the land-lady, "hath told me the same thing. But my husband is always so afraid of papishes. I know a great many papishes that are very honest sort of people and spend their money very freely, and it is always a maxim with me that one man's money is as good as another's."

"Very true, mistress," said the puppet-show man; "I don't care what religion comes, provided the Presbyterians are not uppermost, for they are enemies to puppet-shows."

"And so you would sacrifice your religion to your interest," cries the exciseman, "and are desirous to see popery brought in, are you?"

"Not I, truly," answered the other. "I hate popery as much as any man, but yet it is a comfort to one that one should be able to live under it, which I could not do among Presbyterians. To be sure, every man values his livelihood first, that must be granted; and I warrant if you would confess the truth, you are more afraid of losing your place than anything else, but never fear, friend, there will be an excise under another government as well as under this."

"Why, certainly," replied the exciseman, "I should be a very ill man if I did not honour the king, whose bread I eat. That is no more than natural, as a man may say; for what signifies it to me that there would be an excise-office under another government since my friends would be out and I could expect no better than to follow them. No, no, friend, I shall never be bubbled out of my religion in hopes only of keeping my place under another government, for I should certainly be no better and very probably might be worse."

"Why, that is what I say," cries the landlord, "whenever folks say who knows what may happen. Odsooks! Should not I be a blockhead to lend my money to I know not who because mayhap he may return it again? I am sure it is safe in my own bureau, and there I will keep it."

The attorney's clerk had taken a great fancy to the sagacity of Partridge. Whether this proceeded from the great discernment which the former had into men as well as things, or whether it arose from the sympathy between their minds, for they were both truly Jacobites in principle, they now shook hands heartily and drank bumpers of strong beer to healths which we think proper to bury in oblivion.

These healths were afterwards pledged by all present, and even by my landlord himself, though reluctantly, but he could not withstand the menaces of the clerk, who swore he would never set his foot within his house again if he refused. The bumpers which were swallowed on this occasion soon put an end to the conversation. Here, therefore, we will put an end to the chapter.

IN WHICH FORTUNE SEEMS TO HAVE BEEN IN A BETTER
HUMOUR WITH JONES THAN WE HAVE HITHERTO SEEN HER

As there is no wholesomer, so perhaps there are few
stronger, sleeping potions than fatigue. Of this Jones might
be said to have taken a very large dose, and it operated
very forcibly upon him. He had already slept nine hours,
and might perhaps have slept longer, had he not been awakened by a most violent noise at his chamber-door, where
the sound of many heavy blows was accompanied with
many exclamations of murder. Jones presently leapt from
his bed, where he found the master of the puppet-show be-
labouring the back and ribs of his poor merry-andrew without either mercy or moderation.

Jones instantly interposed on behalf of the suffering party
and pinned the insulting conqueror up to the wall; for the
puppet-show man was no more able to contend with Jones
than the poor parti-coloured jester had been to contend
with this puppet-man.

But though the merry-andrew was a little fellow and not
very strong, he had nevertheless some choler about him. He
therefore no sooner found himself delivered from the enemy
than he began to attack him with the only weapon at
which he was his equal. From this he first discharged a
volley of general abusive words, and thence proceeded to
some particular accusations: "D——n your bl——d, you rascal,"
says he. "I have not only supported you, for you owe all the
money you get to me, but I have saved you from the gallows. Did you not want to rob the lady of her fine riding-
habit no longer ago than yesterday in the back lane here?
Can you deny that you wished to have had her alone in a
wood to strip her, to strip one of the prettiest ladies that
ever was seen in the world? And here you have fallen upon
me and have almost murdered me for doing no harm to a
girl as willing as myself, only because she likes me better
than you."

Jones no sooner heard this than he quitted the master, laying at the same time the most violent injunctions of for-
bearance from any further insult on the merry-andrew,
and then, taking the poor wretch with him into his own

apartment, he soon learnt tidings of his Sophia, whom the fellow as he was attending his master with his drum the day before had seen pass by. He easily prevailed with the lad to show him the exact place, and then, having summoned Partridge, he departed with the utmost expedition.

It was almost eight of the clock before all matters could be got ready for his departure; for Partridge was not in any haste, nor could the reckoning be presently adjusted; and when both these were settled and over, Jones would not quit the place before he had perfectly reconciled all differences between the master and the man.

When this was happily accomplished, he set forwards, and was by the trusty merry-andrew conducted to the spot by which Sophia had passed; and then, having handsomely rewarded his conductor, he again pushed on with the utmost eagerness, being highly delighted with the extraordinary manner in which he had received his intelligence. Of this Partridge was no sooner acquainted than he with great earnestness began to prophesy, and assured Jones that he would certainly have good success in the end; for, he said, two such accidents could never have happened to direct him after his mistress if Providence had not designed to bring them together at last. And this was the first time that Jones lent any attention to the superstitious doctrines of his companion.

They had not gone above two miles when a violent storm of rain overtook them, and as they happened to be at the same time in sight of an ale-house, Partridge with much earnest entreaty prevailed with Jones to enter and weather the storm. Hunger is an enemy (if indeed it may be called one) which partakes more of the English than of the French disposition; for though you subdue this never so often, it will always rally again in time, and so it did with Partridge, who was no sooner arrived within the kitchen than he began to ask the same questions which he had asked the night before. The consequence of this was an excellent cold chine being produced upon the table, upon which not only Partridge but Jones himself made a very hearty breakfast, though the latter began to grow again uneasy, as the people of the house could give him no fresh information concerning Sophia.

Their meal being over, Jones was again preparing to sally, notwithstanding the violence of the storm still continued, but Partridge begged heartily for another mug, and at last, casting his eyes on a lad at the fire, who had entered into the kitchen and who at that instant was looking as earnestly at him, he turned suddenly to Jones and cried, "Master, give me your hand; a single mug shan't serve the turn this bout. Why, here's more news of Madam Sophia come to town. The boy there standing by the fire is the very lad that rode before her. I can swear to my own plaister on his face." "Heavens bless you, sir," cries the boy; "it is your own plaister sure enough; I shall have always reason to remember your goodness, for it hath almost cured me."

At these words Jones started from his chair and, bidding the boy follow him immediately, departed from the kitchen into a private apartment; for so delicate was he with regard to Sophia that he never willingly mentioned her name in the presence of many people, and though he had, as it were, from the overflowings of his heart given Sophia as a toast among the officers, where he thought it was impossible she should be known, yet even there the reader may remember how difficultly he was prevailed upon to mention her surname.

Hard, therefore, was it and, perhaps, in the opinion of many sagacious readers, very absurd and monstrous, that he should principally owe his present misfortune to the supposed want of that delicacy with which he so abounded; for in reality Sophia was much more offended at the freedoms which she thought, and not without good reason, he had taken with her name and character than at any freedoms in which, under his present circumstances, he had indulged himself with the person of another woman; and to say truth, I believe Honour would never have prevailed on her to leave Upton without seeing her Jones had it not been for those two strong instances of a levity in his behaviour, so void of all respect and, indeed, so highly inconsistent with any degree of love and tenderness in great and delicate minds.

But so matters fell out, and so I must relate them; and if any reader is shocked at their appearing unnatural, I cannot help it. I must remind such persons that I am not writing a system but a history, and I am not obliged to reconcile every matter to the received notions concerning truth and nature. But if this was never so easy to do, perhaps it might be more prudent in me to avoid it. For instance, as the fact at present before us now stands without any comment of mine upon it, though it may at first sight offend some readers, yet upon more mature consideration it must please all; for wise and good men may consider what happened to Jones at Upton as a just punishment for his wickedness with regard to women, of which it was indeed the immediate consequence, and silly and bad persons may comfort themselves in their vices by flattering their own hearts that the characters of men are rather owing to accident than to virtue. Now, perhaps the reflections which we should be here inclined to draw would alike contradict both these conclusions, and would show that these incidents contribute only to confirm the great, useful, and uncommon doctrine which it is the purpose of this whole work to inculcate and which we must not fill up our pages by frequently repeating, as an ordinary parson fills his sermon by repeating his text at the end of every paragraph.

We are contented that it must appear, however unhappily Sophia had erred in her opinion of Jones, she had sufficient reason for her opinion, since, I believe, every other young lady would in her situation have erred in the same manner. Nay, had she followed her lover at this very time, and had entered this very ale-house the moment he was departed from it, she would have found the landlord as well acquainted with her name and person as the wench at Upton had appeared to be; for while Jones was examining his boy in whispers in an inner room Partridge, who had no such delicacy in his disposition, was in the kitchen very openly catechizing the other guide who had attended Mrs. Fitzpatrick, by which means the landlord, whose ears were open on all such occasions, became perfectly well acquainted with the tumble of Sophia from her horse, &c., with the mistake concerning Jenny Cameron, with the many consequences of the punch, and, in short, with almost everything which had happened at the inn whence we dispatched our ladies in a coach and six when we last took our leaves of them.

9

CONTAINING LITTLE MORE THAN A FEW ODD OBSERVATIONS

Jones had been absent a full half-hour when he returned into the kitchen in a hurry, desiring the landlord to let him know that instant what was to pay. And now the concern which Partridge felt at being obliged to quit the warm chimney-corner and a cup of excellent liquor was somewhat compensated by hearing that he was to proceed no farther on foot, for Jones by golden arguments had prevailed with the boy to attend him back to the inn whither he had before conducted Sophia; but to this, however, the lad consented upon condition that the other guide would wait for him at the ale-house because, as the landlord at Upton was an intimate acquaintance of the landlord at Gloucester, it might some time or other come to the ears of the latter that his horses had been let to more than one person, and so the boy might be brought to account for money which he wisely intended to put in his own pocket.

We were obliged to mention this circumstance, trifling as it may seem, since it retarded Mr. Jones a considerable time in his setting out; for the honesty of this latter boy was somewhat high—that is, somewhat high-priced—and would indeed have cost Jones very dear had not Partridge, who, as we have said, was a very cunning fellow, artfully thrown in half a crown to be spent at that very ale-house while the boy was waiting for his companion. This half-crown the landlord no sooner got scent of than he opened after it with such vehement and persuasive outcry that the boy was soon overcome and consented to take half a crown more for his stay. Here we cannot help observing that, as there is so much of policy in the lowest life, great men often overvalue themselves on those refinements in imposture in which they are frequently excelled by some of the lowest of the human species.

The horses being now produced, Jones directly leapt into the side-saddle on which his dear Sophia had rid. The lad indeed very civilly offered him the use of his, but he chose the side-saddle, probably because it was softer. Partridge, however, though full as effeminate as Jones, could not bear the thoughts of degrading his manhood; he therefore accepted the boy's offer, and now Jones being mounted on the side-saddle of his Sophia, the boy on that of Mrs. Honour, and Partridge bestriding the third horse, they set forwards on their journey, and within four hours arrived at the inn where the reader hath already spent so much time. Partridge was in very high spirits during the whole way, and often mentioned to Jones the many good omens of his future success which had lately befriended him, and which the reader without being the least superstitious must allow to have been peculiarly fortunate. Partridge was, moreover, better pleased with the present pursuit of his companion than he had been with his pursuit of glory, and from these very omens, which assured the pedagogue of success, he likewise first acquired a clear idea of the amour between Jones and Sophia, to which he had before given very little attention, as he had originally taken a wrong scent concerning the reasons of Jones's departure; and as to what happened at Upton, he was too much frightened just before and after his leaving that place to draw any other conclusions from thence than that Jones was a downright madman—a conceit which was not at all disagreeable to the opinion he before had of his extraordinary wildness, of which, he thought, his behaviour on their quitting Gloucester so well justified all the accounts he had formerly received. He was now, however, pretty well satisfied with his present expedition, and henceforth began to conceive much worthier sentiments of his friend's understanding.

The clock had just struck three when they arrived, and Jones immediately bespoke post-horses, but unluckily there was not a horse to be procured in the whole place; which the reader will not wonder at when he considers the hurry in which the whole nation, and especially this part of it, was at this time engaged, when expresses were passing and repassing every hour of the day and night.

Jones endeavoured all he could to prevail with his former guide to escort him to Coventry, but he was inexorable. While he was arguing with the boy in the inn-yard a person came up to him and, saluting him by his name, inquired how all the good family did in Somersetshire; and now Jones, casting his eyes upon this person, presently discovered him to be Mr. Dowling, the lawyer with whom he had dined at Gloucester, and with much courtesy returned his salutation.

Dowling very earnestly pressed Mr. Jones to go no further that night, and backed his solicitations with many unanswerable arguments, such as that it was almost dark, that the roads were very dirty, and that he would be able to travel much better by daylight; with many others equally good, some of which Jones had probably suggested to himself before, but as they were then ineffectual, so they were still, and he continued resolute in his design even though he should be obliged to set out on foot.

When the good attorney found he could not prevail on Jones to stay, he as strenuously applied himself to persuade the guide to accompany him. He urged many motives to induce him to undertake this short journey, and at last concluded with saying, "Do you think the gentleman won't very well reward you for your trouble?"

Two to one are odds at every other thing as well as at football. But the advantage which this united force hath in persuasion or entreaty must have been visible to a curious observer; for he must have often seen that when a father, a master, a wife, or any other person in authority have stoutly adhered to a denial against all the reasons which a single man could produce, they have afterwards yielded to the repetition of the same sentiments by a second or third person who hath undertaken the cause without attempting to advance anything new in its behalf. And hence, perhaps, proceeds the phrase of seconding an argument or a motion, and the great consequence this is in all assemblies of public debate. Hence, likewise, probably it is that in our courts of law we often hear a learned gentleman (generally a sergeant) repeating for an hour together what another learned gentleman who spoke before him had just been saying.

Instead of accounting for this, we shall proceed in our usual manner to exemplify it in the conduct of the lad above mentioned, who submitted to the persuasions of Mr. Dowling and promised once more to admit Jones into his side-saddle, but insisted on first giving the poor creatures a good bait, saying they had travelled a great ways, and been rid very hard. Indeed, this caution of the boy was needless; for Jones, notwithstanding his hurry and impatience, would have ordered this of himself, for he by no means agreed with the opinions of those who consider animals as mere machines, and when they bury their spurs in the belly of their horse imagine the spur and the horse to have an equal capacity of feeling pain.

While the beasts were eating their corn, or rather were supposed to eat it (for as the boy was taking care of himself in the kitchen, the ostler took great care that his corn should not be consumed in the stable), Mr. Jones at the earnest desire of Mr. Dowling accompanied that gentleman into his room, where they sat down together over a bottle of wine.

IN WHICH MR. JONES AND MR. DOWLING DRINK A BOTTLE TOGETHER

Mr. Dowling, pouring out a glass of wine, named the health of the good Squire Allworthy, adding, "If you please, sir, we will likewise remember his nephew and heir, the young squire; come, sir, here's Mr. Blifil to you, a very pretty young gentleman, and who, I dare swear, will hereafter make a very considerable figure in his country. I have a borough for him myself in my eye."

"Sir," answered Jones, "I am convinced you don't intend to affront me, so I shall not resent it, but I promise you, you have joined two persons very improperly together; for one is the glory of the human species and the other is a rascal who dishonours the name of a man."

Dowling stared at this. He said he thought both the gentlemen had a very unexceptionable character. "As for Squire Allworthy himself," says he, "I never had the happiness to see him, but all the world talks of his goodness. And indeed, as to the young gentleman, I never saw him but once, when I carried him the news of the loss of his mother, and then I was so hurried and drove and tore with the multiplicity of buisness that I had hardly time to converse with him; but he looked so like a very honest gentleman and behaved himself so prettily that I protest I never was more delighted with any gentleman since I was born."

"I don't wonder," answered Jones, "that he should impose upon you in so short an acquaintance, for he hath the cunning of the Devil himself, and you may live with him many years without discovering him. I was bred up with him from my infancy, and we were hardly ever asunder, but it is very lately only that I have discovered half the villainy which is in him. I own I never greatly liked him. I thought he wanted that generosity of spirit which is the sure foundation of all that is great and noble in human nature. I saw a selfishness in him long ago which I despised, but it is lately, very lately, that I have found him capable of the basest and blackest designs; for indeed I have at last found out that he hath taken an advantage of the openness of my own temper and hath concerted the deepest project, by a long train of wicked artifice, to work my ruin, which at last he hath effected."

"Ay! Ay!" cries Dowling. "I protest, then, it is a pity such a person should inherit the great estate of your uncle Allworthy."

"Alas, sir," cries Jones, "you do me an honour to which I have no title. It is true, indeed, his goodness once allowed me the liberty of calling him by a much nearer name, but as this was a voluntary act of goodness only, I can complain of no injustice when he thinks proper to deprive me of this honour, since the loss cannot be more unmerited than the gift originally was. I assure you, sir, I am no relation of Mr. Allworthy, and if the world, who are incapable of setting a true value on his virtue, should think in his behaviour by me he hath dealt hardly by a relation, they do an injustice to the best of men; for I——but I ask your pardon; I shall trouble you with no particulars relating to myself; only as you seemed to think me a relation of Mr. Allworthy, I thought proper to set you right in a matter that might draw some censures upon him, which I promise you I would rather lose my life than give occasion to."

"I protest, sir," cried Dowling, "you talk very much like a man of honour, but instead of giving me any trouble, I protest it would give me great pleasure to know how you came to be thought a relation of Mr. Allworthy's if you are not. Your horses won't be ready this half-hour, and as you have sufficient opportunity, I wish you would tell me how all that happened, for I protest it seems very surprising that you should pass for a relation of a gentleman without being so."

Jones, who in the compliance of his disposition (though not in his prudence) a little resembled his lovely Sophia, was easily prevailed on to satisfy Mr. Dowling's curiosity by relating the history of his birth and education, which he did, like Othello,

> ————even from his boyish years,
> To th' very moment he was bade to tell;

the which to hear, Dowling, like Desdemona, did *seriously incline;*

> He swore 'twas strange, 'twas passing strange;
> 'Twas pitiful, 'twas wondrous pitiful.

Mr. Dowling was indeed very greatly affected with this relation, for he had not divested himself of humanity by being an attorney. Indeed, nothing is more unjust than to carry our prejudices against a profession into private life and to borrow our idea of a man from our opinion of his calling. Habit, it is true, lessens the horror of those actions which the profession makes necessary and consequently habitual, but in all other instances, Nature works in men of all professions alike; nay, perhaps even more strongly with those who give her, as it were, a holiday when they are following their ordinary business. A butcher, I make no doubt, would feel compunction at the slaughter of a fine horse; and though a surgeon can conceive no pain in cutting off a limb, I have known him compassionate a man in a fit of the gout. The common hangman, who hath stretched the necks of hundreds, is known to have trembled at his first operation on a head; and the very professors of human blood, who in their trade of war butcher thousands, not only of their fellow-professors but often of women and children, without remorse, even these, I say, in times of peace, when drums and trumpets are laid aside, often lay aside all their ferocity and become very gentle members of civil society. In the same manner an attorney may feel all the miseries and distresses of his fellow-creatures, provided he happens not to be concerned against them.

Jones, as the reader knows, was yet unacquainted with the very black colours in which he had been represented to Mr. Allworthy, and as to other matters, he did not show them in the most disadvantageous light; for though he was unwilling to cast any blame on his former friend and patron, yet he was not very desirous of heaping too much upon himself. Dowling therefore observed, and not without reason, that very ill offices must have been done him by somebody; "for certainly," cries he, "the squire would never have disinherited you only for a few faults which any young gentleman might have committed. Indeed, I cannot properly say disinherited, for to be sure, by law you cannot claim as heir. That's certain; that nobody need go to counsel for. Yet when a gentleman had in a manner adopted you thus as his own son, you might reasonably have expected some very considerable part if not the whole; nay, if you had expected the whole, I should not have blamed you, for certainly every one is for getting as much as they can, and they are not to be blamed on that account."

"Indeed you wrong me," said Jones; "I should have been contented with very little; I never had any view upon Mr. Allworthy's fortune; nay, I believe I may truly say I never once considered what he could or might give me. This I solemnly declare: if he had done a prejudice to his nephew in my favour, I would have undone it again. I had rather enjoy my own mind than the fortune of another man. What is the poor pride arising from a magnificent house, a numerous equipage, a splendid table, and from all the other advantages or appearances of fortune compared to the warm, solid content, the swelling satisfaction, the thrilling transports, and the exulting triumphs which a good mind enjoys in the contemplation of a generous, virtuous, noble, benevolent action? I envy not Blifil in the prospect of his wealth, nor shall I envy him in the possession of it. I would not think myself a rascal half an hour to exchange situations. I believe, indeed, Mr. Blifil suspected me of the views you mention, and I suppose these suspicions, as they arose from the baseness of his own heart, so they occasioned his baseness to me. But, I thank heaven, I know, I feel—I feel my innocence, my friend; and I would not part with that feeling for the world. For as long as I know I have never done, nor even designed, an injury to any being whatever,

> *Pone me pigris ubi nulla campis*
> *Arbor æstiva recreatur aura,*
> *Quod latus mundi nebulæ, malusque*
> *Jupiter urget.*
>
> *Pone sub curru nimium propinqui*
> *Solis in terra domibus negata;*
> *Dulce ridentem Lalagen amabo,*
> *Dulce loquentem.**

He then filled a bumper of wine and drank it off to the health of his dear Lalage and, filling Dowling's glass like-

* Place me where never summer breeze
Unbinds the glebe or warms the trees;
Where ever-lowering clouds appear,
And angry Jove deforms th' inclement year.

Place me beneath the burning ray,
Where rolls the rapid car of day;
Love and the nymph shall charm my toils,
The nymph who sweetly speaks, and sweetly smiles.
                                        MR. FRANCIS.

wise up to the brim, insisted on his pledging him. "Why, then, here's Miss Lalage's health, with all my heart," cries Dowling. "I have heard her toasted often, I protest, though I never saw her, but they say she's extremely handsome."

Though the Latin was not the only part of this speech which Dowling did not perfectly understand, yet there was somewhat in it that made a very strong impression upon him. And though he endeavoured by winking, nodding, sneering, and grinning to hide the impression from Jones (for we are as often ashamed of thinking right as of thinking wrong), it is certain he secretly approved as much of his sentiments as he understood and really felt a very strong impulse of compassion for him. But we may possibly take some other opportunity of commenting upon this, especially if we should happen to meet Mr. Dowling any more in the course of our history. At present we are obliged to take our leave of that gentleman a little abruptly, in imitation of Mr. Jones, who was no sooner informed by Partridge that his horses were ready than he deposited his reckoning, wished his companion a good night, mounted, and set forward towards Coventry, though the night was dark and it just then began to rain very hard.

11

THE DISASTERS WHICH BEFELL JONES ON HIS DEPARTURE FOR
COVENTRY, WITH THE SAGE REMARKS OF PARTRIDGE

No road can be plainer than that from the place they now were to Coventry, and though neither Jones nor Partridge nor the guide had ever travelled it before, it would have been almost impossible to have missed their way had it not been for the two reasons mentioned in the conclusion of the last chapter.

These two circumstances, however, happening both unfortunately to intervene, our travellers deviated into a much less frequented track, and after riding full six miles, instead of arriving at the stately spires of Coventry, they found themselves still in a very dirty lane, where they saw no symptoms of approaching the suburbs of a large city.

Jones now declared that they must certainly have lost their way, but this the guide insisted upon was impossible, a word which in common conversation is often used not only to signify improbable but often what is really very likely, and sometimes what hath certainly happened: an hyperbolical violence like that which is so frequently offered to the words *infinite* and *eternal*, by the former of which it is usual to express a distance of half a yard, and by the latter, a duration of five minutes. And thus it is as usual to assert the impossibility of losing what is already actually lost. This was, in fact, the case at present; for, notwithstanding all the confident assertions of the lad to the contrary, it is certain they were no more in the right road to Coventry than the fraudulent, griping, cruel, canting miser is in the right road to heaven.

It is not, perhaps, easy for a reader who hath never been in those circumstances to imagine the horror with which darkness, rain, and wind fill persons who have lost their way in the night, and who consequently have not the pleasant prospect of warm fires, dry clothes, and other refreshments to support their minds in struggling with the inclemencies of the weather. A very imperfect idea of this horror will, however, serve sufficiently to account for the conceits which now filled the head of Partridge and which we shall presently be obliged to open.

Jones grew more and more positive that they were out of their road, and the boy himself at last acknowledged he believed they were not in the right road to Coventry, though he affirmed at the same time it was impossible they should have missed the way. But Partridge was of a different opinion. He said when they first set out, he imagined some mischief or other would happen. "Did not you observe, sir," said he to Jones, "that old woman who stood at the door just as you was taking horse? I wish you had given her a small matter, with all my heart, for she said then you might repent it, and at that very instant it began to rain and the wind hath continued rising ever since. Whatever some people may think, I am very certain it is in the power of witches to raise the wind whenever they please. I have seen it happen very often in my time, and if ever I saw a witch in all my life, that old woman was certainly one. I thought so to myself at that very time, and if I had had any halfpence in my pocket, I would have given her some; for to be sure, it is always good to be charitable to those sort of people for fear what may happen, and many a person hath lost his cattle by saving a halfpenny."

Jones, though he was horridly vexed at the delay which

this mistake was likely to occasion in his journey, could not help smiling at the superstition of his friend, whom an accident now greatly confirmed in his opinion. This was a tumble from his horse, by which, however, he received no other injury than what the dirt conferred on his clothes.

Partridge had no sooner recovered his legs than he appealed to his fall as conclusive evidence of all he had asserted, but Jones, finding he was unhurt, answered with a smile, "This witch of yours, Partridge, is a most ungrateful jade and doth not, I find, distinguish her friends from others in her resentment. If the old lady had been angry with me for neglecting her, I don't see why she should tumble you from your horse after all the respect you have expressed for her."

"It is ill jesting," cries Partridge, "with people who have power to do these things, for they are often very malicious. I remember a farrier who provoked one of them by asking her when the time she had bargained with the Devil for would be out, and within three months from that very day, one of his best cows was drowned. Nor was she satisfied with that, for a little time afterwards he lost a barrel of best drink; for the old witch pulled out the spigot and let it run all over the cellar the very first evening he had tapped it to make merry with some of his neighbours. In short, nothing ever thrived with him afterwards; for she worried the poor man so that he took to drinking, and in a year or two his stock was seized, and he and his family are now come to the parish."

The guide and perhaps his horse too were both so attentive to this discourse that, either through want of care or by the malice of the witch, they were now both sprawling in the dirt.

Partridge entirely imputed this fall, as he had done his own, to the same cause. He told Mr. Jones it would certainly be his turn next, and earnestly entreated him to return back, and find out the old woman and pacify her. "We shall very soon," added he, "reach the inn; for though we have seemed to go forward, I am very certain we are in the identical place in which we were an hour ago, and I dare swear if it was daylight, we might now see the inn we set out from."

Instead of returning any answer to this sage advice, Jones was entirely attentive to what had happened to the boy, who received no other hurt than what had before befallen Partridge, and which his clothes very easily bore, as they had been for many years inured to the like. He soon regained his side-saddle and, by the hearty curses and blows which he bestowed on his horse, quickly satisfied Mr. Jones that no harm was done.

12

RELATES THAT MR. JONES CONTINUED HIS JOURNEY, CON-
TRARY TO THE ADVICE OF PARTRIDGE, WITH WHAT HAPPENED
ON THAT OCCASION

They now discovered a light at some distance, to the great pleasure of Jones and to the no small terror of Partridge, who firmly believed himself to be bewitched and that this light was a Jack-with-a-lanthorn, or somewhat more mischievous.

But how were these fears increased when, as they approached nearer to this light (or lights, as they now appeared), they heard a confused sound of human voices; of singing, laughing, and hallooing, together with a strange noise that seemed to proceed from some instruments, but could hardly be allowed the name of music. Indeed, to favour a little the opinion of Partridge, it might very well be called music bewitched.

It is impossible to conceive a much greater degree of horror than what now seized on Partridge, the contagion of which had reached the post-boy, who had been very attentive to many things that the other had uttered. He now therefore joined in petitioning Jones to return, saying he firmly believed what Partridge had just before said: that though the horses seemed to go on, they had not moved a step forwards during at least the last half-hour.

Jones could not help smiling in the midst of his vexation at the fears of these poor fellows. "Either we advance," says he, "towards the lights, or the lights have advanced towards us, for we are now at a very little distance from them; but how can either of you be afraid of a set of people who appear only to be merry-making?"

"Merry-making, sir!" cries Partridge. "Who could be merry-making at this time of night, and in such a place, and such weather? They can be nothing but ghosts or witches, or some evil spirits or other, that's certain."

"Let them be what they will," cries Jones, "I am resolved

to go up to them and inquire the way to Coventry. All witches, Partridge, are not such ill-natured hags as that we had the misfortune to meet with last."

"Oh, Lord, sir," cries Partridge, "there is no knowing what humour they will be in; to be sure, it is always best to be civil to them, but what if we should meet with something worse than witches, with evil spirits themselves? Pray, sir, be advised; pray, sir, do. If you had read so many terrible accounts as I have of these matters, you would not be so foolhardy. The Lord knows whither we have got already, or whither we are going; for sure such darkness was never seen upon earth, and I question whether it can be darker in the other world."

Jones put forwards as fast as he could, notwithstanding all these hints and cautions, and poor Partridge was obliged to follow, for though he hardly dared advance, he dared still less to stay behind by himself.

At length they arrived at the place whence the lights and different noises had issued. This Jones perceived to be no other than a barn, where a great number of men and women were assembled and were diverting themselves with much apparent jollity.

Jones no sooner appeared before the great doors of the barn, which were open, than a masculine and very rough voice from within demanded who was there. To which Jones gently answered, "A friend," and immediately asked the road to Coventry.

"If you are a friend," cries another of the men in the barn, "you had better alight till the storm is over" (for indeed it was now more violent than ever); "you are very welcome to put up your horse, for there is sufficient room for him at one end of the barn."

"You are very obliging," returned Jones, "and I will accept your offer for a few minutes whilst the rain continues; and here are two more who will be glad of the same favour." This was accorded with more goodwill than it was accepted; for Partridge would rather have submitted to the utmost inclemency of the weather than have trusted to the clemency of those whom he took for hobgoblins, and the poor postboy was now infected with the same apprehensions; but they were both obliged to follow the example of Jones, the one because he durst not leave his horse, and the other because he feared nothing so much as being left by himself.

Had this history been writ in the days of superstition, I

should have had too much compassion for the reader to have left him so long in suspense whether Beelzebub or Satan was about actually to appear in person with all his hellish retinue, but as these doctrines are at present very unfortunate and have but few if any believers, I have not been much aware of conveying any such terrors. To say truth, the whole furniture of the infernal regions hath long been appropriated by the managers of playhouses, who seem lately to have lain them by as rubbish, capable only of affecting the upper gallery, a place in which few of our readers ever sit.

However, though we do not suspect raising any great terror on this occasion, we have reason to fear some other apprehensions may here arise in our reader, into which we would not willingly betray him; I mean that we are going to take a voyage into Fairyland and to introduce a set of beings into our history which scarce any one was ever childish enough to believe, though many have been foolish enough to spend their time in writing and reading their adventures.

To prevent, therefore, any such suspicions, so prejudicial to the credit of an historian who professes to draw his materials from nature only, we shall now proceed to acquaint the reader who these people were whose sudden appearance had struck such terrors into Partridge, had more than half frightened the post-boy, and had a little surprised even Mr. Jones himself.

The people then assembled in this barn were no other than a company of Egyptians, or, as they are vulgarly called, gipsies, and they were now celebrating the wedding of one of their society.

It is impossible to conceive a happier set of people than appeared here to be met together. The utmost mirth indeed showed itself in every countenance, nor was their ball totally void of all order and decorum. Perhaps it had more than a country assembly is sometimes conducted with; for these people are subject to a formal government and laws of their own, and all pay obedience to one great magistrate, whom they call their king.

Greater plenty likewise was nowhere to be seen than what flourished in this barn. Here was indeed no nicety nor elegance, nor did the keen appetite of the guests require any. Here was good store of bacon, fowls, and mutton, to which every one present provided better sauce himself than the best and dearest French cook can prepare.

Aeneas is not described under more consternation in the Temple of Juno,

Dum stupet obtutuque hæret defixus in uno,

than was our hero at what he saw in this barn. While he was looking everywhere round him with astonishment a venerable person approached him with many friendly salutations, rather of too hearty a kind to be called courtly. This was no other than the king of the gipsies himself. He was very little distinguished in dress from his subjects, nor had he any regalia of majesty to support his dignity, and yet there seemed (as Mr. Jones said) to be somewhat in his air which denoted authority and inspired the beholders with an idea of awe and respect; though all this was perhaps imaginary in Jones, and the truth may be that such ideas are incident to power and almost inseparable from it.

There was somewhat in the open countenance and courteous behaviour of Jones which, being accompanied with much comeliness of person, greatly recommended him at first sight to every beholder. These were perhaps a little heightened in the present instance by that profound respect which he paid to the king of the gipsies the moment he was acquainted with his dignity, and which was the sweeter to his gipsian majesty as he was not used to receive such homage from any but his own subjects.

The king ordered a table to be spread with the choicest of their provisions for his accommodation, and having placed himself at his right hand, his majesty began to discourse our hero in the following manner:

"Me doubt not, sir, but you have often seen some of my people who are what you call de parties detache, for dey go about everywhere; but me fancy you imagine not we be so considerable body as we be, and maybe you will surprise more when you hear de gipsy be as orderly and well-govern people as any upon face of de earth.

"Me have honour, as me say, to be deir king, and no monarch can do boast of more dutiful subject, ne no more affectionate. How far me deserve deir goodwill, me no say, but dis me can say: dat me never design anyting but to do dem good. Me sall no do boast of dat neider; for what can me do oderwise dan consider of de good of dose poor people who go about all day to give me always de best of what dey get? Dey love and honour me, darefore, because me do love and take care of dem; dat is all; me know no oder reason.

"About a tousand or two tousand year ago, me cannot tell to a year or two, as can neider write nor read, there was great what-you-call—a volution among de gipsy; for dere was de lord gipsy in dose days, and dese lord did quarrel vid one anoder about de place; but de king of de gipsy did demolish dem all and made all his subject equal vid each oder, and since dat time dey have agree very well, for dey no tink of being king; and maybe it be better for dem as dey be, for me assure you it be ver troublesome ting to be king and always to do justice; me have often wish to be de private gipsy when me have been forced to punish my dear friend and relation, for dough we never put to death, our punishments be ver severe. Dey make de gipsy ashamed of demselves, and dat be ver terrible punishment; me ave scarce ever known de gipsy so punish do harm any more."

The king then proceeded to express some wonder that there was no such punishment as shame in other governments. Upon which Jones assured him to the contrary, for that there were many crimes for which shame was inflicted by the English laws, and that it was, indeed, one consequence of all punishment. "Dat be ver strange," said the king; "for me know and hears good deal of your people, dough me no live among dem, and me ave often hear dat sham is de consequence and de cause too of many of your rewards. Are your rewards and punishments, den, de same ting?"

While his majesty was thus discoursing with Jones a sudden uproar arose in the barn, and, as it seems, upon this occasion: the courtesy of these people had by degrees removed all the apprehensions of Partridge, and he was prevailed upon not only to stuff himself with their food but to taste some of their liquors, which by degrees entirely expelled all fear from his composition and in its stead introduced much more agreeable sensations.

A young female gipsy, more remarkable for her wit than her beauty, had decoyed the honest fellow aside, pretending to tell his fortune. Now, when they were alone together in a remote part of the barn, whether it proceeded from the strong liquor, which is never so apt to inflame inordinate desire as after moderate fatigue, or whether the fair gipsy herself threw aside the delicacy and decency of her sex and tempted the youth Partridge with express solicitations, but they were discovered in a very improper manner by the husband of the gipsy, who from jealousy, it seems, had kept a watchful eye over his wife and had dogged her to the place where he found her in the arms of her gallant.

To the great confusion of Jones, Partridge was now hurried before the king, who heard the accusation and likewise the culprit's defence, which was indeed very trifling; for the poor fellow was confounded by the plain evidence which appeared against him and had very little to say for himself. His majesty then, turning towards Jones, said, "Sir, you have hear what dey say; what punishment do you tink your man deserve?"

Jones answered he was sorry for what had happened, and that Partridge should make the husband all the amends in his power. He said he had very little money about him at that time and, putting his hand into his pocket, offered the fellow a guinea. To which he immediately answered he hoped his honour would not think of giving him less than five.

This sum, after some altercation, was reduced to two, and Jones, having stipulated for the full forgiveness of both Partridge and the wife, was going to pay the money when his majesty, restraining his hand, turned to the witness and asked him at what time he had discovered the criminals. To which he answered that he had been desired by the husband to watch the motions of his wife from her first speaking to the stranger, and that he had never lost sight of her afterwards till the crime had been committed. The king then asked if the husband was with him all that time in his lurking-place, to which he answered in the affirmative. His Egyptian majesty then addressed himself to the husband as follows: "Me be sorry to see any gipsy dat have no more honour dan to sell de honour of his wife for money. If you had had de love for your wife, you would have prevented dis matter and not endeavour to make her de whore dat you might discover her. Me do order dat you have no money given you, for you deserve punishment, not reward; me do order, derefore, dat you be de infamous gipsy and do wear pair of horns upon your forehead for one month, and dat your wife be called de whore and pointed at all dat time; for you be de infamous gipsy, but she be no less de infamous whore."

The gipsies immediately proceeded to execute the sentence and left Jones and Partridge alone with his majesty.

Jones greatly applauded the justice of the sentence, upon which the king, turning to him, said, "Me believe you be surprise, for me suppose you have ver bad opinion of my people; me suppose you tink us all de tieves."

"I must confess, sir," said Jones, "I have not heard so favourable an account of them as they seem to deserve."

"Me vil tell you," said the king, "how de difference is between you and us. My people rob your people, and your people rob one anoder."

Jones afterwards proceeded very gravely to sing forth the happiness of those subjects who lived under such a magistrate.

Indeed their happiness appears to have been so complete that we are aware lest some advocate for arbitrary power should hereafter quote the case of those people as an instance of the great advantages which attend that government above all others.

And here we will make a concession which would not perhaps have been expected from us: that no limited form of government is capable of rising to the same degree of perfection or of producing the same benefits to society with this. Mankind have never been so happy as when the greatest part of the then known world was under the dominion of a single master, and this state of their felicity continued during the reigns of five successive princes.[1] This was the true era of the Golden Age, and the only Golden Age which ever had any existence, unless in the warm imaginations of the poets, from the expulsion from Eden down to this day.

In reality, I know but of one solid objection to absolute monarchy. The only defect in which excellent constitution seems to be the difficulty of finding any man adequate to the office of an absolute monarch; for this indispensably requires three qualities very difficult, as it appears from history, to be found in princely natures: first, a sufficient quantity of moderation in the prince to be contented with all the power which is possible for him to have; secondly, enough of wisdom to know his own happiness; and thirdly, goodness sufficient to support the happiness of others when not only compatible with, but instrumental to, his own.

Now, if an absolute monarch with all these great and rare qualifications should be allowed capable of conferring the greatest good on society, it must be surely granted on the

* Nerva, Trajan, Adrian, and the two Antonini.

contrary that absolute power vested in the hands of one who is deficient in them all is likely to be attended with no less a degree of evil.

In short, our own religion furnishes us with adequate ideas of the blessing as well as curse which may attend absolute power. The pictures of heaven and of hell will place a very lively image of both before our eyes; for though the prince of the latter can have no power but what he originally derives from the omnipotent Sovereign in the former, yet it plainly appears from Scripture that absolute power in his infernal dominions is granted to their diabolical ruler. This is indeed the only absolute power which can by Scripture be derived from heaven. If, therefore, the several tyrannies upon earth can prove any title to a divine authority, it must be derived from this original grant to the prince of darkness, and these subordinate deputations must consequently come immediately from him whose stamp they so expressly bear.

To conclude: As the examples of all ages show us that mankind in general desire power only to do harm, and when they obtain it use it for no other purpose, it is not consonant with even the least degree of prudence to hazard an alteration where our hopes are poorly kept in countenance by only two or three exceptions out of a thousand instances to alarm our fears. In this case, it will be much wiser to submit to a few inconveniencies arising from the dispassionate deafness of laws than to remedy them by applying to the passionate open ears of a tyrant.

Nor can the example of the gipsies, though possibly they may have long been happy under this form of government, be here urged, since we must remember the very material respect in which they differ from all other people and to which, perhaps, this their happiness is entirely owing: namely, that they have no false honours among them, and that they look on shame as the most grievous punishment in the world.

13

A DIALOGUE BETWEEN JONES AND PARTRIDGE

The honest lovers of liberty will, we doubt not, pardon that long digression into which we were led at the close of the last chapter to prevent our history from being applied to the use of the most pernicious doctrine which priestcraft had ever the wickedness or the impudence to preach.

We will now proceed with Mr. Jones, who when the storm was over took leave of his Egyptian majesty, after many thanks for his courteous behaviour and kind entertainment, and set out for Coventry, to which place (for it was still dark) a gipsy was ordered to conduct him.

Jones, having by reason of his deviation travelled eleven miles instead of six, and most of those through very execrable roads, where no expedition could have been made in quest of a midwife, did not arrive at Coventry till near twelve. Nor could he possibly get again into the saddle till past two, for post-horses were now not easy to get; nor were the ostler or post-boy in half so great a hurry as himself, but chose rather to imitate the tranquil disposition of Partridge, who, being denied the nourishment of sleep, took all opportunities to supply its place with every other kind of nourishment and was never better pleased than when he arrived at an inn, nor ever more dissatisfied than when he was again forced to leave it.

Jones now travelled post; we will follow him, therefore, according to our custom and to the rules of Longinus, in the same manner. From Coventry he arrived at Daventry; from Daventry at Stratford; and from Stratford at Dunstable, whither he came the next day a little after noon and within a few hours after Sophia had left it; and though he was obliged to stay here longer than he wished, while a smith with great deliberation shoed the post-horse he was to ride, he doubted not but to overtake his Sophia before she should set out from St. Albans, at which place he concluded, and very reasonably, that his lordship would stop and dine.

And had he been right in this conjecture, he most probably would have overtaken his angel at the aforesaid place, but unluckily my lord had appointed a dinner to be prepared for him at his own house in London, and in order to enable him to reach that place in proper time, he had ordered a relay of horses to meet him at St. Albans. When Jones, therefore, arrived there, he was informed that the coach and six had set out two hours before.

If fresh post-horses had been now ready, as they were not, it seemed so apparently impossible to overtake the coach before it reached London that Partridge thought he had now a proper opportunity to remind his friend of a matter which he seemed entirely to have forgotten; what this was the reader will guess when we inform him that Jones had eat nothing more than one poached egg since he had left the ale-house where he had first met the guide returning from Sophia; for with the gipsies he had only feasted his understanding.

The landlord so entirely agreed with the opinion of Mr. Partridge that he no sooner heard the latter desire his friend to stay and dine than he very readily put in his word, and retracting his promise before given of furnishing the horses immediately, he assured Mr. Jones he would lose no time in bespeaking a dinner, which, he said, could be got ready sooner than it was possible to get the horses up from grass and to prepare them for their journey by a feed of corn.

Jones was at length prevailed on, chiefly by the latter argument of the landlord, and now a joint of mutton was put down to the fire. While this was preparing, Partridge, being admitted into the same apartment with his friend or master, began to harangue in the following manner:

"Certainly, sir, if ever man deserved a young lady, you deserve young Madam Western; for what a vast quantity of love must a man have to be able to live upon it without any other food, as you do. I am positive I have eat thirty times as much within these last twenty-four hours as your honour, and yet I am almost famished, for nothing makes a man so hungry as travelling, especially in this cold, raw weather. And yet I can't tell how it is but your honour is seemingly in perfect good health, and you never looked better nor fresher in your life. It must be certainly love that you live upon."

"And a very rich diet too, Partridge," answered Jones. "But did not Fortune send me an excellent dainty yesterday? Dost thou imagine I cannot live more than twenty-four hours on this dear pocket-book?"

"Undoubtedly," cries Partridge, "there is enough in that pocket-book to purchase many a good meal. Fortune sent it to your honour very opportunely for present use, as your honour's money must be almost out by this time."

"What do you mean?" answered Jones. "I hope you don't imagine that I should be dishonest enough, even if it belonged to any other person besides Miss Western——"

"Dishonest!" replied Partridge. "Heaven forbid I should wrong your honour so much; but where's the dishonesty in borrowing a little for present spending, since you will be so well able to pay the lady hereafter? No, indeed, I would have your honour pay it again as soon as it is convenient, by all means; but where can be the harm in making use of it now you want it? Indeed, if it belonged to a poor body, it would be another thing, but so great a lady, to be sure, can never want it, especially now as she is along with a lord, who it can't be doubted will let her have whatever she hath need of. Besides, if she should want a little, she can't want the whole; therefore I would give her a little, but I would be hanged before I mentioned the having found it at first and before I got some money of my own, for London, I have heard, is the very worst of places to be in without money. Indeed, if I had not known to whom it belonged, I might have thought it was the Devil's money and have been afraid to use it; but as you know otherwise, and came honestly by it, it would be an affront to Fortune to part with it all again at the very time when you want it most; you can hardly expect she should ever do you such another good turn, for *Fortuna nunquam perpetuo est bona.* You will do as you please, notwithstanding all I say, but for my part, I would be hanged before I mentioned a word of the matter."

"By what I can see, Partridge," cries Jones, "hanging is a matter *non longe alienum à Scævolæ studiis.*" "You should say *alienus*," says Partridge; "I remember the passage; it is an example under *communis, alienus, immunis, variis casibus serviunt.*" "If you do remember it," cries Jones, "I find you don't understand it; but I tell thee, friend, in plain English, that he who finds another's property and wilfully detains it from the known owner, deserves *in foro conscientiæ* to be hanged no less than if he had stolen it. And as for this very identical bill, which is the property of my angel and was once in her dear possession, I will not deliver it into any hands but her own upon any consideration whatever; no, though I was as hungry as thou art and had no other means to satisfy my craving appetite; this I hope to do before I sleep, but if it should happen otherwise, I charge thee, if thou wouldst not incur my displeasure forever, not to shock me any more by the bare mention of such detestable baseness."

"I should not have mentioned it now," cries Partridge, "if it had appeared so to me, for I'm sure I scorn any wickedness as much as another; but perhaps you know better; and yet I might have imagined that I should not have lived so many years and have taught school so long without being able to distinguish between *fas et nefas;* but it seems we are all to live and learn. I remember my old schoolmaster, who was a prodigious great scholar, used often to say, *"Polly matete cry town is my daskalon."* The English of which, he told us, was that a child may sometimes teach his grandmother to suck eggs. I have lived to a fine purpose, truly, if I am to be taught my grammar at this time of day. Perhaps, young gentleman, you may change your opinion if you live to my years, for I remember I thought myself as wise when I was a stripling of one or two and twenty as I am now. I am sure I always taught *alienus*, and my master read it so before me."

There were not many instances in which Partridge could provoke Jones, nor were there many in which Partridge himself could have been hurried out of his respect. Unluckily, however, they had both hit on one of these. We have already seen Partridge could not bear to have his learning attacked, nor could Jones bear some passage or other in the foregoing speech. And now, looking upon his companion with a contemptuous and disdainful air (a thing not usual with him), he cried, "Partridge, I see thou art a conceited old fool, and I wish thou art not likewise an old rogue. Indeed, if I was as well convinced of the latter as I am of the former, thou shouldst travel no farther in my company."

The sage pedagogue was contented with the vent which he had already given to his indignation, and, as the vulgar phrase is, immediately drew in his horns. He said he was sorry he had uttered anything which might give offence, for that he had never intended it, but *nemo omnibus horis sapit.*

As Jones had the vices of a warm disposition, he was entirely free from those of a cold one, and if his friends must have confessed his temper to have been a little too easily ruffled, his enemies must at the same time have confessed that it as soon subsided; nor did it at all resemble the sea, whose swelling is more violent and dangerous after a storm is over than while the storm itself subsists. He instantly accepted the submission of Partridge, shook him by the hand, and with the most benign aspect imaginable said twenty kind things and at the same time very severely condemned himself, though not half so severely as he will most probably be condemned by many of our good readers.

Partridge was now highly comforted, as his fears of having offended were at once abolished and his pride completely satisfied by Jones having owned himself in the wrong, which submission he instantly applied to what had principally nettled him and repeated in a muttering voice, "To be sure, sir, your knowledge may be superior to mine in some things, but as to the grammar, I think I may challenge any man living. I think, at least, I have that at my finger's end."

If anything could add to the satisfaction which the poor man now enjoyed, he received this addition by the arrival of an excellent shoulder of mutton that at this instant came smoking to the table. On which, having both plentifully feasted, they again mounted their horses and set forward for London.

14

WHAT HAPPENED TO MR. JONES IN HIS JOURNEY FROM ST. ALBANS

They were got about two miles beyond Barnet, and it was now the dusk of the evening, when a genteel-looking man, but upon a very shabby horse, rode up to Jones and asked him whether he was going to London, to which Jones answered in the affirmative. The gentleman replied, "I should be obliged to you, sir, if you will accept of my company, for it is very late and I am a stranger to the road." Jones readily complied with the request, and on they travelled together, holding that sort of discourse which is usual on such occasions.

Of this, indeed, robbery was the principal topic, upon which subject the stranger expressed great apprehensions, but Jones declared he had very little to lose and consequently as little to fear. Here Partridge could not forbear putting in his word. "Your honour," said he, "may think it a little, but I am sure if I had a hundred-pound bank-note in my pocket, as you have, I should be very sorry to lose it; but for my part, I never was less afraid in my life; for we are four of us, and if we all stand by one another, the best man in England can't rob us. Suppose he should have a pistol, he can kill but one of us; and a man can die but once; that's my comfort, a man can die but once."

Besides the reliance on superior numbers, a kind of valour which hath raised a certain nation among the moderns to a high pitch of glory, there was another reason for the extraordinary courage which Partridge now discovered, for he had at present as much of that quality as was in the power of liquor to bestow.

Our company were now arrived within a mile of Highgate when the stranger turned short upon Jones and, pulling out a pistol, demanded that little bank-note which Partridge had mentioned.

Jones was at first somewhat shocked at this unexpected demand; however, he presently recollected himself and told the highwayman all the money he had in his pocket was entirely at his service; and so saying, he pulled out upwards of three guineas and offered to deliver it, but the other answered with an oath, that would not do. Jones answered coolly he was very sorry for it, and returned the money into his pocket.

The highwayman then threatened if he did not deliver the bank-note that moment, he must shoot him, holding his pistol at the same time very near to his breast. Jones instantly caught hold of the fellow's hand, which trembled so that he could scarce hold the pistol in it, and turned the muzzle from him. A struggle then ensued, in which the former wrested the pistol from the hand of his antagonist and both came from their horses on the ground together, the highwayman upon his back and the victorious Jones upon him.

The poor fellow now began to implore mercy of the conqueror, for to say the truth, he was in strength by no means a match for Jones. "Indeed, sir," says he, "I could have had no intention to shoot you, for you will find the pistol was not loaded. This is the first robbery I ever attempted, and I have been driven by distress to this."

At this instant, at about an hundred and fifty yards' distance lay another person on the ground, roaring for mercy in a much louder voice than the highwayman. This was no other than Partridge himself, who, endeavouring to make his escape from the engagement, had been thrown from his horse, and lay flat on his face, not daring to look up and expecting every minute to be shot.

In this posture he lay till the guide, who was no otherwise concerned than for his horses, having secured the stumbling beast, came up to him and told him his master had got the better of the highwayman.

Partridge leapt up at this news, and ran back to the place where Jones stood with his sword drawn in his hand to guard the poor fellow; which Partridge no sooner saw than he cried out, "Kill the villain, sir; run him through the body; kill him this instant."

Luckily, however, for the poor wretch, he had fallen into more merciful hands; for Jones, having examined the pistol and found it to be really unloaded, began to believe all the man had told him before Partridge came up: namely, that he was a novice in the trade and that he had been driven to it by the distress he mentioned, the greatest indeed imaginable: that of five hungry children and a wife lying-in of a sixth, in the utmost want and misery. The truth of all which the highwayman most vehemently asserted and offered to convince Mr. Jones of if he would take the trouble to go to his house, which was not above two miles off, saying that he desired no favour, but upon condition of proving all he had alleged.

Jones at first pretended that he would take the fellow at his word and return with him, declaring that his fate should depend entirely on the truth of his story. Upon this, the poor fellow immediately expressed so much alacrity that Jones was perfectly satisfied with his veracity, and began now to entertain sentiments of compassion for him. He returned the fellow his empty pistol, advised him to think of honester means of relieving his distress, and gave him a couple of guineas for the immediate support of his wife and his family, adding he wished he had more for his sake, but the hundred pound that had been mentioned was not his own.

Our readers will probably be divided in their opinions concerning this action; some may applaud it perhaps as an act of extraordinary humanity, while those of a more saturnine temper will consider it as a want of regard to that justice which every man owes his country. Partridge certainly saw it in that light; for he testified much dissatisfaction on the occasion, quoted an old proverb, and said he should not wonder if the rogue attacked them again before they reached London.

The highwayman was full of expressions of thankfulness and gratitude. He actually dropped tears, or pretended so to do. He vowed he would immediately return home and would never afterwards commit such a transgression; whether he kept his word or no perhaps may appear hereafter.

Our travellers, having remounted their horses, arrived in town without encountering any new mishap. On the road much pleasant discourse passed between Jones and Partridge on the subject of their last adventure, in which Jones expressed a great compassion for those highwaymen who are by unavoidable distress driven, as it were, to such illegal courses as generally bring them to a shameful death. "I mean," said he, "those only whose highest guilt extends no farther than to robbery, and who are never guilty of cruelty nor insult to any person, which is a circumstance that, I must say, to the honour of our country, distinguishes the robbers of England from those of all other nations, for murder is amongst those almost inseparably incident to robbery."

"No doubt," answered Partridge, "it is better to take away one's money than one's life, and yet it is very hard upon honest men that they can't travel about their business without being in danger of these villains. And to be sure, it would be better that all rogues were hanged out of the way than that one honest man should suffer. For my own part, indeed, I should not care to have the blood of any of them on my own hands, but it is very proper for the law to hang them all. What right hath any man to take sixpence from me unless I give it him? Is there any honesty in such a man?"

"No, surely," cries Jones; "no more than there is in him who takes the horses out of another man's stable or who applies to his own use the money which he finds when he knows the right owner."

These hints stopped the mouth of Partridge, nor did he open it again till Jones having thrown some sarcastical jokes on his cowardice, he offered to excuse himself on the inequality of fire-arms, saying, "A thousand naked men are nothing to one pistol, for though it is true it will kill but one at a single discharge, yet who can tell but that one may be himself."

BOOK XIII

CONTAINING THE SPACE OF TWELVE DAYS

1

AN INVOCATION

Come, bright love of fame, inspire my glowing breast: not thee I call, who over swelling tides of blood and tears doth bear the hero on to glory while sighs of millions waft his spreading sails, but thee, fair, gentle maid, whom Mnesis, happy nymph, first on the banks of Hebrus didst produce; thee, whom Maeonia educated, whom Mantua charmed, and who on that fair hill which overlooks the proud metropolis of Britain sat with thy Milton, sweetly tuning the heroic lyre; fill my ravished fancy with the hopes of charming ages yet to come. Foretell me that some tender maid, whose grandmother is yet unborn, hereafter, when under the fictitious name of Sophia she reads the real worth which once existed in my Charlotte, shall from her sympathetic breast send forth the heaving sigh. Do thou teach me not only to foresee but to enjoy; nay, even to feed on future praise. Comfort me by a solemn assurance that when the little parlour in which I sit at this instant shall be reduced to a worse furnished box, I shall be read with honour by those who never knew nor saw me, and whom I shall neither know nor see.

And thou, much plumper dame, whom no airy forms nor phantoms of imagination clothe, whom the well-seasoned beef and pudding richly stained with plums delight; thee, I call; of whom in a *trekschuit* in some Dutch canal the fat *juffrouw* Gelt, impregnated by a jolly merchant of Amsterdam, was delivered; in Grub Street school didst thou suck in the elements of thy erudition. Here hast thou, in thy maturer age, taught poetry to tickle not the fancy but the pride of the patron. Comedy from thee learns a grave and solemn air, while tragedy storms loud and rends th' affrighted theatres with its thunder. To soothe thy wearied limbs in slumber, Alderman History tells his tedious tale; and again to awaken thee, Monsieur Romance performs his surprising tricks of dexterity. Nor less thy well-fed bookseller obeys thy influence. By thy advice the heavy, unread, folio lump, which long had dozed on the dusty shelf piecemealed into numbers, runs nimbly through the nation. Instructed by thee, some books like quacks impose on the world by promising wonders, while others turn beaux and trust all their merits to a gilded outside. Come, thou jolly substance, with thy shining face, keep back thy inspiration but hold forth thy tempting rewards: thy shining, chinking heap; thy quickly convertible bank-bill, big with unseen riches; thy often-varying stock; the warm, the comfortable house; and lastly, a fair portion of that bounteous mother, whose flowing breasts yield redundant sustenance for all her numerous offspring, did not some too greedily and wantonly drive their brethren from the teat. Come thou, and if I am too tasteless of thy valuable treasures, warm my heart with the transporting thought of conveying them to others. Tell me that through thy bounty the prattling babes, whose innocent play hath often been interrupted by my labours, may one time be amply rewarded for them.

And now this ill-yoked pair, this lean shadow and this fat substance, have prompted me to write, whose assistance shall I invoke to direct my pen?

First, Genius; thou gift of heaven, without whose aid in vain we struggle against the stream of Nature. Thou, who dost sow the generous seeds which Art nourishes and brings to perfection, do thou kindly take me by the hand and lead me through all the mazes, the winding labyrinths of Nature. Initiate me into all those mysteries which profane eyes never beheld. Teach me, which to thee is no difficult task, to know mankind better than they know themselves. Remove that mist which dims the intellects of mortals, and causes them to adore men for their art or to detest them for their cunning in deceiving others, when they are in reality the objects only of ridicule for deceiving themselves. Strip off the thin disguise of wisdom from self-conceit, of plenty from avarice, and of glory from ambition. Come, thou that hast inspired thy Aristophanes, thy Lucian, thy Cervantes, thy Rabelais, thy Molière, thy Shakespeare, thy Swift, thy Marivaux, fill my pages with humour till mankind learn the good nature to laugh only at the follies of others, and the humility to grieve at their own.

And thou, almost the constant attendant on true Genius, Humanity, bring all thy tender sensations. If thou hast already disposed of them all between thy Allen and thy Lyttleton, steal them a little while from their bosoms. Not without these the tender scene is painted. From these alone proceed the noble disinterested friendship, the melting love, the generous sentiment, the ardent gratitude, the soft compassion, the candid opinion, and all those strong energies of a good mind which fill the moistened eyes with tears, the glowing cheeks with blood, and swell the heart with tides of grief, joy, and benevolence.

And thou, O Learning (for without thy assistance nothing pure, nothing correct, can Genius produce), do thou guide my pen. Thee, in thy favourite fields, where the limpid, gently rolling Thames washes thy Etonian banks, in early youth I have worshipped. To thee, at thy birchen altar, with true Spartan devotion I have sacrificed my blood. Come, then, and from thy vast, luxuriant stores in long antiquity piled up, pour forth the rich profusion. Open thy Maeonian and thy Mantuan coffers, with whatever else includes thy philosophic, thy poetic, and thy historical treasures, whether with Greek or Roman characters thou hast chosen to inscribe the ponderous chests; give me awhile that key to all thy treasures, which to thy Warburton thou hast entrusted.

Lastly, come, Experience, long conversant with the wise, the good, the learned, and the polite; nor with them only, but with every kind of character, from the minister at his levee to the bailiff in his sponging-house; from the duchess at her drum to the landlady behind her bar. From thee only can the manners of mankind be known, to which the recluse pedant, however great his parts or extensive his learning may be, hath ever been a stranger.

Come all these, and more if possible; for arduous is the task I have undertaken, and without all your assistance will, I find, be too heavy for me to support. But if you all smile on my labours, I hope still to bring them to a happy conclusion.

2

WHAT BEFELL MR. JONES ON HIS ARRIVAL IN LONDON

The learned Dr. Misaubin used to say that the proper direction to him was *To Dr. Misaubin, in the World;* intimating that there were few people in it to whom his great reputation was not known. And, perhaps, upon a very nice examination into the matter, we shall find that this circumstance bears no inconsiderable part among the many blessings of grandeur.

The great happiness of being known to posterity, with the hopes of which we so delighted ourselves in the preceding chapter, is the portion of few. To have the several elements which compose our names, as Sydenham expresses it, repeated a thousand years hence is a gift beyond the power of title and wealth, and is scarce to be purchased unless by the sword and the pen. But to avoid the scandalous imputation while we yet live of being *one whom nobody knows* (a scandal, by the by, as old as the days of Homer *) will always be the envied portion of those who have a legal title either to honour or estate.

From that figure, therefore, which the Irish peer who brought Sophia to town hath already made in this history, the reader will conclude, doubtless, it must have been an easy matter to have discovered his house in London without knowing the particular street or square which he inhabited, since he must have been one *whom everybody knows.* To say the truth, so it would have been to any of those tradesmen who are accustomed to attend the regions of the great, for the doors of the great are generally no less easy to find than it is difficult to get entrance into them. But Jones, as well as Partridge, was an entire stranger in London, and as he happened to arrive first in a quarter of the town the inhabitants of which have very little intercourse with the householders of Hanover or Grosvenor Square (for he entered through Gray's Inn Lane), so he rambled about some time before he could even find his way to those happy mansions where Fortune segregates

* See the second *Odyssey*, verse 175.

from the vulgar those magnanimous heroes, the descendants of ancient Britons, Saxons, or Danes, whose ancestors, being born in better days, by sundry kinds of merit, have entailed riches and honour on their posterity.

Jones, being at length arrived at those terrestrial Elysian Fields, would now soon have discovered his lordship's mansion, but the peer unluckily quitted his former house when he went for Ireland, and as he was just entered into a new one, the fame of his equipage had not yet sufficiently blazed in the neighbourhood; so that after a successless inquiry till the cock had struck eleven, Jones at last yielded to the advice of Partridge and retreated to the Bull and Gate in Holborn, that being the inn where he had first alighted and where he retired to enjoy that kind of repose which usually attends persons in his circumstances.

Early in the morning he again set forth in pursuit of Sophia, and many a weary step he took to no better purpose than before. At last, whether it was that Fortune relented, or whether it was no longer in her power to disappoint him, he came into the very street which was honoured by his lordship's residence, and being directed to the house, he gave one gentle rap at the door.

The porter, who from the modesty of the knock had conceived no high idea of the person approaching, conceived but little better from the appearance of Mr. Jones, who was dressed in a suit of fustian and had by his side the weapon formerly purchased of the sergeant, of which, though the blade might be composed of well-tempered steel, the handle was composed only of brass, and that none of the brightest. When Jones, therefore, inquired after the young lady who had come to town with his lordship, this fellow answered surlily that there were no ladies there. Jones then desired to see the master of the house, but was informed that his lordship would see nobody that morning. And upon growing more pressing, the porter said he had positive orders to let no person in. "But if you think proper," said he, "to leave your name, I will acquaint his lordship; and if you call another time, you shall know when he will see you."

Jones now declared that he had very particular business with the young lady and could not depart without seeing her. Upon which the porter, with no very agreeable voice or aspect, affirmed that there was no young lady in that house, and consequently none could he see; adding, "Sure you are the strangest man I ever met with, for you will not take an answer."

I have often thought that by the particular description of Cerberus, the porter of hell, in the sixth *Aeneid*, Virgil might possibly intend to satirize the porters of the great men in his time; the picture at least resembles those who have the honour to attend the doors of our great men. The porter in his lodge answers exactly to Cerberus in his den, and, like him, must be appeased by a sop before access can be gained to his master. Perhaps Jones might have seen him in that light, and have recollected the passage where the Sibyl, in order to procure an entrance for Aeneas, presents the keeper of the Stygian avenue with such a sop. Jones in like manner now began to offer a bribe to the human Cerberus, which a footman overhearing, instantly advanced and declared if Mr. Jones would give him the sum proposed, he would conduct him to the lady. Jones instantly agreed, and was forthwith conducted to the lodging of Mrs. Fitzpatrick by the very fellow who had attended the ladies thither the day before.

Nothing more aggravates ill success than the near approach to good. The gamester who loses his party at piquet by a single point laments his bad luck ten times as much as he who never came within a prospect of the game. So in a lottery, the proprietors of the next numbers to that which wins the great prize are apt to account themselves much more unfortunate than their fellow-sufferers. In short, these kind of hairbreadth missings of happiness look like the insults of Fortune, who may be considered as thus playing tricks with us and wantonly diverting herself at our expense.

Jones, who more than once already had experienced this frolicsome disposition of the heathen goddess, was now again doomed to be tantalized in the like manner; for he arrived at the door of Mrs. Fitzpatrick about ten minutes after the departure of Sophia. He now addressed himself to the waiting-woman belonging to Mrs. Fitzpatrick, who told him the disagreeable news that the lady was gone, but could not tell him whither; and the same answer he afterwards received from Mrs. Fitzpatrick herself. For as that lady made no doubt but that Mr. Jones was a person detached from her uncle Western in pursuit of his daughter, so she was too generous to betray her.

Though Jones had never seen Mrs. Fitzpatrick, yet he had heard that a cousin of Sophia was married to a gentleman of that name. This, however, in the present tumult of his mind never once recurred to his memory; but when the footman who had conducted him from his lordship's acquainted him with the great intimacy between the ladies and with their calling each other cousin, he then recollected the story of the marriage which he had formerly heard, and as he was presently convinced that this was the same woman, he became more surprised at the answer which he had received and very earnestly desired leave to wait on the lady herself, but she as positively refused him that honour.

Jones, who though he had never seen a court was better bred than most who frequent it, was incapable of any rude or abrupt behaviour to a lady. When he had received, therefore, a peremptory denial, he retired for the present, saying to the waiting-woman that if this was an improper hour to wait on her lady, he would return in the afternoon; and that he then hoped to have the honour of seeing her. The civility with which he uttered this, added to the great comeliness of his person, made an impression on the waiting-woman, and she could not help answering, "Perhaps, sir, you may." And indeed, she afterwards said everything to her mistress which she thought most likely to prevail on her to admit a visit from the handsome young gentleman, for so she called him.

Jones very shrewdly suspected that Sophia herself was now with her cousin, and was denied to him, which he imputed to her resentment of what had happened at Upton. Having, therefore, dispatched Partridge to procure him lodgings, he remained all day in the street, watching the door where he thought his angel lay concealed, but no person did he see issue forth except a servant of the house; and in the evening he returned to pay his visit to Mrs. Fitzpatrick, which that good lady at last condescended to admit.

There is a certain air of natural gentility which it is neither in the power of dress to give nor to conceal. Mr. Jones, as hath been before hinted, was possessed of this in a very eminent degree. He met, therefore, with a reception from the lady somewhat different from what his apparel seemed to demand, and after he had paid her his proper respects, was desired to sit down.

The reader will not, I believe, be desirous of knowing all the particulars of this conversation, which ended very little to the satisfaction of poor Jones. For though Mrs. Fitzpatrick soon discovered the lover (as all women have the eyes of hawks in those matters), yet she still thought it was such a lover as a generous friend of the lady should not betray her to. In short, she suspected this was the very Mr. Blifil from whom Sophia had flown, and all the answers which she artfully drew from Jones concerning Mr. Allworthy's family confirmed her in this opinion. She therefore strictly denied any knowledge concerning the place whither Sophia was gone, nor could Jones obtain more than a permission to wait on her again the next evening.

When Jones was departed, Mrs. Fitzpatrick communicated her suspicion concerning Mr. Blifil to her maid, who answered, "Sure, madam, he is too pretty a man, in my opinion, for any woman in the world to run away from. I had rather fancy it is Mr. Jones." "Mr. Jones," said the lady. "What Jones?" For Sophia had not given the least hint of any such person in all their conversation, but Mrs. Honour had been much more communicative and had acquainted her sister Abigail with the whole history of Jones, which this now again related to her mistress.

Mrs. Fitzpatrick no sooner received this information than she immediately agreed with the opinion of her maid, and, what is very unaccountable, saw charms in the gallant, happy lover which she had overlooked in the slighted squire. "Betty," says she, "you are certainly in the right; he is a very pretty fellow, and I don't wonder that my cousin's maid should tell you so many women are fond of him. I am sorry now I did not inform him where my cousin was, and yet if he be so terrible a rake as you tell me, it is a pity she should ever see him any more; for what but her ruin can happen from marrying a rake and a beggar against her father's consent? I protest, if he be such a man as the wench described him to you, it is but an office of charity to keep her from him, and I am sure it would be unpardonable in me to do otherwise, who have tasted so bitterly of the misfortunes attending such marriages."

Here she was interrupted by the arrival of a visitor, which was no other than his lordship; and as nothing passed at this visit either new or extraordinary or anyways material to this history, we shall here put an end to this chapter.

A PROJECT OF MRS. FITZPATRICK, AND HER VISIT TO LADY BELLASTON

When Mrs. Fitzpatrick retired to rest, her thoughts were entirely taken up by her cousin Sophia and Mr. Jones. She was, indeed, a little offended with the former for the disingenuity which she now discovered. In which meditation she had not long exercised her imagination before the following conceit suggested itself: that could she possibly become the means of preserving Sophia from this man and of restoring her to her father, she should in all human probability by so great a service to the family reconcile to herself both her uncle and her aunt Western.

As this was one of her most favourite wishes, so the hope of success seemed so reasonable that nothing remained but to consider of proper methods to accomplish her scheme. To attempt to reason the case with Sophia did not appear to her one of those methods; for as Betty had reported from Mrs. Honour that Sophia had a violent inclination to Jones, she conceived that to dissuade her from the match was an endeavour of the same kind as it would be very heartily and earnestly to entreat a moth not to fly into a candle.

If the reader will please to remember that the acquaintance which Sophia had with Lady Bellaston was contracted at the house of Mrs. Western, and must have grown at the very time when Mrs. Fitzpatrick lived with this latter lady, he will want no information that Mrs. Fitzpatrick must have been acquainted with her likewise. They were, besides, both equally her distant relations.

After much consideration, therefore, she resolved to go early in the morning to that lady and endeavour to see her, unknown to Sophia, and to acquaint her with the whole affair. For she did not in the least doubt but that the prudent lady, who had often ridiculed romantic love and indiscreet marriages in her conversation, would very readily concur in her sentiments concerning this match and would lend her utmost assistance to prevent it.

This resolution she accordingly executed; and the next morning before the sun, she huddled on her clothes and, at a very unfashionable, unseasonable, unvisitable hour, went to Lady Bellaston, to whom she got access without the least knowledge or suspicion of Sophia, who though not asleep lay at that time awake in her bed, with Honour snoring by her side.

Mrs. Fitzpatrick made many apologies for her early, abrupt visit at an hour when, she said, she should not have thought of disturbing her ladyship but upon business of the utmost consequence. She then opened the whole affair, told all she had heard from Betty, and did not forget the visit which Jones had paid to herself the preceding evening.

Lady Bellaston answered with a smile, "Then you have seen this terrible man, madam; pray, is he so very fine a figure as he is represented? For Etoff entertained me last night almost two hours with him. The wench, I believe, is in love with him by reputation." Here the reader will be apt to wonder, but the truth is that Mrs. Etoff, who had the honour to pin and unpin the Lady Bellaston, had received complete information concerning the said Mr. Jones and had faithfully conveyed the same to her lady last night (or rather that morning) while she was undressing, on which accounts she had been detained in her office above the space of an hour and half.

The lady, indeed, though generally well enough pleased with the narratives of Mrs. Etoff at those seasons, gave an extraordinary attention to her account of Jones, for Honour had described him as a very handsome fellow, and Mrs. Etoff in her hurry added so much to the beauty of his person to her report that Lady Bellaston began to conceive him to be a kind of miracle in nature.

The curiosity which her woman had inspired was now greatly increased by Mrs. Fitzpatrick, who spoke as much in favour of the person of Jones as she had before spoken in dispraise of his birth, character, and fortune.

When Lady Bellaston had heard the whole, she answered gravely, "Indeed, madam, this is a matter of great consequence. Nothing can certainly be more commendable than the part you act, and I shall be very glad to have my share in the preservation of a young lady of so much merit and for whom I have so much esteem."

"Doth not your ladyship think," says Mrs. Fitzpatrick eagerly, "that it would be the best way to write immediately to my uncle and acquaint him where my cousin is?"

The lady pondered a little upon this and thus answered:

"Why, no, madam, I think not. Di Western hath described her brother to me to be such a brute that I cannot consent to put any woman under his power who hath escaped from it. I have heard he behaved like a monster to his own wife; for he is one of those wretches who think they have a right to tyrannize over us, and from such I shall ever esteem it the cause of my sex to rescue any woman who is so unfortunate to be under their power. The business, dear cousin, will be only to keep Miss Western from seeing this young fellow till the good company which she will have an opportunity of meeting here give her a properer turn."

"If he should find her out, madam," answered the other, "your ladyship may be assured he will leave nothing unattempted to come at her."

"But, madam," replied the lady, "it is impossible he should come here—though indeed it is possible he may get some intelligence where she is, and then may lurk about the house. I wish therefore I knew his person."

"Is there no way, madam, by which I could have a sight of him? For otherwise, you know, cousin, she may contrive to see him without my knowledge." Mrs. Fitzpatrick answered that he had threatened her with another visit that afternoon, and that if her ladyship pleased to do her the honour of calling upon her then, she would hardly fail of seeing him between six and seven; and if he came earlier, she would by some means or other detain him till her ladyship's arrival. Lady Bellaston replied she would come the moment she could get from dinner, which she supposed would be by seven at farthest, for that it was absolutely necessary she should be acquainted with his person. "Upon my word, madam," says he, "it was very good to take this care of Miss Western, but common humanity, as well as regard to our family, requires it of us both, for it would be a dreadful match indeed."

Mrs. Fitzpatrick failed not to make a proper return to the compliment which Lady Bellaston had bestowed on her cousin and, after some little immaterial conversation, withdrew; and getting as fast as she could into her chair, unseen by Sophia or Honour, returned home.

WHICH CONSISTS OF VISITING

Mr. Jones had walked within sight of a certain door during the whole day, which though one of the shortest appeared to him to be one of the longest in the whole year. At length, the clock having struck five, he returned to Mrs. Fitzpatrick, who though it was a full hour earlier than the decent time of visiting received him very civilly, but still persisted in her ignorance concerning Sophia.

Jones, in asking for his angel, had dropped the word *cousin*, upon which Mrs. Fitzpatrick said, "Then, sir, you know we are related, and as we are, you will permit me the right of inquiring into the particulars of your business with my cousin." Here Jones hesitated a good while and at last answered he had a considerable sum of money of hers in his hands, which he desired to deliver to her. He then produced the pocket-book and acquainted Mrs. Fitzpatrick with the contents and with the method in which they came into his hands. He had scarce finished his story when a most violent noise shook the whole house. To attempt to describe this noise to those who have heard it would be in vain, and to aim at giving any idea of it to those who have never heard the like would be still more vain, for it may be truly said,

> ——*Non acuta*
> *Sic geminant Corybantes æra.*

The priests of Cybele do not so rattle their sounding brass.

In short, a footman knocked, or rather thundered, at the door. Jones was a little surprised at the sound, having never heard it before, but Mrs. Fitzpatrick very calmly said that as some company were coming, she could not make him any answer now; but if he pleased to stay till they were gone, she intimated she had something to say to him.

The door of the room now flew open and, after pushing in her hoop sideways before her, entered Lady Bellaston, who, having first made a very low curtsy to Mrs. Fitzpatrick and as low a one to Mr. Jones, was ushered to the upper end of the room.

We mention these minute matters for the sake of some country ladies of our acquaintance who think it contrary to the rules of modesty to bend their knees to a man.

The company were hardly well settled before the arrival of the peer lately mentioned caused a fresh disturbance and a repetition of ceremonials.

These being over, the conversation began to be (as the phrase is) extremely brilliant. However, as nothing passed in it which can be thought material to this history, or, indeed, very material in itself, I shall omit the relation; the rather as I have known some very fine, polite conversation grow extremely dull when transcribed into books or repeated on the stage. Indeed, this mental repast is a dainty of which those who are excluded from polite assemblies must be contented to remain as ignorant as they must of the several dainties of French cookery, which are only served at the tables of the great. To say the truth, as neither of these are adapted to every taste, they might both be often thrown away on the vulgar.

Poor Jones was rather a spectator of this elegant scene than an actor in it; for though in the short interval before the peer's arrival Lady Bellaston first and afterwards Mrs. Fitzpatrick had addressed some of their discourse to him, yet no sooner was the noble lord entered than he engrossed the whole attention of the two ladies to himself; and as he took no more notice of Jones than if no such person had been present, unless by now and then staring at him, the ladies followed his example.

The company had now stayed so long that Mrs. Fitzpatrick plainly perceived they all designed to stay out each other. She therefore resolved to rid herself of Jones, he being the visitant to whom she thought the least ceremony was due. Taking therefore an opportunity of a cessation of chat, she addressed herself gravely to him and said, "Sir, I shall not possibly be able to give you an answer to-night as to that business, but if you please to leave word where I may send to you to-morrow . . ."

Jones had natural, but not artificial, good breeding. Instead, therefore, of communicating the secret of his lodgings to a servant, he acquainted the lady herself with it particularly, and soon after very ceremoniously withdrew.

He was no sooner gone than the great personages who had

taken no notice of him present began to take much notice of him in his absence, but if the reader hath already excused us from relating the more brilliant part of this conversation, he will surely be very ready to excuse the repetition of what may be called vulgar abuse; though perhaps it may be material to our history to mention an observation of Lady Bellaston, who took her leave in a few minutes after him, and then said to Mrs. Fitzpatrick at her departure, "I am satisfied on the account of my cousin; she can be in no danger from this fellow."

Our history shall follow the example of Lady Bellaston and take leave of the present company, which was now reduced to two persons, between whom, as nothing passed which in the least concerns us or our reader, we shall not suffer ourselves to be diverted by it from matters which must seem of more consequence to all those who are at all interested in the affairs of our hero.

5

AN ADVENTURE WHICH HAPPENED TO MR. JONES AT HIS LODGINGS, WITH SOME ACCOUNT OF A YOUNG GENTLEMAN WHO LODGED THERE, AND OF THE MISTRESS OF THE HOUSE AND HER TWO DAUGHTERS

The next morning, as early as it was decent, Jones attended at Mrs. Fitzpatrick's door, where he was answered that the lady was not at home, an answer which surprised him the more as he had walked backwards and forwards in the street from break of day, and if she had gone out, he must have seen her. This answer, however, he was obliged to receive; and not only now but to five several visits which he made her that day.

To be plain with the reader, the noble peer had from some reason or other, perhaps from a regard for the lady's honour, insisted that she should not see Mr. Jones, whom he looked on as a scrub, any more, and the lady had complied in making that promise to which we now see her so strictly adhere.

But as our gentle reader may possibly have a better opinion of the young gentleman than her ladyship, and may even have some concern should it be apprehended that during this unhappy separation from Sophia he took up his residence either at an inn or in the street, we shall now give an account of his lodging, which was indeed in a very reputable house and in a very good part of the town.

Mr. Jones, then, had often heard Mr. Allworthy mention the gentlewoman at whose house he used to lodge when he was in town. This person, who, as Jones likewise knew, lived in Bond Street, was the widow of a clergyman, and was left by him at his decease in possession of two daughters and of a complete set of manuscript sermons.

Of these two daughters, Nancy, the elder, was now arrived at the age of seventeen and Betty, the younger, at that of ten.

Hither Jones had dispatched Partridge, and in this house he was provided with a room for himself in the second floor and with one for Partridge in the fourth.

The first floor was inhabited by one of those young gentlemen who in the last age were called men of wit and pleasure about town, and properly enough; for as men are usually denominated from their business or profession, so pleasure may be said to have been the only business or profession of those gentlemen to whom fortune had made all useful occupations unnecessary. Playhouses, coffee-houses, and taverns were the scenes of their rendezvous. Wit and humour were the entertainment of their looser hours, and love was the business of their more serious moments. Wine and the Muses conspired to kindle the brightest flames in their breasts; nor did they only admire, but some were able to celebrate the beauty they admired, and all to judge of the merit of such compositions.

Such, therefore, were properly called the men of wit and pleasure; but I question whether the same appellation may with the same propriety be given to those young gentlemen of our times who have the same ambition to be distinguished for parts. Wit certainly they have nothing to do with. To give them their due, they soar a step higher than their predecessors, and may be called men of wisdom and *virtu* (take heed you do not read virtue). Thus, at an age when the gentlemen above mentioned employed their time in toasting the charms of a woman or in making sonnets in her praise, in giving their opinion of a play at the theatre or of a poem at Will's or Button's, these gentlemen are considering of methods to bribe a corporation, or meditating speeches for the House of Commons, or rather for the magazines. But the science of gaming is that which above all others employs their thoughts. These are the studies of their graver hours, while for their amusements they have the vast circle of connoisseurship, painting, music, statuary, and natural philosophy; or rather *unnatural*, which deals in the wonderful and knows nothing of Nature except her monsters and imperfections.

When Jones had spent the whole day in vain inquiries after Mrs. Fitzpatrick, he returned at last disconsolate to his apartment. Here, while he was venting his grief in private, he heard a violent uproar below-stairs, and soon after a female voice begged him for heaven's sake to come and prevent murder. Jones, who was never backward on any occasion to help the distressed, immediately ran downstairs, when, stepping into the dining-room, whence all the noise issued, he beheld the young gentleman of wisdom and *virtu* just before mentioned pinned close to the wall by his footman, and a young woman standing by wringing her hands and crying out, "He will be murdered! he will be murdered!" And indeed the poor gentleman seemed in some danger of being choked when Jones flew hastily to his assistance and rescued him just as he was breathing his last from the unmerciful clutches of the enemy.

Though the fellow had received several kicks and cuffs from the little gentleman, who had more spirit than strength, he had made it a kind of scruple of conscience to strike his master, and would have contented himself with only choking him, but towards Jones he bore no such respect; he no sooner therefore found himself a little roughly handled by his new antagonist than he gave him one of those punches in the guts which, though the spectators at Broughton's Amphitheatre have such exquisite delight in seeing them, convey but very little pleasure in the feeling.

The lusty youth had no sooner received this blow than he meditated a most grateful return, and now ensued a combat between Jones and the footman, which was very fierce, but short; for this fellow was no more able to contend with Jones than his master had before been to contend with him.

And now Fortune, according to her usual custom, reversed the face of affairs: the former victor lay breathless on the ground, and the vanquished gentleman had recovered breath enough to thank Mr. Jones for his seasonable assistance; he received likewise the hearty thanks of the young woman present, who was indeed no other than Miss Nancy, the eldest daughter of the house.

The footman, having now recovered his legs, shook his head at Jones and with a sagacious look cried, "Oh, d——n me, I'll have nothing more to do with you; you have been upon the stage, or I am d——nably mistaken"; and indeed, we may forgive this his suspicion, for such was the agility and strength of our hero that he was perhaps a match for one of the first-rate boxers, and could with great ease have beaten all the muffled * graduates of Mr. Broughton's school.

His master, foaming with wrath, ordered his man immediately to strip, to which the latter very readily agreed on condition of receiving his wages. This condition was presently complied with, and the fellow was discharged.

And now the young gentleman, whose name was Nightingale, very strenuously insisted that his deliverer should take part of a bottle of wine with him, to which Jones after much entreaty consented, though more out of complaisance than inclination, for the uneasiness of his mind fitted him very little for conversation at this time. Miss Nancy likewise, who was the only female then in the house, her mamma and sister being both gone to the play, condescended to favour them with her company.

When the bottle and glasses were on the table, the gentleman began to relate the occasion of the preceding disturbance.

"I hope, sir," said he to Jones, "you will not from this accident conclude that I make a custom of striking my servants; for I assure you this is the first time I have been guilty of it in my remembrance, and I have passed by many provoking faults in this very fellow before he could provoke me to it; but when you hear what hath happened this evening, you will, I believe, think me excusable. I happened to come home several hours before my usual time, when I found four gentlemen of the cloth at whist by my fire, and my

---

* Lest posterity should be puzzled by this epithet, I think proper to explain it by an advertisement which was published Feb. 1, 1747:
  N.B. Mr. Broughton proposes, with proper assistance, to open an academy at his house in the Haymarket for the instruction of those who are willing to be initiated in the mystery of boxing, where the whole theory and practice of that truly British art, with all the various stops, blows, cross-buttocks, &c., incident to combatants will be fully taught and explained; and that persons of quality and distinction may not be deterred from entering into *a course of these lectures,* they will be given with the utmost tenderness and regard to the delicacy of the frame and constitution of the pupil, for which reason muffles are provided that will effectually secure them from the inconveniency of black eyes, broken jaws, and bloody noses.

Hoyle, sir—my best Hoyle, which cost me a guinea—lying open on the table with a quantity of porter spilt on one of the most material leaves of the whole book. This, you will allow, was provoking; but I said nothing till the rest of the honest company were gone and then gave the fellow a gentle rebuke, who instead of expressing any concern made me a pert answer: that servants must have their diversions as well as other people; that he was sorry for the accident which had happened to the book, but that several of his acquaintance had bought the same for a shilling, and that I might stop as much in his wages if I pleased. I now give him a severer reprimand than before, when the rascal had the insolence to— In short, he imputed my early coming home to— In short, he cast a reflection. He mentioned the name of a young lady in a manner—in such a manner that incensed me beyond all patience, and in my passion I struck him."

Jones answered that he believed no person living would blame him. "For my part," said he, "I confess I should on the last-mentioned provocation have done the same thing."

Our company had not sat long before they were joined by the mother and daughter at their return from the play. And now they all spent a very cheerful evening together; for all but Jones were heartily merry, and even he put on as much constrained mirth as possible. Indeed half his natural flow of animal spirits, joined to the sweetness of his temper, was sufficient to make a most amiable companion, and notwithstanding the heaviness of his heart, so agreeable did he make himself on the present occasion that at their breaking up, the young gentleman earnestly desired his further acquaintance. Miss Nancy was well pleased with him, and the widow, quite charmed with her new lodger, invited him, with the other, next morning to breakfast.

Jones on his part was no less satisfied. As for Miss Nancy, though a very little creature, she was extremely pretty, and the widow had all the charms which can adorn a woman near fifty. As she was one of the most innocent creatures in the world, so she was one of the most cheerful. She never thought nor spoke nor wished any ill, and had constantly that desire of pleasing which may be called the happiest of all desires in this: that it scarce ever fails of attaining its end when not disgraced by affectation. In short, though her power was very small, she was in her heart one of the warmest friends. She had been a most affectionate wife, and was a most fond and tender mother.

As our history doth not, like a newspaper, give great characters to people who never were heard of before, nor will ever be heard of again, the reader may hence conclude that this excellent woman will hereafter appear to be of some importance in our history.

Nor was Jones a little pleased with the young gentleman himself, whose wine he had been drinking. He thought he discerned in him much good sense, though a little too much tainted with town foppery, but what recommended him most to Jones were some sentiments of great generosity and humanity which occasionally dropped from him, and particularly many expressions of the highest disinterestedness in the affair of love. On which subject the young gentleman delivered himself in a language which might have very well become an Arcadian shepherd of old, and which appeared very extraordinary when proceeding from the lips of a modern fine gentleman; but he was only one by imitation, and meant by nature for a much better character.

6

WHAT ARRIVED WHILE THE COMPANY WERE AT BREAKFAST, WITH SOME HINTS CONCERNING THE GOVERNMENT OF DAUGHTERS

Our company brought together in the morning the same good inclinations towards each other with which they had separated the evening before, but poor Jones was extreme disconsolate; for he had just received information from Partridge that Mrs. Fitzpatrick had left her lodging and that he could not learn whither she was gone. This news highly afflicted him, and his countenance as well as his behaviour, in defiance of all his endeavours to the contrary, betrayed manifest indications of a disordered mind.

The discourse turned at present, as before, on love, and Mr. Nightingale again expressed many of those warm, generous, and disinterested sentiments upon this subject which wise and sober men call romantic, but which wise and sober women generally regard in a better light. Mrs. Miller (for so the mistress of the house was called) greatly approved these sentiments, but when the young gentleman appealed to Miss Nancy, she answered only that she believed the gentleman who had spoke the least was capable of feeling the most.

This compliment was so apparently directed to Jones that we should have been sorry had he passed it by unregarded. He made her, indeed, a very polite answer and concluded with an oblique hint that her own silence subjected her to a suspicion of the same kind; for indeed she had scarce opened her lips either now or the last evening.

"I am glad, Nanny," says Mrs. Miller, "the gentleman hath made the observation; I protest I am almost of his opinion. What can be the matter with you, child? I never saw such an alteration. What is become of all your gaiety? Would you think, sir, I used to call her my little prattler? She hath not spoke twenty words this week."

Here their conversation was interrupted by the entrance of a maidservant, who brought a bundle in her hands, which, she said, was delivered by a porter for Mr. Jones. She added that the man immediately went away, saying it required no answer.

Jones expressed some surprise on this occasion and declared it must be some mistake; but the maid persisting that she was certain of the name, all the women were desirous of having the bundle immediately opened, which operation was at length performed by little Betsy with the consent of Mr. Jones; and the contents were found to be a domino, a mask, and a masquerade ticket.

Jones was now more positive than ever in asserting that these things must have been delivered by mistake, and Mrs. Miller herself expressed some doubt and said she knew not what to think. But when Mr. Nightingale was asked, he delivered a very different opinion. "All I can conclude from it, sir," said he, "is that you are a very happy man; for I make no doubt but these were sent you by some lady whom you will have the happiness of meeting at the masquerade."

Jones had not a sufficient degree of vanity to entertain any such flattering imagination, nor did Mrs. Miller herself give much assent to what Mr. Nightingale had said till Miss Nancy having lifted up the domino, a card dropped from the sleeve, in which was written as follows:

To Mr. Jones.

The Queen of the Fairies sends you this;
Use her favours not amiss.

Mrs. Miller and Miss Nancy now both agreed with Mr.

Nightingale; nay, Jones himself was almost persuaded to be of the same opinion. And as no other lady but Mrs. Fitzpatrick, he thought, knew his lodging, he began to flatter himself with some hopes that it came from her and that he might possibly see his Sophia. These hopes had surely very little foundation, but as the conduct of Mrs. Fitzpatrick, in not seeing him according to her promise and in quitting her lodgings, had been very odd and unaccountable, he conceived some faint hope that she (of whom he had formerly heard a very whimsical character) might possibly intend to do him that service in a strange manner which she declined doing by more ordinary methods. To say the truth, as nothing certain could be concluded from so odd and uncommon an incident, he had the greater latitude to draw what imaginary conclusions from it he pleased. As his temper, therefore, was naturally sanguine, he indulged it on this occasion, and his imagination worked up a thousand conceits to favour and support his expectations of meeting his dear Sophia in the evening.

Reader, if thou hast any good wishes towards me, I will fully repay them by wishing thee to be possessed of this sanguine disposition of mind; since, after having read much and considered long on that subject of happiness, which hath employed so many great pens, I am almost inclined to fix it in the possession of this temper, which puts us in a manner out of the reach of Fortune and makes us happy without her assistance. Indeed, the sensations of pleasure it gives are much more constant, as well as much keener, than those which that blind lady bestows, nature having wisely contrived that some satiety and languor should be annexed to all our real enjoyments lest we should be so taken up by them as to be stopped from further pursuits. I make no manner of doubt but that in this light we may see the imaginary future chancellor just called to the bar, the archbishop in crape, and the prime minister at the tail of an opposition more truly happy than those who are invested with all the power and profit of these respective offices.

Mr. Jones having now determined to go to the masquerade that evening, Mr. Nightingale offered to conduct him thither. The young gentleman at the same time offered tickets to Miss Nancy and her mother, but the good woman would not accept them. She said she did not conceive the harm which some people imagined in a masquerade, but that such extravagant diversions were only proper for persons of quality and fortune, and not for young women who were to get their living and could at best hope to be married to a good tradesman. "A tradesman!" cries Nightingale. "You shan't undervalue my Nancy. There is not a nobleman upon earth above her merit." "Oh fie, Mr. Nightingale," answered Mrs. Miller; "you must not fill the girl's head with such fancies; but if it was her good luck" (says the mother with a simper) "to find a gentleman of your generous way of thinking, I hope she would make a better return to his generosity than to give her mind up to extravagant pleasures. Indeed, where young ladies bring great fortunes themselves they have some right to insist on spending what is their own; and on that account, I have heard the gentlemen say a man has sometimes a better bargain with a poor wife than with a rich one. But let my daughters marry whom they will; I shall endeavour to make them blessings to their husbands. I beg, therefore, I may hear of no more masquerades. Nancy is, I am certain, too good a girl to desire to go; for she must remember when you carried her hither last year, it almost turned her head, and she did not return to herself or to her needle in a month afterwards."

Though a gentle sigh which stole from the bosom of Nancy seemed to argue some secret disapprobation of these sentiments, she did not dare openly to oppose them. For as this good woman had all the tenderness, so she had preserved all the authority, of a parent; and as her indulgence to the desires of her children was only restrained by her fears for their safety and future welfare, so she never suffered those commands which proceeded from such fears to be either disobeyed or disputed. And this the young gentleman, who had lodged two years in the house, knew so well that he presently acquiesced in the refusal.

Mr. Nightingale, who grew every minute fonder of Jones, was very desirous of his company that day to dinner at the tavern, where he offered to introduce him to some of his acquaintance; but Jones begged to be excused, as his clothes, he said, were not yet come to town.

To confess the truth, Mr. Jones was now in a situation which sometimes happens to be the case of a young gentleman of much better figure than himself. In short, he had not one penny in his pocket; a situation in much greater credit among the ancient philosophers than among the modern wise men who live in Lombard Street or those who frequent White's Chocolate-House. And, perhaps, the great honours which those philosophers have ascribed to an empty pocket may be one of the reasons of that high contempt in which they are held in the aforesaid street and chocolate-house.

Now, if the ancient opinion that men might live very comfortably on virtue only, be, as the modern wise men just above mentioned pretend to have discovered, a notorious error, no less false is, I apprehend, that position of some writers of romance: that a man can live altogether on love; for however delicious repasts this may afford to some of our senses or appetites, it is most certain it can afford none to others. Those, therefore, who have placed too great a confidence in such writers have experienced their error when it was too late, and have found that love was no more capable of allaying hunger than a rose is capable of delighting the ear or a violin of gratifying the smell.

Notwithstanding, therefore, all the delicacies which love had set before him—namely, the hope of seeing Sophia at the masquerade, on which, however ill-founded his imagination might be, he had voluptuously feasted during the whole day—the evening no sooner came than Mr. Jones began to languish for some food of a grosser kind. Partridge discovered this by intuition and took the occasion to give some oblique hints concerning the bank-bill, and when these were rejected with disdain, he collected courage enough once more to mention a return to Mr. Allworthy.

"Partridge," cries Jones, "you cannot see my fortune in a more desperate light than I see it myself; and I begin heartily to repent that I suffered you to leave a place where you was settled and to follow me. However, I insist now on your returning home; and for the expense and trouble which you have so kindly put yourself to on my account, all the clothes I left behind in your care I desire you would take as your own. I am sorry I can make you no other acknowledgement."

He spoke these words with so pathetic an accent that Partridge, among whose vices ill nature or hardness of heart were not numbered, burst into tears, and after swearing he would not quit him in his distress, he began with the most earnest entreaties to urge his return home. "For heaven's sake, sir," says he, "do but consider; what can your honour do? How is it possible you can live in this town without money? Do what you will, sir, or go wherever you please, I am resolved not to desert you. But pray, sir, consider. Do, pray, sir, for your own sake, take it into your consideration, and I'm sure," says he, "that your own good sense will bid you return home."

"How often shall I tell thee," answered Jones, "that I have no home to return to? Had I any hopes that Mr. Allworthy's doors would be open to receive me, I want no distress to urge me—nay, there is no other cause upon earth which could detain me a moment from flying to his presence; but, alas, that I am forever banished from. His last words were—Oh, Partridge, they still ring in my ears—his last words were, when he gave me a sum of money, what it was I know not, but considerable I'm sure it was—his last words were: 'I am resolved from this day forward on no account to converse with you any more.'"

Here passion stopped the mouth of Jones, as surprise for a moment did that of Partridge; but he soon recovered the use of speech and after a short preface, in which he declared he had no inquisitiveness in his temper, inquired what Jones meant by a considerable sum, he knew not how much; and what was become of the money.

In both these points he now received full satisfaction; on which he was proceeding to comment when he was interrupted by a message from Mr. Nightingale, who desired his master's company in his apartment.

When the two gentlemen were both attired for the masquerade and Mr. Nightingale had given orders for chairs to be sent for, a circumstance of distress occurred to Jones which will appear very ridiculous to many of my readers. This was how to procure a shilling, but if such readers will reflect a little on what they have themselves felt from the want of a thousand pound or, perhaps, of ten or twenty, to execute a favourite scheme, they will have a perfect idea of what Mr. Jones felt on this occasion. For this sum, therefore, he applied to Partridge, which was the first he had permitted him to advance and was the last he intended that poor fellow should advance in his service. To say the truth, Partridge had lately made no offer of this kind; whether it was that he desired to see the bank-bill broke in upon, or that distress should prevail on Jones to return home, or from what other motive it proceeded, I will not determine.

7

CONTAINING THE WHOLE HUMOURS OF A MASQUERADE

Our cavaliers now arrived at that temple where Heydegger, the great *arbiter deliciarum*, the great high priest of pleasure, presides and, like other heathen priests, imposes on his votaries by the pretended presence of the deity when in reality no such deity is there.

Mr. Nightingale, having taken a turn or two with his companion, soon left him and walked off with a female, saying, "Now you are here, sir, you must beat about for your own game."

Jones began to entertain strong hopes that his Sophia was present, and these hopes gave him more spirits than the lights, the music, and the company, though these are pretty strong antidotes against the spleen. He now accosted every woman he saw whose stature, shape, or air bore any resemblance to his angel. To all of whom he endeavoured to say something smart in order to engage an answer, by which he might discover that voice which he thought it impossible he should mistake. Some of these answered by a question in a squeaking voice, "Do you know me?" Much the greater numbers said, "I don't know you, sir," and nothing more. Some called him an impertinent fellow; some made him no answer at all; some said, "Indeed I don't know your voice, and I shall have nothing to say to you"; and many gave him as kind answers as he could wish, but not in the voice he desired to hear.

Whilst he was talking with one of these last (who was in the habit of a shepherdess) a lady in a domino came up to him and, slapping him on the shoulder, whispered him at the same time in the ear, "If you talk any longer with that trollop, I will acquaint Miss Western."

Jones no sooner heard that name than immediately quitting his former companion, he applied to the domino, begging and entreating her to show him the lady she had mentioned if she was then in the room.

The mask walked hastily to the upper end of the innermost apartment before she spoke, and then, instead of answering him, sat down and declared she was tired. Jones sat down by her and still persisted in his entreaties; at last the lady coldly answered, "I imagined Mr. Jones had been a more discerning lover than to suffer any disguise to conceal his mistress from him." "Is she here then, madam?" replied Jones with much vehemence. Upon which the lady cried, "Hush, sir, you will be observed. I promise you upon my honour, Miss Western is not here."

Jones, now taking the mask by the hand, fell to entreating her in the most earnest manner to acquaint him where he might find Sophia; and when he could obtain no direct answer, he began to upbraid her gently for having disappointed him the day before, and concluded, saying, "Indeed, my good fairy queen, I know your majesty very well, notwithstanding the affected disguise of your voice. Indeed, Mrs. Fitzpatrick, it is a little cruel to divert yourself at the expense of my torments."

The mask answered, "Though you have so ingeniously discovered me, I must still speak in the same voice lest I should be known by others. And do you think, good sir, that I have no greater regard for my cousin than to assist in carrying on an affair between you two, which must end in her ruin as well as your own? Besides, I promise you, my cousin is not mad enough to consent to her own destruction if you are so much her enemy as to tempt her to it."

"Alas, madam," said Jones, "you little know my heart when you call me an enemy of Sophia."

"And yet to ruin any one," cries the other, "you will allow, is the act of an enemy, and when by the same act you must knowingly and certainly bring ruin on yourself, is it not folly or madness as well as guilt? Now, sir, my cousin hath very little more than her father will please to give her, very little for one of her fashion. You know him, and you know your own situation."

Jones vowed he had no such design on Sophia, that he would rather suffer the most violent of deaths than sacrifice her interest to his desires. He said he knew how unworthy he was of her, every way; that he had long ago resolved to quit all such aspiring thoughts but that some strange accidents had made him desirious to see her once more, when he promised he would take leave of her forever. "No, madam," concluded he, "my love is not of that base kind which seeks its own satisfaction at the expense of what is most dear to its object. I would sacrifice everything to the possession of my Sophia but Sophia herself."

Though the reader may have already conceived no very sublime idea of the virtue of the lady in the mask, and though possibly she may hereafter appear not to deserve one of the first characters of her sex, yet it is certain these generous sentiments made a strong impression upon her and greatly added to the affection she had before conceived for our young hero.

The lady now, after a silence of a few moments, said she did not see his pretensions to Sophia so much in the light of presumption as of imprudence. "Young fellows," says she, "can never have too aspiring thoughts. I love ambition in a young man, and I would have you cultivate it as much as possible. Perhaps you may succeed with those who are infinitely superior in fortune; nay, I am convinced there are women—but don't you think me a strange creature, Mr. Jones, to be thus giving advice to a man with whom I am so little acquainted, and one with whose behaviour to me I have so little reason to be pleased?"

Here Jones began to apologize and to hope he had not offended in anything he had said of her cousin. To which the mask answered, "And are you so little versed in the sex to imagine you can well affront a lady more than by entertaining her with your passion for another woman? If the fairy queen had had no better opinion of your gallantry, she would scarce have appointed you to meet her at a masquerade."

Jones had never less inclination to an amour than at present; but gallantry to the ladies was among his principles of honour, and he held it as much incumbent on him to accept a challenge to love as if it had been a challenge to fight. Nay, his very love to Sophia made it necessary for him to keep well with the lady, as he made no doubt but she was capable of bringing him into the presence of the other.

He began, therefore, to make a very warm answer to her last speech when a mask in the character of an old woman joined them. This mask was one of those ladies who go to a masquerade only to vent ill nature by telling people rude truths and by endeavouring, as the phrase is, to spoil as much sport as they are able. This good lady, therefore, having observed Jones and his friend, whom she well knew, in close consultation together in a corner of the room, concluded she could nowhere satisfy her spleen better than by interrupting them. She attacked them, therefore, and soon drove them from their retirement; nor was she contented with this, but pursued them to every place which they shifted to avoid her till Mr. Nightingale, seeing the distress of his friend, at last relieved him and engaged the old woman in another pursuit.

While Jones and his mask were walking together about the room, to rid themselves of the teaser, he observed his lady speak to several masks with the same freedom of acquaintance as if they had been barefaced. He could not help expressing his surprise at this, saying, "Sure, madam, you must have infinite discernment, to know people in all disguises." To which the lady answered, "You cannot conceive anything more insipid and childish than a masquerade to the people of fashion, who in general know one another as well here as when they meet in an assembly or a drawing-room; nor will any woman of condition converse with a person with whom she is not acquainted. In short, the generality of persons whom you see here may more properly be said to kill time in this place than in any other, and generally retire from hence more tired than from the longest sermon. To say the truth, I begin to be in that situation myself, and if I have any faculty at guessing, you are not much better pleased. I protest it would be almost charity in me to go home for your sake." "I know but one charity equal to it," cries Jones, "and that is to suffer me to wait on you home." "Sure," answered the lady, "you have a strange opinion of me to imagine that upon such an acquaintance I would let you into my doors at this time o' night. I fancy you impute the friendship I have shown my cousin to some other motive. Confess honestly; don't you consider this contrived interview as little better than a downright assignation? Are you used, Mr. Jones, to make these sudden conquests?" "I am not used, madam," said Jones, "to submit to such sudden conquests, but as you have taken my heart by surprise, the rest of my body hath a right to follow, so you must pardon me if I resolve to attend you wherever you go." He accompanied these words with some proper actions, upon which the lady, after a gentle rebuke and saying their familiarity would be observed, told him she was going to sup with an acquaintance, whither she hoped he would not follow her; "for if you should," said she, "I shall be thought an unaccountable creature, though my friend indeed is not censorious; yet I hope you won't follow me; I protest I shall not know what to say if you do."

The lady presently after quitted the masquerade, and Jones, notwithstanding the severe prohibition he had received, presumed to attend her. He was now reduced to the same dilemma we have mentioned before: namely, the want of a shilling, and could not relieve it by borrowing as before. He therefore walked boldly on after the chair in which his lady rode, pursued by a grand huzza from all the chairmen present, who wisely take the best care they can to discountenance all walking afoot by their betters. Luckily, however, the gentry who attend at the opera-house were too busy to quit their stations, and as the lateness of the hour prevented him from meeting many of their brethren in the street, he proceeded without molestation in a dress which at another season would have certainly raised a mob at his heels.

The lady was set down in a street not far from Hanover Square, where the door being presently opened, she was carried in, and the gentleman without any ceremony walked in after her.

Jones and his companion were now together in a very well-furnished and well-warmed room, when the female, still speaking in her masquerade voice, said she was surprised at her friend, who must absolutely have forgot her appointment; at which after venting much resentment she suddenly expressed some apprehension from Jones, and asked him what the world would think of their having been alone together in a house at that time of night. But instead of a direct answer to so important a question, Jones began to be very important with the lady to unmask, and at length, having prevailed, there appeared not Mrs. Fitzpatrick, but the Lady Bellaston herself.

It would be tedious to give the particular conversation which consisted of very common and ordinary occurrences, and which lasted from two till six o'clock in the morning. It is sufficient to mention all of it that is anywise material to this history. And this was a promise that the lady would endeavour to find out Sophia and in a few days bring him to an interview with her, on condition that he would then take his leave of her. When this was thoroughly settled, and a second meeting in the evening appointed at the same place, they separated; the lady returned to her house, and Jones to his lodgings.

CONTAINING A SCENE OF DISTRESS, WHICH WILL APPEAR VERY EXTRAORDINARY TO MOST OF OUR READERS

Jones, having refreshed himself with a few hours' sleep, summoned Partridge to his presence and, delivering him a bank-note of fifty pounds, ordered him to go and change it. Partridge received this with sparkling eyes, though when he came to reflect farther, it raised in him some suspicions not very advantageous to the honour of his master; to these the dreadful idea he had of the masquerade, the disguise in which his master had gone out and returned, and his having been abroad all night contributed. In plain language, the only way he could possibly find to account for the possession of this note was by robbery, and to confess the truth, the reader, unless he should suspect it was owing to the generosity of Lady Bellaston, can hardly imagine any other.

To clear, therefore, the honour of Mr. Jones and to do justice to the liberality of the lady, he had really received this present from her, who though she did not give much in to the hackney charities of the age, such as building hospitals, &c., was not, however, entirely void of that Christian virtue, and conceived (very rightly I think) that a young fellow of merit without a shilling in the world was no improper object of this virtue.

Mr. Jones and Mr. Nightingale had been invited to dine this day with Mrs. Miller. At the appointed hour, therefore, the two young gentlemen with the two girls attended in the parlour, where they waited from three till almost five before the good woman appeared. She had been out of town to visit a relation, of whom at her return she gave the following account:

"I hope, gentlemen, you will pardon my making you wait; I am sure if you knew the occasion—I have been to see a cousin of mine, about six miles off, who now lies in. It should be a warning to all persons" (says she, looking at her daughters) "how they marry indiscreetly. There is no happiness in this world without a competency. Oh, Nancy, how shall I describe the wretched condition in which I found your poor cousin? She hath scarce lain in a week, and there was she, this dreadful weather, in a cold room without any curtains to her bed, and not a bushel of coals in her house to supply her with fire; her second son, that sweet little fellow, lies ill of a quinsy in the same bed with his mother, for there is no other bed in the house. Poor little Tommy! I believe, Nancy, you will never see your favourite any more, for he is really very ill. The rest of the children are in pretty good health, but Molly, I am afraid, will do herself an injury; she is but thirteen years old, Mr. Nightingale, and yet in my life I never saw a better nurse; she tends both her mother and her brother, and what is wonderful in a creature so young, she shows all the cheerfulness in the world to her mother; and yet I saw her—I saw the poor child, Mr. Nightingale, turn about and privately wipe the tears from her eyes." Here Mrs. Miller was prevented by her own tears from going on, and there was not, I believe, a person present who did not accompany her in them; at length she a little recovered herself and proceeded thus: "In all this distress the mother supports her spirits in a surprising manner. The danger of her son sits heaviest upon her, and yet she endeavours as much as possible to control even this concern, on her husband's account. Her grief, however, sometimes gets the better of all her endeavours, for she was always extravagantly fond of this boy, and a most sensible, sweet-tempered creature it is. I protest I was never more affected in my life than when I heard the little wretch, who is hardly yet seven years old, while his mother was wetting him with her tears, beg her to be comforted. 'Indeed, Mamma,' cried the child, 'I shan't die; God Almighty, I'm sure, won't take Tommy away; let heaven be ever so fine a place, I had rather stay here and starve with you and my papa than go to it.' Pardon me, gentlemen, I can't help it," says she, wiping her eyes; "such sensibility and affection in a child. And yet, perhaps he is least the object of pity, for a day or two will most probably place him beyond the reach of all human evils. The father is indeed most worthy of compassion. Poor man, his countenance is the very picture of horror, and he looks rather like one dead than alive. Oh, heavens, what a scene did I behold at my first coming into the room! The good creature was lying behind the bolster, supporting at once both his child and his wife. He had nothing on but a thin waistcoat, for his coat was spread over the bed to supply the want of blankets. When he rose up at my entrance, I scarce knew him. As comely a man, Mr. Jones, within this fortnight as you ever beheld; Mr. Nightingale hath seen him. His eyes sunk, his face pale, with a long beard. His body shivering with cold and worn with hunger too, for my cousin says she can hardly prevail upon him to eat. He told me himself in a whisper—he told me—I can't repeat it—he said he could not bear to eat the bread his children wanted. And yet, can you believe it, gentlemen? In all this misery, his wife has as good caudle as if she lay in, in the midst of the greatest affluence; I tasted it, and I scarce ever tasted better. The means of procuring her this, he said, he believed was sent him by an angel from heaven; I know not what he meant, for I had not spirits enough to ask a single question.

"This was a love-match, as they call it, on both sides; that is, a match between two beggars. I must indeed say I never saw a fonder couple, but what is their fondness good for but to torment each other?" "Indeed, Mamma," cries Nancy, "I have always looked on my cousin Anderson" (for that was her name) "as one of the happiest of women." "I am sure," says Mrs. Miller, "the case at present is much otherwise; for any one might have discerned that the tender consideration of each other's sufferings makes the most intolerable part of their calamity, both to the husband and the wife. Compared to which hunger and cold, as they affect their own persons only, are scarce evils. Nay, the very children—the youngest, which is not two years old, excepted—feel in the same manner; for they are a most loving family and, if they had but a bare competency, would be the happiest people in the world." "I never saw the least sign of misery at her house," replied Nancy. "I am sure my heart bleeds for what you now tell me." "Oh, child," answered the mother, "she hath always endeavoured to make the best of everything. They have always been in great distress, but indeed, this absolute ruin hath been brought upon them by others. The poor man was bail for the villain his brother, and about a week ago, the very day before her lying-in, their goods were all carried away and sold by an execution. He sent a letter to·me of it by one of the bailiffs, which the·villain never delivered. What must he think of my suffering a week to pass before he heard of me?"

It was not with dry eyes that Jones heard this narrative; when it was ended, he took Mrs. Miller apart with him into another room and, delivering her his purse, in which was the sum of £50, desired her to send as much of it as she thought proper to these poor people. The look which Mrs. Miller gave Jones on this occasion is not easy to be described. She burst into a kind of agony of transport and cried out, "Good heavens! Is there such a man in the world?" But recollecting herself, she said, "Indeed I know one such, but can there be another?" "I hope, madam," cries Jones, "there are many who have common humanity; for to relieve such distresses in our fellow-creatures can hardly be called more." Mrs. Miller then took ten guineas, which were the utmost he could prevail with her to accept, and said she would find some means of conveying them early the next morning, adding that she had herself done some little matter for the poor people, and had not left them in quite so much misery as she found them.

They then returned to the parlour, where Nightingale expressed much concern at the dreadful situation of these wretches, whom indeed he knew, for he had seen them more than once at Mrs. Miller's. He inveighed against the folly of making oneself liable for the debts of others, vented many bitter execrations against the brother, and concluded with wishing something could be done for the unfortunate family. "Suppose, madam," said he, "you should recommend them to Mr. Allworthy? Or what think you of a collection? I will give them a guinea with all my heart."

Mrs. Miller made no answer; and Nancy, to whom her mother had whispered the generosity of Jones, turned pale upon the occasion, though if either of them was angry with Nightingale, it was surely without reason. For the liberality of Jones, if he had known it, was not an example which he had any obligation to follow, and there are thousands who would not have contributed a single halfpenny; as indeed he did not, in effect, for he made no tender of anything, and therefore as the others thought proper to make no demand, he kept his money in his pocket.

I have in truth observed, and shall never have a better opportunity than at present to communicate my observation, that the world are in general divided into two opinions concerning charity, which are the very reverse of each other. One party seems to hold that all the acts of this kind are to be esteemed as voluntary gifts, and however little you give (if indeed no more than your good wishes), you acquire a great degree of merit in so doing. Others, on the contrary, appear to be as firmly persuaded that beneficence is a positive duty, and that whenever the rich fall greatly short of their ability in relieving the distresses of the poor, their pitiful largesses are so far from being meritorious that they have only performed their duty by halves and are in some sense more contemptible than those who have entirely neglected it.

To reconcile these different opinions is not in my power. I shall only add that the givers are generally of the former sentiment, and the receivers are almost universally inclined to the latter.

9

WHICH TREATS OF MATTERS OF A VERY DIFFERENT KIND
FROM THOSE IN THE PRECEDING CHAPTER

In the evening Jones met his lady again, and a long conversation again ensued between them, but as it consisted only of the same ordinary occurrences as before, we shall avoid mentioning particulars, which we despair of rendering agreeable to the reader unless he is one whose devotion to the fair sex, like that of the papists to their saints, wants to be raised by the help of pictures. But I am so far from desiring to exhibit such pictures to the public that I would wish to draw a curtain over those that have been lately set forth in certain French novels, very bungling copies of which have been presented us here under the name of translations.

Jones grew still more and more impatient to see Sophia; and finding after repeated interviews with Lady Bellaston no likelihood of obtaining this by her means, for on the contrary, the lady began to treat even the mention of the name of Sophia with resentment, he resolved to try some other method. He made no doubt but that Lady Bellaston knew where his angel was, so he thought it likely that some of her servants should be acquainted with the same secret. Partridge, therefore, was employed to get acquainted with those servants in order to fish this secret out of them.

Few situations can be imagined more uneasy than that to which his poor master was at present reduced; for besides the difficulties he met with in discovering Sophia, besides the fears he had of having disobliged her, and the assurances he had received from Lady Bellaston of the resolution which Sophia had taken against him and of her having purposely concealed herself from him, which he had sufficient reason to believe might be true, he had still a difficulty to combat which it was not in the power of his mistress to remove, however kind her inclination might have been. This was the exposing of her to be disinherited of all her father's estate, the almost inevitable consequence of their coming together without a consent, which he had no hopes of ever obtaining.

Add to all these the many obligations which Lady Bellaston, whose violent fondness we can no longer conceal, had heaped upon him, so that by her means he was now become one of the best-dressed men about town, and was not only relieved from those ridiculous distresses we have before mentioned but was actually raised to a state of affluence beyond what he had ever known.

Now, though there are many gentlemen who very well reconcile it to their consciences to possess themselves of the whole fortune of a woman without making her any kind of return, yet to a mind the proprietor of which doth not deserve to be hanged nothing is, I believe, more irksome than to support love with gratitude only, especially where inclination pulls the heart a contrary way. Such was the unhappy case of Jones; for though the virtuous love he bore to Sophia, and which left very little affection for any other woman, had been entirely out of the question, he could never have been able to have made an adequate return to the generous passion of this lady, who had, indeed, been once an object of desire, but was now entered at least into the autumn of life, though she wore all the gaiety of youth both in her dress and manner; nay, she contrived still to maintain the roses in her cheeks, but these, like flowers forced out of season by art, had none of that lively, blooming freshness with which Nature at the proper time bedecks her own productions. She had, besides, a certain imperfection which renders some flowers, though very beautiful to the eye, very improper to be placed in a wilderness of sweets, and what above all others is most disagreeable to the breath of love.

Though Jones saw all these discouragements on the one side, he felt his obligations full as strongly on the other; nor did he less plainly discern the ardent passion whence those obligations proceeded, the extreme violence of which if he failed to equal, he well knew the lady would think him ungrateful, and, what is worse, he would have thought himself so. He knew the tacit consideration upon which all her favours were conferred, and as his necessity obliged him to accept them, so his honour, he concluded, forced him to pay the price. This, therefore, he resolved to do, whatever misery it cost him, and to devote himself to her from that great principle of justice by which the laws of some countries oblige a debtor who is no otherwise capable of discharging his debt to become the slave of his creditor.

While he was meditating on these matters he received the following note from the lady:

A very foolish, but a very perverse, accident hath happened since our last meeting, which makes it improper I should see you any more at the usual place. I will, if possible, contrive some other place by to-morrow. In the meantime, adieu.

This disappointment, perhaps, the reader may conclude was not very great, but if it was, he was quickly relieved, for in less than an hour afterwards another note was brought him from the same hand, which contained as follows:

I have altered my mind since I wrote, a change which if you are no stranger to the tenderest of all passions, you will not wonder at. I am now resolved to see you this evening at my own house, whatever may be the consequence. Come to me exactly at seven; I dine abroad, but will be at home by that time. A day, I find, to those that sincerely love seems longer than I imagined.

If you should accidentally be a few moments before me, bid them show you into the drawing-room.

To confess the truth, Jones was less pleased with this last epistle than he had been with the former, as he was prevented by it from complying with the earnest entreaties of Mr. Nightingale, with whom he had now contracted much intimacy and friendship. These entreaties were to go with that young gentleman and his company to a new play which was to be acted that evening and which a very large party had agreed to damn, from some dislike they had taken to the author, who was a friend to one of Mr. Nightingale's acquaintance. And this sort of fun our hero, we are ashamed to confess, would willingly have preferred to the above kind appointment, but his honour got the better of his inclination.

Before we attend him to this intended interview with the lady, we think proper to account for both the preceding notes, as the reader may possibly be not a little surprised at the imprudence of Lady Bellaston in bringing her lover to the very house where her rival was lodged.

First, then, the mistress of the house where these lovers had hitherto met, and who had been for some years a pensioner to that lady, was now become a Methodist, and had that very morning waited upon her ladyship and, after rebuking her very severely for her past life, had positively declared that she would on no account be instrumental in carrying on any of her affairs for the future.

The hurry of spirits into which this accident threw the lady made her despair of possibly finding any other convenience to meet Jones that evening, but as she began a little to recover from her uneasiness at the disappointment, she set her thoughts to work, when luckily it came into her head to propose to Sophia to go to the play, which was immediately consented to and a proper lady provided for her companion. Mrs. Honour was likewise dispatched with Mrs. Etoff on the same errand of pleasure, and thus her own house was left free for the safe reception of Mr. Jones, with whom she promised herself two or three hours of uninterrupted conversation after her return from the place where she dined, which was at a friend's house in a pretty distant part of the town near her old place of assignation, where she had engaged herself before she was well apprised of the revolution that had happened in the mind and morals of her late confidante.

10

A CHAPTER WHICH, THOUGH SHORT, MAY DRAW TEARS FROM SOME EYES

Mr. Jones was just dressed to wait on Lady Bellaston when Mrs. Miller rapped at his door and, being admitted, very earnestly desired his company below-stairs to drink tea in the parlour.

Upon his entrance into the room she presently introduced a person to him, saying, "This, sir, is my cousin, who hath been so greatly beholden to your goodness, for which he begs to return you his sincerest thanks."

The man had scarce entered upon that speech which Mrs. Miller had so kindly prefaced when both Jones and he, looking steadfastly at each other, showed at once the utmost tokens of surprise. The voice of the latter began instantly to falter, and instead of finishing his speech, he sunk down into a chair, crying, "It is so; I am convinced it is so!"

"Bless me, what's the meaning of this?" cries Mrs. Miller. "You are not ill, I hope, cousin? Some water; a dram this instant."

"Be not frightened, madam," cries Jones; "I have almost as much need of a dram as your cousin. We are equally surprised at this unexpected meeting. Your cousin is an acquaintance of mine, Mrs. Miller."

"An acquaintance!" cries the man. "Oh, heaven!"

"Ay, an acquaintance," repeated Jones, "and an honoured acquaintance too. When I do not love and honour the man who dares venture everything to preserve his wife and children from instant destruction, may I have a friend capable of disowning me in adversity."

"Oh you are an excellent young man," cries Mrs. Miller; "yes indeed, poor creature! He hath ventured everything. If he had not had one of the best of constitutions, it must have killed him."

"Cousin," cries the man, who had now pretty well recovered himself, "this is the angel from heaven whom I meant. This is he to whom before I saw you I owed the preservation of my Peggy. He it was to whose generosity every comfort, every support which I have procured for her, was owing. He is indeed the worthiest, bravest, noblest of all human beings. Oh, cousin, I have obligations to this gentleman of such a nature!"

"Mention nothing of obligations," cries Jones eagerly; "not a word, I insist upon it; not a word" (meaning, I suppose, that he would not have him betray the affair of the robbery to any person). "If by the trifle you have received from me I have preserved a whole family, sure pleasure was never bought so cheap."

"Oh, sir," cries the man, "I wish you could this instant see my house. If any person had ever a right to the pleasure you mention, I am convinced it is yourself. My cousin tells me she acquainted you with the distress in which she found us. That, sir, is all greatly removed, and chiefly by your goodness. My children have now a bed to lie on—and they have—they have—eternal blessings reward you for it—they have bread to eat. My little boy is recovered, my wife is out of danger, and I am happy. All, all owing to you, sir, and to my cousin here, one of the best of women. Indeed, sir, I must see you at my house. Indeed my wife must see you and thank you. My children, too, must express their gratitude. Indeed, sir, they are not without a sense of their obligation, but what is my feeling when I reflect to whom I owe that they are now capable of expressing their gratitude. Oh, sir, the little hearts which you have warmed had now been as cold as ice without your assistance!"

Here Jones attempted to prevent the poor man from proceeding, but indeed, the overflowing of his own heart would of itself have stopped his words. And now Mrs. Miller likewise began to pour forth thanksgivings, as well in her own name as in that of her cousin, and concluded with saying she doubted not but such goodness would meet a glorious reward.

Jones answered he had been sufficiently rewarded already. "Your cousin's account, madam," said he, "hath given me a sensation more pleasing than I have ever known. He must be a wretch who is unmoved at hearing such a story; how transporting, then, must be the thought of having happily acted a part in this scene! If there are men who cannot feel the delight of giving happiness to others, I sincerely pity them, as they are incapable of tasting what is in my opinion a greater honour, a higher interest, and a sweeter pleasure than the ambitious, the avaricious, or the voluptuous man can ever obtain."

The hour of appointment being now come, Jones was forced to take a hasty leave, but not before he had heartily shaken his friend by the hand and desired to see him again as soon as possible, promising that he would himself take the first opportunity of visiting him at his own house. He then stepped into his chair and proceeded to Lady Bellaston's, greatly exulting in the happiness which he had procured to this poor family; nor could he forbear reflecting without horror on the dreadful consequences which must have attended them had he listened rather to the voice of strict justice than to that of mercy when he was attacked on the high road.

Mrs. Miller sung forth the praises of Jones during the whole evening, in which Mr. Anderson, while he stayed, so passionately accompanied her that he was often on the very point of mentioning the circumstances of the robbery. However, he luckily recollected himself and avoided an indiscretion which would have been so much the greater as he knew Mrs. Miller to be extremely strict and nice in her principles. He was likewise well apprised of the loquacity of this lady, and yet, such was his gratitude that it had almost got the better both of discretion and shame and made him publish that which would have defamed his own character, rather than omit any circumstances which might do the fullest honour to his benefactor.

11

IN WHICH THE READER WILL BE SURPRISED

Mr. Jones was rather earlier than the time appointed and earlier than the lady, whose arrival was hindered not only by the distance of the place where she dined but by some other cross accidents, very vexatious to one in her situation of mind. He was accordingly shown into the drawing-room, where he had not been many minutes before the door opened and in came—no other than Sophia herself, who had left the play before the end of the first act; for this, as we have already said, being a new play, at which two large parties met, the one to damn and the other to applaud, a violent uproar and an engagement between the two parties had so terrified our heroine that she was glad to put herself under the protection of a young gentleman, who safely conveyed her to her chair.

As Lady Bellaston had acquainted her that she should not be at home till late, Sophia, expecting to find no one in the room, came hastily in and went directly to a glass which almost fronted her without once looking towards the upper end of the room, where the statue of Jones now stood motionless. In this glass it was, after contemplating her own lovely face, that she first discovered the said statue, when, instantly turning about, she perceived the reality of the vision; upon which she gave a violent scream and scarce preserved herself from fainting till Jones was able to move to her and support her in his arms.

To paint the looks or thoughts of either of these lovers is beyond my power. As their sensations from their mutual silence may be judged to have been too big for their own utterance, it cannot be supposed that I should be able to express them; and the misfortune is that few of my readers have been enough in love to feel by their own hearts what passed at this time in theirs.

After a short pause, Jones with faltering accents said, "I see, madam, you are surprised." "Surprised!" answered she. "Oh, heavens! Indeed, I am surprised. I almost doubt whether you are the person you seem." "Indeed," cries he, "my Sophia—pardon me, madam, for this once calling you so—I am that very wretched Jones, whom Fortune after so many disappointments hath at last kindly conducted to you. Oh, my Sophia, did you know the thousand torments I have suffered in this long, fruitless pursuit!" "Pursuit of whom?" said Sophia, a little recollecting herself and assuming a reserved air. "Can you be so cruel to ask that question?" cries Jones. "Need I say of you?" "Of me?" answered Sophia. "Hath Mr. Jones, then, any such important business with me?" "To some, madam," cries Jones, "this might seem an important business" (giving her the pocket-book). "I hope, madam, you will find it of the same value as when it was lost." Sophia took the pocket-book and was going to speak when he interrupted her thus: "Let us not, I beseech you, lose one of these precious moments which Fortune hath so kindly sent us. Oh, my Sophia, I have business of a much superior kind. Thus, on my knees, let me ask your pardon." "My pardon?" cries she. "Sure, sir, after what is past, you cannot expect, after what I have heard——" "I scarce know what I say," answered Jones. "By heavens, I scarce wish you should pardon me! Oh, my Sophia, henceforth never cast away a thought on such a wretch as I am. If any remembrance of me should ever intrude to give a moment's uneasiness to that tender bosom, think of my unworthiness, and let the remembrance of what passed at Upton blot me forever from your mind."

Sophia stood trembling all this while. Her face was whiter than snow, and her heart was throbbing through her stays. But at the mention of Upton a blush arose in her cheeks, and her eyes, which before she had scarce lifted up, were turned upon Jones with a glance of disdain. He understood this silent reproach and replied to it thus: "Oh, my Sophia, my only love, you cannot hate or despise me more for what happened there than I do myself, but yet do me the justice to think that my heart was never unfaithful to you. *That* had no share in the folly I was guilty of; it was even then unalterably yours. Though I despaired of possessing you, nay, almost of ever seeing you more, I doted still on your charming idea and could *seriously* love no other woman. But if my heart had not been engaged, she into whose company I accidentally fell at that cursed place was not an object of serious love. Believe me, my angel, I never have seen her from that day to this, and never intend or desire to see her again." Sophia in her heart was very glad to hear this, but forcing into her face an air of more coldness than she yet had assumed, "Why," said she, "Mr. Jones, do you take the trouble to make a defence where you are not accused? If I thought it worth-while to accuse you, I have a charge of an unpardonable nature indeed." "What is it, for heaven's sake?" answered Jones, trembling and pale, expecting to hear of his amour with Lady Bellaston. "Oh," said she, "how is it possible! Can everything noble and everything base be lodged together in the same bosom?" Lady Bellaston, and the ignominious circumstance of having been *kept*, rose again in his mind and stopped his mouth from any reply. "Could I have expected," proceeded Sophia, "such treatment from you? Nay, from any gentleman, from any man of honour? To have my name traduced in public, in inns, among the meanest vulgar! To have any little favours that my unguarded heart may have too lightly betrayed me to grant boasted of there! Nay, even to hear that you had been forced to fly from my love!"

Nothing could equal Jones's surprise at these words of Sophia; but yet, not being guilty, he was much less embarrassed how to defend himself than if she had touched that tender string at which his conscience had been alarmed. By some examination, he presently found that her supposing him guilty of so shocking an outrage against his love and her reputation was entirely owing to Partridge's talk at the inns before landlords and servants, for Sophia confessed to him it was from them that she received her intelligence. He had no very great difficulty to make her believe that he was entirely innocent of an offence so foreign to his character, but she had a great deal to hinder him from going instantly home and putting Partridge to death, which he more than once swore he would do. This point being cleared up, they soon found themselves so well pleased with each other that Jones quite forgot he had begun the conversation with conjuring her to give up all thoughts of him, and she was in a temper to have given ear to a petition of a very different nature; for before they were aware, they had both gone so far that he let fall some words that sounded like a proposal of marriage. To which she replied that did not her duty to her father forbid her to follow her own inclinations, ruin with him would be more welcome to her than the most affluent fortune with another man. At the mention of the word *ruin* he started, let drop her hand, which he had held for some time, and, striking his breast with his own, cried out, "Oh, Sophia, can I, then, ruin thee? No, by heavens, no! I never will act so base a part. Dearest Sophia, whatever it costs me, I will renounce you; I will give you up; I will tear all such hopes from my heart as are inconsistent with your real good. My love I will ever retain, but it shall be in silence; it shall be at a distance from you; it shall be in some foreign land, from whence no voice, no sigh of my despair, shall ever reach and disturb your ears. And when I am dead——" He would have gone on, but was stopped by a flood of tears which Sophia let fall in his bosom, upon which she leaned without being able to speak one word. He kissed them off, which for some moments she allowed him to do without any resistance, but then, recollecting herself, gently withdrew out of his arms, and to turn the discourse from a subject too tender, and which she found she could not support, bethought herself to ask him a question she had never had time to put to him before: how he came into that room. He began to stammer, and would in all probability have raised her suspicions by the answer he was going to give, when at once the door opened, and in came Lady Bellaston.

Having advanced a few steps, and seeing Jones and Sophia together, she suddenly stopped; when after a pause of a few moments, recollecting herself with admirable presence of mind, she said, though with sufficient indications of surprise both in voice and countenance: "I thought, Miss Western, you had been at the play?"

Though Sophia had had no opportunity of learning of Jones by what means he had discovered her, yet as she had not the least suspicion of the real truth or that Jones and Lady Bellaston were acquainted, so she was very little confounded; and the less as the lady had in all their conversations on the subject entirely taken her side against her father. With very little hesitation, therefore, she went through the whole story of what had happened at the playhouse and the cause of her hasty return.

The length of this narrative gave Lady Bellaston an opportunity of rallying her spirits and of considering in what manner to act. And as the behaviour of Sophia gave her hopes that Jones had not betrayed her, she put on an air of good humour and said, "I should not have broken in so abruptly upon you, Miss Western, if I had known you had company."

Lady Bellaston fixed her eyes on Sophia whilst she spoke these words. To which that poor young lady, having her face overspread with blushes and confusion, answered in a stammering voice, "I am sure, madam, I shall always think the honour of your ladyship's company——" "I hope, at least," cries Lady Bellaston, "I interrupt no business." "No, madam," answered Sophia, "our business was at an end. Your ladyship may be pleased to remember I have often mentioned the loss of my pocket-book, which this gentleman, having very luckily found, was so kind to return to me with the bill in it."

Jones, ever since the arrival of Lady Bellaston, had been ready to sink with fear. He sat kicking his heels, playing with his fingers, and looking more like a fool, if it be possible, than a young booby squire when he is first introduced into a polite assembly. He began, however, now to recover himself, and taking a hint from the behaviour of Lady Bellaston, who, he saw, did not intend to claim any acquaintance with him, he resolved as entirely to affect the stranger on his part. He said ever since he had had the pocket-book in his possession, he had used great diligence in inquiring out the lady whose name was writ in it, but never till that day could be so fortunate to discover her.

Sophia had, indeed, mentioned the loss of her pocket-book to Lady Bellaston, but as Jones for some reason or other had never once hinted to her that it was in his possession, she believed not one syllable of what Sophia now said, and wonderfully admired the extreme quickness of the young lady in inventing such an excuse. The reason of Sophia's leaving the playhouse met with no better credit, and though she could not account for the meeting between these two lovers, she was firmly persuaded it was not accidental.

With an affected smile, therefore, she said, "Indeed, Miss Western, you have had very good luck in recovering your money. Not only as it fell into the hands of a gentleman of honour but as he happened to discover to whom it belonged. I think you would not consent to have it advertised. It was great good fortune, sir, that you found out to whom the note belonged."

"Oh, madam," cries Jones, "it was inclosed in a pocket-book in which the young lady's name was written."

"That was very fortunate indeed," cries the lady. "And it was no less so that you heard Miss Western was at my house, for she is very little known."

Jones had at length perfectly recovered his spirits, and as he conceived he had now an opportunity of satisfying Sophia as to the question she had asked him just before Lady Bellaston came in, he proceeded thus: "Why, madam," answered he, "it was the luckiest chance imaginable I made this discovery. I was mentioning what I had found and the name of the owner the other night to a lady at the masquerade, who told me she believed she knew where I might see Miss Western, and if I would come to her house the next morning, she would inform me. I went according to her appointment, but she was not at home; nor could I ever meet with her till this morning, when she directed me to your ladyship's house. I came accordingly and did myself the honour to ask for your ladyship, and upon my saying that I had very particular business, a servant showed me into this room, where I had not been long before the young lady returned from the play."

Upon his mentioning the masquerade, he looked very slyly at Lady Bellaston without any fear of being remarked by Sophia, for she was visibly too much confounded to make any observations. This hint a little alarmed the lady, and she was silent; when Jones, who saw the agitations of Sophia's mind, resolved to take the only method of relieving her, which was by retiring, but before he did this, he said, "I believe, madam, it is customary to give some reward on these occasions. I must insist on a very high one for my honesty: it is, madam, no less than the honour of being permitted to pay another visit here."

"Sir," replied the lady, "I make no doubt that you are a gentleman, and my doors are never shut to people of fashion."

Jones then, after proper ceremonials, departed, highly to his own satisfaction and no less to that of Sophia, who was terribly alarmed lest Lady Bellaston should discover what she knew already but too well.

Upon the stairs Jones met his old acquaintance Mrs. Honour, who, notwithstanding all she had said against him, was now so well bred to behave with great civility. This meeting proved, indeed, a lucky circumstance, as he communicated to her the house where he lodged, with which Sophia was unacquainted.

12

IN WHICH THE THIRTEENTH BOOK IS CONCLUDED

The elegant Lord Shaftesbury somewhere objects to telling too much truth, by which it may be fairly inferred that, in some cases, to lie is not only excusable but commendable.

And surely there are no persons who may so properly challenge a right to this commendable deviation from truth as young women in the affair of love, for which they may plead precept, education, and, above all, the sanction, nay, I may say the necessity, of custom, by which they are restrained not from submitting to the honest impulses of nature (for that would be a foolish prohibition) but from owning them.

We are not, therefore, ashamed to say that our heroine now pursued the dictates of the above-mentioned right honourable philosopher. As she was perfectly satisfied, then, that Lady Bellaston was ignorant of the person of Jones, so she determined to keep her in that ignorance, though at the expense of a little fibbing.

Jones had not been long gone before Lady Bellaston cried, "Upon my word, a good, pretty, young fellow; I wonder who he is, for I don't remember ever to have seen his face before."

"Nor I neither, madam," cries Sophia; "I must say he behaved very handsomely in relation to my note."

"Yes, and he is a very handsome fellow," said the lady; "don't you think so?"

"I did not take much notice of him," answered Sophia, "but I thought he seemed rather awkward and ungenteel than otherwise."

"You are extremely right," cries Lady Bellaston. "You may see by his manner that he hath not kept good company. Nay, notwithstanding his returning your note and refusing the reward, I almost question whether he is a gentleman. I have always observed there is a something in persons well-born which others can never acquire. I think I will give orders not to be at home to him."

"Nay, sure, madam," answered Sophia, "one can't suspect after what he hath done. Besides, if your ladyship observed him, there was an elegance in his discourse, a delicacy, a prettiness of expression that, that—"

"I confess," said Lady Bellaston, "the fellow hath words —and indeed, Sophia, you must forgive me; indeed you must."

"I forgive your ladyship!" said Sophia.

"Yes, indeed, you must," answered she, laughing, "for I had a horrible suspicion when I first came into the room—I vow you must forgive it, but I suspected it was Mr. Jones himself."

"Did your ladyship indeed?" cries Sophia, blushing and affecting a laugh.

"Yes, I vow I did," answered she; "I can't imagine what put it into my head, for, give the fellow his due, he was genteelly dressed, which I think, dear Sophy, is not commonly the case with your friend."

"This raillery," cries Sophia, "is a little cruel, Lady Bellaston, after my promise to your ladyship."

"Not at all, child," said the lady. "It would have been cruel before, but after you have promised me never to marry without your father's consent, in which you know is implied your giving up Jones, sure you can bear a little raillery on a passion which was pardonable enough in a young girl in the country and of which you tell me you have so entirely got the better. What must I think, my dear Sophy, if you cannot bear a little ridicule even on his dress? I shall begin to fear you are very far gone indeed, and almost question whether you have dealt ingenuously with me."

"Indeed, madam," cries Sophia, "your ladyship mistakes me if you imagine I had any concern on his account."

"On his account?" answered the lady. "You must have mistaken me; I went no farther than his dress, for I would not injure your taste by any other comparison. I don't imagine, my dear Sophy, if your Mr. Jones had been such a fellow as this——"

"I thought," says Sophia, "your ladyship had allowed him to be handsome."

"Whom, pray?" cried the lady, hastily.

"Mr. Jones," answered Sophia—and immediately recollecting herself, "Mr. Jones! No, no, I ask your pardon—I mean the gentleman who was just now here."

"Oh, Sophy! Sophy!" cries the lady. "This Mr. Jones, I am afraid, still runs in your head."

"Then upon my honour, madam," said Sophia, "Mr. Jones is as entirely indifferent to me as the gentleman who just now left us."

"Upon my honour," said Lady Bellaston, "I believe it. Forgive me, therefore, a little innocent raillery, but I promise you I will never mention his name any more."

And now the two ladies separated, infinitely more to the delight of Sophia than of Lady Bellaston, who would willingly have tormented her rival a little longer had not business of more importance called her away. As for Sophia, her mind was not perfectly easy under this first practice of deceit, upon which when she retired to her chamber she reflected with the highest uneasiness and conscious shame. Nor could the peculiar hardship of her situation and the necessity of the case at all reconcile her conduct to her mind, the frame of which was too delicate to bear the thought of having been guilty of a falsehood, however qualified by circumstances. Nor did this thought once suffer her to close her eyes during the whole succeeding night.

BOOK XIV

CONTAINING TWO DAYS

1

AN ESSAY TO PROVE THAT AN AUTHOR WILL WRITE THE BETTER FOR HAVING SOME KNOWLEDGE OF THE SUBJECT ON WHICH HE WRITES

As several gentlemen in these times, by the wonderful force of genius only, without the least assistance of learning, perhaps without being well able to read, have made a considerable figure in the republic of letters, the modern critics, I am told, have lately begun to assert that all kind of learning is entirely useless to a writer, and, indeed, no other than a kind of fetters on the natural spriteliness and activity of the imagination, which is thus weighed down and prevented from soaring to those high flights which otherwise it would be able to reach.

This doctrine, I am afraid, is at present carried much too far; for why should writing differ so much from all other arts? The nimbleness of a dancing-master is not at all prejudiced by being taught to move, nor doth any mechanic, I believe, exercise his tools the worse by knowing how to use them. For my own part, I cannot conceive that Homer or Virgil would have writ with more fire if, instead of being masters of all the learning of their times, they had really been as ignorant as most of the authors of the present age. Nor do I believe that all the imagination, fire, and judgement of Pitt could have produced those orations that have made the senate of England in these our times a rival in eloquence to Greece and Rome if he had not been so well read in the writings of Demosthenes and Cicero as to have transfused their whole spirit into his speeches and, with their spirit, their knowledge too.

I would not here be understood to insist on the same fund of learning in any of my brethren as Cicero persuades us is necessary to the composition of an orator. On the contrary, very little reading is, I conceive, necessary to the poet, less to the critic, and the least of all to the politician. For the first, perhaps, Bysshe's *Art of Poetry* and a few of our modern poets may suffice; for the second, a moderate heap of plays; and for the last, an indifferent collection of political journals.

To say the truth, I require no more than that a man should have some little knowledge of the subject on which he treats, according to the old maxim of law, *Quam quisque norit artem in eâ se exerceat*. With this alone a writer may sometimes do tolerably well; and indeed, without this all the other learning in the world will stand him in little stead.

For instance, let us suppose that Homer and Virgil, Aristotle and Cicero, Thucydides and Livy, could have met all together and have clubbed their several talents to have composed a treatise on the art of dancing; I believe it will be readily agreed they could not have equalled the excellent treatise which Mr. Essex hath given us on that subject, entitled *The Rudiments of Genteel Education*. And indeed, should the excellent Mr. Broughton be prevailed on to set fist to paper, and to complete the abovesaid rudiments by delivering down the true principles of athletics, I question whether the world will have any cause to lament that none of the great writers, either ancient or modern, have ever treated about that noble and useful art.

To avoid a multiplicity of examples in so plain a case and to come at once to my point, I am apt to conceive that one reason why many English writers have totally failed in describing the manners of upper life may possibly be that in reality they know nothing of it.

This is a knowledge unhappily not in the power of many authors to arrive at. Books will give us a very imperfect idea of it, nor will the stage a much better: the fine gentleman formed upon reading the former will almost always turn out a pedant, and he who forms himself upon the latter, a coxcomb.

Nor are the characters drawn from these models better supported. Vanbrugh and Congreve copied Nature, but they who copy them draw as unlike the present age as Hogarth would do if he was to paint a rout or a drum in the dresses of Titian and of Vandyke. In short, imitation here will not do the business. The picture must be after Nature herself. A true knowledge of the world is gained only by conversation, and the manners of every rank must be seen in order to be known.

Now, it happens that this higher order of mortals is not to be seen, like all the rest of the human species, for nothing, in the streets, shops, and coffee-houses; nor are they shown like the upper rank of animals, for so much apiece. In short, this is a sight to which no persons are admitted without one or other of these qualifications: viz., either birth or fortune, or what is equivalent to' both, the honourable profession of a gamester. And, very unluckily for the world, persons so qualified very seldom care to take upon themselves the bad trade of writing, which is generally entered upon by the lower and poorer sort, as it is a trade which many think requires no kind of stock to set up with.

Hence those strange monsters in lace and embroidery, in silks and brocades, with vast wigs and hoops, which under the name of lords and ladies strut the stage, to the great delight of attorneys and their clerks in the pit, and of citizens and their apprentices in the galleries, and which are no more to be found in real life than the centaur, the chimera, or any other creature of mere fiction. But to let my reader into a secret, this knowledge of upper life, though very necessary for the preventing mistakes, is no very great resource to a writer whose province is comedy or that kind of novels which, like this I am writing, is of the comic class.

What Mr. Pope says of women is very applicable to most in this station, who are indeed so entirely made up of form and affectation that they have no character at all, at least, none which appears. I will venture to say the highest life is much the dullest and affords very little humour or entertainment. The various callings in lower spheres produce the great variety of humorous characters, whereas here, except among the few who are engaged in the pursuit of ambition and the fewer still who have a relish for pleasure, all is vanity and servile imitation. Dressing and cards, eating and drinking, bowing and curtsying, make up the business of their lives.

Some there are, however, of this rank upon whom passion exercises its tyranny and hurries them far beyond the bounds which decorum prescribes; of these, the ladies are as much distinguished by their noble intrepidity and a certain superior contempt of reputation from the frail ones of meaner degree as a virtuous woman of quality is by the elegance and delicacy of her sentiments from the honest wife of a yeoman or shopkeeper. Lady Bellaston was of this intrepid character, but let not my country readers conclude from her that this is the general conduct of women of fashion, or that we mean to represent them as such. They might as well suppose that every clergyman was represented by Thwackum or every soldier by Ensign Northerton.

There is not, indeed, a greater error than that which universally prevails among the vulgar, who, borrowing their opinion from some ignorant satirists, have affixed the character of lewdness to these times. On the contrary, I am convinced there never was less of love intrigue carried on among persons of condition than now. Our present women have been taught by their mothers to fix their thoughts only on ambition and vanity, and to despise the pleasures of love as unworthy their regard; and being afterwards by the care of such mothers married without having husbands, they seem pretty well confirmed in the justness of those sentiments; whence they content themselves for the dull remainder of life with the pursuit of more innocent, but I am afraid more childish, amusements, the bare mention of which would ill suit with the dignity of this history. In my humble opinion, the true characteristic of the present *beau-monde* is rather folly than vice, and the only epithet which it deserves is that of *frivolous*.

2

CONTAINING LETTERS AND OTHER MATTERS WHICH ATTEND
AMOURS

Jones had not long been at home before he received the following letter:

I was never more surprised than when I found you was gone. When you left the room, I little imagined you intended to have left the house without seeing me again. Your behaviour is all of a piece and convinces me how much I ought to despise a heart which can dote upon an idiot, though I know not whether I should not admire her cunning more than her simplicity: wonderful both! For though she understood not a word of what passed between us, she yet had the skill, the assurance, the—what shall I call it?—to deny to my face that she knows you or ever saw you before. Was this a scheme laid between you, and have you been base enough to betray me? Oh, how I despise her, you, and all the world, but chiefly myself, for —I dare not write what I should afterwards run mad to read; but remember, I can detest as violently as I have loved.

Jones had but little time given him to reflect on this letter before a second was brought him from the same hand; and this, likewise, we shall set down in the precise words:

When you consider the hurry of spirits in which I must have writ, you cannot be surprised at any expressions in my former note. Yet, perhaps, on reflection, they were rather too warm. At least I would if possible think all owing to the odious playhouse, and to the impertinence of a fool, which detained me beyond my appointment. How easy is it to think well of those we love? Perhaps you desire I should think so. I have resolved to see you to-night, so come to me immediately.
P.S. I have ordered to be at home to none but yourself.
P.S. Mr. Jones will imagine I shall assist him in his defence, for I believe he cannot desire to impose on me more than I desire to impose on myself.
P.S. Come immediately.

To the men of intrigue I refer the determination whether the angry or the tender letter gave the greatest uneasiness to Jones. Certain it is he had no violent inclination to pay any more visits that evening, unless to one single person. However, he thought his honour engaged, and had not this been motive sufficient, he would not have ventured to blow the temper of Lady Bellaston into that flame of which he had reason to think it susceptible, and of which he feared the consequence might be a discovery to Sophia, which he dreaded. After some discontented walks, therefore, about the room, he was preparing to depart when the lady kindly prevented him, not by another letter but by her own presence. She entered the room very disordered in her dress and very discomposed in her looks, and threw herself into a chair, where, having recovered her breath, she said, "You see, sir, when women have gone one length too far, they will stop at none. If any person would have sworn this to me a week ago, I would not have believed it of myself." "I hope, madam," said

Jones, "my charming Lady Bellaston will be as difficult to believe anything against one who is so sensible of the many obligations she hath conferred upon him." "Indeed!" says she. "Sensible of obligations! Did I expect to hear such cold language from Mr. Jones?" "Pardon me, my dear angel," said he, "if after the letters I have received, the terrors of your anger, though I know not how I have deserved it——" "And have I, then," says she with a smile, "so angry a countenance? Have I really brought a chiding face with me?" "If there be honour in man," said he, "I have done nothing to merit your anger. You remember the appointment you sent me—I went in pursuance—" "I beseech you," cried she, "do not run through the odious recital. Answer me but one question and I shall be easy: have you not betrayed my honour to her?" Jones fell upon his knees and began to utter the most violent protestations, when Partridge came dancing and capering into the room like one drunk with joy, crying out, "She's found! She's found! Here, sir, here; she's here—Mrs. Honour is upon the stairs." "Stop her a moment," cries Jones. "Here, madam, step behind the bed; I have no other room nor closet nor place on earth to hide you in; sure never was so damned an accident!" "D—ned indeed!" said the lady as she went to her place of concealment; and presently afterwards in came Mrs. Honour. "Heyday!" says she. "Mr. Jones, what's the matter? That impudent rascal, your servant, would scarce let me come upstairs. I hope he hath not the same reason now to keep me from you as he had at Upton. I suppose you hardly expected to see me, but you have certainly bewitched my lady. Poor dear young lady! To be sure, I loves her as tenderly as if she was my own sister. Lord have mercy upon you if you don't make her a good husband; and to be sure, if you do not, nothing can be bad enough for you." Jones begged her only to whisper, for that there was a lady dying in the next room. "A lady!" cries she. "Ay, I suppose one of your ladies. Oh, Mr. Jones, there are too many of them in the world; I believe we are got into the house of one, for my Lady Bellaston I darst to say is no better than she should be." "Hush! Hush!" cries Jones. "Every word is overheard in the next room." "I don't care a farthing," cries Honour; "I speaks no scandal of any one; but to be sure, the servants make no scruple of saying as how her ladyship meets men at another place— where the house goes under the name of a poor gentlewoman but her ladyship pays the rent; and many's the good thing besides, they say, she hath of her." Here Jones, after expressing the utmost uneasiness, offered to stop her mouth. "Heyday! Why, sure, Mr. Jones, you will let me speak; I speaks no scandal, for I only says what I heard from others, and, thinks I to myself, much good may it do the gentlewoman with her riches if she comes by it in such a wicked manner. To be sure, it is better to be poor and honest." "The servants are villains," cries Jones, "and abuse their lady unjustly." "Ay, to be sure, servants are always villains, and so my lady says, and won't hear a word of it." "No, I am convinced," says Jones, "my Sophia is above listening to such base scandal." "Nay, I believe it is no scandal neither," cries Honour, "for why should she meet men at another house? It can never be for any good; for if she had a lawful design of being courted, as to be sure any lady may lawfully give her company to men upon that account, why, where can be the sense——" "I protest," cries Jones, "I can't hear all this of a lady of such honour and a relation of Sophia; besides, you will distract the poor lady in the next room. Let me entreat you to walk with me downstairs." "Nay, sir, you won't let me speak, I have done. Here, sir, is a letter from my young lady. What would some men give to have this? But, Mr. Jones, I think you are not over and above generous, and yet I have heard some servants say— But I am sure you will do me the justice to own I never saw the colour of your money." Here Jones hastily took the letter and presently after slipped five pieces into her hand. He then returned a thousand thanks to his dear Sophia in a whisper and begged her to leave him to read her letter; she presently departed, not without expressing much grateful sense of his generosity.

Lady Bellaston now came from behind the curtain. How shall I describe her rage? Her tongue was at first incapable of utterance, but streams of fire darted from her eyes, and well indeed they might, for her heart was all in a flame. And now as soon as her voice found way, instead of expressing any indignation against Honour or her own servants, she began to attack poor Jones. "You see," said she, "what I have sacrificed to you; my reputation, my honour—gone forever! And what return have I found? Neglected, slighted, for a country-girl, for an idiot." "What neglect, madam, or what slight," cries Jones, "have I been guilty of?" "Mr. Jones," said she, "it is in vain to dissemble; if you will make me easy, you must entirely give her up, and as a proof of your intention, show me the letter." "What letter, madam?" said

Jones. "Nay, surely," said she, "you cannot have the confidence to deny your having received a letter by the hands of that trollop." "And can your ladyship," cries he, "ask of me what I must part with my honour before I grant? Have I acted in such a manner by your ladyship? Could I be guilty of betraying this poor innocent girl to you, what security could you have that I should not act the same part by yourself? A moment's reflection will, I am sure, convince you that a man with whom the secrets of a lady are not safe must be the most contemptible of wretches." "Very well," said she, "I need not insist on your becoming this contemptible wretch in your own opinion, for the inside of the letter could inform me of nothing more than I know already. I see the footing you are upon." Here ensued a long conversation, which the reader who is not too curious will thank me for not inserting at length. It shall suffice, therefore, to inform him that Lady Bellaston grew more and more pacified, and at length believed, or affected to believe, his protestations that his meeting with Sophia that evening was merely accidental, and every other matter which the reader already knows; and which as Jones set before her in the strongest light, it is plain that she had in reality no reason to be angry with him.

She was not, however, in her heart perfectly satisfied with his refusal to show her the letter, so deaf are we to the clearest reason when it argues against our prevailing passions. She was, indeed, well convinced that Sophia possessed the first place in Jones's affections, and yet, haughty and amorous as this lady was, she submitted at last to bear the second place, or, to express it more properly in a legal phrase, was contented with the possession of that of which another woman had the reversion.

It was at length agreed that Jones should for the future visit at the house; for that Sophia, her maid, and all the servants would place these visits to the account of Sophia, and that she herself would be considered as the person imposed upon.

This scheme was contrived by the lady and highly relished by Jones, who was indeed glad to have a prospect of seeing his Sophia at any rate, and the lady herself was not a little pleased with the imposition on Sophia, which Jones, she thought, could not possibly discover to her for his own sake.

The next day was appointed for the first visit, and then after proper ceremonials the Lady Ballaston returned home.

CONTAINING VARIOUS MATTERS

Jones was no sooner alone than he eagerly broke open his letter and read as follows:

Sir, it is impossible to express what I have suffered since you left this house, and as I have reason to think you intend coming here again, I have sent Honour, though so late at night, as she tells me she knows your lodgings, to prevent you. I charge you by all the regard you have for me not to think of visiting here, for it will certainly be discovered; nay, I almost doubt from some things which have dropped from her ladyship that she is not already without some suspicion. Something favourable perhaps may happen; we must wait with patience, but I once more entreat you, if you have any concern for my ease, do not think of returning hither.

This letter administered the same kind of consolation to poor Jones which Job formerly received from his friends. Besides disappointing all the hopes which he promised to himself from seeing Sophia, he was reduced to an unhappy dilemma with regard to Lady Bellaston; for there are some certain engagements which, as he well knew, do very difficulty admit of any excuse for the failure, and to go after the strict prohibition from Sophia, he was not to be forced by any human power. At length, after much deliberation, which during that night supplied the place of sleep, he determined to feign himself sick; for this suggested itself as the only means of failing the appointed visit without incensing Lady Bellaston, which he had more than one reason of desiring to avoid.

The first thing, however, which he did in the morning was to write an answer to Sophia, which he enclosed in one to Honour. He then dispatched another to Lady Bellaston containing the above-mentioned excuse, and to this he soon received the following answer:

I am vexed that I cannot see you here this afternoon,

but more concerned for the occasion; take great care of yourself and have the best advice, and I hope there will be no danger. I am so tormented all this morning with fools that I have scarce a moment's time to write to you. Adieu.

P.S. I will endeavour to call on you this evening at nine. Be sure to be alone.

Mr. Jones now received a visit from Mrs. Miller, who after some formal introduction began the following speech: "I am very sorry, sir, to wait upon you on such an occasion; but I hope you will consider the ill consequence which it must be to the reputations of my poor girls if my house should once be talked of as a house of ill fame. I hope you won't think me, therefore, guilty of impertinence if I beg you not to bring any more ladies in at that time of night. The clock had struck two before one of them went away." "I do assure you, madam," said Jones, "the lady who was here last night, and who stayed the latest (for the other only brought me a letter), is a woman of very great fashion and my near relation." "I don't know what fashion she is of," answered Mrs. Miller, "but I am sure no woman of virtue, unless a very near relation indeed, would visit a young gentleman at ten at night and stay four hours in his room with him alone; besides, sir, the behaviour of her chairmen shows what she was, for they did nothing but make jests all the evening in the entry, and asked Mr. Partridge in the hearing of my own maid if madam intended to stay with his master all night, with a great deal of stuff not proper to be repeated. I have really a great respect for you, Mr. Jones, upon your own account; nay, I have a very high obligation to you for your generosity to my cousin. Indeed, I did not know how very good you had been till lately. Little did I imagine to what dreadful courses the poor man's distress had driven him. Little did I think when you gave me the ten guineas that you had given them to a highwayman! Oh, heavens! What goodness have you shown! How have you preserved this family! The character which Mr. Allworthy hath formerly given me of you was, I find, strictly true. And indeed, if I had no obligation to you, my obligations to him are such that on his account I should show you the utmost respect in my power. Nay, believe me, dear Mr. Jones, if my daughters and my own reputation were out of the case, I should for your own sake be sorry that so pretty a young gentleman should converse with these women; but if you are resolved to do it, I must beg you to take another lodging, for I do not myself like to have such things carried on under my roof, but more especially upon the account of my girls, who have little, heaven knows, besides their characters to recommend them." Jones started and changed colour at the name of Allworthy. "Indeed, Mrs. Miller," answered he a little warmly, "I do not take this at all kind. I will never bring any slander on your house, but I must insist on seeing what company I please in my own room; and if that gives you any offence, I shall as soon as I am able look for another lodging." "I am sorry we must part then, sir," said she, "but I am convinced Mr. Allworthy himself would never come within my doors if he had the least suspicion of my keeping an ill house." "Very well, madam," said Jones. "I hope, sir," said she, "you are not angry, for I would not for the world offend any of Mr. Allworthy's family. I have not slept a wink all night about this matter." "I am sorry I have disturbed your rest, madam," said Jones, "but I beg you will send Partridge up to me immediately"; which she promised to do, and then with a very low curtsy retired.

As soon as Partridge arrived, Jones fell upon him in the most outrageous manner. "How often," said he, "am I to suffer for your folly, or rather for my own in keeping you? Is that tongue of yours resolved upon my destruction?" "What have I done, sir?" answered affrighted Partridge. "Who was it gave you authority to mention the story of the robbery, or that the man you saw here was the person?" "I, sir?" cries Partridge. "Now, don't be guilty of a falsehood in denying it," said Jones. "If I did mention such a matter," answers Partridge, "I am sure I thought no harm; for I should not have opened my lips if it had not been to his own friends and relations, who, I imagined, would have let it go no farther." "But I have a much heavier charge against you," cries Jones, "than this. How durst you, after all the precautions I gave you, mention the name of Mr. Allworthy in this house?" Partridge denied that he ever had, with many oaths. "How else," said Jones, "should Mrs. Miller be acquainted that there was any connection between him and me? And it is but this moment she told me she respected me on his account." "Oh, Lord, sir," said Partridge, "I desire only to be heard out; and to be sure, never was anything so unfortunate; hear me but out and you will own how wrongfully you have accused me. When Mrs. Honour came downstairs last night, she met me in the entry and asked me when my master had heard from Mr. Allworthy; and to be sure, Mrs. Miller heard the very words, and the moment Madam Honour was gone, she called me into the parlour to her. 'Mr. Partridge,' says she, 'what Mr. Allworthy is that the gentlewoman mentioned? Is it the great Mr. Allworthy of Somersetshire?' 'Upon my word, madam,' says I, 'I know nothing of the matter.' 'Sure,' says she, 'your master is not the Mr. Jones I have heard Mr. Allworthy talk of?' 'Upon my word, madam,' says I, 'I know nothing of the matter.' 'Then,' says she, turning to her daughter Nancy, says she, 'as sure as tenpence, this is the very young gentleman, and he agrees exactly with the squire's description.' The Lord above knows who it was told her, for I am the arrantest villain that ever walked upon two legs if ever it came out of my mouth. I promise you, sir, I can keep a secret when I am desired. Nay, sir, so far was I from telling her anything about Mr. Allworthy that I told her the very direct contrary; for though I did not contradict it at that moment, yet, as second thoughts, they say, are best, so when I came to consider that somebody must have informed her, thinks I to myself I will put an end to the story; and so I went back again into the parlour some time afterwards and says I, 'upon my word,' says I, 'whoever,' says I, 'told you that this gentleman was Mr. Jones? That is,' says I, 'that this Mr. Jones was that Mr. Jones, told you a confounded lie, and I beg,' says I, 'you will never mention any such matter,' says I; 'for my master,' says I, 'will think I must have told you so; and I defy anybody in the house ever to say I mentioned any such word.' To be certain, sir, it is a wonderful thing, and I have been thinking with myself ever since how it was she came to know it; not but I saw an old woman here t'other day a-begging at the door who looked as like her we saw in Warwickshire that caused all that mischief to us. To be sure, it is never good to pass by an old woman without giving her something, especially if she looks at you; for all the world shall never persuade me but that they have a great power to do mischief, and to be sure, I shall never see an old woman again but I shall think to myself, *Infandum, regina, jubes renovare dolorem.*"

The simplicity of Partridge set Jones a-laughing and put a final end to his anger, which had, indeed, seldom any long duration in his mind; and instead of commenting on his defence, he told him he intended presently to leave those lodgings, and ordered him to go and endeavour to get him others.

4

WHICH WE HOPE WILL BE VERY ATTENTIVELY PERUSED BY YOUNG PEOPLE OF BOTH SEXES

Partridge had no sooner left Mr. Jones than Mr. Nightingale, with whom he had now contracted a great intimacy, came to him and after a short salutation said, "So, Tom, I hear you had company very late last night. Upon my soul, you are a happy fellow, who have not been in town above a fortnight and can keep chairs waiting at your door till two in the morning." He then ran on with much commonplace raillery of the same kind till Jones at last interrupted him, saying, "I suppose you have received all this information from Mrs. Miller, who hath been up here a little while ago to give me warning. The good woman is afraid, it seems, of the reputation of her daughters." "Oh, she is wonderfully nice," says Nightingale, "upon that account; if you remember, she would not let Nancy go with us to the masquerade." "Nay, upon my honour, I think she's in the right of it," says Jones. "However, I have taken her at her word and have sent Partridge to look for another lodging." "If you will," says Nightingale, "we may, I believe, be again together; for to tell you a secret, which I desire you won't mention in the family, I intend to quit the house to-day." "What, hath Mrs. Miller given you warning too, my friend?" cries Jones. "No," answered the other, "but the rooms are not convenient enough. Besides, I am grown weary of this part of the town. I want to be nearer the places of diversion, so I am going to Pall Mall." "And do you intend to make a secret of your going away?" said Jones. "I promise you," answered Nightingale, "I don't intend to bilk my lodgings, but I have a private reason for not taking a formal leave." "Not so private," answered Jones, "I promise you; I have seen it ever since the second day of my coming to the house. Here will be some wet eyes on your departure. Poor Nancy, I pity her, faith! Indeed, Jack, you have played the fool with that girl. You have given her a longing which, I am afraid, nothing will ever cure her of." Nightingale answered, "What the devil would you have me do? Would you have me marry her to cure her?" "No," answered Jones, "I would not have had you make love to her, as you have often done in my presence. I have been astonished at the blindness of her mother in never seeing it." "Pugh, see it!" cries Nightingale. "What the devil should she see?" "Why, see," said Jones, "that you have made her daughter distractedly in love with you. The poor girl cannot conceal it a moment; her eyes are never off from you and she always colours every time you come into the room. Indeed, I pity her heartily, for she seems to be one of the best-natured and honestest of human creatures." "And so," answered Nightingale, "according to your doctrine, one must not amuse oneself by any common gallantries with women for fear they should fall in love with us." "Indeed, Jack," said Jones, "you wilfully misunderstand me; I do not fancy women are so apt to fall in love, but you have gone far beyond common gallantries." "What, do you suppose," says Nightingale, "that we have been abed together?" "No, upon my honour," answered Jones, very seriously, "I do not suppose so ill of you; nay, I will go farther, I do not imagine you have laid a regular premeditated scheme for the destruction of the quiet of a poor little creature, or have even foreseen the consequence; for I am sure thou art a very good-natured fellow, and such a one can never be guilty of a cruelty of that kind, but at the same time you have pleased your own vanity without considering that this poor girl was made a sacrifice to it, and while you have had no design but of amusing an idle hour, you have actually given her reason to flatter herself that you had the most serious designs in her favour. Prithee, Jack, answer me honestly: to what have tended all those elegant and luscious descriptions of happiness arising from violent and mutual fondness, all those warm professions of tenderness and generous, disinterested love? Did you imagine she would not apply them? Or, speak ingenuously, did not you intend she should?" "Upon my soul, Tom," cries Nightingale, "I did not think this was in thee. Thou wilt make an admirable parson. So, I suppose, you would not go to bed to Nancy now if she would let you?" "No," cries Jones, "may I be d—ned if I would." "Tom, Tom," answered Nightingale, "last night; remember last night,

'When every eye was closed, and the pale moon

And silent stars shone conscious of the theft.' "

"Lookee, Mr. Nightingale," said Jones, "I am no canting hypocrite, nor do I pretend to the gift of chastity more than my neighbours. I have been guilty with women, I own it, but am not conscious that I have ever injured any; nor would I, to procure pleasure to myself be knowingly the cause of misery to any human being."

"Well, well," said Nightingale, "I believe you, and I am convinced you acquit me of any such thing."

"I do, from my heart," answered Jones, "of having debauched the girl, but not from having gained her affections."

"If I have," said Nightingale, "I am sorry for it, but time and absence will soon wear off such impressions. It is a receipt I must take myself; for to confess the truth to you, I never liked any girl half so much in my whole life; but I must let you into the whole secret, Tom. My father hath provided a match for me with a woman I never saw, and she is now coming to town in order for me to make my addresses to her."

At these words Jones burst into a loud fit of laughter, when Nightingale cried, "Nay, prithee don't turn me into ridicule. The devil take me if I am not half mad about this matter! My poor Nancy! Oh, Jones, Jones, I wish I had a fortune in my own possession."

"I heartily wish you had," cries Jones, "for if this be the case, I sincerely pity you both; but surely you don't intend to go away without taking your leave of her?"

"I would not," answered Nightingale, "undergo the pain of taking leave for ten thousand pound; besides, I am convinced, instead of answering any good purpose it would only serve to inflame my poor Nancy the more. I beg, therefore, you would not mention a word of it to-day, and in the evening or to-morrow morning I intend to depart."

Jones promised he would not; and said upon reflection he thought, as he had determined and was obliged to leave her, he took the most prudent method. He then told Nightingale he should be very glad to lodge in the same house with him, and it was accordingly agreed between them that Nightingale should procure him either the ground floor or the two pair of stairs, for the young gentleman himself was to occupy that which was between them.

This Nightingale, of whom we shall be presently obliged to say a little more, was in the ordinary transactions of life a man of strict honour and, what is more rare among young gentlemen of the town, one of strict honesty too; yet in affairs of love he was somewhat looser in his morals; not that he was even here as void of principle as gentlemen sometimes are, and oftener affect to be, but it is certain he had been guilty of some indefensible treachery to women, and had, in a certain mystery called Making Love, practised many deceits which, if he had used in trade, he would have been counted the greatest villain upon earth.

But as the world, I know not well for what reason, agree to see this treachery in a better light, he was so far from being ashamed of his iniquities of this kind that he gloried in them, and would often boast of his skill in gaining of women and his triumphs over their hearts; for which he had before this time received some rebukes from Jones, who always expressed great bitterness against any misbehaviour to the fair part of the species, who if considered, he said, as they ought to be, in the light of the dearest friends were to be cultivated, honoured, and caressed with the utmost love and tenderness, but if regarded as enemies, were a conquest of which a man ought rather to be ashamed than to value himself upon it.

5

A SHORT ACCOUNT OF THE HISTORY OF MRS. MILLER

Jones this day eat a pretty good dinner for a sick man, that is to say, the larger half of a shoulder of mutton. In the afternoon he received an invitation from Mrs. Miller to drink tea; for that good woman, having learnt either by means of Partridge or by some other means natural or supernatural that he had a connection with Mr. Allworthy, could not endure the thoughts of parting with him in an angry manner.

Jones accepted the invitation; and no sooner was the tea-kettle removed and the girls sent out of the room than the widow, without much preface, began as follows: "Well, there are very surprising things happen in this world, but certainly it is a wonderful business that I should have a relation of Mr. Allworthy in my house and never know anything of the matter. Alas, sir, you little imagine what a friend that best of gentlemen hath been to me and mine. Yes, sir, I am not ashamed to own it; it is owing to his goodness that I did not long since perish for want, and leave my poor little wretches—two destitute, helpless, friendless orphans—to the care, or rather to the cruelty, of the world.

"You must know, sir, though I am now reduced to get my living by letting lodgings, I was born and bred a gentlewoman. My father was an officer of the army and died in a considerable rank, but he lived up to his pay, and as that expired with him, his family at his death became beggars. We were three sisters. One of us had the good luck to die soon after of the smallpox; a lady was so kind as to take the second out of charity, as she said, to wait upon her. The mother of this lady had been a servant to my grandmother, and having inherited a vast fortune from her father, which he had got by pawnbroking, was married to a gentleman of great estate and fashion. She used my sister so barbarously, often upbraiding her with her birth and poverty, calling her in derision a gentlewoman, that I believe she at length broke the heart of the poor girl. In short, she likewise died within a twelvemonth after my father. Fortune thought proper to provide better for me, and within a month from his decease I was married to a clergyman, who had been my lover a long time before and who had been very ill-used by my father on that account; for though my poor father could not give any of us a shilling, yet he bred us up as delicately, considered us, and would have had us consider ourselves, as highly as if we had been the richest heiresses. But my dear husband forgot all this usage, and the moment we were become fatherless he immediately renewed his addresses to me so warmly that I, who always liked and now more than ever esteemed him, soon complied. Five years did I live in a state of perfect happiness with that best of men till at last— Oh, cruel, cruel Fortune that ever separated us, that deprived me of the kindest of husbands and my poor girls of the tenderest parent! Oh, my poor girls, You never knew the blessing which ye lost! I am ashamed, Mr. Jones, of this womanish weakness, but I shall never mention him without tears." "I ought rather, madam," said Jones, "to be ashamed that I do not accompany you." "Well, sir," continued she, "I was now left a second time in a much worse condition than before; besides the terrible affliction I was to encounter, I had now two children to provide for, and was if possible more penniless than ever when that great, that good, that glorious, man, Mr. Allworthy, who had some little acquaintance with my husband, accidentally heard of my distress and immediately writ this letter to me. Here, sir; here it is; I put it into my pocket to show it you. This is the letter, sir; I must and will read it to you.

'MADAM,

'I heartily condole with you on your late grievous loss, which your own good sense and the excellent lessons you must have learnt from the worthiest of men will better enable you to bear than any advice which I am capable of giving. Nor have I any doubt that you, whom I have heard to be the tenderest of mothers, will suffer any immoderate indulgence of grief to prevent you from discharging your duty to those poor infants who now alone stand in need of your tenderness.

'However, as you must be supposed at present to be incapable of much worldly consideration, you will pardon my having ordered a person to wait on you and to pay you twenty guineas, which I beg you will accept till I have the pleasure of seeing you, and believe me to be, madam, &c.'

"This letter, sir, I received within a fortnight after the irreparable loss I have mentioned, and within a fortnight afterwards Mr. Allworthy—the blessed Mr. Allworthy—came to pay me a visit, when he placed me in the house where you now see me, gave me a large sum of money to furnish it, and settled an annuity of £50 a year upon me, which I have constantly received ever since. Judge, then, Mr. Jones, in what regard I must hold a benefactor to whom I owe the preservation of my life, and of those dear children, for whose sake alone my life is valuable. Do not, therefore, think me impertinent, Mr. Jones (since I must esteem one for whom I know Mr. Allworthy hath so much value), if I beg you not to converse with these wicked women. You are a young gentleman and do not know half their artful wiles. Do not be angry with me, sir, for what I said upon account of my house; you must be sensible it would be the ruin of my poor dear girls. Besides, sir, you cannot but be acquainted that Mr. Allworthy himself would never forgive my conniving at such matters, and particularly with you."

"Upon my word, madam," said Jones, "you need make no farther apology, nor do I in the least take anything ill you have said; but give me leave, as no one can have more value than myself for Mr. Allworthy, to deliver you from one mistake, which perhaps would not be altogether for his honour; I do assure you, I am no relation of his."

"Alas, sir," answered she, "I know you are not. I know very well who you are, for Mr. Allworthy hath told me all; but I do assure you, had you been twenty times his son, he could not have expressed more regard for you than he hath often expressed in my presence. You need not be ashamed, sir, of what you are; I promise you no good person will esteem you the less on that account. No, Mr. Jones; the words *dishonourable birth* are nonsense, as my dear, dear husband used to say, unless the word *dishonourable* be applied to the parents, for the children can derive no real dishonour from an act of which they are entirely innocent."

Here Jones heaved a deep sigh and then said, "Since I perceive, madam, you really do know me and Mr. Allworthy hath thought proper to mention my name to you, and since you have been so explicit with me as to your own affairs, I will acquaint you with some more circumstances concerning myself." And these Mrs. Miller having expressed great desire and curiosity to hear, he began and related to her his whole history, without once mentioning the name of Sophia.

There is a kind of sympathy in honest minds by means of which they give an easy credit to each other. Mrs. Miller believed all which Jones told her to be true and expressed much pity and concern for him. She was beginning to comment on the story, but Jones interrupted her; for as the hour of assignation now drew nigh, he began to stipulate for a second interview with the lady that evening, which he promised should be the last at her house, swearing at the same time that she was one of great distinction, and that nothing but what was entirely innocent was to pass between them; and I do firmly believe he intended to keep his word.

Mrs. Miller was at length prevailed on and Jones departed to his chamber, where he sat alone till twelve o'clock, but no Lady Bellaston appeared.

As we have said that this lady had a great affection for Jones, and as it must have appeared that she really had so, the reader may perhaps wonder at the first failure of her appointment, as she apprehended him to be confined by sickness, a season when friendship seems most to require such visits. This behaviour, therefore, in the lady may by some be condemned as unnatural; but that is not our fault, for our business is only to record truth.

6

CONTAINING A SCENE WHICH WE DOUBT NOT WILL AFFECT ALL OUR READERS

Mr. Jones closed not his eyes during all the former part of the night, not owing to any uneasiness which he conceived at being disappointed by Lady Bellaston; nor was Sophia herself, though most of his waking hours were justly to be charged to her account, the present cause of dispelling his slumbers. In fact, poor Jones was one of the best-natured fellows alive and had all that weakness which is called compassion, and which distinguishes this imperfect character from that noble firmness of mind which rolls a man, as it were, within himself and, like a polished bowl, enables him to run through the world without being once stopped by the calamities which happen to others. He could not help, therefore, compassionating the situation of poor Nancy, whose love for Mr. Nightingale seemed to him so apparent that he was astonished at the blindness of her mother, who had more than once the preceding evening remarked to him the great change in the temper of her daughter, "who from being," she said, "one of the liveliest, merriest girls in the world was, on a sudden, become all gloom and melancholy."

Sleep, however, at length got the better of all resistance; and now, as if he had really been a deity, as the ancients imagined, and an offended one too, he seemed to enjoy his dear-bought conquest. To speak simply and without any metaphor, Mr. Jones slept till eleven the next morning, and would perhaps have continued in the same quiet situation much longer had not a violent uproar awakened him.

Partridge was now summoned, who, being asked what was the matter, answered that there was a dreadful hurricane below-stairs, that Miss Nancy was in fits, and that the other sister and the mother were both crying and lamenting over her. Jones expressed much concern at this news, which Partridge endeavoured to relieve, by saying with a smile he fancied the young lady was in no danger of death, for that

Susan (which was the name of the maid) had given him to understand it was nothing more than a common affair. "In short," said he, "Miss Nancy hath had a mind to be as wise as her mother; that's all. She was a little hungry, it seems, and so sat down to dinner before grace was said; and so there is a child coming for the Foundling Hospital." "Prithee leave thy stupid jesting," cries Jones. "Is the misery of these poor wretches a subject of mirth? Go immediately to Mrs. Miller and tell her I beg leave— Stay, you will make some blunder; I will go myself, for she desired me to break-fast with her." He then rose and dressed himself as fast as he could; and while he was dressing, Partridge, notwith-standing many severe rebukes, could not avoid throwing forth certain pieces of brutality, commonly called jests, on this occasion. Jones was no sooner dressed than he walked downstairs, and, knocking at the door, was presently ad-mitted by the maid into the outward parlour, which was as empty of company as it was of any apparatus for eating. Mrs. Miller was in the inner room with her daughter, whence the maid presently brought a message to Mr. Jones that her mistress hoped he would excuse the disappointment, but an accident had happened which made it impossible for her to have the pleasure of his company at breakfast that day; and begged his pardon for not sending him up notice sooner. Jones desired she would give herself no trouble about any-thing so trifling as his disappointment, that he was heartily sorry for the occasion, and that if he could be of any service to her, she might command him.

He had scarce spoke these words when Mrs. Miller, who heard them all, suddenly threw open the door and, coming out to him, in a flood of tears said, "Oh, Mr. Jones, you are certainly one of the best young men alive. I give you a thou-sand thanks for your kind offer of your service, but alas, sir, it is out of your power to preserve my poor girl. Oh, my child, my child! She is undone; she is ruined forever!" "I hope, madam," said Jones, "no villain——" "Oh, Mr. Jones," said she, "that villain who yesterday left my lodgings hath betrayed my poor girl, hath destroyed her. I know you are a man of honour. You have a good, a noble, heart, Mr. Jones. The actions to which I have been myself a witness could proceed from no other. I will tell you all; nay, indeed, it is impossible after what hath happened to keep it a secret. That Nightingale, that barbarous villain, hath undone my daughter. She is—she is— Oh, Mr. Jones, my girl is with child by him, and in that condition he hath deserted her! Here, here, sir, is his cruel letter! Read it, Mr. Jones, and tell me if such another monster lives."

The letter was as follows:

DEAR NANCY,

As I found it impossible to mention to you what I am afraid will be no less shocking to you than it is to me, I have taken this method to inform you that my father insists upon my immediately paying my addresses to a young lady of fortune whom he hath provided for my— I need not write the detested word. Your own good understanding will make you sensible how entirely I am obliged to an obedience by which I shall be forever excluded from your dear arms. The fondness of your mother may encourage you to trust her with the unhappy consequence of our love, which may be easily kept a secret from the world and for which I will take care to provide, as I will for you. I wish you may feel less on this account than I have suffered; but summon all your fortitude to your assistance, and forgive and forget the man whom nothing but the prospect of certain ruin could have forced to write this letter. I bid you forget me; I mean only as a lover, but the best of friends you shall ever find in

Your faithful, though unhappy,

J.N.

When Jones had read this letter, they both stood silent during a minute, looking at each other; at last he began thus: "I cannot express, madam, how much I am shocked at what I have read, yet let me beg you in one particular to take the writer's advice. Consider the reputation of your daughter." "It is gone; it is lost, Mr. Jones," cried she, "as well as her innocence. She received the letter in a roomful of company, and, immediately swooning away upon opening it, the contents were known to every one present. But the loss of her reputation, bad is it is, is not the worst; I shall lose my child; she hath attempted twice to destroy herself already, and though she hath been hitherto prevented, vows she will not outlive it, nor could I myself outlive any accident of that nature. What then will become of my little Betsy, a helpless infant orphan? And the poor little wretch will, I believe, break her heart at the miseries with which she sees her sister and myself distracted, while she is ignorant of the cause. Oh, 'tis the most sensible and best-natured little thing. The barbarous, cruel . . . hath destroyed us all. Oh, my poor children! Is this the reward of all my cares? Is this the fruit of all my prospects? Have I so cheerfully undergone all the labours and duties of a mother? Have I been so tender of their infancy, so careful of their education? Have I been toiling so many years, denying myself even the conveniences of life to provide some little sustenance for them, to lose one or both in such a manner?" "Indeed, madam," said Jones, with tears in his eyes, "I pity you from my soul." "Oh, Mr. Jones," answered she, "even you, though I know the goodness of your heart, can have no idea of what I feel. The best, the kindest, the most dutiful of children. Oh, my poor Nancy, the darling of my soul, the delight of my eyes, the pride of my heart; too much, indeed, my pride, for to those foolish, ambitious hopes arising from her beauty I owe her ruin. Alas, I saw with pleasure the liking which this young man had for her. I thought it an honourable affection, and flattered my foolish vanity with the thoughts of seeing her married to one so much her superior. And a thousand times in my presence, nay, often in yours, he hath endeavoured to soothe and encourage these hopes by the most generous expressions of disinterested love, which he hath always directed to my poor girl, and which I, as well as she, believed to be real. Could I have believed that these were only snares laid to betray the innocence of my child and for the ruin of us all?" At these words little Betsy came running into the room crying, "Dear mamma, for heaven's sake come to my sister, for she is in another fit and my cousin can't hold her." Mrs. Miller immediately obeyed the summons, but first ordered Betsy to stay with Mr. Jones, and begged him to entertain her a few minutes, saying in the most pathetic voice, "Good heaven! Let me preserve one of my children at least."

Jones in compliance with this request did all he could to comfort the little girl, though he was in reality himself very highly affected with Mrs. Miller's story. He told her her sister would be very well again soon; that by taking on in that manner, she would not only make her sister worse but make her mother ill too. "Indeed, sir," says she, "I would not do anything to hurt them for the world. I would burst my heart rather than they should see me cry. But my poor sister can't see me cry. I am afraid she will never be able to see me cry any more. Indeed, I can't part with her; indeed

I can't. And then poor Mamma too, what will become of her? She says she will die too and leave me; but I am resolved I won't be left behind." "And are you not afraid to die, my little Betsy?" said Jones. "Yes," answered she, "I was always afraid to die because I must have left my mamma, and my sister, but I am not afraid of going anywhere with those I love."

Jones was so pleased with this answer that he eagerly kissed the child, and soon after Mrs. Miller returned, saying she thanked heaven Nancy was now come to herself. "And now Betsy," says she, "you may go in, for your sister is better and longs to see you." She then turned to Jones and began to renew her apologies for having disappointed him of his breakfast.

"I hope, madam," said Jones, "I shall have a more exquisite repast than any you could have provided for me. This, I assure you, will be the case if I can do any service to this little family of love. But whatever success may attend my endeavours, I am resolved to attempt it. I am very much deceived in Mr. Nightingale if, notwithstanding what hath happened, he hath not much goodness of heart at the bottom, as well as a very violent affection for your daughter. If this be the case, I think the picture which I shall lay before him will affect him. Endeavour, madam, to comfort yourself and Miss Nancy as well as you can. I will go instantly in quest of Mr. Nightingale, and I hope to bring you good news."

Mrs. Miller fell upon her knees and invoked all the blessings of heaven upon Mr. Jones, to which she afterwards added the most passionate expressions of gratitude. He then departed to find Mr. Nightingale, and the good woman returned to comfort her daughter, who was somewhat cheered at what her mother told her; and both joined in resounding the praises of Mr. Jones.

7

THE INTERVIEW BETWEEN MR. JONES AND MR. NIGHTINGALE

The good or evil we confer on others very often, I believe, recoils on ourselves; for as men of a benign disposition enjoy their own acts of the beneficence equally with those to whom they are done, so there are scarce any natures so entirely diabolical as to be capable of doing injuries without paying themselves some pangs for the ruin which they bring on their fellow-creatures.

Mr. Nightingale, at least, was not such a person. On the contrary, Jones found him in his new lodgings sitting melancholy by the fire and silently lamenting the unhappy situation in which he had placed poor Nancy. He no sooner saw his friend appear than he rose hastily to meet him and after much congratulation said, "Nothing could have been more opportune than this kind visit, for I was never more in the spleen in my life."

"I am sorry," answered Jones, "that I bring news very unlikely to relieve you; nay, what I am convinced must, of all other, shock you the most. However, it is necessary you should know it. Without further preface, then, I come to you, Mr. Nightingale, from a worthy family which you have involved in misery and ruin." Mr. Nightingale changed colour at these words, but Jones, without regarding it, proceeded in the liveliest manner to paint the tragical story with which the reader was acquainted in the last chapter.

Nightingale never once interrupted the narration, though he discovered violent emotions at many parts of it. But when it was concluded, after fetching a deep sigh he said, "What you tell me, my friend, affects me in the tenderest manner. Sure there never was so cursed an accident as the poor girl's betraying my letter. Her reputation might otherwise have been safe and the affair might have remained a profound secret, and then the girl might have gone off never the worse; for many such things happen in this town, and if the husband should suspect a little when it is too late, it will be his wiser conduct to conceal his suspicion both from his wife and the world."

"Indeed, my friend," answered Jones, "this could not have been the case with your poor Nancy. You have so entirely gained her affections that it is the loss of you, and not of her reputation, which afflicts her, and will end in the destruction of her and her family." "Nay, for that matter, I promise you," cries Nightingale, "She hath my affections so absolutely that my wife, whoever she is to be, will have very little share in them." "And is it possible, then," said Jones, "you can think of deserting her?" "Why, what can I do?" answered the other. "Ask Miss Nancy," replied Jones warmy. "In the condition to which you have reduced her, I sincerely think she ought to determine what reparation you shall make her. Her interest alone, and not yours, ought to be your sole consideration. But if you ask me what you shall do, what can you do less," cries Jones, "than fulfil the expectations of her family and her own? Nay, and I sincerely tell you they were mine too ever since I first saw you together. You will pardon me if I presume on the friendship you have favoured me with, moved as I am with compassion for those poor creatures. But your own heart will best suggest to you whether you have never intended, by your conduct, to persuade the mother as well as the daughter into an opinion that you designed honourably; and if so, though there may have been no direct promise of marriage in the case, I will leave to your own good understanding how far you are bound to proceed."

"Nay, I must not only confess what you have hinted," said Nightingale, "but I am afraid even that very promise you mention I have given."- "And can you, after owning that," said Jones, "hesitate a moment?" "Consider, my friend," answered the other; "I know you are a man of honour and would advise no one to act contrary to its rules; if there were no other objection, can I after this publication of her disgrace think of such an alliance with honour?" "Undoubtedly," replied Jones, "and the very best and truest honour, which is goodness, requires it of you. As you mention a scruple of this kind, you will give me leave to examine it. Can you with honour be guilty of having under false pretences deceived a young woman and her family, and of having by these means treacherously robbed her of her innocence? Can you with honour be the knowing, the wilful, nay, I must add the artful, contriver of the ruin of a human being? Can you with honour destroy the fame, the peace, nay, probably both the life and soul too, of this creature? Can honour bear the thought that this creature is a tender, helpless, defenceless young woman? A young woman who loves, who dotes on you, who dies for you; who hath placed the utmost confidence in your promises, and to that confidence hath sacrificed everything which is dear to her? Can honour support such contemplations as these a moment?"

"Common sense, indeed," said Nightingale, "warrants all you say, but yet you well know the opinion of the world is so much the contrary that was I to marry a whore, though my own, I should be ashamed of ever showing my face again."

"Fie upon it, Mr. Nightingale," said Jones; "do not call her by so ungenerous a name; when you promised to marry her she became your wife, and she hath sinned more against prudence than virtue. And what is this world which you would be ashamed to face but the vile, the foolish, and the profligate? Forgive me if I say such a shame must proceed from false modesty, which always attends false honour as its shadow. But I am well assured there is not a man of real sense and goodness in the world who would not honour and applaud the action. But admit no other would, would not your own heart, my friend, applaud it? And do not the warm, rapturous sensations which we feel from the consciousness of an honest, noble, generous, benevolent action convey more delight to the mind than the undeserved praise of millions? Set the alternative fairly before your eyes. On the one side, see this poor, unhappy, tender, believing girl in the arms of her wretched mother, breathing her last. Hear her breaking heart in agonies, sighing out your name, and lamenting, rather than accusing, the cruelty which weighs her down to destruction. Paint to your imagination the circumstances of her fond, despairing parent, driven to madness or, perhaps, to death by the loss of her lovely daughter. View the poor, helpless, orphan infant; and when your mind hath dwelt a moment only on such ideas, consider yourself as the cause of all the ruin of this poor, little, worthy, defenceless family. On the other side, consider yourself as relieving them from their temporary sufferings. Think with what joy, with what transports, that lovely creature will fly to your arms. See her blood returning to her pale cheeks, her fire to her languid eyes, and raptures to her tortured breast. Consider the exultations of her mother, the happiness of all. Think of this little family made by one act of yours completely happy. Think of this alternative, and sure I am mistaken in my friend if it requires any long deliberation whether he will sink these wretches down forever or, by one generous, noble resolution, raise them all from the brink of misery and despair to the highest pitch of human happiness. Add to this but one consideration more: the consideration that it is your duty so to do—that the misery from which you will relieve these poor people is the misery which you yourself have wilfully brought upon them."

"Oh, my dear friend," cries Nightingale, "I wanted not your eloquence to rouse me. I pity poor Nancy from my soul, and would willingly give anything in my power that no familiarities had ever passed between us. Nay, believe me, I had many struggles with my passion before I could prevail with myself to write that cruel letter which hath caused all the misery in that unhappy family. If I had no inclinations to consult but my own, I would marry her to-morrow morning; I would, by heaven; but you will easily imagine how impossible it would be to prevail on my father to consent to such a match; besides, he hath provided another for me, and to-morrow, by his express command, I am to wait on the lady."

"I have not the honour to know your father," said Jones, "but suppose he could be persuaded, would you yourself consent to the only means of preserving these poor people?" "As eagerly as I would pursue my happiness," answered Nightingale, "for I never shall find it in any other woman. Oh, my dear friend, could you imagine what I have felt within these twelve hours for my poor girl I am con-convinced she would not engross all your pity. Passion leads me only to her, and if I had any foolish scruples of honour, you have fully satisfied them; could my father be induced to comply with my desires, nothing would be wanting to complete my own happiness or that of my Nancy."

"Then I am resolved to undertake it," said Jones. "You must not be angry with me in whatever light it may be necessary to set this affair, which you may depend on it could not otherwise be long hid from him; for things of this nature make a quick progress when once they get abroad, as this unhappily hath already. Besides, should any fatal accident follow, as upon my soul I am afraid will unless immediately prevented, the public would ring of your name in a manner which if your father hath common humanity must offend him. If you will therefore tell me where I may find the old gentlemen, I will not lose a moment in the business, which while I pursue, you cannot do a more generous action than by paying a visit to the poor girl. You will find I have not exaggerated in the account I have given of the wretchedness of the family."

Nightingale immediately consented to the proposal; and now, having acquainted Jones with his father's lodging and the coffee-house where he would most probably find him, he hesitated a moment and then said, "My dear Tom, you are going to undertake an impossibility. If you knew my father, you would never think of obtaining his consent. Stay, there is one way: suppose you told him I was already married, it might be easier to reconcile him to the fact after it was done; and upon my honour I am so affected with what you have said, and I love my Nancy so passionately, I almost wish it was done, whatever might be the consequence."

Jones greatly approved the hint and promised to pursue it. They then separated, Nightingale to visit his Nancy and Jones in quest of the old gentleman.

8

WHAT PASSED BETWEEN JONES AND OLD MR. NIGHTINGALE, WITH THE ARRIVAL OF A PERSON NOT YET MENTIONED IN THIS HISTORY

Notwithstanding the sentiment of the Roman satirist which denies the divinity of Fortune, and the opinion of Seneca to the same purpose, Cicero, who was, I believe, a wiser man than either of them, expressly holds the contrary; and certain it is, there are some incidents in life so very strange and unaccountable that it seems to require more than human skill and foresight in producing them.

Of this kind was what now happened to Jones, who found Mr. Nightingale the elder in so critical a minute that Fortune, if she was really worthy all the worship she received at Rome, could not have contrived such another. In short, the old gentleman and the father of the young lady whom he intended for his son had been hard at it for many hours, and the latter was just now gone, and had left the former delighted with the thoughts that he had succeeded in a long contention which had been between the two fathers of the future bride and bridegroom; in which both endeavoured to overreach the other and, as not rarely happens in such cases, both had retreated fully satisfied of having obtained the victory.

This gentleman whom Mr. Jones now visited was what they call a man of the world, that is to say, a man who directs his conduct in this world as one who being fully persuaded there is no other is resolved to make the most of this. In his early years he had been bred to trade, but having acquired a very good fortune, he had lately declined his business, or to speak more properly, had changed it from dealing in goods to dealing only in money, of which he had always a plentiful fund at command and of which he knew very well how to make a very plentiful advantage, sometimes of the necessities of private men and sometimes of those of the public. He had indeed conversed so entirely with money that it may be almost doubted whether he imagined there was any other thing really existing in the world; this at least may be certainly averred: that he firmly believed nothing else to have any real value.

The reader will, I fancy, allow that Fortune could not have culled out a more improper person for Mr. Jones to attack with any probability of success, nor could the whimsical lady have directed this attack at a more unseasonable time.

As money, then, was always uppermost in this gentleman's thoughts, so the moment he saw a stranger within his doors, it immediately occurred to his imagination that such stranger was either come to bring him money or to fetch it from him. And according as one or other of these thoughts prevailed, he conceived a favourable or unfavourable idea of the person who approached him.

Unluckily for Jones, the latter of these was the ascendant at present; for as a young gentleman had visited him the day before with a bill from his son for a play debt, he apprehended at the first sight of Jones that he was come on such another errand. Jones therefore had no sooner told him that he was come on his son's account then the old gentleman, being confirmed in his suspicion, burst forth into an exclamation that he would lose his labour. "Is it then possible, sir," answered Jones, "that you can guess my business?" "If I do guess it," replied the other, "I repeat again to you, you will lose your labour. What, I suppose you are one of those sparks who lead my son into all those scenes of riot and debauchery, which will be his destruction, but I shall pay no more of his bills, I promise you. I expect he will quit all such company for the future. If I had imagined otherwise, I should not have provided a wife for him, for I would be instrumental in the ruin of nobody." "How, sir," said Jones, "and was this lady of your providing?" "Pray, sir," answered the old gentleman, "How comes it to be any concern of yours?" "Nay, dear sir," replied Jones, "be not offended that I interest myself in what regards your son's happiness, for whom I have so great an honour and value. It was upon that very account I came to wait upon you. I can't express the satisfaction you have given me by what you say, for I do assure you your son is a person for whom I have the highest honour. Nay, sir, it is not easy to express the esteem I have for you, who could be so generous, so good, so kind, so indulgent, to provide such a match for your son, a woman who, I dare swear, will make him one of the happiest men upon earth."

There is scarce anything which so happily introduces men to our good liking as having conceived some alarm at their first appearance; when once those apprehensions begin to vanish, we soon forget the fears which they occasioned and look on ourselves as indebted for our present ease to those very persons who at first raised our fears.

Thus it happened to Nightingale, who no sooner found that Jones had no demand on him, as he suspected, than he began to be pleased with his presence. "Pray, good sir," said he, "be pleased to sit down. I do not remember to have ever had the pleasure of seeing you before, but if you are a friend of my son and have anything to say concerning this young lady, I shall be glad to hear you. As to her making him happy, it will be his own fault if she doth not. I have discharged my duty in taking care of the main article. She will bring him a fortune capable of making any reasonable, prudent, sober man happy." "Undoubtedly," cries Jones, "for she is in herself a fortune; so beautiful, so genteel, so sweet-tempered, and so well educated; she is indeed a most accomplished young lady, sings admirably well, and hath a most delicate hand at the harpsichord." "I did not know any of these matters," answered the old gentleman, "for I never saw the lady; but I do not like her the worse for what you tell me, and I am the better pleased with her father for not laying any stress on these qualifications in our bargain. I shall always think it a proof of his understanding. A silly fellow would have brought in these articles as an addition to her fortune, but to give him his due, he never mentioned any such matter, though, to be sure, they are no disparagements to a woman." "I do assure you, sir," cries Jones, "she hath them all in the most eminent degree; for my part, I own I was afraid you might have been a little backward, a little less inclined to the match, for your son told me you had never seen the lady; therefore I came, sir, in that case, to entreat you, to conjure you, as you value the happiness of your son, not to be averse to his match with a woman who hath not only all the good qualities I have mentioned but many more." "If that was your business, sir," said the old gentleman, "we are both obliged to you, and you may be perfectly easy, for I give you my word I was very well satisfied with her fortune." "Sir," answered Jones, "I honour you every moment more and more. To be so easily satisfied, so very moderate on that account, is a proof of the soundness of your understanding as well as the nobleness of your mind." "Not so very moderate, young gentleman, not so very moderate," answered the father. "Still more and more noble," replied Jones, "and give me leave to add sensible, for sure it is little less than madness to consider money as the sole foundation of happiness. Such a woman as this with her little, her nothing, of a fortune." "I find," cries the old gentleman, "you have a pretty just opinion of money, my friend, or else you are better acquainted with the person of the lady than with her circumstances. Why, pray, what fortune do you imagine this lady to have?" "What fortune?" cries Jones. "Why, too contemptible a one to be named for your son." "Well, well, well," said the other, "perhaps he might have done better." "That I deny," said Jones, "for she is one of the best of women." "Ay, ay, but in point of fortune I mean," answered the other. "And yet, as to that now, how much do you imagine your friend is to have?" "How much," cries Jones, "how much! Why, at the utmost, perhaps £200." "Do you mean to banter me, young gentleman?" said the father, a little angry. "No, upon my soul," answered Jones, "I am in earnest; nay, I believe I have gone to the utmost farthing. If I do the lady an injury, I ask her pardon." "Indeed you do," cries the father. "I am certain she hath fifty times that sum, and she shall produce fifty to that before I consent that she shall marry my son." "Nay," said Jones, "it is too late to talk of consent now—if she hath not fifty farthings, your son is married." "My son married!" answered the old gentleman with surprise. "Nay," said Jones, "I thought you was unacquainted with it." "My son married to Miss Harris!" answered he again. "To Miss Harris!" said Jones. "No, sir, to Miss Nancy Miller, the daughter of Mrs. Miller, at whose house he lodged; a young lady who, though her mother is reduced to let lodgings——" "Are you bantering or are you in earnest?" cries the father with a most solemn voice. "Indeed, sir," answered Jones, "I scorn the character of a banterer. I came to you in most serious earnest, imagining, as I find true, that your son had never dared acquaint you with a match so much inferior to him in point of fortune, though the reputation of the lady will suffer it no longer to remain a secret."

While the father stood like one struck suddenly dumb at this news a gentleman came into the room and saluted him by the name of brother.

But though these two were in consanguinity so nearly related, they were in their dispositions almost the opposites to each other. The brother who now arrived had likewise been bred to trade, in which he no sooner saw himself worth £6000 than he purchased a small estate with the greatest part of it and retired into the country, where he married the daughter of an unbeneficed clergyman, a young lady who, though she had neither beauty nor fortune, had recommended herself to his choice entirely by her good humour, of which she possessed a very immoderate share.

With this woman he had during twenty-five years lived a life more resembling the model which certain poets ascribe to the Golden Age than any of those patterns which are furnished by the present times. By her he had four children, but none of them arrived at maturity except only one daughter, whom in vulgar language he and his wife had spoiled; that is, had educated with the utmost tenderness and fondness, which she returned to such a degree that she had actually refused a very extraordinary match with a gentleman a little turned of forty because she could not bring herself to part with her parents.

The young lady whom Mr. Nightingale had intended for his son was a near neighbour of his brother and an acquaintance of his niece, and in reality it was upon the account of this projected match that he was now come to town; not indeed to forward but to dissuade his brother from a purpose which he conceived would inevitably ruin his nephew; for he foresaw no other event from a union with Miss Harris, notwithstanding the largeness of her fortune, as neither her person nor mind seemed to him to promise any kind of matrimonial felicity, for she was very tall, very thin, very ugly, very affected, very silly, and very ill-natured.

His brother therefore no sooner mentioned the marriage of his nephew with Miss Miller than he expressed the utmost satisfaction, and when the father had very bitterly reviled his son and pronounced sentence of beggary upon him, the uncle began in the following manner:

"If you was a little cooler, brother, I would ask you whether you love your son for his sake or for your own. You would answer, I suppose, and so I suppose you think, for his sake; and doubtless it is his happiness which you intended in the marriage you proposed for him.

"Now, brother, to prescribe rules of happiness to others hath always appeared to me very absurd, and to insist on doing this very tyrannical. It is a vulgar error, I know, but it is nevertheless an error. And if this be absurd in other things, it is mostly so in the affair of marriage, the happiness of which depends entirely on the affection which subsists between the parties.

"I have therefore always thought it unreasonable in parents to desire to choose for their children on this occasion, since to force affection is an impossible attempt; nay, so much doth love abhor force that I know not whether through an unfortunate but incurable perverseness in our natures, it may not be even impatient of persuasion.

"It is, however, true that though a parent will not, I think, wisely prescribe, he ought to be consulted on this occasion, and in strictness, perhaps, should at least have a negative voice. My nephew, therefore, I own, in marrying without asking your advice, hath been guilty of a fault. But honestly speaking, brother, have you not a little promoted this fault? Have not your frequent declarations on this subject given him a moral certainty of your refusal where there was any deficiency in point of fortune? Nay, doth not your present anger arise solely from that deficiency? And if he hath failed in his duty here, did not you as much exceed that authority when you absolutely bargained with him for a woman without his knowledge, whom you yourself never saw, and whom if you had seen and known as well as I, it must have been madness in you to have ever thought of bringing her into your family.

"Still, I own my nephew in a fault, but surely it is not an unpardonable fault. He hath acted indeed without your consent in a matter in which he ought to have asked it, but it is in a matter in which his interest is principally concerned; you yourself must and will acknowledge that you consulted his interest only, and if he unfortunately differed from you and hath been mistaken in his notion of happiness, will you, brother, if you love your son, carry him still wider from the point? Will you increase the ill consequences of his simple choice? Will you endeavour to make an event certain misery to him which may accidentally prove so? In a word, brother, because he hath put it out of your power to make his circumstances as affluent as you would, will you distress them as much as you can?"

By the force of the true Catholic faith St. Anthony won upon the fishes. Orpheus and Amphion went a little farther and by the charms of music enchanted things merely inanimate. Wonderful both! But neither history nor fable have ever yet ventured to record an instance of any one who by force of argument and reason hath triumphed over habitual avarice.

Mr. Nightingale, the father, instead of attempting to answer his brother, contented himself with only observing that they had always differed in their sentiments concerning the education of their children. "I wish," said he, "brother, you would have confined your care to your own daughter and never have troubled yourself with my son, who hath, I believe, as little profited by your precepts as by your example"; for young Nightingale was his uncle's godson and had lived more with him than with his father, so that the uncle had often declared he loved his nephew almost equally with his own child.

Jones fell into raptures with this good gentleman; and when after much persuasion they found the father grew still more and more irritated instead of appeased, Jones conducted the uncle to his nephew at the house of Mrs. Miller.

9

CONTAINING STRANGE MATTERS

At his return to his lodgings, Jones found the situation of affairs greatly altered from what they had been in at his departure. The mother, the two daughters, and young Mr. Nightingale were now sat down to supper together when the uncle was at his own desire introduced without any ceremony into the company, to all of whom he was well known, for he had several times visited his nephew at that house.

The old gentleman immediately walked up to Miss Nancy, saluted, and wished her joy, as he did afterwards the mother and the other sister; and lastly, he paid the proper compliments to his nephew with the same good humour and courtesy as if his nephew had married his equal or superior in fortune, with all the previous requisites first performed.

Miss Nancy and her supposed husband both turned pale and looked rather foolish than otherwise upon the occasion, but Mrs. Miller took the first opportunity of withdrawing; and having sent for Jones into the dining-room, she threw herself at his feet and in a most passionate flood of tears called him her good angel, the preserver of her poor little family, with many other respectful and endearing appellations, and made him every acknowledgement which the highest benefit can extract from the most grateful hearts.

After the first gust of her passion was a little over, which, she declared, if she had not vented, would have burst her, she proceeded to inform Mr. Jones that all matters were settled between Mr. Nightingale and her daughter and that they were to be married the next morning; at which Mr. Jones having expressed much pleasure, the poor woman fell again into a fit of joy and thanksgivings, which he at length with difficulty silenced and prevailed on her to return with him back to the company, whom they found in the same good humour in which they had left them.

This little society now passed two or three very agreeable hours together, in which the uncle, who was a very great lover of his bottle, had so well plied his nephew that this latter, though not drunk, began to be somewhat flustered; and now, Mr. Nightingale, taking the old gentleman with him upstairs into the apartment he had lately occupied, unbosomed himself as follows:

"As you have been always the best and kindest of uncles to me, and as you have shown such unparalleled goodness in forgiving this match, which, to be sure, may be thought a little improvident, I should never forgive myself if I attempted to deceive you in anything." He then confessed the truth and opened the whole affair.

"How, Jack!" said the old gentleman. "And are you really, then, not married to this young woman?" "No, upon my honour," answered Nightingale, "I have told you the simple truth." "My dear boy," cries the uncle, kissing him, "I am heartily glad to hear it. I never was better pleased in my life. If you had been married, I should have assisted you as much as was in my power to have made the best of a bad matter, but there is a great difference between considering a thing which is already done and irrecoverable and that which is yet to do. Let your reason have fair play, Jack, and you will see this match in so foolish and preposterous a light that there will be no need of any dissuasive arguments." "How, sir!" replied young Nightingale. "Is there this difference between having already done an act and being in honour engaged to do it?" "Pugh," said the uncle, "honour is a creature of the world's making, and the world hath the power of a creator over it and may govern and direct it as they please. Now you well know how trivial these breaches of contract are thought; even the grossest make but the wonder and conversation of a day. Is there a man who will be afterwards more backward in giving you his sister or daughter? Or is there any sister or daughter who would be more backward to receive you? Honour is not concerned in these engagements." "Pardon me, dear sir," cries Nightingale, "I can never think so; and not only honour but conscience and humanity are concerned. I am well satisfied that was I now to disappoint the young creature, her death would be the consequence, and I should look on myself as her murderer, nay, as her murderer by the cruellest of all methods, by breaking her heart." "Break her heart, indeed! No, no, Jack," cries the uncle, "the hearts of women are not so soon broke; they are tough, boy; they are tough." "But, sir," answered Nightingale, "my own affections are engaged and I never could be happy with any other woman. How often have I heard you say that children should be always suffered to choose for themselves and that you would let my cousin Harriet do so!" "Why, ay," replied the old gentleman, "so I would have them; but then I would have them choose wisely. Indeed, Jack, you must and shall leave this girl." "Indeed, uncle," cries the other, "I must and will have her." "You will, young gentleman?" said the uncle. "I did not expect such a word from you. I should not wonder if you had used such language to your father, who hath always treated you like a dog and kept you at the distance which a tyrant preserves over his subjects, but I, who have lived with you upon an equal footing, might surely expect better usage; but I know how to account for it all: it is all owing to your preposterous education, in which I have had too little share. There is my daughter, now, whom I have brought up as my friend, never doth anything without my advice, nor ever refuses to take it when I give it her." "You have never yet given her advice in an affair of this kind," said Nightingale. "for I am greatly mistaken in my cousin if she would be very ready to obey even your most positive commands in abandoning her inclinations." "Don't abuse my girl," answered the old gentleman with some emotion. "Don't abuse my Harriet. I have brought her up to have no inclinations contrary to my own. By suffering her to do whatever she pleases, I have inured her to a habit of being pleased to do whatever I like." "Pardon me, sir," said Nightingale, "I have not the least design to reflect on my cousin, for whom I have the greatest esteem, and indeed I am convinced you will never put her to so severe a trial or lay such hard commands on her as you would do on me. But, dear sir, let us return to the company, for they will begin to be uneasy at our long absence. I must beg one favour of my dear uncle, which is that he would not say anything to shock the poor girl or her mother." "Oh, you need not fear me," answered he. "I understand myself too well to affront women, so I will readily grant you that favour, and in return I must expect another of you." "There are but few of your commands, sir," said Nightingale, "which I shall not very cheerfully obey." "Nay, sir, I ask nothing," said the uncle, "but the honour of your company home to my lodging that I may reason the case a little more fully with you; for I would if possible have the satisfaction of preserving my family, notwithstanding the headstrong folly of my brother, who in his own opinion is the wisest man in the world."

Nightingale, who well knew his uncle to be as headstrong as his father, submitted to attend him home, and then they both returned back into the room, where the old gentleman promised to carry himself with the same decorum which he had before maintained.

10

A SHORT CHAPTER, WHICH CONCLUDES THE BOOK

The long absence of the uncle and nephew had occasioned some disquiet in the minds of all whom they had left behind them, and the more as during the preceding dialogue the uncle had more than once elevated his voice so as to be heard downstairs; which, though they could not distinguish what he said, had caused some evil foreboding in Nancy and her mother, and indeed even in Jones himself.

When the good company therefore again assembled, there was a visible alteration in all their faces, and the good humour which at their last meeting universally shone forth in every countenance was now changed into a much less agreeable aspect. It was a change, indeed, common enough to the weather in this climate, from sunshine to clouds, from June to December.

This alteration was not, however, greatly remarked by any present; for as every one was now endeavouring to conceal their own thoughts and to act a part, they became all too busily engaged in the scene to be spectators of it. Thus, neither the uncle nor nephew saw any symptoms of suspicion in the mother or daughter, nor did the mother or daughter remark the overacted complaisance of the old man, nor the counterfeit satisfaction which grinned in the features of the young one.

Something like this, I believe, frequently happens where the whole attention of two friends being engaged in the part which each is to act in order to impose on the other, neither sees nor suspects the art practised against himself; and thus, the thrust of both (to borrow no improper metaphor on the occasion) alike takes place.

From the same reason, it is no unusual thing for both parties to be overreached in a bargain, though the one must be always the greater loser, as was he who sold a blind horse and received a bad note in payment. ·

Our company in about half an hour broke up, and the uncle carried off his nephew, but not before the latter had assured Miss Nancy in a whisper that he would attend her early in the morning and fulfil all his engagements.

Jones, who was the least concerned in this scene, saw the most. He did indeed suspect the very fact; for besides observing the great alteration in the behaviour of the uncle, the distance he assumed, and his overstrained civility to Miss Nancy, the carrying off a bridegroom from his bride at that time of night was so extraordinary a proceeding that it could be only accounted for by imagining that young Nightingale had revealed the whole truth, which the apparent openness of his temper and his being flustered with liquor made too probable.

While he was reasoning with himself whether he should acquaint these poor people with his suspicion the maid of the house informed him that a gentlewoman desired to speak with him. He went immediately out and, taking the candle from the maid, ushered his visitant upstairs, who, in the person of Mrs. Honour, acquainted him with such dreadful news concerning his Sophia that he immediately lost all consideration for every other person, and his whole stock of compassion was entirely swallowed up in reflections on his own misery and on that of his unfortunate angel.

What this dreadful matter was, the reader will be informed after we have first related the many preceding steps which produced it; and those will be the subject of the following book.

BOOK XV

In Which the History Advances About Two Days

1

TOO SHORT TO NEED A PREFACE

There are a set of religious, or rather moral, writers who teach that virtue is the certain road to happiness, and vice to misery, in this world. A very wholesome and comfortable doctrine, and to which we have but one objection: namely, that it is not true.

Indeed, if by virtue these writers mean the exercise of those cardinal virtues which, like good housewives, stay at home and mind only the business of their own family, I shall very readily concede the point; for so surely do all these contribute and lead to happiness that I would almost wish, in violation of all the ancient and modern sages, to call them rather by the name of wisdom than by that of virtue; for with regard to this life, no system, I conceive, was ever wiser than that of the ancient Epicureans, who held this wisdom to constitute the chief good, nor foolisher than that of their opposites, those modern epicures, who place all felicity in the abundant gratification of every sensual appetite.

But if by virtue is meant (as I almost think it ought) a certain relative quality which is always busying itself without doors, and seems as much interested in pursuing the good of others as its own, I cannot so easily agree that this is the surest way to human happiness because I am afraid we must then include poverty and contempt, with all the mischiefs which backbiting, envy, and ingratitude can bring on mankind, in our idea of happiness; nay, sometimes perhaps we shall be obliged to wait upon the said happiness to a gaol, since many by the above virtue have brought themselves thither.

I have not now leisure to enter upon so large a field of speculation as here seems opening upon me; my design was to wipe off a doctrine that lay in my way, since while Mr. Jones was acting the most virtuous part imaginable in labouring to preserve his fellow-creatures from destruction, the Devil or some other evil spirit, one, perhaps, clothed in human flesh, was hard at work to make him completely miserable in the ruin of his Sophia.

This, therefore, would seem an exception to the above rule if indeed it was a rule, but as we have in our voyage through life seen so many other exceptions to it, we choose to dispute the doctrine on which it is founded, which we don't apprehend to be Christian, which we are convinced is not true, and which is indeed destructive of one of the noblest arguments that reason alone can furnish for the belief of immortality.

But as the reader's curiosity (if he hath any) must be now awake and hungry, we shall provide to feed it as fast as we can.

2

IN WHICH IS OPENED A VERY BLACK DESIGN AGAINST SOPHIA

I remember a wise old gentleman who used to say, "When children are doing nothing, they are doing mischief." I will not enlarge this quaint saying to the most beautiful part of the creation in general, but so far I may be allowed; that when the effects of female jealousy do not appear openly in their proper colours of rage and fury, we may suspect that mischievous passion to be at work privately, and attempting to undermine what it doth not attack above-ground.

This was exemplified in the conduct of Lady Bellaston, who under all the smiles which she wore in her countenance concealed much indignation against Sophia, and as she plainly saw that this young lady stood between her and the full indulgence of her desires, she resolved to get rid of her by some means or other; nor was it long before a very favourable opportunity of accomplishing this presented itself to her.

The reader may be pleased to remember that when Sophia was thrown into that consternation at the playhouse by the wit and humour of a set of young gentlemen who call themselves the town, we informed him that she had put herself under the protection of a young nobleman, who had very safely conducted her to her chair.

This nobleman, who frequently visited Lady Bellaston, had more than once seen Sophia there since her arrival in town, and had conceived a very great liking to her; which liking, as beauty never looks more amiable than in distress, Sophia had in this fright so increased that he might now without any great impropriety be said to be actually in love with her.

It may easily be believed that he would not suffer so handsome an occasion of improving his acquaintance with the beloved object as now offered itself to elapse, when even good breeding alone might have prompted him to pay her a visit.

The next morning, therefore, after this accident he waited on Sophia with the usual compliments and hopes that she had received no harm from her last night's adventure.

As love, like fire, when once thoroughly kindled is soon blown into a flame, Sophia in a very short time completed her conquest. Time now flew away unperceived, and the noble lord had been two hours in company with the lady before it entered into his head that he had made too long a visit. Though this circumstance alone would have alarmed Sophia, who was somewhat more a mistress of computation at present, she had, indeed, much more pregnant evidence from the eyes of her lover of what passed within his bosom; nay, though he did not make any open declaration of his passion, yet many of his expressions were rather too warm and too tender to have been imputed to complaisance, even in the age when such complaisance was in fashion— the very reverse of which is well known to be the reigning mode at present.

Lady Bellaston had been apprised of his lordship's visit at his first arrival; and the length of it very well satisfied her that things went as she wished and as, indeed, she had suspected the second time she saw this young couple together. This business she rightly, I think, concluded that she should by no means forward by mixing in the company while they were together; she therefore ordered her servants that when my lord was going they should tell him she desired to speak with him, and employed the intermediate time in meditating how best to accomplish a scheme which she made no doubt but his lordship would very readily embrace the execution of.

Lord Fellamar (for that was the title of this young nobleman) was no sooner introduced to her ladyship than she attacked him in the following strain: "Bless me, my lord, are you here yet? I thought my servants had made a mistake and let you go away, and I wanted to see you about an affair of some importance." "Indeed, Lady Bellaston," said he, "I don't wonder you are astonished at the length of my visit; for I have stayed above two hours, and I did not think I had stayed above half a one." "What am I to conclude from thence, my lord?" said she. "The company must be very agreeable which can make time slide away so very deceitfully." "Upon my honour," said he, "the most agreeable I ever saw. Pray tell me, Lady Bellaston, who is this blazing star which you have produced among us all of a sudden?" "What blazing star, my lord?" said she, affecting a surprise. "I mean," said he, "the lady I saw here the other day, whom I had last night in my arms at the playhouse and to whom I have been making that unreasonable visit." "Oh, my cousin Western!" said she. "Why, that blazing star, my lord, is the daughter of a country booby squire, and hath been in town about a fortnight for the first time." "Upon my soul," said he, "I should swear she had been bred in a court; for besides her beauty, I never saw anything so genteel, so sensible, so polite." "Oh, brave!" cries the lady. "My cousin hath you, I find." "Upon my honour," answered he, "I wish she had, for I am in love with her to distraction." "Nay, my lord," said she, "it is not wishing yourself very ill neither, for she is a very great fortune; I assure you she is an only child and her father's estate is a good £3000 a year." "Then I can assure you, madam," answered the lord, "I think her the best match in England." "Indeed, my lord," replied she, "if you like her, I heartily wish you had her." "If you think so kindly of me, madam," said he, "as she is a relation of yours, will you do me the honour to propose it to her father?" "And are you really, then, in earnest?" cries the lady with an affected gravity. "I hope, madam," answered he, "you have a better opinion of me than to imagine I would jest with your ladyship in an affair of this kind." "Indeed, then," said the lady, "I will most readily propose your lordship to her father, and I can, I believe, assure you of his joyful acceptance of the proposal; but there is a bar, which I am almost ashamed to mention, and yet it is one you will never be able to conquer. You have a rival, my lord, and a rival who, though I blush to name him, neither you nor all the world will ever be able to conquer." "Upon my word, Lady Bellaston," cries he, "you have struck a damp to my heart which hath almost deprived me of being." "Fie, my lord," said she, "I should rather hope I had struck fire into you. A lover, and talk of damps in your heart! I rather imagined you would have asked your rival's name that you might have immediately entered the lists with him." "I promise you, madam," answered he, "there are very few things I would not undertake for your charming cousin; but, pray, who is this happy man?" "Why, he is," said she, "what I am sorry to say most happy men with us are: one of the lowest fellows in the world. He is a beggar, a bastard, a foundling, a fellow in meaner circumstances than one of your lordship's footmen." "And is it possible," cried he, "that a young creature with such perfections should think of bestowing herself so unworthily?" "Alas, my lord," answered she, "consider the country—the bane of all young women is the country. There they learn a set of romantic notions of love, and I know not what folly, which this town and good company can scarce eradicate in a whole winter." "Indeed, madam," replied my lord, "your cousin is of too immense a value to be thrown away; such ruin as this must be prevented." "Alas!" cries she. "My lord, how can it be prevented? The family have already done all in their power, but the girl is, I think, intoxicated, and nothing less than ruin will content her. And to deal more openly with you, I expect every day to hear she is run away with him." "What you tell me, Lady Bellaston," answered his lordship, "affects me most tenderly, and only raises my compassion instead of lessening my adoration of your cousin. Some means must be found to preserve so inestimable a jewel. Hath your ladyship endeavoured to reason with her?" Here the lady affected a laugh and cried, "My dear lord, sure you know us better than to talk of reasoning a young woman out of her inclinations? These inestimable jewels are as deaf as the jewels they wear; time, my lord, time is the only medicine to cure their folly, but this is a medicine which I am certain she will not take; nay, I live in hourly horrors on her account. In short, nothing but violent methods will do." "What is to be done?" cries my lord. "What methods are to be taken? Is there any method upon earth?—Oh, Lady Bellaston, there is nothing which I would not undertake for such a reward." "I really know not," answered the lady after a pause; and then, pausing again, she cried out, "Upon my soul, I am at my wit's end on this girl's account. If she can be preserved, something must be done immediately, and as I say, nothing but violent methods will do. If your lordship hath really this attachment to my cousin (and to do her justice, except in this silly inclination, of which she will soon see her folly, she is every way deserving), I think there may be one way; indeed, it is a very disagreeable one and what I am almost afraid to think of. It requires great spirit, I promise you." "I am not conscious, madam," said he, "of any defect there, nor am I, I hope, suspected of any such. It must be an egregious defect indeed which could make me backward on this occasion." "Nay, my lord," answered she, "I am far from doubting you. I am much more inclined to doubt my own courage, for I must run a monstrous risk. In short, I must place such a confidence in your honour as a wise woman will scarce ever place in a man on any consideration." In this point likewise my lord very well satisfied her; for his reputation was extremely clear, and common fame did him no more than justice in speaking well of him. "Well, then," said she, "my lord—I—I vow, I can't bear the apprehension of it. No, it must not be. At least every other method shall be tried. Can you get rid of your engagements and dine here to-day? Your lordship will have an opportunity of seeing a little more of Miss Western. I promise you we have no time to lose. Here will be nobody but Lady Betty and Miss Eagle and Colonel Hampsted and Tom Edwards; they will all go soon—and I shall be at home to nobody. Then your lordship may be a little more explicit. Nay, I will contrive some method to convince you of her attachment to this fellow." My lord made proper compliments, accepted the invitation, and then they parted to dress, it being now past three in the morning, or, to reckon by the old style, in the afternoon.

3

A FURTHER EXPLANATION OF THE FOREGOING DESIGN

Though the reader may have long since concluded Lady Bellaston to be a member (and no inconsiderable one) of the Great World, she was in reality a very considerable member of the *Little World*; by which appellation was distinguished a very worthy and honourable society which not long since flourished in this kingdom.

Among other good principles upon which this society was founded there was one very remarkable; for as it was a rule of an honourable club of heroes who assembled at the close of the late war that all the members should every day fight once at least, so 'twas in this that every member should within the twenty-four hours tell at least one merry fib, which was to be propagated by all the brethren and sisterhood.

Many idle stories were told about this society, which from a certain quality may be, perhaps not unjustly, supposed to have come from the society themselves: as that the Devil was the president, and that he sat in person in an elbow-chair at the upper end of the table; but upon very strict inquiry, I find there is not the least truth in any of those tales, and that the assembly consisted in reality of a set of very good sort of people, and the fibs which they propagated were of a harmless kind and tended only to produce mirth and good humour.

Edwards was likewise a member of this comical society. To him, therefore, Lady Bellaston applied as a proper instrument for her purpose, and furnished him with a fib which he was to vent whenever the lady gave him her cue; and this was not to be till the evening, when all the company but Lord Fellamar and himself were gone and while they were engaged in a rubber at whist.

To this time, then, which was between seven and eight in the evening, we will convey our reader, when Lady Bellaston, Lord Fellamar, Miss Western, and Tom being engaged at whist and in the last game of their rubbers, Tom received his cue from Lady Bellaston, which was, "I protest, Tom, you are grown intolerable lately; you used to tell us all the news of the town and now you know no more of the world than if you lived out of it."

Mr. Edwards then began as follows: "The fault is not mine, madam. It lies in the dullness of the age, that doth nothing worth talking of. Oh, la, though now I think on't, there hath a terrible accident befallen poor Colonel Wilcox. Poor Ned. You know him, my lord; everybody knows him; faith, I am very much concerned for him."

"What is it, pray?" says Lady Bellaston.

"Why, he hath killed a man this morning in a duel, that's all."

His lordship, who was not in the secret, asked gravely whom he had killed. To which Edwards answered, "A young fellow we none of us know, a Somersetshire lad just come to town, one Jones his name is; a near relation of one Mr. Allworthy, of whom your lordship, I believe, hath heard. I saw the lad lie dead in a coffee-house. Upon my soul he is one of the finest corpses I ever saw in my life."

Sophia, who just began to deal as Tom had mentioned that a man was killed, stopped her hand and listened with attention (for all stories of that kind affected her), but no sooner had he arrived at the latter part of the story than she began to deal again, and having dealt three cards to one, and seven to another, and ten to a third, at last dropped the rest from her hand and fell back in her chair.

The company behaved as usually on these occasions. The usual disturbance ensued, the usual assistance was summoned, and Sophia at last, as it is usual, returned again to life, and was soon after at her earnest desire led to her own apartment, where at my lord's request Lady Bellaston acquainted her with the truth, attempted to carry it off as a jest of her own, and comforted her with repeated assurances that neither his lordship nor Tom, though she had taught him the story, were in the true secret of the affair.

There was no farther evidence necessary to convince Lord Fellamar how justly the case had been represented to him by Lady Bellaston, and now at her return into the room, a scheme was laid between those two noble persons, which, though it appeared in no very heinous light to his lordship (as he faithfully promised, and faithfully resolved too, to make the lady all the subsequent amends in his power by marriage), yet many of our readers, we doubt not, will see with just detestation.

The next evening at seven was appointed for the fatal purpose, when Lady Bellaston undertook that Sophia should be alone and his lordship should be introduced to her. The whole family were to be regulated for the purpose, most of the servants dispatched out of the house; and for Mrs. Honour, who to prevent suspicion was to be left with her mistress till his lordship's arrival, Lady Bellaston herself was to engage her in an apartment as distant as possible from the scene of the intended mischief and out of the hearing of Sophia.

Matters being thus agreed on, his lordship took his leave and her ladyship retired to rest, highly pleased with a project of which she had no reason to doubt the success and which promised so effectually to remove Sophia from being any future obstruction to her amour with Jones, by a means of which she should never appear to be guilty even if the fact appeared to the world; but this she made no doubt of preventing by huddling up a marriage, to which she thought the ravished Sophia would easily be brought to consent and at which all the rest of her family would rejoice.

But affairs were not in so quiet a situation in the bosom of the other conspirator; his mind was tossed in all the distracting anxiety so nobly described by Shakespeare:

> Between the acting of a dreadful thing
> And the first motion, all the interim is
> Like a phantasma or a hideous dream.
> The genius and the mortal instruments
> Are then in council; and the state of man,
> Like to a little kingdom, suffers then
> The nature of an insurrection.

Though the violence of his passion had made him eagerly embrace the first hint of this design, especially as it came from a relation of the lady, yet when that friend to reflection, a pillow, had placed the action itself in all its natural black colours before his eyes, with all the consequences which must, and those which might probably, attend it, his resolution began to abate, or rather, indeed, to go over to the other side; and after a long conflict, which lasted a whole night, between honour and appetite, the former at length prevailed, and he determined to wait on Lady Bellaston and to relinquish the design.

Lady Bellaston was in bed, though very late in the morning, and Sophia sitting by her bedside when the servant acquainted her that Lord Fellamar was below in the parlour;

upon which her ladyship desired him to stay, and that she would see him presently, but the servant was no sooner departed than poor Sophia began to entreat her cousin not to encourage the visits of that odious lord (so she called him, though a little unjustly) upon her account. "I see his design," said she, "for he made downright love to me yesterday morning, but as I am resolved never to admit it, I beg your ladyship not to leave us alone together any more and to order the servants that if he inquires for me, I may be always denied to him."

"La, child," says Lady Bellaston, "you country-girls have nothing but sweethearts in your head; you fancy every man who is civil to you is making love. He is one of the most gallant young fellows about town and, I am convinced, means no more than a little gallantry. Make love to you indeed! I wish with all my heart he would, and you must be an arrant mad woman to refuse him."

"But as I shall certainly be that mad woman," cries Sophia, "I hope his visits shall not be intruded upon me."

"Oh, child," said Lady Bellaston, "you need not be so fearful, if you resolve to run away with that Jones, I know no person who can hinder you."

"Upon my honour, madam," cries Sophia, "your ladyship injures me. I will never run away with any man, nor will I ever marry contrary to my father's inclinations."

"Well, Miss Western," said the lady, "if you are not in a humour to see company this morning, you may retire to your own apartment, for I am not frightened at his lordship and must send for him up into my dressing-room."

Sophia thanked her ladyship and withdrew, and presently afterwards Fellamar was admitted upstairs.

4

BY WHICH IT WILL APPEAR HOW DANGEROUS AN ADVOCATE
A LADY IS WHEN SHE APPLIES HER ELOQUENCE TO AN ILL
PURPOSE

When Lady Bellaston heard the young lord's scruples, she treated them with the same disdain with which one of those sages of the law called Newgate solicitors treats the qualms of conscience in a young witness. "My dear lord," said she, "you certainly want a cordial. I must send to Lady Edgely for one of her best drams. Fie upon it! Have more resolution. Are you frightened by the word *rape*? Or are you apprehensive—? Well, if the story of Helen was modern, I should think it unnatural! I mean the behaviour of Paris, not the fondness of the lady, for all women love a man of spirit. There is another story of the Sabine ladies—and that too, I thank heaven, is very ancient. Your lordship, perhaps, will admire my reading, but I think Mr. Hook tells us they made tolerable good wives afterwards. I fancy few of my married acquaintance were ravished by their husbands." "Nay, dear Lady Bellaston," cried he, "don't ridicule me in this manner." "Why, my good lord," answered she, "do you think any woman in England would not laugh at you in her heart, whatever prudery she might wear in her countenance? You force me to use a strange kind of language and to betray my sex most abominably, but I am contented with knowing my intentions are good and that I am endeavouring to serve my cousin; for I think you will make her a husband notwithstanding this, or upon my soul, I would not even persuade her to fling herself away upon an empty title. She should not upbraid me hereafter with having lost a man of spirit, for that his enemies allow this poor young fellow to be."

Let those who have had the satisfaction of hearing reflections of this kind from a wife or a mistress declare whether they are at all sweetened by coming from a female tongue. Certain it is, they sunk deeper into his lordship than anything which Demosthenes or Cicero could have said on the occasion.

Lady Bellaston, perceiving she had fired the young lord's pride, began now like a true orator to rouse other passions to its assistance. "My lord," says she in a graver voice, "you will be pleased to remember you mentioned this matter to me first, for I would not appear to you in the light of one who is endeavouring to put off my cousin upon you. Fourscore thousand pounds do not stand in need of an advocate to recommend them." "Nor doth Miss Western," said he, "require any recommendation from her fortune, for in my opinion, no woman ever had half her charms." "Yes, yes, my lord," replied the lady, looking in the glass; "there have been women with more than half her charms, I assure you; not that I need lessen her on that account: she is a most delicious girl, that's certain, and within these few hours she will be in the arms of one who surely doth not deserve her, though I will give him his due, I believe he is truly a man of spirit."

"I hope so, madam," said my lord, "though I must own he doth not deserve her, for unless heaven or your ladyship disappoint me, she shall within that time be in mine."

"Well spoken, my lord," answered the lady. "I promise you no disappointment shall happen from my side, and within this week I am convinced I shall call your lordship my cousin in public."

The remainder of this scene consisted entirely of raptures, excuses, and compliments, very pleasant to have heard from the parties, but rather dull when related at second hand. Here, therefore, we shall put an end to this dialogue and hasten to the fatal hour when everything was prepared for the destruction of poor Sophia.

But this being the most tragical matter in our whole history, we shall treat it in a chapter by itself.

5

CONTAINING SOME MATTERS WHICH MAY AFFECT, AND
OTHERS WHICH MAY SURPRISE, THE READER

The clock had now struck seven, and poor Sophia, alone and melancholy, sat reading a tragedy. It was *The Fatal Marriage*, and she was now come to that part where the poor distressed Isabella disposes of her wedding-ring.

Here the book dropped from her hand and a shower of tears ran down into her bosom. In this situation she had continued a minute when the door opened and in came Lord Fellamar. Sophia started from her chair at his entrance, and his lordship, advancing forwards and making a low bow, said, "I am afraid, Miss Western, I break in upon you abruptly." "Indeed, my lord," says she, "I must own myself a little surprised at this unexpected visit." "If this visit be unexpected, madam," answered Lord Fellamar, "my eyes must have been very faithless interpreters of my heart when last I had the honour of seeing you; for surely you could not otherwise have hoped to detain my heart in your possession without receiving a visit from its owner." Sophia, confused as she was, answered this bombast (and very properly, I think) with a look of inconceivable disdain. My lord then made another and a longer speech of the same sort.

Upon which Sophia, trembling, said, "Am I really to conceive your lordship to be out of your senses? Sure, my lord, there is no other excuse for such behaviour." "I am indeed, madam, in the situation you suppose," cries his lordship; "and sure you will pardon the effects of a frenzy which you yourself have occasioned, for love hath so totally deprived me of reason that I am scarce accountable for any of my actions." "Upon my word, my lord," said Sophia, "I neither understand your words nor your behaviour." "Suffer me, then, madam," cries he, "at your feet to explain both, by laying open my soul to you and declaring that I dote on you to the highest degree of distraction. O most adorable, most divine creature! What language can express the sentiments of my heart?" "I do assure you, my lord," said Sophia, "I shall not stay to hear any more of this." "Do not," cries he, "think of leaving me thus cruelly; could you know half the torments which I feel, that tender bosom must pity what those eyes have caused." Then, fetching a deep sigh and laying hold of her hand, he ran on for some minutes in a strain which would be little more pleasing to the reader than it was to the lady, and at last concluded with a declaration that if he was master of the world, he would lay it at her feet. Sophia then, forcibly pulling away her hand from his, answered with much spirit, "I promise you, sir, your world and its master I should spurn from me with equal contempt." She then offered to go, and Lord Fellamar, again laying hold of her hand, said, "Pardon me, my beloved angel, freedoms which nothing but despair could have tempted me to take. Believe me, could I have had any hope that my title and fortune, neither of them inconsiderable unless when compared with your worth, would have been accepted, I had in the humblest manner presented them to your acceptance. But I cannot lose you. By heaven, I will sooner part with my soul. You are, you must, you shall be, only mine." "My lord," says she, "I entreat you to desist from a vain pursuit, for upon my honour, I will never hear you on this subject. Let go my hand, my lord, for I am resolved to go from you this moment, nor will I ever see you more." "Then, madam," cries his lordship, "I must make the best use of this moment, for I cannot, nor will, live without you." "What do you mean, my lord?" said Sophia. "I will raise the family." "I have no fear, madam," answered he, "but of losing you, and that I am resolved to prevent the only way which despair points to me." He then caught her in his arms; upon which she screamed so loud that she must have alarmed some one to her assistance had not Lady Bellaston taken care to remove all ears.

But a more lucky circumstance happened for poor Sophia: another noise now broke forth, which almost drowned her cries, for now the whole house rang with "Where is she? D—n me, I'll unkennel her this instant. Show me her chamber, I say. Where is my daughter? I know she's in the house, and I'll see her if she's above-ground. Show me where she is." At which last words the door flew open, and in came Squire Western with his parson and a set of myrmidons at his heels.

How miserable must have been the condition of poor Sophia when the enraged voice of her father was welcome to her ears! Welcome, indeed, it was, and luckily did he come; for it was the only accident upon earth which could have preserved the peace of her mind from being forever destroyed.

Sophia, notwithstanding her fright, presently knew her father's voice, and his lordship, notwithstanding his passion, knew the voice of reason, which peremptorily assured him it was not now a time for the perpetration of his villainy. Hearing, therefore, the voice approach, and hearing likewise whose it was (for as the squire more than once roared forth the word *daughter*, so Sophia in the midst of her struggling cried out upon her father), he thought proper to relinquish his prey, having only disordered her handkerchief and with his rude lips committed violence on her lovely neck.

If the reader's imagination doth not assist me, I shall never be able to describe the situation of these two persons when Western came into the room. Sophia tottered into a chair, where she sat disordered, pale, breathless, bursting with indignation at Lord Fellamar; affrighted, and yet more rejoiced, at the arrival of her father.

His lordship sat down near her, with the bag of his wig hanging over one of his shoulders, the rest of his dress being somewhat disordered and rather a greater proportion of linen than is usual appearing at his bosom. As to the rest, he was amazed, affrighted, vexed, and ashamed.

As to Squire Western, he happened at this time to be overtaken by an enemy which very frequently pursues, and seldom fails to overtake, most of the country-gentlemen in this kingdom. He was, literally speaking, drunk; which circumstance, together with his natural impetuosity, could produce no other effect than his running immediately up to his daughter, upon whom he fell foul with his tongue in the most inveterate manner; nay, he had probably committed violence with his hands had not the parson interposed, saying, "For heaven's sake, sir, animadvert that you are in the house of a great lady. Let me beg you to mitigate your wrath; it should minister a fullness of satisfaction that you have found your daughter, for as to revenge, it belongeth not unto us. I discern great contrition in the countenance of the young lady. I stand assured if you will forgive her, she will repent her of all past offences and return unto her duty."

The strength of the parson's arms had at first been of more service than the strength of his rhetoric. However, his last words wrought some effect and the squire answered, "I'll forgee her if she wull ha' un. If wot ha' un, Sophy, I'll forgee thee all. Why dost unt speak? Shat ha' un? D—n me, shat ha' un? Why dost unt answer? Was ever such a stubborn tuoad?"

"Let me entreat you, sir, to be a little more moderate," said the parson; "you frighten the young lady so that you deprive her of all power of utterance."

"Power of mine a—," answered the squire. "You take her part, then, you do? A pretty parson, truly, to side with an undutiful child. Yes, yes, I will gee you a living with a pox. I'll gee un to the Devil sooner."

"I humbly crave your pardon," said the parson; "I assure your worship I meant no such matter."

My Lady Bellaston now entered the room and came up to the squire, who no sooner saw her than, resolving to follow the instructions of his sister, he made a very civil bow in the rural manner and paid her some of his best compliments. He then immediately proceeded to his complaints and said, "There, my lady cousin, there stands the most undutiful child in the world; she hankers after a beggarly rascal and won't marry one of the greatest matches in all England that we have provided for her."

"Indeed, Cousin Western," answered the lady, "I am persuaded you wrong my cousin. I am sure she hath a better understanding. I am convinced she will not refuse what she must be sensible is so much to her advantage."

This was a wilful mistake in Lady Bellaston, for she well knew whom Mr. Western meant, though perhaps she thought he would easily be reconciled to his lordship's proposals.

"Do you hear there," quoth the squire, "what her ladyship says? All your family are for the match. Come, Sophy, be a good girl and be dutiful, and make your father happy."

"If my death will make you happy, sir," answered Sophia, "you will shortly be so."

"It's a lie, Sophy; it's a d—ned lie, and you know it," said the squire.

"Indeed, Miss Western," said Lady Bellaston, "you injure your father; he had nothing in view but your interest in this match, and I and all your friends must acknowledge the highest honour done to your family in the proposal."

"Ay, all of us," quoth the squire; "nay, it was no proposal of mine. She knows it was her aunt proposed it to me first. Come, Sophy, once more let me beg you to be a good girl and gee me your consent before your cousin."

"Let me give him your hand, cousin," said the lady. "It is the fashion nowadays to dispense with time and long courtships."

"Pugh," said the squire, "what signifies time; won't they have time enough to court afterwards? People may court very well after they have been abed together."

As Lord Fellamar was very well assured that he was meant by Lady Bellaston, so, never having heard nor suspected a word of Blifil, he made no doubt of his being meant by the father. Coming up, therefore, to the squire, he said, "Though I have not the honour, sir, of being personally known to you, yet as I find I have the happiness to have my proposals accepted, let me intercede, sir, in behalf of the young lady that she may not be more solicited at this time."

"You intercede, sir!" said the squire. "Why, who the devil are you?"

"Sir, I am Lord Fellamar," answered he, "and am the happy man whom I hope you have done the honour of accepting for a son-in-law."

"You are a son of a b—," replied the squire, "for all your laced coat. You my son-in-law; and be d—ned to you!"

"I shall take more from you, sir, than from any man," answered the lord, "but I must inform you that I am not used to hear such language without resentment."

"Resent my a—," quoth the squire. "Don't think I am afraid of such a fellow as thee art? Because hast a got a spit there dangling at thy side. Lay by your spit, and I'll give thee enough of meddling with what doth not belong to thee. I'll teach you to father-in-law me. I'll lick thy jacket."

"It's very well, sir," said my lord. "I shall make no disturbance before the ladies. I am very well satisfied. Your humble servant, sir; Lady Bellaston, your most obedient."

His lordship was no sooner gone than Lady Bellaston, coming up to Mr. Western, said, "Bless me, sir, what have you done? You know not whom you have affronted; he is a nobleman of the first rank and fortune, and yesterday made proposals to your daughter, and such as I am sure you must accept with the highest pleasure."

"Answer for yourself, lady cousin," said the squire; "I will have nothing to do with any of your lords. My daughter shall have an honest country-gentleman; I have pitched upon one for her—and she shall ha' un. I am sorry for the trouble she hath given your ladyship, with all my heart." Lady Bellaston made a civil speech upon the word *trouble*, to which the squire answered, "Why that's kind—and I would do as much for your ladyship. To be sure, relations should do for one another. So I wish your ladyship a good night. Come, madam, you must go along with me by fair means or I'll have you carried down to the coach."

Sophia said she would attend him without force, but begged to go in a chair, for she said she should not be able to ride any other way.

"Prithee," cries the squire, "wout unt persuade me canst not ride in a coach, wouldst? That's a pretty thing surely. No, no, I'll never let thee out of my sight any more till art married, that I promise thee." Sophia told him she saw he was resolved to break her heart. "Oh, break thy heart and be d—ned," quoth he, "if a good husband will break it. I don't value a brass varden, not a hapenny, of any undutiful b— upon earth." He then took violently hold of her hand, upon which the parson once more interfered, begging him to use gentle methods. At that, the squire thundered out a curse and bid the parson hold his tongue, saying, "At'n't in pulpit now? When art a-got up there I never mind what dost say; but I won't be priest-ridden, nor taught how to behave myself by thee. I wish your ladyship a good night. Come along, Sophy, be a good girl and all shall be well. Shat ha' un, d—n me, shat ha' un."

Mrs. Honour appeared below-stairs and, with a low curtsy to the squire, offered to attend her mistress, but he pushed her away, saying, "Hold, madam, hold; you come no more near my house." "And will you take my maid away from me?" said Sophia. "Yes, indeed, madam, will I," cries the squire; "you need not fear being without a servant;

I will get you another maid, and a better maid than this, who, I'd lay five pound to a crown, is no more a maid than my grannum. No, no, Sophy, she shall contrive no more escapes, I promise you." He then packed up his daughter and the parson into the hackney-coach, after which he mounted himself and ordered it to drive to his lodgings. In the way thither he suffered Sophia to be quiet, and entertained himself with reading a lecture to the parson on good manners and a proper behaviour to his betters.

It is possible he might not so easily have carried off his daughter from Lady Bellaston had that good lady desired to have detained her, but in reality she was not a little pleased with the confinement into which Sophia was going; and as her project with Lord Fellamar had failed of success, she was well contented that other violent methods were now going to be used in favour of another man.

6

BY WHAT MEANS THE SQUIRE CAME TO DISCOVER HIS DAUGHTER

Though the reader in many histories is obliged to digest much more unaccountable appearances than this of Mr. Western without any satisfaction at all, yet, as we dearly love to oblige him whenever it is in our power, we shall now proceed to show by what method the squire discovered where his daughter was.

In the third chapter, then, of the preceding book, we gave a hint (for it is not our custom to unfold at any time more than is necessary for the occasion) that Mrs. Fitzpatrick, who was very desirous of reconciling herself to her uncle and aunt Western, thought she had a probable opportunity, by the service of preserving Sophia from committing the same crime which had drawn on herself the anger of her family. After much deliberation, therefore, she resolved to inform her aunt Western where her cousin was, and accordingly she writ the following letter, which we shall give the reader at length for more reasons than one:

Honoured madam,

The occasion of my writing this will perhaps make a letter of mine agreeable to my dear aunt for the sake of one of her nieces, though I have little reason to hope it will be so on the account of another.

Without more apology, as I was coming to throw my unhappy self at your feet I met by the strangest accident in the world my cousin Sophy, whose history you are better acquainted with than myself, though alas, I know infinitely too much; enough indeed to satisfy me that unless she is immediately prevented, she is in danger of running into the same fatal mischief which, by foolishly and ignorantly refusing your most wise and prudent advice, I have unfortunately brought on myself.

In short, I have seen the man; nay, I was most part of yesterday in his company, and a charming young fellow I promise you he is. By what accident he came acquainted with me is too tedious to tell you now, but I have this morning changed my lodgings to avoid him, lest he should by my means discover my cousin; for he doth not yet know where she is, and it is advisable he should not till my uncle hath secured her. No time, therefore, is to be lost, and I need only inform you that she is now with Lady Bellaston, whom I have seen, and who hath, I find, a design of concealing her from her family. You know, madam, she is a strange woman; but nothing could misbecome me more than to presume to give any hint to one of your great understanding and great knowledge of the world besides barely informing you of the matter of fact.

I hope, madam, the care which I have shown on this occasion for the good of my family will recommend me again to the favour of a lady who hath always exerted so much zeal for the honour and true interest of us all, and that it may be a means of restoring me to your friendship, which hath made so great a part of my former, and is so necessary to my future, happiness. I am,

with the utmost respect,
honoured madam,
your most dutiful, obliged niece,
and most obedient,
humble servant,
HARRIET FITZPATRICK.

Mrs. Western was now at her brother's house, where she had resided ever since the flight of Sophia in order to administer comfort to the poor squire in his affliction. Of this comfort, which she doled out to him in daily portions, we have formerly given a specimen.

She was now standing with her back to the fire and, with a pinch of snuff in her hand, was dealing forth this daily allowance of comfort to the squire while he smoked his afternoon pipe, when she received the above letter, which she had no sooner read than she delivered it to him, saying, "There, sir, there is an account of your lost sheep. Fortune hath again restored her to you, and if you will be governed by my advice, it is possible you may yet preserve her."

The squire had no sooner read the letter than he leaped from his chair, threw his pipe into the fire, and gave a loud huzza for joy. He then summoned his servants, called for his boots, and ordered the Chevalier and several other horses to be saddled, and that Parson Supple should be immediately sent for. Having done this, he turned to his sister, caught her in his arms, and gave her a close embrace, saying, "Zounds! You don't seem pleased; one would imagine you was sorry I have found the girl."

"Brother," answered she, "the deepest politicians, who see to the bottom, discover often a very different aspect of affairs from what swims on the surface. It is true, indeed, things do look rather less desperate than they did formerly in Holland, when Lewis the Fourteenth was at the gates of Amsterdam, but there is a delicacy required in this matter, which you will pardon me, brother, if I suspect you want. There is a decorum to be used with a woman of figure such as Lady Bellaston, brother, which requires a knowledge of the world superior, I am afraid, to yours."

"Sister," cries the squire, "I know you have no opinion of my parts, but I'll show you on this occasion who is a fool. Knowledge, quotha! I have not been in the country so long without having some knowledge of warrants and the law of the land. I know I may take my own wherever I can find it. Show me my own daughter, and if I don't know how to come at her, I'll suffer you to call me fool as long as I live. There be justices of peace in London as well as in other places."

"I protest," cries she, "you make me tremble for the event of this matter, which, if you will proceed by my advice, you may bring to so good an issue. Do you really imagine, brother, that the house of a woman of figure is to be attacked by warrants and brutal justices of the peace? I will inform you how to proceed. As soon as you arrive in town and have got yourself into a decent dress (for indeed, brother, you have none at present fit to appear in), you must send your compliments to Lady Bellaston and desire leave to wait on her. When you are admitted to her presence, as you certainly will be, and have told her your story, and have made proper use of my name (for I think you only just know one another by sight, though you are relations), I am confident she will withdraw her protection from my niece, who hath certainly imposed upon her. This is the only method. Justices of peace indeed! Do you imagine any such event can arrive to a woman of figure in a civilized nation?"

"D—n their figures," cries the squire; "a pretty civilized nation truly, where women are above the law. And what, must I stand sending a parcel of compliments to a confounded whore that keeps away a daughter from her own natural father? I tell you, sister, I am not so ignorant as you think me. I know you would have women above the law, but it is all a lie; I heard his lordship say at size that no one is above the law. But this of yours is Hanover law, I suppose."

"Mr. Western," said she, "I think you daily improve in ignorance. I protest you are grown an arrant bear."

"No more a bear than yourself, sister Western," said the squire. "Pox! You may talk of your civility an you will, I am sure you never show any to me. I am no bear, no, nor no dog neither, though I know somebody that is something that begins with a *B*, but pox, I will show you I have a-got more good manners than some folks."

"Mr. Western," answered the lady, "you may say what you please, *je vous méprise de tout mon cœur*. I shall not, therefore, be angry. Besides, as my cousin with that odious Irish name justly says, I have that regard for the honour and true interest of my family and that concern for my niece, who is a part of it, that I have resolved to go to town myself upon this occasion; for indeed, indeed, brother, you are not a fit minister to be employed at a polite court. Greenland—Greenland should always be the scene of the tramontane negotiation."

"I thank heaven," cries the squire, "I don't understand you now. You are got to your Hanoverian linguo. However, I'll show you I scorn to be behindhand in civility with you, and as you are not angry for what I have said, so I am not angry for what you have said. Indeed, I have always thought it a folly for relations to quarrel, and if they do now and then give a hasty word, why, people should give and take; for my part I never bear malice, and I take it very kind of you to go up to London, for I never was there but twice in my life, and then I did not stay above a fortnight at a time; and to be sure, I can't be expected to know much of the streets and the folks in that time. I never denied that you knowed all these matters better than I. For me to dispute that would be all as one, as for you to dispute the management of a pack of dogs, or the finding a hare sitting, with me." "Which I promise you," says she, "I never will." "Well, and I promise you," returned he, "that I never will dispute the t'other."

Here, then, a league was struck (to borrow a phrase from the lady) between the contending parties; and now the parson arriving and the horses being ready, the squire departed, having promised his sister to follow her advice, and she prepared to follow him the next day.

But having communicated these matters to the parson on the road, they both agreed that the prescribed formalities might very well be dispensed with, and the squire, having changed his mind, proceeded in the manner we have already seen.

7

IN WHICH VARIOUS MISFORTUNES BEFALL POOR JONES

Affairs were in the aforesaid situation when Mrs. Honour arrived at Mrs. Miller's and called Jones out from the company, as we have before seen; with whom, when she found herself alone, she began as follows:

"Oh, my dear sir, how shall I get spirits to tell you? You are undone, sir, and my poor lady's undone, and I am undone." "Hath anything happened to Sophia?" cries Jones, staring like a madman. "All that is bad," cries Honour. "Oh, I shall never get such another lady! Oh, that I should ever live to see this day!" At these words Jones turned pale as ashes, trembled and stammered, but Honour went on. "Oh, Mr. Jones. I have lost my lady forever." "How! What! For heaven's sake tell me. Oh, my dear Sophia!" "You may well call her so," said Honour; "she was the dearest lady to me. I shall never have such another place."

"D—n your place," cries Jones. "Where is? What, what is become of my Sophia?" "Ay, to be sure," cries she, "servants may be d—ned. It signifies nothing what becomes of them, though they are turned away and ruined ever so much. To be sure, they are not flesh and blood like other people. No, to be sure, it signifies nothing what becomes of them." "If you have any pity, any compassion," cries Jones, "I beg you will instantly tell me what hath happened to Sophia?" "To be sure, I have more pity for you than you have for me," answered Honour; "I don't d—n you because you have lost the sweetest lady in the world. To be sure, you are worthy to be pitied, and I am worthy to be pitied too; for to be sure, if ever there was a good mistress——" "What hath happened," cries Jones in almost a raving fit. "What? What?" said Honour. "Why, the worst that could have happened both for you and for me: her father is come to town and hath carried her away from us both." Here Jones fell on his knees in thanksgiving that it was no worse. "No worse!" repeated Honour. "What could be worse for either of us? He carried her off, swearing she should marry Mr. Blifil— that's for your comfort—and for poor me, I am turned out-of-doors." "Indeed, Mrs. Honour," answered Jones, "you frightened me out of my wits. I imagined some most dreadful sudden accident had happened to Sophia, something compared to which even the seeing her married to Blifil would be a trifle; but while there is life there are hopes, my dear Honour. Women in this land of liberty cannot be married by actual brutal force." "To be sure, sir," said she, "that's true. There may be some hopes for you, but alack-a-day, what hopes are there for poor me? And to be sure, sir, you must be sensible I suffer all this upon your account. All the quarrel the squire hath to me is for taking your part, as I have done, against Mr. Blifil." "Indeed Mrs. Honour," answered he, "I am sensible of my obligations to you and will leave nothing in my power undone to make you amends." "Alas, sir," said she, "what can make a servant amends for the loss of one place but the getting another altogether as good!" "Do not despair, Mrs. Honour," said Jones, "I hope to reinstate you again in the same." "Alack-a-day, sir," said she, "how can I flatter myself with such hopes when I know it is a thing impossible, for the squire is so set against me; and yet, if you should ever have my lady, as to be sure, I now hopes heartily you will, for you are a generous, good-natured gentleman, and I am sure you loves her, and to be sure, she loves you as dearly as her own soul; it is a matter in vain to deny it because as why everybody that is in the least acquainted with my lady must see it; for, poor dear lady, she can't dissemble, and if two people who loves one another a'n't happy, why, who should be so? Happiness don't always depend upon what people has; besides, my lady has enough for both. To be sure, therefore, as one may say, it would be all the pity in the world to keep two such loviers asunder; nay, I am convinced, for my part, you will meet together at last, for if it is to be, there is no preventing it. If a marriage is made in heaven, all the justices of peace upon earth can't break it off. To be sure, I wishes that Parson Supple had but a little more spirit to tell the squire of his wickedness in endeavouring to force his daughter contrary to her liking, but then, his whole dependence is on the squire, and so the poor gentleman, though he is a very religious good sort of man and talks of the badness of such doings behind the squire's back, yet he dares not say his soul is his own to his face. To be sure, I never saw him make so bold as just now; I was afeard the squire would have struck him. I would not have your honour be melancholy, sir, nor despair; things may go better as long as you are sure of my lady, and that I am certain you may be, for she never will be brought to consent to marry any other man. Indeed, I am terribly afeard the squire will do her a mischief in his passion, for he is a prodigious passionate gentleman, and I am afeard, too, the poor lady will be brought to break her heart, for she is as tender-hearted as a chicken; it is pity, methinks, she had not a little of my courage. If I was in love with a young man and my father offered to lock me up, I'd tear his eyes out, but I'd come at him; but then, there's a great fortune in the case, which it is in her father's power either to give her or not; that, to be sure, may make some difference."

Whether Jones gave strict attention to all the foregoing harangue or whether it was for want of any vacancy in the discourse, I cannot determine, but he never once attempted to answer, nor did she once stop till Partridge came running into the room and informed him that the great lady was upon the stairs.

Nothing could equal the dilemma to which Jones was now reduced. Honour knew nothing of any acquaintance that subsisted between him and Lady Bellaston, and she was almost the last person in the world to whom he would have communicated it. In this hurry and distress he took (as is common enough) the worse course, and instead of exposing her to the lady, which would have been of little consequence, he chose to expose the lady to her; he therefore resolved to hide Honour, whom he had but just time to convey behind the bed, and to draw the curtains.

The hurry in which Jones had been all day engaged on account of his poor landlady and her family, the terrors occasioned by Mrs. Honour, and the confusion into which he was thrown by the sudden arrival of Lady Bellaston had altogether driven former thoughts out of his head, so that it never once occurred to his memory to act the part of a sick man, which, indeed, neither the gaiety of his dress nor the freshness of his countenance would have at all supported.

He received her ladyship, therefore, rather agreeably to her desires than to her expectations, with all the good humour he could muster in his countenance and without any real or affected appearance of the least disorder.

Lady Bellaston no sooner entered the room than she squatted herself down on the bed. "So, my dear Jones," said she, "you find nothing can detain me long from you. Perhaps I ought to be angry with you, that I have neither seen nor heard from you all day, for I perceive your distemper would have suffered you to come abroad; nay, I suppose you have not sat in your chamber all day dressed up like a fine lady to see company after a lying-in, but, however, don't think I intend to scold you; for I never will give you an excuse for the cold behaviour of a husband by putting on the ill humour of a wife."

"Nay, Lady Bellaston," said Jones, "I am sure your ladyship will not upbraid me with neglect of duty when I only waited for orders. Who, my dear creature, hath reason to complain? Who missed an appointment last night and left an unhappy man to expect and wish and sigh and languish?"

"Do not mention it, my dear Mr. Jones," cried she. "If you knew the occasion, you would pity me. In short, it is impossible to conceive what women of condition are obliged to suffer from the impertinence of fools in order to keep up the farce of the world. I am glad, however, all your languishing and wishing have done you no harm, for you never looked better in your life. Upon my faith, Jones, you might at this instant sit for the picture of Adonis."

There are certain words of provocation which men of

honour hold can only properly be answered by a blow. Among lovers, possibly there may be some expressions which can only be answered by a kiss. The compliment which Lady Bellaston now made Jones seems to be of this kind, especially as it was attended with a look in which the lady conveyed more soft ideas than it was possible to express with her tongue.

Jones was certainly at this instant in one of the most disagreeable and distressed situations imaginable; for to carry on the comparison we made use of before, though the provocation was given by the lady, Jones could not receive satisfaction, nor so much as offer to ask it, in the presence of a third person, seconds in this kind of duels not being according to the law of arms. As this objection did not occur to Lady Bellaston, who was ignorant of any other woman being there but herself, she waited some time in great astonishment for an answer from Jones, who, conscious of the ridiculous figure he made, stood at a distance, and not daring to give the proper answer, gave none at all. Nothing can be imagined more comic nor yet more tragical than this scene would have been if it had lasted much longer. The lady had already changed colour two or three times, had got up from the bed and sat down again, while Jones was wishing the ground to sink under him or the house to fall on his head, when an odd accident freed him from an embarrassment out of which neither the eloquence of a Cicero nor the politics of a Machiavel could have delivered him without utter disgrace.

This was no other than the arrival of young Nightingale, dead drunk, or rather in that state of drunkenness which deprives men of the use of their reason without depriving them of the use of their limbs.

Mrs. Miller and her daughters were in bed, and Partridge was smoking his pipe by the kitchen fire, so that he arrived at Mr. Jones's chamber door without any interruption. This he burst open and was entering without any ceremony when Jones started from his seat and ran to oppose him, which he did so effectually that Nightingale never came far enough within the door to see who was sitting on the bed.

Nightingale had in reality mistaken Jones's apartment for that in which himself had lodged; he therefore strongly insisted on coming in, often swearing that he would not be kept from his own bed. Jones, however, prevailed over him and delivered him into the hands of Partridge, whom the noise on the stairs soon summoned to his master's assistance.

And now Jones was unwillingly obliged to return to his own apartment, where at the very instant of his entrance he heard Lady Bellaston venting an exclamation, though not a very loud one, and at the same time saw her flinging herself into a chair in a vast agitation, which in a lady of a tender constitution would have been an hysteric fit.

In reality, the lady, frightened with the struggle between the two men, of which she did not know what would be the issue, as she heard Nightingale swear many oaths he would come to his own bed, attempted to retire to her own place of hiding, which to her great confusion she found already occupied by another.

"Is this usage to be borne, Mr. Jones?" cries the lady. "Basest of men! What wretch is this to whom you have exposed me?" "Wretch!" cries Honour, bursting in a violent rage from her place of concealment. "Marry come up! Wretch, forsooth! As poor a wretch as I am, I am honest; that is more than some folks who are richer can say."

Jones, instead of applying himself directly to take off the edge of Mrs. Honour's resentment as a more experienced gallant would have done, fell to cursing his stars and lamenting himself as the most unfortunate man in the world; and presently after, addressing himself to Lady Bellaston, he fell to some very absurd protestations of innocence. By this time the lady, having recovered the use of her reason, which she had as ready as any woman in the world, especially on such occasions, calmly replied, "Sir, you need make no apologies; I see now who the person is. I did not at first know Mrs. Honour; but now I do, I can suspect nothing wrong between her and you, and I am sure she is a woman of too good sense to put any wrong constructions upon my visit to you; I have been always her friend, and it may be in my power to be much more so hereafter."

Mrs. Honour was altogether as placable as she was passionate. Hearing, therefore, Lady Bellaston assume the soft tone, she likewise softened hers. "I'm sure, madam," says she, "I have been always ready to acknowledge your ladyship's friendships to me; sure I never had so good a friend as your ladyship—and to be sure, now I see it is your ladyship that I spoke to, I could almost bite my tongue off for very mad. I, constructions upon your ladyship—to be sure, it doth not become a servant, as I am, to think about such a great lady— I mean I was a servant; for indeed I am nobody's servant now, the more miserable wretch is me. I have lost the best mistress." Here Honour thought fit to produce a shower of tears. "Don't cry, child," says the good lady. "Ways perhaps may be found to make you amends. Come to me to-morrow morning." She then took up her fan, which lay on the ground, and without even looking at Jones walked very majestically out of the room, there being a kind of dignity in the impudence of women of quality, which their inferiors vainly aspire to attain to in circumstances of this nature.

Jones followed her downstairs, often offering her his hand, which she absolutely refused him, and got into her chair without taking any notice of him as he stood bowing below her.

At his return upstairs, a long dialogue passed between him and Mrs. Honour while she was adjusting herself after the discomposure she had undergone. The subject of this was his infidelity to her young lady, on which she enlarged with great bitterness; but Jones at last found means to reconcile her, and not only so, but to obtain a promise of most inviolable secrecy, and that she would the next morning endeavour to find out Sophia and bring him a further account of the proceedings of the squire.

Thus ended this unfortunate adventure to the satisfaction only of Mrs. Honour; for a secret (as some of my readers will perhaps acknowledge from experience) is often a very valuable possession, and that not only to those who faithfully keep it, but sometimes to such as whisper it about till it come to the ears of every one except the ignorant person who pays for the supposed concealing of what is publicly known.

8

SHORT AND SWEET

Notwithstanding all the obligations she had received from Jones, Mrs. Miller could not forbear in the morning some gentle remonstrances for the hurricane which had happened the preceding night in his chamber. These were, however, so gentle and so friendly, professing, and indeed truly, to aim at nothing more than the real good of Mr. Jones himself that he, far from being offended, thankfully received the admonition of the good woman, expressed much concern for what had passed, excused it as well as he could, and promised never more to bring the same disturbances into the house.

But though Mrs. Miller did not refrain from a short expostulation in private at their first meeting, yet the occasion of his being summoned downstairs that morning was of a much more agreeable kind, being indeed to perform the office of a father to Miss Nancy, and to give her in wedlock to Mr. Nightingale, who was now ready dressed and full as sober as many of my readers will think a man ought to be who receives a wife in so imprudent a manner.

And here perhaps it may be proper to account for the escape which this young gentleman had made from his uncle, and for his appearance in the condition in which we have seen him the night before.

Now, when the uncle had arrived at his lodgings with his nephew, partly to indulge his own inclinations (for he dearly loved his bottle) and partly to disqualify his nephew from the immediate execution of his purpose, he ordered wine to be set on the table, with which he so briskly plied the young gentleman that this latter, who though not much used to drinking did not detest it so as to be guilty of disobedience or of want of complaisance by refusing, was soon completely finished.

Just as the uncle had obtained this victory and was preparing a bed for his nephew, a messenger arrived with a piece of news which so entirely disconcerted and shocked him that he in a moment lost all consideration for his nephew, and his whole mind became entirely taken up with his own concerns.

This sudden and afflicting news was no less than that his daughter had taken the opportunity of almost the first moment of his absence and had gone off with a neighbouring young clergyman, against whom, though her father could have had but one objection, namely, that he was worth nothing, yet she had never thought proper to communicate her amour even to that father, and so artfully had she managed that it had never been once suspected by any till now that it was consummated.

Old Mr. Nightingale no sooner received this account than in the utmost confusion he ordered a post-chaise to be instantly got ready, and having recommended his nephew to the care of a servant, he directly left the house, scarce knowing what he did nor whither he went.

The uncle thus departed, when the servant came to attend the nephew to bed, had waked him for that purpose, and had at last made him sensible that his uncle was gone, he, instead of accepting the kind offices tendered him, insisted on a chair being called; with this the servant, who had received no strict orders to the contrary, readily complied, and thus, being conducted back to the house of Mrs. Miller, he had staggered up to Mr. Jones's chamber, as hath been before recounted.

This bar of the uncle being now removed (though young Nightingale knew not as yet in what manner) and all parties being quickly ready, the mother, Mr. Jones, Mr. Nightingale, and his love stepped into a hackney-coach, which conveyed him to Doctors' Commons, where Miss Nancy was, in vulgar language, soon made an honest woman, and the poor mother became, in the purest sense of the word, one of the happiest of all human beings.

And now Mr. Jones, having seen his good offices to that poor woman and her family brought to a happy conclusion, began to apply himself to his own concerns; but here, lest many of my readers should censure his folly for thus troubling himself with the affairs of others and lest some few should think he acted more disinterestedly than indeed he did, we think proper to assure our reader that he was so far from being unconcerned in this matter that he had indeed a very considerable interest in bringing it to that final consummation.

To explain this seeming paradox at once: he was one who could truly say with him in Terence, *"Homo sum; humani nihil a me alienum puto."* He was never an indifferent spectator of the misery or happiness of any one, and he felt either the one or the other in greater proportion as he himself contributed to either. He could not, therefore, be the instrument of raising a whole family from the lowest state of wretchedness to the highest pitch of joy without conveying great felicity to himself, more, perhaps, than worldly men often purchase to themselves by undergoing the most severe labour, and often by wading through the deepest iniquity.

Those readers who are of the same complexion with him will perhaps think this short chapter contains abundance of matter, while others may probably wish, short as it is, that it had been totally spared as impertinent to the main design, which I suppose they conclude is to bring Mr. Jones to the gallows, or if possible, to a more deplorable catastrophe.

9

CONTAINING LOVE-LETTERS OF SEVERAL SORTS

Mr. Jones at his return home found the following letters lying on his table, which he luckily opened in the order they were sent:

LETTER I

Surely I am under some strange infatuation; I cannot keep my resolutions a moment, however strongly made or justly founded. Last night I resolved never to see you more; this morning I am willing to hear if you can, as you say, clear up this affair. And yet, I know that to be impossible. I have said everything to myself which you can invent. Perhaps not. Perhaps your invention is stronger. Come to me, therefore, the moment you receive this. If you can forge an excuse, I almost promise you to believe it. Betrayed to— I will think no more. Come to me directly. This is the third letter I have writ; the two former are burnt. I am almost inclined to burn this too. I wish I preserve my senses. Come to me presently.

LETTER II

If you ever expect to be forgiven, or even suffered within my doors, come to me this instant.

LETTER III

I now find you was not at home when my notes came to your lodgings. The moment you receive this let me see you—I shall not stir out, nor shall anybody be let in but yourself. Sure nothing can detain you long.

Jones had just read over these three billets when Mr. Nightingale came into the room. "Well, Tom," said he, "any news from Lady Bellaston after last night's adventure?" (for it was now no secret to anyone in that house who the lady was). "The Lady Bellaston?" answered Jones very gravely. "Nay, dear Tom," cries Nightingale, "don't be so reserved to your friends. Though I was too drunk to see her last night, I saw her at the masquerade. Do you think I am ignorant who the Queen of the Fairies is?" "And did you really then know the lady at the masquerade?" said Jones. "Yes, upon my soul, did I," said Nightingale, "and have given you twenty hints of it since, though you seemed always so tender on that point that I would not speak plainly. I fancy, my friend, by your extreme nicety in this matter, you are not so well acquainted with the character of the lady as with her person. Don't be angry, Tom, but upon my honour you are not the first young fellow she hath debauched. Her reputation is in no danger, believe me."

Though Jones had no reason to imagine the lady to have been of the vestal kind when his amour began, yet as he was thoroughly ignorant of the town and had very little acquaintance in it, he had yet no knowledge of that character which is vulgarly called a demi-rep; that is to say, a woman who intrigues with every man she likes under the name and appearance of virtue, and who, though some over-nice ladies will not be seen with her, is visited (as they term it) by the whole town; in short, whom everybody knows to be what nobody calls her.

When he found, therefore, that Nightingale was perfectly acquainted with his intrigue, and began to suspect that so scrupulous a delicacy as he had hitherto observed was not quite necessary on the occasion, he gave a latitude to his friend's tongue and desired him to speak plainly what he knew or had ever heard of the lady.

Nightingale, who in many other instances was rather too effeminate in his disposition, had a pretty strong inclination to tittle-tattle. He had no sooner, therefore, received a full liberty of speaking from Jones than he entered upon a long narrative concerning the lady, which, as it contained many particulars highly to her dishonour, we have too great a tenderness for all women of condition to repeat. We would cautiously avoid giving an opportunity to the future commentators on our works of making any malicious application, and of forcing us to be against our will the author of scandal, which never entered into our head.

Jones, having very attentively heard all that Nightingale had to say, fetched a deep sigh, which the other observing, cried, "Hey-day! Why, thou art not in love, I hope! Had I imagined my stories would have affected you, I promise you should never have heard them." "Oh, my dear friend," cries Jones, "I am so entangled with this woman that I know not how to extricate myself. 'In love' indeed! No, my friend, but I am under obligations to her, and very great ones. Since you know so much, I will be very explicit with you. It is owing perhaps solely to her that I have not before this wanted a bit of bread. How can I possibly desert such a woman? And yet I must desert her or be guilty of the blackest treachery to one who deserves infinitely better of me than she can, a woman, my Nightingale, for whom I have a passion which few can have an idea of. I am half distracted with doubts how to act." "And is this other, pray, an honourable mistress?" cries Nightingale. "Honourable?" answered Jones. "No breath ever yet durst sully her reputation. The sweetest air is not purer, the limpid stream not clearer, than her honour. She is all over, both in mind and body, consummate perfection. She is the most beautiful creature in the universe, and yet she is mistress of such noble, elevated qualities that though she is never from my thoughts, I scarce ever think of her beauty but when I see it." "And can you, my good friend," cries Nightingale, "with such an engagement as this upon your hands, hesitate a moment about quitting such a——" "Hold," said Jones, "no more abuse of her; I detest the thought of ingratitude." "Pooh!" answered the other. "You are not the first upon whom she hath conferred obligations of this kind. She is remarkably liberal where she likes; though, let me tell you, her favours are so prudently bestowed that they should rather raise a man's vanity than his gratitude." In short, Nightingale proceeded so far on this head and told his friend so many stories of the lady, which he swore to the truth of, that he entirely removed all esteem for her from the breast of Jones, and his gratitude was lessened in proportion. Indeed, he began to look on all the favours he had received rather as wages than benefits, which not only depreciated her but himself too in his own conceit, and put him quite out of humour with both. From this disgust, his mind by a natural transition turned towards Sophia: her virtue, her purity, her love to him, her sufferings on his account, filled all his thoughts and made his commerce with Lady Bellaston appear still more odious. The result of all was that though his turning himself out of her *service*, in which light he now saw his affair with her, would be the loss of his bread, yet he determined to quit her if he could but find a handsome pretence; which having communicated to his friend, Nightingale considered a little and then said, "I have it, my boy; I have found out a sure method: propose marriage to her, and I would venture hanging upon the success." "Marriage!" cries Jones. "Ay, propose marriage," answered Nightingale, "and she will declare off in a moment. I knew a young fellow whom she kept formerly, who made the offer to her in earnest, and was presently turned off for his pains."

Jones declared he would not venture the experiment. "Perhaps," said he, "she may be less shocked at this proposal from one man than from another. And if she should take me at my word, where am I then? Caught in my own trap and undone forever." "No," answered Nightingale, "not if I can give you an expedient by which you may at any time get out of the trap." "What expedient can that be?" replied Jones. "This," answered Nightingale. "The young fellow I mentioned, who is one of the most intimate acquaintances I have in the world, is so angry with her for some ill offices she hath since done him that I am sure he would without any difficulty give you a sight of her letters; upon which you may decently break with her and declare off before the knot is tied if she should really be willing to tie it, which I am convinced she will not."

After some hesitation, Jones, upon the strength of this assurance, consented, but as he swore he wanted the confidence to propose the matter to her face, he wrote the following letter, which Nightingale dictated:

Madam,
    I am extremely concerned that by an unfortunate engagement abroad I should have missed receiving the honour of your ladyship's commands the moment they came, and the delay which I must now suffer of vindicating myself to your ladyship greatly adds to this misfortune. Oh, Lady Bellaston, what a terror have I been in for fear your reputation should be exposed by these perverse accidents. There is one only way to secure it. I need not name what that is. Only permit me to say that as your honour is as dear to me as my own, so my sole ambition is to have the glory of laying my liberty at your feet, and believe me when I assure you I can

never be made completely happy without you generously bestow on me a legal right of calling you mine forever. I am, madam, with most profound respect, your ladyship's most obliged, obedient, humble servant,

THOMAS JONES

To this she presently returned the following answer:

Sir,

When I read over your serious epistle, I could from its coldness and formality have sworn that you had already the legal right you mention; nay, that we had for many years composed that monstrous animal a husband and wife. Do you really, then, imagine me a fool? Or do you fancy yourself capable of so entirely persuading me out of my senses that I should deliver my whole fortune into your power in order to enable you to support your pleasures at my expense. Are these the proofs of love which I expected? Is this the return for— But I scorn to upbraid you, and am in great admiration of your profound respect.

P.S. I am prevented from revising; perhaps I have said more than I meant. Come to me at eight this evening.

Jones, by the advice of his privy council, replied:

Madam,

It is impossible to express how much I am shocked at the suspicion you entertain of me. Can Lady Bellaston have conferred favours on a man whom she could believe capable of so base a design? Or can she treat the most solemn tie of love with contempt? Can you imagine, madam, that if the violence of my passion in an unguarded moment overcame the tenderness which I have for your honour, I would think of indulging myself in the continuance of an intercourse which could not possibly escape long the notice of the world, and which, when discovered, must prove so fatal to your reputation? If such be your opinion of me, I must pray for a sudden opportunity of returning those pecuniary obligations which I have been so unfortunate to receive at your hands, and for those of a more tender kind, I shall remain, &c.

And so concluded in the very words with which he had concluded the former letter.

The lady answered as follows:

I see you are a villain, and I despise you from my soul. If you come here I shall not be at home.

Though Jones was well satisfied with his deliverance from a thraldom which those who have ever experienced it will, I apprehend, allow to be none of the lightest, he was not, however, perfectly easy in his mind. There was in this scheme too much of fallacy to satisfy one who utterly detested every species of falsehood or dishonesty, nor would he indeed have submitted to put it in practice had he not been involved in a distressful situation, where he was obliged to be guilty of some dishonour either to the one lady or the other; and surely the reader will allow that every good principle, as well as love, pleaded strongly in favour of Sophia.

Nightingale highly exulted in the success of his stratagem, upon which he received many thanks and much applause from his friend. He answered, "Dear Tom, we have conferred very different obligations on each other. To me you owe the regaining your liberty; to you I owe the loss of mine. But if you are as happy in the one instance as I am in the other, I promise you we are the two happiest fellows in England."

The two gentlemen were now summoned down to dinner, where Mrs. Miller, who performed herself the office of cook, had exerted her best talents to celebrate the wedding of her daughter. This joyful circumstance she ascribed principally to the friendly behaviour of Jones; her whole soul was fired with gratitude towards him, and all her looks, words, and actions were so busied in expressing it that her daughter and even her new son-in-law were very little the objects of her consideration.

Dinner was just ended when Mrs. Miller received a letter, but as we have had letters enough in this chapter, we shall communicate the contents in our next.

10

CONSISTING PARTLY OF FACTS, AND PARTLY OF OBSERVATIONS UPON THEM

The letter, then, which arrived at the end of the preceding

chapter was from Mr. Allworthy, and the purport of it was his intention to come immediately to town with his nephew, Blifil, and a desire to be accommodated with his usual lodgings, which were the first floor for himself and the second for his nephew.

The cheerfulness which had before displayed itself in the countenance of the poor woman was a little clouded on this occasion. This news did indeed a good deal disconcert her. To requite so disinterested a match with her daughter by presently turning her new son-in-law out of doors appeared to her very unjustifiable on the one hand; and on the other, she could scarce bear the thoughts of making any excuse to Mr. Allworthy, after all the obligations received from him, for depriving him of lodgings which were indeed strictly his due; for that gentleman, in conferring all his numberless benefits on others, acted by a rule diametrically opposite to what is practised by most generous people. He contrived on all occasions to hide his beneficence not only from the world but even from the object of it. He constantly used the words *lend* and *pay*, instead of *give*, and by every other method he could invent always lessened the favours he conferred with his tongue while he was heaping them with both his hands. When he settled the annuity of £50 a year, therefore, on Mrs. Miller, he told her it was in consideration of always having her first floor when he was in town (which he scarce ever intended to be), but that she might let it at any other time, for that he would always send her a month's warning. He was now, however, hurried to town so suddenly that he had no opportunity of giving such notice, and this hurry probably prevented him, when he wrote for his lodgings, adding, "if they were then empty"; for he would most certainly have been well satisfied to have relinquished them on a less sufficient excuse than what Mrs. Miller could now have made.

But there are a sort of persons who, as Prior excellently well remarks, direct their conduct by something

> Beyond the fixed and settled rules
> Of vice and virtue in the schools;
> Beyond the letter of the law.

To these, it is so far from being sufficient that their defence would acquit them at the Old Bailey that they are not even contented though conscience, the severest of all judges, should discharge them. Nothing short of the fair and honourable will satisfy the delicacy of their minds, and if any of their actions fall short of this mark, they mope and pine, are as uneasy and restless as a murderer who is afraid of a ghost or of the hangman.

Mrs. Miller was one of these. She could not conceal her uneasiness at this letter, with the contents of which she had no sooner acquainted the company and given some hints of her distress than Jones, her good angel, presently relieved her anxiety. "As for myself, madam," said he, "my lodging is at your service at a moment's warning; and Mr. Nightingale, I am sure, as he cannot yet prepare a house fit to receive his lady, will consent to return to his new lodging, whither Mrs. Nightingale will certainly consent to go." With which proposal both husband and wife instantly agreed.

The reader will easily believe that the cheeks of Mrs. Miller began again to glow with additional gratitude to Jones, but perhaps it may be more difficult to persuade him that Mr. Jones, having in his last speech called her daughter Mrs. Nightingale (it being the first time that agreeable sound had ever reached her ears), gave the fond mother more satisfaction and warmed her heart more towards Jones than his having dissipated her present anxiety.

The next day was then appointed for the removal of the new-married couple and of Mr. Jones, who was likewise to be provided for in the same house with his friend. And now the serenity of the company was again restored, and they passed the day in the utmost cheerfulness, all except Jones, who though he outwardly accompanied the rest in their mirth felt many a bitter pang on the account of his Sophia, which were not a little heightened by the news of Mr. Blifil's coming to town (for he clearly saw the intention of his journey), and what greatly aggravated his concern was that Mrs. Honour, who had promised to inquire after Sophia and to make her report to him early the next evening, had disappointed him.

In the situation that he and his mistress were in at this time, there were scarce any grounds for him to hope that he should hear any good news, yet he was as impatient to see Mrs. Honour as if he had expected she would bring him a letter with an assignation in it from Sophia, and bore the disappointment as ill. Whether this impatience arose from that natural weakness of the human mind which makes it desirous to know the worst and renders uncertainty the most intolerable of pains, or whether he still flattered himself with some secret hopes, we will not determine. But that it might be the last, whoever has loved cannot but know. For of all the powers exercised by this passion over our minds, one of the most wonderful is that of supporting hope in the midst of despair. Difficulties, improbabilities, nay, impossibilities, are quite overlooked by it, so that to any man extremely in love may be applied what Addison says of Caesar:

> The Alps, and Pyrenaeans sink before him!

Yet it is equally true that the same passion will sometimes make mountains of mole-hills and produce despair in the midst of hope; but these cold fits last not long in good constitutions. Which temper Jones was now in, we leave the reader to guess, having no exact information about it, but this is certain: that he had spent two hours in expectation when, being unable any longer to conceal his uneasiness, he retired to his room, where his anxiety had almost made him frantic when the following letter was brought him from Mrs. Honour, with which we shall present the reader *verbatim et literatim*:

Sir,

I shud sartenly haf kaled on you a cordin too mi promiss haddunt itt bin that hur lashipp prevent mee, for too bee sur, sir, you nose very well that evere persun must luk furst at ome, and sartenly such anuther offar mite not ave ever hapned, so as I shud ave bin justly to blam had I not excepted of it when her laship was so veri kind as to offar to mak mee hur one uman without mi ever askin any such thing; to bee sur, shee is won of thee best ladis in thee wurld, and pepil who sase to the kontrari must bee veri wiket pepil in thare harts. To be sur, if ever I ave sad anything of that kine it as bin thru ignorens and I am hartili sorri for it. I nose your onor to be a genteelman of more onur and onesty, if I ever said ani such thing, to repete it to hurt a pore servant that as alwais ad thee gratest respect in thee world for ure onour. To bee sur, won shud kepe wons tung within one's teeth, for no boddi nose what may hapen; and too bee sur, if ani boddi ad tolde mee yester-

day that I shud haf bin in so gud a plase to day, I shud
not haf beleeved it; for too bee sur, I never was a dremd
of any such thing, nor shud I ever have soft after ani
other bodi's plase, but as her laship wass so kine of her
one a cord too give it mee without askin, to be sure,
Mrs. Etoff herself nor no other bodi can blam mee for
exceptin such a thing when it fals in mi waye. I beg
ure onur not too menshon ani thing of what I haf sad,
for I wish ure onur all thee gud luk in thee wurld;
and I don't cuestion butt thatt u wil haf Madam Sofia
in the end, butt ass to miself ure onur nose I kant bee
of ani farder sarvis to u in that matar, nou bein under
thee cumand off anuthar parson and nott mi one mistress. I begg ure onur to say nothing of what past, and
belive me to be, sir, ure onur's umble sarvant to
cumand till deth,

HONOUR BLACKMORE.

Various were the conjectures which Jones entertained on
this step of Lady Bellaston, who in reality had little farther
design than to secure within her own house the repository
of a secret, which she chose should make no farther progress than it had made already; but mostly she desired to
keep it from the ears of Sophia, for though that young
lady was almost the only one who would never have repeated it again, her ladyship could not persuade herself of
this, since as she now hated poor Sophia with most implacable hatred, she conceived a reciprocal hatred to herself
to be lodged in the tender breast of our heroine, where no
such passion had ever yet found an entrance.

While Jones was terrifying himself with the apprehension
of a thousand dreadful machinations and deep political designs, which he imagined to be at the bottom of the promotion of Honour, Fortune, who hitherto seems to have been
an utter enemy to his match with Sophia, tried a new method
to put a final end to it by throwing a temptation in his
way which in his present desperate situation it seemed unlikely he should be able to resist.

11

CONTAINING CURIOUS, BUT NOT UNPRECEDENTED, MATTER

There was a lady, one Mrs. Hunt, who had often seen Jones
at the house where he lodged, being intimately acquainted

with the women there and, indeed, a very great friend to Mrs. Miller. Her age was about thirty, for she owned six and twenty; her face and person very good, only inclining a little too much to be fat. She had been married young by her relations to an old Turkey merchant, who, having got a great fortune, had left off trade. With him she lived without reproach but not without pain, in a state of great self-denial, for about twelve years, and her virtue was rewarded by his dying and leaving her very rich. The first year of her widowhood was just at an end, and she had passed it in a good deal of retirement, seeing only a few particular friends and dividing her time between her devotions and novels, of which she was always extremely fond. Very good health, a very warm constitution, and a great deal of religion made it absolutely necessary for her to marry again, and she resolved to please herself in her second husband, as she had done her friends in the first. From her the following billet was brought to Jones:

Sir,

From the first day I saw you I doubt my eyes have told you too plainly that you were not indifferent to me, but neither my tongue nor my hand should have ever avowed it had not the ladies of the family where you lodged given me such a character of you and told me such proofs of your virtue and goodness as convince me you are not only the most agreeable but the most worthy of men. I have also satisfaction to hear from them that neither my person, understanding, or character are disagreeable to you. I have a fortune sufficient to make us both happy, but which cannot make me so without you. In thus disposing of myself, I know I shall incur the censure of the world, but if I did not love you more than I fear the world, I should not be worthy of you. One only difficulty stops me: I am informed you are engaged in a commerce of gallantry with a woman of fashion. If you think it worth-while to sacrifice that to the possession of me, I am yours; if not, forget my weakness and let this remain an eternal secret between you and

ARABELLA HUNT.

At the reading of this Jones was put into a violent flutter. His fortune was then at a very low ebb, the source being stopped from which hitherto he had been supplied. Of all he had received from Lady Bellaston not above five guineas remained, and that very morning he had been dunned by a tradesman for twice that sum. His honourable mistress was in the hands of her father and he had scarce any hopes ever to get her out of them again. To be subsisted at her expense from that little fortune she had independent of her father went much against the delicacy both of his pride and his love. This lady's fortune would have been exceeding convenient to him, and he could have no objection to her in any respect. On the contrary, he liked her as well as he did any woman except Sophia. But to abandon Sophia and marry another, that was impossible; he could not think of it upon any account. Yet why should he not, since it was plain she could not be his? Would it not be kinder to her than to continue her longer engaged in a hopeless passion for him? Ought he not to do so in friendship to her? This notion prevailed some moments, and he had almost determined to be false to her from a high point of honour, but that refinement was not able to stand very long against the voice of nature, which cried in his heart that such friendship was treason to love. At last he called for pen, ink, and paper, and writ as follows to Mrs. Hunt:

Madam,

It would be but a poor return to the favour you have done me to sacrifice any gallantry to the possession of you, and I would certainly do it, though I were not disengaged, as at present I am, from any affair of that kind. But I should not be the honest man you think me if I did not tell you that my affections are engaged to another, who is a woman of virtue and one that I never can leave. though it is probable I shall never possess her. God forbid that in return of your kindness to me, I should do you such an injury as to give you my hand when I cannot give my heart. No. I had much rather starve than be guilty of that. Even though my mistress were married to another, I would not marry you unless my heart had entirely effaced all impressions of her. Be assured that your secret was not more safe in your own breast than in that of your most obliged and grateful, humble servant,

T. JONES.

When our hero had finished and sent this letter, he went to his scrutoire, took out Miss Western's muff, kissed it several times, and then strutted some turns about his room with more satisfaction of mind than ever any Irishman felt in carrying off a fortune of £50,000.

12

A DISCOVERY MADE BY PARTRIDGE

While Jones was exulting in the consciousness of his integrity Partridge came capering into the room, as was his custom when he brought, or fancied he brought, any good tidings. He had been dispatched that morning by his master with orders to endeavour, by the servants of Lady Bellaston or by any other means, to discover whither Sophia had been conveyed, and he now returned and with a joyful countenance told our hero that he had found the lost bird. "I have seen, sir," says he, "Black George, the gamekeeper, who is one of the servants whom the squire hath brought with him to town. I knew him presently, though I have not seen him these several years; but you know, sir, he is a very remarkable man, or to use a purer phrase, he hath a most remarkable beard, the largest and blackest I ever saw. It was some time, however, before Black George could recollect me." "Well, but what is your good news?" cries Jones. "What do you know of my Sophia?" "You shall know presently, sir," answered Partridge; "I am coming to it as fast as I can. You are so impatient, sir, you would come at the infinitive mood before you can get to the imperative. As I was saying, sir, it was some time before he recollected my face." "Confound your face," cries Jones; "what of my Sophia?" "Nay, sir," answered Partridge, "I know nothing more of Madam Sophia than what I am going to tell you, and I should have told you all before this if you had not interrupted me; but if you look so angry at me, you will frighten all of it out of my head, or to use a purer phrase, out of my memory. I never saw you look so angry since the day we left Upton, which I shall remember if I was to live a thousand years." "Well, pray go on in your own way," said Jones; "you are resolved to make me mad, I find." "Not for the world," answered Partridge; "I have suffered enough for that already, which as I said I shall bear in my remembrance the longest day I have to live." "Well, but Black George?" cries Jones. "Well, sir, as I was saying, it was a long time before he could recollect me, for indeed I am very much altered since I saw him. *Non sum qualis eram.* I have had troubles in the world, and nothing alters a man so much as grief. I have heard it will change the colour of a man's hair in a night. However, at last, know me he did, that's sure enough, for we are both of an age and were at the same charity school. George was a great dunce, but no matter for that; all men do not thrive in the world according to their learning. I am sure I have reason to say so, but it will be all one a thousand years hence. Well, sir—where was I? Oh, well, we no sooner knew each other than after many hearty shakes by the hand, we agreed to go to an ale-house and take a pot, and by good luck the beer was some of the best I have met with since I have been in town. Now, sir, I am coming to the point; for no sooner did I name you, and told him that you and I came to town together and had lived together ever since, than he called for another pot and swore he would drink to your health; and indeed he drank your health so heartily that I was over-joyed to see there was so much gratitude left in the world. And after we had emptied that pot, I said I would be my pot too, and so we drank another to your health, and then I made haste home to tell you the news."

"What news?" cries Jones. "You have not mentioned a word of my Sophia!" "Bless me! I had like to have forgot that. Indeed, we mentioned a great deal about young Madam Western, and George told me all: that Mr. Blifil is coming to town in order to be married to her. 'He had best make haste, then,' says I, 'or somebody will have her before he comes; and indeed,' says I, 'Mr. Seagrim, it is a thousand pities somebody should not have her, for he certainly loves her above all the women in the world. I would have both you and she know that it is not for her fortune he follows her; for I can assure you as to matter of that there is another lady, one of much greater quality and fortune than she can pretend to, who is so fond of somebody that she comes after him day and night.'"

Here Jones fell into a passion with Partridge for having, as he said, betrayed him, but the poor fellow answered he had mentioned no name. "Besides, sir," said he, "I can assure you, George is sincerely your friend, and wished Mr. Blifil at the devil more than once; nay, he said he would do any-thing in his power upon earth to serve you, and so I am convinced he will. Betray you, indeed! Why, I question whether you have a better friend than George upon earth except myself, or one that would go farther to serve you."

"Well," says Jones, a little pacified, "you say this fellow, who I believe indeed is enough inclined to be my friend, lives in the same house with Sophia?"

"In the same house!" answered Partridge. "Why, sir, he is one of the servants of the family, and very well dressed, I promise you, he is; if it was not for his black beard you would hardly know him."

"One service, then, at least he may do me," says Jones. "Sure he can certainly convey a letter to my Sophia."

"You have hit the nail *ad unguem*," cries Partridge. "How came I not to think of it? I will engage he shall do it upon the very first mentioning."

"Well, then," said Jones, "do you leave me at present and I will write a letter which you shall deliver to him to-morrow morning, for I suppose you know where to find him."

"Oh, yes, sir," answered Partridge, "I shall certainly find him again; there is no fear of that. The liquor is too good for him to stay away long. I make no doubt but he will be there every day he stays in town."

"So you don't know the street, then, where my Sophia is lodged?" cries Jones.

"Indeed, sir, I do," said Partridge.

"What is the name of the street?" cries Jones.

"The name, sir; why here, sir, just by," answered Partridge, "not above a street or two off. I don't indeed know the very name; for as he never told me, if I had asked, you know, it might have put some suspicion into his head. No, no, sir, let me alone for that. I am too cunning for that, I promise you."

"Thou art most wonderfully cunning indeed," replied Jones; "however, I will write to my charmer, since I believe you will be cunning enough to find him to-morrow at the ale-house."

And now, having dismissed the sagacious Partridge, Mr. Jones sat himself down to write, in which employment we shall leave him for a time. And here we put an end to the fifteenth book.

BOOK XVI

1

OF PROLOGUES

I have heard of a dramatic writer who used to say he would rather write a play than a prologue; in like manner, I think, I can with less pains write one of the books of this history than the prefatory chapter to each of them.

To say the truth, I believe many a hearty curse hath been devoted on the head of that author who first instituted the method of prefixing to his play that portion of matter which is called the prologue, and which at first was part of the piece itself; but of latter years hath had usually so little connexion with the drama before which it stands that the prologue to one play might as well serve for any other. Those, indeed, of more modern date seem all to be written on the same three topics: viz., an abuse of the taste of the town, a condemnation of all contemporary authors, and an eulogium on the performance just about to be represented. The sentiments in all these are very little varied, nor is it possible they should; and indeed I have often wondered at the great invention of authors who have been capable of finding such various phrases to express the same thing.

In like manner I apprehend, some future historian (if any one shall do me the honour of imitating my manner) will, after much scratching his pate, bestow some good wishes on my memory for having first established these several initial chapters, most of which, like modern prologues, may as properly be prefixed to any other book in this history as to that which they introduce, or indeed to any other history as to this.

But however authors may suffer by either of these inventions, the reader will find sufficient emolument in the one as the spectator hath long found in the other.

First, it is well known that the prologue serves the critic for an opportunity to try his faculty of hissing and to tune his catcall to the best advantage, by which means I have known those musical instruments so well prepared that they have been able to play in full concert at the first rising of the curtain.

The same advantages may be drawn from these chapters, in which the critic will be always sure of meeting with something that may serve as a whetstone to his noble spirit, so that he may fall with a more hungry appetite for censure on the history itself. And here his sagacity must make it needless to observe how artfully these chapters are calculated for that excellent purpose, for in these we have always taken care to intersperse somewhat of the sour or acid kind in order to sharpen and stimulate the said spirit of criticism.

Again, the indolent reader, as well as spectator, finds great advantage from both these; for as they are not obliged either to see the one or read the others, and both the play and the book are thus protracted, by the former they have a quarter of an hour longer allowed them to sit at dinner, and by the latter they have the advantage of beginning to read at the fourth or fifth page instead of the first; a matter by no means of trivial consequence to persons who read books with no other view than to say they have read them, a more general motive to reading than is commonly imagined, and from which not only law books and good books, but the pages of Homer and Virgil, of Swift and Cervantes, have been often turned over.

Many other are the emoluments which arise from both these, but they are for the most part so obvious that we shall not at present stay to enumerate them, especially since it occurs to us that the principal of merit of both the prologue and the preface is that they be short.

2

We must now convey the reader to Mr. Western's lodgings,
which were in Piccadilly, where he was placed by the recommendation of the landlord at the Hercules Pillars at Hyde
Park Corner; for at the inn, which was the first he saw on
his arrival in town, he placed his horses, and in those
lodgings, which were the first he heard of, he deposited himself.

Here, when Sophia alighted from the hackney-coach which
brought her from the house of Lady Bellaston, she desired
to retire to the apartment provided for her, to which her father very readily agreed and whither he attended her himself. A short dialogue, neither very material nor pleasant to
relate minutely, then passed between them; in which he
pressed her vehemently to give her consent to the marriage
with Blifil, who, as he acquainted her, was to be in town in a
few days, but instead of complying, she gave a more peremptory and resolute refusal than she had ever done before.
This so incensed her father that after many bitter vows that
he would force her to have him whether she would or no,
he departed from her with many hard words and curses,
locked the door, and put the key into his pocket.

While Sophia was left with no other company than what
attend the closest state prisoner: namely, fire and candle,
the squire sat down to regale himself over a bottle of wine
with his parson and the landlord of the Hercules Pillars,
who, as the squire said, would make an excellent third man
and could inform them of the news of the town and how
affairs went; for to be sure, says he, he knows a great deal,
since the horses of many of the quality stand at his house.

In this agreeable society, Mr. Western passed that evening
and great part of the succeeding day, during which period
nothing happened of sufficient consequence to find a place in
this history. All this time Sophia passed by herself; for
her father swore she should never come out of her chamber
alive unless she first consented to marry Blifil, nor did he
ever suffer the door to be unlocked unless to convey her
food, on which occasions he always attended himself.

The second morning after his arrival, while he and the parson were at breakfast together on a toast and tankard, he was informed that a gentleman was below to wait on him.

"A gentleman!" quoth the squire. "Who the devil can he be? Do, doctor, go down and see who 'tis. Mr. Blifil can hardly be come to town yet. Go down, do, and know what his business is."

The doctor returned with an account that it was a very well-dressed man, and by the ribbon in his hat he took him for an officer of the army; that he said he had some particular business, which he could deliver to none but Mr. Western himself.

"An officer!" cried the squire. "What can any such fellow have to do with me? If he wants an order for baggage-waggons, I am no justice of peace here, nor can I grant a warrant. Let un come up, then, if he must speak to me."

A very genteel man now entered the room, who, having made his compliments to the squire and desired the favour of being alone with him, delivered himself as follows:

"Sir, I come to wait upon you by the command of my lord Fellamar, but with a very different message from what I suppose you expect after what passed the other night."

"My lord who?" cries the squire. "I never heard the name o' un."

"His lordship," said the gentleman, "is willing to impute everything to the effect of liquor, and the most trifling acknowledgement of that kind will set everything right; for as he hath the most violent attachment to your daughter, you, sir, are the last person upon earth from whom he would resent an affront, and happy is it for you both that he hath given such public demonstrations of his courage as to be able to put up an affair of this kind without danger of any imputation on his honour. All he desires, therefore, is that you will before me make some acknowledgement; the slightest in the world will be sufficient; and he intends this afternoon to pay his respects to you in order to obtain your leave of visiting the young lady on the footing of a lover."

"I don't understand much of what you say, sir," said the squire; "but I suppose by what you talk about my daughter that this is the lord which my cousin, Lady Bellaston, mentioned to me, and said something about his courting my daughter. If so be that how that be the case—you may give my service to his lordship and tell un the girl is disposed of already."

"Perhaps, sir," said the gentleman, "you are not sufficiently apprised of the greatness of this offer. I believe such a person, title, and fortune would be nowhere refused."

"Lookee, sir," answered the squire, "to be very plain, my daughter is bespoke already, but if she was not, I would not marry her to a lord upon any account; I hate all lords; they are a parcel of courtiers and Hanoverians, and I will have nothing to do with them."

"Well, sir," said the gentleman, "if that is your resolution, the message I am to deliver to you is that my lord desires the favour of your company this morning in Hyde Park."

"You may tell my lord," answered the squire, "that I am busy and cannot come. I have enough to look after at home and can't stir abroad on any account."

"I am sure, sir," quoth the other, "you are too much a gentleman to send such a message; you will not, I am convinced, have it said of you that after having affronted a noble peer, you refuse him satisfaction. His lordship would have been willing from his great regard to the young lady to have made up matters in another way, but unless he is to look on you as a father, his honour will not suffer his putting up such an indignity as you must be sensible you offered him."

"I offered him!" cries the squire. "It is a d—ned lie; I never offered him anything."

Upon these words the gentleman returned a very short verbal rebuke, and this he accompanied at the same time with some manual remonstrances, which no sooner reached the ears of Mr. Western than that worthy squire began to caper very briskly about the room, bellowing at the same time with all his might, as if desirous to summon a greater number of spectators to behold his agility.

The parson, who had left great part of the tankard unfinished, was not retired far; he immediately attended, therefore, on the squire's vociferation, crying, "Bless me, sir, what's the matter?" "Matter?" quoth the squire. "Here's a highwayman, I believe, who wants to rob and murder me— for he hath fallen upon me with that stick there in his hand, when I wish I may be d—ned if I gid un the least provocation."

"How, sir," said the captain; "did you not tell me I lied?"

"No, as I hope to be saved," answered the squire. "I

believe I might say, ' 'Twas a lie that I had offered any affront to my lord,' but I never said the word *you lie*. I understand myself better, and you might have understood yourself better than to fall upon a naked man. If I had had a stick in my hand, you would not have dared strike me. I'd have knocked thy lanthorn jaws about thy ears. Come down into yard this minute and I'll take a bout with thee at single-stick for a broken head, that I will, or I will go into naked room and box thee for a bellyful. At unt half a man, at unt, I'm sure."

The captain with some indignation replied, "I see, sir, you are below my notice, and I shall inform his lordship you are below his. I am sorry I have dirtied my fingers with you." At which words he withdrew, the parson interposing to prevent the squire from stopping him, in which he easily prevailed, as the other, though he made some efforts for the purpose, did not seem very violently bent on success. However, when the captain was departed, the squire sent many curses and some menaces after him, but as these did not set out from his lips till the officer was at the bottom of the stairs, and grew louder and louder as he was more and more remote, they did not reach his ears or at least did not retard his departure.

Poor Sophia, however, who in her prison heard all her father's outcries from first to last, began now first to thunder with her foot and afterwards to scream as loudly as the old gentleman himself had done before, though in a much sweeter voice. These screams soon silenced the squire and turned all his consideration towards his daughter, whom he loved so tenderly that the least apprehension of any harm happening to her threw him presently into agonies; for except in that single instance in which the whole future happiness of her life was concerned, she was sovereign mistress of his inclinations.

Having ended his rage against the captain with swearing he would take the law of him, the squire now mounted upstairs to Sophia, whom as soon as he had unlocked and opened the door he found all pale and breathless. The moment, however, that she saw her father, she collected all her spirits, and catching him hold by the hand, she cried passionately, "Oh, my dear sir, I am almost frightened to death; I hope to heaven no harm hath happened to you." "No, no," cries the squire, "no great harm. The rascal hath not hurt me much, but rat me if I don't ha' the laa o' un." "Pray, dear sir," says she, "tell me what's the matter; who is it that hath insulted you?" "I don't know the name o' un," answered Western; "some officer fellow, I suppose, that we are to pay for beating us, but I'll make him pay this bout if the rascal hath got anything, which I suppose he hath not. For thof he was dressed out so vine, I question whether he hath got a voot of land in the world." "But, dear sir," cries she, "what was the occasion of your quarrel?" "What should it be, Sophy," answered the squire, "but about you, Sophy? All my misfortunes are about you; you will be the death of your poor father at last. Here's a varlet of a lord, the Lord knows who, forsooth! who hath a-taan a liking to you, and because I would not gi un my consent, he sent me a kallenge. Come, do be a good girl, Sophy, and put an end to all your father's troubles; come, do, consent to ha' un; he will be in town within this day or two; do but promise me to marry un as soon as he comes and you will make me the happiest man in the world, and I will make you the happiest woman; you shall have the finest clothes in London and the finest jewels and a coach and six at your command. I promised Allworthy already to give up half my estate. Odrabbet it! I should hardly stick at giving up the whole." "Will my papa be so kind," says she, "as to hear me speak?" "Why wout ask, Sophy," cries he, "when dost know that I had rather hear thy voice than the music of the best pack of dogs in England? Hear thee, my dear little girl, I hope I shall hear thee as long as I live, for if I was ever to lose that pleasure, I would not gee a brass varden to live a moment longer. Indeed, Sophy, you do not know how I love you; indeed you don't, or you never could have run away and left your poor father, who hath no other joy, no other comfort upon earth, but his little Sophy." At these words the tears stood in his eyes, and Sophia (with the tears streaming from hers) answered, "Indeed, my dear papa, I know you have loved me tenderly, and heaven is my witness how sincerely I have returned your affection, nor could anything but an apprehension of being forced into the arms of this man have driven me to run from a father whom I love so passionately that I would with pleasure sacrifice my life to his happiness; nay, I have endeavoured to reason myself into doing more, and had almost worked up a resolution to endure the most miserable of all lives to comply with your inclination. It was that resolution alone to which I could not force my mind; nor can I ever." Here the squire began to look wild and the foam appeared at his lips, which Sophia observing begged to be heard out, and then proceeded: "If my father's life, his health, or any real happiness of his was at stake, here stands your resolved daughter; may heaven blast me if there is a misery I would not suffer to preserve you. No, that most detested, most loathsome of all lots would I embrace. I would give my hand to Blifil for your sake." "I tell thee it will preserve me," answers the father; "it will gee me health, happiness, life, everthing. Upon my soul I shall die if dost refuse me; I shall break my heart, I shall, upon my soul." "Is it possible," says she, "you can have such a desire to make me miserable?" "I tell thee noa," answered he loudly; "my whole desire is to make thee happy; me! D—n me if there is a thing upon earth I would not do to see thee happy!" "And will not my dear papa allow me to have the least knowledge of what will make me so? If it be true that happiness consists in opinion, what must be my condition when I shall think myself the most miserable of all the wretches upon earth?" "Better think yourself so," said he, "than know it by being married to a poor, bastardly vagabond." "If it will content you, sir," said Sophia, "I will give you the most solemn promise never to marry him nor any other one while my papa lives, without his consent. Let me dedicate my whole life to your service; let me be again your poor Sophy and my whole business and pleasure be, as it hath been, to please and divert you." "Lookee, Sophy," answered the squire, "I am not to be choused in this manner. Your aunt Western would then have reason to think me the fool she doth. No, no, Sophy; I'd have you to know I have a-got more wisdom and know more of the world than to take the word of a woman in a matter where a man is concerned." "How, sir, have I deserved this want of confidence?" said she. "Have I ever broke a single promise to you? Or have I ever been found guilty of a falsehood from my cradle?" "Lookee, Sophy," cries he, "that's neither here nor there. I am determined upon this match, and have him you shall, d—n me if shat unt. D—n me if shat unt, though dost hang thyself the next morning." At repeating which words he clinched his fist, knit his brows, bit his lips, and thundered so loud that the poor, afflicted, terrified Sophia sunk trembling into her chair, and had not a flood of tears come immediately to her relief, perhaps worse had followed.

Western beheld the deplorable condition of his daughter with no more contrition or remorse than the turnkey of

Newgate feels at viewing the agonies of a tender wife when taking her last farewell of her condemned husband; or rather, he looked down on her with the same emotions which arise in an honest, fair tradesman who sees his debtor dragged to prison for £10 which, though a just debt, the wretch is wickedly unable to pay. Or, to hit the case still more nearly, he felt the same compunction with a bawd when some poor innocent whom she hath ensnared into her hands falls into fits at the first proposal of what is called seeing company. Indeed, this resemblance would be exact was it not that the bawd hath an interest in what she doth and the father, though perhaps he may blindly think otherwise, can in reality have none in urging his daughter to almost an equal prostitution.

In this condition he left his poor Sophia, and, departing with a very vulgar observation on the effect of tears, he locked the room and returned to the parson, who said everything he durst in behalf of the young lady, which though perhaps it was not quite so much as his duty required, yet was it sufficient to throw the squire into a violent rage and into many indecent reflections on the whole body of the clergy, which we have too great an honour for that sacred function to commit to paper.

3

WHAT HAPPENED TO SOPHIA DURING HER CONFINEMENT

The landlady of the house where the squire lodged had begun very early to entertain a strange opinion of her guests. However, as she was informed that the squire was a man of a vast fortune and she had taken care to exact a very extraordinary price for her rooms, she did not think proper to give any offence; for though she was not without some concern for the confinement of poor Sophia, of whose great sweetness of temper and affability the maid of the house had made so favourable a report, which was confirmed by all the squire's servants, yet she had much more concern for her own interest than to provoke one whom, as she said, she perceived to be a very hastish kind of a gentleman.

Though Sophia eat but little, yet she was regularly served with her meals; indeed, I believe if she had liked any one rarity, that the squire, however angry, would have spared neither pains nor cost to have procured it for her, since however strange it may appear to some of my readers, he really doted on his daughter, and to give her any kind of pleasure was the highest satisfaction of his life.

The dinner hour being arrived, Black George carried her up a pullet, the squire himself (for he had sworn not to part with the key) attending the door. As George deposited the dish some compliments passed between him and Sophia (for he had not seen her since she left the country, and she treated every servant with more respect than some persons show to those who are in a very slight degree their inferiors); Sophia would have had him take the pullet back, saying she could not eat, but George begged her to try, and particularly recommended her to the eggs, of which he said it was full.

All this time the squire was waiting at the door, but George was a great favourite with his master, as his employment was in concerns of the highest nature: namely, about the game, and was accustomed to take many liberties. He had officiously carried up the dinner, being, as he said, very desirous to see his young lady; he made, therefore, no scruple of keeping his master standing above ten minutes while civilities were passing between him and Sophia, for which he received only a good-humoured rebuke at the door when he returned.

The eggs of pullets, partridges, pheasants, &c., were, as George well knew, the most favourite dainties of Sophia. It was, therefore, no wonder that he who was a very good-natured fellow should take care to supply her with this kind of delicacy at a time when all the servants in the house were afraid she would be starved, for she had scarce swallowed a single morsel in the last forty hours.

Though vexation hath not the same effect on all persons as it usually hath on a widow, whose appetite it often renders sharper than it can be rendered by the air on Bansted Downs or Salisbury Plain, yet the sublimest grief, notwithstanding what some people may say to the contrary, will eat at last. And Sophia herself after some little consideration began to dissect the fowl, which she found to be as full of eggs as George had reported it.

But if she was pleased with these, it contained something which would have delighted the Royal Society much more; for if a fowl with three legs be so invaluable a curiosity, when perhaps time hath produced a thousand such, at what price shall we esteem a bird which so totally contradicts all the laws of animal economy as to contain a letter in its belly? Ovid tells us of a flower into which Hyacinthus was metamorphosed that bears letters on its leaves, which Virgil recommended as a miracle to the Royal Society of his day, but no age nor nation hath ever recorded a bird with a letter in its maw.

But though a miracle of this kind might have engaged all the *Académies des Sciences* in Europe, and perhaps in a fruitless inquiry, yet the reader by barely recollecting the last dialogue which passed between Messieurs Jones and Partridge will be very easily satisfied from whence this letter came, and how it found its passage into the fowl.

Sophia, notwithstanding her long fast and notwithstanding her favourite dish was there before her, no sooner saw the letter than she immediately snatched it up, tore it open, and read as follows:

Madam,

Was I not sensible to whom I have the honour of writing, I should endeavour, however difficult, to paint the horrors of my mind at the account brought me by Mrs. Honour, but as tenderness alone can have any true idea of the pangs which tenderness is capable of feeling, so can this most amiable quality, which my Sophia possesses in the most eminent degree, sufficiently inform her what her Jones must have suffered on this melancholy occasion. Is there a circumstance in the world which can heighten my agonies when I hear of any misfortune which hath befallen you? Surely there is one only, and with that I am accursed. It is, my Sophia, the dreadful consideration that I am myself the wretched cause. Perhaps I here do myself too much honour, but none will envy me an honour which costs me so extremely dear. Pardon me this presumption, and pardon me the greater still if I ask you whether my advice, my assistance, my presence, my absence, my death, or my tortures can bring you any relief? Can the most perfect admiration, the most watchful observance, the most ardent love, the most melting tenderness, the most resigned submission to your will, make you amends for what you are to sacrifice to my happiness? If they can, fly, my lovely angel, to those arms which are ever open to receive and protect you, and to which, whether you bring yourself alone or the riches of the world with you, is in my opinion an alternative not worth regarding. If, on the contrary, wisdom shall predominate and, on the most mature reflection, inform you that the sacrifice is too great, and if there be no way left to reconcile you to your father and restore the peace of your dear mind but by abandoning me, I conjure you, drive me forever from your thoughts, exert your resolution, and let no compassion for my sufferings bear the least weight in that tender bosom. Believe me, madam, I so sincerely love you better than myself that my great and principal end is your happiness. My first wish (why would not Fortune indulge me in it?) was, and pardon me if I say still is, to see you every moment the happiest of women; my second wish is to hear you are so, but no misery on earth can equal mine while I think you owe an uneasy moment to him who is,

Madam,

In every sense, and to every purpose,

Your devoted

THOMAS JONES.

What Sophia said or did or thought upon this letter, how often she read it or whether more than once, shall all be left to our reader's imagination. The answer to it he may, perhaps, see hereafter, but not at present; for this reason among others: that she did not now write any, and that for several good causes, one of which was this: she had no paper, pen, nor ink.

In the evening, while Sophia was meditating on the letter she had received or on something else, a violent noise from below disturbed her meditations. This noise was no other than a round bout at altercation between two persons. One of the combatants, by his voice, she immediately distinguished to be her father, but she did not so soon discover the shriller pipes to belong to the organ of her aunt Western, who was just arrived in town, and having by means of one of her servants, who stopped at the Hercules Pillars, learnt where her brother lodged, she drove directly to his lodgings.

We shall therefore take our leave at present of Sophia and, with our usual good breeding, attend her ladyship.

4

The squire and the parson (for the landlord was now otherwise engaged) were smoking their pipes together when the arrival of the lady was first signified. The squire no sooner heard her name than he immediately ran down to usher her upstairs; for he was a great observer of such ceremonials, especially to his sister, of whom he stood more in awe than of any other human creature, though he never would own this nor did he perhaps know it himself.

Mrs. Western, on her arrival in the dining-room, having flung herself into a chair, began thus to harangue: "Well, surely no one ever had such an intolerable journey. I think the roads, since so many turnpike acts, are grown worse than ever. La, brother, how could you get into this odious place? No person of condition, I dare swear, ever set foot here before." "I don't know," cries the squire; "I think they do well enough; it was landlord recommended them. I thought as he knew most of the quality, he could best show me where to get among um." "Well, and where's my niece?" says the lady. "Have you been to wait upon Lady Bellaston yet?" "Ay, ay," cries the squire, "your niece is safe enough; she is upstairs in chamber." "How," answered the lady, "is my niece in this house and doth she not know of my being here?" "No, nobody can well get to her," says the squire, "for she is under lock and key. I have her safe; I vetched her from my lady cousin the first night I came to town and I have taken care o' her ever since; she is as secure as a fox in a bag, I promise you." "Good heaven!" returned Mrs. Western. "What do I hear! I thought what a fine piece of work would be the consequence of my consent to your coming to town yourself; nay, it was indeed your own headstrong will, nor can I charge myself with having ever consented to it. Did you not promise me, brother, that you would take none of these headstrong measures? Was it not by those headstrong measures that you forced my niece to run away from you in the country? Have you a mind to oblige her to take such another step?" "Z—ds and the Devil," cries the squire, dashing his pipe on the ground, "did ever mortal hear the like? When I expected you would have commended me for all I have done, to be fallen upon in this manner!" "How, brother!" said the lady. "Have I ever given you the least reason to imagine I should commend you for locking up your daugther? Have I not often told you that women in a free country are not to be treated with such arbitrary power? We are as free as the men, and I heartily wish I could not say we deserve that freedom better. If you expect I should stay a moment longer in this wretched house, or that I should ever own you again as my relation, or that I should ever trouble myself again with the affairs of your family, I insist upon it that my niece be set at liberty this instant." This she spoke with so commanding an air, standing with her back to the fire with one hand behind her and a pinch of snuff in the other, that I question whether Thalestris at the head of her Amazons ever made a more tremendous figure. It is no wonder, therefore, that the poor squire was not proof against the awe which she inspired. "There!" he cried, throwing down the key. "There it is; do whatever you please. I intended only to have kept her up till Blifil came to town, which can't be long, and now if any harm happens in the meantime, remember who is to be blamed for it."

"I will answer it with my life," cried Mrs. Western, "but I shall not intermeddle at all unless upon one condition, and that is, that you will commit the whole entirely to my care without taking any one measure yourself unless I shall eventually appoint you to act. If you ratify these preliminaries, brother, I yet will endeavour to preserve the honour of your family; if not, I shall continue in a neutral state."

"I pray you, good sir," said the parson, "permit yourself this once to be admonished by her ladyship; peradventure, by communing with young Madam Sophia, she will effect more than you have been able to perpetrate by more rigorous measures."

"What dost thee open upon me?" cries the squire. "If thee dost begin to babble, I shall whip thee in presently."

"Fie, brother," answered the lady, "is this language to a clergyman? Mr. Supple is a man of sense and gives you the best advice, and the whole world, I believe, will concur in his opinion; but I must tell you I expect an immediate answer to my categorical proposals. Either cede your daughter to my disposal or take her wholly to your own surprising discretion, and then I here, before Mr. Supple, evacuate the garrison and renounce you and your family forever."

"I pray you, let me be a mediator," cries the parson; "let me supplicate you."

"Why, there lies the key on the table," cries the squire. "She may take un up if she pleases; who hinders her?"

"No, brother," answered the lady, "I insist on the formality of its being delivered me with a full ratification of all the concessions stipulated."

"Why, then, I will deliver it to you. There 'tis," cries the squire. "I am sure, sister, you can't accuse me of ever denying to trust my daughter to you. She hath a-lived wi' you a whole year and muore to a time without my ever zeeing her."

"And it would have been happy for her," answered the lady, "if she had always lived with me. Nothing of this kind would have happened under my eye."

"Ay, certainly," cries he; "I only am to blame."

"Why, you are to blame, brother," answered she. "I have been often obliged to tell you so and shall always be obliged to tell you so. However, I hope you will now amend and gather so much experience from past errors as not to defeat my wisest machinations by your blunders. Indeed, brother, you are not qualified for these negotiations. All your whole scheme of politics is wrong. I once more, therefore, insist that you do not intermeddle. Remember only what is past."

"Z—ds and bl—d, sister," cries the squire, "what would you have me say? You are enough to provoke the Devil."

"There, now," said she, "just according to the old custom. I see, brother, there is no talking to you. I will appeal to Mr. Supple, who is a man of sense, if I said anything which could put any human creature into a passion, but you are so wrong-headed every way."

"Let me beg you, madam," said the parson, "not to irritate his worship."

"Irritate him?" said the lady. "Sure you are as great a fool as himself. Well, brother, since you have promised not to interfere, I will once more undertake the management of my niece. Lord have mercy upon all affairs which are under the directions of men. The head of one woman is worth a thousand of you." And now, having summoned a servant to show her to Sophia, she departed, bearing the key with her.

She was no sooner gone than the squire (having first shut

the door) ejaculated twenty "bitches" and as many hearty curses against her, not sparing himself for having ever thought of her estate; but added, "Now one hath been a slave so long, it would be pity to lose it at last for want of holding out a little longer. The bitch can't live forever, and I know I am down for it upon the will."

The parson greatly commended this resolution, and now the squire, having ordered in another bottle, which was his usual method when anything either pleased or vexed him, did by drinking plentifully of this medicinal julep so totally wash away his choler that his temper was become perfectly placid and serene when Mrs. Western returned with Sophia into the room. The young lady had on her hat and capuchin, and the aunt acquainted Mr. Western that she intended to take her niece with her to her own lodgings. "For indeed, brother," says she, "these rooms are not fit to receive a Christian soul in."

"Very well, madam," quoth Western, "whatever you please. The girl can never be in better hands than yours, and the parson here can do me the justice to say that I have said fifty times behind your back that you was one of the most sensible women in the world."

"To this," cries the parson, "I am ready to bear testimony."

"Nay, brother," says Mrs. Western, "I have always, I'm sure, given you as favourable a character. You must own you have a little too much hastiness in your temper, but when you will allow yourself time to reflect, I never knew a man more reasonable."

"Why, then, sister, if you think so," said the squire, "here's your good heath with all my heart. I am a little passionate sometimes, but I scorn to bear any malice. Sophy, do you be a good girl and do everything your aunt orders you."

"I have not the least doubt of her," answered Mrs. Western. "She hath had already an example before her eyes in the behaviour of that wretch her cousin Harriet, who ruined herself by neglecting my advice. Oh, brother, what think you? You was hardly gone out of hearing when you set out for London, when who should arrive but that impudent fellow with the odious Irish name—that Fitzpatrick. He broke in abruptly upon me without notice or I would not have seen him. He ran on a long, unintelligible story about his wife, to which he forced me to give him a hearing, but I made him very little answer and delivered him the letter from his wife, which I bid him answer himself. I suppose the wretch will endeavour to find us out, but I beg you will not see her, for I am determined I will not."

"I zee her?" answered the squire. "You need not fear me. I'll ge no encouragement to such undutiful wenches. It is well for the fellow, her husband, I was not at huome. Od rabbit it, he should have taken a dance through the horse-pond, I promise un. You zee, Sophy, what undutifulness brings volks to do. You have an example in your own family."

"Brother," cries the aunt, "you need not shock my niece by such odious repetitions. Why will you not leave everything entirely to me?" "Well, well; I wull, I wull," said the squire.

And now Mrs. Western, luckily for Sophia, put an end to the conversation by ordering chairs to be called. I say luckily; for had it continued much longer, fresh matter of dissension would most probably have arisen between the brother and sister, between whom education and sex made the only difference; for both were equally violent and equally positive; they had both a vast affection for Sophia and both a sovereign contempt for each other.

5

IN WHICH JONES RECEIVES A LETTER FROM SOPHIA, AND GOES TO A PLAY WITH MRS. MILLER AND PARTRIDGE

The arrival of Black George in town and the good offices which that grateful fellow had promised to do for his old benefactor greatly comforted Jones in the midst of all the anxiety and uneasiness which he had suffered on the account of Sophia; from whom by the means of the said George he received the following answer to his letter, which Sophia, to whom the use of pen, ink, and paper was restored with her liberty, wrote the very evening when she departed from her confinement:

Sir,

As I do not doubt your sincerity in what you write, you will be pleased to hear that some of my afflictions are at an end by the arrival of my aunt Western, with whom I am at present and with whom I enjoy all the liberty I can desire. One promise my aunt hath insisted on my making, which is that I will not see or converse with any person without her knowledge and consent. This promise I have most solemnly given and shall most inviolably keep, and though she hath not expressly forbidden me writing, yet that must be an omission from forgetfulness, or this, perhaps, is included in the word *conversing*. However, as I cannot but consider this as a breach of her generous confidence in my honour, you cannot expect that I shall after this continue to write myself or to receive letters without her knowledge. A promise is with me a very sacred thing and to be extended to everything understood from it, as well as to what is expressed by it, and this consideration may, perhaps, on reflection afford you some comfort. But why should I mention a comfort to you of this kind? For though there is one thing in which I can never comply with the best of fathers, yet am I firmly resolved never to act in defiance of him or to take any step of consequence without his consent. A firm persuasion of this must teach you to divert your thoughts from what Fortune hath (perhaps) made impossible. This your own interest persuades you. This may reconcile you, I hope, to Mr. Allworthy, and if it will, you have my injunctions to pursue it. Accidents have laid some obligations on me; your good intentions probably more. Fortune may, perhaps, be sometimes kinder to us both than at present. Believe this: that I shall always think of you as I think you deserve, and am,

Sir,

Your obliged, humble servant,

SOPHIA WESTERN.

I charge you write to me no more—at present at least; and accept this, which is now of no service to me, which I know you must want, and think you owe the trifle only to that fortune by which you found it.*

A child who hath just learnt his letters would have spelt this letter out in less time than Jones took in reading it. The sensations it occasioned were a mixture of joy and grief, somewhat like what divide the mind of a good man when he peruses the will of his deceased friend, in which a large

---

* Meaning, perhaps, the bank-bill for £100.

legacy, which his distresses make the more welcome, is bequeathed to him. Upon the whole, however, he was more pleased than displeased, and indeed the reader may probably wonder that he was displeased at all; but the reader is not quite so much in love as was poor Jones, and love is a disease which, though it may in some instances resemble a consumption (which it sometimes causes), in others proceeds in direct opposition to it, and particularly in this: that it never flatters itself or sees any one symptom in a favourable light.

One thing gave him complete satisfaction, which was that his mistress had regained her liberty and was now with a lady where she might at least assure herself of a decent treatment. Another comfortable circumstance was the reference which she made to her promise of never marrying any other man; for however disinterested he might imagine his passion, and notwithstanding all the generous overtures made in his letter, I very much question whether he could have heard a more afflicting piece of news than that Sophia was married to another, though the match had been never so great and never so likely to end in making her completely happy. That refined degree of Platonic affection which is absolutely detached from the flesh and is, indeed, entirely and purely spiritual is a gift confined to the female part of the creation, many of whom I have heard declare (and doubtless with great truth) that they would with the utmost readiness resign a lover to a rival when such resignation was proved to be necessary for the temporal interest of such lover. Hence, therefore, I conclude that this affection is in nature, though I cannot pretend to say I have ever seen an instance of it.

Mr. Jones having spent three hours in reading and kissing the aforesaid letter, and being at last in a state of good spirits from the last-mentioned considerations, he agreed to carry an appointment which he had before made into execution. This was to attend Mrs. Miller and her younger daughter into the gallery of the playhouse, and to admit Mr. Partridge as one of the company. For as Jones had really that taste for humour which many affect, he expected to enjoy much entertainment in the criticisms of Partridge, from whom he expected the simple dictates of nature, unimproved indeed, but likewise unadulterated, by art.

In the first row, then, of the first gallery did Mr. Jones, Mrs. Miller, her youngest daughter, and Partridge take their places. Partridge immediately declared it was the finest place he had ever been in. When the first music was played he said it was a wonder how so many fiddlers could play at one time without putting one another out. While the fellow was lighting the upper candles he cried out to Mrs. Miller, "Look, look, madam, the very picture of the man in the end of the Common-Prayer Book, before the Gunpowder-Treason service." Nor could he help observing with a sigh when all the candles were lighted that here were candles enough burnt in one night to keep an honest poor family for a whole twelvemonth.

As soon as the play, which was *Hamlet, Prince of Denmark*, began, Partridge was all attention, nor did he break silence till the entrance of the ghost; upon which he asked Jones what man that was in the strange dress, "something," said he, "like what I have seen in a picture. Sure it is not armour, is it?" Jones answered, "That is the ghost." To which Partridge replied with a smile, "Persuade me to that, sir, if you can. Though I can't say I ever actually saw a ghost in my life, yet I am certain I should know one if I saw him better than that comes to. No, no, sir, ghosts don't appear in such dresses as that, neither." In this mistake, which caused much laughter in the neighbourhood of Partridge, he was suffered to continue till the scene between the ghost and Hamlet, when Partridge gave that credit to Mr. Garrick which he had denied to Jones, and fell into so violent a trembling that his knees knocked against each other. Jones asked him what was the matter and whether he was afraid of the warrior upon the stage. "Oh la, sir," said he, "I perceive now it is what you told me. I am not afraid of anything, for I know it is but a play, and if it was really a ghost, it could do one no harm at such a distance and in so much company; and yet, if I was frightened, I am not the only person." "Why, who," cries Jones, "dost thou take to be such a coward here besides thyself?" "Nay, you may call me coward if you will, but if that little man there upon the stage is not frightened, I never saw any man frightened in my life. Ay, ay; go along with you! Ay, to be sure! Who's fool then? Will you? Lud have mercy upon such foolhardiness! Whatever happens, it is good enough for you. Follow you? I'd follow the Devil as soon. Nay, perhaps it is the Devil—for they say he can put on what likeness he pleases. Oh, here he is again! No farther! No, you have gone far enough already, farther than I'd have gone for all the King's dominions." Jones offered to speak but Partridge cried, "Hush, hush, dear sir, don't you hear him!" And during the whole speech of the ghost he sat with his eyes fixed partly on the ghost and partly on Hamlet, and with his mouth open, the same passions which succeeded each other in Hamlet succeeding likewise in him.

When the scene was over Jones said, "Why, Partridge, you exceed my expectations. You enjoy the play more than I conceived possible." "Nay, sir," answered Partridge, "if you are not afraid of the Devil, I can't help it; but to be sure, it is natural to be surprised at such things, though I know there is nothing in them. Not that it was the ghost that surprised me neither, for I should have known that to have been only a man in a strange dress, but when I saw the little man so frightened himself, it was that which took hold of me." "And dost thou imagine, then, Partridge," cries Jones, "that he was really frightened?" "Nay, sir," said Partridge, "did not you yourself observe afterwards, when he found out it was his own father's spirit and how he was murdered in the garden, how his fear forsook him by degrees and he was struck dumb with sorrow, as it were, just as I should have been had it been my own case. But hush! Oh la! What noise is that? There he is again. Well, to be certain, though I know there is nothing at all in it, I am glad I am not down yonder where those men are." Then, turning his eyes again upon Hamlet, "Ay, you may draw your sword; what signifies a sword against the power of the Devil?"

During the second act Partridge made very few remarks. He greatly admired the fineness of the dresses, nor could he help observing upon the King's countenance. "Well," said he, "how people may be deceived by faces? *Nulla fides fronti* is, I find, a true saying. Who would think by looking in the King's face that he had ever committed a murder?" He then inquired after the ghost, but Jones, who intended he should be surprised, gave him no other satisfaction than that he might possibly see him again soon, and in a flash of fire.

Partridge sat in fearful expectation of this, and now, when the ghost made his next appearance, Partridge cried out, "There, sir, now; what say you now? Is he frightened now or no? As much frightened as you think me, and to be sure, nobody can help some fears; I would not be in so bad a condition as what's-his-name, Squire Hamlet, is there for all the world. Bless me! What's become of the spirit? As I am a living soul, I thought I saw him sink into the earth." "Indeed, you saw right," answered Jones. "Well, well," cries Partridge, "I know it is only a play; and besides, if there was anything in all this, Madam Miller would not laugh so, for as to you, sir, you would not be afraid, I believe, if the Devil was here in person. There, there—ay, no wonder you are in such a passion; shake the vile, wicked wretch to pieces. If she was my own mother, I should serve her so. To be sure, all duty to a mother is forfeited by such wicked doings. Ay, go about your business; I hate the sight of you."

Our critic was now pretty silent till the play which Hamlet introduces before the King. This he did not at first understand till Jones explained it to him; but he no sooner entered into the spirit of it than he began to bless himself that he had never committed murder. Then, turning to Mrs. Miller, he asked her if she did not imagine the King looked as if he was touched; "though he is," said he, "a good actor and doth all he can to hide it. Well, I would not have so much to answer for as that wicked man there hath, to sit upon a much higher chair than he sits upon. No wonder he run away; for your sake I'll never trust an innocent face again."

The grave-digging scene next engaged the attention of Partridge, who expressed much surprise at the number of skulls thrown upon the stage. To which Jones answered that it was one of the most famous burial-places about town. "No wonder, then," cries Partridge, "that the place is haunted. But I never saw in my life a worse grave-digger. I had a sexton when I was clerk that should have dug three graves while he is digging one. The fellow handles a spade as if it was the first time he had ever had one in his hand. Ay, ay, you may sing. You had rather sing than work, I believe." Upon Hamlet's taking up the skull, he cried out, "Well, it is strange to see how fearless some men are; I never could bring myself to touch anything belonging to a dead man on any account. He seemed frightened enough, too, at the ghost, I thought. *Nemo omnibus horis sapit.*"

Little more worth remembering occurred during the play, at the end of which Jones asked him which of the players he had liked best. To this he answered with some appearance of indignation at the question, "The King, without doubt." "Indeed, Mr. Partridge," says Mrs. Miller, "you are not of the same opinion with the town, for they are all agreed that Hamlet is acted by the best player who was ever on the stage." "He the best player!" cries Partridge with a contemptuous sneer. "Why, I could act as well as he myself. I am sure if I had seen a ghost, I should have looked in the very same manner and done just as he did. And then, to be sure, in that scene, as you called it, between him and his mother, where you told me he acted so fine, why, Lord help me, any man, that is, any good man, that had had such a mother would have done exactly the same. I know you are only joking with me, but indeed, madam, though I was never at a play in London, yet I have seen acting before in the country; and the King for my money: he speaks all his words distinctly, half as loud again as the other. Anybody may see he is an actor."

While Mrs. Miller was thus engaged in conversation with Partridge a lady came up to Mr. Jones, whom he immediately knew to be Mrs. Fitzpatrick. She said she had seen him from the other part of the gallery and had taken that opportunity of speaking to him, as she had something to say which might be of great service to himself. She then acquainted him with her lodgings and made him an appointment the next day in the morning, which upon recollection she presently changed to the afternoon; at which time Jones promised to attend her.

Thus ended the adventure at the playhouse, where Partridge had afforded great mirth not only to Jones and Mrs. Miller but to all who sat within hearing, who were more attentive to what he said than to anything that passed on the stage.

He durst not go to bed all that night for fear of the ghost, and for many nights after, sweated two or three hours before he went to sleep, with the same apprehensions, and waked several times in great horrors, crying out, "Lord have mercy upon us! There it is!"

6

IN WHICH THE HISTORY IS OBLIGED TO LOOK BACK

It is almost impossible for the best parent to observe an exact impartiality to his children even though no superior merit should bias his affection, but sure a parent can hardly be blamed when that superiority determines his preference.

As I regard all the personages of this history in the light of my children, so I must confess the same inclination of partiality to Sophia, and for that I hope the reader will allow me the same excuse, from the superiority of her character.

This extraordinary tenderness which I have for my heroine never suffers me to quit her any long time without the utmost reluctance. I could now, therefore, return impatiently to inquire what hath happened to this lovely creature since her departure from her father's, but that I am obliged first to pay a short visit to Mr. Blifil.

Mr. Western, in the first confusion into which his mind was cast upon the sudden news he received of his daughter, and in the first hurry to go after her, had not once thought of sending any account of the discovery to Blifil. He had not gone far, however, before he recollected himself, and accordingly stopped at the very first inn he came to and dispatched away a messenger to acquaint Blifil with his having found Sophia, and with his firm resolution to marry her to him immediately if he would come up after him to town.

As the love which Blifil had for Sophia was of that violent kind which nothing but the loss of her fortune or some such accident could lessen, his inclination to the match was not at all altered by her having run away, though he was obliged to lay this to his own account. He very readily, therefore, embraced this offer. Indeed, he now proposed the gratification of a very strong passion besides avarice by marrying this young lady, and this was hatred; for he concluded that matrimony afforded an equal opportunity of satisfying either hatred or love, and this opinion is very probably verified by much experience. To say the truth, if we are to judge by the ordinary behaviour of married persons to each other, we shall perhaps be apt to conclude that the generality seek the indulgence of the former passion only in their union of everything but of hearts.

There was one difficulty, however, in his way, and this arose from Mr. Allworthy. That good man, when he found by the departure of Sophia (for neither that nor the cause of it could be concealed from him) the great aversion which she had for his nephew, began to be seriously concerned that he had been deceived into carrying matters so far. He by no means concurred with the opinions of those parents who think it as immaterial to consult the inclinations of their children in the affair of marriage as to solicit the good pleasure of their servants when they intend to take a journey, and who are, by law or decency at least, withheld often from using absolute force. On the contrary, as he esteemed the institution to be of the most sacred kind, he thought every preparatory caution necessary to preserve it holy and inviolate, and very wisely concluded that the surest way to effect this was by laying the foundation in previous affection.

Blifil, indeed, soon cured his uncle of all anger on the score of deceit by many vows and protestations that he had been deceived himself, with which the many declarations of Western very well tallied; but now to persuade Allworthy to consent to the renewing his addresses was a matter of such apparent difficulty that the very appearance was sufficient to have deterred a less enterprising genius, but this young gentleman so well knew his own talents that nothing within the province of cunning seemed to him hard to be achieved.

Here, then, he represented the violence of his own affection and the hopes of subduing aversion in the lady by perseverance. He begged that in an affair on which depended all his future repose he might at least be at liberty to try all fair means for success. Heaven forbid, he said, that he should ever think of prevailing by any other than the most gentle methods. "Besides, sir," said he, "if they fail, you may then (which will be surely time enough) deny your consent." He urged the great and eager desire which Mr. Western had for the match, and lastly, he made great use of the name of Jones, to whom he imputed all that had happened and from whom, he said, to preserve so valuable a young lady was even an act of charity.

All these arguments were well seconded by Thwackum, who dwelt a little stronger on the authority of parents than Mr. Blifil himself had done. He ascribed the measures which Mr. Blifil was desirous to take to Christian motives; "and though," says he, "the good young gentleman hath mentioned charity last, I am almost convinced it is his first and principal consideration."

Square, possibly, had he been present, would have sung to the same tune, though in a different key, and would have discovered much moral fitness in the proceeding, but he was now gone to Bath for the recovery of his health.

Allworthy, though not without reluctance, at last yielded to the desires of his nephew. He said he would accompany him to London, where he might be at liberty to use every honest endeavour to gain the lady. "But I declare," said he, "I will never give my consent to any absolute force being put on her inclinations, nor shall you ever have her unless she can be brought freely to compliance."

Thus did the affection of Allworthy for his nephew betray the superior understanding to be triumphed over by the inferior, and thus is the prudence of the best of heads often defeated by the tenderness of the best of hearts.

Blifil, having obtained this uphoped-for acquiescence in his uncle, rested not till he carried his purpose into execution. And as no immediate business required Mr. Allworthy's presence in the country, and little preparation is necessary to men for a journey, they set out the very next day and arrived in town that evening, when Mr. Jones, as we have seen, was diverting himself with Partridge at the play.

The morning after his arrival Mr. Blifil waited on Mr. Western, by whom he was most kindly and graciously received and from whom he had every possible assurance (perhaps more than was possible) that he should very shortly be as happy as Sophia could make him; nor would the squire suffer the young gentleman to return to his uncle till he had, almost against his will, carried him to his sister.

7

IN WHICH MR. WESTERN PAYS A VISIT TO HIS SISTER, IN COMPANY WITH MR. BLIFIL

Mrs. Western was reading a lecture on prudence and matrimonial politics to her niece when her brother and Blifil broke in with less ceremony than the laws of visiting require. Sophia no sooner saw Blifil than she turned pale and almost lost the use of all her faculties, but her aunt, on the contrary, waxed red and, having all her faculties at command, began to exert her tongue on the squire.

"Brother," said she, "I am astonished at your behaviour. Will you never learn any regard to decorum? Will you still look upon every apartment as your own, or as belonging to one of your country tenants? Do you think yourself at liberty to invade the privacies of women of condition without the least decency or notice?" "Why, what a pox is the matter now?" quoth the squire. "One would think I had caught you at—" "None of your brutality, sir, I beseech you," answered she. "You have surprised my poor niece so, that she can hardly, I see, support herself. Go, my dear, retire, and endeavour to recruit your spirits, for I see you have occasion." At which words Sophia, who never received a more welcome command, hastily withdrew.

"To be sure, sister," cries the squire, "you are mad, when I have brought Mr. Blifil here to court her, to force her away."

"Sure, brother," says she, "you are worse than mad, when you know in what situation affairs are, to— I am sure, I ask Mr. Blifil pardon, but he knows very well to whom to impute so disagreeable a reception. For my own part, I am sure, I shall always be very glad to see Mr. Blifil, but his own good sense would not have suffered him to proceed so abruptly had you not compelled him to it."

Blifil bowed and stammered and looked like a fool, but Western, without giving him time to form a speech for the purpose, answered, "Well, well, I am to blame if you will; I always am, certainly; but come, let the girl be fetched back again or let Mr. Blifil go to her. He's come up on purpose, and there is no time to be lost."

"Brother," cries Mrs. Western, "Mr. Blifil, I am confident, understands himself better than to think of seeing my niece any more this morning, after what hath happened. Women are of a nice contexture, and our spirits when disordered are not to be recomposed in a moment. Had you suffered Mr. Blifil to have sent his compliments to my niece and to have desired the favour of waiting on her in the afternoon, I should possibly have prevailed on her to have seen him, but now I despair of bringing about any such matter."

"I am very sorry, madam," cried Blifil, "that Mr. Western's extraordinary kindness to me, which I can never enough acknowledge, should have occasioned——" "Indeed, sir," said she, interrupting him, "you need make no apologies; we all know my brother so well."

"I don't care what anybody knows of me," answered the squire. "But when must he come to see her? For consider, I tell you, he is come up on purpose, and so is Allworthy." "Brother," said she, "whatever message Mr. Blifil thinks proper to send to my niece shall be delivered to her, and I suppose she will want no instructions to make a proper answer. I am convinced she will not refuse to see Mr. Blifil at a proper time." "The devil she won't!" answered the squire. "Odsbud! Don't we know— I say nothing, but some volk are wiser than all the world. If I might have had my will, she had not run away before, and now I expect to hear every moment she is guone again. For as great a fool as some volk think me, I know very well she hates—" "No matter, brother," replied Mrs. Western; "I will not hear my niece abused. It is a reflection on my family. She is an honour to it and she will be an honour to it, I promise you. I will pawn my whole reputation in the world on her conduct. I shall be glad to see you, brother, in the afternoon, for I have somewhat of importance to mention to you. At present, Mr. Blifil as well as you must excuse me, for I am in haste to dress." "Well, but," said the squire, "do appoint a time." "Indeed," said she, "I can appoint no time. I tell you I will see you in the afternoon." "What the devil would you have me do?" cries the squire, turning to Blifil. "I can no more turn her than a beagle can turn an old hare. Perhaps she will be in a better humour in the afternoon." "I am condemned, I see, sir, to misfortune," answered Blifil, "but I shall always own my obligations to you." He then took a ceremonious leave of Mrs. Western, who was altogether as ceremonious on her part, and then they departed, the squire muttering to himself with an oath that Blifil should see his daughter in the afternoon.

If Mr. Western was little pleased with this interview, Blifil was less. As to the former, he imputed the whole behaviour of his sister to her humour only and to her dissatisfaction at the omission of ceremony in the visit, but Blifil saw a little deeper into things. He suspected somewhat of more consequence from two or three words which dropped from the lady, and to say the truth, he suspected right, as will appear when I have unfolded the several matters which will be contained in the following chapter.

8

SCHEMES OF LADY BELLASTON FOR THE RUIN OF JONES

Love had taken too deep a root in the mind of Lord Fellamar to be plucked up by the rude hands of Mr. Western. In the heat of resentment he had indeed given a commission to Captain Egglane, which the captain had far exceeded in the execution; nor had it been executed at all had his lordship been able to find the captain after he had seen Lady Bellaston, which was in the afternoon of the day after he had received the affront, but so industrious was the captain in the discharge of his duty that having after long inquiry found out the squire's lodgings very late in the evening, he sat up all night at a tavern that he might not miss the squire in the morning, and by that means missed the revocation which my lord had sent to his lodgings.

In the afternoon, then, next after the intended rape of Sophia, his lordship, as we have said, made a visit to Lady Bellaston, who laid open so much of the character of the squire that his lordship plainly saw the absurdity he had been guilty of in taking any offence at his words, especially as he had those honourable designs on his daughter. He then unbosomed the violence of his passion to Lady Bellaston, who readily undertook the cause and encouraged him with certain assurance of a most favourable reception from all the elders of the family, and from the father himself when he should be sober and should be made acquainted with the nature of the offer made to his daughter. The only danger, she said, lay in the fellow she had formerly mentioned, who though a beggar and a vagabond had by some means or other, she knew not what, procured himself tolerable clothes, and passed for a gentleman. "Now," says she, "as I have for the sake of my cousin made it my business to inquire after this fellow, I have luckily found out his lodgings"; with which she then acquainted his lordship. "I am thinking, my lord," added she, "for this fellow is too mean for your personal resentment, whether it would not be possible for your lordship to contrive some method of having him pressed and sent on board a ship. Neither law nor conscience forbid this project; for the fellow, I promise you, however well dressed, is but a vagabond, and as proper as any fellow in the streets to be pressed into the service, and as for the conscientious part, surely the preservation of a young lady from such ruin is a most meritorious act; nay, with regard to the fellow himself, unless he could succeed (which heaven forbid) with my cousin, it may probably be the means of preserving him from the gallows and, perhaps, may make his fortune in an honest way."

Lord Fellamar very heartily thanked her ladyship for the part which she was pleased to take in the affair, upon the success of which his whole future happiness entirely depended. He said he saw at present no objection to the pressing scheme and would consider of putting it in execution. He then most earnestly recommended to her ladyship to do him the honour of immediately mentioning his proposals to the family, to whom, he said, he offered a *carte blanche,* and would settle his fortune in almost any manner they should require. And after uttering many ecstasies and raptures concerning Sophia, he took his leave and departed, but not before he had received the strongest charge to beware of Jones and to lose no time in securing his person where he should no longer be in a capacity of making any attempts to the ruin of the young lady.

The moment Mrs. Western was arrived at her lodgings, a card was dispatched with her compliments to Lady Bellaston, who no sooner received it than with the impatience of a lover she flew to her cousin, rejoiced at this fair opportunity which beyond her hopes offered itself; for she was much better pleased with the prospect of making the proposals to a woman of sense, and who knew the world, than to a gentleman whom she honoured with the appellation of Hottentot, though indeed from him she apprehended no danger of a refusal.

The two ladies being met, after very short previous ceremonials fell to business, which was, indeed, almost as soon concluded as begun; for Mrs. Western no sooner heard the name of Lord Fellamar than her cheeks glowed with pleasure, but when she was acquainted with the eagerness of his passion, the earnestness of his proposals, and the generosity of his offer, she declared her full satisfaction in the most explicit terms.

In the progress of their conversation, their discourse turned to Jones, and both cousins very pathetically lamented the unfortunate attachment which both agreed Sophia had to that young fellow, and Mrs. Western entirely attributed it to the folly of her brother's management. She concluded, however, at last with declaring her confidence in the good understanding of her niece, who though she would not give up her affection in favour of Blifil will, "I doubt not," says she, "soon be prevailed upon to sacrifice a simple inclination to the addresses of a fine gentleman, who brings her both a title and a large estate; for indeed," added she, "I must do Sophy the justice to confess, this Blifil is but a hideous kind of fellow, as you know, Bellaston, all country-gentlemen are, and hath nothing but his fortune to recommend him."

"Nay," said Lady Bellaston, "I don't, then, so much wonder at my cousin, for I promise you this Jones is a very agreeable fellow, and hath one virtue which the men say is a great recommendation to us. What do you think, Di—I shall certainly make you laugh; nay, I can hardly tell you myself for laughing—will you believe that the fellow hath had the assurance to make love to me? But if you should be inclined to disbelieve it, here is evidence enough: his own handwriting, I assure you." She then delivered her cousin the letter with the proposals of marriage, which, if the reader hath a desire to see, he will find already on record in the fifteenth book of this history.

"Upon my word, I am astonished," said Mrs. Western; "this is indeed a masterpiece of assurance. With your leave, I may possibly make some use of this letter." "You have my full liberty," cries Lady Bellaston, "to apply it to what purpose you please. However, I would not have it shown to any but Miss Western, nor to her unless you find occasion." "Well, and how did you use the fellow?" returned Mrs. Western. "Not as a husband," said the lady. "I am not married, I promise you, my dear. You know, Di, I have tried the comforts once already, and once I think is enough for any reasonable woman."

This letter Lady Bellaston thought would certainly turn the balance against Jones in the mind of Sophia, and she was emboldened to give it up, partly by her hopes of having him instantly dispatched out of the way and partly by having secured the evidence of Honour, who, upon sounding her, she saw sufficient reason to imagine was prepared to testify whatever she pleased.

But perhaps the reader may wonder why Lady Bellaston, who in her heart hated Sophia, should be so desirous of promoting a match which was so much to the interest of the young lady. Now, I would desire such readers to look carefully into human nature, page almost the last, and there he will find in scarce-legible characters that women, notwithstanding the preposterous behaviour of mothers, aunts, &c., in matrimonial matters, do in reality think it so great a misfortune to have their inclinations in love thwarted that they imagine they ought never to carry enmity higher than upon these disappointments; again, he will find it written, much about the same place, that a woman who hath once been pleased with the possession of a man will go above half-way to the Devil to prevent any other woman from enjoying the same.

If he will not be contented with these reasons, I freely confess I see no other motive to the actions of that lady unless we will conceive she was bribed by Lord Fellamar, which for my own part I see no cause to suspect.

Now, this was the affair which Mrs. Western was preparing to introduce to Sophia by some prefatory discourse on the folly of love, and on the wisdom of legal prostitution for hire, when her brother and Blifil broke abruptly in upon her, and hence arose all that coldness in her behaviour to Blifil, which though the squire, as was usual with him, imputed to a wrong cause, infused into Blifil himself (he being a much more cunning man) a suspicion of the real truth.

9

IN WHICH JONES PAYS A VISIT TO MRS. FITZPATRICK

The reader may now perhaps be pleased to return with us to Mr. Jones, who at the appointed hour attended on Mrs. Fitzpatrick; but before we relate the conversation which now passed, it may be proper, according to our method, to return a little back and to account for so great an alteration of behaviour in this lady, that from changing her lodging principally to avoid Mr. Jones, she had now industriously, as hath been seen, sought this interview.

And here we shall need only to resort to what happened the preceding day, when, hearing from Lady Bellaston that Mr. Western was arrived in town, she went to pay her duty to him at his lodgings at Piccadilly, when she was received with many scurvy compellations too coarse to be repeated and was even threatened to be kicked out of doors. From hence an old servant of her aunt Western, with whom she was well acquainted, conducted her to the lodgings of that lady, who treated her not more kindly but more politely, or to say the truth, with rudeness in another way. In short, she returned from both plainly convinced not only that her scheme of reconciliation had proved abortive but that she must forever give over all thoughts of bringing it about by any means whatever. From this moment, desire of revenge only filled her mind, and in this temper meeting Jones at the play, an opportunity seemed to her to occur of effecting this purpose.

The reader must remember that he was acquainted by Mrs. Fitzpatrick, in the account she gave of her own story, with the fondness Mrs. Western had formerly shown for Mr. Fitzpatrick at Bath, from the disappointment of which Mrs. Fitzpatrick derived the great bitterness her aunt had expressed toward her. She had, therefore, no doubt but that the good lady would as easily listen to the addresses of Mr. Jones as she had done to the other, for the superiority of charms was clearly on the side of Mr. Jones, and the advance which her aunt had since made in age, she concluded (how justly I will not say), was an argument rather in favour of her project than against it.

Therefore, when Jones attended after a previous declaration of her desire of serving him, arising, as she said, from a firm assurance how much she should by so doing oblige Sophia, and after some excuses for her former disappointment, and after acquainting Mr. Jones in whose custody his mistress was, of which she thought him ignorant, she very explicitly mentioned her scheme to him and advised him to make sham addresses to the older lady in order to procure an easy access to the younger, informing him at the same time of the success which Mr. Fitzpatrick had formerly owed to the very same stratagem.

Mr. Jones expressed great gratitude to the lady for the kind intentions towards him which she had expressed, and indeed testified, by this proposal, but besides intimating some diffidence of success from the lady's knowledge of his love to her niece, which had not been her case in regard to Mr. Fitzpatrick, he said he was afraid Miss Western would never agree to an imposition of this kind, as well from her utter detestation of all fallacy as from her avowed duty to her aunt.

Mrs. Fitzpatrick was a little nettled at this; and indeed if it may not be called a lapse of the tongue, it was a small deviation from politeness in Jones, and into which he would scarce have fallen had not the delight he felt in praising Sophia hurried him out of all reflection, for this commendation of one cousin was more than a tacit rebuke on the other.

"Indeed, sir," answered the lady, with some warmth, "I cannot think there is anything easier than to cheat an old woman with a profession of love when her complexion is amorous, and though she is my aunt, I must say there never was a more lecherous one than her ladyship. Can't you pretend that the despair of possessing her niece, from her being promised to Blifil, has made you turn your thoughts towards her? As to my cousin Sophia, I can't imagine her to be such a simpleton as to have the least scruple on such an account or to conceive any harm in punishing one of these hags for the many mischiefs they bring upon families by their tragi-comic passions, for which I think it is pity they were not punishable by law. I had no such scruple myself, and yet I hope my cousin Sophia will not think it an affront when I say she cannot detest every real species of falsehood more than her cousin Fitzpatrick. To my aunt indeed I pretend no duty, nor doth she deserve any. However, sir, I have given you my advice, and if you decline pursuing it, I shall have the less opinion of your understanding, that's all."

Jones now clearly saw the error he had committed and exerted his utmost power to rectify it, but he only faltered and fluttered into nonsense and contradiction. To say the truth, it is often safer to abide by the consequences of the first blunder than to endeavour to rectify it; for by such endeavours we generally plunge deeper instead of extricating ourselves, and few persons will on such occasions have the good nature which Mrs. Fitzpatrick displayed to Jones by saying with a smile, "You need attempt no more excuses, for I can easily forgive a real lover, whatever is the effect of fondness for his mistress."

She then renewed her proposal and very fervently recommended it, omitting no argument which her invention could suggest on the subject; for she was so violently incensed against her aunt that scarce anything was capable of affording her equal pleasure with exposing her, and, like a true woman, she would see no difficulties in the execution of a favourite scheme.

Jones, however, persisted in declining the undertaking, which had not indeed the least probability of success. He easily perceived the motives which induced Mrs. Fitzpatrick to be so eager in pressing her advice. He said he would not deny the tender and passionate regard he had for Sophia, but was so conscious of the inequality of their situations that he could never flatter himself so far as to hope that so divine a young lady would condescend to think on one so unworthy; nay, he protested he could scarce bring himself to wish she should. He concluded with a profession of generous sentiments, which we have not at present leisure to insert.

There are some fine women (for I dare not here speak in too general terms) with whom self is so predominant that they never detach it from any subject, and as vanity is with them a ruling principle, they are apt to lay hold of whatever praise they meet with and, though the property of others, convey it to their own use. In the company of these ladies it is impossible to say anything handsome of another woman which they will not apply to themselves; nay, they often improve the praise they seize: as, for instance, if her beauty, her wit, her gentility, her good humour, deserve so much commendation, what do I deserve who possess those qualities in so much more eminent a degree?

To these ladies a man often recommends himself while he is commending another woman, and while he is expressing ardour and generous sentiments for his mistress, they are considering what a charming lover this man would make to them, who can feel all this tenderness for an inferior degree of merit. Of this, strange as it may seem, I have seen many instances besides Mrs. Fitzpatrick, to whom all this really happened, and who now began to feel a somewhat for Mr. Jones, the symptoms of which she much sooner understood than poor Sophia had formerly done.

To say the truth, perfect beauty in both sexes is a more irresistible object than it is generally thought, for notwithstanding some of us are contented with more homely lots, and learn by rote (as children to repeat what gives them no idea) to despise outside and to value more solid charms, yet I have always observed at the approach of consummate beauty that these more solid charms only shine with that kind of lustre which the stars have after the rising of the sun.

When Jones had finished his exclamations, many of which would have become the mouth of Oroöndates himself, Mrs. Fitzpatrick heaved a deep sigh, and taking her eyes off from Jones, on whom they had been some time fixed, and dropping them on the ground, she cried, "Indeed, Mr. Jones, I pity you, but it is the curse of such tenderness to be thrown away on those who are insensible of it. I know my cousin better than you, Mr. Jones, and I must say any woman who makes no return to such a passion and such a person is unworthy of both."

"Sure, madam," said Jones, "you can't mean——"
"Mean?" cries Mrs. Fitzpatrick. "I know not what I mean. There is something, I think, in true tenderness bewitching; few women ever meet with it in men, and fewer still know how to value it when they do. I never heard such truly

noble sentiments, and I can't tell how it is but you force one to believe you. Sure she must be the most contemptible of women who can overlook such merit."

The manner and look with which all this was spoke infused a suspicion into Jones, which we don't care to convey in direct words to the reader. Instead of making any answer, he said, "I am afraid, madam, I have made too tiresome a visit," and offered to take his leave.

"Not at all, sir," answered Mrs. Fitzpatrick. "Indeed I pity you, Mr. Jones; indeed I do; but if you are going, consider of the scheme I have mentioned. I am convinced you will approve it, and let me see you again as soon as you can. To-morrow morning if you will, or at least some time to-morrow. I shall be at home all day."

Jones then, after many expressions of thanks, very respectfully retired, nor could Mrs. Fitzpatrick forbear making him a present of a look at parting, by which if he had understood nothing, he must have had no understanding in the language of the eyes. In reality it confirmed his resolution of returning to her no more, for faulty as he hath hitherto appeared in this history, his whole thoughts were now so confined to his Sophia that I believe no woman upon earth could have now drawn him into an act of inconstancy.

Fortune, however, who was not his friend, resolved, as he intended to give her no second opportunity, to make the best of this, and accordingly produced the tragical incident which we are now in sorrowful notes to record.

10

THE CONSEQUENCE OF THE PRECEDING VISIT

Mr. Fitzpatrick, having received the letter before mentioned from Mrs. Western, and being by that means acquainted with the place to which his wife was retired, returned directly to Bath and thence the day afterwards set forward to London.

The reader hath been already often informed of the jealous temper of this gentleman. He may likewise be pleased to remember the suspicion which he had at Upton conceived of Jones upon his finding him in the room with Mrs. Waters, and though sufficient reasons had afterwards appeared entirely to clear that suspicion, yet now reading so handsome a character of Mr. Jones from his wife caused him to reflect that she likewise was in the inn at the same time, and jumbled together such a confusion of circumstances in a head which was naturally none of the clearest that the whole produced that green-eyed monster mentioned by Shakespeare in his tragedy of *Othello*.

And now, as he was inquiring in the street after his wife, and had just received directions to the door, unfortunately Mr. Jones was issuing from it.

Fitzpatrick did not yet recollect the face of Jones; however, seeing a young, well-dressed fellow coming from his wife, he made directly up to him and asked him what he had been doing in that house. "For I am sure," said he, "you must have been in it, as I saw you come out of it."

Jones answered very modestly that he had been visiting a lady there. To which Fitzpatrick replied, "What business have you with the lady?" Upon which Jones, who now perfectly remembered the voice, features, and indeed coat, of the gentleman, cried out, "Ha, my good friend! Give me your hand; I hope there is no ill blood remaining between us upon a small mistake which happened so long ago."

"Upon my soul, sir," said Fitzpatrick, "I don't know your name, nor your face." "Indeed, sir," said Jones, "neither have I the pleasure of knowing your name, but your face I very well remember to have seen before at Upton, where a foolish quarrel happened between us, which, if it is not made up yet, we will now make up over a bottle."

"At Upton!" cried the other. "Ha! Upon my soul, I believe your name is Jones." "Indeed," answered he, "it is." "Oh, upon my soul," cries Fitzpatrick, "you are the very man I wanted to meet. Upon my soul, I will drink a bottle with you presently, but first I will give you a great knock over the pate. There is for you, you rascal. Upon my soul, if you do not give me satisfaction for that blow, I will give you another." And then, drawing his sword, puts himself in a posture of defence, which was the only science he understood.

Jones was a little staggered by the blow, which came somewhat unexpectedly, but presently recovering himself, he also drew, and though he understood nothing of fencing, pressed on so boldly upon Fitzpatrick that he beat down his guard and sheathed one-half of his sword in the body of the said gentleman, who had no sooner received it than he stepped backwards, dropped the point of his sword, and, leaning upon it, cried, "I have satisfaction enough; I am a dead man."

"I hope not," cries Jones, "but whatever be the consequence, you must be sensible you have drawn it upon yourself." At this instant a number of fellows rushed in and seized Jones, who told them he should make no resistance and begged some of them at least would take care of the wounded gentleman.

"Ay," cries one of the fellows, "the wounded gentleman will be taken care enough of, for I suppose he hath not many hours to live. As for you, sir, you have a month at least good yet." "D—n me, Jack," said another, "he hath prevented his voyage; he's bound to another port now"; and many other such jests was our poor Jones made the subject of by these fellows, who were indeed the gang employed by Lord Fellamar and had dogged him into the house of Mrs. Fitzpatrick, waiting for him at the corner of the street when this unfortunate accident happened.

The officer who commanded this gang very wisely concluded that his business was now to deliver his prisoner into the hands of the civil magistrate. He ordered him, therefore, to be carried to a public-house, where, having sent for a constable, he delivered him to his custody.

The constable, seeing Mr. Jones very well dressed and hearing that the accident had happened in a duel, treated his prisoner with great civility, and at his request dispatched a messenger to inquire after the wounded gentleman, who was now at a tavern under the surgeon's hands. The report brought back was that the wound was certainly mortal and there were no hopes of life. Upon which the constable informed Jones that he must go before a justice. He answered, "Wherever you please; I am indifferent as to what happens to me, for though I am convinced I am not guilty of murder in the eye of the law, yet the weight of blood I find intolerable upon my mind."

Jones was now conducted before the justice, where the surgeon who dressed Mr. Fitzpatrick appeared and deposed that he believed the wound to be mortal, upon which the prisoner was committed to the Gatehouse. It was very late at night, so that Jones would not send for Partridge till the next morning, and as he never shut his eyes till seven, so it was near twelve before the poor fellow, who was greatly frightened at not hearing from his master so long, received a message which almost deprived him of his being when he heard it.

He went to the Gatehouse with trembling knees and a beating heart, and was no sooner arrived in the presence of Jones than he lamented the misfortune that had befallen him with many tears, looking all the while frequently about him in great terror, for as the news now arrived that Mr. Fitzpatrick was dead, the poor fellow apprehended every minute that his ghost would enter the room. At last he delivered him a letter, which he had like to have forgot, and which came from Sophia by the hands of Black George.

Jones presently dispatched every one out of the room and, having eagerly broke open the letter, read as follows:

You owe the hearing from me again to an accident which I own surprises me. My aunt hath just now shown me a letter from you to Lady Bellaston, which contains a proposal of marriage. I am convinced it is your own hand; and what more surprises me is that it is dated at the very time when you would have me imagine you was under such concern on my account. I leave you to comment on this fact. All I desire is that your name may never more be mentioned to

S.W.

Of the present situation of Mr. Jones's mind, and of the pangs with which he was now tormented, we cannot give the reader a better idea than by saying his misery was such that even Thwackum would almost have pitied him. But bad as it is, we shall at present leave him in it, as his good genius (if he really had any) seems to have done. And here we put an end to the sixteenth book of our history.

BOOK XVII

CONTAINING THREE DAYS

1

· CONTAINING A PORTION OF INTRODUCTORY WRITING

When a comic writer hath made his principal characters as
happy as he can or when a tragic writer hath brought them
to the highest pitch of human misery, they both conclude
their business to be done and that their work is come to a
period.

Had we been of the tragic complexion, the reader must
allow we were now very nearly arrived at this period, since
it would be difficult for the Devil or any of his representa-
tives on earth to have contrived much greater torments for
poor Jones than those in which we left him in the last
chapter; and as for Sophia, a good-natured woman would
hardly wish more uneasiness to a rival than what she must
at present be supposed to feel. What, then, remains to complete the tragedy but a murder or two and a few moral
sentences?

But to bring our favourites out of their present anguish
and distress, and to land them at last on the shore of happiness, seems a much harder task, a task indeed so hard that
we do not undertake to execute it. In regard to Sophia, it is
more than probable that we shall somewhere or other provide a good husband for her in the end, either Blifil, or my
lord, or somebody else, but as to poor Jones, such are the
calamities in which he is at present involved, owing to his
imprudence, by which if a man doth not become a felon to
the world he is at least a *felo de se*, so destitute is he now
of friends and so persecuted by enemies that we almost

despair of bringing him to any good, and if our reader delights in seeing executions, I think he ought not to lose any time in taking a first row at Tyburn.

This I faithfully promise: that notwithstanding any affection which we may be supposed to have for this rogue, whom we have unfortunately made our hero, we will lend him none of that supernatural assistance with which we are entrusted upon condition that we use it only on very important occasions. If he doth not, therefore, find some natural means of fairly extricating himself from all his distresses, we will do no violence to the truth and dignity of history for his sake; for we had rather relate that he was hanged at Tyburn (which may very probably be the case) than forfeit our integrity or shock the faith of our reader.

In this the ancients had a great advantage over the moderns. Their mythology, which was at that time more firmly believed by the vulgar than any religion is at present, gave them always an opportunity of delivering a favourite hero. Their deities were always ready at the writer's elbow to execute any of his purposes, and the more extraordinary the intervention was, the greater was the surprise and delight of the credulous reader. Those writers could with greater ease have conveyed a hero from one country to another, nay from one world to another, and have brought him back again than a poor circumscribed modern can deliver him from a gaol.

The Arabians and Persians had an equal advantage in writing their tales, from the genii and fairies, which they believe in as an article of their faith, upon the authority of the Koran itself. But we have none of these helps. To natural means alone are we confined; let us try, therefore, what by these means may be done for poor Jones, though to confess the truth, something whispers me in the ear that he doth not yet know the worst of his fortune, and that a more shocking piece of news than any he hath yet heard remains for him in the unopened leaves of fate.

2

THE GENEROUS AND GRATEFUL BEHAVIOUR OF MRS. MILLER

Mr. Allworthy and Mrs. Miller were just sat down to breakfast when Blifil, who had gone out very early that morning, returned to make one of the company.

He had not been long seated before he began as follows, "Good lord! My dear uncle, what do you think hath happened? I vow I am afraid of telling it you for fear of shocking you with the remembrance of ever having shown any kindness to such a villain." "What is the matter, child?" said the uncle. "I fear I have shown kindness in my life to the unworthy more than once. But charity doth not adopt the vices of its objects." "Oh, sir," returned Blifil, "it is not without the secret direction of Providence that you mention the word *adoption*. Your adopted son, sir, that Jones, that wretch whom you nourished in your bosom, hath proved one of the greatest villains upon earth." "By all that's sacred, 'tis false," cries Mrs. Miller. "Mr. Jones is no villain. He is one of the worthiest creatures breathing, and if any other person had called him villain, I would have thrown all this boiling water in his face." Mr. Allworthy looked very much amazed at this behaviour. But she did not give him leave to speak before, turning to him, she cried, "I hope you will not be angry with me; I would not offend you, sir, for the world, but indeed I could not bear to hear him called so." "I must own, madam," said Allworthy very gravely, "I am a little surprised to hear you so warmly defend a fellow you do not know." "Oh, I do know him, Mr. Allworthy," said she, "indeed I do; I should be the most ungrateful of all wretches if I denied it. Oh, he hath preserved me and my little family, and we have all reason to bless him while we live. And I pray heaven to bless him and turn the hearts of his malicious enemies. I know, I find, I see, he hath such." "You surprise me, madam, still more," said Allworthy. "Sure you must mean some other. It is impossible you should have any such obligations to the man my nephew mentions." "Too surely," answered she, "I have obligations to him of the greatest and tenderest kind. He hath been the preserver of me and mine. Believe me, sir, he hath been abused, grossly abused, to you; I know he hath, or you, whom I know to be all goodness and honour, would not after the many kind and tender things I have heard you say of this poor helpless child have so disdainfully called him fellow. Indeed, my best of friends, he deserves a kinder appellation from you had you heard the good, the kind, the grateful things which I have heard him utter of you. He never mentions your name but with a sort of adoration. In this very room I have

755

seen him on his knees, imploring all the blessings of heaven upon your head. I do not love that child there better than he loves you."

"I see, sir, now," said Blifil, with one of those grinning sneers with which the Devil marks his best beloved, "Mrs. Miller really doth know him. I suppose you will find she is not the only one of your acquaintance to whom he hath exposed you. As for my character, I perceive by some hints she hath thrown out he hath been very free with it, but I forgive him." "And the Lord forgive you, sir," says Mrs. Miller. "We have all sins enough to stand in need of His forgiveness."

"Upon my word, Mrs. Miller," said Allworthy, "I do not take this behaviour of yours to my nephew kindly, and I do assure you, as any reflections which you cast upon him must come only from that wickedest of men, they would only serve, if that were possible, to heighten my resentment against him; for I must tell you, Mrs. Miller, the young man who now stands before you hath ever been the warmest advocate for the ungrateful wretch whose cause you espouse. This, I think, when you hear it from my own mouth, will make you wonder at so much baseness and ingratitude."

"You are deceived, sir," answered Mrs. Miller. "If they were the last words which were to issue from my lips, I would say you were deceived, and I once more repeat it: the Lord forgive those who have deceived you. I do not pretend to say the young man is without faults, but they are the faults of wildness and of youth, faults which he may, nay, which I am certain he will, relinquish, and if he should not, they are vastly overbalanced by one of the most humane, tender, honest hearts that ever man was blessed with."

"Indeed, Mrs. Miller," said Allworthy, "had this been related of you, I should not have believed it." "Indeed, sir," answered she, "you will believe everything I have said, I am sure you will; and when you have heard the story which I shall tell you (for I will tell you all), you will be so far from being offended that you will own (I know your justice so well) that I must have been the most despicable and most ungrateful of wretches if I had acted any other part than I have."

"Well, madam," said Allworthy, "I shall be very glad to hear any good excuse for a behaviour which I must confess I think wants an excuse. And now, madam, will you be pleased to let my nephew proceed in his story without interruption? He would not have introduced a matter of slight consequence with such a preface. Perhaps even this story will cure you of your mistake."

Mrs. Miller gave tokens of submission, and then Mr. Blifil began thus: "I am sure, sir, if you don't think proper to resent the ill usage of Mrs. Miller, I shall easily forgive what affects me only. I think your goodness hath not deserved this indignity at her hands." "Well, child," said Allworthy, "but what is this new instance? What hath he done of late?" "What," cries Blifil, "notwithstanding all Mrs. Miller hath said, I am very sorry to relate, and what you should never have heard from me had it not been a matter impossible to conceal from the whole world. In short, he hath killed a man; I will not say murdered, for perhaps it may not be so construed in law, and I hope the best for his sake."

Allworthy looked shocked and blessed himself, and then, turning to Mrs. Miller, he cried, "Well, madam, what say you now?"

"Why, I say, sir," answered she, "that I never was more concerned at anything in my life; but if the fact be true, I am convinced the man, whoever he is, was in fault. Heaven knows there are many villains in this town who make it their business to provoke young gentlemen. Nothing but the greatest provocation could have tempted him, for of all the gentlemen I ever had in my house, I never saw one so gentle or so sweet-tempered. He was beloved by every one in the house and every one who came near it."

While she was thus running on, a violent knocking at the door interrupted the conversation and prevented her from proceeding further or from receiving any answer; for as she concluded this was a visitor to Mr. Allworthy, she hastily retired, taking with her her little girl, whose eyes were all over blubbered at the melancholy news she heard of Jones, who used to call her his little wife, and not only gave her many playthings but spent whole hours in playing with her himself.

Some readers may, perhaps, be pleased with these minute circumstances, in relating of which we follow the example of Plutarch, one of the best of our brother historians; and others, to whom they may appear trivial, will we hope at least pardon them, as we are never prolix on such occasions.

THE ARRIVAL OF MR. WESTERN, WITH SOME MATTERS
CONCERNING THE PATERNAL AUTHORITY

Mrs. Miller had not long left the room when Mr. Western
entered, but not before a small wrangling bout had passed
between him and his chairmen; for the fellows, who had
taken up their burden at the Hercules Pillars, had conceived
no hopes of having any future good customer in the squire,
and they were, moreover, farther encouraged by his generosity (for he had given them of his own accord sixpence
more than their fare); they therefore very boldly demanded
another shilling, which so provoked the squire that he not
only bestowed many hearty curses on them at the door but
retained his anger after he came into the room, swearing
that all the Londoners were like the court and thought of
nothing but plundering country-gentlemen. "D——n me," says
he, "if I won't walk in the rain rather than get into one of
their hand-barrows again. They have jolted me more in a
mile than Brown Bess would in a long fox-chase."

When his wrath on this occasion was a little appeased,
he resumed the same passionate tone on another. "There,"
says he, "there is fine business forwards now. The hounds
have changed at last, and when we imagined we had a fox
to deal with, od rat it, it turns out to be a badger at last."

"Pray, my good neighbour," said Allworthy, "drop your
metaphors and speak a little plainer." "Why, then," says the
squire, "to tell you plainly, we have been all this time afraid
of a son of a whore of a bastard of somebody's, I don't
know who, not I. And now here is a confounded son of a
whore of a lord, who may be a bastard too for aught I
know or care, for he shall never have a daughter of mine
by my consent. They have beggared the nation, but they
shall never beggar me. My land shall never be sent over
to Hanover."

"You surprise me much, my good friend," said Allworthy.
"Why, zounds! I am surprised myself," answered the squire;
"I went to zee sister Western last night according to her
own appointment, and there I was a-had into a whole
roomful of women. There was my lady cousin Bellaston and
my Lady Betty and my Lady Catharine and my Lady

I-don't-know-who; d—n me if ever you catch me among such a kennel of hoop-petticoat b—s. D—n me, I'd rather be run by my own dogs, as one Acton was, that the story-book says was turned into a hare, and his own dogs killed un and eat un. Od rabbit it, no mortal was ever run in such a manner: if I dodged one way, one had me; if I offered to clap back, another snapped me. 'Oh, certainly one of the greatest matches in England,' says one cousin" (here he attempted to mimic them). "'A very advantageous offer indeed,' cries another cousin (for you must know they be all my cousins, thof I never zeed half o' um before). 'Surely, says that fat a—se b—, my Lady Bellaston, 'cousin, you must be out of your wits to think of refusing such an offer.'"

"Now I begin to understand," says Allworthy; "some person hath made proposals to Miss Western, which the ladies of the family approve but is not to your liking."

"My liking!" said Western. "How the devil should it? I tell you it is a lord, and those are always volks whom you know I always resolved to have nothing to do with. Did unt I refuse a matter of vorty years' purchase now for a bit of land which one o' um had a mind to put into a park, only because I would have no dealings with lords; and dost think I would marry my daughter zu? Besides, ben't I engaged to you, and did I ever go off any bargain when I had promised?"

"As to that point, neighbour," said Allworthy, "I entirely release you from any engagement. No contract can be binding between parties who have not a full power to make it at the time, nor ever afterwards acquire the power of fulfilling it."

"Slud, then!" answered Western. "I tell you I have power and I will fulfil it. Come along with me directly to Doctors' Commons; I will get a licence, and I will go to sister and take away the wench by force, and she shall ha' un or I will lock her up and keep her upon bread and water as long as she lives."

"Mr. Western," said Allworthy, "shall I beg you will hear my full sentiments on this matter?" "Hear thee! Ay, to be sure, I will," answered he. "Why, then, sir," cries Allworthy, "I can truly say without a compliment either to you or the young lady that when this match was proposed, I embraced it very readily and heartily from my regard to you both. An alliance between two families so nearly neighbours, and between whom there had always existed so mutual an intercourse and good harmony, I thought a most desirable event, and with regard to the young lady, not only the concurrent opinion of all who knew her but my own observation assured me that she would be an inestimable treasure to a good husband. I shall say nothing of her personal qualifications, which certainly are admirable; her good nature, her charitable disposition, her modesty, are too well known to need any panegyric; but she hath one quality which existed in a high degree in that best of women, who is now one of the first of angels, which, as it is not of a glaring kind, more commonly escapes observation; so little indeed is it remarked that I want a word to express it. I must use negatives on this occasion. I never heard anything of pertness or what is called repartee out of her mouth, no pretence to wit, much less to that kind of wisdom which is the result only of great learning and experience, the affectation of which in a young woman is as absurd as any of the affectations of an ape. No dictatorial sentiments, no judicial opinions, no profound criticisms. Whenever I have seen her in the company of men, she hath been all attention, with the modesty of a learner, not the forwardness of a teacher. You'll pardon me for it, but I once, to try her only, desired her opinion on a point which was controverted between Mr. Thwackum and Mr. Square. To which she answered with much sweetness, 'You will pardon me, good Mr. Allworthy; I am sure you cannot in earnest think me capable of deciding any point in which two such gentlemen disagree.' Thwackum and Square, who both alike thought themselves sure of a favourable decision, seconded my request. She answered with the same good humour, 'I must absolutely be excused, for I will affront neither so much as to give my judgement on his side.' Indeed, she always showed the highest deference to the understandings of men, a quality absolutely essential to the making a good wife. I shall only add that as she is most apparently void of all affectation, this deference must be certainly real."

Here Blifil sighed bitterly; upon which Western, whose eyes were full of tears at the praise of Sophia, blubbered out, "Don't be chicken-hearted, for shat ha' her; d—n me, shat ha' her if she was twenty times as good."

"Remember your promise, sir," cried Allworthy; "I was not to be interrupted." "Well, shat unt," answered the squire, "I won't speak another word."

"Now, my good friend," continued Allworthy, "I have

dwelt so long on the merit of this young lady, partly as I really am in love with her character and partly that fortune (for the match in that light is really advantageous on my nephew's side) might not be imagined to be my principal view in having so eagerly embraced the proposal. Indeed, I heartily wished to receive so great a jewel into my family, but though I may wish for many good things, I would not therefore steal them or be guilty of any violence or injustice to possess myself of them. Now, to force a woman into a marriage contrary to her consent or approbation is an act of such injustice and oppression that I wish the laws of our country could restrain it, but a good conscience is never lawless in the worst-regulated state, and will provide those laws for itself which the neglect of legislators hath forgotten to supply. This is surely a case of that kind; for is it not cruel, nay, impious, to force a woman into that state against her will, for her behaviour in which she is to be accountable to the highest and most dreadful court of judicature and to answer at the peril of her soul? To discharge the matrimonial duties in an adequate manner is no easy task, and shall we lay this burden upon a woman while we at the same time deprive her of all that assistance which may enable her to undergo it? Shall we tear her very heart from her while we enjoin her duties to which a whole heart is scarce equal? I must speak very plainly here: I think parents who act in this manner are accessaries to all the guilt which their children afterwards incur and, of course, must, before a just judge, expect to partake of their punishment; but if they could avoid this, good heaven, is there a soul who can bear the thought of having contributed to the damnation of his child?

"For these reasons, my best neighbour, as I see the inclinations of this young lady are most unhappily averse to my nephew, I must decline any further thoughts of the honour you intended him, though I assure you I shall always retain the most grateful sense of it."

"Well, sir," said Western (the froth bursting forth from his lips the moment they were uncorked), "you cannot say but I have heard you out, and now I expect you'll hear me; and if I don't answer every word o't, why, then, I'll consent to gee the matter up. First, then, I desire you to answer me one question: did not I beget her? Did not I beget her? Answer me that. They say, indeed, it is a wise father that knows his own child, but I am sure I have the best title to her, for I bred her up. But I believe you will allow me to be her father; and if I be, am I not to govern my own child? I ask you that: am I not to govern my own child? And if I am to govern her in other matters, surely I am to govern her in this, which concerns her most. And what am I desiring all this while? Am I desiring her to do anything for me? To give me anything? Zu much on t'other side that I am only desiring her to take away half my estate now and t'other half when I die. Well, and what is it all vor? Why is unt it to make her happy? It's enough to make one mad to hear volks talk; if I was going to marry myself, then she would ha' reason to cry and to blubber, but on the contrary, han't I offered to bind down my land in zuch a manner that I could not marry if I would, seeing as narro' woman upon earth would ha' me. What the devil in hell can I do more? I contribute to her damnation! Zounds! I'd zee all the world d—d bevore her little vinger should be hurt. Indeed, Mr. Allworthy, you must excuse me, but I am surprised to hear you talk in zuch a manner, and I must say, take it how you will, that I thought you had more sense."

Allworthy resented this reflection only with a smile, nor could he, if he would have endeavoured it, have conveyed into that smile any mixture of malice or contempt. His smiles at folly were, indeed, such as we may suppose the angels bestow on the absurdities of mankind.

Blifil now desired to be permitted to speak a few words. "As to using any violence on the young lady, I am sure I shall never consent to it. My conscience will not permit me to use violence on any one, much less on a lady for whom, however cruel she is to me, I shall always preserve the purest and sincerest affection, but yet I have read that women are seldom proof against perseverance. Why may I not hope, then, by such perseverance at last to gain those inclinations in which for the future I shall, perhaps, have no rival; for as for this lord, Mr. Western is so kind to prefer me to him, and sure, sir, you will not deny but that a parent hath at least a negative voice in these matters; nay, I have heard this very young lady herself say so more than once, and declare that she thought children inexcusable who married in direct opposition to the will of their parents. Besides, though the other ladies of the family seem to favour the pretensions of my lord, I do not find the lady herself is inclined to give him any countenance; alas, I am too well assured she is not; I am too sensible that wickedest of men remains uppermost in her heart."

"Ay, ay, so he does," cries Western.

"But surely," says Blifil, "when she hears of this murder which he hath committed, if the law should spare his life——"

"What's that?" cries Western. "Murder! Hath he committed a murder, and is there any hopes of seeing him hanged? Tol de rol, tol lol de rol." Here he fell a-singing and capering about the room.

"Child," says Allworthy, "this unhappy passion of yours distresses me beyond measure. I heartily pity you and would do every fair thing to promote your success."

"I desire no more," cries Blifil. "I am convinced my dear uncle hath a better opinion of me than to think that I myself would accept of more."

"Lookee," says Allworthy, "you have my leave to write, to visit, if she will permit it—but I insist on no thoughts of violence. I will have no confinement, nothing of that kind attempted."

"Well, well," cries the squire, "nothing of that kind shall be attempted; we will try a little longer what fair means will effect, and if this fellow be but hanged out of the way—tol lol de rol. I never heard better news in my life; I warrant everything goes to my mind. Do, prithee, dear Allworthy, come and dine with me at the Hercules Pillars; I have bespoke a shoulder of mutton roasted, and a spare-rib of pork, and a fowl and egg-sauce. There will be nobody but ourselves unless we have a mind to have the landlord, for I have sent Parson Supple down to Basingstoke after my tobacco-box, which I left at an inn there, and I would not lose it for the world, for it is an old acquaintance of above twenty years' standing. I can tell you, landlord is a vast comical bitch; you will like un hugely."

Mr. Allworthy at last agreed to this invitation, and soon after the squire went off, singing and capering at the hopes of seeing the speedy tragical end of poor Jones.

When he was gone, Mr. Allworthy resumed the aforesaid subject with much gravity. He told his nephew he wished with all his heart he would endeavour to conquer a passion "in which I cannot," says he, "flatter you with any hopes of succeeding. It is certainly a vulgar error that aversion in a woman may be conquered by perseverance. Indifference may, perhaps, sometimes yield to it, but the usual triumphs gained by perseverance in a lover are over caprice, prudence, affectation, and often an exorbitant degree of levity, which excites women not overwarm in their constitutions to indulge their vanity by prolonging the time of courtship even when they are well enough pleased with the object and resolve (if they ever resolve at all) to make him a very pitiful amends in the end. But a fixed dislike, as I am afraid this is, will rather gather strength than be conquered by time. Besides, my dear, I have another apprehension, which you must excuse. I am afraid this passion which you have for this fine young creature hath her beautiful person too much for its object, and is unworthy of the name of that love which is the only foundation of matrimonial felicity. To admire, to like, and to long for the possession of a beautiful woman without any regard to her sentiments towards us is, I am afraid, too natural, but love, I believe, is the child of love only; at least I am pretty confident that to love the creature who we are assured hates us is not in human nature. Examine your heart, therefore, thoroughly, my good boy, and if upon examination you have but the least suspicion of this kind, I am sure your own virtue and religion will impel you to drive so vicious a passion from your heart and your good sense will soon enable you to do it without pain."

The reader may pretty well guess Blifil's answer, but if he should be at a loss, we are not at present at leisure to satisfy him, as our history now hastens on to matters of higher importance and we can no longer bear to be absent from Sophia.

4

AN EXTRAORDINARY SCENE BETWEEN SOPHIA AND HER AUNT

The lowing heifer and the bleating ewe in herds and flocks may ramble safe and unregarded through the pastures. These are, indeed, hereafter doomed to be the prey of man, yet many years are they suffered to enjoy their liberty undisturbed. But if a plump doe be discovered to have escaped from the forest and to repose herself in some field or grove, the whole parish is presently alarmed, every man is ready to set his dogs after her; and if she is preserved from the rest by the good squire, it is only that he may secure her for his own eating.

I have often considered a very fine young woman of fortune and fashion when first found strayed from the pale of her nursery to be in pretty much the same situation with this doe. The town is immediately in an uproar; she is hunted from park to play, from court to assembly, from assembly to her own chamber, and rarely escapes a single season from the jaws of some devourer or other; for if her friends protect her from some, it is only to deliver her over to one of their own choosing, often more disagreeable to her than any of the rest; while whole herds or flocks of other women securely and scarce regarded traverse the park, the play, the opera, and the assembly, and though for the most part at least they are at last devoured, yet for a long time do they wanton in liberty, without disturbance or control.

Of all these paragons, none ever tasted more of this persecution than poor Sophia. Her ill stars were not contented with all that she had suffered on account of Blifil; they now raised her another pursuer, who seemed likely to torment her no less than the other had done. For though her aunt was less violent, she was no less assiduous in teasing her than her father had been before.

The servants were no sooner departed after dinner than Mrs. Western, who had opened the matter to Sophia, informed her that she expected his lordship that very afternoon and intended to take the first opportunity of leaving her alone with him. "If you do, madam," answered Sophia with some spirit, "I shall take the first opportunity of leaving him by himself." "How, madam!" cries the aunt. "Is this the return you make me for my kindness in relieving you from your confinement at your father's?" "You know, madam," said Sophia, "the cause of that confinement was a refusal to comply with my father in accepting a man I detested, and will my dear aunt, who hath relieved me from that distress, involve me in another, equally bad?" "And do you think, then, madam," answered Mrs. Western, "that there is no difference between my lord Fellamar and Mr. Blifil?" "Very little, in my opinion," cries Sophia, "and if I must be condemned to one, I would certainly have the merit of sacrificing myself to my father's pleasure." "Then my pleasure, I find," said the aunt, "hath very little weight with you, but that consideration shall not move me.

I act from nobler motives. The view of aggrandizing my family, of ennobling yourself, is what I proceed upon. Have you no sense of ambition? Are there no charms in the thoughts of having a coronet on your coach?" "None, upon my honour," said Sophia. "A pincushion upon my coach would please me just as well." "Never mention honour," cries the aunt. "It becomes not the mouth of such a wretch. I am sorry, niece, you force me to use these words, but I cannot bear your grovelling temper; you have none of the blood of the Westerns in you. But however mean and base your own ideas are, you shall bring no imputation on mine. I will never suffer the world to say of me that I encouraged you in refusing one of the best matches in England, a match which besides its advantage in fortune would do honour to almost any family, and hath indeed in title the advantage of ours." "Surely," says Sophia, "I am born deficient and have not the senses with which other people are blessed; there must be certainly some sense which can relish the delights of sound and show which I have not; for surely mankind would not labour so much nor sacrifice so much for the obtaining, nor would they be so elate and proud with possessing, what appeared to them, as it doth to me, the most insignificant of all trifles."

"No, no, miss," cries the aunt, "you are born with as many senses as other people, but I assure you, you are not born with a sufficient understanding to make a fool of me or to expose my conduct to the world. So I declare this to you upon my word, and you know, I believe, how fixed my resolutions are: unless you agree to see his lordship this afternoon, I will with my own hands deliver you to-morrow morning to my brother and will never henceforth interfere with you nor see your face again." Sophia stood a few moments silent after this speech, which was uttered in a most angry and peremptory tone, and then, bursting into tears, she cried, "Do with me, madam, whatever you please; I am the most miserable, undone wretch upon earth; if my dear aunt forsakes me, where shall I look for a protector?" "My dear niece," cries she, "you will have a very good protector in his lordship, a protector whom nothing but a hankering after that vile fellow Jones can make you decline." "Indeed, madam," said Sophia, "you wrong me. How can you imagine, after what you have shown me, if I had ever any such thoughts that I should not banish them forever. If it will satisfy you, I will receive

766

the sacrament upon it, never to see his face again." "But child, dear child," said the aunt, "be reasonable; can you invent a single objection?" "I have already, I think, told you a sufficient objection," answered Sophia. "What?" cries the aunt. "I remember none." "Sure, madam," said Sophia, "I told you he had used me in the rudest and vilest manner." "Indeed, child," answered she, "I never heard you or did not understand you. But what do you mean by this rude, vile manner?" "Indeed, madam," said Sophia, "I am almost ashamed to tell you. He caught me in his arms, pulled me down upon the settee, and thrust his hand into my bosom, and kissed it with such violence that I have the mark upon my left breast at this moment." "Indeed!" said Mrs. Western. "Yes, indeed, madam," answered Sophia; "my father luckily came in at that instant or heaven knows what rudeness he intended to have proceeded to." "I am astonished and confounded," cries the aunt. "No woman of the name of Western hath been ever treated so since we were a family. I would have torn the eyes of a prince out if he had attempted such freedoms with me. It is impossible; sure, Sophia, you must invent this to raise my indignation against him." "I hope, madam," said Sophia, "you have too good an opinion of me to imagine me capable of telling an untruth. Upon my soul, it is true." "I should have stabbed him to the heart had I been present," returned the aunt. "Yet surely he could have no dishonourable design; it is impossible; he durst not; besides, his proposals show he had not, for they are not only honourable but generous. I don't know; the age allows too great freedoms. A distant salute is all I would have allowed before the ceremony. I have had lovers formerly, not so long ago neither; several lovers, though I never would consent to marriage and I never encouraged the least freedom. It is foolish custom and what I never would agree to. No man kissed more of me than my cheek. It is as much as one can bring oneself to give lips up to a husband, and indeed, could I ever have been persuaded to marry, I believe I should not have soon been brought to endure so much." "You will pardon me, dear madam," said Sophia, "if I make one observation: you own you have had many lovers, and the world knows it even if you should deny it. You refused them all and, I am convinced, one coronet at least among them." "You say true, dear Sophy," answered she; "I had once the offer of a title." "Why, then," said Sophia, "will you not suffer me to refuse this one?" "It is true, child," said she, "I have refused the offer of a title, but it was not so good an offer; that is, not so very, very good an offer——" "Yes, madam," said Sophia, "but you have had very great proposals from men of vast fortunes. It was not the first, nor the second, nor the third advantageous match that offered itself." "I own it was not," said she. "Well, madam," continued Sophia, "and why may not I expect to have a second, perhaps better than this? You are now but a young woman, and I am convinced would not promise to yield to the first lover of fortune, nay, or of title too. I am a very young woman and sure I need not despair." "Well, my dear, dear Sophy," cries the aunt, "what would you have me say?" "Why, I only beg that I may not be left alone, at least this evening; grant me that, and I will submit if you think after what is passed I ought to see him in your company." "Well, I will grant it," cries the aunt. "Sophy, you know I love you and can deny you nothing. You know the easiness of my nature; I have not always been so easy. I have been formerly thought cruel, by the men, I mean. I was called the cruel Parthenissa. I have broke many a window that has had verses to the cruel Parthenissa in it. Sophy, I was never so handsome as you, and yet I had something of you formerly. I am a little altered. Kingdoms and states, as Tully Cicero says in his *Epistles,* undergo alterations, and so much the human form." Thus run she on for near half an hour upon herself and her conquests and her cruelty till the arrival of my lord, who, after a most tedious visit, during which Mrs. Western never once offered to leave the room, retired not much more satisfied with the aunt than with the niece. For Sophia had brought her aunt into so excellent a temper that she consented to almost everything her niece said, and agreed that a little distant behaviour might not be improper to so forward a lover.

Thus Sophia, by a little well-directed flattery, for which surely none will blame her, obtained a little ease for herself, and at least put off the evil day. And now we have seen our heroine in a better situation than she hath been for a long time before, we will look a little after Mr. Jones, whom we left in the most deplorable situation that can well be imagined.

MRS. MILLER AND MR. NIGHTINGALE VISIT JONES IN THE PRISON

When Mr. Allworthy and his nephew went to meet Mr. Western, Mrs. Miller set forwards to her son-in-law's lodgings in order to acquaint him with the accident which had befallen his friend Jones, but he had known it long before from Partridge (for Jones when he left Mrs. Miller had been furnished with a room in the same house with Mr. Nightingale). The good woman found her daughter under great affliction on account of Mr. Jones, whom having comforted as well as she could, she set forwards to the Gatehouse, where she heard he was, and where Mr. Nightingale was arrived before her.

The firmness and constancy of a true friend is a circumstance so extremely delightful to persons in any kind of distress that the distress itself, if it be only temporary and admits of relief, is more than compensated by bringing this comfort with it. Nor are instances of this kind so rare as some superficial and inaccurate observers have reported. To say the truth, want of compassion is not to be numbered among our general faults. The black ingredient which fouls our disposition is envy. Hence our eye is seldom, I am afraid, turned upward to those who are manifestly greater, better, wiser, or happier than ourselves without some degree of malignity, while we commonly look downwards on the mean and miserable with sufficient benevolence and pity. In fact, I have remarked that most of the defects which have discovered themselves in the friendships within my observation have arisen from envy only, a hellish vice, and yet one from which I have known very few absolutely exempt. But enough of a subject which if pursued would lead me too far.

Whether it was that Fortune was apprehensive lest Jones should sink under the weight of his adversity and that she might thus lose any future opportunity of tormenting him, or whether she really abated somewhat of her severity towards him, she seemed a little to relax her persecution by sending him the company of two faithful friends, and what is perhaps more rare, a faithful servant. For Partridge, though he had many imperfections, wanted not fidelity, and though fear would not suffer him to be hanged for his master, yet the world, I believe, could not have bribed him to desert his cause.

While Jones was expressing great satisfaction in the presence of his friends Partridge brought an account that Mr. Fitzpatrick was still alive, though the surgeon declared that he had very little hopes. Upon which Jones fetching a deep sigh, Nightingale said to him, "My dear Tom, why should you afflict yourself so upon an accident which, whatever be the consequence, can be attended with no danger to you and in which your conscience cannot accuse you of having been in the least to blame? If the fellow should die, what have you done more than taken away the life of a ruffian in your own defence? So will the coroner's inquest certainly find it, and then you will be easily admitted to bail; and though you must undergo the form of a trial, yet it is a trial which many men would stand for you for a shilling." "Come, come, Mr. Jones," says Mrs. Miller, "cheer yourself up. I knew you could not be the aggressor, and so I told Mr. Allworthy, and so he shall acknowledge too before I have done with him."

Jones gravely answered that whatever might be his fate, he should always lament the having shed the blood of one of his fellow-creatures as one of the highest misfortunes which could have befallen him. "But I have another misfortune of the tenderest kind. Oh, Mrs. Miller, I have lost what I held most dear upon earth." "That must be a mistress," said Mrs. Miller. "But come, come, I know more than you imagine" (for indeed Partridge had blabbed all), "and I have heard more than you know. Matters go better, I promise you, than you think, and I would not give Blifil sixpence for all the chance which he hath of the lady."

"Indeed, my dear friend, indeed," answered Jones, "you are an entire stranger to the cause of my grief. If you was acquainted with the story, you would allow my case admitted of no comfort. I apprehend no danger from Blifil. I have undone myself." "Don't despair," replied Mrs. Miller; "you know not what a woman can do, and if anything be in my power, I promise you I will do it to serve you. It is my duty. My son, my dear Mr. Nightingale, who is so kind to tell me he hath obligations to you on the same account, knows it is my duty. Shall I go to the lady myself? I will say anything to her you would have me say."

"Thou best of women," cries Jones, taking her by the hand, "talk not of obligations to me; but as you have been so kind to mention it, there is a favour which, perhaps, may be in your power. I see you are acquainted with the lady (how you came by your information I know not) who sits, indeed, very near my heart. If you could contrive to deliver this" (giving her a paper from his pocket), "I shall forever acknowledge your goodness."

"Give it me," said Mrs. Miller. "If I see it not in her own possession before I sleep, may my next sleep be my last. Comfort yourself, my good young man; be wise enough to take warning from past follies and I warrant all shall be well, and I shall yet see you happy with the most charming young lady in the world, for so I hear from every one she is."

"Believe me, madam," said he, "I do not speak the common cant of one in my unhappy situation. Before this dreadful accident happened, I had resolved to quit a life of which I was become sensible of the wickedness as well as folly. I do assure you, notwithstanding the disturbances I have unfortunately occasioned in your house, for which I heartily ask your pardon, I am not an abandoned profligate. Though I have been hurried into vices, I do not approve a vicious character, nor will I ever from this moment deserve it."

Mrs. Miller expressed great satisfaction in these declarations, in the sincerity of which she averred she had an entire faith; and now the remainder of the conversation passed in the joint attempts of that good woman and Mr. Nightingale to cheer the dejected spirits of Mr. Jones, in which they so far succeeded as to leave him much better comforted and satisfied than they found him; to which happy alteration nothing so much contributed as the kind undertaking of Mrs. Miller to deliver his letter to Sophia, which he despaired of finding any means to accomplish; for when Black George produced the last from Sophia, he informed Partridge that she had strictly charged him on pain of having it communicated to her father not to bring her any answer. He was, moreover, not a little pleased to find he had so warm an advocate to Mr. Allworthy himself in this good woman, who was in reality one of the worthiest creatures in the world.

After about an hour's visit from the lady (for Nightingale had been with him much longer), they both took their leave, promising to return to him soon; during which Mrs. Miller said she hoped to bring him some good news from his mistress, and Mr. Nightingale promised to inquire into the state of Mr. Fitzpatrick's wound, and likewise to find out some of the persons who were present at the rencounter.

The former of these went directly in quest of Sophia, whither we likewise shall now attend her.

6

IN WHICH MRS. MILLER PAYS A VISIT TO SOPHIA

Access to the young lady was by no means difficult, for as she lived now on a perfect friendly footing with her aunt, she was at full liberty to receive what visitants she pleased.

Sophia was dressing when she was acquainted that there was a gentlewoman below to wait on her; as she was neither afraid nor ashamed to see any of her own sex, Mrs. Miller was immediately admitted.

Curtsies and the usual ceremonials between women who are strangers to each other being passed, Sophia said, "I have not the pleasure to know you, madam." "No, madam," answered Mrs. Miller, "and I must beg pardon for intruding upon you. But when you know what has induced me to give you this trouble, I hope——" "Pray, what is your business, madam?" said Sophia with a little emotion. "Madam, we are not alone," replied Mrs. Miller in a low voice. "Go out, Betty," said Sophia.

When Betty was departed, Mrs. Miller said, "I was desired, madam, by a very unhappy young gentleman to deliver you this letter." Sophia changed colour when she saw the direction, well knowing the hand, and after some hesitation said, "I could not conceive, madam, from your appearance that your business had been of such a nature. Whomever you brought this letter from, I shall not open it. I should be sorry to entertain an unjust suspicion of any one, but you are an utter stranger to me."

"If you will have patience, madam," answered Mrs. Miller, "I will acquaint you who I am and how I came by that letter." "I have no curiosity, madam, to know anything," cries Sophia, "but I must insist on your delivering that letter back to the person who gave it you."

Mrs. Miller then fell upon her knees, and in the most passionate terms implored her compassion, to which Sophia answered, "Sure, madam, it is surprising you should be so very strongly interested in the behalf of this person. I would not think, madam——" "No, madam," says Mrs. Miller, "you shall not think anything but the truth. I will tell you all, and you will not wonder that I am interested. He is the best-natured creature that ever was born." She then began and related the story of Mr. Anderson. After this she cried, "This, madam, this is his goodness, but I have much more tender obligations to him. He hath preserved my child." Here, after shedding some tears, she related everything concerning that fact, suppressing only those circumstances which would have most reflected on her daughter, and concluded with saying, "Now, madam, you shall judge whether I can ever do enough for so kind, so good, so generous a young man; and sure he is the best and worthiest of all human beings."

The alterations in the countenance of Sophia had hitherto been chiefly to her disadvantage and had inclined her complexion to too great paleness, but she now waxed redder if possible than vermilion and cried, "I know not what to say; certainly, what arises from gratitude cannot be blamed. But what service can my reading his letter do your friend, since I am resolved never——" Mrs. Miller fell again to her entreaties and begged to be forgiven, but she could not, she said, carry it back. "Well, madam," says Sophia, "I cannot help it if you will force it upon me. Certainly you may leave it, whether I will or no." What Sophia meant or whether she meant anything, I will not presume to determine, but Mrs. Miller actually understood this as a hint, and presently, laying the letter down on the table, took her leave, having first begged permission to wait again on Sophia, which request had neither assent nor denial.

The letter lay upon the table no longer than till Mrs. Miller was out of sight, for then Sophia opened and read it.

This letter did very little service to his cause; for it consisted of little more than confessions of his own unworthiness and bitter lamentations of despair, together with the most solemn protestations of his unalterable fidelity to Sophia, of which, he said, he hoped to convince her if he had ever more the honour of being admitted to her presence; and that he could account for the letter to Lady Bellaston in such a manner that though it would not entitle him to her forgiveness, he hoped at least to obtain it from her mercy; and concluded with vowing that nothing was ever less in his thoughts than to marry Lady Bellaston.

Though Sophia read the letter twice over with great attention, his meaning still remained a riddle to her, nor could her invention suggest to her any means to excuse Jones. She certainly remained very angry with him, though indeed Lady Bellaston took up so much of her resentment that her gentle mind had but little left to bestow on any other person.

That lady was most unluckily to dine this very day with her aunt Western, and in the afternoon they were all three by appointment to go together to the opera, and thence to Lady Thomas Hatchet's drum. Sophia would have gladly been excused from all, but she would not disoblige her aunt; and as to the arts of counterfeiting illness, she was so entirely a stranger to them that it never once entered into her head. When she was dressed, therefore, down she went, resolved to encounter all the horrors of the day; and a most disagreeable one it proved, for Lady Bellaston took every opportunity very civilly and slyly to insult her; to all which her dejection of spirits disabled her from making any return, and indeed, to confess the truth, she was at the very best but an indifferent mistress of repartee.

Another misfortune which befell poor Sophia was the company of Lord Fellamar, whom she met at the opera, and who attended her to the drum. And though both places were too public to admit of any particularities, and she was farther relieved by the music at the one place and by the cards at the other, she could not, however, enjoy herself in his company; for there is something of delicacy in women which will not suffer them to be even easy in the presence of a man whom they know to have pretensions to them which they are disinclined to favour.

Having in this chapter twice mentioned a drum, a word which our posterity, it is hoped, will not understand in the sense it is here applied, we shall, notwithstanding our present haste, stop a moment to describe the entertainment here meant, and the rather as we can in a moment describe it.

A drum, then, is an assembly of well-dressed persons of both sexes, most of whom play at cards and the rest do nothing at all, while the mistress of the house performs the part of the landlady at an inn and, like the landlady of an

inn, prides herself in the number of her guests, though she
doth not always, like her, get anything by it.

No wonder, then, as so much spirits must be required to
support any vivacity in these scenes of dullness, that we
hear persons of fashion eternally complaining of the want
of them—a complaint confined entirely to upper life. How
insupportable must we imagine this round of impertinence
to have been to Sophia at this time; how difficult must she
have found it to force the appearance of gaiety into her
looks when her mind dictated nothing but the tenderest sorrow and when every thought was charged with tormenting
ideas.

Night, however, at last restored her to her pillow, where
we will leave her to soothe her melancholy at least, though
incapable, we are afraid, of rest, and shall pursue our history, which, something whispers us, is now arrived at the
eve of some great event.

7

A PATHETIC SCENE BETWEEN MR. ALLWORTHY AND MRS. MILLER

Mrs. Miller had a long discourse with Mr. Allworthy at his
return from dinner, in which she acquainted him with
Jones's having unfortunately lost all which he was pleased
to bestow on him at their separation, and with the distresses
to which that loss had subjected him, of all which she had
received a full account from the faithful retailer Partridge.
She then explained the obligations she had to Jones; not
that she was entirely explicit with regard to her daughter;
for though she had the utmost confidence in Mr. Allworthy
and though there could be no hopes of keeping an affair
secret which was unhappily known to more than half a
dozen, yet she could not prevail with herself to mention
those circumstances which reflected most on the chastity of
poor Nancy, but smothered that part of her evidence as
cautiously as if she had been before a judge and the girl
was now on her trial for the murder of a bastard.

Allworthy said there were few characters so absolutely
vicious as not to have the least mixture of good in them.
"However," says he, "I cannot deny but that you had some
obligations to the fellow, bad as he is, and I shall therefore

excuse what hath passed already, but must insist you never mention his name to me more; for I promise you it was upon the fullest and plainest evidence that I resolved to take the measures I have taken." "Well, sir," says she, "I make not the least doubt but time will show all matters in their true and natural colours, and that you will be convinced this poor young man deserves better of you than some other folks that shall be nameless."

"Madam," cries Allworthy, a little ruffled, "I will not hear any reflections on my nephew, and if you ever say a word more of that kind, I will depart from your house that instant. He is the worthiest and best of men, and I once more repeat it to you: he hath carried his friendship to this man to a blameable length by too long concealing facts of the blackest dye. The ingratitude of the wretch to this good young man is what I most resent; for, madam, I have the greatest reason to imagine he had laid a plot to supplant my nephew in my favour and to have disinherited him."

"I am sure, sir," answered Mrs. Miller, a little frightened (for though Mr. Allworthy had the utmost sweetness and benevolence in his smiles, he had great terror in his frowns), "I shall never speak against any gentleman you are pleased to think well of. I am sure, sir, such behaviour would very little become me, especially when the gentleman is your nearest relation, but, sir, you must not be angry with me, you must not indeed, for my good wishes to this poor wretch. Sure I may call him so now, though once you would have been angry with me if I had spoke of him with the least disrespect. How often have I heard you call him your son? How often have you prattled to me of him with all the fondness of a parent? Nay, sir, I cannot forget the many tender expressions, the many good things, you have told me of his beauty and his parts and his virtues, of his good nature and generosity. I am sure, sir, I cannot forget them, for I find them all true. I have experienced them in my own cause. They have preserved my family. You must pardon my tears, sir; indeed you must, when I consider the cruel reverse of fortune which this poor youth, to whom I am so much obliged, hath suffered. When I consider the loss of your favour, which I know he valued more than his life, I must, I must, lament him. If you had a dagger in your hand ready to plunge into my heart, I must lament the misery of one whom you have loved and I shall ever love."

Allworthy was pretty much moved with this speech, but

it seemed not to be with anger; for after a short silence, taking Mrs. Miller by the hand, he said very affectionately to her, "Come, madam, let us consider a little about your daughter. I cannot blame you for rejoicing in a match which promises to be advantageous to her, but you know this advantage in a great measure depends on the father's reconciliation. I know Mr. Nightingale very well, and have formerly had concerns with him; I will make him a visit and endeavour to serve you in this matter. I believe he is a worldly man, but as this is an only son and the thing is now irretrievable, perhaps he may in time be brought to reason. I promise you I will do all I can for you."

Many were the acknowledgements which the poor woman made to Allworthy for this kind and generous offer, nor could she refrain from taking this occasion again to express her gratitude towards Jones, "to whom," said she, "I owe the opportunity of giving you, sir, this present trouble." Allworthy gently stopped her, but he was too good a man to be really offended with the effects of so noble a principle as now actuated Mrs. Miller, and indeed, had not this new affair inflamed his former anger against Jones, it is possible he might have been a little softened towards him by the report of an action which malice itself could not have derived from an evil motive.

Mr. Allworthy and Mrs. Miller had been above an hour together when their conversation was put an end to by the arrival of Blifil and another person, which other person was no less than Mr. Dowling, the attorney, who was now become a great favourite with Mr. Blifil, and whom Mr. Allworthy at the desire of his nephew had made his steward; and had likewise recommended him to Mr. Western, from whom the attorney received a promise of being promoted to the same office upon the first vacancy, and in the meantime was employed in transacting some affairs which the squire then had in London in relation to a mortgage.

This was the principal affair which then brought Mr. Dowling to town; therefore he took the same opportunity to charge himself with some money for Mr. Allworthy and to make a report to him of some other business; in all which, as it was of much too dull a nature to find any place in this history, we will leave the uncle, nephew, and their lawyer concerned and resort to other matters.

CONTAINING VARIOUS MATTERS

Before we return to Mr. Jones, we will take one more view of Sophia.

Though that young lady had brought her aunt into great good humour by those soothing methods which we have before related, she had not brought her in the least to abate of her zeal for the match with Lord Fellamar. This zeal was now inflamed by Lady Bellaston, who had told her the preceding evening that she was well satisfied from the conduct of Sophia, and from her carriage to his lordship, that all delays would be dangerous, and that the only way to succeed was to press the match forward with such rapidity that the young lady should have no time to reflect, and be obliged to consent while she scarce knew what she did. In which manner, she said, one-half of the marriages among people of condition were brought about. A fact very probably true, and to which, I suppose, is owing the mutual tenderness which afterwards exists among so many happy couples.

A hint of the same kind was given by the same lady to Lord Fellamar, and both these so readily embraced the advice that the very next day was at his lordship's request appointed by Mrs. Western for a private interview between the young parties. This was communicated to Sophia by her aunt, and insisted upon in such high terms that, after having urged everything she possibly could invent against it without the least effect, she at last agreed to give the highest instance of complaisance which any young lady can give, and consented to see his lordship.

As conversations of this kind afford no great entertainment, we shall be excused from reciting the whole that passed at this interview, in which, after his lordship had made many declarations of the most pure and ardent passion to the silent, blushing Sophia, she at last collected all the spirits she could raise, and with a trembling low voice said, "My lord, you must be yourself conscious whether your former behaviour to me hath been consistent with the professions you now make." "Is there," answered he, "no way by which I can atone for madness? What I did, I am afraid, must have too plainly convinced you that the violence of love had deprived me of my senses." "Indeed, my lord," said she, "it is in your power to give me a proof of an affection which I much rather wish to encourage and to which I should think myself more beholden." "Name it, madam," said my lord, very warmly. "My lord," says she, looking down upon her fan, "I know you must be sensible how uneasy this pretended passion of yours hath made me." "Can you be so cruel to call it pretended?" says he. "Yes, my lord," answered Sophia, "all professions of love to those whom we persecute are most insulting pretences. This pursuit of yours is to me a most cruel persecution; nay, it is taking a most ungenerous advantage of my unhappy situation." "Most lovely, most adorable charmer, do not accuse me," cries he, "of taking an ungenerous advantage while I have no thoughts but what are directed to your honour and interest and while I have no view, no hope, no ambition, but to throw myself, honour, fortune, everything, at your feet." "My lord," says she, "it is that fortune and those honours which give you the advantage of which I complain. These are the charms which have seduced my relations, but to me they are things indifferent. If your lordship will merit my gratitude, there is but one way——" "Pardon me, divine creature," said he, "there can be none. All I can do for you is so much your due and will give me so much pleasure that there is no room for your gratitude." "Indeed, my lord," answered she, "you may obtain my gratitude, my good opinion, every kind thought and wish which it is in my power to bestow; nay, you may obtain them with ease, for sure to a generous mind it must be easy to grant my request. Let me beseech you, then, to cease a pursuit in which you can never have any success. For your own sake as well as mine I entreat this favour, for sure you are too noble to have any pleasure in tormenting an unhappy creature. What can your lordship propose but uneasiness to yourself by a perseverance which, upon my honour, upon my soul, cannot, shall not, prevail with me, whatever distresses you may drive me to." Here my lord fetched a deep sigh and then said, "Is it, then, madam, that I am so unhappy to be the object of your dislike and scorn, or will you pardon me if I suspect there is some other?" Here he hesitated, and Sophia answered with some spirit, "My lord, I shall not be accountable to you for the reasons of my conduct. I am obliged to your lordship for the generous offer you have made; I own it is beyond either my deserts or expectations, yet I hope, my lord, you will not insist on my reasons when I declare I cannot accept it." Lord Fellamar returned much to this, which we do not perfectly understand, and perhaps it could not all be strictly reconciled either to sense or grammar, but he concluded his ranting speech with saying that if she has pre-engaged herself to any gentleman, however unhappy it would make him, he should think himself bound in honour to desist. Perhaps my lord laid too much emphasis on the word *gentleman;* for we cannot else well account for the indignation with which he inspired Sophia, who in her answer seemed greatly to resent some affront he had given her.

While she was speaking, with her voice more raised than usual, Mrs. Western came into the room, the fire glaring in her cheeks and the flames bursting from her eyes. "I am ashamed," says she, "my lord, of the reception which you have met with. I assure your lordship we are all sensible of the honour done us, and I must tell you, Miss Western, the family expect a different behaviour from you." Here my lord interfered on behalf of the young lady, but to no purpose; the aunt proceeded till Sophia pulled out her handkerchief, threw herself into a chair, and burst into a violent fit of tears.

The remainder of the conversation between Mrs. Western and his lordship, till the latter withdrew, consisted of bitter lamentations on his side and on hers of the strongest assurances that her niece should and would consent to all he wished. "Indeed, my lord," says she, "the girl hath had a foolish education, neither adapted to her fortune nor her family. Her father, I am sorry to say it, is to blame for everything. The girl hath silly country notions of bashfulness. Nothing else, my lord, upon my honour; I am convinced she hath a good understanding at the bottom, and will be brought to reason."

This last speech was made in the absence of Sophia, for she had sometime before left the room with more appearance of passion than she had ever shown on any occasion; and now his lordship, after many expressions of thanks to Mrs. Western, many ardent professions of passion which nothing could conquer, and many assurances of perseverance, which Mrs. Western highly encouraged, took his leave for this time.

Before we relate what now passed between Mrs. Western and Sophia, it may be proper to mention an unfortunate accident which had happened and which had occasioned the return of Mrs. Western with so much fury, as we have seen.

The reader, then, must know that the maid who at present attended on Sophia was recommended by Lady Bellaston, with whom she had lived for some time in the capacity of a comb-brush; she was a very sensible girl and had received the strictest instructions to watch her young lady very carefully. These instructions, we are sorry to say, were communicated to her by Mrs. Honour, into whose favour Lady Bellaston had now so ingratiated herself that the violent affection which the good waiting-woman had formerly borne to Sophia was entirely obliterated by that great attachment which she had to her new mistress.

Now, when Mrs. Miller was departed, Betty (for that was the name of the girl), returning to her young lady, found her very attentively engaged in reading a long letter, and the visible emotions which she betrayed on that occasion might have well accounted for some suspicions which the girl entertained, but indeed they had yet a stronger foundation, for she had overheard the whole scene which passed between Sophia and Mrs. Miller.

Mrs. Western was acquainted with all this matter by Betty, who, after receiving many commendations and some rewards for her fidelity, was ordered that if the woman who brought the letter came again, she should introduce her to Mrs. Western herself.

Unluckily, Mrs. Miller returned at the very time when Sophia was engaged with his lordship. Betty, according to order, sent her directly to the aunt, who, being mistress of so many circumstances relating to what had passed the day before, easily imposed upon the poor woman to believe that Sophia had communicated the whole affair, and so pumped everything out of her which she knew relating to the letter and relating to Jones.

This poor creature might indeed be called simplicity itself. She was one of that order of mortals who are apt to believe everything which is said to them, to whom nature hath neither indulged the offensive nor defensive weapons of deceit, and who are consequently liable to be imposed upon by any one who will only be at the expense of a little falsehood for that purpose. Mrs. Western, having drained Mrs. Miller of all she knew, which indeed was but little, but which was sufficient to make the aunt suspect a great deal, dismissed her with assurances that Sophia would not see her, that she would send no answer to the letter nor ever receive another; nor did she suffer her to depart without a handsome lecture on the merits of an office to which she could afford no better name than that of procuress. This discovery had greatly discomposed her temper, when, coming into the apartment next to that in which the lovers were, she overheard Sophia very warmly protesting against his lordship's addresses. At which the rage already kindled burst forth, and she rushed in upon her niece in a most furious manner, as we have already described, together with what passed at that time till his lordship's departure.

No sooner was Lord Fellamar gone than Mrs. Western returned to Sophia, whom she upbraided in the most bitter terms for the ill use she had made of the confidence reposed in her, and for her treachery in conversing with a man with whom she had offered but the day before to bind herself in the most solemn oath never more to have any conversation. Sophia protested she had maintained no such conversation. "How, how, Miss Western!" said the aunt. "Will you deny your receiving a letter from him yesterday?" "A letter, madam!" answered Sophia, somewhat surprised. "It is not very well-bred, miss," replies the aunt, "to repeat my words. I say a letter, and I insist upon your showing it me immediately." "I scorn a lie, madam," said Sophia; "I did receive a letter, but it was without my desire and indeed I may say against my consent." "Indeed, indeed, miss," cries the aunt, "you ought to be ashamed of owning you had received it at all, but where is the letter? For I will see it."

To this peremptory demand Sophia paused some time before she returned an answer, and at last only excused herself by declaring she had not the letter in her pocket, which was indeed true; upon which her aunt, losing all manner of patience, asked her niece this short question: whether she would resolve to marry Lord Fellamar or no. To which she received the strongest negative. Mrs. Western then replied with an oath, or something very like one, that she would early the next morning deliver her back into her father's hands.

Sophia then began to reason with her aunt in the following manner: "Why, madam, must I of necessity be forced to marry at all? Consider how cruel you would have thought it in your own case and how much kinder your parents were in leaving you to your liberty. What have I done to forfeit this liberty? I will never marry contrary to my father's consent nor without asking yours. And when I ask the consent of either improperly, it will be then time enough to force some other marriage upon me." "Can I bear to hear this," cries Mrs. Western, "from a girl who hath now a letter from a murderer in her pocket?" "I have no such letter, I promise you," answered Sophia; "and if he be a murderer, he will soon be in no condition to give you any further disturbance." "How, Miss Western," said the aunt, "have you the assurance to speak of him in this manner, to own your affection for such a villain, to my face!" "Sure, madam," said Sophia, "you put a very strange construction on my words." "Indeed, Miss Western," cries the lady, "I shall not bear this usage; you have learnt of your father this manner of treating me; he hath taught you to give me the lie. He hath totally ruined you by his false system of education, and please heaven, he shall have the comfort of its fruits; for once more I declare to you that to-morrow morning I will carry you back. I will withdraw all my forces from the field, and remain henceforth like the wise King of Prussia in a state of perfect neutrality. You are both too wise to be regulated by my measures, so prepare yourself, for to-morrow morning you shall evacuate this house."

Sophia remonstrated all she could, but her aunt was deaf to all she said. In this resolution, therefore, we must at present leave her, as there seems to be no hopes of bringing her to change it.

9

WHAT HAPPENED TO MR. JONES IN THE PRISON

Mr. Jones passed above twenty-four melancholy hours by himself, unless when relieved by the company of Partridge, before Mr. Nightingale returned; not that this worthy young man had deserted or forgot his friend, for indeed he had been much the greatest part of the time employed in his service.

He had heard upon inquiry that the only persons who had seen the beginning of the unfortunate rencounter were a crew belonging to a man-of-war which then lay at Deptford.

To Deptford, therefore, he went in search of this crew, where he was informed that the men he sought after were all gone ashore. He then traced them from place to place till at last he found two of them drinking together with a third person at a hedge-tavern near Aldersgate.

Nightingale desired to speak with Jones by himself (for Partridge was in the room when he came in). As soon as they were alone, Nightingale, taking Jones by the hand, cried, "Come, my brave friend, be not too much dejected at what I am going to tell you; I am sorry I am the messenger of bad news, but I think it my duty to tell you." "I guess already what that bad news is," cries Jones. "The poor gentleman, then, is dead." "I hope not," answered Nightingale. "He was alive this morning, though I will not flatter you; I fear from the accounts I could get that his wound is mortal. But if the affair be exactly as you told it, your own remorse would be all you would have reason to apprehend, let what would happen; but forgive me, my dear Tom, if I entreat you to make the worst of your story to your friends. If you disguise anything to us, you will only be an enemy to yourself."

"What reason, my dear Jack, have I ever given you," said Jones, "to stab me with so cruel a suspicion?" "Have patience," cries Nightingale, "and I will tell you all. After the most diligent inquiry I could make, I at last met with two of the fellows who were present at this unhappy accident, and I am sorry to say they do not relate the story so much in your favour as you yourself have told it." "Why, what do they say?" cries Jones. "Indeed, what I am sorry to repeat, as I am afraid of the consequence of it to you. They say that they were at too great a distance to overhear any words that passed between you, but they both agree that the first blow was given by you." "Then, upon my soul," answered Jones, "they injure me. He not only struck me first, but struck me without the least provocation. What should induce those villains to accuse me falsely?" "Nay, that I cannot guess," said Nightingale, "and if you yourself and I who am so heartily your friend cannot conceive a reason why they should belie you, what reason will an indifferent court of justice be able to assign why they should not believe them? I repeated the question to them several times, and so did another gentleman who was present, who, I believe, is a seafaring man, and who really acted a very friendly part by you; for he begged them often to consider that there was the life of a man in the case, and asked them over and over if they were certain, to which they both answered that they were and would abide by their evidence upon oath. For heaven's sake, my dear friend, recollect yourself; for if this should appear to be the fact, it will be your business to think in time of making the best of your interest. I would not shock you, but you know, I believe, the severity of the law, whatever verbal provocations may have been given you." "Alas, my friend," cries Jones, "what interest hath such a wretch as I? Besides, do you think I would even wish to live with the reputation of a murderer? If I had any friends (as, alas, I have none), could I have the confidence to solicit them to speak in the behalf of a man condemned for the blackest crime in human nature? Believe me, I have no such hope, but I have some reliance on a throne still greatly superior, which will, I am certain, afford me all the protection I merit."

He then concluded with many solemn and vehement protestations of the truth of what he had at first asserted.

The faith of Nightingale was now again staggered, and began to incline to credit his friend, when Mrs. Miller appeared and made a sorrowful report of the success of her embassy, which when Jones had heard, he cried out most heroically, "Well, my friend, I am now indifferent as to what shall happen, at least with regard to my life, and if it be the will of heaven that I shall make an atonement with that for the blood I have spilt, I hope the divine goodness will one day suffer my honour to be cleared, and that the words of a dying man at least will be believed, so far as to justify his character."

A very mournful scene now passed between the prisoner and his friends, at which, as few readers would have been pleased to be present, so few, I believe, will desire to hear it particularly related. We will, therefore, pass on to the entrance of the turnkey, who acquainted Jones that there was a lady without who desired to speak with him when he was at leisure.

Jones declared his surprise at this message. He said he knew no lady in the world whom he could possibly expect to see there. However, as he saw no reason to decline seeing any person, Mrs. Miller and Mr. Nightingale presently took their leave, and he gave orders to have the lady admitted.

If Jones was surprised at the news of a visit from a lady, how greatly was he astonished when he discovered this lady to be no other than Mrs. Waters! In this astonishment, then, we shall leave him awhile in order to cure the surprise of the reader, who will likewise, probably, not a little wonder at the arrival of this lady.

Who this Mrs. Waters was the reader pretty well knows; what she was he must be perfectly satisfied. He will, therefore, be pleased to remember that this lady departed from Upton in the same coach with Mr. Fitzpatrick and the other Irish gentleman, and in their company travelled to the Bath.

Now, there was a certain office in the gift of Mr. Fitzpatrick at that time vacant: namely, that of a wife; for the lady who had lately filled that office had resigned or at least deserted her duty. Mr. Fitzpatrick, therefore, having thoroughly examined Mrs. Waters on the road, found her extremely fit for the place, which on their arrival at Bath he presently conferred upon her, and she without any scruple accepted. As husband and wife this gentleman and lady continued together all the time they stayed at Bath, and as husband and wife they arrived together in town.

Whether Mr. Fitzpatrick was so wise a man as not to part with one good thing till he had secured another, which he had at present only a prospect of regaining, or whether Mrs. Waters had so well discharged her office that he intended still to retain her as principal and to make his wife (as is often the case) only her deputy, I will not say; but certain it is, he never mentioned his wife to her, never communicated to her the letter given him by Mrs. Western, nor ever once hinted his purpose of repossessing his wife; much less did he ever mention the name of Jones. For though he intended to fight with him wherever he met him, he did not imitate those prudent persons who think a wife, a mother, a sister, or sometimes a whole family the safest seconds on these occasions. The first account, therefore, which she had of all this was delivered to her from his lips after he was brought home from the tavern where his wound had been dressed.

As Mr. Fitzpatrick, however, had not the clearest way of telling a story at any time, and was now, perhaps, a little more confused than usual, it was some time before she discovered that the gentleman who had given him this wound was the very same person from whom her heart had received a wound, which, though not of a mortal kind, was yet so deep that it had left a considerable scar behind it. But no sooner was she acquainted that Mr. Jones himself was the man who had been committed to the Gatehouse for this supposed murder than she took the first opportunity of committing Mr. Fitzpatrick to the care of his nurse, and hastened away to visit the conqueror.

She now entered the room with an air of gaiety, which received an immediate check from the melancholy aspect of poor Jones, who started and blessed himself when he saw her. Upon which she said, "Nay, I do not wonder at your surprise; I believe you did not expect to see me, for few gentlemen are troubled here with visits from any lady, unless a wife. You see the power you have over me, Mr. Jones. Indeed, I little thought when we parted at Upton that our next meeting would have been in such a place." "Indeed, madam," says Jones, "I must look upon this visit as kind; few will follow the miserable, especially to such dismal habitations." "I protest, Mr. Jones," says she, "I can hardly persuade myself you are the same agreeable fellow I saw at Upton. Why, your face is more miserable than any dungeon in the universe. What can be the matter with you?" "I thought, madam," said Jones, "as you knew of my being here, you knew the unhappy reason." "Pugh," says she, "you have pinked a man in a duel, that's all." Jones expressed some indignation at this levity and spoke with the utmost contrition for what had happened. To which she answered, "Well, then, sir, if you take it so much to heart, I will relieve you; the gentleman is not dead, and I am pretty confident is in no danger of dying. The surgeon, indeed, who first dressed him was a young fellow and seemed desirous of representing his case to be as bad as possible that he might have the more honour from curing him, but the King's surgeon hath seen him since and says, unless from a fever, of which there are at present no symptoms, he apprehends not the least danger of life." Jones showed great satisfaction in his countenance at this report, upon which she affirmed the truth of it, adding, "By the most extraordinary accident in the world I lodge at the same house and have seen the gentleman, and I promise you he doth you justice and says, whatever be the consequence, that he was entirely the aggressor and that you was not in the least to blame."

Jones expressed the utmost satisfaction at the account which Mrs. Waters brought him. He then informed her of many things which she well knew before, as who Mr. Fitzpatrick was, the occasion of his resentment, &c. He likewise told her several facts of which she was ignorant, as the adventure of the muff and other particulars, concealing only the name of Sophia. He then lamented the follies and vices of which he had been guilty, every one of which, he said, had been attended with such ill consequences that he should be unpardonable if he did not take warning and quit those vicious courses for the future. He lastly concluded with assuring her of his resolution to sin no more lest a worse thing should happen to him.

Mrs. Waters with great pleasantry ridiculed all this as the effects of low spirits and confinement. She repeated some witticisms about the Devil when he was sick, and told him she doubted not but shortly to see him at liberty and as lively a fellow as ever; "and then," says she, "I don't question but your conscience will be safely delivered of all these qualms that it is now so sick in breeding."

Many more things of this kind she uttered, some of which it would do her no great honour, in the opinion of some readers, to remember; nor are we quite certain but that the answers made by Jones would be treated with ridicule by others. We shall therefore suppress the rest of this conversation, and only observe that it ended at last with perfect innocence, and much more to the satisfaction of Jones than of the lady; for the former was greatly transported with the news she had brought him, but the latter was not altogether so pleased with the penitential behaviour of a man whom she had at her first interview conceived a very different opinion of from what she now entertained of him.

Thus, the melancholy occasioned by the report of Mr. Nightingale was pretty well effaced, but the dejection into which Mrs. Miller had thrown him still continued. The account she gave so well tallied with the words of Sophia herself in her letter that he made not the least doubt but that she had disclosed the letter to her aunt and had taken a fixed resolution to abandon him. The torments this thought gave him were to be equalled only by a piece of news which Fortune yet had in store for him, and which we shall communicate in the second chapter of the ensuing book.

BOOK XVIII

1

A FAREWELL TO THE READER

We are now, reader, arrived at the last stage of our long journey. As we have therefore travelled together through so many pages, let us behave to one another like fellow-travellers in a stage-coach who have passed several days in the company of each other, and who, notwithstanding any bickerings or little animosities which may have occurred on the road, generally make all up at last and mount for the last time into their vehicle with cheerfulness and good humour; since after this one stage it may possibly happen to us, as it commonly happens to them, never to meet more.

As I have here taken up this simile, give me leave to carry it a little farther. I intend, then, in this last book to imitate the good company I have mentioned in their last journey. Now, it is well known that all jokes and raillery are at this time laid aside; whatever characters any of the passengers have for the jest's sake personated on the road are now thrown off, and the conversation is usually plain and serious.

In the same manner, if I have now and then in the course of this work indulged any pleasantry for thy entertainment, I shall here lay it down. The variety of matter, indeed, which I shall be obliged to cram into this book will afford no room for any of those ludicrous observations which I have elsewhere made, and which may sometimes, perhaps, have prevented thee from taking a nap when it was beginning to steal upon thee. In this last book thou wilt find nothing (or at most very little) of that nature. All will be plain narrative only, and indeed, when thou hast perused the many great events which this book will produce, thou wilt think the number of pages contained in it scarce sufficient to tell the story.

And now, my friend, I take this opportunity (as I shall have no other) of heartily wishing thee well. If I have been an entertaining companion to thee, I promise thee it is what I have desired. If in anything I have offended, it was really without any intention. Some things, perhaps, here said may have hit thee or thy friends, but I do most solemnly declare they were not pointed at them. I question not but thou hast been told among other stories of me that thou wast to travel with a very scurrilous fellow; but whoever told thee so did me an injury. No man detests and despises scurrility more than myself, nor hath any man more reason, for none has ever been treated with more; and what is a very severe fate, I have had some of the abusive writings of those very men fathered upon me, who in other of their works have abused me themselves with the utmost virulence.

All these works, however, I am well convinced will be dead long before this page shall offer itself to thy perusal; for however short the period may be of my own performances, they will most probably outlive their own infirm author and the weakly productions of his abusive contemporaries.

2

CONTAINING A VERY TRAGICAL INCIDENT

While Jones was employed in these unpleasant meditations, with which we left him tormenting himself, Partridge came stumbling into the room with his face paler than ashes, his eyes fixed in his head, his hair standing on end, and every limb trembling. In short, he looked as he would have done had he seen a spectre, or had he, indeed, been a spectre himself.

Jones, who was little subject to fear, could not avoid being somewhat shocked at this sudden appearance. He did indeed himself change colour, and his voice a little faltered while he asked him what was the matter.

"I hope, sir," said Partridge, "you will not be angry with me. Indeed, I did not listen, but I was obliged to stay in the outward room. I am sure I wish I had been a hundred miles off rather than have heard what I have heard." "Why, what is the matter?" said Jones. "The matter, sir? Oh, good heaven!" answered Partridge. "Was that woman who is just gone out the woman who was with you at Upton?" "She was, Partridge," cries Jones. "And did you really, sir, go to bed with that woman?" said he trembling. "I am afraid what passed between us is no secret," said Jones. "Nay, but pray, sir, for heaven's sake, sir, answer me," cries Partridge. "You know I did," cries Jones. "Why, then, the Lord have mercy upon your soul and forgive you," cries Partridge, "but as sure as I stand here alive, you have been abed with your own mother."

Upon these words, Jones became in a moment a greater picture of horror than Partridge himself. He was, indeed, for some time struck dumb with amazement, and both stood staring wildly at each other. At last his words found way, and in an interrupted voice he said, "How! How! What's this you tell me?" "Nay, sir," cries Partridge, "I have not breath enough left to tell you now—but what I have said is most certainly true: that woman who now went out is your own mother. How unlucky was it for you, sir, that I did not happen to see her at that time to have prevented it. Sure the Devil himself must have contrived to bring about this wickedness."

"Sure," cries Jones, "Fortune will never have done with me till she hath driven me to distraction. But why do I blame Fortune? I am myself the cause of all my misery. All the dreadful mischiefs which have befallen me are the consequences only of my own folly and vice. What thou hast told me, Partridge, hath almost deprived me of my senses. And was Mrs. Waters, then—but why do I ask? For thou must certainly know her. If thou hast any affection for me, nay, if thou hast any pity, let me beseech thee to fetch this miserable woman back again to me. Oh, good heavens! Incest —with a mother! To what am I reserved?" He then fell into the most violent and frantic agonies of grief and despair, in which Partridge declared he would not leave him, but at last, having vented the first torrent of passion, he came a little to himself; and then, having acquainted Partridge that he would find this wretched woman in the same house where the wounded gentleman was lodged, he dispatched him in quest of her.

If the reader will please to refresh his memory by turning to the scene at Upton in the ninth book, he will be apt to admire the many strange accidents which unfortunately prevented any interview between Partridge and Mrs. Waters when she spent a whole day there with Mr. Jones. Instances of this kind we may frequently observe in life, where the greatest events are produced by a nice train of little circumstances, and more than one example of this may be discovered by the accurate eye in this our history.

After a fruitless search of two or three hours, Partridge returned back to his master without having seen Mrs. Waters. Jones, who was in a state of desperation at his delay, was almost raving mad when he brought him this account. He was not long, however, in this condition before he received the following letter:

Sir,

Since I left you, I have seen a gentleman from whom I have learnt something concerning you which greatly surprises and affects me, but as I have not at present leisure to communicate a matter of such high importance, you must suspend your curiosity till our next meeting, which shall be the first moment I am able to see you. Oh, Mr. Jones, little did I think when I passed that happy day at Upton, the reflection upon which is like to embitter all my future life, who it was to whom I owed such perfect happiness. Believe me to be ever sincerely your unfortunate

J. WATERS.

P.S. I would have you comfort yourself as much as possible, for Mr. Fitzpatrick is in no manner of danger; so that whatever other grievous crimes you may have to repent of, the guilt of blood is not among the number.

Jones, having received the letter, let it drop (for he was unable to hold it, and indeed had scarce the use of any one of his faculties). Partridge took it up and, having received consent by silence, read it likewise; nor had it upon him a less sensible effect. The pencil and not the pen should describe the horrors which appeared in both their countenances. While they both remained speechless the turnkey entered the room, and without taking any notice of what sufficiently discovered itself in the faces of them both, acquainted Jones that a man without desired to speak with him. This person was presently introduced, and was no other than Black George.

As sights of horror were not so usual to George as they were to the turnkey, he instantly saw the great disorder which appeared in the face of Jones. This he imputed to the accident that had happened, which was reported in the very worst light in Mr. Western's family; he concluded, therefore, that the gentleman was dead and that Mr. Jones was in a fair way of coming to a shameful end. A thought which gave him much uneasiness; for George was of a compassionate disposition and notwithstanding a small breach of friendship which he had been overtempted to commit, was in the main not insensible of the obligations he had formerly received from Mr. Jones.

The poor fellow, therefore, scarce refrained from a tear at the present sight. He told Jones he was heartily sorry for his misfortunes and begged him to consider if he could be of any manner of service. "Perhaps, sir," said he, "you may want a little matter of money upon this occasion; if you do, sir, what little I have is heartily at your service."

Jones shook him very heartily by the hand and gave him many thanks for the kind offer he had made, but answered he had not the least want of that kind. Upon which George began to press his services more eagerly than before. Jones again thanked him, with assurances that he wanted nothing which was in the power of any man living to give. "Come, come, my good master," answered George, "do not take the matter so much to heart. Things may end better than you imagine; to be sure, you ant the first gentleman who hath killed a man and yet come off." "You are wide of the matter, George," said Partridge; "the gentleman is not dead nor like to die. Don't disturb my master at present, for he is troubled about a matter in which it is not in your power to do him any good." "You don't know what I may be able to do, Mr. Partridge," answered George. "If his concern is about my young lady, I have some news to tell my master." "What do you say, Mr. George?" cried Jones. "Hath anything lately happened in which my Sophia is concerned? My Sophia! How dares such a wretch as I mention her so profanely." "I hope she will be yours yet," answered George. "Why, yes, sir, I have something to tell you about her. Madam Western has just brought Madam Sophia home, and there hath been a terrible to-do. I could not possibly learn

793

the very right of it, but my master he hath been in a vast big passion and so was Madam Western, and I heard her say as she went out of doors into her chair that she would never set her foot in master's house again. I don't know what's the matter, not I, but everything was very quiet when I came out; but Robin, who waited at supper, said he had never seen the squire for a long while in such good humour with young madam; that he kissed her several times, and swore she should be her own mistress and he would never think of confining her any more. I thought this news would please you and so I slipped out, though it was so late, to inform you of it." Mr. Jones assured George that it did greatly please him; for though he should never more presume to lift his eyes towards that incomparable creature, nothing could so much relieve his misery as the satisfaction he should always have in hearing of her welfare.

The rest of the conversation which passed at the visit is not important enough to be here related. The reader will therefore forgive us this abrupt breaking off, and be pleased to hear how this great goodwill of the squire towards his daughter was brought about.

Mrs. Western, on her first arrival at her brother's lodging, began to set forth the great honours and advantages which would accrue to the family by the match with Lord Fellamar, which her niece had absolutely refused; in which refusal, when the squire took the part of his daughter, she fell immediately into the most violent passion and so irritated and provoked the squire that neither his patience nor his prudence could bear any longer; upon which there ensued between them both so warm a bout at altercation that perhaps the regions of Billingsgate never equalled it. In the heat of this scolding, Mrs. Western departed, and had consequently no leisure to acquaint her brother with the letter which Sophia received, which might have possibly produced ill effects; but to say the truth, I believe it never once occurred to her memory at this time.

When Mrs. Western was gone, Sophia, who had been hitherto silent, as well indeed from necessity as inclination, began to return the compliment which her father had made her in taking her part against the aunt by taking his likewise against the lady. This was the first time of her so doing, and it was in the highest degree acceptable to the squire. Again, he remembered that Mr. Allworthy had insisted on an entire relinquishment of all violent means, and indeed, as he made no doubt but that Jones would be hanged, he did not in the least question succeeding with his daughter by fair means; he now therefore once more gave a loose to his natural fondness for her, which had such an effect on the dutiful, grateful, tender, and affectionate heart of Sophia that had her honour given to Jones and something else, perhaps, in which he was concerned been removed, I much doubt whether she would not have sacrificed herself to a man she did not like to have obliged her father. She promised him she would make it the whole business of her life to oblige him, and would never marry any man against his consent, which brought the old man so near to his highest happiness that he was resolved to take the other step and went to bed completely drunk.

3

ALLWORTHY VISITS OLD NIGHTINGALE; WITH A STRANGE
DISCOVERY THAT HE MADE ON THAT OCCASION

The morning after these things had happened, Mr. Allworthy went according to his promise to visit old Nightingale, with whom his authority was so great that after having sat with him three hours, he at last prevailed with him to consent to see his son.

Here an accident happened of a very extraordinary kind; one indeed of those strange chances whence very good and grave men have concluded that Providence often interposes in the discovery of the most secret villainy in order to caution men from quitting the paths of honesty, however warily they tread in those of vice.

Mr. Allworthy at his entrance into Mr. Nightingale's saw Black George; he took no notice of him, nor did Black George imagine he had perceived him. However, when their conversation on the principal point was over, Allworthy asked Nightingale whether he knew one George Seagrim, and upon what business he came to his house. "Yes," answered Nightingale, "I know him very well, and a most extraordinary fellow he is, who in these days hath been able to hoard up £500 from renting a very small estate of £30 a year." "And is this the story which he hath told you?" cries Allworthy. "Nay, it is true, I promise you," said Nightingale, "for I have the money now in my own hands in five bank-bills, which I am to lay out either in a mortgage or in some purchase in the north of England." The bank-bills were no sooner produced at Allworthy's desire than he blessed himself at the strangeness of the discovery. He presently told Nightingale that these bank-bills were formerly his, and then acquainted him with the whole affair. As there are no men who complain more of the frauds of business than highwaymen, gamesters, and other thieves of that kind, so there are none who so bitterly exclaim against the frauds of gamesters, &c., as usurers, brokers, and other thieves of this kind; whether it be that the one way of cheating is a discountenance or reflection upon the other, or that money, which is the common mistress of all cheats, makes them regard each other in the light of rivals, but Nightingale no sooner heard the story than he exclaimed against the fellow in terms much severer than the justice and honesty of Allworthy had bestowed on him.

Allworthy desired Nightingale to retain both the money and the secret till he should hear farther from him, and if he should in the meantime see the fellow, that he would not take the least notice to him of the discovery which he had made. He then returned to his lodgings, where he found Mrs. Miller in a very dejected condition on account of the information she had received from her son-in-law. Mr. Allworthy with great cheerfulness told her that he had much good news to communicate, and with little further preface acquainted her that he had brought Mr. Nightingale to consent to see his son, and did not in the least doubt to effect a perfect reconciliation between them, though he found the father more soured by another accident of the same kind which had happened in his family. He then mentioned the running away of the uncle's daughter, which he had been told by the old gentleman, and which Mrs. Miller and her son-in-law did not yet know.

The reader may suppose Mrs. Miller received this account with great thankfulness and no less pleasure, but so uncommon was her friendship to Jones that I am not certain whether the uneasiness she suffered for his sake did not overbalance her satisfaction at hearing a piece of news tending so much to the happiness of her own family; nor whether even this very news, as it reminded her of the obligations she had to Jones, did not hurt as well as please her, when her grateful heart said to her, "While my own family is happy, how miserable is the poor creature to whose generosity we owe the beginning of all this happiness."

Allworthy, having left her a little while to chew the cud (if I may use that expression) on these first tidings, told her he had still something more to impart, which he believed would give her pleasure. "I think," said he, "I have discovered a pretty considerable treasure belonging to the young gentleman, your friend; but perhaps, indeed, his present situation may be such that it will be of no service to him." The latter part of the speech gave Mrs. Miller to understand who was meant and she answered with a sigh, "I hope not, sir." "I hope so too," cries Allworthy, "with all my heart, but my nephew told me this morning he had heard a very bad account of the affair." "Good heaven, sir," said she. "Well, I must not speak, and yet it is certainly very hard to be obliged to hold one's tongue when one hears——" "Madam," said Allworthy, "you may say whatever you please; you know me too well to think I have a prejudice against any one, and as for that young man, I assure you I should be heartily pleased to find he could acquit himself of everything, and particularly of this sad affair. You can testify the affection I have formerly borne him. The world, I know, censured me for loving him so much. I did not withdraw that affection from him without thinking I had the justest cause. Believe me, Mrs. Miller, I should be glad to find I have been mistaken." Mrs. Miller was going eagerly to reply when a servant acquainted her that a gentleman without desired to speak with her immediately. Allworthy then inquired for his nephew, and was told that he had been for some time in his room with the gentleman who used to come to him and whom Mr. Allworthy, guessing rightly to be Mr. Dowling, he desired presently to speak with him.

When Dowling attended, Allworthy put the case of the bank-notes to him without mentioning any name, and asked in what manner such a person might be punished. To which Dowling answered he thought he might be indicted on the Black Act, but said as it was a matter of some nicety, it would be proper to go to counsel. He said he was to attend counsel presently upon an affair of Mr. Western's, and if Mr. Allworthy pleased, he would lay the case before them. This was agreed to, and then Mrs. Miller, opening the door, cried, "I ask pardon, I did not know you had company," but Allworthy desired her to come in, saying he had finished his business. Upon which Mr. Dowling withdrew and Mrs. Miller introduced Mr. Nightingale the younger, to return thanks for the great kindness done him by Allworthy, but she had scarce patience to let the young gentleman finish his speech before she interrupted him, saying, "Oh, sir, Mr. Nightingale brings great news about poor Mr. Jones; he hath been to see the wounded gentleman, who is out of all danger of death, and what is more, declares he fell upon poor Mr. Jones himself and beat him. I am sure, sir, you would not have Mr. Jones be a coward. If I was a man myself, I am sure if any man was to strike me I should draw my sword. Do pray, my dear, tell Mr. Allworthy, tell him all yourself." Nightingale then confirmed what Mrs. Miller had said, and concluded with many handsome things of Jones, who was, he said, one of the best-natured fellows in the world and not in the least inclined to be quarrelsome. Here Nightingale was going to cease when Mrs. Miller again begged him to relate all the many dutiful expressions he had heard him make use of towards Mr. Allworthy. "To say the utmost good of Mr. Allworthy," cries Nightingale, "is doing no more than strict justice, and can have no merit in it; but indeed I must say no man can be more sensible of the obligations he hath to so good a man than is poor Jones. Indeed, sir, I am convinced the weight of your displeasure is the heaviest burden he lies under. He hath often lamented it to me, and hath as often protested in the most solemn manner he had never been intentionally guilty of any offence towards you; nay, he hath sworn he would rather die a thousand deaths than he would have his conscience upbraid him with one disrespectful, ungrateful, or undutiful thought towards you. But I ask pardon, sir, I am afraid I presume to intermeddle too far in so tender a point." "You have spoke no more than what a Christian ought," cries Mrs. Miller. "Indeed, Mr. Nightingale," answered Allworthy, "I applaud your generous friendship and I wish he may merit it of you. I confess I am glad to hear the report you bring from this unfortunate gentleman, and if that matter should turn out to be as you represent it (and indeed I doubt nothing of what you say), I may perhaps in time be brought to think better than lately I have of this young man; for this good gentlewoman here, nay, all who know me, can witness that I loved him as dearly as if he had been my own son. Indeed, I have considered him as a child sent by Fortune to my care. I still remember the innocent, the helpless, situation in which I found him. I feel the tender pressure of his little hands at this moment. He was my darling, indeed he was." At which words he ceased, and the tears stood in his eyes.

As the answer which Mrs. Miller made may lead us into fresh matters, we will here stop to account for the visible alteration in Mr. Allworthy's mind and the abatement of his anger to Jones. Revolutions of this kind, it is true, do frequently occur in histories and dramatic writers for no other reason than because the history or play draws to a conclusion, and are justified by authority of authors, yet though we insist upon as much authority as any author whatever, we shall use this power very sparingly, and never but when we are driven to it by necessity, which we do not at present foresee will happen in this work.

This alteration, then, in the mind of Mr. Allworthy was occasioned by a letter he had just received from Mr. Square, and which we shall give the reader in the beginning of the next chapter.

4

CONTAINING TWO LETTERS IN VERY DIFFERENT STYLES

"MY WORTHY FRIEND,

"I informed you in my last that I was forbidden the use of the waters, as they were found by experience rather to increase than lessen the symptoms of my distemper. I must now acquaint you with a piece of news which, I believe, will afflict my friends more than it hath afflicted me: Dr. Harrington and Dr. Brewster have informed me that there is no hopes of my recovery.

"I have somewhere read that the great use of philosophy is to learn to die. I will not therefore so far disgrace mine as to show any surprise at receiving a lesson which I must be thought to have so long studied. Yet, to say the truth, one page of the Gospel teaches this lesson better than all the volumes of ancient or modern philosophers. The assurance it gives of another life is a much stronger support to a good mind than all the consolations that are drawn from the necessity of nature, the emptiness or satiety of our enjoyments here, or any other topic of those declamations which are sometimes capable of arming our minds with a stubborn patience in bearing the thoughts of death, but never of raising them to a real contempt of it, and much less of making us think it a real good. I would not here be understood to throw the horrid censure of atheism or even the absolute denial of immortality on all who are called philosophers. Many of that sect, as well ancient as modern, have from the light of reason discovered some hopes of a future state, but in reality that light was so faint and glimmering and the hopes were so uncertain and precarious that it may be justly doubted on which side their belief turned. Plato himself concludes his *Phaedon* with declaring that his best arguments amount only to raise a probability, and Cicero himself rather to profess an inclination to believe than any actual belief in the doctrines of immortality. As to myself, to be very sincere with you, I never was much in earnest in this faith till I was in earnest a Christian.

"You will perhaps wonder at the latter expression, but I assure you it hath not been till very lately that I could with truth call myself so. The pride of philosophy had intoxicated my reason, and the sublimest of all wisdom appeared to me, as it did to the Greeks of old, to be foolishness. God hath, however, been so gracious to show me my error in time and to bring me into the way of truth before I sunk into utter darkness forever.

"I find myself beginning to grow weak; I shall therefore hasten to the main purpose of this letter.

"When I reflect on the actions of my past life, I know of nothing which sits heavier upon my conscience than the injustice I have been guilty of to that poor wretch, your adopted son. I have not, indeed, only connived at the villainy of others, but been myself active in injustice towards him. Believe me, my dear friend, when I tell you, on the word of a dying man, he hath been basely injured. As to the principal fact, upon the misrepresentation of which you discarded him. I solemnly assure you he is innocent. When you lay upon your supposed death-bed, he was the only person in the house who testified any real concern, and what happened afterwards arose from the wildness of his joy on your recovery, and, I am sorry to say it, from the baseness of another person (but it is my desire to justify the innocent and to accuse none). Believe me, my friend, this young man hath the noblest generosity of heart, the most perfect capacity for friendship, the highest integrity, and, indeed, every virtue which can ennoble a man. He hath some faults, but among them is not to be numbered the least want of duty or gratitude towards you. On the contrary, I am satisfied when you dismissed him from your house, his heart bled for you more than for himself.

"Worldly motives were the wicked and base reasons of my concealing this from you so long; to reveal it now I can have no inducement but the desire of serving the cause of truth, of doing right to the innocent, and of making all the amends in my power for a past offence. I hope this declaration, therefore, will have the effect desired and will restore this deserving young man to your favour, the hearing of which while I am yet alive will afford the utmost consolation to, sir, your most obliged, obedient, humble servant,

THOMAS SQUARE."

The reader will after this scarce wonder at the revolution so visibly appearing in Mr. Allworthy, notwithstanding he received from Thwackum by the same post another letter of a very different kind, which we shall here add, as it may possibly be the last time we shall have occasion to mention the name of that gentleman.

"Sir,
"I am not at all surprised at hearing from your worthy nephew a fresh instance of the villainy of Mr. Jones, the atheist's young pupil. I shall not wonder at any murders he may commit, and I heartily pray that your own blood may not seal up his final commitment to the place of wailing and gnashing of teeth.

"Though you cannot want sufficient calls to repentance for the many unwarrantable weaknesses exemplified in your behaviour to this wretch, so much to the prejudice of your own lawful family and of your character. I say, though these may sufficiently be supposed to prick and goad your conscience at this season, I would yet be wanting to my duty if I spared to give you some admonition in order to bring you to a due sense of your errors. I therefore pray you seriously to consider the judgement which is likely to overtake this wicked villain, and let it serve at least as a warning to you that you may not for the future despise the advice of one who is so indefatigable in his prayers for your welfare.

"Had not my hand been withheld from due correction, I had scourged much of this diabolical spirit out of a boy of whom from his infancy I discovered the Devil had taken such entire possession; but reflections of this kind now come too late.

"I am sorry you have given away the living of Westerton so hastily. I should have applied on that occasion earlier had I thought you would not have acquainted me previous to the disposition. Your objection to pluralities is being righteous overmuch. If there were any crime in the practice, so many godly men would not agree to it. If the vicar of Aldergrove should die (as we hear he is in a declining way), I hope you will think of me, since I am certain you must be convinced of my most sincere attachment to your highest welfare—a welfare to which all worldly considerations are as trifling as the small tithes mentioned in Scripture are when compared to the weighty matters of the law.

"I am, sir, your faithful, humble servant,

ROGER THWACKUM."

This was the first time Thwackum ever wrote in this authoritative style to Allworthy, and of this he had afterwards sufficient reason to repent, as in the case of those who mistake the highest degree of goodness for the lowest degree of weakness. Allworthy had, indeed, never liked this man. He knew him to be proud and ill-natured; he also knew that his divinity itself was tinctured with his temper and such as in many respects he himself did by no means approve, but he was at the same time an excellent scholar and most indefatigable in teaching the two lads. Add to this the strict severity of his life and manners, an unimpeached honesty, and a most devout attachment to religion. So that upon the whole, though Allworthy did not esteem nor love the man, yet he could never bring himself to part with a tutor to the boys who was both by learning and industry extremely well qualified for his office, and he hoped that as they were bred up in his own house and under his own eye, he should be able to correct whatever was wrong in Thwackum's instructions.

IN WHICH THE HISTORY IS CONTINUED

Mr. Allworthy in his last speech had recollected some tender ideas concerning Jones, which had brought tears into the good man's eyes. This Mrs. Miller observing, said, "Yes, yes, sir, your goodness to this poor young man is known, notwithstanding all your care to conceal it, but there is not a single syllable of truth in what those villains said. Mr. Nightingale hath now discovered the whole matter. It seems these fellows were employed by a lord, who is a rival of poor Mr. Jones, to have pressed him on board a ship. I assure them I don't know who they will press next. Mr. Nightingale here hath seen the officer himself, who is a very pretty gentleman, and hath told him all, and is very sorry for what he undertook, which he would never have done had he known Mr. Jones to have been a gentleman, but he was told that he was a common strolling vagabond."

Allworthy stared at all this and declared he was a stranger to every word she said. "Yes, sir," answered she, "I believe you are. It is a very different story, I believe, from what those fellows told the lawyer."

"What lawyer, madam? What is it you mean?" said Allworthy. "Nay, nay," said she, "this is so like you to deny your own goodness, but Mr. Nightingale here saw him." "Saw whom, madam?" answered he. "Why, your lawyer, sir," said she, "that you so kindly sent to inquire into the affair." "I am still in the dark, upon my honour," said Allworthy. "Why, then, do you tell him, my dear sir," cries she. "Indeed, sir," said Nightingale, "I did see that very lawyer who went from you when I came into the room at an ale-house in Aldersgate, in company with two of the fellows who were employed by Lord Fellamar to press Mr. Jones and who were by that means present at the unhappy rencounter between him and Mr. Fitzpatrick." "I own, sir," said Mrs. Miller, "when I saw this gentleman come into the room to you, I told Mr. Nightingale that I apprehended you had sent him thither to inquire into the affair." Allworthy showed marks of astonishment in his countenance at this news, and was, indeed, for two or three minutes struck dumb by it. At last, addressing himself to Mr. Nightingale, he said, "I must confess myself, sir, more surprised at what you tell me than I have ever been before at anything in my whole life. Are you certain this was the gentleman?" "I am most certain," answered Nightingale. "At Aldersgate?" cries Allworthy. "And was you in company with this lawyer and the two fellows?" "I was, sir," said the other, "very near half an hour." "Well, sir," said Allworthy, "and in what manner did the lawyer behave? Did you hear all that passed between him and the fellows?" "No, sir," answered Nighingale, "they had been together before I came. In my presence the lawyer said little, but after I had several times examined the fellows, who persisted in a story directly contrary to what I had heard from Mr. Jones and what I find by Mr. Fitzpatrick was a rank falsehood, the lawyer then desired the fellows to say nothing but what was the truth, and seemed to speak so much in favour of Mr. Jones that when I saw the same person with you, I concluded your goodness had prompted you to send him thither." "And did you not send him thither?" says Mrs. Miller. "Indeed I did not," answered Allworthy, "nor did I know he had gone on such an errand till this moment." "I see it all!" said Mrs. Miller. "Upon my soul, I see it all! No wonder they have been closeted so close lately. Son Nightingale, let me beg you run for these fellows immediately—find them out if they are aboveground. I will go myself." "Dear madam," said Allworthy, "be patient, and do me the favour to send a servant upstairs to call Mr. Dowling hither if he be in the house, or if not, Mr. Blifil." Mrs. Miller went out muttering something to herself and presently returned with an answer that Mr. Dowling was gone, but that "the t'other," as she called him, was coming.

Allworthy was of a cooler disposition than the good woman, whose spirits were all up in arms in the cause of her friend. He was not, however, without some suspicions which were near akin to hers. When Blifil came into the room, he asked him with a very serious countenance and with a less friendly look than he had ever before given him whether he knew anything of Mr. Dowling's having seen any of the persons who were present at the duel between Jones and another gentleman.

There is nothing so dangerous as a question which comes by surprise on a man whose business it is to conceal truth or to defend falsehood. For which reason those worthy personages whose noble office it is to save the lives of their fellow-creatures at the Old Bailey take the utmost care, by frequent previous examination, to divine every question which may be asked their clients on the day of trial, that they may be supplied with proper and ready answers, which the most fertile invention cannot supply in an instant. Besides, the sudden and violent impulse on the blood occasioned by these surprises occasions frequently such an alteration in the countenance that the man is obliged to give evidence against himself. And such, indeed, were the alterations which the countenance of Blifil underwent from this sudden question that we scarce blame the eagerness of Mrs. Miller, who immediately cried out, "Guilty, upon my honour! Guilty, upon my soul!"

Mr. Allworthy sharply rebuked her for this impetuosity, and then, turning to Blifil, who seemed sinking into the earth, he said, "Why do you hesitate, sir, at giving me an answer? You certainly must have employed him, for he would not of his own accord, I believe, have undertaken such an errand, and especially without acquainting me."

Blifil then answered, "I own, sir, I have been guilty of an offence; yet may I hope your pardon?" "My pardon?" said Allworthy very angrily. "Nay, sir," answered Blifil, "I knew you would be offended, yet surely my dear uncle will forgive the effects of the most amiable of human weaknesses. Compassion for those who do not deserve it, I own, is a crime, and yet it is a crime from which you yourself are not entirely free. I know I have been guilty of it in more than one instance to this very person, and I will own I did send Mr. Dowling, not on a vain and fruitless inquiry, but to discover the witnesses and to endeavour to soften their evidence. This, sir, is the truth, which though I intended to conceal from you I will not deny."

"I confess," said Nightingale, "this is the light in which it appeared to me from the gentleman's behaviour."

"Now, madam," said Allworthy, "I believe you will once in your life own you have entertained a wrong suspicion and are not so angry with my nephew as you was."

Mrs. Miller was silent; for though she could not so hastily be pleased with Blifil, whom she looked upon to have been the ruin of Jones, yet in this particular instance he had imposed upon her as well as the rest, so entirely had the Devil stood his friend. And indeed, I look upon the vulgar observation that "the Devil often deserts his friends and leaves them in the lurch" to be a great abuse on that gentleman's character. Perhaps he may sometimes desert those who are only his cup acquaintance, or who, at most, are but half his, but he generally stands by those who are thoroughly his servants and helps them off in all extremities till their bargain expires.

As a conquered rebellion strengthens a government, or as health is more perfectly established by recovery from some diseases, so anger when removed often gives new life to affection. This was the case of Mr. Allworthy; for Blifil having wiped off the greater suspicion, the lesser, which had been raised by Square's letter, sunk, of course, and was forgotten, and Thwackum, with whom he was greatly offended, bore alone all the reflections which Square had cast on the enemies of Jones.

As for that young man, the resentment of Mr. Allworthy began more and more to abate towards him. He told Blifil he did not only forgive the extraordinary efforts of his good nature but would give him the pleasure of following his example. Then, turning to Mrs. Miller with a smile which would have become an angel, he cried, "What say you, madam; shall we take a hackney-coach and all of us together pay a visit to your friend? I promise you it is not the first visit I have made in a prison."

Every reader, I believe, will be able to answer for the worthy woman, but they must have a great deal of good nature and be well acquainted with friendship who can feel what she felt on this occasion. Few, I hope, are capable of feeling what now passed in the mind of Blifil, but those who are will acknowledge that it was impossible for him to raise any objection to this visit. Fortune, however, or the gentleman lately mentioned above, stood his friend and prevented his undergoing so great a shock; for at the very instant when the coach was sent for, Partridge arrived and, having called Mrs. Miller from the company, acquainted her with the dreadful accident lately come to light, and hearing Mr. Allworthy's intention, begged her to find some means of stopping him. "For," says he, "the matter must at all hazards be kept a secret from him, and if he should now go, he will find Mr. Jones and his mother, who arrived just as I left him, lamenting over one another the horrid crime they have ignorantly committed."

The poor woman, who was almost deprived of her senses

at this dreadful news, was never less capable of invention than at present. However, as women are much readier at this than men, she bethought herself of an excuse and, returning to Allworthy, said, "I am sure, sir, you will be surprised at hearing any objection from me to the kind proposal you just now made, and yet I am afraid of the consequence of it if carried immediately into execution. You must imagine, sir, that all the calamities which have lately befallen this poor young fellow must have thrown him into the lowest dejection of spirits, and now, sir, should we all on a sudden fling him into such a violent fit of joy, as I know your presence will occasion, it may, I am afraid, produce some fatal mischief, especially as his servant, who is without, tells me he is very far from being well."

"Is his servant without?" cries Allworthy. "Pray call him hither. I will ask him some questions concerning his master."

Partridge was at first afraid to appear before Mr. Allworthy, but was at length persuaded after Mrs. Miller, who had often heard his whole story from his own mouth, had promised to introduce him.

Allworthy recollected Partridge the moment he came into the room, though many years had passed since he had seen him. Mrs. Miller therefore might have spared here a formal oration, in which indeed she was somewhat prolix; for the reader, I believe, may have observed already that the good woman among other things had a tongue always ready for the service of her friends.

"And are you," said Allworthy to Partridge, "the servant of Mr. Jones?" "I can't say, sir," answered he, "that I am regularly a servant, but I live with him, an't please your honour, at present. *Non sum qualis eram,* as your honour very well knows."

Mr. Allworthy then asked him many questions concerning Jones, as to his health and other matters; to all which Partridge answered without having the least regard to what was, but considered only what he would have things appear, for a strict adherence to truth was not among the articles of this honest fellow's morality or his religion.

During this dialogue Mr. Nightingale took his leave, and presently after, Mrs. Miller left the room, when Allworthy likewise dispatched Blifil, for he imagined that Partridge when alone with him would be more explicit than before company. They were no sooner left in private together than Allworthy began as in the following chapter.

IN WHICH THE HISTORY IS FARTHER CONTINUED

"Sure, friend," said the good man, "you are the strangest of all human beings. Not only to have suffered as you have formerly for obstinately persisting in a falsehood, but to persist in it thus to the last, and to pass thus upon the world for the servant of your own son? What interest can you have in all this? What can be your motive?"

"I see, sir," said Partridge, falling down upon his knees, "that your honour is prepossessed against me and resolved not to believe anything I say, and therefore, what signifies my protestations? But yet, there is One above who knows that I am not the father of this young man."

"How!" said Allworthy. "Will you yet deny what you was formerly convicted of upon such unanswerable, such manifest, evidence? Nay, what a confirmation is your being now found with this very man of all which twenty years ago appeared against you. I thought you had left the country; nay, I thought you had been long since dead. In what manner did you know anything of this young man? Where did you meet with him unless you had kept some correspondence together? Do not deny this; for I promise you it will greatly raise your son in my opinion to find that he hath such a sense of filial duty as privately to support his father for so many years."

"If your honour will have patience to hear me," said Partridge, "I will tell you all." Being bid go on, he proceeded thus: "When your honour conceived that displeasure against me, it ended in my ruin soon after; for I lost my little school, and the minister, thinking, I suppose, it would be agreeable to your honour, turned me out from the office of clerk, so that I had nothing to trust to but the barber's shop, which in a country place like that is a poor livelihood; and when my wife died (for till that time I received a pension of £12 a year from an unknown hand, which indeed I believe was your honour's own, for nobody that ever I heard of doth these things besides)—but as I was saying, when she died, this pension forsook me, so that now, as I owed two or three small debts which began to be troublesome to me (particularly one,* which an attorney brought up by law-charges from 15s. to near £30), and as I found all my usual means of living had forsook me, I packed up my little all as well as I could and went off.

"The first place I came to was Salisbury, where I got into the service of a gentleman belonging to the law, and one of the best gentleman that ever I knew; for he was not only good to me, but I know a thousand good and charitable acts which he did while I stayed with him, and I have known him often refuse business because it was paltry and oppressive." "You need not be so particular," said Allworthy. "I know this gentleman, and a very worthy man he is, and an honour to his profession." "Well, sir," continued Partridge, "from hence I removed to Lymington, where I was above three years in the service of another lawyer, who was likewise a very good sort of a man and, to be sure, one of the merriest gentlemen in England. Well, sir, at the end of the three years I set up a little school and was likely to do well again had it not been for a most unlucky accident. Here I kept a pig; and one day, as ill fortune would have it, this pig broke out and did a trespass, I think they call it, in a garden belonging to one of my neighbours, who was a proud, revengeful man and employed a lawyer, one—one—I can't think of his name; but he sent for a writ against me and had me to 'size. When I came there, Lord have mercy upon me—to hear what the counsellors said! There was one that told my lord a parcel of the confoundedest lies about me: he said that I used to drive my hogs into other folks' gardens and a great deal more, and at last he said he hoped I had at last brought my hogs to a fair market. To be sure, one would have thought that instead of being owner only of one poor little pig, I had been the greatest hog-merchant in England. Well——" "Pray," said Allworthy, "do not be so particular. I have heard nothing of your son yet." "Oh, it was a great many years," answered Partridge, "before I saw my son, as you are pleased to call him. I went over to Ireland after this and taught school at Cork (for that one suit ruined

* This is a fact which I knew happen to a poor clergyman in Dorsetshire by the villainy of an attorney who, not contented with the exorbitant costs to which the poor man was put by a single action, brought afterwards another action on the judgement, as it was called—a method frequently used to oppress the poor and bring money into the pockets of attorneys, to the great scandal of the law, of the nation, of Christianity, and even of human nature itself.

me again, and I lay seven years in Winchester gaol)."
"Well," said Allworthy, "pass that over till your return to England." "Then, sir," said he, "it was about half a year ago that I landed at Bristol, where I stayed some time, and, not finding it do there, and hearing of a place between that and Gloucester, where the barber was just dead, I went thither, and there I had been about two months when Mr. Jones came thither." He then gave Allworthy a very particular account of their first meeting and of everything, as well as he could remember, which had happened from that day to this, frequently interlarding his story with panegyrics on Jones and not forgetting to insinuate the great love and respect which he had for Allworthy. He concluded with saying, "Now, sir, I have told your honour the whole truth." And then repeated a most solemn protestation that he was no more the father of Jones than of the Pope of Rome, and imprecated the most bitter curses on his head if he did not speak truth.

"What am I to think of this matter?" cries Allworthy. "For what purpose should you so strongly deny a fact which I think it would be rather your interest to own?" "Nay, sir," answered Partridge (for he could hold no longer), "if your honour will not believe me, you are like soon to have satisfaction enough. I wish you had mistaken the mother of this young man as well as you have his father." And now, being asked what he meant, with all the symptoms of horror both in his voice and countenance, he told Allworthy the whole story, which he had a little before expressed such desire to Mrs. Miller to conceal from him.

Allworthy was almost as much shocked at this discovery as Partridge himself had been while he related it. "Good heavens!" says he. "In what miserable distresses do vice and imprudence involve men! How much beyond our designs are the effects of wickedness sometimes carried!" He had scarce uttered these words when Mrs. Waters came hastily and abruptly into the room. Partridge no sooner saw her than he cried, "Here, sir, here is the very woman herself. This is the unfortunate mother of Mr. Jones; I am sure she will acquit me before your honour. Pray, madam——"

Mrs. Waters, without paying any regard to what Partridge said and almost without taking any notice of him, advanced to Mr. Allworthy. "I believe, sir, it is so long since I had the honour of seeing you that you do not recollect me." "Indeed," answered Allworthy, "you are so very much altered on many accounts that had not this man already acquainted me who you are, I should not have immediately called you to my remembrance. Have you, madam, any particular business which brings you to me?" Allworthy spoke this with great reserve, for the reader may easily believe he was not well pleased with the conduct of this lady, neither with what he had formerly heard nor with what Partridge had now delivered.

Mrs. Waters answered, "Indeed, sir, I have very particular business with you, and it is such as I can only impart to yourself. I must desire, therefore, the favour of a word with you alone, for I assure you what I have to tell you is of the utmost importance."

Partridge was then ordered to withdraw, but before he went, he begged the lady to satisfy Mr. Allworthy that he was perfectly innocent. To which she answered, "You need be under no apprehension, sir; I shall satisfy Mr. Allworthy very perfectly of that matter."

Then Partridge withdrew, and that passed between Mr. Allworthy and Mrs. Waters which is written in the next chapter.

7

CONTINUATION OF THE HISTORY

Mrs. Waters remaining a few moments silent, Mr. Allworthy could not refrain from saying, "I am sorry, madam, to perceive by what I have since heard that you have made so very ill a use——" "Mr. Allworthy," says she, interrupting him, "I know I have faults, but ingratitude to you is not one of them. I never can nor shall forget your goodness, which I own I have very little deserved, but be pleased to waive all upbraiding me at present, as I have so important an affair to communicate to you concerning this young man, to whom you have given my maiden name of Jones."

"Have I, then," said Allworthy, "ignorantly punished an innocent man, in the person of him who hath just left us? Was he not the father of the child?" "Indeed he was not," said Mrs. Waters. "You may be pleased to remember, sir, I formerly told you, you should one day know; and I acknowledge myself to have been guilty of a cruel neglect in not having discovered it to you before. Indeed I little knew how necessary it was." "Well, madam," said Allworthy, "be pleased to proceed." "You must remember, sir," said she, "a young fellow whose name was Summer." "Very well," cries Allworthy. "He was the son of a clergyman of great learning and virtue for whom I had the highest friendship." "So it appeared, sir," answered she, "for I believe you bred the young man up and maintained him at the University, where, I think, he had finished his studies when he came to reside at your house; a finer man, I must say, the sun never shone upon, for besides the handsomest person I ever saw, he was so genteel and had so much wit and good breeding." "Poor gentleman," said Allworthy, "he was indeed untimely snatched away, and little did I think he had any sins of this kind to answer for, for I plainly perceive you are going to tell me he was the father of your child."

"Indeed, sir," answered she, "he was not." "How?" said Allworthy. "To what, then, tends all this preface?" "To a story, sir," said she, "which I am concerned it falls to my lot to unfold to you. Oh, sir, prepare to hear something which will surprise you, will grieve you." "Speak," said Allworthy, "I am conscious of no crime and cannot be afraid to hear." "Sir," said she, "that Mr. Summer, the son of your friend, educated at your expense, who after living a year in the house as if he had been your own son died there of the smallpox, was tenderly lamented by you and buried as if he had been your own; that Summer, sir, was the father of this child." "How!" said Allworthy. "You contradict yourself." "That I do not," answered she. "He was indeed the father of this child, but not by me." "Take care, madam," said Allworthy, "do not to shun the imputation of any crime be guilty of falsehood. Remember there is One from whom you can conceal nothing and before whose tribunal falsehood will only aggravate your guilt." "Indeed, sir," says she, "I am not his mother, nor would I now think myself so for the world." "I know your reason," said Allworthy, "and shall rejoice as much as you find it otherwise, yet you must remember you yourself confessed it before me." "So far what I confessed," said she, "was true: that these hands conveyed the infant to your bed, conveyed it thither at the command of its mother; at her commands I afterwards owned it, and thought myself by her generosity nobly rewarded, both for my secrecy and my shame." "Who could this woman be?" said Allworthy. "Indeed I tremble to name her," answered Mrs. Waters. "By all this preparation I am to guess that she was a relation of mine," cried he. "Indeed she was a near one." At which words Allworthy started, and she continued: "You had a sister, sir." "A sister!" repeated he, looking aghast. "As there is truth in heaven," cries she, "your sister was the mother of that child you found between your sheets." "Can it be possible?" cries he. "Good heavens!" "Have patience, sir," said Mrs. Waters, "and I will unfold to you the whole story. Just after your departure for London, Miss Bridget came one day to the house of my mother. She was pleased to say she had heard an extraordinary character of me, for my learning and superior understanding to all the young women there, so she was pleased to say. She then bid me come to her to the great house, where, when I attended, she employed me to read to her. She expressed great satisfaction in my reading, showed great kindness to me, and made me many presents. At last she began to catechize me on the subject of secrecy, to which I gave her such satisfactory answers that at last, having locked the door of her room, she took me into her closet and then, locking that door likewise, she said she should convince me of the vast reliance she had on my integrity by communicating a secret in which her honour, and consequently her life, was concerned. She then stopped, and after a silence of a minute, during which she often wiped her eyes, she inquired of me if I thought my mother might safely be confided in. I answered I would stake my life on her fidelity. She then imparted to me the great secret which laboured in her breast and which, I believe, was delivered with more pains than she afterwards suffered in child-birth. It was then contrived that my mother and myself only should attend at the time and that Mrs. Wilkins should be sent out of the way, as she accordingly was, to the very furthest part of Dorsetshire to inquire the character of a servant; for the lady had turned away her own maid near three months before, during all which time I officiated about her person upon trial, as she said, though, as she afterwards declared, I was not sufficiently handy for the place. This and many other such things which she used to say of me were all thrown out to prevent any suspicion which Wilkins might hereafter have when I was to own the child, for she thought it could never be believed she would venture to hurt a young woman with whom she had entrusted such a secret. You may be assured, sir, I was well paid for all these affronts, which, together with being informed of the occasion of them, very well contented me. Indeed the lady had a greater suspicion of Mrs. Wilkins than of any other person, not that she had the least aversion to the gentlewoman, but she thought her incapable of keeping a secret, especially from you, sir; for I have often heard Miss Bridget say that if Mrs. Wilkins had committed a murder, she believed she would acquaint you with it. At last the expected day came and Mrs. Wilkins, who had been kept a week in readiness, and put off from time to time upon some pretence or other, that she might not return too soon, was dispatched. Then the child was born, in the presence only of myself and my mother, and was by my mother conveyed to her own house, where it was privately kept by her till the evening of your return, when I by the command of Miss Bridget conveyed it into the bed where you found it. And all suspicions were afterwards laid asleep by the artful conduct of your sister in pretending ill will to the boy, and that any regard she showed him was out of mere complaisance to you."

Mrs. Waters then made many protestations of the truth of this story and concluded by saying, "Thus, sir, you have at last discovered your nephew, for so I am sure you will hereafter think him, and I question not but he will be both an honour and a comfort to you under that appellation."

"I need not, madam," said Allworthy, "express my astonishment at what you have told me, and yet surely you would not, and could not, have put together so many circumstances to evidence an untruth. I confess I recollect some passages relating to that Summer which formerly gave me a conceit that my sister had some liking to him. I mentioned it to her; for I had such a regard to the young man, as well on his own account as on his father's, that I should have willingly consented to a match between them, but she expressed the highest disdain of my unkind suspicion, as she called it, so that I never more spoke on the subject. Good heaven! Well! The Lord disposeth all things. Yet sure it was a most unjustifiable conduct in my sister to carry this secret with her out of the world." "I promise you, sir," said Mrs. Waters, "she always professed a contrary intention, and frequently told me she intended one day to communicate it to you. She said, indeed, she was highly rejoiced that her plot had succeeded so well and that you had of your own accord taken such a fancy to the child that it was yet unnecessary to make any express declaration. Oh, sir, had that lady lived to have seen this poor young man turned like a vagabond from your house; nay, sir, could she have lived to hear that you had yourself employed a lawyer to prosecute him for a murder of which he was not guilty. Forgive me, Mr. Allworthy, I must say it was unkind. Indeed you have been abused; he never deserved it of you." "Indeed, madam," said Allworthy, "I have been abused by the person, whoever he was, that told you so." "Nay, sir," said she, "I would not be mistaken; I did not presume to say you were guilty of any wrong. The gentleman who came to me proposed no such matter; he only said, taking me for Mr. Fitzpatrick's wife, that if Mr. Jones had murdered my husband, I should be assisted with any money I wanted to carry on the prosecution by a very worthy gentleman who, he said, was well apprised what a villain I had to deal with. It was by this man I found out who Mr. Jones was, and this man, whose name is Dowling, Mr. Jones tells me, is your steward. I discovered his name by a very odd accident, for he himself refused to tell it me; but Partridge, who met him at my lodgings the second time he came, knew him formerly at Salisbury."

"And did this Mr. Dowling," says Allworthy with great astonishment in his countenance, "tell you that I would assist in the prosecution?" "No, sir," answered she, "I will not charge him wrongfully. He said I should be assisted, but he mentioned no name. Yet you must pardon me, sir, if from circumstances I thought it could be no other." "Indeed, madam," says Allworthy, "from circumstances I am too well convinced it was another. Good heaven! By what wonderful means is the blackest and deepest villainy sometimes discovered! Shall I beg you, madam, to stay till the person you have mentioned comes, for I expect him every minute; nay, he may be, perhaps, already in the house."

Allworthy then stepped to the door in order to call a servant, when in came not Mr. Dowling, but the gentleman who will be seen in the next chapter.

8

FURTHER CONTINUATION

The gentleman who now arrived was no other than Mr. Western. He no sooner saw Allworthy than, without considering in the least the presence of Mrs. Waters, he began to vociferate in the following manner: "Fine doings at my house! A rare kettle of fish I have discovered at last; who the devil would be plagued with a daughter?" "What's the matter, neighbour?" said Allworthy. "Matter enough," answered Western, "when I thought she was a-just coming to; nay, when she had in a manner promised me to do as I would ha' her, and when I was a-hoped to have had nothing more to do than to have sent for the lawyer and finished all. What do you think I have found out? That the little b— hath bin playing tricks with me all the while and carrying on a correspondence with that bastard of yours. Sister Western, whom I have quarrelled with upon her account, sent me word o't, and I ordered her pockets to be searched when she was asleep, and here I have got un signed with the son of a whore's own name. I have not had patience to read half o't, for 'tis longer than one of Parson Supple's sermons, but I find plainly it is all about love, and indeed what should it be else? I have packed her up in chamber again, and to-morrow morning down she goes into the country unless she consents to be married directly, and there she shall live in a garret upon bread and water all her days; and the sooner such a b— breaks her heart, the better, though, d—n her, that I believe is too tough. She will live long enough to plague me." "Mr. Western," answered Allworthy, "you know I have always protested against force and you yourself consented that none should be used." "Ay," cries he, "that was only upon condition that she would consent without. What the devil and Doctor Faustus, shan't I do what I will with my own daughter, especially when I desire nothing but her own good?" "Well, neighbour," answered Allworthy, "if you will give me leave, I will undertake once to argue with the young lady." "Will you?" said Western. "Why, that is kind now and neighbourly, and mayhap you will do more than I have been able to do with her; for I promise you she hath a very good opinion of you." "Well, sir," said Allworthy, "if you will go home and release the young lady from her captivity, I will wait upon her within this half-hour." "But suppose," said Western, "she should run away with un in the meantime? For Lawyer Dowling tells me there is no hopes of hanging the fellow at last, for that the man is alive and like to do well, and that he thinks Jones will be out of prison again presently." "How!" said Allworthy. "What, did you employ him, then, to inquire or to do anything in that matter?" "Not I," answered Western; "he mentioned it to me just now of his own accord." "Just now!" cries Allworthy. "Why, where did you see him, then? I want much to see Mr. Dowling." "Why, you may see un an you will presently at my lodgings, for there is to be a meeting of lawyers there this morning about a mortgage. Icod! I shall lose two or dree thousand pounds, I believe, by that honest gentleman, Mr. Nightingale." "Well, sir," said Allworthy, "I will be with you within the half-hour." "And do for once," cries the squire, "take a fool's advice: never think of dealing with her by gentle methods; take my word for it, those will never do. I have tried um long enough. She must be frightened into it; there is no other way. Tell her I'm her father, and of the horrid sin of disobedience and of the dreadful punishment of it in t'other world; and then tell her about being locked up all her life in a garret in this, and be kept only on bread and water." "I will do all I can," said Allworthy, "for I promise you, there is nothing I wish for more than an alliance with this amiable creature." "Nay, the girl is well enough for matter o' that," cries the squire. "A man may go farther and meet with worse meat; that I may declare o' her, thof she be my own daughter. And if she will but be obedient to me, there is narrow a father within a hundred miles o' the place that loves a daughter better than I do; but I see you are busy with the lady here, so I will go huome and expect you, and so your humble servant."

As soon as Mr. Western was gone Mrs. Waters said, "I see, sir, the squire hath not the least remembrance of my face. I believe, Mr. Allworthy, you would not have known me neither. I am very considerably altered since that day when you so kindly gave me that advice, which I had been happy had I followed." "Indeed, madam," cries Allworthy, "it gave me great concern when I first heard the contrary." "Indeed, sir," says she, "I was ruined by a very deep scheme of villainy, which if you knew, though I pretend not to think it would justify me in your opinion, it would at least mitigate my offence and induce you to pity me; you are not now at leisure to hear my whole story, but this I assure you: I was betrayed by the most solemn promises of marriage; nay, in the eye of heaven I was married to him; for after much reading on the subject I am convinced that particular ceremonies are only requisite to give a legal sanction to marriage, and have only a worldly use in giving a woman the privileges of a wife, but that she who lives constant to one man after a solemn private affiance, whatever the world may call her, hath little to charge on her own conscience." "I am sorry, madam," said Allworthy, "you made so ill a use of your learning. Indeed it would have been well that you had been possessed of much more or had remained in a state of ignorance. And yet, madam, I am afraid you have more than this sin to answer for." "During his life," answered she, "which was above a dozen years, I most solemnly assure you I had not. And consider, sir, on my behalf, what is in the power of a woman stripped of her reputation and left destitute, whether the good-natured world will suffer such a stray sheep to return to the road of virtue, even if she was never so desirous. I protest, then, I would have chose it had it been in my power, but necessity drove me into the arms of Captain Waters, with whom, though still unmarried, I lived as a wife for many years and went by his name. I parted with this gentleman at Worcester on his march against the rebels, and it was then I accidentally met with Mr. Jones, who rescued me from the hands of a villain. Indeed, he is the worthiest of men. No young gentleman of his age is, I believe, freer from vice and few have the twentieth part of his virtues; nay, whatever vices he hath had, I am firmly persuaded he hath now taken a resolution to abandon them." "I hope he hath," cries Allworthy, "and I hope he will preserve that resolution. I must say I have still the same hopes with regard to yourself. The world, I do agree, are apt to be too unmerciful on these occasions, yet time and perseverance will get the better of this their disinclination, as I may call it, to pity; for though they are not like heaven ready to receive a penitent sinner, yet a continued repentance will at length obtain mercy even with the world. This you may be assured of, Mrs. Waters: that whenever I find you are sincere in such good intentions, you shall want no assistance in my power to make them effectual."

Mrs. Waters fell now upon her knees before him, and in a flood of tears made him many most passionate acknowledgements of his goodness, which, as she truly said, savoured more of the divine than human nature.

Allworthy raised her up and spoke in the most tender manner, making use of every expression which his invention could suggest to comfort her, when he was interrupted by the arrival of Mr. Dowling, who, upon his first entrance

818

seeing Mrs. Waters, started and appeared in some confusion; from which he soon recovered himself as well as he could, and t ien said he was in the utmost haste to attend counsel at Mr. Western's lodgings, but, however, thought it his duty to call and acquaint him with the opinion of counsel upon the case which he had before told him; which was that the conversion of the moneys in that case could not be questioned in a criminal cause, but that an action of trover might be brought, and if it appeared to the jury to be the moneys of plaintiff, that plaintiff would recover a verdict for the value.

Allworthy without making any answer to this bolted the door, and then, advancing with a stern look to Dowling, he said, "Whatever be your haste, sir, I must first receive an answer to some questions. Do you know this young lady?" "That lady, sir?" answered Dowling with great hesitation. Allworthy, then, with the most solemn voice, said, "Look you, Mr. Dowling, as you value my favour or your continuance a moment longer in my service, do not hesitate nor prevaricate, but answer faithfully and truly to every question I ask. Do you know this lady?" "Yes, sir," said Dowling, "I have seen the lady." "Where, sir?" "At her own lodgings." "Upon what business did you go thither, sir, and who sent you?" "I went, sir, to inquire, sir, about Mr. Jones." "And who sent you to inquire about him?" "Who, sir? Why, sir, Mr. Blifil sent me." "And what did you say to the lady concerning that matter?" "Nay, sir, it is impossible to recollect every word." "Will you please, madam, to assist the gentleman's memory?" "He told me, sir," said Mrs. Waters, "that if Mr. Jones had murdered my husband, I should be assisted by any money I wanted to carry on the prosecution by a very worthy gentleman, who was well apprised what a villain I had to deal with. These, I can safely swear, were the very words he spoke." "Were these the words, sir?" said Allworthy. "I cannot charge my memory exactly," cries Dowling, "but I believe I did speak to that purpose." "And did Mr. Blifil order you to say so?" "I am sure, sir, I should not have gone on my own accord, nor have willingly exceeded my authority in matters of this kind. If I said so, I must have so understood Mr. Blifil's instructions." "Look you, Mr. Dowling," said Allworthy, "I promise you before this lady that whatever you have done in this affair by Mr. Blifil's order I will forgive, provided you now tell me strictly the truth; for I believe what you say: that you would not have acted of your own accord and without authority in this matter. Mr. Blifil, then, likewise sent you to examine the two fellows at Aldersgate?" "He did, sir." "Well, and what instructions did he then give you? Recollect as well as you can, and tell me as near as possible the very words he used." "Why, sir, Mr. Blifil sent me to find out the persons who were eyewitnesses of this fight. He said he feared they might be tampered with by Mr. Jones or some of his friends. He said blood required blood, and that not only all who concealed a murderer but those who omitted anything in their power to bring him to justice were sharers in his guilt. He said he found you was very desirous of having the villain brought to justice, though it was not proper you should appear in it." "He did so?" says Allworthy. "Yes, sir," cries Dowling, "I should not, I am sure, have proceeded such lengths for the sake of any other person living but your worship." "What lengths, sir?" said Allworthy. "Nay, sir," cries Dowling, "I would not have your worship think I would on any account be guilty of subordination of perjury, but there are two ways of delivering evidence. I told them, therefore, that if any offers should be made them on the other side, they should refuse them, and that they might be assured they should lose nothing by being honest men and telling the truth. I said we were told that Mr. Jones had assaulted the gentleman first, and that if that was the truth, they should declare it; and I did give them some hints that they should be no losers." "I think you went lengths indeed," cries Allworthy. "Nay, sir," answered Dowling, "I am sure I did not desire them to tell an untruth, nor should I have said what I did unless it had been to oblige you." "You would not have thought, I believe," says Allworthy, "to have obliged me had you known that this Mr. Jones was my own nephew." "I am sure, sir," answered he, "it did not become me to take any notice of what I thought you desired to conceal." "How!" cries Allworthy. "And did you know it then?" "Nay, sir," answered Dowling, "if your worship bids me speak the truth, I am sure I shall do it. Indeed, sir, I did know it; for they were almost the last words which Madam Blifil ever spoke, which she mentioned to me as I stood alone by her bedside, when she delivered me the letter I brought your worship from her." "What letter?" cries Allworthy. "The letter, sir," answered Dowling, "which I brought from Salisbury and which I delivered into the hands of Mr. Blifil." "Oh, heavens!" cries Allworthy. "Well, and what were the words? What did my sister say to you?" "She took me by the hand," answered he, "and as she delivered me the letter said, 'I scarce know what I have written. Tell my brother Mr. Jones is his nephew. He is my son. Bless him,' says she, and then fell backward, as if dying away. I presently called in the people, and she never spoke more to me, and died within a few minutes afterwards." Allworthy stood a minute silent, lifting up his eyes, and then, turning to Dowling, said, "How came you, sir, not to deliver me this message?" "Your worship," answered he, "must remember that you was at that time ill in bed, and being in a violent hurry, as indeed I always am, I delivered the letter and message to Mr. Blifil, who told me he would carry them both to you, which he hath since told me he did, and that your worship, partly out of friendship to Mr. Jones and partly out of regard to your sister, would never have it mentioned, and did intend to conceal it from the world; and therefore, sir, if you had not mentioned it to me first, I am certain I should never have thought it belonged to me to say anything of the matter, either to your worship or any other person."

We have remarked somewhere already that it is possible for a man to convey a lie in the words of truth; this was the case at present, for Blifil had in fact told Dowling what he now related, but had not imposed upon him, nor indeed had imagined he was able so to do. In reality the promises which Blifil had made to Dowling were the motives which had induced him to secrecy, and as he very plainly saw he should not be able to keep them, he thought proper now to make this confession, which the promises of forgiveness— joined to the threats, the voice, the looks of Allworthy, and the discoveries he had made before—extorted from him, who was, besides, taken unawares and had no time to consider of evasions.

Allworthy appeared well satisfied with this relation and, having enjoined strict silence as to what had passed on Dowling, conducted that gentleman himself to the door lest he should see Blifil, who was returned to his chamber, where he exulted in the thoughts of his last deceit on his uncle and little suspected what had since passed below-stairs.

As Allworthy was returning to his room he met Mrs. Miller in the entry, who with a face all pale and full of terror said to him, "Oh, sir, I find this wicked woman hath been with you and you know all; yet do not on this account abandon the poor young man. Consider, sir, he was ignorant it was his own mother, and the discovery itself will most probably break his heart without your unkindness."

"Madam," says Allworthy, "I am under such an astonishment at what I have heard that I am really unable to satisfy you, but come with me into my room. Indeed, Mrs. Miller, I have made surprising discoveries, and you shall soon know them."

The poor woman followed him, trembling, and now Allworthy, going up to Mrs. Waters, took her by the hand, and then, turning to Mrs. Miller, said, "What reward shall I bestow upon this gentlewoman for the services she hath done me? Oh, Mrs. Miller, you have a thousand times heard me call the young man to whom you are so faithful a friend, my son. Little did I then think he was indeed related to me at all. Your friend, madam, is my nephew; he is the brother of that wicked viper which I have so long nourished in my bosom. She will herself tell you the whole story and how the youth came to pass for her son. Indeed, Mrs. Miller, I am convinced that he hath been wronged and that I have been abused—abused by one whom you too justly suspected of being a villain. He is, in truth, the worst of villains."

The joy which Mrs. Miller now felt bereft her of the power of speech, and might perhaps have deprived her of her senses, if not of life, had not a friendly shower of tears come reasonably to her relief. At length, recovering so far from her transport as to be able to speak, she cried, "And is my dear Mr. Jones, then, your nephew, sir? And not the son of this lady? And are your eyes opened to him at last? And shall I live to see him as happy as he deserves?" "He certainly is my nephew," says Allworthy, "and I hope all the rest." "And is this the dear good woman, the person," cries she, "to whom all this discovery is owing?" "She is indeed," says Allworthy. "Why, then," cried Mrs. Miller, upon her knees, "may heaven shower down its choicest blessings upon her head, and for this one good action forgive her all her sins, be they never so many."

Mrs. Waters then informed them that she believed Jones would very shortly be released, for that the surgeon was gone in company with a nobleman to the justice who committed him in order to certify that Mr. Fitzpatrick was out of all manner of danger, and to procure the prisoner his liberty.

Allworthy said he should be glad to find his nephew there at his return home, but that he was then obliged to go on some business of consequence. He then called to a servant to fetch him a chair and presently left the two ladies together.

Mr. Blifil, hearing the chair ordered, came downstairs to attend upon his uncle, for he was never deficient in such acts of duty. He asked his uncle if he was going out, which is a civil way of asking a man where he is going; to which the other making no answer, he again desired to know when he would be pleased to return. Allworthy made no answer to this neither till he was just getting into his chair, and then, turning about, he said: "Harkee, sir, do you find out before my return the letter which your mother sent me on her death-bed." Allworthy then departed, and left Blifil in a situation to be envied only by a man who is just going to be hanged.

9

A FURTHER CONTINUATION

Allworthy took an opportunity whilst he was in the chair of reading the letter from Jones to Sophia which Western delivered him, and there were some expressions in it concerning himself which drew tears from his eyes. At length he arrived at Mr. Western's, and was introduced to Sophia.

When the first ceremonies were past and the gentleman and lady had taken their chairs, a silence of some minutes ensued, during which the latter, who had been prepared for the visit by her father, sat playing with her fan and had every mark of confusion both in her countenance and behaviour. At length Allworthy, who was himself a little disconcerted, began thus: "I am afraid, Miss Western, my family hath been the occasion of giving you some uneasiness, to which, I fear, I have innocently become more instrumental than I intended. Be assured, madam, had I at first known how disagreeable the proposals had been, I should not have suffered you to have been so long persecuted. I hope, therefore, you will not think the design of this visit is to trouble you with any further solicitations of that kind, but entirely to relieve you from them."

"Sir," said Sophia, with a little modest hesitation, "this behaviour is most kind and generous, and such as I could expect only from Mr. Allworthy; but as you have been so kind to mention this matter, you will pardon me for saying it hath indeed given me great uneasiness and hath been the occasion of my suffering much cruel treatment from a father who was till that unhappy affair the tenderest and fondest of all parents. I am convinced, sir, you are too good and generous to resent my refusal of your nephew. Our own inclinations are not in our power, and whatever may be his merit, I cannot force them in his favour." "I assure you, most amiable young lady," said Allworthy, "I am capable of no such resentment, had the person been my own son and had I entertained the highest esteem for him. For you say truly, madam, we cannot force our own inclinations; much less can they be directed by another." "Oh, sir," answered Sophia, "every word you speak proves you deserve that good, that great, that benevolent, character the whole world allows you. I assure you, sir, nothing less than the certain prospect of future misery could have made me resist the commands of my father." "I sincerely believe you, madam," replied Allworthy, "and I heartily congratulate you on your prudent foresight, since by so justifiable a resistance you have avoided misery indeed." "You speak now, Mr. Allworthy," cries she, "with a delicacy which few men are capable of feeling, but surely, in my opinion, to lead our lives with one to whom we are indifferent must be a state of wretchedness—perhaps that wretchedness would be even increased by a sense of the merits of an object to whom we cannot give our affections. If I had married Mr. Blifil——" "Pardon my interrupting you, madam," answered Allworthy, "but I cannot bear the supposition. Believe me, Miss Western, I rejoice from my heart; I rejoice in your escape. I have discovered the wretch, for whom you have suffered all this cruel violence from your father, to be a villain." "How, sir!" cries Sophia. "You must believe this surprises me." "It hath surprised me, madam," answered Allworthy, "and so it will the world. But I have acquainted you with the real truth." "Nothing but truth," says Sophia, "can, I am convinced, come from the lips of Mr. Allworthy. Yet, sir, such sudden, such unexpected, news—discovered, you say—may villainy be ever so!" "You will soon enough hear the story," cries Allworthy. "At present let us not mention so detested a name. I have another matter of a very serious nature to propose. Oh, Miss Western, I know your vast worth, nor can I so easily part with the ambition of being allied to it. I have a near relation, madam, a young man whose character is, I am convinced, the very opposite to that of this wretch, and whose fortune I will make equal to what his was to have been. Could I, madam, hope you would admit a visit from him?" Sophia after a minute's silence answered, "I will deal with the utmost sincerity with Mr. Allworthy. His character and the obligation I have just received from him demand it. I have determined at present to listen to no such proposals from any person. My only desire is to be restored to the affection of my father and to be again the mistress of his family. This, sir, I hope to owe to your good offices. Let me beseech you, let me conjure you by all the goodness which I and all who know you have experienced; do not the very moment when you have released me from one persecution, do not engage me in another as miserable and as fruitless." "Indeed, Miss Western," replied Allworthy, "I am capable of no such conduct, and if this be your resolution, he must submit to the disappointment, whatever torments he may suffer under it." "I must smile now, Mr. Allworthy," answered Sophia, "when you mention the torments of a man whom I do not know and who can consequently have so little acquaintance with me." "Pardon me, dear young lady," cries Allworthy, "I begin now to be afraid he hath had too much acquaintance for the repose of his future days, since, if ever man was capable of a sincere, violent, and noble passion, such, I am convinced, is my unhappy nephew's for Miss Western." "A nephew of yours! Mr. Allworthy," answered Sophia, "it is surely strange I never heard of him before." "Indeed, madam," cries Allworthy, "it is only the circumstance of his being my nephew to which you are a stranger, and which till this day was a secret to me. Mr. Jones, who has long loved you, he, he is my nephew!" "Mr. Jones your nephew, sir?" cries Sophia. "Can it be possible?" "He is indeed, madam," answered Allworthy. "He is my own sister's son—as such I shall always own him, nor am I ashamed of owning him. I am much more ashamed of my past behaviour to him, but I was as ignorant of his merit as of his birth. Indeed, Miss Western, I have used him cruelly. Indeed, I have." Here the good man wiped his eyes, and after a short pause proceeded: "I never shall be able to reward him for his sufferings without your assistance. Believe me, most amiable young lady, I must have a great esteem of that offering which I make to your worth. I know he hath been guilty of faults, but there is great goodness of heart at the bottom. Believe me, madam, there is." Here he stopped, seeming to expect an answer, which he presently received from Sophia, after she had a little recovered herself from the hurry of spirits into which so strange and sudden information had thrown her: "I sincerely wish you joy, sir, of a discovery in which you seem to have such satisfaction. I doubt not but you will have all the comfort you can promise yourself from it. The young gentleman hath certainly a thousand good qualities, which makes it impossible he should not behave well to such an uncle." "I hope, madam," said Allworthy, "he hath those good qualities which must make him a good husband. He must, I am sure, be of all men the most abandoned if a lady of your merit should condescend——" "You must pardon me, Mr. Allworthy," answered Sophia, "I cannot listen to a proposal of this kind. Mr. Jones, I am convinced, hath much merit, but I shall never receive Mr. Jones as one who is to be my husband. Upon my honour, I never will." "Pardon me, madam," cries Allworthy, "if I am a little surprised after what I have heard from Mr. Western. I hope the unhappy young man hath done nothing to forfeit your good opinion if he had ever the honour to enjoy it. Perhaps he may have been misrepresented to you, as he was to me. The same villainy may have injured him everywhere. He is no murderer, I assure you, as he hath been called." "Mr. Allworthy," answered Sophia, "I have told you my resolution. I wonder not at what my father hath told you, but whatever his apprehensions or fears have been, if I know my heart, I have given no occasion for them, since it hath always been a fixed principle with me never to have married without his consent. This is, I think, the duty of a child to a parent, and this, I hope, nothing could ever have prevailed with me to swerve from. I do not, indeed, conceive that the authority of any parent can oblige us to marry in direct opposition to our inclinations. To avoid a force of this kind, which I had reason to suspect, I left my father's house and sought protection elsewhere. This is the truth of my story, and if the world or my father carry my intentions any farther, my own conscience will acquit me." "I hear you, Miss Western," cries Allworthy with admiration. "I admire the justness of your sentiments, but surely there is more in this. I am cautious of offending you, young lady, but am I to look on all which I have hitherto heard or seen as a dream only? And have you suffered so much cruelty from your father on the account of a man to whom you have been always absolutely indifferent?" "I beg, Mr. Allworthy," answered Sophia, "you will not insist on my reasons. Yes, I have suffered indeed; I will not, Mr. Allworthy, conceal—I will be very sincere with you—I own I had a great opinion of Mr. Jones—I believe—I know I have suffered for my opinion—I have been treated cruelly by my aunt as well as by my father, but that is now past—I beg I may not be farther pressed; for whatever hath been, my resolution is now fixed. Your nephew, sir, hath many virtues—he hath great virtues, Mr. Allworthy. I question not but he will do you honour in the world and make you happy." "I wish I could make him so, madam," replied Allworthy, "but that I am convinced is only in your power. It is that conviction which hath made me so earnest a solicitor in his favour." "You are deceived; indeed, sir, you are deceived," said Sophia. "I hope not by him. It is sufficient to have deceived me. Mr. Allworthy, I must insist on being pressed no farther on this subject. I should be sorry—nay, I will not injure him in your favour. I wish Mr. Jones very well. I sincerely wish him well, and I repeat again to you, whatever demerit he may have to me, I am certain he hath many good qualities. I do not disown my former thoughts, but nothing can ever recall them. At present there is not a man on earth whom I would more resolutely reject than Mr. Jones, nor would the addresses of Mr. Blifil himself be less agreeable to me."

Western had been long impatient for the event of this conference and was just now arrived at the door to listen, when, having heard the last sentiments of his daughter's heart, he lost all temper and, bursting open the door in a rage, cried out, "It is a lie. It is a d—ned lie. It is all owning to that d—ned rascal Juones, and if she could get at un, she'd ha'un any hour of the day." Here Allworthy interposed, and addressing himself to the squire with some anger in his look, he said, "Mr. Western, you have not kept your word with me. You promised to abstain from all violence." "Why, so I did," cries Western, "as long as it was possible, but to hear a wench telling such confounded lies— Zounds! Doth she think if she can make vools of other volk, she can make one of me? No, no, I know her better than thee dost." "I am sorry to tell you, sir," answered Allworthy, "it doth not appear by your behaviour to this young lady that you know her at all. I ask pardon for what I say, but I think our intimacy, your own desires, and the occasion justify me. She is your daughter, Mr. Western, and I think she doth honour to your name. If I was capable of envy, I should sooner envy you on this account than any other man whatever." "Od rabbit it," cries the squire, "I wish she was thine with all my heart—wouldst soon be glad to be rid of the trouble o' her." "Indeed, my good friend," answered Allworthy, "you yourself are the cause of all the trouble you complain of. Place that confidence in the young lady which she so well deserves and I am certain you will be the happiest father on earth." "I, confidence in her!" cries the squire. " 'Sblood! What confidence can I place in her when she won't do as I would ha' her? Let her gi but her consent to marry as I would ha' her, and I'll place as much confidence in her as wouldst ha' me." "You have no right, neighbour," answered Allworthy, "to insist on any such consent. A negative voice your daughter allows you, and God and Nature have thought proper to allow you no more." "A negative voice?" cries the squire. "Ay! Ay! I'll show you what a negative voice I ha'. Go along, go into your chamber; go, you stubborn——" "Indeed, Mr. Western," said Allworthy, "indeed, you use her cruelly. I cannot bear to see this. You shall, you must, behave to her in a kinder manner. She deserves the best of treatment." "Yes, yes," said the squire, "I know what she deserves; now she's gone I'll show you what she deserves. See here, sir; here is a letter from my cousin, my Lady Bellaston, in which she is so kind to gi me to understand that the fellow is got out of prison again, and here she advises me to take all the care I can o' the wench. Odzookers! Neighbour Allworthy, you don't know what it is to govern a daughter."

The squire ended his speech with some compliments to his own sagacity, and then Allworthy, after a formal preface, acquainted him with the whole discovery which he had made concerning Jones, with his anger to Blifil, and with every particular which hath been disclosed to the reader in the preceding chapters.

Men over-violent in their dispositions are for the most part as changeable in them. No sooner, then, was Western informed of Mr. Allworthy's intention to make Jones his heir than he joined heartily with the uncle in every commendation of the nephew, and became as eager for her marriage with Jones as he had before been to couple her to Blifil.

Here Mr. Allworthy was again forced to interpose and to relate what had passed between him and Sophia, at which he testified great surprise.

The squire was silent a moment and looked wild with astonishment at this account. At last he cried out, "Why, what can be the meaning of this, neighbour Allworthy? Vond o' un she was, that I'll be sworn to. Odzookers! I have hit o't. As sure as a gun, I have hit o' the very right o't. It's all along o' zister. The girl hath got a hankering after this son of a whore of a lord. I vound 'em together at my cousin, my Lady Bellaston's. He hath turned the head o' her, that's certain. But d——n me if he shall ha' her—I'll ha' no lords nor courtiers in my vamily."

Allworthy now made a long speech, in which he repeated his resolution to avoid all violent measures, and very earnestly recommended gentle methods to Mr. Western as those by which he might be assured of succeeding best with his daughter. He then took his leave and returned back to Mrs. Miller, but was forced to comply with the earnest entreaties of the squire in promising to bring Mr. Jones to visit him that afternoon, that he might, as he said, "make all matters up with the young gentleman." At Mr. Allworthy's departure Western promised to follow his advice in his behaviour to Sophia, saying, "I don't know how 'tis, but d——n me, Allworthy, if you don't make me always do just as you please. And yet I have as good an estate as you, and am in the commission of the peace as well as yourself."

10

WHEREIN THE HISTORY BEGINS TO DRAW TOWARDS A
CONCLUSION

When Allworthy returned to his lodgings, he heard Mr. Jones was just arrived before him. He hurried therefore instantly into an empty chamber, whither he ordered Mr. Jones to be brought to him alone.

It is impossible to conceive a more tender or moving scene than the meeting between the uncle and nephew (for Mrs. Waters, as the reader may well suppose, had at her last visit discovered to him the secret of his birth). The first agonies of joy which were felt on both sides are indeed beyond my power to describe: I shall not therefore attempt it. After

Allworthy had raised Jones from his feet, where he had prostrated himself, and received him into his arms, "Oh, my child," he cried, "how have I been to blame! How have I injured you! What amends can I ever make you for those unkind, those unjust, suspicions which I have entertained, and for all the sufferings they have occasioned to you?" "Am I not now made amends?" cries Jones. "Would not my sufferings if they had been ten times greater have been now richly repaid? Oh, my dear uncle, this goodness, this tenderness, overpowers, unmans, destroys me! I cannot bear the transports which flow so fast upon me. To be again restored to your presence, to your favour; to be once more thus kindly received by my great, my noble, my generous, benefactor." "Indeed, child," cries Allworthy, "I have used you cruelly." He then explained to him all the treachery of Blifil, and again repeated expressions of the utmost concern for having been induced by that treachery to use him so ill. "Oh, talk not so," answered Jones. "Indeed, sir, you have used me nobly. The wisest man might be deceived as you were, and under such a deception the best must have acted just as you did. Your goodness displayed itself in the midst of your anger, just as it then seemed. I owe everything to that goodness of which I have been most unworthy. Do not put me on self-accusation by carrying your generous sentiments too far. Alas, sir, I have not been punished more than I have deserved, and it shall be the whole business of my future life to deserve that happiness you now bestow on me; for believe me, my dear uncle, my punishment hath not been thrown away upon me; though I have been a great, I am not a hardened, sinner; I thank heaven I have had time to reflect on my past life, where, though I cannot charge myself with any gross villainy, yet I can discern follies and vices too sufficient to repent and to be ashamed of, follies which have been attended with dreadful consequences to myself, and have brought me to the brink of destruction." "I am rejoiced, my dear child," answered Allworthy, "to hear you talk thus sensibly; for as I am convinced hypocrisy (good heaven, how I have been imposed on by it in others!) was never among your faults, so I can readily believe all you say. You now see, Tom, to what dangers imprudence alone may subject virtue (for virtue, I am now convinced, you love in a great degree). Prudence is indeed the duty which we owe to ourselves, and if we will be so much our own enemies as to neglect it, we are not to wonder if the world is deficient in discharging their duty to us, for when a man lays the foundation of his own ruin, others will, I am afraid, be too apt to build upon it. You say, however, you have seen your errors, and will reform them. I firmly believe you, my dear child; and therefore, from this moment you shall never be reminded of them by me. Remember them only yourself so far as for the future to teach you the better to avoid them, but still remember, for your comfort, that there is this great difference between those faults which candour may construe into imprudence and those which can be deduced from villainy only. The former, perhaps, are even more liable to subject a man to ruin, but if he reform, his character will at length be totally retrieved; the world, though not immediately, will in time be reconciled to him, and he may reflect, not without some mixture of pleasure, on the dangers he hath escaped; but villainy, my boy, when once discovered is irretrievable; the stains which this leaves behind, no time will wash away. The censures of mankind will pursue the wretch, their scorn will abash him in public, and if shame drives him into retirement, he will go to it with all those terrors with which a weary child who is afraid of hobgoblins retreats from company to go to bed alone. Here his murdered conscience will haunt him. Repose, like a false friend, will fly from him. Wherever he turns his eyes, horror presents itself; if he looks backward, unavailable repentance treads on his heels; if forward, incurable despair stares him in the face; till, like a condemned prisoner confined in a dungeon, he detests his present condition and yet dreads the consequence of that hour which is to relieve him from it. Comfort yourself, I say, my child, that this is not your case, and rejoice with thankfulness to Him who hath suffered you to see your errors before they have brought on you that destruction to which a persistence in even those errors must have led you. You have deserted them, and the prospect now before you is such that happiness seems in your own power." At these words Jones fetched a deep sigh; upon which, when Allworthy remonstrated, he said, "Sir, I will conceal nothing from you; I fear there is one consequence of my vices I shall never be able to retrieve. Oh, my dear uncle, I have lost a treasure——" "You need say no more," answered Allworthy; "I will be explicit with you: I know what you lament; I have seen the young lady and have discoursed with her concerning you. This I must insist on, as an earnest of your sincerity in all you have said and of the steadfastness of your resolution, that you obey me in one instance. To abide entirely by the determination of the young lady, whether it shall be in your favour or no. She hath already suffered enough from solicitations which I hate to think of; she shall owe no further constraint to my family; I know her father will be as ready to torment her now on your account as he hath formerly been on another, but I am determined she shall suffer no more confinement, no more violence, no more uneasy hours." "Oh, my dear uncle," answered Jones, "lay, I beseech you, some command on me in which I shall have some merit in obedience. Believe me, sir, the only instance in which I could disobey you would be to give an uneasy moment to my Sophia. No, sir, if I am so miserable to have incurred her displeasure beyond all hope of forgiveness, that alone, with the dreadful reflection of causing her misery, will be sufficient to overpower me. To call Sophia mine is the greatest and now the only additional blessing which heaven can bestow; but it is a blessing which I must owe to her alone." "I will not flatter you, child," cries Allworthy. "I fear your case is desperate; I never saw stronger marks of an unalterable resolution in any person than appeared in her vehement declarations against receiving your addresses, for which, perhaps, you can account better than myself." "Oh, sir, I can account too well!" answered Jones. "I have sinned against her beyond all hope of pardon, and guilty as I am, my guilt unfortunately appears to her in ten times blacker than the real colours. Oh, my dear uncle, I find my follies are irretrievable, and all your goodness cannot save me from perdition."

A servant now acquainted them that Mr. Western was below-stairs, for his eagerness to see Jones could not wait till the afternoon. Upon which Jones, whose eyes were full of tears, begged his uncle to entertain Western a few minutes till he a little recovered himself; to which the good man consented and, having ordered Mr. Western to be shown into a parlour, went down to him.

Mrs. Miller no sooner heard that Jones was alone (for she had not yet seen him since his release from prison) than she came eagerly into the room and, advancing towards Jones, wished him heartily joy of his new-found uncle and his happy reconciliation, adding, "I wish I could give you joy on another account, my dear child, but anything so inexorable I never saw." Jones with some appearance of surprise asked her what she meant. "Why, then," says she, "I have been with your young lady, and have explained all matters to her as they were told me by my son, Nightingale. She can have no longer any doubt about the letter, that I am certain, for I told her my son, Nightingale, was ready to take his oath, if she pleased, that it was all his own invention and the letter of his inditing. I told her the very reason of sending the letter ought to recommend you to her the more, as it was all upon her account and a plain proof that you was resolved to quit all your profligacy for the future; that you had never been guilty of a single instance of infidelity to her since your seeing her in town. I am afraid I went too far there, but heaven forgive me, I hope your future behaviour will be my justification. I am sure I have said all I can, but all to no purpose. She remains inflexible. She says she had forgiven many faults on account of youth, but expressed such detestation of the character of a libertine that she absolutely silenced me. I often attempted to excuse you, but the justness of her accusation flew in my face. Upon my honour, she is a lovely woman, and one of the sweetest and most sensible creatures I ever saw. I could have almost kissed her for one expression she made use of. It was a sentiment worthy of Seneca or of a bishop. 'I once fancied, madam,' said she, 'I had discovered great goodness of heart in Mr. Jones, and for that I own I had a sincere esteem, but an entire profligacy of manners will corrupt the best heart in the world; and all which a good-natured libertine can expect is that we should mix some grains of pity with our contempt and abhorrence.' She is an angelic creature, that is the truth on't." "Oh, Mrs. Miller," answered Jones, "can I bear to think I have lost such an angel?" "Lost! No," cries Mrs. Miller, "I hope you have not lost her yet. Resolve to leave such vicious courses and you may yet have hopes; nay, if she should remain inexorable, there is another young lady, a sweet pretty young lady, and a swinging fortune, who is absolutely dying for love of you. I heard of it this very morning and I told it to Miss Western; nay, I went a little beyond the truth again, for I told her you had refused her; but indeed I knew you would refuse her. And here I must give you a little comfort: when I mentioned the young lady's name, who is no other than the pretty Widow Hunt, I thought she turned pale, but when I said you had refused her, I will be sworn her face was all over scarlet in an instant; and these were her very words: 'I will not deny but that I believe he has some affection for me.' "

Here the conversation was interrupted by the arrival of Western, who could no longer be kept out of the room even by the authority of Allworthy himself, though this, as we have often seen, had a wonderful power over him.

Western immediately went up to Jones crying out, "My old friend Tom, I am glad to see thee, with all my heart. All past must be forgotten. I could not intend any affront to thee because, as Allworthy here knows, nay, dost know it thyself, I took thee for another person, and where a body means no harm, what signifies a hasty word or two? One Christian must forget and forgive another." "I hope, sir," said Jones, "I shall never forget the many obligations I have had to you, but as for any offence towards me, I declare I am an utter stranger——" "A't," says Western, "then give me thy fist; a't as hearty an honest cock as any in the kingdom. Come along with me; I'll carry thee to thy mistress this moment." Here Allworthy interposed, and the squire, being unable to prevail either with the uncle or nephew, was after some litigation obliged to consent to delay introducing Jones to Sophia till the afternoon; at which time Allworthy, as well in compassion to Jones as in compliance with the eager desires of Western, was prevailed upon to promise to attend at the tea-table.

The conversation which now ensued was pleasant enough, and with which, had it happened earlier in our history, we would have entertained our reader, but as we have now leisure only to attend to what is very material, it shall suffice to say that matters being entirely adjusted as to the afternoon visit, Mr. Western again returned home.

11

THE HISTORY DRAWS NEARER TO A CONCLUSION

When Mr. Western was departed, Jones began to inform Mr. Allworthy and Mrs. Miller that his liberty had been procured by two noble lords, who, together with two surgeons and a friend of Mr. Nightingale's, had attended the magistrate by whom he had been committed, and by whom, on the surgeons' oaths that the wounded person was out of all manner of danger from this wound, he was discharged.

One only of these lords, he said, he had ever seen before,

and that no more than once, but the other had greatly surprised him by asking his pardon for an offence he had been guilty of towards him, occasioned, he said, entirely by his ignorance who he was.

Now, the reality of the case with which Jones was not acquainted till afterwards was this: The lieutenant whom Lord Fellamar had employed according to the advice of Lady Bellaston to press Jones as a vagabond into the sea-service, when he came to report the event which we have before seen to his lordship, spoke very favourably of the behaviour of Mr. Jones on all accounts and strongly assured that lord that he must have mistaken the person, for that Jones was certainly a gentleman; insomuch that his lordship, who was strictly a man of honour and would by no means have been guilty of an action which the world in general would have condemned, began to be much concerned for the advice which he had taken.

Within a day or two after this, Lord Fellamar happened to dine with the Irish peer, who in a conversation upon the duel acquainted his company with the character of Fitzpatrick, to which indeed he did not do strict justice, especially in what related to his lady. He said she was the most innocent, the most injured, woman alive, and that from compassion alone he had undertaken her cause. He then declared an intention of going the next morning to Fitzpatrick's lodgings in order to prevail with him, if possible, to consent to a separation from his wife, who, the peer said, was in apprehensions for her life if she should ever return to be under the power of her husband. Lord Fellamar agreed to go with him, that he might satisfy himself more concerning Jones and the circumstances of the duel, for he was by no means easy concerning the part he had acted. The moment his lordship gave a hint of his readiness to assist in the discovery of the lady, it was eagerly embraced by the other nobleman, who depended much on the authority of Lord Fellamar, as he thought it would greatly contribute to awe Fitzpatrick into a compliance; and perhaps he was in the right, for the poor Irishman no sooner saw these noble peers had undertaken the cause of his wife than he submitted, and articles of separation were soon drawn up and signed between the parties.

Fitzpatrick had been so well satisfied by Mrs. Waters concerning the innocence of his wife with Jones at Upton, or perhaps from some other reasons was now become so indifferent to that matter, that he spoke highly in favour of Jones to Lord Fellamar, took all the blame upon himself, and said the other had behaved very much like a gentleman and a man of honour; and upon that lord's further inquiry concerning Mr. Jones, Fitzpatrick told him he was nephew to a gentleman of very great fashion and fortune, which was the account he had just received from Mrs. Waters after her interview with Dowling.

Lord Fellamar now thought it behoved him to do everything in his power to make satisfaction to a gentleman whom he had so grossly injured, and, without any consideration of rivalship (for he had now given over all thoughts of Sophia), determined to procure Mr. Jones's liberty, being satisfied as well from Fitzpatrick as his surgeon that the wound was not mortal. He therefore prevailed with the Irish peer to accompany him to the place where Jones was confined, to whom he behaved as we have already related.

When Allworthy returned to his lodgings, he immediately carried Jones into his room and then acquainted him with the whole matter, as well what he had heard from Mrs. Waters as what he had discovered from Mr. Dowling.

Jones expressed great astonishment and no less concern at this account, but without making any comment or observation upon it. And now a message was brought from Mr. Blifil, desiring to know if his uncle was at leisure that he might wait upon him. Allworthy started and turned pale, and then in a more passionate tone than I believe he had ever used before bid the servant tell Blifil he knew him not. "Consider, dear sir," cries Jones in a trembling voice. "I have considered," answered Allworthy, "and you yourself shall carry my message to the villain. No one can carry him the sentence of his own ruin so properly as the man whose ruin he hath so villainously contrived." "Pardon me, dear sir," said Jones; "a moment's reflection will, I am sure, convince you of the contrary. What might perhaps be but justice from another tongue would from mine be insult. And to whom? My own brother and your nephew. Nor did he use me so barbarously. Indeed, that would have been more inexcusable than anything he hath done. Fortune may tempt men of no very bad dispositions to injustice, but insults proceed only from black and rancorous minds, and have no temptations to excuse them. Let me beseech you, sir, to do nothing by him in the present height of your anger. Consider, my dear uncle, I was not myself condemned unheard." Allworthy stood silent a moment, and then, embracing Jones, he said with tears gushing from his eyes, "Oh, my child, to what goodness have I been so long blind!"

Mrs. Miller entering the room at that moment, after a gentle rap which was not perceived, and seeing Jones in the arms of his uncle, the poor woman, in an agony of joy, fell upon her knees and burst forth into the most ecstatic thanksgivings to heaven for what had happened. Then, running to Jones, she embraced him eagerly, crying, "My dearest friend, I wish you joy a thousand and a thousand times of this blest day." And next Mr. Allworthy himself received the same congratulations. To which he answered, "Indeed, indeed, Mrs. Miller, I am beyond expression happy." Some few more raptures having passed on all sides, Mrs. Miller desired them both to walk down to dinner in the parlour, where she said there were a very happy set of people assembled, being indeed no other than Mr. Nightingale and his bride, and his cousin Harriet with her bridegroom.

Allworthy excused himself from dining with the company, saying he had ordered some little thing for him and his nephew in his own apartment, for that they had much private business to discourse of, but would not resist promising the good woman that both he and Jones would make part of her society at supper.

Mrs. Miller then asked what was to be done with Blifil. "For indeed," says she, "I cannot be easy while such a villain is in my house." Allworthy answered he was as uneasy as herself on the same account. "Oh," cries she, "if that be the case, leave the matter to me; I'll soon show him the outside of my doors, I warrant you. Here are two or three lusty fellows below-stairs." "There will be no need of any violence," cries Allworthy. "If you will carry him a message from me, he will, I am convinced, depart of his own accord." "Will I?" said Mrs. Miller. "I never did anything in my life with a better will." Here Jones interfered and said he had considered the matter better and would, if Mr. Allworthy pleased, be himself the messenger. "I know," says he, "already enough of your pleasure, sir, and I beg leave to acquaint him with it by my own words. Let me beseech you, sir," added he, "to reflect on the dreadful consequences of driving him to violent and sudden despair. How unfit, alas, is this poor man to die in his present situation." This suggestion had not the least effect on Mrs. Miller. She left the room, crying, "You are too good, Mr. Jones, infinitely too good to live in this world." But it made a deeper impression on Allworthy. "My good child," said he, "I am equally astonished at the goodness of your heart and the quickness of your understanding. Heaven indeed forbid that this wretch should be deprived of any means or time for repentance. That would be a shocking consideration indeed. Go to him, therefore, and use your own discretion; yet do not flatter him with any hopes of my forgiveness, for I shall never forgive villainy farther than my religion obliges me, and that extends not either to our bounty or our conversation."

Jones went up to Blifil's room, whom he found in a situation which moved his pity, though it would have raised a less amiable passion in many beholders. He had cast himself on his bed, where he lay abandoning himself to despair and drowned in tears; not in such tears as flow from contrition and wash away guilt from minds which have been seduced or surprised into it unawares against the bent of their natural dispositions, as will sometimes happen from human frailty, even to the good; no, these tears were such as the frighted thief sheds in his cart and are, indeed, the effects of that concern which the most savage natures are seldom deficient in feeling for themselves.

It would be unpleasant and tedious to paint this scene in full length. Let it suffice to say that the behaviour of Jones was kind to excess. He omitted nothing which his invention could supply to raise and comfort the drooping spirits of Blifil before he communicated to him the resolution of his uncle that he must quit the house that evening. He offered to furnish him with any money he wanted, assured him of his hearty forgiveness of all he had done against him, that he would endeavour to live with him hereafter as a brother, and would leave nothing unattempted to effectuate a reconciliation with his uncle.

Blifil was at first sullen and silent, balancing in his mind whether he should yet deny all; but finding at last the evidence too strong against him, he betook himself at last to confession. He then asked pardon of his brother in the most vehement manner, prostrated himself on the ground, and kissed his feet; in short, he was now as remarkably mean as he had been before remarkably wicked.

Jones could not so far check his disdain but that it a little discovered itself in his countenance at this extreme servility. He raised his brother the moment he could from the ground and advised him to bear his afflictions more like a man, repeating at the same time his promises that he would do all in his power to lessen them; for which Blifil, making many professions of his unworthiness, poured forth a profusion of thanks; and then, he having declared he would immediately depart to another lodging, Jones returned to his uncle.

Among other matters Allworthy now acquainted Jones with the discovery which he made concerning the £500 bank-notes. "I have," said he, "already consulted a lawyer, who tells me to my great astonishment that there is no punishment for a fraud of this kind. Indeed, when I consider the black ingratitude of this fellow towards you, I think a highwayman, compared to him, is an innocent person."

"Good heavens!" says Jones. "Is it possible? I am shocked beyond measure at this news. I thought there was not an honester fellow in the world. The temptation of such a sum was too great for him to withstand, for smaller matters have come safe to me through his hand. Indeed, my dear uncle, you must suffer me to call it weakness rather than ingratitude, for I am convinced the poor fellow loves me and hath done me some kindnesses which I can never forget; nay, I believe he hath repented of this very act; for it is not above a day or two ago, when my affairs seemed in the most desperate situation, that he visited me in my confinement and offered me any money I wanted. Consider, sir, what a temptation to a man who had tasted such bitter distress it must be to have a sum in his possession which must have put him and his family beyond any future possibility of suffering the like."

"Child," cries Allworthy, "you carry this forgiving temper too far. Such mistaken mercy is not only weakness but borders on injustice, and is very pernicious to society, as it encourages vice. The dishonesty of this fellow I might perhaps have pardoned, but never his ingratitude. And give me leave to say, when we suffer any temptation to atone for dishonesty itself, we are as candid and merciful as we ought to be, and so far I confess I have gone; for I have often pitied the fate of a highwayman when I have been on the grand jury, and have more than once applied to the judge on the behalf of such as have had any mitigating circumstances in their case; but when dishonesty is attended with any blacker crime, such as cruelty, murder, ingratitude, or the like, compassion and forgiveness then become faults. I am convinced the fellow is a villain, and he shall be punished, at least as far as I can punish him."

This was spoke with so stern a voice that Jones did not think proper to make any reply; besides, the hour appointed by Mr. Western now drew so near that he had barely time left to dress himself. Here, therefore, ended the present dialogue, and Jones retired to another room, where Partridge attended according to order with his clothes.

Partridge had scarce seen his master since the happy discovery. The poor fellow was unable either to contain or express his transports. He behaved like one frantic, and made almost as many mistakes while he was dressing Jones as I have seen made by Harlequin in dressing himself on the stage.

His memory, however, was not in the least deficient. He recollected how many omens and presages of this happy event, some of which he had remarked at the time, but many more he now remembered; nor did he omit the dreams he had dreamt the evening before his meeting with Jones, and concluded with saying, "I always told your honour something boded in my mind that you would one time or other have it in your power to make my fortune." Jones assured him that this boding should as certainly be verified with regard to him as all the other omens had been to himself, which did not a little add to all the raptures which the poor fellow had already conceived on account of his master.

12

APPROACHING STILL NEARER TO THE END

Jones, being now completely dressed, attended his uncle to Mr. Western's. He was, indeed, one of the finest figures ever beheld, and his person alone would have charmed the greater part of womankind; but we hope it hath already appeared in this history that Nature when she formed him did not totally rely, as she sometimes doth, on this merit only to recommend her work.

Sophia, who, angry as she was, was likewise set forth to the best advantage, for which I leave my female readers to account, appeared so extremely beautiful that even Allworthy when he saw her could not forbear whispering

Western that he believed she was the finest creature in the world. To which Western answered in a whisper overheard by all present, "So much the better for Tom. For d——n me if he shan't ha' the tousling her." Sophia was all over scarlet at these words, while Tom's countenance was altogether as pale, and he was almost ready to sink from his chair.

The tea-table was scarce removed before Western lugged Allworthy out of the room, telling him he had business of consequence to impart and must speak to him that instant in private before he forgot it.

The lovers were now alone, and it will, I question not, appear strange to many readers that those who had so much to say to one another when danger and difficulty attended their conversation, and who seemed so eager to rush into each other's arms when so many bars lay in their way, now that with safety they were at liberty to say or do whatever they pleased should both remain for some time silent and motionless; insomuch that a stranger of moderate sagacity might have well concluded they were mutually indifferent; but so it was, however strange it may seem; both sat with their eyes cast downwards on the ground and for some minutes continued in perfect silence.

Mr. Jones during this interval attempted once or twice to speak, but was absolutely incapable, muttering only, or rather sighing out, some broken words, when Sophia at length, partly out of pity to him and partly to turn the discourse from the subject which she knew well enough he was endeavouring to open, said, "Sure, sir, you are the most fortunate man in the world in this discovery." "And can you really, madam, think me so fortunate," said Jones, sighing, "while I have incurred your displeasure?" "Nay, sir," says she, "as to that, you best know whether you have deserved it." "Indeed, madam," answered he, "you yourself are as well apprised of all my demerits. Mrs. Miller has acquainted you with the whole truth. Oh, my Sophia, am I never to hope for forgiveness?" "I think, Mr. Jones," said she, "I may almost depend on your own justice and leave it to yourself to pass sentence on your own conduct." "Alas, madam," answered he, "it is mercy, and not justice, which I implore at your hands. Justice I know must condemn me—yet not for the letter I sent to Lady Bellaston. Of that I most solemnly declare you have had a true account." He then insisted much on the security given him by Nightingale of a fair pretence for breaking off if, contrary to their expectations, her ladyship should have accepted his offer, but confessed that he had been guilty of a great indiscretion to put such a letter as that into her power, "which," said he, "I have dearly paid for in the effect it has upon you." "I do not, I cannot," says she, "believe otherwise of that letter than you would have me. My conduct, I think, shows you clearly I do not believe there is much in that. And yet, Mr. Jones, have I not enough to resent? After what passed at Upton, so soon to engage in a new amour with another woman, while I fancied, and you pretended, your heart was bleeding for me! Indeed, you have acted strangely. Can I believe the passion you have professed to me to be sincere? Or if I can, what happiness can I assure myself of with a man capable of so much inconstancy?" "Oh, my Sophia," cries he, "do not doubt the sincerity of the purest passion that ever inflamed a human breast. Think, most adorable creature, of my unhappy situation, of my despair. Could I, my Sophia, have flattered myself with the most distant hopes of being ever permitted to throw myself at your feet, in the manner I do now, it would not have been in the power of any other woman to have inspired a thought which the severest chastity could have condemned. Inconstancy, to you! Oh, Sophia, if you can have goodness enough to pardon what is past, do not let any cruel future apprehensions shut your mercy against me. No repentance was ever more sincere. Oh, let it reconcile me to my heaven in this dear bosom." "Sincere repentance, Mr. Jones," answered she, "will obtain the pardon of a sinner, but it is from One who is a perfect judge of that sincerity. A human mind may be imposed on, nor is there any infallible method to prevent it. You must expect, however, that if I can be prevailed on by your repentance to pardon you, I will at least insist on the strongest proof of its sincerity." "Oh, name any proof in my power," answered Jones eagerly. "Time," replied she, "time, Mr. Jones, can alone convince me that you are a true penitent and have resolved to abandon these vicious courses which I should detest you for, if I imagined you capable of persevering in them." "Do not imagine it," cries Jones. "On my knees I entreat, I implore, your confidence, a confidence which it shall be the business of my life to deserve." "Let it, then," said she, "be the business of some part of your life to show me you deserve it. I think I have been explicit enough in assuring you that when I see you merit my confidence, you will obtain it. After what is past, sir, can you expect I should take you upon your word?"

He replied, "Don't believe me upon my word; I have a better security, a pledge, for my constancy which it is impossible to see and to doubt." "What is that?" said Sophia, a little surprised. "I will show you, my charming angel," cried Jones, seizing her hand and carrying her to the glass. "There, behold it there, in that lovely figure, in that face, that shape, those eyes, that mind which shines through those eyes; can the man who shall be in possession of these be inconstant? Impossible, my Sophia! They would fix a Dorimant, a Lord Rochester. You could not doubt it if you could see yourself with any eyes but your own." Sophia blushed and half smiled, but, forcing again her brow into a frown, "If I am to judge," said she, "of the future by the past, my image will no more remain in your heart when I am out of your sight than it will in this glass when I am out of the room." "By heaven, by all that is sacred," said Jones, "it never was out of my heart. The delicacy of your sex cannot conceive the grossness of ours, nor how little one sort of amour has to do with the heart." "I will never marry a man," replied Sophia very gravely, "who shall not learn refinement enough to be as incapable as I am myself of making such a distinction." "I will learn it," said Jones. "I have learnt it already. The first moment of hope that my Sophia might be my wife taught it me at once, and all the rest of her sex from that moment became as little the objects of desire to my sense as of passion to my heart." "Well," said Sophia, "the proof of this must be from time. Your situation, Mr. Jones, is now altered, and I assure you I have great satisfaction in the alteration. You will now want no opportunity of being near me and convincing me that your mind is altered too." "Oh, my angel," cries Jones, "how shall I thank thy goodness? And are you so good to own that you have a satisfaction in my prosperity? Believe me, believe me, madam, it is you alone have given a relish to that prosperity, since I owe to it the dear hope— Oh, my Sophia, let it not be a distant one. I will be all obedience to your commands. I will not dare to press anything further than you permit me. Yet let me entreat you to appoint a short trial. Oh, tell me when I may expect you will be convinced of what is most solemnly true." "When I have gone voluntarily thus far, Mr. Jones," said she, "I expect not to be pressed. Nay, I will not." "Oh, don't look unkindly thus, my Sophia," cries he. "I do not, I dare not, press you. Yet permit me at least once more to beg you would fix the period. Oh, consider the impatience of love." "A twelvemonth, perhaps," said she. "Oh, my Sophia," cries he, "you have named an eternity." "Perhaps it may be something sooner," says she; "I will not be teased. If your passion for me be what I would have it, I think you may now be easy." "Easy, Sophia, call not such exulting happiness as mine by so cold a name. Oh, transporting thought! Am I not assured that the blessed day will come when I shall call you mine; when fears shall be no more; when I shall have that dear, that vast, that exquisite, ecstatic delight of making my Sophia happy?" "Indeed, sir," said she, "that day is in your own power." "Oh, my dear, my divine angel," cried he, "these words have made me mad with joy. But I must, I will, thank those dear lips which have so sweetly pronounced my bliss." He then caught her in his arms and kissed her with an ardour he had never ventured before.

At this instant Western, who had stood some time listening, burst into the room, and with his hunting voice and phrase cried out, "To her, boy, to her, go to her. That's it, little honeys, oh, that's it. Well! What, is it all over? Hath she appointed the day, boy? What shall it be, to-morrow or next day? It shan't be put off a minute longer than next day, I am resolved." "Let me beseech you, sir," says Jones, "don't let me be the occasion——" "Beseech mine a—," cries Western, "I thought thou had'st been a lad of higher mettle than to give way to a parcel of maidenish tricks. I tell thee 'tis all flim-flam. Zoodikers! She'd have the wedding to-night with all her heart. Wouldst not, Sophy? Come, confess, and be an honest girl for once. What, art dumb? Why dost not speak?" "Why should I confess, sir," says Sophia, "since it seems you are so well acquainted with my thoughts?" "That's a good girl," cries he. "And dost consent, then?" "No indeed, sir," says Sophia, "I have given no such consent." "And wunt nut ha' un, then, to-morrow nor next day?" says Western. "Indeed, sir," says she, "I have no such intention." "But I can't tell thee," replied he, "why hast nut, only because thou dost love to be disobedient and to plague and vex thy father." "Pray, sir ——" said Jones interfering. "I tell thee thou a't a puppy," cries he. "When I forbid her, then it was all nothing but sighing and whining and languishing and writing; now I am vor thee, she is against thee. All the spirit of contrary, that's all. She is above being guided and governed by her father, that is the whole truth on't. It is only to disoblige and contradict me." "What would my papa have me do?" cries Sophia. "What would I have thee do?" says he. "Why, gi un thy hand this moment." "Well, sir," said Sophia, "I will obey you. There is my hand, Mr. Jones." "Well, and will you consent to ha' un to-morrow morning?" says Western. "I will be obedient to you, sir," cries she. "Why, then, to-morrow morning be the day," cries he. "Why, then, to-morrow morning shall be the day, Papa, since you will have it so," says Sophia. Jones then fell upon his knees and kissed her hand in an agony of joy, while Western began to caper and dance about the room, presently crying out, "Where the devil is Allworthy? He is without now, a-talking with that d——d lawyer Dowling when he should be minding other matters." He then sallied out in quest of him and very opportunely left the lovers to enjoy a few tender minutes alone.

But he soon returned with Allworthy, saying, "If you won't believe me, you may ask her yourself. Hast nut gi'n thy consent, Sophy, to be married to-morrow?" "Such are your commands, sir," cries Sophia, "and I dare not be guilty of disobedience." "I hope, madam," cries Allworthy, "my nephew will merit so much goodness, and will be always as sensible as myself of the great honour you have done my family. An alliance with so charming and so excellent a young lady would indeed be an honour to the greatest in England." "Yes," cries Western, "but if I had suffered her to stand shill I shall I, dilly-dally, you might not have had that honour yet awhile; I was forced to use a little fatherly authority to bring her to." "I hope not, sir," cries Allworthy. "I hope there is not the least constraint." "Why, there," cries Western, "you may bid her unsay all again if you will. Dost repent heartily of thy promise, dost not, Sophy?" "Indeed, Papa," cries she, "I do not repent, nor do I believe I ever shall, of any promise in favour of Mr. Jones." "Then, nephew," cries Allworthy, "I felicitate you most heartily, for I think you are the happiest of men. And, madam, you will give me leave to congratulate you on this joyful occasion; indeed, I am convinced you have bestowed yourself on one who will be sensible of your great merit and who will at least use his best endeavours to deserve it." "His best endeavours!" cries Western. "That he will, I warrant un. Harkee,

Allworthy, I'll bet thee five pound to a crown we have a boy to-morrow nine months; but prithee, tell me what wut ha'? Wut ha' Burgundy, Champagne, or what? For please Jupiter, we'll make a night on't." "Indeed, sir," said Allworthy, "you must excuse me; both my nephew and I were engaged before I suspected this near approach of his happiness." "Engaged!" quoth the squire. "Never tell me. I won't part with thee to-night upon any occasion. Shalt sup here, please the lord Harry." "You must pardon me, my dear neighbour," answered Allworthy; "I have given a solemn promise, and that you know I never break." "Why, prithee, who art engaged to?" cries the squire. Allworthy then informed him, as likewise of the company. "Odzookers!" answered the squire. "I will go with thee and so shall Sophy; for I won't part with thee to-night, and it would be barbarous to part Tom and the girl." This offer was presently embraced by Allworthy, and Sophia consented, having first obtained a private promise from her father that he would not mention a syllable concerning her marriage.

13: Chapter the Last

IN WHICH THE HISTORY IS CONCLUDED

Young Nightingale had been that afternoon by appointment to wait on his father, who received him much more kindly than he expected. There likewise he met his uncle, who was returned to town in quest of his new-married daughter.

This marriage was the luckiest incident which could have happened to the young gentleman, for these brothers lived in a constant state of contention about the government of their children, both heartily despising the method which each other took. Each of them, therefore, now endeavoured as much as he could to palliate the offence which his own child had committed and to aggravate the match of the other. This desire of triumphing over his brother, added to the many arguments which Allworthy had used, so strongly operated on the old gentleman that he met his son with a smiling countenance and actually agreed to sup with him that evening at Mrs. Miller's.

As for the other, who really loved his daughter with the

most immoderate affection, there was little difficulty in inclining him to a reconciliation. He was no sooner informed by his nephew where his daughter and her husband were than he declared he would instantly go to her. And when he arrived there, he scarce suffered her to fall upon her knees before he took her up and embraced her with a tenderness which affected all who saw him, and in less than a quarter of an hour was as well reconciled to both her and her husband as if he had himself joined their hands.

In this situation were affairs when Mr. Allworthy and his company arrived to complete the happiness of Mrs. Miller, who no sooner saw Sophia than she guessed everything that had happened, and so great was her friendship to Jones that it added not a few transports to those she felt on the happiness of her own daughter.

There have not, I believe, been many instances of a number of people met together where every one was so perfectly happy as in this company. Amongst whom the father of young Nightingale enjoyed the least perfect content; for notwithstanding his affection for his son, notwithstanding the authority and the arguments of Allworthy, together with the other motive mentioned before, he could not so entirely be satisfied with his son's choice; and perhaps the presence of Sophia herself tended a little to aggravate and heighten his concern, as a thought now and then suggested itself that his son might have had that lady or some such other. Not that any of the charms which adorned either the person or mind of Sophia created the uneasiness; it was the contents of her father's coffers which set his heart a-longing. These were the charms which he could not bear to think his son had sacrificed to the daughter of Mrs. Miller.

The brides were both very pretty women, but so totally were they eclipsed by the beauty of Sophia that had they not been two of the best-tempered girls in the world, it would have raised some envy in their breasts; for neither of their husbands could long keep his eyes from Sophia, who sat at the table like a queen receiving homage, or rather like a superior being receiving adoration from all around her. But it was an adoration which they gave, not which she exacted; for she was as much distinguished by her modesty and affability as by all her other perfections.

The evening was spent in much true mirth. All were happy, but those the most who had been most unhappy before. Their former sufferings and fears gave such a relish to their felicity as even love and fortune in their fullest flow could not have given without the advantage of such a comparison. Yet, as great joy, especially after a sudden change and revolution of circumstances, is apt to be silent and dwells rather in the heart than on the tongue, Jones and Sophia appeared the least merry of the whole company. Which Western observed with great impatience, often crying out to them, "Why dost not talk, boy! Why dost look so grave! Hast lost thy tongue, girl! Drink another glass of wine, sha't drink another glass." And the more to enliven her he would sometimes sing a merry song, which bore some relation to matrimony and the loss of a maidenhead. Nay, he would have proceeded so far on that topic as to have driven her out of the room if Mr. Allworthy had not checked him, sometimes by looks and once or twice by a "Fie, Mr. Western!" He began, indeed, once to debate the matter and assert his right to talk to his own daughter as he thought fit, but as nobody seconded him he was soon reduced to order.

Notwithstanding this little restraint, he was so pleased with the cheerfulness and good humour of the company that he insisted on their meeting the next day at his lodgings. They all did so; and the lovely Sophia, who was now in private become a bride too, officiated as the mistress of the ceremonies, or, in the polite phrase, did the honours of the table. She had that morning given her hand to Jones in the chapel at Doctors' Commons, where Mr. Allworthy, Mr. Western, and Mrs. Miller were the only persons present.

Sophia had earnestly desired her father that no others of the company who were that day to dine with him should be acquainted with her marriage. The same secrecy was enjoined to Mrs. Miller, and Jones undertook for Allworthy. This somewhat reconciled the delicacy of Sophia to the public entertainment, which in compliance with her father's will she was obliged to go to, greatly against her own inclinations. In confidence of this secrecy she went through the day pretty well till the squire, who was now advanced into the second bottle, could contain his joy no longer, but, filling out a bumper, drank a health to the bride. The health was immediately pledged by all present, to the great confusion of our poor blushing Sophia and the great concern of Jones upon her account. To say truth, there was not a person present made wiser by this discovery; for Mrs. Miller had whispered it to her daughter, her daughter to her husband, her husband to his sister, and she to all the rest.

Sophia now took the first opportunity of withdrawing with the ladies, and the squire sat in to his cups, in which he was by degrees deserted by all the company, except the uncle of young Nightingale, who loved his bottle as well as Western himself. These two, therefore, sat stoutly to it during the whole evening, and long after that happy hour which had surrendered the charming Sophia to the eager arms of her enraptured Jones.

Thus, reader, we have at length brought our history to a conclusion, in which, to our great pleasure, though contrary perhaps to thy expectation, Mr. Jones appears to be the happiest of all humankind; for what happiness this world affords equal to the possession of such a woman as Sophia I sincerely own I have never yet discovered.

As to the other persons who have made any considerable figure in this history, as some may desire to know a little more concerning them, we will proceed in as few words as possible to satisfy their curiosity.

Allworthy hath never yet been prevailed upon to see Blifil, but he hath yielded to the importunity of Jones, backed by Sophia, to settle £200 a year upon him; to which Jones hath privately added a third. Upon this income he lives in one of the northern counties about 200 miles distant from London, and lays up £200 a year out of it in order to purchase a seat in the next Parliament from a neighbouring borough, which he has bargained for with an attorney there. He is also lately turned Methodist, in hopes of marrying a very rich widow of that sect whose estate lies in that part of the kingdom.

Square died soon after he writ the before-mentioned letter; and as to Thwackum, he continues at his vicarage. He hath made many fruitless attempts to regain the confidence of Allworthy or to ingratiate himself with Jones, both of whom he flatters to their faces and abuses behind their backs. But in his stead, Mr. Allworthy hath lately taken Mr. Abraham Adams into his house, of whom Sophia is grown immoderately fond and declares he shall have the tuition of her children.

Mrs. Fitzpatrick is separated from her husband and retains the little remains of her fortune. She lives in reputation at the polite end of the town, and is so good an economist that she spends three times the income of her fortune without running in debt. She maintains a perfect intimacy with the lady of the Irish peer, and in acts of friendship to her repays all the obligations she owes to her husband.

Mrs. Western was soon reconciled to her niece, Sophia, and hath spent two months together with her in the country. Lady Bellaston made the latter a formal visit at her return to town, where she behaved to Jones as to a perfect stranger, and with great civility wished him joy on his marriage.

Mr. Nightingale hath purchased an estate for his son in the neighbourhood of Jones, where the young gentleman, his lady, Mrs. Miller, and her little daughter reside, and the most agreeable intercourse subsists between the two families.

As to those of lower account, Mrs. Waters returned into the country, had a pension of £60 a year settled upon her by Mr. Allworthy, and is married to Parson Supple, on whom, at the instance of Sophia, Western hath bestowed a considerable living.

Black George, hearing the discovery that had been made, run away and was never since heard of; and Jones bestowed the money on his family, but not in equal proportions, for Molly had much the greatest share.

As for Partridge, Jones hath settled £50 a year on him, and he hath again set up a school, in which he meets with much better encouragement than formerly; and there is now a treaty of marriage on foot between him and Miss Molly Seagrim, which through the mediation of Sophia is likely to take effect.

We now return to take leave of Mr. Jones and Sophia, who within two days after their marriage attended Mr. Western and Mr. Allworthy into the country. Western hath resigned his family seat and the greater part of his estate to his son-in-law, and hath retired to a lesser house of his in another part of the country which is better for hunting. Indeed, he is often as a visitant with Mr. Jones, who as well as his daughter hath an infinite delight in doing everything in their power to please him. And this desire of theirs is attended with such success that the old gentleman declares he was never happy in his life till now. He hath here a parlour and ante-chamber to himself, where he gets drunk with whom he pleases, and his daughter is still as ready as formerly to play to him whenever he desires it; for Jones hath assured her that, as next to pleasing her, one of his highest satisfactions is to contribute to the happiness of the old man, so the great duty which she expresses and performs to her father renders her almost equally dear to him with the love which she bestows on himself.

Sophia hath already produced him two fine children, a boy and a girl, of whom the old gentleman is so fond that he spends much of his time in the nursery, where he declares the tattling of his little grand-daughter, who is above a year and half old, is sweeter music than the finest cry of dogs in England.

Allworthy was likewise greatly liberal to Jones on the marriage, and hath omitted no instance of showing his affection to him and his lady, who love him as a father. Whatever in the nature of Jones had a tendency to vice has been corrected by continual conversation with this good man and by his union with the lovely and virtuous Sophia. He has also, by reflection on his past follies, acquired a discretion and prudence very uncommon in one of his lively parts.

To conclude, as there are not to be found a worthier man and woman than this fond couple, so neither can any be imagined more happy. They preserve the purest and tenderest affection for each other, an affection daily increased and confirmed by mutual endearments and mutual esteem. Nor is their conduct towards their relations and friends less amiable than towards one another. And such is their condescension, their indulgence, and their beneficence to those below them that there is not a neighbour, a tenant, or a servant who doth not most gratefully bless the day when Mr. Jones was married to his Sophia.

FINIS.

APPENDIX

The text printed below is a major revision of the following passage in Book VIII, Chapter 14, starting in the sixteenth paragraph.

". . . For my own part, I had been for some time very seriously affected with the danger to which the Protestant religion was so visibly exposed under a popish prince, and thought the apprehension of it alone sufficient to justify that insurrection; for no real security can ever be found against the persecuting spirit of popery when armed with power except the depriving it of that power, as woeful experience presently showed. You know how King James behaved after getting the better of this attempt: how little he valued either his royal word, or coronation oath, or the liberties and rights of his people. But all had not the sense to foresee this at first, and therefore the Duke of Monmouth was weakly supported; yet all could feel when the evil came upon them, and therefore all united at last to drive out that king against whose exclusion a great party among us had so warmly contended during the reign of his brother, and for whom they now fought with such zeal and affection."

"What you say," interrupted Jones, "is very true; and it has often struck me as the most wonderful thing I ever read of in history that so soon after this convincing experience, which brought our whole nation to join so unanimously in expelling King James for the preservation of our religion and liberties, there should be a party among us mad enough to desire the placing his family again on the throne." "You are not in earnest!" answered the old man. "There can be no such party. As bad an opinion as I have of mankind, I cannot believe them infatuated to such a degree! There may be some hot-headed papists led by their priests to engage in this desperate cause and think it a holy war; but that Protestants, that members of the Church of England, should be such apostates, such *felos de se,* I cannot believe it. No, no, young man, unacquainted as I am with what has passed in the world for these last thirty years, I cannot be so imposed upon as to credit so foolish a tale;

but I see you have a mind to sport with my ignorance." "Can it be possible," replied Jones, "that you have lived so much out of the world as not to know that during that time there have been two rebellions in favour of the son of King James, one of which is now actually raging in the very heart of this kingdom?" At these words the old gentleman started up and, in a most solemn tone of voice, conjured Jones by his Maker to tell him if what he said was really true; which the other as solemnly affirming, he walked several turns about the room in a profound silence, then cried, then laughed, and at last fell down on his knees and blessed God in a loud thanksgiving prayer for having delivered him from all society with human nature, which could be capable of such monstrous extravagances. After which, being reminded by Jones that he had broke off his story, he resumed it again in this manner:

"As mankind in the days I was speaking of was not yet arrived to that pitch of madness which I find they are capable of now, and which, to be sure, I have only escaped by living alone and at a distance from the contagion, there was a considerable rising in favour of Monmouth, and my principles strongly inclining me to take the same part, I determined to join him; and Mr. Watson from different motives concurring in the same resolution (for the spirit of a gamester will carry a man as far upon such an occasion as the spirit of patriotism), we soon provided ourselves with all necessaries, and went to the Duke at Bridgewater.

"The unfortunate event of this enterprise you are, I conclude, as well acquainted with as myself. . . ."

The third edition omits with the exception of a single sentence the following passage after the second paragraph of Chapter 15, in Book VIII:

"As for my own part, I passed through all these nations as you perhaps may have done through a crowd at a show, jostling to get by them, holding my nose with one hand, and defending my pockets with the other, without speaking a word to any of them while I was pressing on to see what I wanted to see, which, however entertaining it might be in itself, scarce made me amends for the trouble the company gave me."

"Did you not find some of the nations among which you

travelled less troublesome to you than others?" said Jones. "Oh, yes," replied the old man; "the Turks were much more tolerable to me than the Christians, for they are men of profound taciturnity and never disturb a stranger with questions. Now and then, indeed, they bestow a short curse upon him, or spit in his face as he walks the streets, but then they have done with him; and a man may live an age in their country without hearing a dozen words from them. But of all the people I ever saw, heaven defend me from the French. With their damned prate and civilities, and doing the honour of their nation to strangers (as they are pleased to call it), but indeed setting forth their own vanity, they are so troublesome that I had infinitely rather pass my life with the Hottentots than set my foot in Paris again. They are a nasty people, but their nastiness is mostly *without;* whereas in France and some other nations that I won't name, it is all *within,* and makes them stink much more to my reason than that of Hottentots does to my nose.

"Thus, sir, I have ended the history of my life; for as to all that series of years during which I have lived retired here, it affords no variety to entertain you, and may be almost considered as one day. The retirement has been so complete that I could hardly have enjoyed a more absolute solitude in the deserts of the Thebais than here in the midst of this populous kingdom. As I have no estate, I am plagued with no tenants or stewards; my annuity is paid me pretty regularly, as indeed it ought to be, for it is much less than what I might have expected in return for what I gave up. Visits I admit none; and the old woman who keeps my house knows that her place entirely depends upon her saving me all the trouble of buying the things that I want, keeping off all solicitation or business from me, and holding her tongue whenever I am within hearing. As my walks are all by night, I am pretty secure in this wild, unfrequented place from meeting any company. Some few persons I have met by chance and sent them home heartily frightened, as from the oddness of my dress and figure they took me for a ghost or a hobgoblin. But what has happened to-night shows that even here I cannot be safe from the villainy of men, for without your assistance I had not only been robbed but very probably murdered."

AFTERWORD

If we leave out Defoe's narratives, *Robinson Crusoe* and *Moll Flanders*—and I think we should—*Tom Jones,* which was published in 1749, is the second great novel. The first, Richardson's *Clarissa Harlowe,* preceded it by only a year.

It is a commonplace that the birth of the novel had to await the development of a suitable reading public, but we should remember that *Tom Jones* was certainly not written for the masses. Fielding's readers would not be those who bought *Robinson Crusoe* in edition costing a few pennies, even though his publisher aimed at a larger audience than that which could afford poetry and those "vast French romances, neatly gilt" of which Pope had spoken. The reader of this new edition has probably paid for it about what he spends on an ordinary lunch. The six volumes of the first edition of *Tom Jones* cost 18 shillings at a time when this was the weekly pay of a skilled craftsman and twice that of a laborer—enough money, as Ian Watt has said, to feed a family for a week or two. There were circulating libraries, of course, and they enabled people to read novels that they could not afford to buy. But it is obvious that a book like *Tom Jones* was written to tempt middle-class pockets and middle-class tastes.

Fielding was the son of a general and the great-grandson of the Earl of Denbigh; one grandfather was a judge, the other an archdeacon. He went to Eton and later, at thirty, to the University of Leiden. He had, in short, the birth and education of a gentleman, though from an early age he got his living in the rough world of the London theater, where he learned a lot about dialogue and plotting. He might never have turned to the novel had not the success of Richardson's *Pamela* prompted him to write the skit *Shamela* (1741) and then *Joseph Andrews* (1742). He was poor and lived by his pen, producing in a short life many plays, a great mass of journalism, and pamphlets on legal and social issues. (In his later years he was famous also as a magistrate.) He had, in short, a public to please, much literary skill, and a knowledge of the world. Out of this blend of need, interest, and skill came *Tom Jones*, the work, he tells us, of a thousand hours, snatched from the journalism of three years.

Fielding was anything but a careless writer. He knew what he wanted to do and understood the novelty of his plans, as the essays prefacing each of the eighteen books of the novel and the Preface to *Joseph Andrews* repeatedly explain. He believed that the novel was a prose descendant of the epic, especially of that neglected branch of epic, the comic. He thought it his business to entertain, but was conventional enough to believe he had also a duty to morality. Fielding's moral views when considered in isolation are not of special interest, but they are an integral part of *Tom Jones* and help to shape the plot. His epic ambitions were, when it came to the point, somewhat less formative than his dramatic skill, but they nevertheless affect the shape of all three of his novels. "It becomes an author generally to divide a book, as it does a butcher to joint his meat, for such assistance is of great help to both the reader and the carver," he says in *Joseph Andrews*. So *Tom Jones* has eighteen books, six for the beginning, six for the middle, and six for the end, the three parts as recommended by Aristotle. The first six give the causes of the action (the open nature of Tom, illustrated by examples; his growing differences with Blifil; the enmity of Thwackum and Square; the alienation from Mr. Allworthy; the beginnings of Tom's love for Sophia, and their separation). The second, or middle, six books are both the consequence of the first six and the agency by which the resolutions of the last six are to be brought about. They deal with the wanderings of Jones on the road to London, the flight of Sophia, and the pursuit by Squire Western. The last six bring upon Jones the apparently disastrous consequences of all the actions previously described; some are attributable to his own lapses from virtue, some to the machinations of Blifil, and some to general ill fortune. When he is in prison, perhaps about to be hanged, he hears the news that Sophia has finally rejected him for his base conduct in the Bellaston affair and, thus reduced to his lowest point, has to face the possibility of his having committed incest. But this last discovery also brings about the peripeteia, or change of fortune; and it is through Jenny Jones, now known as Mrs. Waters, and from the timely deathbed repentance of Square that the truth of his birth emerges. There follow immediately his restoration to the favor of Allworthy and Sophia, and the discomfiture of Blifil.

However much the total merit of *Tom Jones* may be debated, there can be little argument about the mechanical efficiency of the plot, and few have begrudged it the high praise of Coleridge: "What a master of composition Fielding was! Upon my word, I think the *Oedipus Tyrannus,* the *Alchemist,* and *Tom Jones,* the three most perfect plots ever planned." Scholars and critics have attempted to analyze this wonderfully many-layered arrangement of incidents, but it has always evaded full description. And much of the reader's pleasure in *Tom Jones* comes from his recognition of the complexity of the design, its capacity to surprise him without recourse to improbabilities, and the test it provides for his own wits. Consider, for example, the lawyer, Dowling, whose brief, busy appearances may seem merely part of the general hustle and bustle until at the climax, when Blifil tries for the last time to finish Tom off, he is suddenly and plausibly revealed as a principal agent of the plot. Or think of the skill with which Mrs. Miller is used; without her there would not only be lacking a strong advocate for Tom when Allworthy is most obdurate against him; there would also be no means of gathering together in one London house with Allworthy everybody who knows the secret of Tom's birth.

Perhaps we can best make this point about Fielding's careful planning by looking at a single passage—the one in Book IX that describes the events at Upton. Occurring exactly halfway through the novel, this is a plot-node of extraordinary complexity. Jones, having rescued Mrs. Waters (whose real identity we shall not discover for hundreds of pages) from the assault of Northerton, arrives with her at the inn (IX.3). There follows a battle, in which Partridge is wounded by Susan. The soldiers enter, and identify Mrs. Waters. She is prevailed upon to go out and change into a dress the landlady will lend her; Partridge returns, having mended his nose. We think nothing at the time of Mrs. Waters' temporary absence; but of course if Partridge and Mrs. Waters had met, the cat would have been out of the bag, since she is really Jenny Jones, his wife, and the supposed mother of Tom. Their eventual meeting, at the beginning of Book XVIII, seems, by creating a suspicion of incest, only to complete Jones's misery, but this is only a step toward the restoring of his fortunes when Jenny confesses the whole truth. Fielding, indeed, cannot forbear to draw attention to his cleverness. "If the reader will please to refresh his memory," he says in XVIII.2, "by turning to the scene at Upton in the ninth book, he will be apt to admire the many strange accidents which unfortunately prevented any interview between Partridge and Mrs. Waters when she spent a whole day there with Mr. Jones." Later that night Mrs. Waters takes Jones to her bed. In the kitchen, Partridge reveals Tom's relation to Allworthy. Meanwhile, Captain Fitzpatrick comes in search of his wife, and mistakenly supposes her to be in bed with Tom; she is indeed in the inn, but he seeks her no further. Then Sophia arrives at the inn, intending to rest before continuing her journey. Partridge tells Honour, her maid, of Tom's presence; Sophia sends Honour to fetch him, but Partridge stops her, explaining that he is in bed with another woman. Sophia professes herself "very easy," but bursts into tears, and has her muff placed on Tom's bed as a reproach. (Fielding expects you to remember this muff from IV.14 and V.3, but inserts a little reminder in IX.5.) Tom finds the muff; Mr. Western arrives, just missing Sophia; and Mrs. Waters leaves with Captain Fitzpatrick.

Out of all this comes the supposed incest; Sophia's annoyance at the free use she thinks Jones has made of her name; and Fitzpatrick's discomfiture, which later gives rise to the denouement in London when Jones wounds the Captain. Out of it also comes the negative result that if Partridge had not had the nosebleed, which prevented his meeting Mrs. Waters, the truth about Tom would have come out in the presence of Western and Sophia at this early stage. There are other consequences, such as the meeting of Sophia and her cousin Mrs. Fitzpatrick, which produces a subplot corresponding to that of the Man of the Hill. And while he is so concentratedly designing the Upton events to justify later developments Fielding carefully ensures that no one should seem to arrive at the inn simply for the plotter's convenience. Every arrival is fully motivated, sometimes, as with Sophia and Western, retrospectively: "Though the reader, in many histories, is obliged to digest much more unaccountable appearances than this of Mr. Western, without any satisfaction at all, yet, as we dearly love to oblige him whenever it is in our power, we shall now proceed to show by what method the squire discovered where his daughter was:" For the machinery of epic and the easy coincidences of romance, Fielding substitutes an appearance of causality proper to this new kind of fiction, with its hardheaded bourgeois view of what constitutes realism and plausibility. Well might Fielding, at the opening of Book X, warn the reader "not too hastily to condemn any of the incidents . . . as impertinent and foreign to our main design" simply because he does not "immediately conceive in what manner such incident may conduce to that design." See this great creation as a whole, he somewhat opprobriously warns his critics, before you "presume to find fault with any of its parts. . . ."

It is worth noting that the two plots that Coleridge ranks with that of *Tom Jones*—*Oedipus Rex* and *The Alchemist*—both belong to the drama. The plotting of Fielding's novel was clearly the product of his dramatic experience, and the organization of such scenes as the Upton episode has prompted reasonable comparisons with the famous discovery scene in Sheridan's *The School for Scandal*. This indicates an affinity, in the mid-eighteenth century, between the audience for plays and the audience for novels; but we have not outgrown their delight in plausible surprise, and no one will be shocked to hear that one of the great modern masters of plot, Graham Greene, regards *Tom Jones* as the kind of novel "he would like to be able to write."

Mr. Greene, however, does not mean that the Swiss precision of the plotting is the only virtue of the book; in fact, he believes that plot can spoil a novel if it damages "the mythical center." What distinguishes the novel from other literary forms is that it normally possesses a higher degree of faithfulness to everyday reality, combined with more or less formal interest. It is, as it were, bounded on one side by the newspaper and on the other by the fable. Thus its formal tidiness is often inferior to what might be expected of a good play—indeed some great novels, such as *Clarissa* and *Anna Karenina,* do not have this kind of neatness at all. The novel deals in more detail with the actual complexities of life than any other genre, and some novels of an extreme "realist" cast sacrifice nearly all "myth" and "form" to this detailed verisimilitude.

Tom Jones has verisimilitude, but it also has its highly wrought plot. Perhaps that is why it does not give one the full sense of actual life—real, unpredictable, not subject to mechanical patterning—that is to be had from the very greatest novels, such as *The Idiot* and *Anna Karenina.* But it is far from being *mere* plot. Indeed the plot—so complex, involving so many sharply differentiated portraits drawn from "the original book of nature" (however much affected by existing theatrical types), and so faithful to fact that it checks with the almanac for 1745—itself presupposes certain assumptions on the author's part about the nature of reality and personality. So, indeed, does the style—witty, good-natured, worldly—and even the flights of mock-epic prose must have seemed consistent with a realistic view of the world. It is Fielding's own claim that his work has "historic integrity" and that this distinguishes it from "those idle romances which are filled with monsters, the productions not of Nature but of distempered brains" (IV.l). His book is not, he adds, quite plain fact; for that you must read the newspaper. And of course his own frequent intrusions into the story, both in the prefatory chapters and elsewhere, prevent the novel from even having the appearance of a straightforward chronicle of events; for they draw attention to the nature of the artifice, not without hope of applause for its perfection.

Obviously Fielding saw that all his elaborate preparations, his schemes to depress and abuse Jones by every trick of malice and ill fortune, might be said to depend upon his "myth" of normal, young, well-born manhood—a beautiful young man with his heart in the right place, plotted against by the odious Blifil and other detestable opponents. And this is not a context in which we could expect to find profound studies of personality. Fielding sees people and causes from a frankly personal and limited point of view. Innkeepers, doctors, lawyers, coachmen, soldiers—all exist within the bounds of preestablished types. Partridge has a long romance-ancestry; Squire Western, though realized with wonderful freshness, is a development of a type already presented by Fielding in the theater. Allworthy, "a human being replete with benevolence," has a morality name. Thwackum, whose main pleasure is stated in his name, exists largely to emphasize the contrast between his bitter predestinarian divinity and Tom's good heart; Square, whose name mockingly refers to the emblem of Temperance, is less evil, but exists to indicate a philosophical deviation from the same norm; for, unlike Fielding's, his myth has no place for human vice, regarding it as an accidental deformity and part of the great plan: "all partial evil, universal good," he says with Pope, a view Fielding expressly detested as necessarily hypocritical. Hypocrisy was to Fielding the most hateful of vices; he even includes a Quaker in *Tom Jones* in order to express his contempt for one form of it; he speaks of "the pernicious principles of Methodism," holding that sect to be the enemy of good sense because it encouraged "enthusiasm"; and the book is full of strong anti-Jacobite feeling because here, at both the religious and the political levels, was another sect he abhorred.

Technically speaking, Fielding's ethic is based on a modified Pelagianism*, a belief that, as Dr. Harrison puts it in Fielding's last novel, *Amelia*, "there do remain, dispersed in the soil of human nature, diverse seeds of goodness, of benignity, of ingenuity, which being cherished, excited, and quickened by good culture, do . . . thrust out flowers very lovely, yield fruits very pleasant of virtue and goodness." In a sense, *Tom Jones* is about the "quickening" of these seeds in its hero, who for all his warm blood invariably shows signs of true "benevolence." Tom, for all his lapses, is infinitely preferable to the chilly, perfidious Blifil. True, he has to learn that the sins of the flesh meet with retribution. But though they bring him near disaster, we do not feel that the author takes them too seriously. Fielding was writing ironically when he made Lady Booby, in *Joseph Andrews*, ask, "Did ever mortal hear of a *man's* virtue?"; yet he was sufficiently of his age to subscribe with some geniality to something like this double standard. There is a touch of "the man of feeling" about Tom when he deplores the plight to which base loves have reduced the Man of the Hill or when he urges Nightingale to do the proper thing by his girl, Nancy; but Molly ceases to be a worry to Tom once he discovers that she has been promiscuous.

The truth is that most of the disasters that beset Tom arise less from his own errors than from ill luck, the malice of others, or the many indiscretions of Partridge. He is not credited with any very intense spiritual sensitivity, and his reactions of woe or wonder sometimes have a hollow note. But in saying that, one has in mind the great novels of spiritual education that followed Fielding—and learned not only from him but also from Richardson: *Emma*, for instance, and *Middlemarch*, and the *The Portrait of a Lady*. Tom has a good heart, and Fielding credits his readers with similar health. "What can be more innocent than the indulgence of a natural appetite?" asks Jones. He does no harm by intention, and is charitable and right-minded about sexual ethics even when he is the paid lover of Lady Bellaston. The long

---

* See the excellent study by Martin C. Battestin, *The Moral Basis of Fielding's Art* (Middletown, Conn.: Wesleyan University Press, 1959).

and short of Fielding's ethical position is in VI.1. He asks the reader to accept it. If he will not, says Fielding, he might as well put the book away. But insofar as it argues for the possibility that "benevolence" can be associated with sex, who would deny that something of the kind must be true?

In his life as in his books, Fielding combined a warm ethical Christianity—reflected in his deep concern for avoidable social evils—with a hatred of liars and hypocrites and some degree of tolerance toward those who think of love as "the desire of satisfying a voracious appetite with a certain quantity of delicate human flesh." His world is Hogarth's, but it is also Richardson's. Fielding differs from Richardson by dealing with sexual conduct and misconduct primarily as social phenomena, though they indicate the absence or presence of "benevolence" in the characters. This is a matter for comedy; whereas Richardson's intense, even morbid, exploration of spiritual states requires tragedy: the slow death of Clarissa.

This says no more than that the morality of *Tom Jones* is shallow in comparison with that of the greatest novels of the world. It would be priggish thus to end an afterword on a book that must assuredly have given so much pleasure to the reader. The truth is that there are few works of art so perfectly made, so perfectly of their period, yet possessing the energy and high spirits and good humor to transcend it. And if more words are needed in defense of *Tom Jones*, it is sufficient to add that it opened a whole new territory in which the comic genius of Dickens could build his cities. In this book Fielding combined the epic and the dramatic, thereby creating the dominant literary form of our time, even if we no longer call it the "prosai-comi-epic," but simply the "novel."

FRANK KERMODE
UNIVERSITY OF MANCHESTER

A NOTE ON THE TEXT

This new edition is based on the third of 1749, which provides a good text, requiring a minimum of emendation. It has been largely brought up to date in spelling, punctuation, etc., but great care has been taken to preserve what could be obscured or even lost altogether in modernizing too inflexibly: Fielding's deliberate and often comic use of puns, Somersetshire dialect, unusual idioms, and other linguistic features. His personal preference for the forms *hath* and *doth* has also been respected, and on some occasions his use of italic type for emphasis has been restored. Some passages from the first edition of 1749 are given above in an appendix; these were later omitted or revised.

SELECTED BIBLIOGRAPHY

OTHER WORKS BY HENRY FIELDING

The Temple Beau, 1730   Play
Tom Thumb, A Tragedy, 1730   Play
The Coffee-House Politician, 1730   Play
The Grub-Street Opera, 1731   Play
Don Quixote in England, 1734   Play
*An Old Man Taught Wisdom, or
   The Virgin Unmask'd,* 1735   Play
Pasquin, 1736   Play
An Apology for the Life of Mrs. Shamela Andrews, 1741
   Satire
Joseph Andrews, 1742   Novel
Jonathan Wild, 1743   Novel
Amelia, 1751   Novel
Journal of a Voyage to Lisbon, 1755   Travel

SELECTED BIOGRAPHY AND CRITICISM

Battestin, Martin C. *The Moral Basis of Fielding's Art: A Study of Joseph Andrews.* Middletown, Conn.: Wesleyan University Press, 1959.

Blanchard, F. T. *Fielding the Novelist: A Study in Historical Criticism.* New Haven: Yale University Press, 1926.

Cordasco, Francesco. *Henry Fielding: Critical Studies, 1895-1946.* New York: Long Island University Press, 1948.

Cross, Wilbur Lucius. *The History of Henry Fielding.* 3 vols. New Haven: Yale University Press, 1918.

Dudden, Homes. *Henry Fielding: His Life, Works and Times.* 2 vols. New York: Oxford University Press, Inc., 1952.

Pringle, Patrick. *Hue and Cry: The Story of Henry and John Fielding and Their Bow Street Runners.* New York: William Morrow & Company, Inc., 1955.

Watt, Ian. *Rise of the Novel: Studies in Defoe, Richardson, and Fielding.* Berkeley: University of California Press, 1957.

Willcocks, M. P. *A True-Born Englishman: Being the Life of Henry Fielding.* New York: The Macmillan Company, 1948.